I0632142

SUNSET SEALS

The Series

Books 5–8

SHARON HAMILTON

SHARON HAMILTON'S BOOK LIST

SEAL BROTHERHOOD BOOKS

SEAL BROTHERHOOD SERIES

Accidental SEAL Book 1
Fallen SEAL Legacy Book 2
SEAL Under Covers Book 3
SEAL The Deal Book 4
Cruisin' For A SEAL Book 5
SEAL My Destiny Book 6
SEAL of My Heart Book 7
Fredo's Dream Book 8
SEAL My Love Book 9
SEAL Encounter Prequel to Book 1
SEAL Endeavor Prequel to Book 2
Ultimate SEAL Collection Vol. 1 Books 1-4 /2 Prequels
Ultimate SEAL Collection Vol. 2 Books 5-7

SEAL BROTHERHOOD LEGACY SERIES

Watery Grave Book 1
Honor The Fallen Book 2
Grave Injustice Book 3
Deal With The Devil Book 4

BAD BOYS OF SEAL TEAM 3 SERIES

SEAL's Promise Book 1
SEAL My Home Book 2
SEAL's Code Book 3
Big Bad Boys Bundle Books 1-3

BAND OF BACHELORS SERIES

Lucas Book 1
Alex Book 2
Jake Book 3
Jake 2 Book 4
Big Band of Bachelors Bundle

BONE FROG BROTHERHOOD SERIES

New Year's SEAL Dream Book 1

SEALed At The Altar Book 2

SEALed Forever Book 3

SEAL's Rescue Book 4

SEALed Protection Book 5

Bone Frog Brotherhood Superbundle

BONE FROG BACHELOR SERIES

Bone Frog Bachelor Book 0.5

Unleashed Book 1

Restored Book 2

Revenge Book 3

SUNSET SEALS SERIES

SEALed at Sunset Book 1

Second Chance SEAL Book 2

Treasure Island SEAL Book 3

Escape to Sunset Book 4

The House at Sunset Beach Book 5

Second Chance Reunion Book 6

Love's Treasure Book 7

Finding Home Book 8

Sunset SEALs Duet #1

Sunset SEALs Duet #2

LOVE VIXEN

Bone Frog Love

SHADOW SEALS

Shadow of the Heart

Shadow Warrior

SILVER SEALS SERIES

SEAL Love's Legacy

SLEEPER SEALS SERIES

Bachelor SEAL

STAND ALONE BOOKS & SERIES

SEAL's Goal: The Beautiful Game

Nashville SEAL: Jameson

True Blue SEALS Zak

Paradise: In Search of Love

Love Me Tender, Love You Hard

NOVELLAS

SEAL You In My Dreams Magnolias and Moonshine

PARANORMALS

GOLDEN VAMPIRES OF TUSCANY SERIES

Honeymoon Bite Book 1

Mortal Bite Book 2

Christmas Bite Book 3

Midnight Bite Book 4

THE GUARDIANS

Heavenly Lover Book 1

Underworld Lover Book 2

Underworld Queen Book 3

Redemption Book 4

FALL FROM GRACE SERIES

Gideon: Heavenly Fall

NOVELLAS

SEAL Of Time Trident Legacy

All of Sharon's books are available on Audible, narrated by the talented J.D. Hart.

Print Edition

ABOUT THE BUNDLE

The House at Sunset Beach

SEAL Team 3 member Andy Carr is liking his Florida digs – the call of the seabirds and the roaring of the ocean at his back door. Sunset Beach is also the place where he found his soulmate, Aimee, rescuing her from an abusive relationship with another teammate – a sticky situation that nearly lost him his Trident.

But they've embarked on renovating the little house at Sunset she found while they were falling in love, and this house means more to them than just glass, wood, and sheetrock.

Andy begins to reconsider his membership in the Trident Club and is called in another direction as Aimee also searches the bars and halfway houses for her long-lost brother after her ghost sighting of him.

He vows to protect her until his last day on earth, but Aimee can run into trouble all her own, especially when he's gone overseas.

Now that they've found the perfect love and the perfect house to consider laying down roots and raising a family, will echoes from their past destroy the harmony of their romance? Andy always fights to win, but what if he loses?

Second Chance Reunion

A baby given up for adoption…
This second chance couple learns the true meaning of Family…

Like the Brotherhood…no one gets left behind.

As the daughter they gave up for adoption 12 years ago comes back into their lives, Damon and Martel plan their June wedding and Martel's move to San Diego.

But this new second chance has a rocky start with ST3's disappointing mission to Mexico Damon is held responsible for.

Martel struggles with giving up a job and house she loves at the beach in Florida for an unknown future in Coronado with her fiance's career hanging in the balance.

Do they have the grit to keep it tight when enemies keep springing up at every turn?

Love's Treasure

Love Blooms. Danger Looms.

One year has passed since Navy SEAL Ned Silver found the love of his life, his mermaid, Madison, in the beautiful waters of Florida's Gulf Coast. The two of them have embarked on two great adventures: a love affair worthy of Poseidon himself, and a thrilling underwater discovery of a long-lost Spanish Galleon possibly worth millions.

As they explore the depths of their relationship, frolicking in the warm waters littered with ghosts of dreams lost and shipwrecks abundant, dangerous secrets are revealed. Ned wonders if being a Navy SEAL really is his higher calling, or is he now being drawn to remain at Madison's side in Florida, giving up the Coronado lifestyle and his buddies on Team 3. Just as his father did some twenty plus years ago, Ned has found love and adventure to fill a lifetime, and a treasure more valuable than gold or silver, to protect...

If he can fight his way to the finish line.

Finding Home

A life of service to the SEAL Brotherhood and his country to protect the innocent. A life of honor finding and exposing victims of human trafficking—and finding love in the middle!

A year has passed after the dangerous adventures Navy SEAL Jason Kealoha, a Pacific Islander by birth and investigative reporter Kiley Worthington have endured while helping to shut down a human trafficking ring operating out of a stolen cruise ship.

They settle into the white sugar sand beaches of the Florida Gulf Coast, as the place their love was born, and as a refuge from her work in Portland and his Coronado SEAL Team 3. But going forward proves to be more difficult than they originally planned, when danger and characters from their past cast their shadows on their love and idyllic sun-drenched world.

They both have to choose what will be their most important priorities, and will be different for both of them.

This is Book 8, which wraps up the Sunset SEALs series. Readers might enjoy reading Escape to Sunset, which is Book 4, and introduces this couple.

AUTHOR'S NOTE

I always dedicate my SEAL Brotherhood books to the brave men and women who defend our shores and keep us safe. Without their sacrifice, and that of their families—because a warrior's fight always includes his or her family—I wouldn't have the freedom and opportunity to make a living writing these stories. They sometimes pay the ultimate price so we can debate, argue, go have coffee with friends, raise our children and see them have children of their own.

One of my favorite tributes to warriors resides on many memorials, including one I saw honoring the fallen of WWII on an island in the Pacific:

"When you go home
Tell them of us, and say
For your tomorrow,
We gave our today."

These are my stories created out of my own imagination. Anything that is inaccurately portrayed is either my mistake, or done intentionally to disguise something I might have overheard over a beer or in the corner of one of the hangouts along the Coronado Strand.

I support two main charities. Navy SEAL/UDT Museum operates in Ft. Pierce, Florida. Please learn about this wonderful museum, all run by active and former SEALs and their friends and families, and who rely on public support, not that of the U.S. Government. www.navysealmuseum.org

IF YOU GOT ANY CLOSER, YOU WOULD HAVE TO ENLIST

I also support Wounded Warriors, who tirelessly bring together the warrior as well as the family members who are just learning to deal with their soldier's condition and have nowhere to turn. It is a long path to becoming well, but I've seen first-hand what this organization does for its warriors and the families who love them. Please give what your heart tells you is right. If you cannot give, volunteer at one of the many service centers all over the United States. Get involved. Do something meaningful for someone who gave so much of themselves, to families who have paid the price for your freedom. You'll find a family there unlike any other on the planet. www.woundedwarriorproject.org

TABLE OF CONTENTS

THE HOUSE AT SUNSET BEACH

Sunset SEALs Book 5

SHARON HAMILTON

CHAPTER 1

Christmas Week 1980

HANK BORGES SCANNED the living room at the house he'd rented at Sunset Beach on the Florida Gulf Coast. It didn't feel like Christmas. The sun was too bright, the temperature too warm. No Christmas tree lit up the room. The balmy weather felt like an early morning in the middle of the summer in New York City.

More crumpled pieces of paper lay around him than acceptable pages of his manuscript stacked neatly in a box on his right, making him a human hamster standing in a nest of failure. It might've made him chuckle except for the fact that this sea of rejected words scattered all over the floor meant he was failing. Failing to get this book out on time.

Christmas didn't have anything to do with it.

Bah humbug.

As a successful science fiction author of some thirty widely acclaimed bestselling novels, he had a reputation and following much envied by the literary world. He was lucky enough to have fans and fans of fans—sons and daughters, grandson of fans—who had read him over his nearly twenty-year career, which had ignited his sophomore year in college as a struggling psychology major.

He'd taken an elective creative writing course and fell in love with his sensual teacher, Miss Cohn, a child Holocaust survivor whose shapely legs and beautiful lips were so oddly mismatched to the numbers tattooed into her forearm. Most of Hank's friends were going to sock hops and dance parties, learning the Twist and the Mashed Potatoes, screaming over Elvis Presley. Hank's passions lay elsewhere, between the pages of his favorite futuristic fantasy novels.

She couldn't have been more than ten years his senior. He almost stalked her, finding places he could run into her until she agreed to talk to him about his writing—without scaring her, of course. She was a beautiful, fragile creature, and Hank's heart was completely enchanted. The rest of the world disappeared when he thought about her.

"Aliens? You wish to write about aliens?" she'd said in her slight German accent. Her honey-brown hair drifted across her face as she lifted it back behind her ear. Her smile set his heart on fire.

Did she know?

"I love reading science fiction," he'd stammered.

He watched her brown eyes widen, was distracted with the crease at the right side of her upper lip. She waited for him to elaborate.

"What is most important I think is if *you* think I have any talent. I have this"—he hesitated to speak the words but did anyhow—"this *passion* for writing now. You've inspired me, Miss Cohn."

She actually blushed, her long dark lashes caressing the top of her cheeks as she looked down demurely. He'd always wondered how something so horrible could happen to such a delicate creature. He wondered how God could be so cruel. And was it wrong that he was attracted to her? Maybe he'd burn in hell for his crime of sitting in her presence, the strength of her womanhood and her resiliency infusing him with something more than admiration. It was a genuine, major first crush. His father would beat the crap out of him if he ever found out.

She was forbidden fruit. She was not only his teacher, but she was also Jewish, something his Italian Catholic father would never tolerate.

But when had Hank ever done what he was supposed to do? He always skirted the edge of something naughty. He never laid a hand on her that summer. But he loved her nonetheless, as she edited his first fledgling pages and made story suggestions that made him dive into lost weekends with his typewriter. She was a part of every book heroine he wrote after that. They all had brown eyes and big lips. They all had a deep crease at the side of those lips where her flesh mated in a half-smile.

His agent said it was a fluke. But fluke or no, Hank never went back to college. He never found out what became of her, and it filled him with regret.

Now there were two motion pictures based on his book series and three others optioned and in the works. He was contracted for at least two—and hopefully three—books for his publisher this year, but due to an editorial dust-up late last year, he'd canceled one publishing date and bought out his contract, costing him nearly thirty thousand dollars. Then he had rescheduled with a new imprint. That set him back a good two books, yet he was still behind for the new publisher. He told himself he was too good—too experienced—to be dealing with this, but here he was.

This is rookie madness. He gave himself a quick imaginary kick in the seat of the pants and shouted internally, "Get over it!"

But as he stared at the grinning face of his IBM Selectric typewriter, he identified what was happening. He had a full-blown case of writer's block. The phrase made his bowels churn.

Standing up to stretch, he walked to the sliding glass door, crunching on balls of wadded paper as he did so. This sweet little beach house was the refuge he rented every time he wrote a new book. This house at Sunset Beach had always been his lucky charm. It was sort of his secret weapon. Well, not a weapon exactly, his secret dose of vitamins. This little place at Sunset Beach overlooking the tiny waves and the sugary sand had always been inspirational to him. The words always seem to flow, and the stories just kept coming.

But this time was different. As if he had a defective muffler, the words choked like chunks of carbon caught in a filter, causing pressure and an invisible black cloud. He told himself he was too talented to have writer's block.

But that's exactly where he was. He was blocked, tethered to this royal blue typewriter. The contract he was in danger of blowing off would cost him a lot more than the first one he'd bought back. It was money his soon-to-be ex-wife had already spent on God knows what. He was backing out on his marital contract with her, too, and at an even greater cost. His demanding wife back in New York City, his children, and his adoring fans were waiting with bated breath for his new release for all sorts of reasons.

Sadly, it was beginning to look like he was going to fail again! And just like the grand schemes in his epic novels, his failure would sweep over his career like an epidemic. He feared that he would never be able to write a book again. That no one would want to read his novels. Maybe no one wanted to read him now. Maybe that's why it was so difficult for him to write.

"Christ! What the hell am I doing with my life?"

But not one of the menageries of characters in his head answered him. The sliding glass door fogged up and then cleared, revealing a beautiful, sunny day at the beach. Life was perfect for everyone else in the world, even the imaginary world, except him.

How he wished he could play in the sand like the people he watched through the window. They didn't seem to have a care in the world. Children and their family members parked under umbrellas and on lawn chairs. Groups of young men spread out on towels viewing groups of young women also spread out on towels. There was generous sharing of suntan lotion. Everyone had sunglasses. Some had floppy hats, which Hank would have to wear, because he hadn't been outside on the beach one day since he'd arrived a month ago.

Well, maybe it was time for him to venture outside, face the ocean, face the sand, face his would-be fans—as if they knew how famous he was. Maybe it was time to get baked like a lobster, wear Noxzema on his nose, and don a floppy hat. Or perhaps, like his main characters, Captain Sampson and his alcoholic blue vampire android second-in-command, he should down a half a bottle of scotch, hit the warp speed, and boomerang to another galaxy in his drunken stupor. Maybe then, as he ached in his sunburned state, he might be able to write again. It might take something like that for him to be able to perform. It would be like lighting himself on fire.

He shuddered. This was bad. Very bad indeed.

Hank's estranged wife was out shopping for townhouses in very expensive neighborhoods, anticipating a settlement that would put her up in style for the rest of her life. He didn't mind paying child support, as he figured was owed, and he appreciated that his wife agreed to have full custody of the girls so that he could visit on special holidays. After all, he was Hank Borges, the famous science fiction author. He felt uncomfortable being daddy and always had.

He loved his girls, but he didn't think he was very good for them, and according to his wife, he wasn't. It just seemed a lot easier to go along with the program she'd devised, albeit expensive. There were wars he could win and wars he never would win. This one was the latter. He'd take a chance that, when the girls became young adults and began to raise families of their own, they would appreciate him more.

Hank shed his pajamas and donned a T-shirt and a pair of swimming trunks, along with a pair of zoris. He put on a red beach hat that he had found at the grocery store one year, flattened and floppy. He'd packed it in his suitcase every year he came to Sunset Beach, and although he never used it, it did look well-worn just from the packing.

Like my writing career, he thought.

At the doorway, he stepped out as if he had complete snorkel gear, flippers, and a mouthpiece stuck in his piehole. He felt ridiculous in this get up, but he proceeded to the beach anyway.

He was headed for a little slice of sugary white sand beach between a group of young men and a little group of pretty twenty-something girls working in the sand on their knees. In their bikinis and ponytails, they were obviously college-age girls, down for a weekend or a week during the holidays, shedding their family and traditions, like Hank was.

It was a cliche just like so much of what he'd written this morning and tossed away, but the girls wore ice cream colors and all with different coloring. One girl was a brunette with an equally bronzed light coffee mocha complexion. One girl was red haired; another was a very light blonde. The young lady farthest away had mahogany-colored hair with pale peach skin and a long ponytail that extended all the way down her backside to her waist.

"Ladies," he said as he passed them.

They were constructing a sandcastle, all four of them pouring buckets of sandy water to smooth over surfaces. They had built turrets and windows and a ramp as well as an archway entrance that would all dissolve in the oncoming surf later on in the evening.

He removed his zoris and walked toward the ocean. The water was lukewarm, not freezing cold as it would have been up north, and not like how he remembered the water in Santa Cruz that disastrous summer when he brought the wife and girls. Maybe it was the close proximity to the three females in his little clan, but Santa Cruz didn't do anything for his psyche. The wind was too cold, and so was the water. The smell of cotton candy from the Boardwalk made him want to vomit, and remnants of it stuck to his pages, to the fingers, to the keys, and the bottoms of his shoes. Using the bathroom was problematic, so he frequently had to water the ice plant with his own urine. He decided right then and there that Florida would be the only place in the universe he'd be able to write. And he needed to be alone. Complete peace and quiet. Just him and Captain Sampson and Mega Blue.

Except for this time. For a whole month, he'd been unable to write, to even get more than ten pages typed up that he didn't toss as amateur attempts like one of his students.

The first week he was here, he felt this creeping sense of dread overtaking him, like the black plague infecting his fingers and his face and his brain, making him scramble his ideas and unable to put one word in front of the other without making any sense whatsoever. Everything he wrote was awful. It was third-grade level. It was worse than what he would tease his other author friends of reading in someone else's manuscript. Amateurish. Not at all like Hank Borges, the famous science fiction author, would do.

But the ocean didn't see this. The ocean treated him just like any other person who stood up to his white knees in the surf. The sun was right smack in the middle of his forehead, his sunglasses barely able to keep out the glare and the floppy hat not helping. He turned to the side so he wouldn't damage his eyes. Apparently, he would need a different pair. These he'd picked up at the beach store. And it was obvious they were only worth the dollar that he paid for them.

The four girls ran over into the surf, splashed water on each other, and laughed, getting the sand off their legs, their arms, their shoulders, and trying to see who could put the most water on their friends. Their total lack of common sense was thrilling to him. He liked watching them. They laughed freely, throwing their heads back and screaming when the water was tossed in their faces. They slipped, sitting in the water, kicking, splashing water with their toes, and doing everything that a three-year-old might do, except they were in their early twenties. And they were so attractive that Hank felt like asking them what their secret was—if they swallowed some elixir or if, because of their youth, they had discovered the source of happiness.

Was it that he was unhappy? Was he unhappy because his wife didn't want to have anything to do with him? His girls seemed more preoccupied with things at school than things Daddy would talk to them about, except when he brought them lavish gifts. Was it that he had turned that terrible four-oh-plus age and thought perhaps not only his writing career could be over but his desire and need for romance might be gone as well? Maybe his dick was all shriveled up from lack of use. His few further attempts at dating were shameful and embarrassing. He had a performance issue in the bedroom, something he'd never experienced before.

Just like my writing, he thought.

Hank felt the splash of water on his side and whipped around to object. The young woman in front of him gave him a wide smile, her pink lipstick an attractive distraction against her peachy skin. She had Latin coloring, as if she was Italian or Cuban or South American, perhaps Brazilian. His mind wandered to all kinds of exotic places as he stared at her dripping wet, her smile wide below sparkling deep brown eyes and her long ponytail wet and dripping. Crystalline drops of water hung from her ear lobes. She was breathing heavy. Her ample chest made it impossible for him not to come alive as a man even though he'd kind of pictured himself as an old lady with the floppy hat and the pink skin from his lack of sunshine. She clearly was ten times healthier than he was. Who was he to tell her not to splash him, he thought.

"I'm sorry. That was an accident."

He didn't believe a word she said, but he was charmed by her attitude anyway so decided to play along.

"It's quite all right, miss. I think I deserved it a bit."

She angled her head and looked at him, scrunching up her eyebrows and the top of her nose. "Why do you say that?"

"Because, my dear, I'm working on a book, and it's not happening. I'm frustrated, and you guys looked like you were having so much fun I decided maybe I'd indulge a little bit in your energies. So here I am, ready to receive the ocean and all your laughter and smiles and playful attitudes. I need something right now. This book is never going to get written unless I shift something."

"Then you should dunk. You definitely should dunk," said the young black woman. With her hands on her hips, her toe tapped on the wet sand and created a puddle beneath the ball. Her frown was mischievous but serious.

"Dunking's just the best," said the red head.

He was enjoying feeling ganged up on. It was exactly what he deserved. He'd been such a worm, a white, fleshy, flabby worm sitting in that living room trying to write a ridiculous space drama with a little bit of romance added in. The romance was definitely not happening in the book, but even the plot eluded him, and he had a structured list taped to the wall showing chapter by chapter what he should write. Problem was, it was like he was required to write in Russian or Spanish or something, because he had no clue how to structure his English sentences so that they made sense even to himself.

The brunette with the brownie-colored eyes stuck out her lower lip and gave him an empathetic look. "It's not really that bad, is it?"

"Oh, it is. It definitely is." He turned to face the ocean as if willing to take it all on. The entire Gulf of Mexico and all the sharks, the fish, the shells, everything—he'd take it all. He deserved an avalanche of saltwater. He should be dragged out to sea and drowned like a dead fish.

"I'm a mess." He chanced a quick glance to his right to see her looking at him with one eye squinted. "Don't you think?"

"I think you're right. You're one of those men that my mother said never to spend any time with. Not as a teacher, not as a camp counselor, and certainly not as a stranger on the beach. But I'm so sorry you're going through all this. I have no idea what you really mean. And like Estelle said, if you run out of options, I'd just jump in the water and get wet and then go right back up to the house and do whatever it is that you need to do. Put one finger in front of the other, and put together your work. That's what I would do anyway. And if that doesn't work, well, you could always slit your wrists."

It was shocking that she would even consider saying something like this to him, a complete stranger. What if he was teetering on the edge of suicide? It showed a total lack of understanding of the ways of the world. People were fragile. People in New York were especially fragile. And when they were running away to the Florida beach, well, they were definitely, looking for a change.

He watched her backside bounce deliciously along with the screams and giggles of the other three friends. They ran down the beach several houses and then up through a beach access ramp and he lost them into the parking lot or the sea of houses beyond. None of them even turned around to wave good-bye.

It had been a delightful encounter. Maybe she was right. He looked at the ocean, sat, and watched as the water came up to within a foot of his toes. He got up, scrambling to his feet, and walked into the water up to his knees. He sat down and inhaled, squealing to himself as the water covered his lower torso and then splashed up his chest. The right side of his face got wet, and it soaked his backside. He took one more wave, then stood up, and searched for his zoris, repositioned his hat, and ran toward his back patio. He grabbed a towel overhanging one of the chairs, dusted off, left his zoris and the towel outside to dry, opened the sliding glass door, and closed it behind him.

He walked around the table to stare at the blue IBM Selectric typewriter that grinned up at him, the keyboard forming gray teeth. He imagined hearing the beast of a machine chuckling at him, taunting him, daring him to just try to get a story out of it. He turned the little toggle switch to on, heard it buzz as the little ball in the center of the machine whirred to life, twisting itself quickly and then settling down. The tick, tick, tick of the machine continued. He sat gently in his wet trunks, dried his hands on his chest, and then started to write.

'That summer would change his life forever. Just one trip to the green waters and yellow beaches of Scion, the mythical healing beach on the fourth planet of the Recovery Galaxy. He knew that all the energy he received from the ocean would help restore his wounds and make the upcoming bat-

tle his to own. He was conqueror of the worlds of Scion. But he'd been ousted.

Now was his chance to come back with revenge, and this time, he'd win the war.'

Hank re-read his words and liked them. He'd found his mark, his place on the stage, and now he felt the words would flow.

Her name was Carmen, and Hank got so that if he didn't see her playing on the beach, the day was somehow less brilliant. The words were flowing from his fingertips, and he often rehearsed some of the chapters in his mind as he walked the beach. But he always looked for Carmen. He was planning to stay at the house on Sunset until the 1st of February, or until he finished the book. The girls were going back to college after New Year's.

The girls bought him a small Christmas tree and decorated it with shells.

As the days went by, Carmen had decided to not go back to school with her other three friends and remained at the house five doors up from his, taking a job at one of the local coffee shops. She'd explained to him that she needed a break from school, that her parents were divorcing and money was tight, so she wanted to stay away from the family, earn her own, let the beach heal her insides, and just give the family thing a rest. He felt sorry for her. But he was secretly glad to have the company. Talking to her was good for his daily word count.

"Going through a divorce is difficult. But in the long run, it's better to be with someone you love than to stay together for the sake of not saying that you failed at marriage. People don't like to get divorced, because it does feel like failure." His advice over coffee one day didn't seem to faze Carmen.

"Well, in their case, my brother and I felt they should get divorced a long time ago. Of course, they didn't see that."

"Give them time. Your parents are going to need you. It's always wonderful when your kids appreciate you, no matter what kinds of stupid mistakes you've made."

"So you've been divorced and made mistakes?"

"Does God brush his teeth?"

"Big mistakes or little mistakes?"

"Every kind of mistake there is to make. And then a few more. And I'm just entering the divorce phase of my life. I think it's a rite of passage or something."

"You don't seem like that kind of a man."

"I don't know what kind of man I am. But I'll be very poor if I don't finish this book."

He liked talking to her in the afternoons, and a couple of times, they talked long into the sunset. He never tired of watching the orange and purple sky, the way the sun melted into the horizon. Everyone along the beach came out to watch. Some dressed in their colorful bell bottoms and halter tops, others in their cutoffs. Still other people walked out in slacks and shirts, removing their lace up shoes and socks, not really prepared for the beach. Those were Miami Vice types. It took all kinds. But the beach was a leveler, some common ground where everybody performed their little drama in front of the sun, the sky, the wind, the birds, and everybody else. And the truth was, nobody really cared.

As the weeks went by eventually Hank asked Carmen if he could buy her dinner, and she turned him down. But she did agree to have lunch with him on one or two occasions. Finally, she relented and agreed to let him take her out to a fancy seafood restaurant. Hank told himself it wasn't a date because she was twenty years younger than he was. And he was fairly sure Carmen didn't view him as boyfriend-type material. He just liked the way he felt around her, and he liked the innocent way she looked up at him. She laughed at his jokes even though he'd told them thousands of times before. But unlike his former wife and his two daughters, she found him funny and fascinating and didn't neglect to tell him so often.

There came a time when the talk got slightly more serious. He was able to ask her about her family and about her growing up. And he was struck by how strong she was, being raised in a relatively poor family out West. Her parents had worked around and for a large farming outfit and had scraped together enough to send Carmen to college. But it weighed on her heavily, the cost of that college.

It happened one night when he wasn't paying attention. The sunset was especially beautiful, and after most of the people had left the beach, he and Carmen were still standing there looking at where the sun had been. The glow had long faded, and the shadows of early evening had covered everything, turning it a light gray, purple color. When the stars started to come out, he watched the angle of her neck and the way her eyes sparkled in the darkness, and it seemed so natural to reach over, take her in his arms, and kiss her. She didn't fight him, but she was nervous because he felt her shake. She didn't seem to know what to do with her hands, but he did.

One thing led to another, and he whispered in her ear that he'd like to take her to his house. Would she, please?

She said yes.

That night, they breached the chasm of their two worlds in one of the most beautiful lovemaking sessions he'd ever had. It left him drunk with lust, craving for more. He didn't even realize until later, when she told him, that he had been her first.

She let her house go and stayed with him until the 1st of February. They had always talked about the fact that Carmen would go back to California and he would return to New York. They talked about how maybe, someday, they'd come back to Sunset Beach and spend another week or two or a couple of months there together again, and they promised to stay in touch. He said he'd write her letters and took her address. She promised to answer his letters and to buy his new book when it came out.

But as the weeks went by, the book that Hank wrote ranked as a bestseller, and he became involved in the promotion, the book tours, the signings, and the publicity. He intended to write her, and then he caught himself thinking that perhaps she was better off without him. The age difference didn't matter in the bedroom. But he'd had a life, and he was going to have to deal with the mistakes of his past. He had daughters who were ten years younger than she was. He was a responsible father and businessman, and he belonged where he had grown up in New York City. Carmen had her whole life ahead of her, and Hank didn't want to take that life like he'd taken her virginity.

It wasn't until many years later that they met again.

And then, they were inseparable.

CHAPTER 2

Christmas Eve Day 2020
Wedding Day

ANDY CARR WOKE up in the guest bedroom, upstairs, because Aimee had invited several of her girlfriends to spend the night, and he knew what their chitchat would do to his sleep pattern.

Today was the wedding day. The date had been postponed twice, both times due to his deployment schedule. But he was now officially detached from SEAL Team 3, ready to report to his Team 4 group at Little Creek in five days. It didn't leave much time for a honeymoon, so like the wedding itself, they postponed that too.

Last night, he'd given Aimee a gentle peck on the cheek, knowing that chances for one last encounter before the big day, while they were both single, was out of the question. She was buried beneath the gifts and her girlfriends, all spread over their king-sized bed. He didn't begrudge their getting caught up. A couple of them had come a great distance to be there for her.

Eventually, the magpie voices stopped, and he fell blissfully asleep, the caressing sounds of the sea in the distance. It was still there in the morning.

But this morning, things were happening downstairs in the

kitchen. He'd been told the caterers were coming early. The big day was upon them.

He pushed open the master bedroom door and found their vacant bed, still scattered with opened presents and remnants of wrapping paper and bows. With a glance to their closet, he noticed Aimee's green running shoes were gone, and that's when he saw her leading a pack of ladies running down the beach. Even as they ran, they chattered, sparking and delighting everyone they passed by, as if the whole beach was celebrating too.

The house was half-painted on the inside. Although they'd tried to finish everything beforehand, only half the walls were covered in sheetrock. During the remodeling, they'd discovered more than the usual defects in plumbing and long-neglected air conditioning and electrical lines. Then it needed a new roof after the big storm earlier this fall, which took an unexpected chunk out of their savings since the roof had to be tied down and upgraded to hurricane standards. Every window, due to the storm ratings, cost three times what a normal window would cost elsewhere.

But it was their house, with creative touches and brightly colored furniture pieces they'd purchased second-hand and customized to their beach theme. Just about the only thing they didn't change was the color on the outside—*passionate Chinese red*, as Aimee called it. That had been close to the color when Aimee first spotted it a year ago.

The railing bordering the stairwell leading downstairs was made with pieces of ocean-worn branches and lumber, cut together in a hap-hazard design and then polyurethaned to a high polish.

Andy cinched up his pajama bottoms and skipped downstairs bare-chested and barefoot, greeting four catering staff unloading their supplies, catching a couple of the ladies off-guard. One even curtsied, as if he were some prince from a foreign land.

"We've got coffee for you, Mr. Carr," said one of them.

"Thank God." He squinted and saw her nametag. "Gwen. You're a lifesaver."

She blushed and handed him a mug, but without his half-and-half. Before he could object, someone else brought the half-gallon container over and poured easily a quarter cup into his coffee.

"Better. All's right with the world now."

"You nervous?" asked one of the cooks, beginning to arrange plastic containers filled with appetizers. A pair of men were carrying out the folded tent for the ceremony, along with some white chairs. The florist delivered three large sprays of loose, colorful flowers to be used for displays.

Andy took stock of how he felt. "Not really. I think I know what I'm getting into. We've been living together as much as we can over the past year. I'll be stationed in Little Creek now, so it will be better. Closer."

Those who looked up gave an appreciative smile, but no one stopped to really pay any attention to him. He brought his mug outside and walked toward the water to intercept Aimee and her girlfriends.

He found them approaching from the left. He remembered the day he first saw her running on the beach in her green Nikes, how he'd felt unsure if she'd allow him to be close, and how relieved he'd been when he discovered she was softening her hard stance against him. She got closer, and he studied her fresh face and her shapely form as he let her vision warm him all the way down to his toes. He was such a lucky man. He'd almost lost her, and now she would be his forever.

She was grinning at him as she attempted to run right past him, her friends in tow. He grabbed her and planted a morning kiss first on her neck and then squarely on her lips, spilling his coffee on her in the process. Aimee jumped back to avoid additional spillage but leaned into him and gave him another quick kiss.

"You're dangerous this morning, Mr. Carr."

"I'm a lethal warrior, a force for good. Just come closer and I'll show you, Mrs. Carr."

"Not quite. Soon, but not quite."

He quickly set his mug down in the sand and ran after her as she attempted to escape. He lifted her in his arms and ran into the surf, dropping her. At the last moment, she pulled on his drawstring, bringing him crashing down into the water, his waistband slipping to expose one of his butt cheeks. The ladies howled. Andy didn't care. Wet or dry or half-naked, he wasn't going to stop kissing her until he was good and ready to.

They made use of a long shower afterwards, in preparation for their wedding clothes, where they could be intimate in private. Her silky skin and lavender eyes begged him to be ardent yet gentle on this special day. Her cheeks were bright pink as she came for him, as her succulent lips coaxed him on and moaned her pleasure. It was the perfect way to begin the festivities.

THE DAY WAS perfect, and at sunset, they took their vows. As he kissed his new bride, his fingers slid into her hair, which had been done up with pins, flowers, and miniature combs. He messed with the intricate strands and decorations, sending a couple long ringlets down her back. He got a cross look, but the audience loved it.

He winked. "You should know better by now, sweetheart. I like your hair long and sexy," he whispered.

"Thank goodness we had all the pictures taken before the ceremony," she replied, taking his hand and leading him out to the audience, who gave them a standing ovation.

He went along with the obligatory smearing of frosting on her nose and upper lip. Then he lovingly kissed it off. He made her cry with his toast to the lovely lavender beauty who would share his life forever. Even Cory's presence couldn't dampen his day. He still didn't let him dance with Aimee, however.

His new LPO, David Peterson, came down for the occasion with two other SEALs from Team 4, a gesture Andy appreciated. He'd only had a brief workup with them and was still learning everyone's names. His former LPO, Kyle Lansdowne, had helped Andy get the job when Team 4 lost their most senior medic and was short for their next deployment.

S.O. Peterson was a much younger LPO than Kyle and had been promoted fast. Andy'd been told the heavy turnover on the team had resulted from some recent injuries and two difficult deployments in Afghanistan and Sudan, but their main arena was usually South America. It felt like the Navy was trying to find a place to stick Team 4, which was pure folly, of course. Kyle told him not to worry, that the Team was well-trained and would sync quickly around him. Andy had learned to trust Kyle's judgment on his placement and not to ask too many questions, but it was something he thought about as the days grew closer to their deployment.

"I'm looking for great things from you, Andy," Peterson began. "Heard you're prone to heroic acts, and that's saying a bit since Team 3 is legendary for doing some pretty crazy shit," he continued as he clasped Andy's hand enough to cause a little pain.

"Most of that happened before I came on board, but we had our share. I've certainly heard the stories, sir."

"I'm counting on you to give us Africa intel. Even humanitarian security can be deadly."

Andy's personal opinion was that the African arena was more deadly than the Middle East, and certainly South America in general with more warring factions and less control by the governments left penniless by strings of dictators who basically extracted all the country's wealth and foreign aid given to help stabilize the region. All it seemed to do was enable them to buy arms and hire mercenaries who were schooled in combating European and Africacorp troops.

Andy shook his other two teammates' hands as he answered his LPO carefully. "That's the thing. Learning who you can trust. Get that wrong, and it's all over."

Peterson gave Andy a quick stare, laced with a dash or two of panic. Andy felt his stomach rumble and then pushed it out of his consciousness, searching the sunset and hoping he'd have thousands more of them to come. Aimee was speaking animatedly over the laughter and happy conversation, oblivious to all this. That's exactly where he wanted her to stay.

"Got an older brother who served with a couple of your old guys, Andy. He sends his regards," said S.O. Dallas Grant, who was their explosives expert and had only eight fingers to prove it.

"You bet. He still in?"

Grant examined his toes. "There aren't too many one-armed sharpshooters on the Teams, Carr. But when I get home, he can still hunt and shoot better than I can with two arms."

The four men laughed nervously. Peterson nodded in Cory's direction. "You had your hands full there, Andy. Thanks for helping him get straight."

Andy shrugged. "We try not to leave anyone behind. We'll see. But I'd give him some space, if I were you, sir."

Peterson nodded, and then they all turned, blending into the wedding crowd. As Andy watched them disappear, he realized these guys were mere babies. He'd noticed even their senior guys, who didn't come today, were young as well. He hoped that didn't pose a problem.

Aimee's friend Shelley was all over him to dance, so he obliged her. With her silky blonde hair and good looks, this happy schoolteacher, a native of Florida, had once been his blind date when Cory was with Aimee. If Andy's bride had wanted a wedding party, Shelley would have made a stunning Maid of Honor. He knew she was still working on hooking up with a SEAL but didn't like how many times she asked for his help. He smiled anyway and gave her a thumbs-up, which brought on an honest blush that was kind of cute.

Thankfully, the music ended quickly, and she was called to the side. Andy went in search of his wife. He snuck up behind her, pulling her into his chest and placing a series of delicate kisses on her bare shoulder as she cooed and dropped her conversation with a couple of her friends.

Her lavender eyes took stock of his smiling face, telling him she loved the sight of him. It was something every man needed to see, especially an elite warrior. More than words or thank yous, they needed to loom large in their lady's life. He hoped he never stopped making her pulse drive up, making her blush with his words and deeds, that she always felt safe in his arms and at his side, even when he wasn't around to reassure her. He hoped he never stopped seeing the effect he had on her. He hoped he never stopped feeling her melt as he took her for his own, whether in the middle of a crowd or in their bedroom at night. He wanted all of her, forever.

"I never want this to end, Andy," she gushed.

"It will never end, sweetheart."

"I want to keep celebrating forever." She moved her arms up, resting on his shoulders as his hands gripped her waist.

"Just being with you is a celebration, Aimee. I'm the luckiest man alive. Truly. The luckiest. You make everything beautiful."

"It's so nice we could share the magic of this place with everyone—all our friends."

"Magic," he whispered as he kissed her. "Forever."

"The magic will bring you home to me," she answered with a sigh. "It will pull you back here, to the Gulf."

"No, you pull me back here. Because this is where you are."

"And I'll always be on the beach waiting for you or running or eating pancakes, until you come home again."

He pressed his forehead against hers and hoped he wasn't showing his apprehension for the new deployment and the new team. That warm glow where Aimee lived in his heart expanded inside his chest and eclipsed his worries.

Nothing would interfere with his perfect day.

CHAPTER 3

Christmas Day

AIMEE FINGERED THE ribbons on several of the packages that remained unopened from the sunset reception last night. The barefoot beach wedding had been perfect. It was ordered that no one wore shoes so dancing in the sand in her long wedding gown was a challenge, and her calves and thighs were paying the price for her fun. But long after the orange glow of the dying sun had disappeared, the glow in her heart remained.

All of a sudden, her eyes teared up, impeding her from being able to read the card from one of the gifts. Wiping her eyes, she decided some coffee might help. Her belly gurgled—the lack of sleep their lovemaking had caused was just another happy consequence of being so madly, hopelessly in love. She floated to the kitchen, turned water on the stove, scooped coffee into the French press, and waited for her pot to boil.

She heard Andy's footsteps on the stairs.

His sinfully god-like body was bare-chested. He wore his brand-new Christmas boxers she'd given him last night. She hoped she looked half as good as he did this morning.

"Morning, Mrs. Carr," he said, pinning her against the refrigerator and planting a long languid kiss on her caffeine-starved lips.

"Good morning yourself, Mr. Carr. I didn't expect you to be up and awake before noon, knowing how you like your beauty rest."

"The bed was empty and cold. Can't sleep when it's that way. You slipped out rather stealth, my dear. What is your secret mission?"

"Coffee." She poured the boiling water into the carafe while she foraged for half-and-half in the packed refrigerator. "I'm hoping someone comes over today. There's so much food here, we could feed everyone on the beach all day long."

"Not a bad idea," Andy said as he accepted the cream she poured into his favorite Navy SEAL mug. He poured coffee for both of them and followed her to the living room couch with a view of the sugary white sand beach and the new day beyond.

Aimee would go for a run later, but right now, it just felt good to be lazy on the couch with the fresh coffee and her handsome new husband. She wrapped herself tighter in her robe, tucked her legs under her, and sipped, watching Andy's Adam's apple move deliciously up and down as he swallowed his coffee.

He pointed to the table still covered with gifts. "Should I bring some of these over so we can finish opening them?"

Aimee yawned before she could say a thing, which caused her to start laughing when Andy noticed the lack of sleep was affecting her. She took another sip and then sighed. "I like just sitting here next to you right now. I'm beginning to wonder if this coffee is going to do its thing. What did we get, two, maybe three hours of sleep last night?"

Andy wiggled his eyebrows. "Less than that, I think. But who's counting?" He slipped his hand inside her robe and gently caressed her right breast. His coffee was precariously held in his other hand.

"Careful, Andy. You're deadly with the coffee spills…"

"I just get distracted." He shifted his weight closer to her and adjusted his crotch.

She took his mug, holding them both up in the air while Andy licked and fondled each of her breasts, which were bared for him. The familiar ache for him brought fine beads of perspiration to her upper lip while she watched his head reach lower as his tongue traveled to her belly button. When he came up for air, his eyes were deep navy blue. His lips begged to be kissed. He quickly removed the coffee impediment, slipped down his boxers, revealing how ready he was, and pressed her gently back onto the leather couch.

"Oh, Mrs. Carr, I could get used to this," he whispered in her ear as he slipped inside her. The leather couch groaned as he maneuvered his hips back and forth, his hand gently pressing on her rear, pushing her up into him deeper.

But Aimee couldn't think of anything to say except, "Yessss."

AFTER BREAKFAST, SHE started to go over the gifts again. She brought three over to the couch as Andy joined her. He took the card, opened it, and read, "From Jasper Kornblum, Esq." Andy said, holding up his card. "Hope you have a century of happiness here together."

"That's Carmen's attorney. I didn't see him at the reception, but he must have come."

She tore open the light silver wrapping paper covering a large white box.

"I talked to him a few minutes. He's a nice old guy. I usually don't like attorneys."

"Me neither. Necessary evil," she answered, pulling a crystal bowl out from tissue and bubble wrap inside the box. "This is gorgeous. Perfect fruit bowl. Waterford. Expensive." She held the cut crystal up to the light. Tiny shards of rainbows radiated all over the walls of the living room and above.

"Very nice. I didn't know you invited him," said Andy, taking the bowl from her fingers and placing it on the gift table.

"I sent one to Carmen Hernandez, his client. I didn't expect her to come or to send him. I just wanted her to know we were getting married here. This house meant so much to her, or so we were told."

"But this is from him, not her, right?" asked Andy.

"Well, I'd say she already gave us a gift. She agreed to sell us this house. Maybe we could visit her sometime."

Andy gathered up the wrapping paper and packing and then took a seat next to Aimee. "From the sounds of it, she's not doing too well. You'd better go while I'm overseas because he said she didn't have long."

"That's too bad. Of course. I'll do that. What else did he say?"

"He said he'd be calling on us soon, that he had some papers he wanted to discuss, when the time came. Kind of a cryptic answer, if you ask me."

"Oh geez. I hope nothing is wrong with the title."

"You got insurance, though, right?"

"I did."

"Well, we should be okay then. He didn't look like it was a problem, just wanted to pay his respects and to tell us he'd be in touch. I kind of like the guy."

Andy found it easy to like almost anybody, Aimee noted to herself. But he also was a good judge of character, and if there was some malicious intent, Andy would have picked up on it right away.

They continued opening up packages. Aimee was careful to add these to her list for thank-you notes.

A brief knock on the door startled them both. Andy ran over

and waved at the departing delivery truck driver who had just dropped a box on their doorstep.

"On Christmas Day?" Aimee was shocked. "Who is it from?"

Andy squinted at the label. "Della Fortunati. It's from Nashville." He held the box up and shrugged.

"Oh, she was my agent when I sold my parent's home there. How lovely. And for the record, I didn't invite her."

"Well, it's still nice. Here." He handed the preprinted delivery box to her and then retrieved a pair of scissors from the kitchen so she could get past all the plastic tape covering nearly every square inch of the box.

Aimee sliced through the seams and opened the flaps. Inside was a note.

Aimee,

The Andersons found these upstairs in the attic of your mother's home. Somehow, when you and I were cleaning everything out, we missed this. Sorry. But I took a brief look at it and knew these were things you'd want to have.

—Della

Beneath the note were several stacks of old pictures of their family. Aimee was fascinated to examine the ones when she and Logan were grade school age. Her parents looked so young then. There were a couple of her report cards, a Father's Day drawing she'd made, a Christmas ornament Logan had made, and some folded papers, including Aimee's birth certificate.

"This is really cool, Andy. I've never seen some of these."

"How nice they forwarded them on. Now I know you won't be bored when I'm gone. These will take you two days to go through, if I know you well enough."

Aimee was overjoyed and didn't know where to start looking

through everything. She was tickled that part of her family history, which had scattered after the death of her parents and the disappearance of her brother Logan, was chronicled here. Intact. Preserved just for her. Examining one photo of Logan in a basketball jersey, a tall, skinny kid with a big smile, she realized he didn't resemble the troubled young man who was now living on the streets, battling his addiction demons. She was grateful for the hand-up. This gave her more impetus to go looking for him again.

She handed the box to Andy, who was frowning as he placed it on the table. Aimee opened another package.

Over dinner, Andy had been quiet. Aimee thought perhaps the three-plus short days they had left was beginning to get to him, so she didn't want to put any attention on it and hoped it would just pass. But the longer it went on, no matter how many times she tried to engage Andy in light conversation, he was guarded. It wasn't something she was used to. She'd finally decided to bring it up, and then he began to speak.

"Aimee, we're always supposed to have this talk with our wives and parents before deployment. Just so you know, they had me write a letter to you, and if something happens, you'll get it."

"Andy, don't. Can't we wait a couple of days to talk about this?"

"I was going to. But these photographs you were sent got me thinking."

"Okay."

"We weren't married before when I went off, so I didn't prepare you well enough. That's on me. And you know life is fragile. We never know if we might step into something totally unforeseen, even with all the best planning and intel. So you know the drill. Something happens to me, you go on, and you try, if you can, to pick another Team guy. And they'll be coming too."

"Andy, I've been told this. Christy had a good talk with me last time. I really don't want to go into it right now."

"Just hear me out, and then you can be mad, if you want to. It's about what you do when I'm out of the US. You watch for odd things, people who get interested in you. Be careful of what you say to others, especially about me, or anything about what I do for a living."

"I know this."

"And you stick with the wives you know, even though they won't have husbands who are deployed. My new LPO is not much older than I am, and I haven't met his wife, but they are newly married. Help her out, if you can, because she's no Christy Lansdowne."

"I will. You'll leave contact information?"

"Yes, we have a sheet with the other names to stay in touch with, like a phone tree, but you have the old Team 3 guys and gals, so use them too."

"I will." Aimee could see there was still something else.

"I hesitated to bring this up, but I want you to hear me on this, Aimee." Andy took her hands in his and, across the table, squeezed them. "About looking for Logan. I'm going to ask you not to go doing that."

"Why?"

"Because it's dangerous. He might be dangerous. He might be hanging with dangerous people. You have to take extra precautions to be safe, okay?"

"But I'm not going to be searching through homeless shelters or walking the streets, Andy. I might want to check in with the clinic where he was staying, you know, talk to his old doctor."

"He said he'd contact you if he heard anything. But please, don't go anywhere or do anything on your own that could possibly put yourself in danger. And it's not because I don't think you're savvy and smart. I just won't be here to jump in if it was needed. You never know with these kinds of things." He squeezed her hands again. "Like I said earlier, life is fragile."

Her eyes watered as she began to see how concerned he was for her safety. The reality that they'd be separated for what could be several months began to dawn on her. She was missing him already. But she also didn't know how to reassure him that she'd be smart and she'd be safe.

"Andy, I love you for caring about my safety. I really do. But don't worry. I won't do anything stupid or anything that would put myself in any danger."

"You remember what the doctor said. He told you not to go looking for Logan. He even said it wasn't safe. That if you saw him, don't expect he'd be well enough to have interaction without you being in danger. Remember, honey?"

Aimee had fought the doctor's words that day just as she was fighting Andy's words now. But she didn't want him to worry, even though she knew nothing would ever stop her from looking for her brother. She didn't want Andy leaving with that concern. She didn't want to lie, either.

"I promise to be safe, Andy. Thank you for reminding me. I'll be smart. You'll see. No worries there."

"So you'll give me your word you won't go on a scavenger hunt for Logan?"

She hesitated just long enough to cause Andy to give a worried sigh.

"Aimee, I have to have your word. Especially no streaking out on your own."

"I promise. If the doctor calls me, I'll bring Shelley. If I run into Logan, which I don't think I will, but if I do, I won't try to approach him."

"Because you tried to before, remember?"

"Yes, I know. I won't do that again."

"Okay, sweetheart. Thank you. Please, do this for me."

"I will. I promise. You have to promise to come back to me all in one piece, okay?"

"Remember the magic. The magic will bring me home. You'll see."

CHAPTER 4

THE SEPARATION FROM Aimee was more difficult than Andy expected—for him. Aimee cried but held herself together when he denied her request to travel to Little Creek to see him off. He'd told her it was part of his concern that she not take long trips alone, at least until he was back in the States. He promised her the mission was expected to only take sixty days, which was a bit of a white lie, since it was more than possible it could extend another two to four months.

He figured that was the source of his upset and, like he always did on missions, got himself into game mode as he'd been trained. Lots of things happened at home when they were gone. This was just a little trip, a little lie, he told himself.

He'd started making a list of things he'd have to pick up at the Team building, since the Gulf Coast wasn't exactly the place he could obtain gear for the trip. He'd gotten his African immunizations some six months ago when he deployed with Team 3. He was relieved that he wouldn't have those sore arms as he bounced around in transport planes on the way over. On top of everything else, he was grateful for this little break.

But the days went by quickly, and the two of them did half of what they'd planned on doing before his leaving. Of course, that was partly his fault, since they did spend a lot of time in the bedroom, not that Aimee minded. He didn't think getting married would make him feel differently about having sex with her, but it did. This time it was serious. They were a forever couple, not just dating or even living together. He reveled in the celebration of their vows and their love every time he thought about that day. Just like the first day he met her in Cory's rented bungalow, he knew she'd be a part of his life in the future. Now he had all her future, as long as he did his job and came back safe.

And maybe that's why it was harder for him to leave. He had more to lose. He'd become a SEAL as a dumb single guy obsessed with equipment, gear, dangerous stuff, things he could fix, and things he could blow up. Having Aimee in his life eclipsed them all.

The long good-bye kiss was over. He stood nervously in front of her silently weeping form. "Hey, it's going to be okay. Just keep close to the wives," he whispered to the top of her head. "And get some sleep."

She chuckled into his chest. The tension was gone.

He placed his fingers over her lips so she wouldn't say good-bye, which was a rule for him, gave her a wink, and hopped into his truck for the twelve-hour drive up north that would take him all night long. As he backed out the driveway into the beach trail road, he reminded her, "I'll call you before I take off, sweetheart."

He waved and watched her wave in response through his rear-view mirror.

Gulf Boulevard was bathed in that familiar orange glow. He stopped several times to make way for groups of beachgoers who had crossed the road originally to stand at the surf's edge, some with cooler wagons, umbrellas, and folded beach chairs in tow.

This was the end of the year already! An unusually warm December when a third of the country was under a blanket of snow and howling winds. Andy thought it was fitting to leave Sunset

Beach at this time of day, with the warm sun and ocean breeze in his face.

The time of magic. He knew it would still be there when he returned.

ANDY ARRIVED AT base just as the sun was re-appearing. The first thing he noticed was the frigid temperature. Anywhere else but Florida, December would be one of the coldest months. He missed his Hawaiian trunks and flip flops already. He was going to pick up another heavy water-resistant jacket for the trip over, since sometimes the transports were drafty, and they usually flew at night. December was one of West Africa's warmer and wettest months.

He reported to the Team building, one of the first to arrive. Peterson greeted him with a warm handshake. "Happy to see you, Andy. I knew I didn't have to worry, but I wouldn't have blamed you if you went AWOL on me. New bride, beautiful beaches. Nice warm weather." He shook his head, suddenly at a loss for words.

"Nah, and miss all the fun in Africa? The bugs and snakes the size of a VW bus and that red clay that stalls anything within a hundred feet? No way, man."

Peterson took it well and slapped him on the back. "You're right. We were made for this shit, weren't we?"

"Hell yeah!" Andy noted the charts and maps laid out for his presentation later in the morning. "Looks like you're finishing your homework. I'll let you to it, then."

"I'm thinking you drove straight through. Am I right?" he asked Andy.

"Yessir. I did."

"So you go over there where we've got a couple cots and some blankets. The showers are in the corner as well if you want to freshen up. We're starting at nine hundred, so you got about two hours to yourself. Can't promise breakfast, but something's coming just before, if you're hungry. Or you can run over to Beck Hall for some grub."

Andy weighed the value of a shower against getting some rest, something to eat, or a new jacket. He decided he could make do without the breakfast and maybe bum a jacket off another Team Guy. "Thanks. I think I'll just do that."

He ambled over to the dark corner, tossed his bag on a folded pile of blankets, snatched a fresh tee shirt and shorts from his bag, collected his shave kit, and headed to the showers.

In five minute's time, he had completed his triple S routine and tucked himself between two scratchy brown blankets, finding the oversized cot a perfect fit. He pretended the blowers up in the roof rafters were ocean sounds and was hard asleep in seconds.

Mumbled conversation and a latrine flushing woke him up. In the shadows, he quickly donned his jeans and a long-sleeved flannel shirt, straightened his gear, and walked into the lighted room filled with about twenty Team Guys. He shook hands with Archie Nolan and Dallas Grant, who had accompanied his LPO to his wedding.

Dallas pointed to a tray of bagels and cream cheese, fresh fruit, and coffee nearby. "Grab some fixin's, if you're hungry."

As he made his way back to a seat next to Dallas and Archie, Peterson began his presentation. The lights dimmed, as a map of Nigeria and the surrounding area came into view on a large screen.

"This is going to be my first trip to West Africa, but some of you who have come from other teams, like Andy here, are more familiar with the geography and people. We've seen some major instability in both Nigeria and Benin over the past few years, and heavy violence erupted last year which required Uncle Sam's help, some of it seen and some unseen. And there are some bigger players on the horizon destabilizing the area."

Andy had heard it before. He'd seen first-hand the destruction left behind by local militia groups who had formed in the vacuum created by governments who were unable to exert peaceful control over the region. It's what made this part of the world so dangerous. New militia groups, along with leaders with grand plans of country domination and asset control, were popping up all the time, their loyalties sometimes murky.

"We've got a group of Western journalists and aid workers being held captive by a small army that crossed into Nigeria earlier this month, but they are aligned with a rebel leader in Benin who is launching opposition to the duly-elected President. We aren't interested in the politics. We don't care who these groups are, except that we have to find a way to get our American aid workers and two Dutch journalists out without creating an outright civil war."

Peterson didn't give anyone time to react. It didn't take many words to paint the picture of what a mess the factions had made of two countries, threatening to be a powder keg to draw in several others.

"Most of these militias are fighters from neighboring countries who are just trying to make a few bucks to send home to their families, anyway. Freelancers. So there's no real political agenda here and not a real religious or ethnic one, either, which is a shame. Benin is one of the oldest independent nations in Africa and had a flourishing democracy until recently."

Peterson scanned the room and then continued. "We think there are still six people, four males and two females, being held. We aren't sure about their physical condition, but reports say, so far, they are uninjured but no doubt suffering at the hands of the guards. No ransom demands are being made. They are a grass roots and poorly funded missionary group from the Pacific

Northwest, part of a megachurch ministry that had no business being there. But we don't always get the smart ones. They do require rescuing, and State has pushed us to act."

Andy was intrigued by the Dutch journalists, so he raised his hand.

"Andy?"

"Sir, the journalists. What publication are they from?"

"From what we've been able to make out, they were along for the publicity, recording all the good works the aid workers were doing with a camera crew. They brought a ton of Bibles to hand out, all sponsored by a huge church fellowship. It was to be for some documentary coming up. But we don't really know, Andy."

"You have a reason for asking?" Dallas Grant barked, even though he was sitting right next to Andy.

"Well, we uncovered elements of human smuggling in the Canaries and at Cape Verde on Team 3. I wasn't on all those missions, but we did nab a couple of Dutchmen who were involved in some heavy trafficking of young girls. They had a ring that extended well into Nigeria."

"I imagine State is looking into that," said Peterson. "If you have contacts, help me out, Andy. One of the issues here is that everyone works together for a bit, and then they're all for themselves, and they go to war and resurface somewhere else. It's a revolving door."

Andy completely agreed.

Peterson outlined some logistics of the trip over and indicated they'd be leaving at dusk so that they'd have the cover of darkness when they landed at a recently fortified base created in neighboring Niger.

When the meeting broke up, he asked Dallas Grant, who was about Andy's size, if he had an extra jacket he could borrow for the trip. Dallas led him over to his duty locker and pulled out a bag with a brand-new Trident Concept water-repellant jacket with all the zipper pockets and compartments a frog could ever want. Before he handed it to Andy, Dallas pulled the tags off.

"I can't take this. It's way too nice, and it's brand new."

"Sure you can. I haven't had time to customize it, and it will drive me crazy if I can't reach my gear quickly when we're in the field. You take it. I can get another one when I get back."

"I'm paying for it, though."

"If you insist," Dallas said, shrugging his shoulders.

"Thanks, man. I'm seriously stoked."

"Well, don't complain if the zippers are stiff or the angle is wrong for your hands. I gotta get my stash without thinking too much about it. You might want to shoot me later."

"Not a chance. I'll bring a needle and thread and work on it when we arrive if we have time."

"Okay by me, Dolly Madison. Say, if you're good to go, wanna grab a burger? It will be a long time before we'll see anything that fat and juicy again, trust me."

"McCoy's? Cory used to rave about it all the time!"

"Yup. All the bacon and avocados and horseradish you can stand. Of course, in Cory's case, we had to limit the beer and other stuff, but the two of us spent quite a lot of time getting our carb load back when he was here."

"Done deal. Say no more, but you better drive. I'm all turned around."

Before they left the building, Andy gave Peterson a couple of names.

"If you have time, Kyle can get you those numbers. You'll want to talk to them."

"I'm all over this. I've heard of this Sven guy. You deployed with him?"

"Former Norwegian FSK. You won't get a better guide. And,

last I checked, the Kelly and Sven were kind of an item, but you didn't hear it from me. Kelly has good instincts."

"Thanks. I'm calling him now."

Dallas inserted himself. "Excuse me, Peterson, want us to bring you back a burger?"

"Now why in the Hell would I turn that down? Thanks." He started to dig into his back pocket, and Dallas stopped him.

"We'll catch you when we get back."

Both Cory and Dallas had been right. Even though Andy knew he'd be comatose in an hour, the burger was everything he'd hoped for. He relished getting ketchup all over his chin, which he cleanly wiped off. Inside of five days, he'd have a full beard. The fries were hand cut and gigantic wedges smothered in barbeque and rock salt. They each washed it down with a draft, which wasn't exactly regulation, but Andy knew it would help him catch a little more shuteye before the boarding.

"How is Cory doing, anyhow? I tried to talk to him at the wedding, but he wasn't having it," posed Dallas. "And I didn't want to ask in front of our LPO."

"He's working things out, or says he is. I keep my eye on him a bit, especially around Aimee."

"Fuck yeah."

"He sort of avoids me too. But he told me he'd stopped drinking, so I'm hoping that's the case. Haven't seen him acting out much. He'll always be over the top. But you know how the Navy is about injuries, so I suspect he's headed for a drop. I hope not, though."

"Yeah. That would be a shame. Hellofa fun guy, though. Just would never trust him with my daughter—if I had one!"

Back at the team building, Dallas brought Peterson's burger and onion rings, and the two of them headed for the back corner. Andy checked his phone and didn't see a message from Aimee, so laid back and covered his eyes and forehead with the backside of his old Fresno State baseball cap as Dallas hunkered down on the cot adjacent after putting in his ear pods.

Several hours later, as the Team walked across the tarmac to the waiting transport, Andy pulled out his cell and dialed Aimee.

"Hey, you."

"Hey yourself," Andy said as he kept walking. "Can you hear me?"

"Not really well. Would you mind asking the pilot to turn off those engines I hear in the background?"

"Cute. I don't want to get on his bad side or he's liable to drop me over the Atlantic."

"Good thinking. So you're about to board?"

"Yup."

"And are you going to some place familiar?"

She was clever with the light interrogation.

"God no," he lied. He hoped this wasn't going to start becoming a habit. But security on their cell phones had been drilled into them, and Aimee should have known better. He told himself she'd asked for it. "Still, not a safe place. I'll tell you all about the beaches when I get back home."

"You're lying."

"I'm not telling." He loved their banter. "So, sweetheart, do me a favor and take off all your clothes right now."

"I'm almost naked. In my underwear."

"Well, definitely take off those panties, then. You don't need them. I want you sleeping butt naked in my bed tonight."

"Our bed, handsome."

"On second thought, maybe I could bribe this guy to fly me back to Florida. What do you say?"

"In your dreams, cowboy."

"I'd take a ride. A nice slow one, right about now."

"And we could take turns who's on top. I'm all rested. Frisky as Hell."

"I'm getting the message loud and clear. I'm not going to be able to sit down in a couple seconds."

"Awww. Poor baby. I have a cure for that."

"You do. You definitely do. So hold that thought. Stay safe. Keep the doors and windows locked. And when I get home, plan on not wearing a stitch for at least a couple of weeks, okay?"

"It's a deal. I can't wait. And let the magic pull you back, Andy. I need you here. Now and always."

"Same thing, sweetheart. Love you forever."

"Forever it is. I'll be waiting. Naked."

CHAPTER 5

THE NEXT MORNING, Aimee dressed and put on her running shoes and made it to the beach before her mood and her will changed. She knew the physical exercise would do her good, and she wasn't wrong.

It was a bit foggy this morning, unlike the several days prior, which were exceptionally clear and warm. The old fisherman was already out in his lawn chair, his windbreaker pulled tight around his body and the hood tied with a black cord framing his reddened face. He was working on a beer. His pole was secured in the plastic stake dug a foot deep in the semi-wet sand as he watched the tip for a bob or tug. The line going out into the surf was taut, waiting to snag something to go into his blue plastic bucket that was bigger than the bait he kept swimming there.

He was a regular, and Aimee suspected he ate fish for breakfast nearly every morning.

"Morning," she said as she passed him.

"God bless. You have a good day now," he answered.

Two ladies rode motorized fat tire bicycles and followed the shore in tandem, chattering away, waving to her, and then going right back to their animated conversation. Another group of young couples ran in a pod of a dozen or so at a pretty good clip. Aimee focused on the smooth stretch of beach ahead and didn't pay them much attention. She wasn't there to make friends and didn't need the distraction.

She was thinking about the pictures and other treasures in the box that had been left on Christmas Day. It was a snapshot into her parent's life when things were happy, before Logan disappeared. She had spent late into the night searching all their faces as if she could determine what had happened to change their family dynamic so. But she came away with nothing. The wide smiles and affectionate poses belied the future that would engulf them all in sorrow.

The mystery of her family was more than just Logan and his mental illness. There was something else there, she thought, as she flipped through the pictures. But she couldn't put her finger on it.

Her timer on her watch went off. She turned and headed back home.

After her shower, she made a smoothie and sat watching the ocean while she drank her breakfast and dried her hair with a towel. A silver flash of the crystal bowl caught her eye, and she retrieved the attorney's card and her cell phone, dialing.

Mr. Kornblum's secretary answered in a sweet voice and let Aimee know he wasn't expected in the office until this afternoon. She left her phone number for a return call.

Pulling out her beach-themed thank-you notes, she began composing a message to the older attorney, thanking him for the beautiful bowl, adding how the cutting in the crystal sides lit up the room in color and light.

She sat back and looked at her note.

"Kind of dumb," she murmured. "Too girly for him," she continued. She was going to rip it up and start again when she changed her mind and decided to embellish it instead.

We've always loved how the sun bounces off the walls of this house, spreading different colors, depending on the time of day. This lovely piece of crystal will be well used and goes so perfectly with the magic and drama we find here. We call it our magic.

She smiled. It was kind of corny, but she decided to send it anyway. Labeling the envelope with the information from the card, she pressed her heart stamp on the outside, sealed it, and placed it on the small table by the front door to mail.

Aimee kept her grandmother's old desk in the corner of her bedroom. She pulled down the front partition, revealing cubbies stuffed with little keepsakes and office supplies she'd gathered. She even had some old paperclips and labels that had to be licked, curled and yellowed in their original boxes. As a child, she remembered how fascinated she was to explore all these simple treasures and was often scolded for not leaving her grandmother's things alone.

This morning, she pulled out the brown envelope that held a copy of her title papers and a copy of the life estate that had been created for the previous owner. Somewhere, she'd written down the name of the complex where Mrs. Hernandez resided in Sarasota. She found it in the lower right corner of the letter from Mr. Kornblum, effectively accepting her verbal offer to purchase the house and outlining the terms of the sale.

Our Lady of Light.

She loved the name. Most things in Florida were named after palm tree, or ocean breezes with words like *paradise* sprinkled in the middle. But Our Lady of Light was distinctly different. The previous owner might have chosen it because of the name.

She searched her cell for a phone number and dialed it.

"May I speak to one of your residents, a Carmen Hernandez, please?"

"Miss Hernandez is in the critical care wing of our facility, and she does not take phone calls. I'm sorry. Are you a relative?"

"No, a family friend. What are visiting hours?"

"I'm afraid you'll have to get the family's permission to see her. Let me put you through to the other side."

Without asking for approval, Aimee was placed on hold. A male attendant answered the phone next.

"Can I help you?"

"I'm wanting to visit Mrs. Carmen Hernandez. How do I make an appointment?" she asked.

"Are you family?"

"Family friend. She knows me through correspondence."

"I'm afraid you'll need family permission to see her. None of our patients here are allowed visitors unless with a family member."

"I see." Aimee knew she wouldn't get a satisfactory answer, but she had to ask the question anyway. "How is she doing?"

"We can't give that information out."

"But is she getting stronger, better, or—"

"Generally, this facility is end of life care. It's mostly hospice patients here. Miss Hernandez is in that category, which is all I can tell you. She has good days and bad days—I think you can read between the lines."

"Yes, thank you."

She inhaled to avoid the flood of tears that were threatening. She was overwhelmed with sadness that she hadn't thought to visit the woman before now. Perhaps it was too late. Aimee was filled with regret.

She picked up the life estate document, bound in a dark brown book cover. She skimmed over the boiler plate until she came to more of the meat of the document.

I, Hank Borges, bequeath my sole separate property to Miss

*Carmen Hernandez for as long as she shall live, along with a stipend of...*It was several thousand dollars a month he had provided for her. As Aimee read on, she discovered the home was delivered to her free and clear, without a mortgage, and that a maintenance fund was set up for care of the landscaping and for repairs as required. That struck Aimee as odd, since the house had fallen into such disrepair when she found it a year ago.

What happened? Who was Hank Borges? The name was slightly familiar to Aimee, but she couldn't pinpoint why.

She got out her laptop and looked up Hank Borges, resident of Sunset Beach but formerly from Manhattan. His biography was short. His obituary from 1998 was long.

Popular science fiction author of some eighty novels made famous by such motion pictures as the Red Planet and The Soul of The Moon, she read.

There was a picture taken of him on a sunny day, the wind blowing through his nearly white hair, with the unmistakable backdrop of a white sand beach and ocean. Aimee wondered if it was taken here, at this very house, but the detail was slightly fuzzy and hard to make out.

So Hank Borges perhaps had lived here at one time too. Were they married? If so, why did the attendant call her Miss Hernandez?

Aimee read further about his life in New York and a notation that he'd become even more prolific when he retired and moved to the Florida Gulf Coast, which had always been his writing inspiration. He had doubled his production of books and was in the middle of finishing a novel on the day of his death at seventy-two.

But there wasn't any mention of a Carmen Hernandez or a wife or companion. And maybe, she thought, that was what he wanted. Perhaps that was their silent arrangement.

Now Aimee was intrigued and even more upset with herself for perhaps missing the chance to meet this mystery woman, who obviously meant something to the famous author.

She knew Mr. Kornblum would have the answers she sought.

Aimee took the sheets off the bed and ran several loads of laundry while she toyed with the idea of driving down to Sarasota to see if she could somehow sneak in an audience with the elderly lady who used to own this home.

She was vacuuming and nearly didn't hear her phone ring in time. Jasper Kornblum had returned her call.

"I'm glad you like the bowl. My wife is much better at picking out wedding gifts, so I'm afraid I can't take any credit for it. She has nice tastes."

"Oh, I'm sorry I missed her as well."

"No, no. I came alone. I just was curious to see what you'd done with the place so I could report to Carmen. We didn't want to impose."

"You totally could have brought her. I wish you had. We had plenty, as I'm sure you saw."

"It was a perfect day for the perfect couple." He cleared his throat. "So what can I do for you?"

"Andy has just left for overseas. But I was wondering if I could arrange a meeting with Mrs. Hernandez—"

"*Miss* Hernandez. She never married."

"Oh. Well, Andy said you told him she's not doing very well. I'm afraid I neglected to reach out before, but I wanted to thank her for letting us buy the house. I took the liberty of calling Our Lady of Light, and they've told me I have to be family. Can you arrange a meeting?"

"She's not going to recover, Aimee. Between you and me, her demise could happen any day now."

"Then all the more reason to try to see her sooner. Can you authorize this?"

"I can, but I won't unless her doctor says it wouldn't be too risky. She's very frail. Everything is being done to keep her comfortable, but she sleeps most of the day. Let me see if I can reach him, and then I'll let you know. What's your schedule like?"

"I'm open. My primary job is to do some painting and coordinate workmen we've scheduled. I could be available anytime, really."

"Okay, little lady. Let me see what I can arrange. I'm sure she'd want to meet you. But, unfortunately, she might not even know you're there. I saw her two weeks ago and was surprised how far down she had gone. But she's a fighter. I'll ring you back as soon as I find out, okay?"

"Thank you, Mr. Kornblum. You have a nice day."

"You as well, Aimee."

After he hung up, Aimee was disappointed she hadn't asked about Hank Borges. She made a mental note to do so the next conversation.

On the internet, she looked up Mr. Borges' books and found most of them out of print, but several copies were available used. She ordered three and saw that they'd be arriving in just two days.

Just before dinner she received the call she'd been hoping for. Jasper Kornblum agreed to pick her up in the morning and drive her himself to Sarasota where they might be able to visit Miss Hernandez. He cautioned her about getting too excited for much conversation.

Aimee knew it was going to be hard getting herself to sleep tonight. She couldn't wait for her new adventure.

But before she drifted off, she said a little prayer for Andy on the other side of the world somewhere. Her evenings meant his day was just beginning.

She sent a little magic his way.

CHAPTER 6

THE LANDING WAS far from perfect, and the many potholes in the hastily created landing strip set out in the middle of rural Niger meant the entire team sighed in relief when at last the engines were cut and their forward bumpy momentum stopped.

Peterson stood at the doorway, which had to be unsecured. He banged on the steel frame several times, and then Andy heard the distinctive whir and buzz-buzz of the electric drill removing all the rivets securing the door.

The blast of hot hair and the smell of swamp overwhelmed them all, even though it was still before sunrise. Several coughed. Andy pulled his bandana up over his nose and mouth, turned his baseball cap backwards, and unzipped his jacket. In a matter of minutes, he'd be roasting like a hot dog in a bun, but now wasn't the time to strip down and perhaps overlook some of his gear.

Peterson had jumped from the plane nearly four feet and sorely complained.

"Holy shit storm assignment from Hell."

Their LPO's words set Andy's nerves on edge. He was used to Kyle's swearing on missions but not first jump out of the gate. He read no humor in the faces of all the men on the team who waited their turn to exit the transport. An uneasy lull fell over the crowd.

Several voices in an African dialect Andy didn't recognize

chattered orders and recommendations as a stairway was dragged to the opening for everyone else to use. It had four wheels attached to it, but one of them was missing, so the action required four strong men to position.

Andy was familiar with the sunglass-encased stern faces dressed in khaki fatigues that many of the African and Coalition-trained forces wore. Smiles were very expensive and usually not trusted. He got the vibe right away that pissing contests were to be avoided, if they valued their life. It was never lost on him that he was a guest in someone else's country, and the presence of a SEAL platoon wasn't always good news for the locals. The alliances were complicated and far too complex for him to understand, and as Peterson said, this wasn't about politics. As long as the rental fees for the privilege of conducting some kind of operation here were paid, all was well. Everything had a price. Even free wasn't.

And all of it was totally out of their control. They had to trust the system that sometimes got it horribly wrong. This one had been feeling this way to Andy since the moment they left the base in Virginia.

They heard a diesel bus drone in the distance as two yellowing headlights moved toward them. Another four-door Russian-made Humvee-type vehicle followed behind. As the rear taillights on the bus flashed, Andy could see that the other vehicle was missing a door. It seemed anything that came in fours was missing something. A wheel here, a door there. As long as it wasn't too important, they'd have to live with things like this. He guessed some local leader had needed that door more than the militia group did.

Peterson and two of the other Team guys were instructed to go with the driver in the truck, while everyone else piled into the bus. Andy was pleasantly surprised at the cleanliness of the inside, with the exception of a rear bathroom, again without a door, which seemed to be a common theme, and stunk like a dead animal. Everyone avoided the rear as much as possible. Windows were opened, those that worked, anyhow. The men kept their masks on not for sanitation but to avoid the noxious smell.

Andy took a seat by himself and Dallas took the one behind him, each resting their packs beside them. Dallas managed to finally get the window between them open to a four-inch crack as the diesel engine kicked in, and a cloud of black smoke was visible out the rear window as they pulled away. They watched as their LPO struck out ahead, disappearing in the low-lying bushes on a well-worn trail that could almost be called a road, just as their transport quickly turned the opposite direction and took off into the night sky.

Their leader's truck was probably easier to see through the red clay dust billowing behind them because of the brake lights. The road was relatively smooth and straight, which alleviated one of Andy's fears of maneuverability. The driver ground the gears frequently and didn't appear to be very experienced overcorrecting to avoid potholes and occasionally a long-dead animal.

He glanced at Dallas, checking his phone. The screen illuminated his face and beard that was new since the wedding. Andy's would be matching him in about as much time.

"Get anything?" he asked.

"Nothing I trust." Dallas flipped off the phone. "Probably shouldn't have fired it up, but I just wanted to know how isolated we are," he added.

"Wanna take turns with trying to catch few more Z's?" Andy asked him.

"No, you go ahead. I'm good. My nerves are fried. Every trip to Africa, it gets worse. I hate this place, truth be told," he whispered.

Andy nodded his complete understanding. When he'd agreed to sign on to Team 4, he had hoped that Africa wasn't going to be one of the destinations. "Crude and bumpy as it is, way better to come this way than do a drop. The way this place changes almost daily, no telling where it's safe, even if you embed with locals. I'm sure I don't have to tell you that, Dallas."

"No, you're right. That's how we lost our medic in Venezuela on that evacuation. The whole thing went to shit after that."

"Was Cory with you guys then?"

"Nope, that was the time before. That one didn't turn out so well, either." Dallas leaned over the seat and was very careful with his whisper, coming close enough to Andy's ear he could feel his Teammate's hot breath. "I'm beginning to think #4 is my unlucky number. At least for this crew, it is. Half this group is trying to transfer out."

Andy's bowels nearly gave way. This was not what he wanted to hear. He'd heard talk about how some Teams just didn't gel well. Often times a change in leadership was required before anyone developed the confidence in each other they required to be able to work as one cohesive unit. He wondered if the young LPO was that impediment.

But now wasn't the time to be second-guessing his new leader, either.

"I think Peterson's okay, Dallas. Doesn't help when the team is being shoved all over the globe."

"He shouldn't have told the guys it was his first trip."

"We aren't stupid. Everyone would have figured it out. I think he's okay. Besides, you're scaring me, and now I won't be able to sleep, either. So knock it off."

"Yeah, I do that sometimes. Apologies. We just need some cohesive muscle memory and then we'll be fine. But if the leader doesn't lead, that's how mistakes happen when other people try to step up to fill the void. I think he's a nice enough guy, plenty smart, and a critical thinker. But he lacks a little confidence, and that gets worn like a badge on his shirt for all to see."

"Better than some of those junior officers with all the schooling and no practical tactical training in the field. And if they're not smart enough to know that, even though they're ranked, they better listen to their Chief first or ask for suggestions, the whole Team loses otherwise."

"I agree with you there."

Andy was glad he'd recommended Sven and Kelly to Peterson. Now he was thinking he should have recommended a couple more.

As the pink glow of sunrise began to develop, the green plain ushered in some beautiful scenery, especially when they passed by small lakes that peppered the area. They encountered gazelles and several massive flocks of pelican-like birds that did more of a waterski landing on those bodies of water, wings flapping and causing quite a splash. Large white clouds rose in the pinkish-blue sky of morning.

At last, they approached several villages in a row, as the road became wider and more littered with donkey-driven carts or small lorries. Occasionally, a covered troop transport passed them. Every one of the men who were awake studied those very carefully, and it appeared all of them were empty—a good sign there weren't troop movements on the rise.

Traffic increased to a steady stream of two-way passage until they came to a fairly large city. None of the buildings were over three stories tall, mostly patched with layers of corrugated metal and cement material. The ground floors of most buildings were open-air shops with vendors like one giant flea market. Now they saw scooters passing them, one with a young boy clutching a small goat behind an older man, perhaps his father.

Brightly painted schools with no doors or windows were buzzing with children beginning to congregate on the grounds. Young boys kicked around a rag-covered, makeshift soccer ball. Several women and girls appeared in headdress, reminding Andy that half the population was Muslim.

Peterson had said they wouldn't be stopping along the way so they could get across the border to Benin quickly and to their proposed compound without interference and without attracting too much notice. But Andy knew hundreds of pairs of eyes had seen them—they all knew the Americans were here, because the team certainly wasn't Chinese, and Russians used their own drivers. But Andy agreed., It was a good idea to get to their base as soon as they could.

He rifled through his pack and dug out a granola bar and a bottle of water, letting the bouncing bus lull him into being a tourist for a bit more. His stomach liked the nourishment. His eyes found the people and the colorful images fascinating.

They arrived at a checkpoint guarding the border. It was well-fortified on both sides, so at each gate, young men no older than high school age in the US walked up and down the length of the bus and the truck ahead of them with Peterson, holding semi-automatic rifles and peering into the windows as they grilled the driver with questions. He showed a sheaf of papers, which were carefully checked.

Andy made sure he didn't make eye contact with any of the border patrol. Random hot spots were common, but the fact that there were twenty of them made for more interesting scrutiny and was less likely to cause a fight. Again, he realized they'd been seen. Eyes observed and tongues would be wagging.

As they made it through the Benin checkpoint, he was struck by the number of uniformed children walking to school. The couple of towns they passed through looked slightly more prosperous. Signs in French were everywhere, unlike Niger. There were more shops and more little open-air eating places where barbeque was made over firepits made of oil barrels or rings of stone. Women and young girls wrapped themselves in colorful fabric. Several taller buildings had been built in the downtown area of one of the towns. The largest structure with bars on the outside, Andy took for a local jail.

Just outside of the town of Kandi they entered a complex of small cottages and one large central building looking like an old school dormitory, just past a rural cemetery on a slight upslope. Outside, the perimeter was fenced in concrete and boulders and a gate made of corrugated metal, which was manually opened when they approached.

"Home sweet home, I guess," mumbled Dallas.

It had all the elements Andy was hoping for. The windows had glass. The top of the dorm building was littered with several air conditioners, past and present victims of the African heat. Three of them looked like recent installations, so he realized they'd have relief of some sort. The perimeter had a defensible wall. But better still was the fact that the complex was atop a slight swale, and anyone's approach, if by road anyway, could be easily followed.

As a base camp, Andy had to admit it was one of the best he'd seen. For his fourth deployment to this part of the world, it could have been a lot worse.

The men were housed in the common area, on cots. Private rooms with doors were relegated to their equipment and other things that needed to be guarded twenty-four hours a day on rotation. Andy was happy with this. Afterall, he was more concerned about losing their electronics and ammunition than privacy. As long as they could quietly set up a triage room as Peterson had instructed, where some of his medical supplies could be held in locked storage closets, they had a fighting chance of survival even if the worst were to happen.

It was always good to look out for the worst and not to get too complacent or bored when it didn't show up. Because that's when it always did. Nothing could shoot a .50 Cal hole in a Team's confidence faster than not being prepared for the totally unpreparable.

He slept in their new medical unit while Dallas watched the doorway from their bunks. The last thing Andy thought about before he dozed off was how he now felt like that one big hot dog waiting to be covered in chili, onions, and melted cheese. He could feel the bush talking back to him. Somewhere a pod of monkeys howled, and a jungle dog answered without fear.

CHAPTER 7

JASPER KORNBLUM KNOCKED on Aimee's front door right at the strike of nine o'clock, just as he'd promised. He was dressed in a white suit with a bolero tie. With his white hair, moustache, and well-trimmed beard, he resembled a slim and well-built Colonel Sanders. His steel blue eyes bored into her and caused a slight involuntary shiver.

"Jasper Kornblum, at your service, Mrs. Carr." His hand shot out, bridging the gap between them.

"Nice to meet you. Come in. I'm nearly ready. Can I offer you coffee?" Aimee said as she stepped aside and widened the doorway opening.

Mr. Kornblum appeared to be in his sixties, with sharp eyes that soaked in every detail of their living room. "No coffee please, but I would take a glass of water, if I can trouble you for it." He was still scanning the artwork on the walls and the detail on their unconventional stairway railing as he spoke.

Aimee fetched him a juice glass of filtered water from the counter and retreated to the bedroom to finish fixing her hair. She wore it twisted up in a swirled braid, something she hoped would keep her cooler for the hour-long drive to Sarasota.

She grabbed her shoulder bag and joined him in the living room. He pointed to the beach.

"That was the perfect spot for a wedding, and what a beautiful evening for it. Christmas Eve."

The comment warmed Aimee's heart. "Thank you. We thought so. Wanted to make it memorable for everyone."

"I regret not meeting your parents."

That familiar tug at her heart appeared and just as suddenly obeyed her internal command to disappear. "They're both gone. Would have been hard to meet them." She said it with a straight face, and it caused the older attorney to furrow his brow.

"I'm sorry. I thought that was Andy's parents."

"No, they were there." She hoisted her shoulder bag and took the water glass from Mr. Kornblum. "Shall we go?"

As they sped down the two-lane boulevard toward the freeway entrance, she felt like softening her earlier frostiness at the mention of her deceased parents.

"I want to thank you again for the beautiful bowl, Mr. Kornblum. Really a lovely cut crystal pattern. Sends rainbows all over the room during the day."

"Good light. That house always had good light."

"So you saw it before when Mrs. Hernandez lived there?"

"Miss Hernandez, dear. She never married."

"I remember now… But didn't she live there with someone who left it for her as a life estate?"

"That's true. But they never married."

"Who was he?"

"Hank Borges. Famous science fiction writer. My understanding is that they were both very happy there, eventually. I only met him once."

"Is he any good?" she asked. "I've ordered a couple of his old paperbacks."

"That's all you can find now—old, used paperbacks. I understand they are a collector's item."

"Then I must have gotten a good deal. I think I paid thirty cents for one of them."

Mr. Kornblum chuckled. "Well, I've been misinformed. I stand corrected, Mrs. Carr."

"You can call me Aimee, please."

"And you can call me Jasper."

That made her wrinkle her nose.

"Or Mr. Kornblum, whatever makes you feel comfortable."

"It's just that—" Aimee stopped before could think how to finish her sentence.

"I'm so old? That what you mean? I'm probably older than your father. Or your father was."

That was it exactly, she mentally confirmed. "I try to be respectful of my elders. Just the way I was raised, Mr. Kornblum."

"I don't mind, child."

Several miles of freeway passed before the attorney began another conversation. "I've told you that Carmen is not well at all. They are telling me she may not even be conscious for our meeting. I'm afraid she's in her final days, so I don't want you to be shocked, Aimee."

"I understand." Thoughts of her mother's slow, painful passing and the guilt she felt when she finally died haunted her. She was more familiar with the process than she'd ever wanted to be. "It's my fault I didn't think to reach out to her before. It's what I should have done."

"She was used to not having anyone around her. Not like there was a big family to be there during this stay. Carmen was a very private person, from what others have told me. And Hank wanted to make sure the estate protected her after he was gone. You see, he had a family, while she did not. He was afraid the family would try to claim the house as their inheritance, even though it was set out in his will as going to Miss Hernandez."

"An ex-wife, then?"

"Daughters. Two still alive. The former Mrs. Borges is gone."

"And should I be ready for a visit sometime?"

"I'd say not. That's been so long ago, and with their mother gone, the girls don't have any interest in fighting her old battles." He squeezed his steering wheel tightly and added, "Or so I've been told. But there is the issue of some of Hank's book titles being left to Carmen and not the family. But the bulk of his estate went to the family."

"So how long did they live there?"

"You mean together in the house at Sunset?"

"Yes."

"About ten years. Until Hank's death."

Aimee wanted to ask but felt it was bad manners. Mr. Kornblum saved her the question.

"He died in a hospital, in case you were curious," he whispered. "It was very quick, a stroke." He followed it up with a kind smile and then went back to focusing on the road.

It felt like he was pausing, trying to elicit questions from her, and that made her quiet all of a sudden. Part of the excitement of the trip had left her, and now she experienced some foreboding sadness.

"I'm glad you asked to see her. I was going to make an appointment to discuss some things about Carmen's estate anyway. We can do that now, if you like."

"What things?" Aimee asked.

"Miss Hernandez is a very wealthy woman. And she's going to be leaving a large portion of her assets to you, Aimee."

"And my husband."

"Yes, because you are married. But you found the house. You fell in love with it. You made the offer and purchased it before your marriage. She's going to return the money you paid for it to you and then some."

"What?"

"You're going to inherit a significant fortune, Aimee. She has no one else to leave it to. There are some designated charities, of course, but the bulk of it will go to you."

"I'm flabbergasted." Aimee felt her hands shake. Her heart was pounding in her chest. She wished Andy was with her to hear all the news. "She doesn't even know me. We've never met, right?"

"I believe you're right, but I can't say for sure. She was very private, as I've said before. But she read a lot. Followed events. Even when she was moved to the hospital, she stayed current on things. She knew I was going to the wedding, and she had wanted to hear all about it."

Aimee wondered why the woman had developed such an interest in her.

"She also wrote novels under a pen name. She wrote romance from that beach house and did quite well. Maybe even eclipsed Hank's work."

"Really? What under what name?"

"Callie Harmon."

"Oh my gosh! I have read several of her novels. She wrote some very steamy stuff. I stumbled upon them when I first moved to Florida because it was all about the area. I love her books."

"Well, that's a good thing." When Aimee didn't answer, he added, "She's left her entire literary works rights to you, my dear."

"No way."

"I have the paperwork with me for you to review, if you like. I'm not allowed to give you the entire contents of the will, of course, but just wanted you to be prepared. And I thought you should know when you meet her."

Aimee was lost in thought. What sort of thing would she say to Miss Hernandez now that she knew all this information? Did this woman do some sort of study on her? Or why would she leave her estate to a complete stranger?

"You're asking yourself why," he said with a wry smile.

"Exactly. I've got to hand it to you. You're quite a mind reader. Do you have an answer for me?"

"Only a guess."

"Which is?"

"I think she wanted to leave her money to someone who loved the house as much as she did. Someone who wouldn't want to tear it down and build a McMansion on it, like so many others do in the area. That's not a deed restriction when she sold you the property, but it is in the will. Even if the house gets destroyed in a hurricane or other disaster, it has to be rebuilt to the original floorplan and footprint as a promise and condition of accepting the money."

Aimee was thinking about the magic that seemed to live in the house. Some of her friends had called her crazy, but now she understood her intuition had put her on the right track.

"She didn't want to spoil the magic. There is magic there," she whispered.

"And so you understand."

But do I? Do I really understand?

THE ASSISTED LIVING section of the Our Lady of Light residences did feel like a hospital. Aimee felt a slight shortness of breath, and in her gasping, she didn't finish sentences and lost her train of thought. So much of her experience walking into this place reminded her of those sad days she came to be by her mother's side as she lay dying. It was the reason she avoided hospitals altogether.

Though the company running the facility tried very hard, with the use of pastel colors and soft lighting inside the rooms, it still had a familiar hospital odor that made Aimee begin to clench her teeth and squeeze her palms into fists. They were greeted by a male attendant who showed them to Carmen Hernandez' room.

She was dressed in a brightly colored, flowered housecoat. Her hair was combed, and her makeup was done. Even her nails were freshly painted bright red. Aimee had expected a much older woman, someone with gaunt cheeks sunken in, lips a light purple, with a face emerging from a nest of gray hair.

This woman before her had graying temples and plenty of streaks of light color, but her haircut was recent, and she looked so healthy, Aimee wondered if there hadn't been some mistake. She was fully conscious and gave a wide smile to the two of them as they entered the room.

"There you are, dear!" Carmen said, clasping her hands together. That's when Aimee saw the IV attached to the back of her right hand, connected to a hanging bag of clear liquid next to the bed.

"You look wonderful today. I'm impressed," said Mr. Kornblum. "Whatever they're doing, you look twenty years younger, Carmen."

"Oh, nonsense. A little rouge and lipstick, some foundation, and anyone can look more youthful. It's a trick, Jasper. You know it's a trick."

"But they said—" he began to object.

"*They* don't have anything to do with it. I have good days and bad days. Today is a good day. A special day. Aimee has come to see me at last."

"And I'm so sorry it took me so long. I feared I'd made a huge mistake by not coming sooner."

"Ah, but it is the magic. The magic of love. You know about this, don't you, Aimee?" she said with a sweet smile.

Aimee blushed. It was as if this strange woman knew exactly what her insides were screaming. She felt a real connection to her.

"The truth is, they have a special cocktail that makes me feel like your age, Aimee. And right after you leave, they'll whisk me into the shower, get me back into my hospital gown, and deliver another bag. That one will have all the bad stuff, and I'll be sick for three days, maybe a week. I'm getting very tired of it."

Aimee had been told she had Stage IV breast cancer. Unlike her mother, who wasted away and nearly lost all her hair even without any cancer drugs, Carmen Hernandez's hair was very healthy and thick.

"Come, pull up this chair and let's chat. Jasper, did you tell her about the inheritance?"

While Aimee dragged the armchair closer, Jasper sat on the edge of the bed.

"I did indeed. Not all the details. Perhaps you'd like to do that yourself, Carmen."

Suddenly, her demeanor shifted, and she became distracted, frowning at her lap. "I'm going to be sick. Jasper, call the nurse."

While the attorney went in search of help, Carmen whispered to Aimee, "I had to speak to you in private. Forgive me." She winked.

Aimee took her outstretched hand and felt familiar coldness there. "I am so grateful for everything you've already done, Miss Hernandez. For selling me the house. It truly is a special place. I love the light and—"

"The magic? You feel the magic too?" Carmen asked, squeezing her hand.

"Something like that. Tell me what it was like."

"Well, I lived there for twenty years, a little more. Hank was only there half that time, unfortunately. But he used to call it his secret weapon. He couldn't write anywhere else after he had his first few novels published. So he purchased the home and left it vacant when he wasn't there. The first time I walked inside, I felt the power of the magic. Good magic. It's the kind of magic that comes from the heart, Aimee. I think you feel it too."

She nodded her agreement and let the older woman continue.

"It's something that has to be protected. You must never tear it down or all the power will be gone. I've had offers, and I've turned down a lot of money to sell to a builder who would tear it down and replace it with something huge, but—"

Mr. Kornblum and a nurse rushed into the room.

"I'm going to have to ask you two to leave. She cannot tolerate this," the nurse said, quickly separating their hand-holding then checking her pulse, her eyes, and the drip on the bag at the side. "Miss Hernandez, you know you have to be careful. Your immune system is running on empty; your iron count is dangerously low, and we are preparing for that emergency iron infusion this afternoon."

"I know all that. Just give me a few more minutes," the older woman objected.

"Just a few. Five minutes max." The nurse moved to the other side of the bed, making notes on a whiteboard hanging on the wall. "You want something for the nausea?"

"No. I'm fine." She inhaled deeply, as if drawing strength. Aimee saw a slight green tint to her color—something the makeup failed to hide. Carmen continued, "All right then," she sighed. "Just before Hank's passing, I discovered my love of writing as well. He was delighted. He started editing my work and encouraging me to write more and more. I'd just finished my first rough draft when he suddenly left us."

She wiped a tear from her cheek and stared down at her lap.

"I've ordered some of his books, Miss Hernandez. Now I plan on reading all of yours as well." Aimee was hoping it would cheer her up. "Mr. Kornblum told me about them on the way down here."

"Romance. You love romance?"

"I do."

"You believe in the Happily Ever After?" she asked as if it was a strange idol placed on a church mantlepiece.

"Absolutely, I do."

Suddenly, Carmen grabbed Aimee's hand again. "You know what this means?" She searched Aimee's face, but Aimee wasn't sure what answer the older woman was looking for.

"Tell me," Aimee said, rubbing her thumb over the bony knuckles of Carmen's left hand.

"It means I will live forever, that's what it means. As long as someone is reading my books, I'll always be there. Hank and I will always be there at that house at Sunset Beach. But you have to keep reading. Love stories. Forget his science fiction books. Read love stories, Aimee."

"I will." She felt hot tears begin to form again at the tops of her cheekbones and then spill over the ledge and drop onto her lap. The sadness was overwhelming. Aimee wondered if there was some form of dementia developing, perhaps an early stage and wondered which affliction would overtake her first—her cancer or the dementia. She decided to feed the illusion of a dying woman by telling her about her own experience.

"You are so right, Carmen. The house *is* magic. Something lives there that you can feel. I completely understand."

"Powered by love, Aimee. Don't forget that." The older woman's gaze was unwavering.

"Of course."

The nurse began to roll her eyes and motioned for them to head toward the doorway. "I think she's had enough."

"Oh, not nearly enough. There is never enough love," Carmen

added stubbornly, still seeking Aimee's attention.

"We got the message, Carmen," said Mr. Kornblum. "Trust me, Aimee's not going to forget this. You can tell her more about the magic next time."

Carmen leaned forward and whispered to her, "Next time you see me, I'll be with Hank. I promise. I trust that you will keep us alive."

Her comment caused Aimee's spine to stiffen with the bittersweet notion that life was finite but that love was eternal. That was the message Carmen had been trying to tell her. Then she thought about Andy, so far away, the part about the finiteness of life striking a huge, gaping wound in her heart. More tears washed down her cheeks. Her eyes were now red and sore.

"There is more of the story. He's coming back, Aimee."

"Who?" asked Mr. Kornblum, his face wrinkled in a scowl.

"They both are. Hank and Andy. They're coming back, and they'll never leave us again!"

CHAPTER 8

THE TEAM PILED into the bus, along with their three Africacorps "handlers," which was a nice way of describing the government spies. Peterson had briefed them on the fact that a thriving oil drilling business was being protected and was the private concern of the new president and several of his top generals. Andy suspected they were also into other concerns, namely drugs and girls.

So the SEALs needed to thread the needle between the government forces aided by their Africacorp and coalition well-equipment troops and the ragtag, rebel militia group having their way with villages and animal poaching that was suspected of holding the missionaries and journalists. The SEALs were only allowed to travel on designated roads in certain areas, just to make sure they didn't get a glimpse of something Uncle Sam wouldn't like that might end the partnership with the US Special Forces.

But everyone expected to see the worst.

Andy noticed right away that the rear lavatory had been cleaned up overnight. However, it still was missing a door. And just before they fired up the engine in the rusty white beast, someone noted a tire had gone flat. It was an hour before a replacement tire could be located and they could get on their way.

The driver was going to let them off at the edge of a protected forest, a site being built with UNESCO funds for creation of a nature preserve of endangered species. The region was targeted by a recent IUCN Red List paper, calling out one particular species of blue baboon, well on its way to extinction. It was thought that the militia group was also responsible for poaching various other species as well, for transport to private zoos that illegally purchased the animals as breeding stock. Several old camps had been identified with use of drone footage. The SEALs single focus was for the rescue of the workers and not the animals.

The two Nigerian guides took the tip of the spear, slashing a wide path for the rest of the team to follow. Dallas and Andy were soon drenched in sweat as the party crossed a tall grassy savannah, heading into a dark jungle forest. They could hear the sounds of screaming and howling monkeys and baboons. The foliage was alive with tiny yellow birds and large black-winged duck-like creatures who were nesting in the trees above and frequently divebombed the group, coming quite close to knocking hats off and sending men sprawling onto the jungle floor to avoid contact.

Andy was glad he'd brought a healthy supply of repellant and knew, without it, he'd not get a wink of sleep.

The guides stopped, using binoculars to search the treetops ahead and consulting one another as to the best route to take. Peterson wasn't getting any respect from them, and each time their LPO asked for clarification and translation, he was completely ignored.

It was painful for Andy to watch. Dallas rolled his eyes.

"If he doesn't shut up, they're gonna gag him. I've seen it done," Dallas whispered.

Two hours into their hike, Andy took a drink of water and shared some with Dallas and Conley Brown, a medic first timer. He poured water on his shemagh and wrapped it around his neck and head, tying it under his chin. Then he replaced his Fresno

State Bulldogs baseball cap securely on the wet headdress, the bill facing down his backside. His black gloves were full of stickers, but so far had managed to keep his hands from sustaining little cuts from the stubborn brush.

The group slowly moved forward while Andy mentally checked his pockets, adjusted the medic pack on his shoulders, and felt the reassuring bulge of his sidearm and KA-BAR. Conley walked beside him as they followed behind Dallas.

"You've been here three or four times, Andy?"

"Three. Well, I'm not sure I call the Canaries or Cape Verde part of the African continent. Way different terrain, but I've been along the coast, seen the villages there. The islands are rocks, old volcanos, and really tough terrain. We took on a lot of ankle and knee injuries hiking those hills," he answered.

Conley nodded. His light pink baby's bottom skin was getting cut up and was slightly sunburned. Andy tried not to stare, but he didn't see that the boy had developed a beard yet. He'd heard about some Team Guys who lied about their age, and Conley looked younger than that even.

"You best get some sunscreen on those cheeks and lather up your nose. Make you look like a lifeguard and the girls will love it," Andy mumbled in the kid's direction.

"Yeah, I think I wiped it all off." He stopped, quickly pulling out a Warrior Wipe, which was a repellant and sunscreen all in one, and wiping across his forehead, around his cheeks, and over his nose.

"Careful of your eyes. You don't want to get any stuff in there or—"

"Argh." Conley groaned. "God dammit. Too late. Mother*fucker*. Every time I do that, I feel like pissing my pants."

Andy just nodded and didn't make much of it.

"Sonofabitch that stuff stings."

"Yeah, but your eyeballs won't burn now. Thank the SEAL gods for that."

"Fuck that."

"Use your water. I got an irrigator we can use when we stop for tea and crackers." Andy grinned and wondered if he had bugs stuck in his teeth.

The sound of a chainsaw and the crack of a falling tree pierced the area, getting the guides excited. They pointed off to where the sound was coming on the right, and their conversation bubbled over as their pace increased.

Another sound of the chainsaw preceded the sight of a large tree falling very close to where they were walking, followed by the screeching sounds of chimps or baboons being displaced. They could hear multiple tools pounding and chopping wood, or perhaps nailing boards together. A campfire was burning, and the smell of food cooking filled Andy's nose, making him hungry.

Several minutes later, they encountered a clearing busy with nearly a dozen local villagers working shirtless in the filtered light of the hot sun. They were building small enclosures for animals, setting up fences, and raising crisscrossed beams lashed together that would be covered in canvas or perhaps plastic membrane. A pile of metal corrugated material lay twisted and haphazardly stacked to the side. Several large dormitory-type structures were located on the other side of the clearing, made out of concrete and animal dung blocks, open glassless windows covered with canvas rags.

Peterson was shaking hands with a European-looking officer. Andy figured he was attached to the UN crew for security.

Out of one of the buildings walked Sven Tolar, who was washing his hands with a rag, smiling and heading right for Andy.

"So now my new friend is my enemy," he said in his clipped

Norwegian accent. "Are you responsible for this posting?" He glanced at Peterson and the officer and shook Andy's glove and sticker-encrusted hand.

"Guilty as charged. Don't knock my clock out, Sven. But I have to say I'm really glad to see you."

"And I'm very glad to be alive, to be seen!"

"This here's Dallas, Conley. Peterson over there is the LPO. Who's your guy?"

"That's Gunnar Fucktard. Former circus performer."

Andy must have looked horrified.

"They building a zoo or breeding ground?" Andy asked.

"Who knows? They're protecting the blue baboons here. It's a humanitarian mission. They're supposedly beautiful creatures, near extinct. This place is supposed to be a research center, someday a tourist destination, so they say."

Peterson joined them. "You must be Sven Tolar," he said, extending his hand.

"At your service, Chief."

"You get here today?" he asked.

"Yesterday. I came in with some supplies and reinforcements and a cook, but we got to travel by truck. How come you guys hiked in? There's a road just a half click away."

Peterson shrugged.

"See, they're messing with you, Peterson. They've been watching you the whole time," whispered Sven so others wouldn't hear.

"And that's why Andy here recommended you."

Gunnar began shouting orders to the Team to unpack their loads in one of the two block buildings.

"Chief, don't let him do that. He works for you, not the other way around."

"My men are tired. I'll dance with him later. Right now, I want to check in with the Headshed and let the guys rest up."

"Have you heard anything about the journalists, Sven?" asked Andy.

Dallas and Conley eagerly listened for an answer.

"Some of the crew I came in with said they saw some strangers in town. There's a small town, called Benot, with a school, some government buildings and shops, a jail, and an Africacorps detachment about twenty minutes away by truck. But they could have been hired workers brought in to work on the dam. They've been seeing a lot of that lately. But they weren't from here, that's for sure."

"State's sending a bird overhead tonight. Any armed groups other than the Africacorps?" asked Peterson.

"Not yet. Gunnar and I are not quite talking that friendly yet. He's going to try to put your guys to work building latrines and finishing the pens and tree clearing, since your salaries don't come out of his expenses."

Peterson followed the men inside the dorms. Sven pulled Andy aside. "How's Kyle, and how's Tucker? He get that lady of his knocked up again?"

"Kyle's great. Aimee and I got married."

"I heard. Congrats. You sure about this?"

"Best thing I've done so far."

"She's a nice girl. You still working on that house?"

"Of course. Kind of a money pit. But she's in love with that place." Andy continued, "Team 3 went on a training so the guys who were going to come, Kyle included, didn't make it. I thought perhaps you'd be with them."

"I took a little tour of my own up to see Kelly in Portland. I'd been gone nearly a month before I came here."

"And?" Andy was hoping Sven and Kelly had rekindled their little affair they'd started during the last mission to the Canaries.

Dallas and Conley broke away and headed for the building.

"She turned me down, Andy," Sven whispered. Andy stopped in his tracks.

"Why would she go do something stupid like that? You guys were perfect for each other."

"I think Jenna's long recovery has had a lot to do with it. I keep thinking she'll be back, but she doesn't want this life now."

Andy didn't have to ask if Sven was ready for the same. At some point in his career, he knew that risking it all, leaving Aimee—and maybe kids—behind might not be his priority. It was something every SEAL had to deal with at the end of the last mission. Kyle had told him about guys who came to talk to him, and he told Andy he could almost see that spear lodged in their chest—the blade engraved with the words 'I quit.' The biggest problem with quitting was facing the fear of what would come next. Would they ever find something else that excited them as much as working with brothers who would die for each other?

"She's still young. Maybe she'll come to her senses," he said, placing a hand on Sven's shoulder.

"She's kinda getting used to her father-in-law's good wine and comfortable digs. And she deserves it, Andy. She'll get bored in time. And she's working with Jenna, who is still traumatized. I think she wants to help Colin with his new venture, too, the security company. The one Tucker's thinking about."

"Tucker isn't ready yet." Andy was certain of this.

"I told Kyle they should send Tucker over with me. Not sure what happened. Your Peterson is going to need help, Andy. You know that, right?"

"Tell me about it."

"Even before I left Coronado to visit the Rileys, there was talk about this team being a real fuckup. Now why would Kyle put you here with these guys?"

"Because I wanted to stay in Little Creek, closer to Aimee.

They lost their senior medic, and Kyle thought it would be big shoes to fit into and would help me advance up the ladder."

Sven let his lower lip peel forward and shook his head, a scowl forming. "Watch yourself. Peterson is no Lansdowne. Kyle runs a pretty tight crew. Even the wives are tight, like sisters."

"Yup. That's the way it's done."

"You guys have had a run of bad luck." Sven squinted then tapped Andy in the middle of his chest, thinking as he did so. "Nah. I think once you guys get your sea legs, you'll be fine. What you frogs need is a couple of good firefights, and you'll be right as rain. You'll be communicating without saying a word, like Team 6. You'll be finishing each other's sentences before long. You'll get there," he said as he winked.

"Good to hear you say that, Sven. All the same, I'm fuckin' glad you're here."

"Shoot. I wouldn't miss this for anything. They actually *pay* me to have this kind of fun."

They both laughed.

Sven added, "What a life, right? I'm sure as hell no carpenter, and they better not put me on fence detail."

"And I'm not going to go training baboons who can tear my arms out of my sockets. I don't care how endangered they are."

"Hell, I'll help them become even more endangered if they touch one hair on your head," Sven chuckled.

Andy felt like some of his jitters were floating away, just by trash talking with a man who had faced years more wartime challenges and close calls than anyone else he knew. For a while this morning and yesterday, he'd felt like he and Dallas were the only two seniors on the crew.

Which didn't bode well for a good outcome.

But with Sven by his side, at least they had a fighting chance to come out in one piece. Aimee had called it magic, the magic of their love story, and thought it would keep him safe. What it really was, Andy thought, was courage to bust through anything coming after him and to never give up. There would be lots of blood and dust.

He wanted to walk through his front door back at Sunset Beach on his own two feet, not delivered in a pine box.

No pixie dust anywhere.

CHAPTER 9

AIMEE'S INSIDES WERE jumbled all the way home. Mr. Kornblum was smart enough to leave her alone. She'd been worried she'd say something to him she'd regret later on. Her foul mood continued, aggravated by late afternoon traffic. A downpour descended upon the car as they sped down the freeway. The bridge over to the Gulf was gleaming in the fresh rain like a giant silver arch. The sun was so bright, even through all the rain, that it hurt her eyes.

Mr. Kornblum flipped her visor down, and that did give some relief.

As they traveled to the bottom of the arch, the car slowed to make the right-hand turn to Gulf Boulevard. Here the traffic was just as crowded, but only single lane in each direction and at a considerably slower speed. He successfully dodged pedestrians who were either crossing the road to view the sunset or coming home from a day on the sand.

The attorney cleared his throat. "Can I offer you a drink, or perhaps I can treat you to an early dinner? Not sure about you, but that hospital sandwich we had for lunch wasn't all that satisfying."

"I should be the one taking you to dinner. You did all the driving. I'm not being a very good guest."

"I don't mind, dearie. You have a lot to take in. And you're facing it all on your own with Andy being overseas." He let that sink in a bit and then added, "How long will he be gone again?"

"This one has no set time limit. Could be a few weeks or up to four months. We just never know." Aimee knew it wasn't the time or distance away from Andy that worried her. It was the fact that it was a new team, and Andy had said he had to find his place. He'd also confided in her that Africa continued to be one of the most dangerous places to be deployed. But she couldn't share any of that, and maybe that's what had her tangled up in the hammock of the rotten mood. "I say the dinner's on me. You pick the place, though. Pick what you want. I'm not sure how hungry I'll be."

"Very well. Seafood? Crab?"

She nodded and then blushed at the memory of some of their early dinners out, after their love affair had flamed to perfection—the steamy nights, butter and crab all over her body, and the effects of her margarita sparking her libido. Whatever the day's concerns were, Andy could always work it out of her, leaving her feeling soft, pliable, and well-loved. She missed his tenderness. Right now, the world was looking like it was going to smack her in the eye and laugh at her cruelly.

He was pulling into Crabby Bill's and the usual scene, no matter if it was Tuesday or Saturday night. There were the early diners who came to meet their retired friends, Snowbirds from up north, taking advantage of the specials and driving themselves carefully home in their golf carts. Later would come the younger couples and some families, who would play darts or listen to the guitar player singing for tips and beer. And then the party scene started in earnest around eight, groups of couples or single men and women standing across the room from each other, judging the pickings or dancing to the music of a western combo.

If he'd have given her the space, she would have apologized and given some excuse for the way she was reacting, but she couldn't think of the words to say.

What am I feeling?

But as they were shown to a table outside on the shell-strewn patio in a corner near the parking lot, Aimee realized the noise of the early evening would probably preclude any discussions they were to have. She was okay with it.

Force of habit with a touch of melancholy allowed her the space to order her favorite strawberry margarita. Mr. Kornblum ordered a beer.

"Well, Aimee, I'd say we were pretty lucky. Carmen was having one of her good days. I'd say, the best I've seen her."

"I was expecting someone way more infirmed, especially for someone under hospice care. I've seen people walking around all over the place who look dead compared to her. She's very sharp. At least she was, until the end when she was talking about Hank coming back to her. Doesn't it usually work that she would go join him? And she mentioned Andy—"

"It happens at this stage, Aimee. I had a long conversation with her on the phone one day. I actually think she forgot who I was. Perhaps might have mistaken me for Hank. She was prattling on about everything she'd done that day, and of course, none of it was true. She doesn't drive any longer. She certainly doesn't go swimming in the ocean any longer."

"But she used to."

"Yup. She's very convincing, so it's hard to really know where she's coming from. She's describing the place she's traveling to, like another one of her adventures. They used to meet up over the years before they lived together. And then she'd go back to California, and he'd return to New York. Boy would I like to be a fly on the wall in those days." He smiled into his glass and took a long swig of his beer.

"I've had a little experience with my parents' estate when they passed. And it was important that we documented everything while my mother was well enough to be considered of sound mind. Don't you worry about that with Carmen?"

"I think she knows what she's doing. We've kept our business meetings very short, and I only proceed when I'm certain all the marbles are in place. I also usually get a witness to everything she signs, someone who isn't on my payroll. And I've never been asked to do anything that I felt was bad for her or for someone else. It is her desire that you inherit her money, Aimee. She could give it all away to charity, but she wants you to use it. To have it to enjoy."

"As long as the house remains the same size."

"That's a requirement. You can modernize it, but you can't tear it down. And if it's damaged in a hurricane, and it has been damaged over the years, it has to be rebuilt to the same size it is now."

"I think I understand better what she meant by doing that. Almost like the house captured, trapped something there that will escape if it's torn down." She sipped her drink, closed her eyes, and pretended Andy was home, sitting right in front of her. But of course, he wasn't there when she opened her eyes.

"I set it up today so you can go back on your own and visit, if you like."

Aimee was touched by his gesture. "Why is she doing all of this? Has she told you? Why me?"

"Because you loved the house in its dilapidated condition and have now restored her to the beauty it was when she lived there. When they lived there. In a way, she's put you on a mission—a mission to explore inside yourself what the house brings out of you. Almost as if it's an old friend and not just a physical house at all. She's treating it like a sentient being, in a way."

"Do you know the history of the property? Is there something else I'm not aware of? Some backstory?"

He shrugged. "You'd have to ask her. All I know is that they were very happy there. It was his touchstone, a place where his creative energy could expand, where he could write his books. I'm guessing she wants the same for you. She found her writing ability there. Maybe you have some talent you haven't explored yet. Who knows?"

On the way home, Mr. Kornblum surprised her with his comment.

"You haven't asked me how much money is in her estate, Aimee. Aren't you curious?"

"I don't want to know." It was out before she could retract it. "Neither one of us came from real money. I have to honestly say I've never chased it, either."

He gave a belly laugh. "Boy, young lady, I don't run across many people like you. It's usually the first thing anyone asks."

"I just want to know why."

He walked her to the front door and extended his hand. "Nice to spend some time with you today, Aimee. I hope you get all your questions answered, and if I can help in any way, just give me a ring."

"Thanks, I will. You've been very generous with your time."

"I still work for Carmen. She asked me to prepare you and was delighted when you wanted to meet her. I hope that, when the time comes, I can help you manage your estate as well, but that's entirely up to you. So, you see, there is a bit of a selfish motive there. I am an attorney, after all."

She laughed, feeling comfortable around him. "Well, we've made a good start then. Thanks again."

Aimee watched him pull out from the driveway, back up, and then wave to her as he exited to find the road back to Tampa. She dialed her front door code and took a step across the threshold but stumbled on something at her feet. She found a small brown box—so small, in fact, that she'd missed it entirely when she started inside. The box was tied with a piece of white ribbon about a quarter-inch wide, ending in a bow.

Aimee shook the box, and it rattled. She examined the underside and all the edges to see if there was a note or some sort of notation written anywhere indicating where it had come from. She turned around and searched the alleyway and didn't find any curious onlookers. When she untied the ribbon, she found a small bracelet made from objects she'd seen on the beach over the past year she'd lived there.

There were several shells, mostly white, but many with colors of yellow, purple, and rose. Where a hole had developed along its journey to her hands, someone had used a piece of wire and twisted it carefully to attach the shells to the bracelet. There was a smooth turquoise piece of sea glass with wire crisscrossing and encapsulating it and then attaching it to the rest of the strand. A pink piece of lacey calcified coral, a smooth black pebble, and a yellow and clear cat's eye marble, all with tiny holes inserted in them, were attached to the rest of the strand. As she examined the objects, she also found a partial bottle cap and an orange plastic fish charm, as well as a green plastic coffee cup stopper.

Someone had installed a clasp between two charms, and when Aimee opened it up and placed the bracelet around her wrist, it fit perfectly. She snapped it closed and held her hand out in front of her, shaking the little pieces so lovingly stitched together.

On her heel, she whirled around to face the alleyway again.

"Is anyone out there?" she called, her voice echoing against the concrete carport pad and bouncing against the walls of the place next door. "Hello? Did you make this for me?"

Listening for any sign of life, she walked out to the alleyway and first looked to her right and then her left.

"I'd like to say thank you. It's very beautiful," her voice echoed to the silent houses and cars nearby. "Very unusual, and everything looks like you found them here on this beach, which makes it even more special. Won't you come out and talk to me? I'd like to personally thank you for it."

But no one answered.

On her steps back to her still-opened front door, she examined the box inside to determine if there had been any clue left as to who either the artist or the giver was. But just like the silent alleyway, she found no clue as to who had left this gift for her.

One last time, she studied the garage and alleyway from her porch. "Thank you. It's beautiful. I'll take good care of it."

Aimee set the box on the coffee table, kicked off her shoes, and was on her way to the kitchen for some water when something caught her eye. Through the living room sliding glass door, she saw where someone had drawn a heart in the sand. Inside were two names:

Aimee and Andy.

When she saw how her name was spelled, using the proper spelling her mother had given her, not a more common way to spell Aimee, she knew all of a sudden who had made this bracelet for her, meant as a wedding present.

Logan!

She scanned the beach in both directions as the orange glow of sunset covered everyone and the stiff peaks of purple clouds slowly bloomed in the sky. It was impossible to see everyone's faces, but no one looked in her direction. Retrieving her cell from her jacket pocket, she took a quick picture of the heart and their names drawn on her patio.

Aimee ran to their bedroom and pulled out two of Andy's long-sleeved work shirts she'd hung up from the dryer and didn't need ironing. She folded them into a small square, one on top of the other, then added a pair of his jeans, rejecting Andy's paint jeans and opting for a decent pair with no holes in them. She got out an old pair of running shoes he'd recently complained about and two pairs of thick socks, two pairs of briefs, and two white V-necked T-shirts. She also found a light-weight jacket that would make a good windbreaker and could be worn in warm weather. She removed a small tube of toothpaste and a toothbrush she'd gotten from her dentist at her last cleaning, still wrapped in plastic.

Everything was neatly folded and placed in one of her shopping bags. She added a bar of soap, some liquid hand sanitizer, two apples, two bananas, and a half loaf of wheat bread. She also found a small unopened mango juice container and two water bottles.

The bag was heavy as Aimee lifted it to her door and set it down on the doormat. To the empty carport and alleyway beyond, she shouted, "Thank you. Please accept these as my appreciation. I will leave more food tomorrow, if you like this. Please stay safe and warm, Logan." Her voice faltered as her eyes filled with tears. "Just remember that I love you. That Mom and Dad always loved you until their last day. Let me help you, Logan. Let *me* be *your* big sister for a change. I want to help."

Everything was still eerily quiet, but she felt someone was watching her all the same. Andy's words and those of the doctor she'd spoken to at the hospital where Logan had been in detox came shouting out to her.

Be careful. He could be dangerous. Don't do anything stupid. He may not be the big brother you once knew.

And Andy had made her promise she'd do that, made her promise she'd not try to contact him or go looking for him while he was gone. But that was before Logan reached out from the near dead of the streets and touched her heart by making something with his own hands. And he also showed her that perhaps he knew about the wedding, for how else could it explain the heart drawing in the sand?

This means there is hope. This means a part of him I've loved all those years still remain.

Aimee left the bag on the mat, closed her front door, and locked it. She wasn't stupid. Of course, she should lock all her doors and windows and take every precaution available to her. She also had another idea. She called her teacher friend, Shelley.

"How *was* the meeting, Aimee? And have you heard from Andy yet since he's been gone?" She was always direct and didn't sugarcoat anything.

"Not since he got there. I might hear tonight. But, Shelley, after I got home seeing Carmen Hernandez, I got a beautiful package left for me on my doorstep. It's a bracelet made from found things at the beach. Shells, a bottle cap, a marble, pieces of coral. It's really beautiful and a little crude, but he made it with his own hands."

"Who made it?"

"Logan. I know it was Logan."

"Oh dear, did you see him lurking around your door or something?"

"No. And that's a little unkind, don't you think?"

"Well, he does have a drug and alcohol problem. You don't want to mess around with that, Aimee. I thought Andy made you promise—"

"Yes, he did. But I'm being careful."

"You still keep the gun beside your bed?"

"Yup, in the bedside table. Just like when I was living in the bungalow last summer. But, Shelley, I think this is a really good sign. I think it was a call for help."

"You're not qualified. He needs professional help."

"But he's my brother. He reached out to me. Am I supposed to just turn my back on him?"

"You're not turning your back on him. You're getting him the help he needs. He doesn't need a friend who likes his jewelry. He has much larger issues. You don't know how sick he is, and I'm pretty sure Andy would be upset if he thought you were trying to encourage him."

Aimee wiped the thought out of her mind, refusing to listen to that little voice of doubt coming from the back of her head. "You should see the bracelet. It's so unusual."

Shelley's voice became quiet. Then she asked the question Aimee didn't want to answer. "So what did you do, Aimee?" Shelley knew her all too well.

"I gave him some clothes. Well, I didn't see him, of course. But I gave him a couple pairs of Andy's old jeans, still in good shape. A couple shirts, some underwear, a pair of running shoes, and toiletries—soap and toothpaste."

"Unbelievable," Shelley sighed into the phone.

"I've locked all my doors and windows. Just to be sure."

"Um hum." Shelley was unusually quiet while Aimee also told her about the bananas, waters, the mango juice, and hand sanitizer.

"I just wanted to help, that's all. Wouldn't you do the same? What if it was one of your kids, living on the street? Wouldn't you do something?"

"I'd call the cops."

"No, you wouldn't. I know you, Shelley. You're just as kind-hearted as I am."

"There's a reason they tell you not to give the people at the grocery store money. They buy drugs and alcohol with it."

"I didn't give him any money."

"Oh. My. God. I should hope not."

"I gave him clothes and stuff that would be good for him."

"You know you're wasting your time justifying what you did."

Aimee felt her anger brewing and didn't appreciate Shelley's lack of compassion.

"You're a fucking snob, Shelley." She immediately regretted the outburst.

"Oh yeah? So, answer me this one question, Aimee. Why did you call me? Why even check the windows and doors? You know you were acting a little reckless. What would happen if he knocked on your door? If he showed up on your patio?"

"Well, he already did that."

"Oh, Jesus. I can't believe I'm hearing this. Now I'm going to call the cops."

"No, it wasn't like that. He made a drawing in the sand. A heart. Inside, it had Andy and my names in it. He was telling me he knew about the wedding. Shelley, this gives me hope. Hope that my brother, whatever faults he has and no matter what health issues are going on with him, has a good, healthy part of him that remains. I want to appeal to that good side, that healthy part of him, not treat him like a criminal or street urchin. I think you're heartless, Shelley."

Aimee could hear her heavy breathing and knew Shelley was biting her tongue.

"And I'm sorry about the part about you being a snob. That was unkind of me."

In a very measured voice, Shelley revealed her thoughts. "Aimee, this isn't Disneyland, my friend. You have to start living in the real world, not the one you want it to be. Let the people who are professionals do their job. You need to get out of the way, even if you think you're being cruel."

"But—"

"Just imagine this. What would happen to him if he caused you harm? What if you encouraged him too soon, made a judgment about what he was thinking and who he was, when in actuality that didn't begin to describe who he's become, Aimee? And, if he really wanted to gain access to your house, wouldn't he have a pretty easy time breaking your sliding glass door down? He could do it with a lawn chair or one of your bricks on the patio. Are you telling me you'd shoot him? Or would you hesitate?"

"I think you're making more out of this than needs to be."

"So ask yourself honestly the answers to those questions. And the real reason you called me? You wanted to feel safe. You'd better check your gut, Aimee. And I think you should come over and stay with me tonight, and then let's go call Social Services or that doctor you met with and ask them what to do. Because, if you think you can help him on your own, you might make everything worse."

CHAPTER 10

FIRST LIGHT OF day, Andy requested he be able to call Aimee on his cell. Peterson asked him to wait until they had a day in the city of Benot, which had been planned for tomorrow.

"Not as worried about the technology of a group finding you as I am your bubble showing up in someone's internet preferences here, and then that information gets relayed to someone else who can cause us a problem. And I'm the only one authorized to use the SAT phone," Peterson said.

Andy could see it was hard for him to tell him no.

"So am I on the team doing some reconnaissance in the jungle or working the equipment?"

"Did you get your triage set up?"

"All done, sir. Your new man, Conley Brown. He's got a good head on his shoulders. He organizes like it's *DIY Benin Jungle, Season 4*. I can tell they've put those guys through some still drills to have them work that fast. I don't remember being taught that."

"He's been around it all his life. His mother is a Navy doc, stationed right now in Djibouti."

"No shit?"

"That's what I'm told. He's serious about not being a *One and Done*. Plans to get his twenty in."

"He's a good candidate for it," agreed Andy. "So you didn't

answer my question."

"Well, if you're not needed with the setup, then sure, I'd like you and Sven to take several guys and head south to a plain, a small savannah atop Mont Sokbaro. It's a day trip. You'll be on your own overnight, come back tomorrow morning. We got drone footage of some local trails. We need to check on something that showed up."

"You're gonna want it painted?"

"Only if you identify something. I'll give you the com so we can do a three-way with our friendlies in the sky. What our bird can see, so can others. I don't need them to know we're looking there, if you get my drift."

"Understood."

"You want me to pick the team?"

"Yessir. I'm not quite up to date on the skillset."

"Head back to the bunker and get Sven packing. I'll meet you there with my list, and I'll send others I see over there. Make sure Conley knows he's not to be giving Viagra to the locals, okay? And no animal medicine in our surgery, got it?"

"Fuck no. You think—"

"Gunnar Larssen is a bullshitter from way back. We gotta work with him, but if I catch anything dirty on him, I'm reporting it. He has a huge authority complex. He's going to be envious of some of your equipment, particularly the disinfectants and antibiotics and painkillers. All the expensive stuff."

"Must be something in the water, sir."

"I'm not tracking, Andy."

"Seems like everyone is trying to seize power, using other resources to get it, or get one over on everyone else."

"We're talking centuries of uprisings and violence. They squander their freedoms fighting for everything. No one is strong enough to overcome it. So Uncle Sam, the Chinese, Russians, we all add our powder to the mix and wham! Someone gets power who shouldn't have. One thing's for certain, it isn't about the blue baboons or the people or even about the ecosphere. It's all about power and who has it and who doesn't."

Andy didn't have much to say, except to internally notice Peterson actually understood a lot more about the dynamics of Western Africa than he let on. It was running a Team he was light on. He wasn't sure if that was a good thing or not.

"Sir, can I recommend someone to you?"

"Go ahead. I got turned down for several I said were critical. Who?"

"You need Tucker Hudson. You need Fredo, Danny Begay, and his cousin who is a SWCC boat guy, if we'll be doing anything on the Niger River. Armando and T.J. would be good too. But Tucker. He's the key. He's like the glue. Second time around for him, and the man is tough. Sven is great, but he's not American-grown, and that makes a difference. The men trust Tucker. And you need a couple of bullies standing up or silencing Mr. Larssen. Fredo has a way of using humor to knock a guy off his perch. Is Gunnar even military any longer?"

"Supposed to be strictly on the UN payroll. But we don't know who else has him by the balls. I'm really not happy to have to work with him, and I've not even been here a day."

Peterson drew a line in the red dusty soil. "Tucker's expecting a little one any day, Kyle told me. And he doesn't want to miss the birth. You know how that is. It's not his time up, so for a special duty, he's got to be willing."

"That's too bad. How much longer?"

"He didn't tell me. I think soon. But this is baby #2, so anything goes. You know that."

"Indeed, I do."

"Well, maybe Brandy and the kid will cooperate, and he can

get out of night feedings and come join the circus over here, sir."

"Wouldn't that be something?"

Several minutes later, Andy and Sven were trading equipment and admiring their packs. It was a common thing to do, show customization for little compartments used to stash their tools of choice. Like tattoos, showing off their gear or some cool feature they'd stitched into their bags—toolbelts to protect and hold that gear—was a pastime. Almost like a pissing contest, and it helped spend hours of waiting or non-sleep when they were just too wired.

Dallas' shadow completely filled the doorway. Behind him, stood Archie Nolan, Kit Holmes, Connor Lannahan, and Qwanme Jones. Jones was the only one bigger and taller than Dallas, having just taken leave of a lucrative football career to join up with the Teams after his little brother was killed in Afghanistan some five years prior. Andy made the introductions to Sven, getting help from the team filling in the blanks.

Peterson arrived last.

"Dallas, you're point man on this, and I want you right next to him, Sven. We got four of you who speak French, which will have to do. Benin has some fifty dialects and ethnic languages, and we'd not be ready until the next century if we had to be fluent in any of them."

The team grumbled agreement.

"Last night, we got some good drone footage of a nice grassy area." He pulled out a map of West Africa, pointing to a northern central region of Benin. "This here is Mont Sokbaro, and it's a favorite for excursions to capture baboons, chimps, and some Western African Gorillas, mostly for poaching breeders for zoos, since it's a big no-no to capture underage or females with little ones. They identified a couple sites here and here." Peterson showed two lighted areas taken with night vision photography.

"You need to check out both camps, determine if they're civilian or militia or *otherwise*. They have the advantage of heavy tree coverage, so a night drop was deemed unfeasible. But they can't hide everything."

Off to the side of both areas were square-shaped perimeter structures, probably stone and block, and inside the heat signature showed a dotting of humans, either troops overnighting or the kidnap victims.

"Quite common here is the kidnapping of school-age children for ransom. But aid workers? Those are greatly prized," Peterson said and set his jaw, grinding his teeth. "One thing you don't see are vehicles. No roads here. Lots of rough turf. Even though the mountain forms a nice plateau, it's still too rough for an airstrip. So figure everyone who's here has hiked up, same as you. And if there are prisoners or children, you have to figure they would have suffered under the laborious journey."

The men passed around the IR black and white photos, occasionally pointing to mountain trails or other items of interest.

Sven had a question. "So other than the guys left back at base, who are our backups?"

"We're to call State first then the Africacorps. They earn a decent wage here and come from all over Central Africa, but they can easily be hired by the militias, who pay a lot better. And, of course, they'll be more motivated to fight to save their own farms and communities. When those guys desert, they take their guns and equipment and maps with them."

One of the men asked if anyone had taken direct responsibility for the aid workers abduction.

Sven was quick to answer. "New groups sprouting up all the time. These aid workers are like cash cows to them. They are easy targets, usually have family somewhere who care about them and can pay up. Even the municipal police are sometimes in on it or try to take over someone else's operation."

"And from what the Headshed told me, the Africacorps guys go home whenever violence starts erupting back at home, unless they're conscripted criminals. They'll work for the highest bidder, so don't count on them." Sven was all program now, not an ounce of frivolity in his tone of voice.

Andy asked the crowd if anyone had more questions or had noted something they hadn't noticed. The room was silent.

"These guys aren't evil, the ones who cause all this mayhem. They're opportunity players and generally not well trained. But some of them have served alongside our Special Forces, and they notice everything. Do not show photographs, maps, or do anything to make them think we're a forward guard of some small invasion or rescue army. They switch sides frequently, depending on who is paying. They'd prefer peace, but war is way more profitable. After generations in a row now of destabilizing wars, most of them have not known what peace even looks like."

Andy added, "And you're not going to win their hearts and minds by being a nice guy. They play rough and hard, and they are constantly looking for opportunity to remove certain things from your possession. So we should stay in twos. No lone wolf forays into the bush. You're liable not to come back."

Peterson handed Jones the com and watched as it was slipped into a padded pocket on the footballer's backpack. He handed Dallas and Andy each a SAT phone. Sven didn't attempt to hide his disapproval that he didn't get one. Qwanme passed out Invisios to everyone. They tested batteries on everything they brought and then announced the party's departure in thirty minutes.

The jungle gave some relief from the scalding sun, except for small clearings which sometimes were just naturally dried-up finger lakes or places where a building or residence had once stood. As they began to climb at the base of the four-hundred foot "hill" that shouldn't have been called Mont anything, Andy turned around to look at where they'd been. The sweeping vistas here were unlike anything else he'd seen in Northwest Africa. Thin fingers of light smoke drifted around in spots on the valley floor carrying with it the scent of barbeque.

At a distance, the whole plain below looked like some National Geographic special on the landscape of an underpopulated land famous for shipping more slaves to England and the Eastern United States than just about anywhere else. Yet it looked so serene and peaceful.

After several grueling hours, by midafternoon, they had reached what would have been a summit if Mont Sokbaro hadn't blown its top centuries ago. What lay in the area before them was a lush, green valley overpopulated with vines and twisting trees covering up the jagged edges of the crater's rim. Their feet padded across the red loamy soil easily five hundred feet deep that had at one time covered the entire area. Steam emanated from the red clay, indicating an abundance of moisture and the bio breakdown of dead branches and trees.

At an abandoned school or government building of some kind, they stopped to take refreshment, study the maps again, and set up a temporary night camp.

Andy's calves were burning, and his ankles were sore from little stumbles that caused him to bring all his weight down on a turned foot. It was going to feel good to stop, and maybe they'd let him have just ten minutes of meditation before they'd prepare their evening meal. He knew the instant spaghetti was going to taste damned good. He'd even lick the damned container, he was so hungry.

CHAPTER 11

"HAVE YOU MADE the call yet?" Shelley asked.

Aimee had gotten up late, still in a rotten mood. They tried to talk when she arrived at Shelley's house last night. She probably had too much wine, and then she began the worry about what had been wafting around the back of her head now for the past twenty-four hours.

No call from Andy.

She knew it was entirely unrealistic to hear from him so soon. He'd warned her of this. She'd been through it once already since they'd gotten together, but it still didn't help her courage. Shelley was a good friend, but she trusted Andy's advice, especially when it came to street smarts. He had, after all, been a great help to Cory—the SEAL she'd been dating, Andy's best friend—before Andy came out to visit and they fell in love.

Cory would be the *last* person she'd ask for advice, even though he was well familiar with drug and alcohol addiction.

She felt like she was freefalling, in limbo. Her once perfect world might still be perfect, but now the edges of that story were lightly singed. Nothing was as it appeared. Plus, she wondered about her trust in attorney Jasper Kornblum. What was she to think about the estate and inheriting money she never asked for? And why was she chosen? She still had no answer to that.

It was like a great big five-thousand-piece puzzle dumped on the table without a picture to follow. Parts of the whole thing lay scattered in front of her. Where should she start? What was the information she needed to make a correct decision? Should she contact her ladies on Andy's new team for support, people she hadn't even met, like she would have on his old Team 3? What would they think about her having a drug-addicted homeless brother? Shelley wanted her to call the police, but what if that meant an extra layer of violence on her brother just at the time when he was trying to reach out?

"Aimee, I asked you a question," Shelley demanded. Her hardness wasn't necessary, and it rankled her.

"Shelley, would you just stop pushing me? I can't figure anything out when I'm under pressure."

"What's to figure out? You're in danger, Aimee."

That really started the fires of hell. She stood, pointing to her best friend. "Dammit, Shelley, I said back off!"

Shelley whirled around then retreated to the kitchen where she proceeded to empty the dishwasher and bang pots and pans together, making a heroic gesture to let her know she was put out too.

Aimee didn't feel she owed an apology to anyone. It would have been the "nice" thing to do, but she just didn't feel like it. At the moment, she didn't care if Shelley thought she was being selfish or that her bratty behavior came as the result of her feeling entitled. Shelley's own story had been ragged and a bit raw, and she'd seen a much more difficult slice of life than Aimee had.

But that still was no excuse.

She peered around the corner and watched Shelley brew more coffee and wash her hands in the sink. Her friend looked up at her while drying her hands in the dishtowel, discarding it with a toss onto the countertop. She crossed her arms and waited for an apology Aimee knew she expected, but she would not give.

"I'm going to go back home and make my calls there. I think I will be more relaxed. I know you mean well, but I can't stand you hovering over me while I do it. You're right to be concerned about me and Logan. I get that. But I can't think straight here. I just can't."

"No one's holding you against your will, Aimee. I'm fine with you leaving any fucking time you want. And I'll probably be here the next time you call in a panic."

"I *wasn't* in a panic."

"You knew and still know you're in danger. Don't try to do this alone, Aimee. I know I've said it a dozen times by now. That's not a healthy way to do it."

"But I have to do it my way, Shelley."

"Okay, suit yourself. But if I can't get hold of you, I'm calling the cops."

It was a standoff, a compromise. And they didn't lose their friendship over it. It was as good as Aimee could get today from her best friend.

When she returned to her place, the bag with the clothes and food items were gone. Nothing was left in its place. She remembered that she'd promised to give more food next time, so she set her overnight bag down and began making a sandwich for Logan. Then she added another one. Anxious to get this easy decision out of the way, she wrapped them up, added more apples and one last banana, some waters again, and a couple granola bars. At the last minute, she slipped in two disinfectant wipes Andy always brought with him on fishing trips and on deployment.

She set the brown lunch bag on the doormat and locked the door.

The sand message had dried, and the edges partially collapsed. She went out onto the beach on a very mild winter day without a cloud in the sky. The warm sand felt good on her bare feet, and she vowed to get back into her running routine again. It did help her make decisions and sort out her concerns in life.

Maybe that's the problem.

Her cell phone pinged, and she didn't recognize the number. She scrolled for something from Andy and found none. Then she looked up her directory and called Dr. Denby at the Sunshine Palms Treatment Center.

It took nearly two minutes before Denby came on the line.

"How are you, Aimee? Anything new about your brother?"

"I'm good. Andy and I got married on Christmas Eve. Andy's on deployment, but oddly enough, I think Logan is reaching out to me."

"Really? How?"

"I think he made me a bracelet from stuff we find at the beach. Shells, rocks, pieces of wire. He left it in a box on my doorstep."

"So he knows where you live?"

"Apparently."

"And how do you know it's Logan?"

"Well—" She wasn't going to tell him it was a hunch or that it looked like something Logan would make, but that was the truth. Then she remembered the heart drawn in the sand. "He drew a heart with Andy and my names in it on my back patio, in the sand. He spelled my name correctly, Dr. Denby, which almost never happens. But I think this was a wedding present to me. I took as a sign he was reaching out." She examined the charms hanging around her wrist. "Very carefully done. Beautiful. Like he put his heart into it."

"Well, Aimee, I have to admit we don't usually see that. Usually, the kind of contact families have with their member is ransacking the home, stealing stuff, begging for money, or promising to get clean. Money for a bus ticket to a rehab place they have no intention of visiting. Very sad. But I have to warn you."

"Yes, I knew this was coming."

"Well, Logan can be very charming when he's in control. I saw a glimpse of it a time or two. But I really worry about all the damage living on the street has permanently done to his body. And these patients don't usually have an epiphany and all of a sudden get clean on their own."

"But couldn't this be the first step?"

"Possible. Anything is possible. But you have to be prepared for the opposite as well. Don't put too much faith in it. And now we have the problem of him knowing where you live. And you live alone now?"

"Yes."

"See, that's a problem. He didn't show up when your husband was around, so that's a red flag in my book, Aimee. And I have to tell you to please be very careful."

She sighed, flopping her body onto the buttery yellow leather couch and watching the waves outside. "I gave him some clothes and a little bit of food." She expected a scolding.

"I see," Dr. Denby said calmly. "It would be harmless if you weren't so vulnerable. One thing they do, Aimee, and they do it really well, is calculate whom they can use to get what they need. They're experts at taking advantage, look for opportunities to do so. The moral code is corrupted, overpowered by years of abuse. You can't assume they think straight or even care as much as you think they do. And they'll use that, too. Use it against you to get what they want."

"But I can afford to help him, just a little bit. I'm not giving him money. I gave him some clothes, some water bottles, fruit, and sandwiches. No money. I know better than that."

"So you're training a wild dog or cat, trying to coax him into your world. That usually doesn't work out very well. You have to be careful, and I'd recommend not doing any of that going forward."

"But what do I do?"

"I think you need to go down to the police department and have a discussion, so they have a file on you and on him. Just in case you call with a problem. And you should tell them that, as far as you know, he's not been violent with anyone and you don't suspect he has a weapon. That's very important. How you call for help can make the difference between life or death for him. The police are charged with your safety, even at the expense of his. It's how they're trained."

"So I should make a complaint, then?"

"It's called an incident report. You can recommend that he be given another stay here, if you like, something other than going to jail if he acts out or violates the law. He may not know any longer where his own boundaries are, or yours either."

"I feel so helpless."

"You'd be doing him a service to report it, Aimee. I think your husband would want you to do the same, especially since you're alone. And can I recommend something else?"

"What?"

"Get a dog. Get a grown dog who will be protective and will bark when someone's around."

Aimee immediately thought that would be a good idea. "Where would I go?"

"There's a no-kill shelter not far from you. I can text you the phone number. Sometimes you have to pay vet fees if they're a rescue or were abandoned. And the neuter or spay fee. It's a good way to get a friendly, watchful friend."

"They don't allow dogs on our beach, but there's a dog park nearby. I like that suggestion, doctor."

"Good. But you also should make that report, and I'd do it today. And don't leave anything else on your stoop. You have to ask yourself what if it isn't Logan, but someone using him and his identify somehow to get something from you."

"Okay, I'll do it this morning. Can I have them call you?"

"No, they won't do that. You can mention that I've treated him before, and I might get a call if they pick him up, but no guarantees. They're very busy, and if he's broken the law, I most definitely won't be called. Nor will you."

Dr. Denby also gave her the phone number of a local NAMI chapter and encouraged her to start to attend meetings to learn about mental illness.

"You will find fellowship amongst the other families who have dealt with this heartbreaking situation. These are people you can talk to about things no other person would begin to understand. You will learn from them, Aimee. Give them a shot."

"Thank you."

After her phone call, she checked the front porch and found the brown paper bag gone.

CHAPTER 12

DALLAS AWAKENED ANDY, putting his finger up to his lips to indicate they needed to be quiet. Andy couldn't figure out where he was at first. The dark night was the blackest he'd ever seen, showing there wasn't an incandescent light within twenty miles of the camp.

But the moon shone bright enough to see the silvery outlines of expressionless faces, packs, boots, cots, and tall bushes tossing from side to side in the stiff African savannah breeze.

Dallas pointed to his own ear, so Andy retrieved his Invisio to be able to hear what their point man whispered.

"There's a large encampment on the other side of the clearing. Sven and I took our NV goggles, and the whole place lit up. I'm going to paint the corners. Give Peterson a call and let him know we have at least sixty count. We gotta get close, get some pictures, and get the hell out of here tonight."

"Roger that," he whispered and dialed.

"Holy shit. Combatants or prisoners?" Peterson demanded, as Dallas stepped into the huddle a few paces in front of Andy.

"Don't know yet. We're getting in close to give you some markers. Make sure they send that bird up tonight."

"No, it's planned. They might already be there."

Dallas gave him the hurry-up sign. "Gotta go. We're not staying tonight, so look for us, and if you hear something, that would be bad news."

"Godspeed. That phone has a locator. Make sure it stays on so the men upstairs will know."

"Roger that."

Dallas indicated they follow single file behind him. Archie and Kit came next, their very white skin reflecting off the moon. Andy tapped Kit on the back and handed him a jar of face paint they took turns using as they followed the trail. Qwanme grinned, pushing Andy's hand away to turn down the goop, as he called it, his big white teeth reflecting in the limited light. His skin was already darker than the night sky.

Monkeys occasionally called out and were answered, as if they also had a perimeter that was guarded. With their NV goggles, they could see eyes staring back at them from the bushes, following their progression.

Two guards were sitting on two flat rocks, slumped over and snoring loudly, facing one another, their rifles slung across their shoulders. One had a long-sleeved hooded sweatshirt in a dark color. The other one wore some kind of soccer jersey from a team Andy didn't recognize.

A bonfire burned a short distance away, blinding them at first, then illuminating the walls of the old school or storage building without doors or windows. Inside, they heard coughing sporadically, and in one case, Andy was sure it was that of a child. Sven turned and faced him.

"Children," he whispered.

Dallas used three fingers to indicate the others were to run perimeter in the other direction and take pictures. Immediately, the two of them turned and headed the opposite direction, toward the backside of the structures, flipping to infrared.

"Watch out for animals."

At first, Andy wasn't sure what he meant. But all of a sudden, they heard a donkey bray not far away. They froze in place until several minutes passed to make sure it wasn't a defensive trumpeting of their position.

Dallas retrieved the tubes of paint from his pack and turned on his scanner so he could see where he poured the paint laced with iron and other metal shavings. He slowly walked along the outer wall of the building. This specialized marking would enable the drones to pick up the signal without problem. He squeezed the bottle, which looked like a ketchup container, sending bits of liquid out in front nearly two feet. A clear and odorless liquid, in daylight, it wouldn't be visible without a scanner like he had tonight.

Andy followed behind to watch for signs of another sentry, turning to face backwards often to check for someone following them. He snapped pictures silently, sending them to Peterson for the upload. He was trying to lean into an open window to take a picture of what looked like young children when he heard the sounds of water falling and realized he was standing not more than three feet away from a little boy peeing in the night. He completely froze and let the kid do his business.

It was all over in less than a minute. The kid, probably scared of the dark, ran back inside the large room and disappeared into the sea of bodies. Dallas returned, and they waited until it sounded like no one else had awakened and then snapped shots of the blackness inside the open window they hoped would reveal something when properly projected.

Dallas pointed a reverse course to head back where they started, shooting everything, including boulders and felled trees.

When they met up with the other group, Kit Holmes was eager to tell them something. He got close, whispering, "Found some ammunition crates and spent rounds, even some .50 cal, as well as empty C4 containers, lying around. Looks like they brought in a pygmy railroad car by helicopter and dropped it here. All locked up. I'm betting they're storing some serious firepower there."

"That's good intel. Somebody's been practicing."

"A training camp?" Archie asked.

Dallas shrugged. "How about you?" he asked Sven.

"I'm guessing yes. This isn't a garrison. I want to see the pictures when we get back."

"Nobody saw any evidence of our hostages, then?" Andy posed.

The collective shaking of heads was disappointing, but part of the job was eliminating possibilities.

They returned to their base, quickly retrieved everything, covered up all indication anyone had been there, and quietly crept through the lip of the crater and down the side. Medium-sized rocks rolled down the sides of the hill, several men sliding on their butts when they almost took a twisted-ankle fall. It took them nearly an hour to come down the sides that took only half that time on the climb.

At the bottom, they removed their sweaty helmets and stopped for a water break, releasing a collective sigh that no one was injured and the element of surprise was still on their side.

An hour later, they stumbled into camp, just as the horizon was beginning to blush. It was nearly four. Andy was looking forward to a little sleep before their next round.

Peterson grinned as he collected the two phones. "Great work, gents. I think we made some fans tonight."

Qwanme took possession of the delicate Invisios so he could disinfect, clean, and store them for next use.

"Can't wait to hear what they make of the pictures. Did you see any vehicles up there?" Peterson asked.

"No, sir," answered Dallas. "I think they're dropping in supplies. The crater wall going up is so rocky and treacherous it's a natural barrier. No way could you haul anything heavy in there, so I think it's dropped by chopper."

"Did they all look like kids?"

"Couldn't see," answered Andy. "Might have been a mixed group, but I didn't see any girls. Did you guys?"

Kit and Connor shook their heads.

"Saw spent cartridges all over the place," Sven added. "I think it's like a little training camp. Little boys volunteered or abducted to train. They get them old enough to be able to hold and shoot without it sending them back on their butts. An army of children." Sven spat into the night.

"How was *your* day? Train any baboons?" Andy asked Peterson.

"Gunnar had a fit when he discovered his labor crew was gone. You owe the boys who stayed behind some serious bank. And you should have seen Conley. He was patching up scrapes and bruises and took care of someone's ingrown toenail. Pretty disgusting stuff."

"Yeah, well, when you're trained to operate, you operate," said Andy, laughing to himself. He'd have to give Conley kudos for his good behavior. "And no baboons located or brought into surgery."

"They have to get the pens built first," added Sven. "But you don't want to hear all that screaming all night long. The pack will follow a captured member for miles and make everyone miserable. They make such a ruckus."

"I'm gonna take a shower and get this shit off my face. Can I get some shut-eye?" Archie asked.

Peterson nodded and gave the all clear to the group, who scattered. He stepped up to Andy. "You want to go into town today?"

It wasn't the first thing Andy was looking forward to. But the unspoken benefit of that mission was a chance to call Aimee. And he needed to do that.

"Can I get a couple of hours in?"

"Sure. Take three or four. Get some grub and then we'll take off. Today, we'll travel by truck."

"I'd like that, sir."

Andy was headed to his cot when Peterson called him out. "Hey, Andy. You did good today. I made sure to tell Kyle you were a very welcome addition here. I think with you on the Team, we're about to change our luck, and I told him so."

"Thank you, sir. But Kyle's not the one I have to impress. I'd appreciate a good word with the Lt. Commander, sir."

"I'll do that."

As Andy tried to leave, Peterson interrupted him again. He hated like hell when someone didn't know when the conversation was over. He was tired, wet, and a little sore. He'd have been happier with a firefight. Sven had been right about that.

"Sir?"

"Do you still think we need Tucker and some of the other guys?"

"Couldn't hurt. I think you're going to have to split the team up into groups to find where they're holding them. It's a huge area we have to search. If it will speed up the mission, I'm all for it. I mean, I think it would be smart to do that."

"I'm glad you said that, because they're on their way. They'll be here in two days."

"Tucker must be a new papa again. That's great." Andy was elated but knew Tucker was sacrificing much to tag along.

Still, it was good news. Things were about to get interesting, which either meant they'd pull off a huge rescue mission or things would go all to hell. But it would be nice to do it with some of his buds.

CHAPTER 13

AIMEE WENT TO the Pinellas County Sheriff's Department and filed an incident report, like Dr. Denby had suggested. One of the deputies knew Andy and several other guys on other teams she didn't know. She felt it brought a little extra diligence on their part. They explained that with the report on file, any responding officers hopefully would access it and thus have better detail on her brother. That meant there was a greater chance less force would be used in any apprehension. She thanked them, got cards and cell phone numbers, and was promised house patrols on a regular basis, particularly at night.

She called Shelley on her way over to the clinic in Largo where she was going to attend a NAMI meeting, which Dr. Denby had also suggested, texting her the location and the fact that there was a day meeting she might be able to make.

"You were right, Shelley. And I just wanted you to know Dr. Denby put it in terms I could understand. I'm sorry if I was a bit testy with you."

"My bedside manner sucks sometimes. And maybe I just don't have the big heart like you do, but I was worried about you. Still am, Aimee. But you're on the right track."

"Thanks. So no cop-calling, okay? I'm going to be in that meeting, so don't panic."

Shelley laughed. "I'm going over to the school to start getting the classroom set up for after break. You want to catch dinner somewhere, or do you need some space?"

"No, actually, I was thinking the same thing. I'll text you when I'm done. Let's make it an early dinner, okay?"

"You got it. Can I ask you if Andy has called?"

Aimee sighed into the phone, feeling that tiny stab of pain and worry again. "Not yet. It's still early. I'm not worried," she lied.

"Okay, I promise not to ask again. See you later."

She had an hour before the meeting began, so she visited the Rose Hill Shelter. It was a training school for vet techs, and she'd driven by it hundreds of times and never thought about adoption before.

The reception area was sterile, and of course, there was the unmistakable smell of animals, even though it was clean and the floor buffed to a shiny patina. The walls were papered with posters of missing pets and stories of how abandoned dogs and cats had been adopted—some of them with major injuries—and went on to have a happy, normal life afterwards. Aimee drew strength and hope from the many stories advertised there.

A young, uniformed technician asked her to come forward when her name was called.

"I'd like to inquire about seeing some of your dogs who need good homes. I've never done this before. What's the process?"

"Do you have a preference for size of dog?"

"I would think a larger one. I don't want a puppy. They're cute, but I think too much work for me."

"Have you had a dog before?"

"When I was growing up. Our family had a lab-mix of some kind. Her name was Cookie. My parents had her for about ten years."

The tech went on to explain the process and told her that

many of the dogs who were deemed receptive had gone through simple obedience training and were housebroken. Many of the dogs had been left behind by elderly people undergoing life changes, so it wasn't uncommon to find a dog already very well behaved and desiring human companionship.

The hardest part of the meeting was seeing the variety of dog population in cages. Aimee wanted to take them all. One by one, she put her fingers up to the cage and spoke with several. The technician let her interact with three who she felt a connection with, so she had a short playtime in one of the rooms.

There was a beautiful golden retriever mix named Sandy who looked like she had the youth and energy to be able to take on runs. Her bark was loud, but she was also very playful. The dog had been spayed already and hadn't been in the shelter long. She went over the dog's records with the tech, and Aimee was hopeful Andy would be okay with her decision.

Sandy sat in front of her as she explained her situation to the young girl. "I need to check with my husband first, and I should get a call in the next few days. I want to be sure he's okay with having a dog, since this isn't anything we've talked about. Can I reserve her for a few days? Get back to you?"

Sandy put a paw on her lap as if she understood. She was begging to be taken home.

"I can call you if someone else comes in and wants to adopt her. We do charge a fee, so if you pay the deposit, I can give you first right. But if we don't hear back from you within a few hours, then we'll release the dog to someone else. I think she's very adoptable and won't be here long, so don't take too much time."

As Aimee said good-bye, Sandy's mournful expression broke her heart. She knew the look the dog gave her as she was being led back to her cage was something she'd never forget. She was already connected and ready to take the plunge.

The clinic in Largo was an outpatient drop-in space servicing runaways and teens. She smelled fresh coffee brewing and knew that usually meant a meeting was about to begin so followed her nose to a large classroom with chairs around several long tables. About a dozen people had already arrived, some in pairs and some singles.

Aimee was greeted and given a name badge after being introduced to several of the regular attendees. By the time the meeting coordinator arrived, nearly all the seats had been filled.

She was introduced again as a newcomer attending on behalf of her brother. Aimee was grateful she didn't have to go into details of her relationship with Logan with a room full of strangers. She listened to stories from parents, siblings, and even spouses of people affected by various forms of mental illness. Some were kids living on the street that parents hadn't seen for many years. Others were trying to cope with a family member living in their house, disrupting other family or worse, stealing and abusing others. One couple had a daughter diagnosed with a severe mental illness they had dealt with for several years, only to have their other child, a son, diagnosed with the same disease recently.

Aimee heard the stories of mothers who loved their sons and daughters but were afraid of their own children. They had stories of sending them to expensive rehab clinics. People had lost homes trying to pay for their kids' addiction issues over and over again until the family was nearly homeless themselves.

She heard one tale of a mother who hadn't seen her son for ten years but looked for him everywhere. She'd volunteered at homeless shelters, just to be able to have some sight of him, but never had and was still waiting.

It was an eye-opening experience for her. The room was filled with hope and realism, but she found a family of people there who were going through exactly what she was with Logan.

The coordinator asked her, finally, if she wanted to share about her experiences.

"My brother, Logan, has been homeless for over twelve years now, maybe longer, I don't know. We grew up in California, so when I moved here, I was surprised to see him working in a restaurant one night. But I could never get in touch with him. He was fired the night I saw him, and when I looked into where he was staying, he'd left his program and was back out on the street."

She showed them the gift he had left her. A couple of ladies were crying as she told her story. Then she talked about how conflicted she was about what to do with his reaching out and got more personal stories, all mixed, of how that had worked out for others in the room.

"Main thing is to make sure you don't put yourself in harm's way, Aimee," the coordinator said. "I think, from what you've heard today, you can expect that it will be a long bumpy road. Even when they clean up, they are still very flawed. You have to understand it's a long process and sometimes without a perfect ending."

Aimee was grateful for the honesty. She walked away knowing that there weren't one-size-fits-all solutions to these problems and that if she was going to bring Logan into their lives together, it was a long row to hoe. It was important to her that she let Andy know what she'd discovered so it could be a joint description.

But the funny thing was that, of all the stories that were told, all the questions anyone had in the group, everyone was completely aligned that Aimee should adopt Sandy and not wait for Andy's permission.

She took a class schedule and learned about a series of lectures given by various health professionals, helping to bring mental illness the attention it deserved, and vowed she'd attend as many of them as she could.

On the way home, she nearly went by the shelter and picked Sandy up but held to her conviction that she ask Andy first.

All during dinner with her friend, she thought about the golden dog who had so stolen her heart. The more she thought about it, the more convinced she became that adopting Sandy was the right thing to do. Shelley was happy to hear about the group and the classes.

"But I'm going to insist that you not stay home alone until you get that dog, Aimee. You're welcome to stay with me."

"I'm fine, Shelley, really."

"There you go again. Then invite me over. Honestly, Aimee, I won't sleep a wink if you don't."

"Okay. I'm in the mood for some romantic movies anyway. We'll get out the Kleenex and have a good cry tonight."

"Oh dear. That bad?"

"Well, you're inviting yourself. Are you sure you want to come?"

"Maybe we should work on a puzzle."

"Nope, it's going to be the Romance Channel. I want to learn about broken hearts that are mended, things that turn out in the end just the way we want them to. I've had enough reality for one day. And then I'm going to cry myself to sleep and dream of my husband."

Shelley shook her head in mock disgust. Finally, she added, with a wry smile, "Okay, but if you touch me, I'll slap you so hard you'll see stars."

CHAPTER 14

THE ROAD TO Benot twisted through some beautiful scenery, showing sparkling lakes and little villages tucked into the foliage along the edges. Life was simple there. The colorful patterns of dresses and headdresses the ladies wore fascinated Andy. They passed by women working in the fields or drying animal skins and boiling fabric in huge oil drum kettles. Everywhere there was a healthy population of chickens and toddlers.

Peterson had told them their cover was that they were helping to set up a clinic in the town, given a charter through a church charity in the United States. Sven thought that approach was a sound one. They were out scouting for locations to set up shop.

"Everything in the big city needs permission. This way we find out who is running it. Who is afraid of whom, who the good guys are and who are not so good."

Sven had taken the seat next to Andy.

"So you heard Tucker's coming?"

"Yup. Armando, Fredo, and Kelly are on their way, too, with a couple guys from Colin Riley's new concern. I'm anxious to talk to them, see how they're doing."

"So you and Kelly might patch things up?" Andy asked.

"We'll see. I haven't spoken to her. I'm keeping a low profile. But I'm glad she's coming. She has the best kind of connections."

"So is she still independent?"

"She got her credentials back. Can't explain how she got them in such quick order, because normally, they take weeks. Somebody high up must have pulled some strings."

"Maybe Riley had something to do with it."

Sven wrinkled his nose. "State is sometimes difficult. They aren't elected officials who could use a campaign donation. So I don't think Riley has the pull there. But this mission got on someone's radar, so I'm grateful."

"Those diplomatic connections might come in handy."

"I hope we don't need them, but yes." Sven watched a group of young girls walking home from school, all in a dark blue and white uniform. Two nuns sat drinking a can of soda nearby, under the shade of an umbrella.

"You don't see many of those here, do you?" Andy asked Sven.

"Not hardly. Used to be heavily Catholic, but not so much now. Everything takes a back seat to politics these days. They've lost so many clergy in the past few years. And the UN cannot make up the shortfall, but they're trying."

"So will we be welcomed here?"

"Hard to say. First, we'll try it without Kelly. If we strike out, we'll come back with her and let her work her magic." Sven winked and gave a belly laugh. Andy knew he was looking forward to the reunion and the magic she might bring to his life too.

Peterson turned in the front seat, addressing them. "Andy, I promised you a call home. What about you, Sven?"

"Thanks, sir. I'm good."

His LPO handed Andy the phone. "Wait until we come to a stop. I'll give you about five minutes privacy, and then you join us. Got it?"

"Thanks, man."

The quaintness of the countryside was soon diluted with evidence of a city coming up. The road widened and was littered with abandoned cars, a dead chicken that had been run over, and scooters buzzing in and around traffic everywhere, making the driving especially challenging. Andy's neck was beginning to hurt from the jerking movements of their truck. He'd gotten some bites on his legs that itched badly and were swollen. He was going to look for some Benadryl as soon as he could safely get his kit out.

Several taller buildings clustered around a central location of the town with a fountain at the intersection of two main roads. Children played in the pool, splashing cars and tossing water through opened truck windows and at pedestrian traffic passing by. The red clay from the dusty non-paved thoroughfare had scattered silt everywhere. Andy was beginning to taste it.

The driver pulled into a parking lot outside a commercial bank building several stories tall. Peterson directed the other two trucks to pull up alongside them while everyone got out, adjusted their packs, and stretched their legs. The driver had promised to watch their stuff, but no one was buying it.

Andy dialed Aimee's number. If it was noon in Africa, it would be around five in the morning Florida time. But she picked her phone up after two rings.

"God, it's good to hear your voice, sweetheart," Andy started.

"Me too, Andy. I kept telling myself to be patient. It wasn't working. So glad you called."

"Listen, I've only been given five minutes so let's make it count. I'm good, it's hot, the food is mostly what we packed in here, so far there is no end in sight, but I'm safe. Settling in. Anything eventful going on there?"

"Oh, God, where do I start?"

"Uh-oh. Hope that doesn't mean Cory's making a nuisance of himself."

"No. Haven't seen him, but I think Logan has been reaching

out to me. Made me a bracelet and left it on the doorstep. I gave him some of your old clothes."

"Is that necessary? I mean, not that I'm in love with the clothes, but do you think that's wise?"

"I've been told that it's not. And you'll be happy to know Shelley and Dr. Denby got me to file a police report."

"You're welcome, Andy," Shelley's voice shouted from the other side of the room.

"Shelley's staying over? That's smart. Tell her thanks."

"I'm learning about mental illness. Dr. Denby suggested a group, and I attended the first meeting today."

"This isn't one of those twelve-step programs now, is it?"

"No, it's a support group."

"Okay. So you filed a police report. And what else? How does Logan look?"

"I haven't seen him, Andy. I just know it's him."

"Okay, that explains why Shelley's there."

"I want to ask you something. I want to adopt a dog. It was suggested since I'm alone so much. But I wanted to get your approval first."

"He better be potty trained."

"I found a really nice golden Lab mix. I think she'd be a good running companion too. But mainly it's for my safety. I don't know how he found out where we live, but with a loyal dog, I'd feel safer."

"I'm cool with it." Andy saw Peterson give him the wrap-up signal. "Hey, I gotta go. I'll try to call back in a couple of days. But promise me you'll not encourage him to hang around the house, Aimee, okay? Not without me there."

"Do you know how long?"

"No clue."

"One more quick question. If I need to talk to someone, do I call your LPO's wife on Team 4 or—"

"Call Christy. What do you need to talk about?"

"I don't know. There's a lot more going on. Met with Carmen Hernandez and her attorney—"

"Problems? Okay, look, I'm really getting pressured. But call Christy. Use her. They aren't on deployment yet, so you can even talk to Kyle if you want."

"Thanks. Go save the day."

"Working on it."

Peterson banged on the window and yelled from behind the glass, "Carr! I need your butt out here now."

Andy was embarrassed Aimee had to hear that. He also didn't think it was very smart for him to make such a spectacle or draw attention to them.

"Sorry, Andy. Love you. Be safe."

"Love you, sweetheart. Sleep naked, but not when Shelley's over there."

She was still laughing when Andy hung up.

Peterson grabbed the phone back. "Next time, three minutes, then maybe you'll be done in five."

"Sorry. You know how it is with that first phone call home."

They divided into two groups of six. Andy stayed with Sven, and Dallas went with Peterson. They were to work the perimeter of the town center, looking for a space large enough for a three-office clinic, or that was the ruse. But while they were checking out vacant buildings for lease, they were observing the population, other shops, and who ran them.

"Everything okay at home?" Sven asked.

"More or less. Being married is complicated. It's good, don't get me wrong, but Aimee gets into things, and I'd just feel better being there."

"That's always the way it happens. Shit explodes sometimes at home."

"This wasn't that bad, but—well, that's a talk for another time when I don't have to concentrate."

They took pictures of storefronts but also got shots of the local Guarda police and license plates of some expensive cars slowly traveling through the downtown area. Even the shops on the ground floor were of interest. Several times they found a group of military-aged males gathering in the back of some of these shops or walking together on the opposite street. The team observed what kind of vehicles they drove and who they talked to.

The two groups met back near their parked trucks. Sven had a plan to talk to the local Commissioner of Health, so while the rest of the team waited, he and Andy and Peterson walked up the steps to a three-story government office. At the side, in a taller wing, was the local jail, evident by the bars on the windows. Faces appeared between the bars along with hands and forearms as the prisoners watched the streets below.

Inside, the building was air conditioned, which was so welcome that Andy closed his eyes and took in a deep breath of cool, clean air free of red clay dust. Sven had already opened the frosted glass door to Amadi Sabi's office, the Commissioner of Health.

They were lucky to find Mr. Sabi sitting behind his desk, the reception area of his office vacant. He motioned for them to enter, saying something in his local Benin tongue. As they entered through the doorway, he switched to French, having sized them up to be Europeans.

Sven spoke up, responding in French, and asked if he spoke English.

"Yes. Yes, I do. You are English then?"

"I'm Norwegian, but these two are from the States, yes. Allow me to introduce you. This is Dr. Carr and Dr. Peterson. We are here from the Southern Baptist Africa Project. We've been given a mandate to find a suitable location to set up a mobile clinic. We'll need a base office, and Benot is centrally located."

"Please, sit down," he said graciously. There was only one chair across from his desk, so Peterson took it. Andy hoped they didn't look too rough around the edges, since they had been literally camping in the bush for four days. Sven continued the discussion.

"We understand this is a safe area?" he floated to Mr. Sabi, trying to calculate the rise he'd get out of the gentleman.

Sabi laughed deep and long—almost a guttural growl—shaking his head. "If you wanted safe, well, then you'd have to go back to the States. But even there it isn't safe. Here in Africa, we are very grateful for what the rest of the world can do to help us. We welcome you with open arms. I can probably find some surplus properties you can rent directly from this office, saving you from having to deal with crooked leasing agents in town. How does that sound?"

"Well, what I meant was, we'd like to make a presence here, expand if we could. Perhaps build a hospital," Sven proposed.

"You have such strength?"

"We do a lot of fundraising. For the right cause, yes."

"I cannot promise you a site for a hospital, but if you want to operate a clinic, you would have to do so under my office auspices. And we wouldn't want to interfere with the World Health projects in the area, either. For instance, we wouldn't want to build a clinic right next to another one, would we? We'd like to serve the entire country."

"That makes sense, Mr. Sabi. Where would be the greatest need in the safest area?"

"Look, doctor—what did you say your name was?"

"I am not a doctor. Sven Tolar."

"Mr. Tolar from Norway, the safest place is one that is well guarded. You see, the way we work here is that we provide you with a good location at a relatively cheap price, but you will have to hire security to ensure the integrity of the project and keep the doors open. Many of our police and fire departments work extra duty as guards in banks, hospitals, clinics, and sometimes schools or traveling with businessmen and officials from all around the world."

"So what you're telling me is that the location isn't as important, as long as we have the budget for the security, right?"

"Exactly."

"And what if we were to bring our own security?" Peterson injected.

"Of course, but they would work under our people, who are highly trained and specialize in knowing everything there is to know about security here. You wouldn't want to do it on your own. It's not recommended, and I don't think I could get the permits for it, either."

Andy felt Sven had come to the end of his useful conversation. In one hand, Sabi had a sheaf of papers at least a quarter inch thick.

"So you wish we should fill out the paperwork?" Andy asked, leaning forward to accept the stack of forms.

"Please, doctor," he said, handing them to Andy.

When Peterson stood, Mr. Sabi did as well, shaking their hands one by one. "Gentlemen, I look forward to our partnership going forward. Please, use me as your resource. I will help you get whatever you need. I will be your partner, standing in the shadows, making things happen for you. All worries about security and safety should by now be put to rest. *N'est pas*?"

CHAPTER 15

SHELLEY WAS OFF to her classroom prep, so the two parted company and went their separate ways. Aimee couldn't wait to go get Sandy. On the way, she stopped for a set of stainless steel dog bowls in their own stand, bought dog treats, and some expensive gourmet frozen raw dog food with venison and salmon, along with some kibbles. She also bought a yellow jeweled collar she hoped would fit, with a yellow leash to match. The pet store owner recommended a good shampoo for a longer-haired dog, and she passed on the conditioner.

The whole bill was just under two hundred dollars. She swallowed hard and gave her credit card.

With the new leash and collar clutched in her hand, she ran up the steps and into the reception area. A new clerk was at the front desk.

"I'm here to pick up Sandy."

"Sandy? Let me check to see if she's still here. We had a couple in here yesterday afternoon, and I thought they adopted her."

Aimee was crestfallen.

"But I paid the deposit. She said they would hold her for me for a few days and call me first if—"

"I see that she's been adopted. I'm so sorry."

"But—" Aimee's eyes began to overflow. She looked down at

the leash and the collar and felt the pangs deep in her heart. "I *paid* for her."

"No one pays, Miss."

It was a snooty answer, but Aimee knew she had it coming. Suddenly, the helpful tech looked ugly and cruel. Aimee wanted to climb over the counter and go check for herself to make sure the dog was really gone. But then she'd have to see all those other lonesome faces behind bars—sweet animals she couldn't afford to take home.

The tech was waiting for Aimee to say something further.

"Can't you double check with your colleague who was here yesterday? Do you actually have adoption paperwork processed?"

The girl's eyes narrowed. "I don't have access to the director's office, and he keeps all the adoption files there. But yes, I see that her fee was paid and—"

"But *I* paid the fee. *I* did it," Aimee insisted.

"It happens all the time. Some people come in and pay for an animal and then just never come pick it up." Her eyebrows, that tiny strip of over-plucked hair above her eyes, rose into her bangs.

Aimee was horrified. "Can you check to see if she's still here?"

Just then, the girl from yesterday entered the reception area, wearing a rubber apron and gloves. She pushed the hair from her forehead with her forearm and greeted Aimee.

"I'd shake your hand, but—"

"She's come for Sandy," the other tech whispered.

"Yes, and I got her all bathed for you. I had a feeling you'd be by. And since we've had so much interest in her, I knew someone would be taking her soon if you didn't. So I pulled her paperwork."

Aimee nearly fainted with relief.

"That's why she doesn't show up on the list," the tech said to the other girl.

"Okay, well, then I'm going to go get the exercise group going. Can you finish with her?"

"Of course." The tech smiled at Aimee. "I'm so sorry about that. I can see you were close to a meltdown. That bodes well for Sandy."

"I couldn't stop thinking about her. I talked to my husband early this morning, and he was fine with it. I knew she'd be popular."

"You made a wise choice, although we try to get the right homes for all our animals here. Some of our most injured ones, the ones who need the most care and love, seem to find the most loving homes. It's really a labor of love working here. There are special people all over the Largo area—they even come from out of state to check out our dogs. Sandy's profile just went up on our website yesterday, and we've had lots of calls. But that just means another nice dog will be adopted, so it's all good."

"Thank you for what you do. When I have an opportunity, and I can't do it now, I'd love to make a donation to your shelter. You're a non-profit?

"Yes, and since we're aligned with the school, we keep our fees low since it is offset a bit by part of their tuition, so it helps." She removed her rubber gloves and apron, tossing them in a towel bin in the corner. "Now, let's get the paperwork done, and then we'll see if the pretty girl is all ready for you. I don't want to put her in your car if she's still wet."

"I don't care. I honestly don't." Aimee knew Andy would have something to say about the condition of the car afterwards, but that was a hurdle she'd have to mount later. Right now, all she wanted to do was get Sandy to her home and get her adjusted seamlessly.

The tech helped Aimee fill out the adoption paperwork. She

was given a form she'd have to fill out to get her dog license, but the fee was included in her payment. In her paperwork was a list of vets in the area and a copy of what shots she'd had, and she was up to date. There was an extra copy so Aimee could send it in with the license form.

"Can I ask you a favor? If I fill this out, can you send it in for me? That way I know it will be done correctly. Add the shot records too?"

"Absolutely." She began filling in several boxes and then turned it over to Aimee to put her address and signature at the bottom. "I'll include a copy of the license charge, and you might want to put in your cell number."

"Oh, good idea." Aimee added that.

"One more thing? Go to one of those pet stores that has the address tags, and fill in your address and your phone number, in case she gets lost. It helps. She's going to be a little skittish at first since everything's new, so you should get this done on your way home. Your license should be mailed to you within a week or so."

"Thank you so much!"

"Okay, well, I'm going to get your girl, see if she's ready."

Aimee handed her the leash and the collar.

"Oh, this is cute. A jeweled collar. I can tell she's going to be spoiled."

"No doubt about it."

The tech disappeared behind a swinging door while Aimee tapped her foot. She heard her stomach growl and realized she hadn't eaten anything for breakfast. Someone else came into the room behind her, which set off a little bell summoning an attendant, but Aimee couldn't take her eyes off that little crack in the door, waiting.

At last, she heard the tech's voice behind the door. "That's a good girl. Now, let's go outside and meet your new mommy, shall we?"

Right on cue, Sandy barked. Aimee was so thrilled she nearly wet her pants. Sandy burst through the door, and ran right for her, yanking the leash from the tech's hand. She put her paws on the counter and barked again.

Aimee leaned forward. "We're going to have to teach you about that, but are you ready to go home?"

The dog fed on the excitement of the moment. Aimee figured she was conditioned by the sight of the leash and not necessarily going home with her. But she'd take whatever she could get. She reached over the countertop and grabbed the leash as the tech popped up the countertop to allow Sandy to enter the reception area. But Sandy was headed straight for the door, no doubt excited to be taken for a walk.

The tech followed behind, all the paperwork stuck in a plastic bag, along with some instructions and a couple dog treats. Aimee opened the second door, and Sandy jumped up on the seat without being coaxed.

"You're going to need to get a seat cover. This dog is going to shed," said the young girl.

"I know it. And I'm going to need a dog bed too. I tried to think of everything. I'll get it on the way home."

The tech gave a loving rub to Sandy's jowl, patted her head, and accepted the paw she was presented, shaking it. "Good-bye, Sandy. Have fun in your new home."

Aimee closed the door, and by the time she went around to the driver's seat, Sandy had already occupied it. She slid herself in and ordered the dog to go to the back seat, which she did. With a thumbs-up, Aimee drove out of the parking lot and headed for the pet store on the way home.

After another two-hundred-dollar shopping spree, even

with the pet store owner giving her a ten percent discount on her new purchases, Aimee and Sandy were finally home. She attached her leash and tried not to let her pull too hard, yanking it back sharply to get the dog to heel. She figured it wasn't too soon to begin training. Once inside the door, she unclipped the leash and let the dog roam the house, while she brought in the food, the dog bed, and the treats.

When Aimee entered the living room, she didn't see Sandy anywhere.

"Sandy? Where are you?"

Did I leave the door open?

Dropping her items, she ran up the stairs to the master bedroom. Sandy had nestled herself in the pillows of her bed. That's when Aimee knew she could take the dog bed back. That's where the dog was used to sleeping when she had an owner who loved her.

"Well, if that's the way it's going to be, Sandy, I'll be fine with it. But you're going to have to sell Andy on the idea. He's going to be your biggest problem."

Sandy angled her head, listening, as if she understood fully.

CHAPTER 16

ANDY HELPED THE cranky UN project manager to build sheds and enclosures for his new undertaking. He put up with the eccentric former zookeeper, but it wasn't long before he realized the man really did know quite a bit about primates. The long-term mission wasn't as important as helping to gain his trust and support today. They were using the jungle outpost as their new base, even though they had a perfectly good one closer to the Northern border. They owed him something.

The photographs that had been taken proved that indeed there was a training camp for young boys at the top of Mont Sokbaro. What wasn't clear was who was paying for this, and without complaints of kidnappings or the abuse of the children, the folks in Norfolk decided it was something they shouldn't insert themselves in. At least for now.

That suited Andy fine.

So the search remained for the hostages, and every day now that it wasn't resolved was creating a lot of tension. The upper brass decided the Team should remain at Gunnar's encampment but continue to work their way outward in all directions, like the spokes of a wheel. They swept through the grassy savannah lands, trying to get information from some of the smaller villages since the larger towns were proving to be dry holes. These were mostly farmers who tended small plots and sold their goods locally at the markets. Life was simple, and it was also very tough. They had a natural distrust of newcomers and strangers who often brought so much violence with them.

It was a good decision, based on good intel, and Andy agreed it could yield fruit, given enough time.

They had a two-day window until Tucker and Kelly arrived, along with several others from Kyle's SEAL Team 3. That reunion was to be back at the stone-walled villa near Kandi and the Niger border where they'd been taken their first day here.

Sometimes drone footage would highlight something interesting, and they'd send a party the next day, but no one was coming up with any actionable result… until the day they were supposed to leave for the rendezvous up North. A girls' school in Benot had been attacked, and two teachers and a half dozen girls were taken. From the way the attack occurred, Peterson, Sven, and Dallas were convinced it was the same group.

"They came in with guns blazing, killing the local police who were moonlighting as guards at the school. Once the protectors were gone, they were able to grab at random," said Peterson. "We're to go looking for them."

"What about Tucker and the others we're supposed to meet?" asked Andy.

"I guess we'll be late, then," said Peterson. "This takes priority now. We'll get up there as soon as we can."

"Or maybe a few of us could go up and bring them down to meet us here," Sven added.

"Yeah, it doesn't make much sense to have people who can help sitting on their hands," said Dallas.

"Problem as I see it is, we can't spare anybody." Peterson's jaw was set. He was about to make a big mistake, and all three of the others knew it.

This was one of those times where an LPO earned his creds or lost the confidence of the team. Andy knew there were always dangers to every decision. Picking the right choice to navigate the best one was hard but what a good leader had to learn to do.

"Look, why don't Sven and I go up there and get them? We take one truck. Sven knows the road. We can get back down here quickly if we don't hike like we did coming in." Andy was hoping Peterson would buy it but could already see he was set against splitting the Team up any further.

"Not what I'd do. You're gonna have to stick with me for a bit. We'll get up there, and just a couple of days won't make that much difference."

Dallas spat on the ground but held his tongue.

Andy thought about the choice again and what was about to be done and decided to lay it on the line. He didn't want to give Peterson a challenge to his authority, but he knew it was a mistake. Convinced Tucker and Kelly, as well as the others they brought, would double their chances of a successful mission, he had to speak out.

"I'm going to ask you to consider something, sir." Andy saw Peterson's eyes go red with anger and then settle down, as the fear factor started percolating.

"All right. Let's hear it. But then I decide, and that's the end of it, agreed?"

Everyone nodded their heads.

"Sven and I are part of the Team but newbies. We add an extra element to the mix. The guys haven't worked with us much yet. You've already got a full squad. You've got Conley and several others who speak French. You met with Mr. Sabi—it would be easy to add someone to that conversation. But if we stay and it doesn't work out how we think it should—say we engage and it gets heavy—you think any of us would be able to send two out to get the rest of the team that, at that point, we'd sorely need? But if we delay and you guys do general information gathering and not execute the spear until we have a full force, we'll have better intel and a whole lot more firepower. It's just nuts to have them waiting up there."

Silence took over the group. Dallas jumped in.

"Two more won't be as effective as the seven we have on the way. Weakest link in that plan is, what happens if you or Sven get into trouble? Then we're totally cut off, and the groups stay separated or go in blind."

Andy nodded at the obvious flaw in his plan and got Sven's attention. "What do you think?" he asked the Norwegian.

"I like it. Can we take one of the Gunnar's guys? Part of his corps? Might give us legitimacy."

"You're gonna get that bastard to give up one of his men? What planet are you on, Sven?" Peterson was livid with that suggestion.

Sven coolly tilted his head and smiled. Andy knew he'd already thought about the solution.

"Well, we tell him that we're going up to get Uncle Sam's money and his State Department liaison, who will be very grateful for his assistance and might make a serious donation to his cause. It could lighten his heavy financial burden a bit."

Dallas began to chuckle. Andy had a hard time keeping a straight face, so he looked at his boots.

"You son of a bitch. How do you know they're bringing in cash?" Peterson demanded.

"Because that's part of what Kelly does. And she's got the backing of a billionaire. I was in on the rescue of his daughter last year. He'd do just about anything to find these guys. If she doesn't bring some in, she can get it quickly."

It was a beautiful plan. Andy could see that Peterson was hesitant to make a decision.

"You know in your gut it's the only way, sir. It risks only two of us, but damn if it doesn't increase the odds by double. I'm willing to put my life on the line for it. Sven here is dumb enough to do anything."

Dallas started to laugh.

Andy continued, "Besides, you can always say Sven talked you into it later, if you have to."

"But I don't want to have that conversation with the Headshed."

"With all due respect, sir, I don't know a good LPO who hasn't," grumbled Dallas.

Andy had been told stories about Kyle. "As legendary as Lansdowne is, there was a time in his career he thought he was going to be written up and stuck on a desk, or worse. It was a real rough patch, and it lasted months."

"I heard about that," whispered Dallas. "I think my brother was on the team when that went down."

Sven put his arm on Peterson's shoulder. "There are no safe choices, only good ones. You're about to make a really good one, Peterson. And us three are going to help you carry it out. Put your trust in us."

It started as a gentle nod of his head, but within seconds, Peterson was completely focused on saying yes. "Hell, let's go for it."

It wouldn't have been appropriate to cheer, but Andy thought he heard one echoing out over the lush savannah grasslands of Benin, something he might have heard in any football stadium back home.

One of the things he'd been taught by SEALs who had gone before him was that it was a very good idea to make your LPO look damn smart, and that kudos and promotions always ran downward to the benefit of the men underneath. Not to mention, this was the Brotherhood. A team was supposed to cover all the aspects of a mission, making up for little weaknesses that would inevitably pop up. They were prepared to do the impossible. It was what their training was all about. It was what the Trident meant, after all. If the roles were reversed and Andy was the LPO, they'd all do the same for him.

CHAPTER 17

AIMEE TOOK SANDY out for a run on Gulf Boulevard, eventually winding up at the nearby dog park. There, she was able to let her off the leash and let her run freely, playing with several others.

She checked her cell and returned a call to Mr. Kornblum.

"I'm afraid I have some bad news. Carmen passed away last night. It was very peaceful, I'm told."

Aimee's nerve endings were stunned as this new bombshell scattered at her feet. She sat forward, clutching the phone to her ear so she could hear better.

"But she looked so—" It was hard to accept after only knowing her for such a short time. Her passing brought on a wave of regret. Although she'd been told this might happen, it wasn't something she expected so soon.

"I know. I was a little surprised myself. But the doctors had been warning me all along this could happen. But, like you, I was not expecting it for perhaps weeks. So now I have the task of administering her trust, filing notices and distributing her assets according to her will. And that involves you, Aimee, as the sole beneficiary. Is it possible you could meet me in the office tomorrow or sometime this week?"

"Gosh, everything is so rushed these days for me—changing so fast I can hardly keep track. I just met her, and now she's gone. I'm being selfish, I know."

"Not at all, Aimee. Perfectly normal. But I'm glad you acted when you did. Take your time, if you like. There isn't any time requirement, but it's always more prudent to do it sooner than later. Sometimes, in these cases, people start coming out of the woodwork, claiming they're entitled to a piece of the estate. I have no such knowledge of anyone like that, but I never say never. However, the will is pretty bullet-proof, if I do say so myself."

"Oh gosh. I didn't think of that. Really?"

"Happens all the time. But that's not your worry. It's mine to protect. Just remember, this is what she wanted, Aimee."

She gulped in air. "Okay, I could be there tomorrow if—" She looked at Sandy playing. She didn't dare leave her in the house alone. It was too soon.

"If what?"

"I adopted a dog, and I've just picked her up today. Would it be possible for me to bring her with me? I don't trust that she can be left in my house alone."

"What kind of dog?"

"She's big. Retriever mix. But well behaved. I don't think she'd cause a problem."

"I don't see why not. I have clients with service dogs all the time. So tomorrow, shall we say ten o'clock?"

Aimee knew she didn't have to check her calendar. Several of her workmen were just coming back from visiting their families out of state, and no one had called her about coming back just yet. "I'll be there."

She ran with Sandy farther down the boulevard then reversed course and came back to her house. The dog was mildly distracted with the traffic, but overall, she did very well on her first day out. She nearly drained her water dish, so Aimee knew to be on the lookout for her first accident.

The mail came, and books she'd ordered arrived in their brown packaging. Two were Hank Borges books, dog-eared with covers curling up. She sat down bringing her coffee into the living room as Sandy jumped up on the leather couch, nestling beside her as if she'd grown up there.

"Do you like science fiction, Sandy? This man"—she held up the book—"used to write books in this very house. He probably wrote this one here. Should we look?"

Sandy's ears were alert, waiting to listen to more of the story.

Opening the cover page, Aimee read the dedication.

'This book is dedicated to C, who knows the outer space of my interior better than anyone else in this galaxy. There are epic travels we will take one day, and they will be glorious journeys of the heart. Just think what we can discover when we leave our temporal bodies and free ourselves into the Heavens.'

H—

Inside the back-cover flap was the familiar black and white picture of Borges standing barefoot on the beach just like the one outside her living room window. She flipped back to the dedication page and then turned through the list of his books and testimonials, looking for something about or for Carmen, but at last came to the title page and then the start of the book.

The Prince of Scion.

'It was the summer that would change his life forever. Just one trip to the green waters and yellow beaches of Scion, the mythical healing beach on the fourth planet of the Recovery Galaxy. He knew that all the energy he received from the ocean would help restore his wounds and make the upcom-

ing battle his to own. He was conqueror of the worlds of Scion. But he'd been ousted.

Now was his chance to come back, with revenge, and this time, he'd win the war.'

Aimee continued reading the story until past the brightest part of the day and then until the sun began to set. She patted Sandy on the head and walked out on the beach, clutching Hank Borges' book in her left hand. Checking back at her house, she saw Sandy sitting there just inside the window, watching like a sentry.

The crowds were smaller today with the air crisp and colder than usual. The waves barely made a noise as they lapped upon the smooth, wet sand surface. She waved to the fisherman who was out there every day sitting in his lawn chair, often drinking beers in the morning. She watched as a pod of dolphin swam by, heading south, taking turns breaching the waterline and then diving back in. There was hardly an audience to revel in their beauty.

She'd not been spending much time outside the last few days. The wedding and then Andy's sudden departure made the past week feel like a marathon. They'd spent so much time planning everything. Then, in a whoosh, it was all over, and she was alone, like the first time she came to Sunset Beach. Then there was poor Carmen and the bracelet that Logan had left for her. So much had happened there was not enough time to tell Andy about it all.

And now things were about to change again. She thought about Logan and what he was doing, even regretting that she'd filed the police report.

It seemed the whole world was pulling her in a direction not of her choosing. She started the walk, of course, facing the path, but forces unseen were guiding her deeper into the forest, away from former routines, the world she thought she knew so well.

Is this how a new bride feels?

Aimee knew that most brides didn't have to say good-bye to their new husbands not even a week after the marriage. Maybe that's what was causing all her confusion. Everything in her world had begun to shift. It almost felt like she didn't have any control in the matter.

As the sun melted into the horizon, she said her little prayer for Andy, wishing he could feel the pull of the magic of this place, that golden tether bringing him back home safe to her. It would all be over soon, and then they'd be together once again, to jumpstart their future—until the next mission, of course.

Maybe in time this would begin to feel routine.

Aimee fed Sandy again, prepared herself some soup, and then took her new friend out for one last potty before bed. Back inside, she made sure everything downstairs was locked. Sandy followed her up the stairs where she jumped back up on the king-sized mattress and waited for her to shower and dress for bed.

She took the book with her, adjusted the pillows and with Sandy by her side, tried to finish the story. She fell away into a green oceans of Scion dream, wondering what was to become of the prince's blue vampire second-in-command. Would he find a happily ever after, or was this not going to be a romance?

SANDY'S BARK AWAKENED Aimee around one o'clock A.M. She clamored to her feet, grabbing her robe. Sandy was at the open doorway to the master, clearly barking at something downstairs. She stepped next to the dog then came out onto the balcony overlooking the living room area, checked for movement, and didn't find anything of interest.

"What did you hear, girl?" she asked as she petted the top of her head. Sandy stood on all fours, wagging her tail, but didn't appear to want to go downstairs.

"Should we try it?" Aimee called out, "Is there anyone there?"

Her voice echoed throughout the great room. They both listened carefully. There was no answer.

Andy kept a gun in the nightstand drawer and a baseball bat in the guest bedroom, which she passed on her way to the landing. If this were Logan as she believed, she didn't want to shoot him. Decision made, she grabbed the baseball bat and, with Sandy by her side, made her way silently down the stairs, barefoot and vigilant, her arm raised high, just in case.

As she approached the front entryway, Sandy whined, which made Aimee stop.

"Who's there? Is there someone out there?"

Again, there was no answer. She pointed to the door and asked Sandy to go check it out. The dog ran right up to it, barked several times, and sat looking at it, perfectly still, listening.

The hair on the back of her neck began to spike. She felt sweat running down her armpits and her mouth was chalky and parched.

"Who's there?" she shouted and waited, hearing nothing. Aimee approached the door and put her ear to it. She heard nothing but the sounds of an occasional car on Gulf Boulevard. A bundle of leaves blew around outside in a sudden gust. The door was still locked. She glanced around the room and, after determining she was alone, reached for the door and turned the handle, unlocking it.

Sandy came to standing position, wagging her tail.

"Who is it, girl? Do you know who it is?"

She continued wagging her tail, anxious for her to open the door. And so she did.

The dog burst out into the carport several feet, stopped, and sniffed the air. Aimee had followed her onto the stoop but, again, saw and heard nothing out of the ordinary. Afraid Sandy would run off or find a cat to chase, she called to her, and both of them headed back toward the front door.

On the doorstep, she stepped on something sharp. At first, Aimee thought she'd cut her foot on a piece of glass, but when she looked down, there was a small, curled shell, not more than three inches long and in perfect condition. She glanced over her shoulder at the carport area one last time then followed Sandy through the doorway.

At the last minute, Aimee replaced the shell back on the mat where she'd found it and safely secured them both inside.

CHAPTER 18

ANDY AND SVEN, along with their UN consort, left before nightfall so they could clear a good distance between them and the UNESCO project. It was assumed there was less hostile activity north, especially if they stayed away from the border with Nigeria and the Niger River, but fingerlings and tributaries formed lakes and smaller rivers throughout the region. It was much faster to navigate these areas in the truck. Plus, they had the benefit of a heater if it rained, which was sometimes a luxury in these parts. Gunnar was a stickler on getting the best equipment possible. All of his four-door trucks were less than a year old, with full on satellite radio and air conditioning too.

Classic maneuvers of some of these militia groups was to raid in one country and then cross over the border into another where there was no jurisdiction or where there was less cooperation. There was also the possibility that they'd run into one of these, either fleeing one country or just arriving in another. They would be heavily armed and ruthless, working by their own rules of engagement and more or less autonomous.

Their driver, Adaze, was Nigerian by birth, but his mother was from Benin. Sven had selected him because he seemed to be more friendly than some of the others. Plus, he was fluent in French. It turned out that he had an uncle he stayed with for several years as a youth in Paris. Sven and Andy could only understand about half of what he said, but he painted quite a picture for them both, chasing girls and getting into small-time trouble until the family sent him back.

He told them it had always been a dream of his to join the police force, but working for the UN, while perhaps as dangerous, was a worthier steppingstone for a better life for him and young son. His wife had died after the baby was born, so while on assignment, his son was cared for by his mother's family nearby. He tried to go home as much as possible.

Andy determined he'd been a good pick for two reasons. He seemed genuinely honest about doing good things for his mother's country, and he had good local connections they could rely on.

He told them he was already putting out feelers to some of his family to help the Americans find the hostages. He noted that because the militia group was so hard to find, they obviously had either money to hole up somewhere or had bought themselves some powerful connections.

"Either way, it smells like money," he said in his heavily-accented English, holding his fingers up to his nose. "But they can't hide forever from the *little* people. They can control many but not all the *little* people."

That confirmed what Andy wanted to believe, that most the population was tired of the carnage and wars. They had never aspired to collecting huge sums of money, because it wasn't as valuable as their freedom was. In most cases, the more westernized part of the population had huge appetites for goods from Europe and the U.S. A pair of Nikes would sell for more than a month's salary, but in many portions of the country, it was more a status symbol than having two or three wives.

Sven laughed at that, disagreeing with him. "You should see

the Norwegian girls, Adaze. If you had one of them as a wife, you wouldn't say that, my friend."

They had a spirited discussion on the value of women. Andy didn't agree with either one of them but held his tongue.

Adaze lifted the cuff on his pantleg and revealed he wore Nikes. "Gift from Gunnar."

He laughed easily, which was refreshing. "I am going to pass them down to my son."

Andy wondered how many shoes he'd discarded, just thrown away and never bothered to take to the Salvation Army, because it was something he'd have to get in the car and do. One of the best things about his travel was that he'd become very grateful for how he got to live, especially when he compared it to people trying to live and raise families in a war zone.

They were stopped at a police checkpoint which was the only indication that there had been some militia activity in the area. A European businessman had been killed in a kidnapping attempt, Adaze told them. This was information he obtained from the guards. His credentials were an easy ticket through the checkpoint, with an admonishment to be careful, signed off with a peace symbol for benefit of the Americans.

It was an easy cover to say they were American contractors, and most probably believed them, since SEALs didn't normally travel in such small groups. But Sven had been right, having Adaze with them did give them better creds.

As they were driving away from the roadblock, Adaze noticed they had picked up a tail. Someone in a lorry converted to a makeshift camper was following a good distance away.

"Shall I burn some rubber?" he asked and then gave them a belly laugh.

Before Sven could give permission, he'd floored it and left the entire countryside covered in red dust. With only the major highways paved, burning rubber on a dirt thoroughfare was nearly impossible, but he gave it a good try. After they took a fork in the road, they slowed back down to a cruising speed. They were making excellent time and might arrive before it was too dark outside. That was the hope, anyway. They might even beat Tucker and the rest of the crew coming in.

They stopped for a quick bite to eat at a palapa-covered open firepit kitchen run by a local family their driver knew. Andy tasted some of the hottest chicken he'd ever had, and he wondered how long it might take before his tongue and cheeks would stop throbbing afterwards.

Sven wasn't affected at all. Adaze had dared them to use some of his friend's "special green sauce," but they both declined while he piled it on. Only after he finished did he tell them it worked as a good barrier for fire ants and other pesky bugs.

"Good to know," Sven had said, shaking his head.

This part of the trip was downhill, and they were nearing the outskirts of Kandi, a fairly large city in the province. Instead of arriving from the North, Tucker and the team were arriving direct from France on a chartered flight provided for by Mr. Riley, right into Kandi. Their transport was already taken care of, so Adaze avoided the main center and headed up the hill toward their complex.

By foot, this had taken a day, but with the truck, they made it in merely five hours.

The first thing Andy remarked was that several of the men stationed at the complex had been pulled off the job. No one was guarding the gate in front, and while nothing appeared out of the ordinary, no one was paying attention like when they'd stayed there before.

He noticed the room he'd set up had been ransacked a bit. He was glad he'd not left any of the expensive medications and equipment, but some of the non-essential medical supplies had been used. Several dirty and bloody bandages remained on the floor. Worst thing about it was that no one knew or would admit to who had done this.

Sven pressed one of the guards Andy recognized from before. “This place was bought and paid for by Uncle Sam. What the hell happened? Where are your men?”

Adaze drifted into the crowd, making like he was looking for some food and water, but he’d promised to listen to what the others were saying in non-English dialogue. Andy figured it wouldn’t be safe for him to focus too much on his actions and just trust the affable UN soldier.

The man with the dark glasses and stoic features was extremely tight-lipped, indicating he understood little of what Sven was asking, which they both knew was only part of the truth. He did look under extreme duress.

“They will be back. Tat’s all I can say, Sam.” He used the term “Sam” in addressing all the Americans. Andy didn’t get that it was used as a sign of disrespect.

While Sven spoke with the guard and two others who had come over to help with this little situation, Andy retreated to the room he’d set up for a treatment and possibly surgery center, if needed. He hoped that Tucker and the rest brought more supplies, because being spread so thin between the two camps was taking a toll on what services he could provide. But it was important to be ready and, since this was to be closest to the eventual extraction site, the most necessary.

He’d left a small, locked metal locker the Team sometimes used for storing explosives, and that had now disappeared. It contained vials of antibiotic and a few for pain. Even though it was heavy, Andy now wished he tried somehow to take it along with him. He was good on disinfectant, tape, sterile sutures, and still had a dozen bags of saline for emergency hydration. He'd wrapped a set of surgery tools, including a small saw and several scalpels in a baggie, and had wrapped the roll of garbage bags around it so it had remained undetected. He was relieved to find that it was still there.

They heard a truck pull up, and Andy saw two young local women, both dressed in scrubs, jump out of the back, pulling large backpacks behind them. Sven knew one of the ladies and helped her with her things.

"Andy! Good news!"

When he rushed outside, Sven was the happiest he'd looked in days.

"Flora and I used to work at the mission in Nigeria back in the day." He had his arm around her chubby shoulder as she put her palm up to her face, embarrassed. "She has the best hands and demeanor, Andy. I used to call her Florence Nightingale."

"Nice to meet you," Andy nodded to both of them.

Sven walked them over to one of the other rooms that was being used for food storage. Diku, the guard who appeared to be in charge, shouted instructions and soon a couple of folding cots were installed in the cool cinderblock room. A piece of blue plastic tarp was installed over the doorway to give the women privacy.

Andy headed back to the surgery. Sven followed him inside.

"So what do you think?" he asked Sven.

"I'm delighted with the nurses. Not quite sure on the story about the men and vehicles missing, but it could be as he said. They might have been needed elsewhere. We need Adaze's take on things."

"I'm sure he'll be over soon. I agree it was a stroke of genius bringing him along. We want to make sure they don't understand we trust him, right?"

"My thoughts exactly. So what's going on with the medical

supplies?"

"Lost my antibiotics and some painkiller vials. I still have the pills with me. Still got good surgery tools, disinfectant, saline, but someone came in here and helped themselves to bandages and shit, but nothing we can't live without. I'm sure hoping Tucker will be bringing me more morphine and antibiotics."

"Roger that." Sven scratched his chin. "What are you thinking?"

Andy looked outside, trying to find Adaze. "I want to hear from the driver first, but I'm thinking I should call Peterson and let him know some of these guys went MIA. How did the ladies show up?"

"Diku said someone local asked for them to help out. Flora is here visiting family, and she was conscripted to come up here. She didn't know who ordered it, but the director of her mission in Nigeria knew she was here and sent her over."

The two men stared at each other.

"Which means word has gotten out we're here," Andy muttered to a nodding Sven.

"It does. God, that's what I hate about this place. You just don't know if they're trying to help you or hurt you. Now, if we had fifty guys, well, we'd get a perimeter set up, you know, go to town. But here, out in the bush, we're on our own."

"Well, we are trying not to become a target."

"Which means they can't arrive too soon. We gotta get the hell out before they're told it's just us."

"Agreed. So let me know what Adaze says, and I'm going to keep working here. Can you grab me some food?"

"I'll go find him and, yes, bring you back something. You got waters?"

"Hell yes."

A few minutes later, Andy had the room straightened and had

done a quick clean. He covered surfaces he wanted to stay relatively sterile, knowing he'd have to do it all over again, but it was also a way to track if someone had messed with his stuff. All the garbage was stuffed into a white bag, tied, and left outside. He opted not to burn the bloody bandages out of expediency.

Sven brought a paper plate filled with some fried banana-like foods, some local squash, and a skewer of some variety of small fish. A ball of white rice was set in the middle of the plate for use in eating with his fingers.

"Eat up. Then we'll talk," Sven whispered.

All of it, thankfully, was not very spicy and satisfied his stomach. It was gone in mere seconds.

"So here's the deal. Word went out about the kidnapping down south. The crew here, when they heard about it, thought it was one of us, and some went to investigate and give assistance. I hate to think the poor bastard lost his life because of us, but he was traveling the same route we were, but we'd stopped, remember? He had a German bodyguard, for all the good it did him, and he had a local driver. The coincidence is stunning, Andy."

"Holy shit. Do you suppose they know about Tucker and them arriving today?"

"Who knows? This crew probably does. Let's hope they get here quick so we can get out before they figure out they got the wrong guy."

"They probably figured out that a rescue attempt might be made. They were expecting something, right?" Andy asked.

"Maybe. Hard to say. But I'm thinking we need to act fast and then get out of this place. We got one chance. Not like we can hole up for the right time."

"Right."

"I told Adaze to stay with the men and learn everything he can. I'm going to order him around and warned him about it, not treat him as a friend so he's more useful to us."

"I completely agree. So I need to call Peterson, then?"

"Yes, do it from the ladies' place. No one needs to see you with that SAT phone."

Andy crossed the center of the complex on his way to the ladies' place. He noted that there had been posted guards on the front gate, which pleased him. He gave a casual wave to Diku, more as a show he had confidence whatever had been amiss was now repaired. He got a small nod of the head back in return.

"Flora," he called out to the blue tarp covering their doorway.

"Yes, sir. You can come in, if you like."

Andy pulled the screen back and found the other nurse lying on her back, rubbing her belly. He hadn't noticed before, but she was several months pregnant. He admired her all the more for working so hard, riding in the back of a truck while in this condition. He gave her a confident smile and a thumbs-up then tapped his belly. She giggled, rolled to her side, and covered her face just as Flora had done earlier.

The protector in him rose up, grabbed his heart, and gave it a squeeze. He was in awe that these two willing countrywomen would put themselves and their unborn families in danger to help the mission. It reminded him of the humanity he shared with every peace-loving person around the globe. It was why he did what he did.

A force for good.

"You want something?" Flora asked.

"Did you bring any antibiotics? Mine seemed to walk away while we were on the trail."

"I have a little in my kit, sir, but only a very little. We don't travel with drugs, usually, less dangerous that way."

"I understand. Well, I'm out completely. I'll see if I can get you more when we meet up with our friends."

"Yes, I was told this is an important mission."

"Flora, I'm sure Sven told you we're trying to do this in secret, or as much as possible."

Her smile widened. "I understand, sir, but this is Africa, sir. Even the birds and the trees talk. They whisper. Impossible to do anything in secret here."

Andy was counting on that very thing.

"So you know we're looking for these bad people. You know about the hostages."

"Yes, and I have asked my mother's people for help. Gossip is a big-time interest in my tiny village. Not all the peoples here think you are the enemy. They will be careful, sir."

"Don't do anything stupid, though. Don't risk more than you can afford to. We want you to be safe as well."

"Thank you," she said as she put her hands together in prayer and bowed. "We will do our best. We always do. God is in charge, even though there would be others who think they are." She winked at Andy, leaning in, whispering, "Even though there are those who think otherwise."

"You are Catholic, both of you?" he asked.

"No, sir. We are Free Will Baptist. But I work for a Catholic charity. I don't speak about it, and you mustn't either."

Andy was so grateful for a helpful soul he could have hugged her, which would have completely ruined everything.

"So, Flora, I have to make a phone call."

"You want me to leave?"

"No, but I want you to close your ears."

"I understand, sir."

She showed Andy a chair and then turned, leaned over her co-worker, and began whispering, the two of them giggling like two small schoolgirls.

Peterson picked up before it rang.

"Give me a SitRep."

Andy could tell the stress was getting to him.

"We're back at the Kandi base. We've lost some men here, and they got into some of my medical supplies, but it's all fixed now. I'm stripped of antibiotic and pain meds. We're awaiting Tucker and them to arrive. You have any idea when?"

"Shouldn't be too long from now. So your drive was uneventful? Thank God you're safe. When we heard about the other attempted kidnapping, we feared the worst."

"Kind of a daily occurrence, I'd say. Here's the thing. The guy was a Dutch or Belgian businessman traveling with his German bodyguard in a small vehicle like we were in, and they had a local driver. Sven and I think the group thought they were us. That's the biggest takeaway and what has us concerned."

"Roger that. I'm going to send this upstairs. They're tracking the phone, so if you lose it, use your regular phone in an emergency. Somehow, you have to get a signal and let us know. And I'm asking for more drones, see if we can follow your group as you head south."

"Right. That's good to know. As soon as they arrive, we're taking off. I just don't feel safe here, especially since the area was expecting us. We were followed for a bit at a checkpoint, but our driver lost him, we think."

"Did he work out, then?"

"Couldn't have been more perfect. We're trying to make sure he's not compromised."

"Okay, so let me know when you're on the road. I'll see if I can get some help with the meds up there."

"There are a couple of nurses from Nigeria. Sven knows one of them. It's great to have them, but did our guys send them?"

"Not that I know of, but I better ask. Can they be trusted to receive the meds?"

"I'd say so, yes. And send a couple protection details for them too. One of them is pregnant. They're defenseless without any of us around."

"Okay. Let's keep this short. Check back on your departure."

"Thanks, Peterson. See? The plan worked."

"Don't count your chickens just yet, Andy. That's bad luck."

Before Andy could give an answer, Peterson added, "But thanks. I appreciate the support. Just get down here safely. It feels like things are escalating, and I'm in agreement. We need to make a move and get out."

He patted Flora's shoulder after hanging up. "Thanks."

Not halfway across the camp, he heard the sounds of several vehicles approaching. The dust was so heavy he couldn't tell who they were until he saw the huge, hulking form of Tucker jumping off the back of a small flatbed, carrying a pack that probably weighed as much as he did. On any normal man, the pack would have tipped him on his ass. But this was Tucker.

And Tucker, fresh from becoming a new father, was ready to get back in the fray.

God bless America!

CHAPTER 19

LAST NIGHT'S EVENT with Sandy's alert, while exactly what she should have done, left Aimee shaken, and she found it difficult to sleep afterwards. Hank Borges' book was no comfort to her. In fact, she couldn't even read any of her favorite go-to romance novels at all. She attempted to watch TV but found no interest in anything. She threw the remote to the foot of her bed and just lay back, staring at the ceiling, giving Sandy a light pet until sleep finally overtook her.

She should have been excited, she thought as she walked outside with the rear seat cover. Still at her toes, the shell lay perfect in its odd placement, a reminder, again, that things were not normal. Everything seemed to be spinning out of control. The shell incident only underscored that, far from calming her nerves or making her look forward to some communication with Logan. She realized there was a danger that these little gifts were not his work at all but someone else's, messing with her mind.

Dr. Denby, Andy, and Shelley were right. Every one of them were right.

She vowed that she'd give the Sheriff's department a visit on the way home.

Sandy watched the passing traffic for a few minutes then settled down into the seat, her paws outstretched with her head resting atop them. The dog was quickly becoming the bright spot of her day. She could only imagine how tense she would have been without her companionship. The instant bond she made that day at the shelter was indeed something she could trust and gave her some small sense of protection.

The traffic was congested this morning, so when she arrived at Mr. Kornblum's office, she was a whole ten minutes late. She grabbed the leash, and she and Sandy jogged into the large modern building, darting into the third-floor elevator before someone downstairs told her the dog wouldn't be allowed.

Jasper Kornblum's office wasn't as big or expansive as she'd imagined. He had a secretary seated in the tiny lobby and a conference room beyond with a beautiful view of downtown Tampa. There wasn't the buzzing around of associates or customers waiting like she'd seen in some offices. No one offered her an espresso or a glass of champagne, although today, she could use some alcohol.

Mr. Kornblum appeared and was interested in being introduced to Sandy, who gave him her paw.

"Nice pup. She's got a lovely coat, too. How's she with the housebreaking, or did she come already trained?"

"She's good. She's had a run with me. Bought her a dog bed, which I have to return because she prefers to sleep on my bed. So I guess I'm going to cave on that one until Andy comes home. He may not be so pleased."

Mr. Kornblum had a thick file under his arm, directing her to the conference room. He asked his receptionist to bring a small bowl of water for the dog and two coffees.

"Cream for me. Lots of it," instructed Aimee.

She showed Sandy a sunny corner and had her sit then took a chair across the polished black conference table from Mr. Kornblum. He spread out two files, opening the first and pulling out documents clipped together in several batches, pink arrows affixed to some of the pages.

He lay a single sheet of paper in front of her and turned it around so she could read it.

"These are the instructions from Carmen I prepared about six months ago when she was diagnosed as terminal." He slipped another piece of paper beneath it, while Aimee read the verbiage.

It was very short, indicating it was her desire to leave all her worldly goods to Aimee Greer. "But I'm Aimee Carr now."

"The formal legal instructions and the documents you'll sign take that into account. This was her notarized proof of her desire to leave everything to you."

He let her complete the paragraph and then flipped the page over to reveal a list of items that filled most the page.

"And this is an inventory of what you have inherited."

At first, she focused on the pink arrow at the bottom, but then she began to read. There was a list of four accounts, two with a savings bank and two with a brokerage firm in Sarasota. The total of the stock value, dated today, and bank accounts amounted to over two million dollars.

Her first reaction was to cover her mouth, since her jaw had dropped to nearly touch her chest. Mr. Kornblum's amused expression made her think, at first, he was playing a cruel trick on her.

"This can't be," she mumbled. "I'm—"

The receptionist brought in two mugs of coffee and lay a glass bowl in front of Sandy, who immediately and very sloppily slurped her way to emptying it.

"I'll get more," the receptionist chuckled.

"I think we're fine, Hailey."

Aimee was in shock and kept reading the first few lines of assets over and over again, making sure she hadn't misunderstood a decimal point or two.

"She's leaving all this to me? She has no family, no one else she wants to leave money to? I mean, I'm not interfering with some family member's inheritance plans, am I?"

"She had no offspring or siblings. Her parents are gone. Hank left her the house and the bulk of his last twenty-five books' sales to her. And she had some success on her own. Quite a bit of success. She was a shrewd investor, lived a very simple life, and saved like there was no tomorrow. I think in many ways, she was a lot like you, Aimee. Her needs were small, and she really didn't enjoy spending money. She liked saving it."

"I thought, when you told me, that perhaps we could get a new car or pay for some of the construction we've been saving for to complete on the house, but this—this is nowhere near what I thought it could be. I don't know what to say."

"Say thank you. Say it to her."

Aimee teared up immediately. Mr. Kornblum slid the tissues over to her and waited, his hands folded in front of him. Sandy had been alerted to Aimee's tears and walked over to sit next to her. It made her laugh that the dog had already developed the sense that she was emotional.

"So how does this work, then?"

"Well, I have several papers you will need to sign, and we'll have Hailey notarize. You'll want to meet with the bank representatives so they can explain what has to happen on their end, their paperwork. You'll be given access to her jewelry in a safe deposit box. The contents are listed here." He tapped a list of contents, which included two gold bands, two cocktail rings, a tennis bracelet, and a child's heart-shaped locket.

"What's this?"

"Apparently, there's a letter of explanation in the box. I wasn't given any information about it."

"But did she have a daughter?"

"No, she's signed affidavits that she had no children of her own. That's stipulated in the will and all the estate documents. I'm afraid that mystery you're going to have to work out on your own."

"I don't know what to do." Aimee was wondering how Andy would take the news and wondering if she should wait to tell him after he got home. She didn't want to distract him from the importance of his mission.

"Why don't we start by signing the paperwork? Then I can file the proper notices and give you authorization to have access. It will take about thirty days to complete the process, but after that time, you'll be able to access everything and do what you like with it. I do suggest you meet with the portfolio managers at the two brokerage houses. I usually tell people to just leave things where they are at, until you decide what your plans are for the money. They can help you strategize an exit plan, if you need it. This is also a good time to interview them and figure out for yourself whom you want to continue working with. Maybe wait until Andy returns, but you're not required to. This is your money, Aimee. She knew about your wedding plans, but it's your sole separate property."

"I wouldn't think of doing anything without Andy's input."

"Of course. I would be the same way, Aimee."

"Do I have to decide anything now?"

"Well, you can decide to refuse the money. You can do that. But all we need today is your signature." He handed her a pen. "And tell your face to smile. Trust me, this is a good thing. She'd want to see you happy."

Suddenly, an idea popped into her head. "Her funeral? Can I pay for her funeral?"

"No, that's already been taken care of. It wasn't anticipated there would be many in attendance, so she prepaid for a small service and asked that her ashes be spread at the beach. I can have them released to you, if you like."

The idea of sprinkling the contents of Carmen's life into the bay filled her with sadness. "I couldn't—" She broke down in tears again, resting her head on her forearms. Mr. Kornblum grabbed one of her hands and squeezed.

"It's going to take time to get used to this. This is a gift, Aimee. Nothing you need to feel guilty of or sad about. It was her way of celebrating her life by sharing it with you, you and Andy and whomever else you want to. In time, that's the way you'll see it, I'm sure."

"When? When is the funeral?"

"In three days."

"I want to go," she mumbled, wiping the streaks of tears from her cheeks with his Kleenex.

"I'll be there too. I'm bringing my wife, as well. I think we'll be the only ones, but you never know."

"Can we wait for Andy?"

"No. But you can have another service, if you like. Maybe he could help you spread the ashes. I think he'd want to help you with that."

He was right, of course. She stared at the pen, still clutched in her fingers, and began to look for pages with pink arrows at the bottom.

She'd been right all along. That house at Sunset Beach was magic. Everything that flowed from it was magic. Her life had been forever altered the day she found it and fell in love with it and the man who gave her the confidence to go after it. What if Andy had said no? What if her mother hadn't left her the money to purchase it? What if she'd decided it was too old and in need of too much repair and should be torn down? What if she had never come to the Florida Gulf Coast and walked the beach? That's where her life had begun. That's when it all started.

Magic. Pure magic!

CHAPTER 20

SVEN WAS THE first on the team to greet Tucker. The two men had an extreme bear hug. Tucker towered over Sven by several inches and was probably double his body size, but it made no difference. Sven tried to pick him up anyway.

They'd arrived in brand new white four-door pickups, which left room in the back for backpacks and equipment. Tucker had ridden there with the equipment. Kelly Fielding made her way out of the passenger's seat of the first truck. Fredo, Danny Begay, Armando, T.J. Talbot, and Jake Green all exited the second vehicle. T.J. and Danny approached Andy.

"How's it going, kid?" T.J. was grinning, carrying a large backpack with a red cross on it. "I understand from the Headshed that you are short on antibiotics. I got y'all fixed up kid, and some painkillers too." He shoved the backpack into Andy's belly.

"Cool." Andy slipped the pack over his shoulder. "Okay, I got mine. Where's all the rest for you guys?"

Fredo punched him in the arm. "Nice one, bro. You holding up okay?"

"Of course. Got good mentors," Andy answered.

The new team members were still getting unloaded. They had brought along two extra guards, plus the drivers. Diku greeted the Africacorps troops warmly, as did several of the compound guards under his command.

Their temporary meet and greet was halted as Sven drew the SEALs into a circle and explained their dire situation.

"Look, guys. I'm not going to sugarcoat it at all. We're in kind of a shitstorm here. I'm sure you know that Peterson and the rest of the team, Andy's team, are holed up down south with the UNESCO project and Gunner Larssen's men. They're okay but probably not very secure. That's why you guys are here."

Tucker was the first to respond. "Just lay it out, Sven. Please tell us what you want us to do and we're here for you."

"Well, Andy and I came back here to double check the compound, and it appears that they partially abandoned the site, and some of the medical was used by unknowns. We really aren't sure—still trying to figure that out. These guys have worked pretty hard," he pointed to Diku, who was having his own private conversation with his colleagues.

"I think they're honest. Apparently, half this team headed south to investigate the kidnapping of the European businessman, and I guess everyone here thought it was us. We need to get south quickly before they figure out they got the wrong guys, and if the whole area thinks that one of this ambushed team murdered by this militia group was us, then good for us. But they won't take long to figure out who they really got. We need to get to safety and to Peterson and his group before they get cut off. We think the militia group that murdered the businessman is the same group that has the hostages."

"Good on you, Andy. You guys risked your butts to get up here," T.J. barked.

"So, you're saying we got to get out of Dodge then. Is that right?" asked Fredo.

"That's what we're saying Fredo." Andy was sure everyone got the message.

"So how do we do this? You got any thoughts on whose trucks we take and when we leave?" asked Tucker.

Andy stepped forward and answered him. "I think we need three trucks. We got two, but we may need one of yours. Or we can take a third here. But we got to go right away. As in *now*."

"Okay then, so no need to unload." Armando picked his bag up and headed back to the truck.

"T.J., you and I need to meet with a couple of nurses who showed up this afternoon. I want to make sure they've got some meds for our return trip. And I need to give them instructions. So, let's go on up there, and then we'll all meet you back here, but get ready to roll out of here like in ten minutes, okay?"

The team was used to these sorts of excursions where they had little time to decompress, rest up, or refresh themselves after a long flight and trip over. But this was what it was all about. And if it was urgent, it was urgent.

On the way across the courtyard to the nurses' room, Andy whispered to T.J., "Truth is, T.J., I've got to call Peterson, and I need to do it where no one will see me. What you can do is introduce yourself to the nurses, have Flora and her assistant meet you in the surgery center we set up, and you can unload some of your vials of antibiotics and maybe three or four pain meds, some morphine, whatever you brought."

"Sure thing. How did these ladies show up?"

"You know, T.J., this is Africa. I have no fucking clue who sent them, but they were sent by someone in the Archdiocese in Nigeria. They work for a Catholic charities group. Their coordinator over there is a Frenchman. We don't have any contact with him, but Sven knows Flora, and he trusts her. So the bottom line is someone knows we might need medical assistance, which is a whole other problem."

"I got ya. So, they're staying here?"

"Yeah, unfortunately. I can't really take these women into combat. They're not trained, and I'd be afraid we'd spend a lot of resources protecting them. But we have a couple of extra guards on their way over, or at least I requested it, to protect them. We're going to take some of these guys, but we have to leave some behind, obviously, to man the compound. This will be where we come back to after our mission, and then we'll head up north to get the transport out of Niger. But somebody's got to stay here and protect the campsite and the nurses. And I need a little bit of medical supplies here, just for giggles."

"Giggles?"

"God, T.J., I'm running out of words here. It's just a big clusterfuck. But we're doing the best we can."

"I'd say, my man, you're doing pretty damn good."

He knocked on the outside of the building and called through the blue plastic sheet to the nurses. Flora pulled aside the screen and invited them in.

"Flora, this is T.J. Talbot. He's a medic from Team 3, and I've served with him. He's going to take you over to the surgery and help restock some antibiotics and a little bit of other stuff, too, so you tell him what you think we are going to need. Okay?"

"Sure thing, Andy." She looked up at the tall medic and curtsied in front of him, which Andy thought was funny. T.J. tried to cover his smile with his hand, but both ladies were embarrassed and giggled like schoolgirls.

"Nice to meet you." Flora pushed her assistant in front, who also curtsied, and greeted T.J. with a very soft handshake.

The two nurses left, and T.J. followed behind carrying the medic pack. Andy retrieved his SAT phone and dialed Peterson.

"Tell me they got there safely, Andy," Peterson barked.

"Yes, sir, they did. We didn't get any of Collin's guys, but we got seven, including Kelly Fielding. We got Fredo and Danny,

Armando, and, of course, Tucker. Plus, we have T.J. and Jake Green, so we got a good group. I'm grateful for the medical supplies that T.J. brought."

"That's good. I'm glad they got that together. So, when are you leaving?"

"We're going to go now, even though it's dark. Any intel to say that the roads are not passable or there's some kind of hazard ahead?" Andy asked.

"We're going to have you traced, and we will notify you if we find any activity. It's easier for us to track at night, so although it's going to be more dangerous for you, I'd prefer it. But be careful. And you got local drivers there, so hopefully they can get around anything that might come up. I'll make sure the guys who have the eyes in the sky give us a major heads-up in case something forms."

"Thanks, Peterson. One thing I didn't mention before was that several of the drivers have family in the area, and the word has gone out to them to bring back any local intel. Several of them have told us that there doesn't appear to be anything going on here, so we think they're either headed your direction or they're even farther south than you. But I hope we don't run into anybody, and if so, you know we'll deal."

"Okay then, so I'm going to assume you're on the road in like less than ten, right?"

"You would be correct. We'll see you in about five, six hours?"

"No, I think it will be closer to sunrise. But you stay safe, hear?"

"Absolutely."

Andy left the storage room and headed over to the surgery where T.J. was still instructing Flora on several items that he brought for her. He stashed a few things in bins that were mislabeled to throw off anybody who might be looking for antibiotics or the pain meds, and they all agreed that most of the supplies needed to be taken on the road, since they had nearly twenty-five men to take care of. Andy told Flora that two guards were on their way over to give them extra protection, and then there would be at least five remaining behind to man the complex. He authorized her to do minor triage and first aid for any of the men in the compound but not to encourage locals to come in and seek medical attention, as might happen.

"Just tell them you're a privately contracted clinic, if you have to say anything," he added.

Andy and T.J. approached the trucks again. Sven had coordinated who was going to stay behind in the complex and who was going to go with the group. Diku wanted to go, and he promised his second-in-command would take good care of the nurses and guard the complex. With some hesitation, Sven agreed after checking with Andy.

"I just want to make it so that they have enough protection for now, and I hope this guy isn't going to leave. Diku, we can't have this place abandoned while we're gone. I trust that, if you stayed, that wouldn't happen. I'm going to be really pissed if these guys abandon their post."

Diku shook his head. "No, man. They good. They good men."

Sven pulled Andy aside. "I think they can be paid a little something. What do you think?" he whispered.

"You mean Kelly brought it?"

Sven nodded.

"Then I'd say yeah. Give them something. I'm sure it doesn't have to be much."

Sven brought Kelly over, and the three of them discussed payment.

"Here's what I propose," Kelly said. "I got hundred-dollar packets and five-hundred-dollar packets. I'd like to give the guards that stay a hundred-dollar packet. I think that's good money to them."

"Hell yeah," Sven said.

"I think that's half a year's salary," said Andy.

"So, I'm going to recommend giving a fiver to Diku, and tell him he'll get a bonus when the mission is successfully rendezvoused with the other team? You okay with that?"

"Absolutely." said Andy. Sven nodded. "Another five hundred to Sven for Adaze too."

"Completely agree," said Sven.

"Okay then, give me two minutes with Diku, and I'll make sure he gets his men paid."

Two vehicles were loaded from the compound. One was the four-door pickup that they had arrived in, and one was a delivery van that would seat several more and carry most of their equipment. It was decided that the vehicles that picked up the team at the airport would return.

With several local guards staying behind, that left five to accompany the team, and although it was a little light, Andy was grateful they could communicate with, Diku and their driver, Adaze. The others were just for extra firepower, should it be needed. It also added more legitimacy, since they were traveling in UNESCO trucks. If there was not a local contingent, somebody along the way would notice.

They began their journey just before the stroke of midnight. Before they left, Diku had his man distribute water and a small package of sweet potatoes, chicken, and leafy green vegetables of some kind, wrapped in a rice ball. It didn't taste great, but Andy was grateful for the nourishment. The water was heavenly.

With any luck, they'd be meeting up with Peterson and his team before morning.

CHAPTER 21

AIMEE DECIDED TO drop by Shelley's school and found her car in the parking lot, so she took Sandy and knocked on her classroom door. Latin jazz music played loudly in the room, so when no one answered, she knocked a little harder.

Shelley's unmade-up face was quite the sight. She had a red bandana around her head, cutoff jeans, and a halter top t-shirt. Aimee laughed when she thought Shelley did not quite have the appearance of a respectable schoolteacher.

"Just wanted to introduce you to Sandy."

Shelley kneeled and eyed Sandy's face straight on. "What a beautiful puppy. She's a girl?"

"Well, she's not a puppy. She's full grown, and she's spayed. It's Sandy. Sandy meet Shelley."

Sandy put her paw on Shelley's knee as if understanding the formal introduction.

"Aw, you are such a good girl. You're going to keep my friend Aimee safe? Is that right?"

The dog's ears went into alert, and then she looked up at Aimee.

Shelley stood, arching her back with her hands on her hips. "So I don't think you've seen my classroom this year. I'm right in the middle of preparing a module on the oceans, which is the study they're going to do for the next three months. You see?"

She pointed to a wall that was filled with cut-out pictures of fish, looking like a huge kelp forest window with various sea creatures big and small. A list of vocabulary terms was listed on the side. It was a colorful display of Shelley's creative abilities.

"We do this so that by the time the whales start moving, the kids will have some context. Most of the kids around here know quite a bit about sea life, because they live here. But many of them don't know about the migrations and why they happen, and it's, I think, my favorite module." She examined her handiwork, turned to Aimee, and smiled.

"That's fantastic Shelley," Aimee said. She was really a talented teacher, Aimee thought, and wondered what it would have been like to have a teacher like her growing up.

"So we got the introduction out of the way. What are you really here for? Have you heard from Andy?" Shelley's direct questions shouldn't have been a surprise to Aimee by now, but they still caught her off guard.

"You promised you weren't going to ask me that again."

"You're right. I'm sorry." Shelley put both hands up in the air and shook her head. "I forget, and I know you'll forgive me."

"Of course. But I do have some other news, and I would be bursting to tell Andy, but I'll just have to do it when he calls me. I got a call yesterday that Carmen Hernandez passed away suddenly. The attorney asked me to come into his office this morning to go over some paperwork. And it turns out she has left me some money."

Shelley stared at her, her eyes getting wide. "How *much* money?"

Aimee rocked her head from side to side, fidgeting with what she should tell her. "A lot. I mean, Shelley, it's a lot."

"Oh my gosh!"

"I don't want you to breathe a word about this with anybody. I don't want a soul to know, for obvious reasons."

"Done!" Shelley said, crossing her heart.

"It gives Andy and I some flexibility in what we do with the house, and other things too."

"I'd say so. Then why aren't you, like, jumping for joy?"

"Because I just don't feel this money is mine. I mean, I didn't earn it. I'm not a relative of hers. I only got to meet her one time."

"What do you mean? It's what she wanted, Aimee."

"It just doesn't feel right yet. I don't understand why she chose me. It's like one of those things you always hear growing up. '*If it's too good to be true it is.*' I just somehow can't fathom that it's real. I mean, this will change our lives for the remainder of the time we're here. I can do things that I never thought I could do before. And it opens up a whole set of choices, that I just—Now I've got all these decisions I have to make."

"You *have to* make?" Shelley asked with a scowl.

"No, it's just that I want to be a good steward of it."

"Oh, for Christ's sakes, Aimee, enjoy it. I think she gave you the money because you fell in love with her place. You were perhaps the daughter she never had. I think she wanted you and Andy to be happy. It made her happy knowing that. I wouldn't question it any further. I would enjoy it. Why can't you just do that, Aimee?"

"I guess because I feel like I don't deserve it."

"Listen to yourself, Aimee. Just listen to what you're saying. That's nonsense. You have to embrace it and accept it and live your life to the fullest. You're given an opportunity to do something that, like you said, others can't do. So this is your chance. I mean, in a way, it's kind of your new job, right?"

Aimee thought about it for a minute and understood the logic.

"It just hasn't sunk home yet."

Shelley grabbed her and gave Aimee a bear hug. "You are such a big doofus, Aimee. I think you're one of the most honest, wonderful, and loving people I've ever met in my entire life. I can't wait to see what you do with that money. *You deserve it.*"

Armed with that bit of encouragement from Shelley, Aimee took Sandy to the dog park on the way home. She stared down at her cell phone, wishing she could get a call from Andy. She had not remembered being so anxious last time he was on deployment, but that was before they got married. She wondered why that would change things, and then she started to think about all the other changes that had occurred in her life.

The money was certainly something that was occupying her mind, but Logan and his reaching out to her were also issues.

And it all came at the same time when she was worried for Andy's mission and safe return. She decided to just accept what was here today and have faith that Andy would call her soon. She'd try to focus on some of the things she might want to accomplish with her new inheritance.

They arrived home, and Aimee fixed Sandy her dinner early. She sat in front of the TV with the dog at her side, eating a rice bowl. She was going to turn in early and watched the weather report, which indicated there was going to be a huge storm arriving in the evening. Outside, she repositioned the chairs, secured a table, and made sure that the umbrellas were tucked to the side of the house so that any wind that would accompany the storm wouldn't damage them.

She checked all the doors and windows, making sure they were properly closed and locked, brought her dishes into the kitchen, and then took Sandy upstairs so she could read in bed. As she continued with Hank's story, the wind started howling, Sandy's ears peaking at the sound of thunder and lightning. It was going to be a wild night, she thought. But she was used to them now, even though this was an unusually late storm.

Out of her bedroom window, she could see white caps in the bay already and hear the fronds of trees slapping against the side of the house and the wet road from Gulf Boulevard as traffic brought people home.

She turned off the light and decided to turn in. Again, she stared at the ceiling. She thought about the magic of the house. She thought about her future, filled with possibilities, and then drifted off to sleep.

It was sometime late in the evening when Sandy started to bark again, startling her. She slipped on her robe, decided to take the baseball bat, and followed the dog downstairs. Sandy headed straight for the front door.

"Sandy, is someone there?" Then she yelled through the door, "If you're out there, I can't talk to you. You can't come by. You have to leave me alone. Please stop."

She listened for a sign, but with the howling of the wind and weather outside, she did not want to open the door. She didn't turn on any of the lights and moved to the kitchen window to see if she could detect anyone outside the front door area, but the area appeared clear. Sandy wanted to go out, but Aimee discouraged her. "I'll take you in a few hours, in the morning. When it's not so miserable and dark outside."

Just then, several thunderous roars shook the whole house. It felt as if lightning had struck right in front of her or perhaps nearby on the beach as she'd seen from time to time. She stared out the sliding glass door, and all she could see were raindrops flowing horizontally. Sandy ran over to the sliding glass door as another huge bolt of lightning went off. Aimee could see in that flash of light the figure of a man, leaning into the window. She jumped back, calling for Sandy. Another bolt of lightning illuminated the patio, and the area was clear.

Had she imagined this? Was there really somebody out there? Or was it just her mind playing tricks on her?

She looked at the cell phone in her hand and decided she needed to give Shelley a call first. Then she corrected herself and called the Pinellas County Sherriff's Office.

The clerk who answered the phone was made aware of the fact that there had been an incident report on file, and Aimee asked her to look it up so she could give further detail. She asked if it would be possible for an officer to come over and check the grounds, making sure that Logan or whoever the person was wasn't still in the area. She told the clerk that she feared for her life.

The dispatcher agreed to send someone over.

In less than ten minutes, two flashing police cars drove up through her carport. She opened the door and let them inside. Both of them were dressed in yellow rain slickers, water dribbling down their faces.

"Mrs. Carr?"

"Yes, I'm the one who called."

"You reported a suspicious person?"

"Yes, I did. Please come in." She handed them a tea towel for their hands and face.

"Thanks, ma'am. Much appreciated. So tell me what he looked like."

"He was wearing a hoodie that looked like it was soaking wet, and he was tall, thin. He could be my brother. The last time I saw him close was many years ago, but I think I've had a sighting since, and this person looked like the man I saw in the parking lot a year ago. Maybe he wanted to come inside and get out of the rain, and—"

"No, ma'am. If he's leaning up next to the window, that's

breaking the law. Especially in the middle of the night. You were right to call us."

"So you'll do a search and then come back and let me know what you find?"

"Yes, ma'am, just give us a few minutes, and we'll be right back."

The two officers left their lights flashing as they began searching the area with flashlights. Aimee closed the front door. Sandy sat at her side.

The storm continued to rage with intermittent thunder and lightning, which made her jump every time she heard it. Sandy's head was whipping from side to side checking the front door and then the back sliding glass door at every thunderous noise. "That's a good girl. This will all be over soon, I hope. The good guys are here, Sandy."

Several minutes later, she heard another knock at the door and opened to the two officers.

"Ma'am, we haven't found anything, but it looks like you have some footprints on your patio and perhaps some prints on the sliding glass door. It's probably not too much we can do tonight. But I'm going to recommend that we keep a patrol car here for the night just cruising back and forth on the street and throughout the neighborhoods. That would probably make you feel a little more secure, right?"

"Oh, absolutely. Thank you so much, officer."

A squawking noise came over a little loudspeaker affixed to the officer's chest. He answered the call and stepped to the side to have a private conversation with a dispatcher.

When he returned, he addressed her. "It appears that you have some neighbors nearby who report a break-in. They're outside. Mind if I let them in to talk?"

"Not at all. Please do!"

The officer opened the door, and a middle-aged couple emerged in their pajamas, with rain slickers on and boots.

The woman started first. "We live just four houses up. We came back to Florida this afternoon. We've had the place rented, and everything was cleaned for us after the last tenant. But when we got here and we walked in, it looked like somebody had been living in the house. We found a side door unlocked, but nothing's really damaged or anything."

"Why do you say someone's been living there?"

"Well, they left a backpack and an old smelly sleeping bag in the living room. So when I saw the flashing lights and saw the activity over here, we just thought we should come over and tell you. We were going to go down to the police department in the morning and report it."

"How long has it been vacant?"

She looked up at her partner, who answered, "It's been three and a half weeks, almost four weeks."

"Other than the sleeping bag and backpack, how could you tell that somebody had been living there?" the officer asked.

"Because whomever it was broke into our owner pantry, which we hadn't unlocked yet. We had a bunch of items stored for us; granola bars, Gatorade, waters, things like that. It looks like whomever has been living there has been living off the juice and waters and snacks in the owner closet. There wasn't anything in the refrigerator, and he didn't touch anything else, except he left a mess on the kitchen."

"Food and things? What kind of mess?"

"Some kind of a project. He got out one of our toolboxes and had pliers and things all over the table with shells and crap."

Aimee ran to the kitchen counter and picked up the charm bracelet that had been left for her. "Did it look like this? Like some of these things?"

"Exactly. So that's what he was doing. There was wire and shells and all kinds of garbage—you know, stuff you find on the beach. It looked like he was making something. Something exactly like that."

Several minutes later, the neighbors left after exchanging phone numbers with Aimee They invited her to call them anytime if she had anymore sightings. Everyone was happy that there would be a patrol car out front, which might deter anybody who was still in the area. The neighbors left. Aimee needed to add one more bit of information for the report.

"I need to give you the phone number for Dr. Denby. It's already in the report, but I want to be sure you have it in case he shows up tonight. If this is indeed my brother, Logan, Dr. Denby treated him at his center in Sarasota. I think he would be agreeable to taking him back, if you find him. Maybe take him directly there, instead of jail or wherever you put these guys."

"Well, that's a problem. Because breaking and entering is against the law. It's a misdemeanor unless something major was stolen or broken. But it's still against the law, and we aren't allowed to just pick someone up and then release them to a nonsecure facility. More than likely, he'd have to be held overnight. But I can certainly put that in the file, and if we do apprehend him this evening on our shift, I can make sure that message gets to them. You might want to alert your doctor friend to what's happened here. I assume he knows that you've had some contact with him?"

"Yes, he knows all about it. He suggested his name be given out."

"Then I would give him a call and let him know. Who knows? Maybe he'll show himself. It's hard to say with these guys, though. Especially with the long history of drug and alcohol abuse. You know they aren't thinking straight. And you're right to not let him into your home. You do have to treat him like a threat. And now he's not only a threat to you, but he's a threat to other people and their property as well, and that's the real problem. When they start spiraling out of control, they become a danger to not only themselves but everybody around them. So please do not have any contact with him if he tries to approach you."

It was going to be another one of those nights, where she would be tossing, listening to the thunder and lightning, seeing the flashing lights glow through her windows, and thinking about being on the edge between Aimee's old life and her new life. She wished Andy would call.

There was just no getting around it. She needed to talk to her husband.

CHAPTER 22

THE TWO TRUCKS barreled down the roadway, winding through parts of the outer city of Kandi and back out into the stretches of highway headed to the lake region. They crossed over numerous bridges that were not guarded, which was one of the advantages of traveling at night. Andy made a quick call to check that the tracking birds were following him and got confirmation from Peterson that yes, indeed, they were being watched.

Diku and Adaze were the perfect drivers for this type of excursion, because both had spent time in Benin and had family currently living in several of the nearby villages. So if a road was washed out, they knew all the back ways to get around it. In fact, Andy figured they might even have a leg up on some of the militiamen who came over the Nigerian border.

All along the way, they kept their eyes peeled for lorries with troop transport or large bands of militia. The little villages they crossed through and around were quiet with very little lighting, mostly bonfires occasionally seen out in the fields. Some field hands did do work at night, processing and boxing, but nearly everything was shut down at dark.

The roads were so full of ruts and the diesel motors so loud that conversation was limited. Andy and several others took the time to catch a few Zs. He had been on the road for two days straight with very little sleep.

About an hour into the trip, Andy's SAT phone pinged.

"We got a sighting of maybe twenty to thirty men who've just flown in from a remote village in Nigeria, arriving in a couple of birds of unknown origin. If you could try to swing by and snap some photographs, we're going to see if anybody is headed your way. Norfolk wants to have eyes on the ground."

"Roger that."

Andy gave the instructions about the group, and Adaze maneuvered around some of the back alleyways of a small town, knowing a facility in that area that could house helicopters and possibly drop and store troops. It was an old hangar that had been used for farming operations, crop dusting, and delivery of materials, but the military often used it in the past. The militias did, as well. They parked in front of an abandoned school yard, anxious to get in the middle of the fray.

Sven suggested that Andy and the others stay in the trucks with the drivers while he took Tucker, T.J., Fredo, and two other SEALs to investigate and hopefully get pictures for the men upstairs. They disappeared into the night without making a sound, as if the blackness swallowed them whole.

Roughly fifteen minutes later, the group returned, wasting no time to get back on the road. Sven took to uploading some of their photos, and Andy verified with Peterson afterward that they'd been received.

"I'll get you back a report," Peterson barked. "Your assessment of the group?"

Sven leaned over and spoke into the phone. "Sir, they look like recruits of some kind, but they're bedded down for the night in a bunker nearby. And I don't see any trucks nearby, so they're not going anywhere, at least not tonight. It could be that they're getting ready for some kind of an operation or exercise, but they look private, like possibly guards for some Benin military operation. The uniforms are non-descript, so I don't know for sure, but they don't look like militia. And with the militia, you'd see the trucks with the .50s on the back, and I just don't see it. I see nothing but passenger vehicles over there."

"Okay then. Carry on. Get yourself south, and we'll check in later when we have some results for you."

About forty minutes later, Peterson pinged again.

"We got a road closure up ahead. It's a full-on blockade. You want to avoid it, no option. They tell me there's lots of troops and trucks, and it doesn't look good."

"Will do." Andy thought about the pictures. "Hey, Peterson, they say anything about the pics?"

"Negative. No interest."

After he disconnected, Adaze indicated he knew a long way around the checkpoint that would carry them in a wide loop but would probably delay their return a good half hour.

"We may have to go through some rice fields. Maybe we go through fingerlings," Adaze said. "But I think it is the safest way. We won't get stuck with these brand-new trucks, and we'll avoid the road closure. Something must have happened to cause all this interest at this time of night."

Sven looked at T.J. and Tucker, all of them nodding to themselves. It was obvious something had happened back there, but without firsthand information and without being directed to inquire further, they were happy to avoid it.

Andy thought the truck was going to tilt on its side as they headed off a small embankment and through a tiny rivulet. The heavy vehicle came up the other side and almost hit a water buffalo standing right there, the headlights blinding him temporarily. Adaze was quick to maneuver around the beast. "You don't want to hit one of those. They got friends, and they come after you. I've seen them chase a truck for ten kilometers." He laughed, but the rest of the team was quiet.

It took several bumpy roads before they returned to the wide red highway headed straight south to Benot. The road wasn't paved, but it had been frequently used and had been rocked on several occasions. The potholes were minimum, and the closer they got to the city, the faster they were able to travel. The road widened slightly and allowed for a second lane of travel.

It was an easy stretch to get back. They arrived at Benot through the town center and passed by several of the downtown offices and buildings they had been scoping the day before.

The sun had just started sending rose-colored shards of light into the sky, which highlighted soaring purple and gray thunder clouds, threatening a storm they said was on the way.

When they pulled up to the compound at the UNESCO site, Andy was surprised at the quantity of work that had been completed by the men left behind. They had constructed a whole lodge house, which could serve as a dining hall, meeting hall/bunkhouse. They'd filled in the walls with a small forest of cut pine logs. They had built corrals and pens and had managed to build a block latrine and storage unit with massive wooden doors that could be locked and secured, a perfect place to store their ammunition, supplies, or things they didn't want animals and other curious villagers to get into.

Gunnar came running out of one of the little cabins, holding a lantern. He had a smile that extended nearly from ear to ear.

"My friends, my friends, welcome, welcome to the sanctuary!"

Peterson appeared out of the dark and made the introductions, ordering the men to take up shelter in various cabins that Gunnar provided for them. Another cabin was assigned to Diku, Adaze, and the other Africacorps men.

Peterson called for a meeting in the lodge building in ten

minutes.

Kit, Connor, and Dallas greeted the new men from Team 3. After everyone took seats, several brought over local dishes that had been prepared, heating them with microwaves and sending them down the communal table. While they munched on finger food, Peterson took the floor. He pinned a map to the wall and began discussions about hotspots in several regions, indicating where there had been some recent sightings of interest.

"We have two locations that we're most curious about. One of them is actually an old gentleman's club that had been set up during the European days. It had been owned until recently by a very eccentric Dutch businessman, who maintained a quasi-brothel there. However, he's gone, and it appears either relatives or someone he sold the property to is now running it. If they're holed up there, then the hostages are probably not going to be in terrible condition, because the buildings and the grounds have been well maintained, and it won't be like sleeping out in the bush. It could also explain why we haven't seen these people because they're staying put. It is usually well-fortified and guarded."

"The other place we're looking at is a school that was in session until recently. The local leaders had had problems with kidnappings and children missing, so they closed the school for the rest of the year. There are several classrooms, offices, and a large auditorium, and any one of those facilities could also hold a number of hostages, as well as house militia men."

"How many men are at each of these locations? Do the drones tell us that?" Tucker wanted to know.

"We have multiple sightings at the school. However, right now, not many at the villa. So our decision was to check out the school first and see who's there. It could be that they are using both spaces, but probably not."

Fredo asked if it was determined that the girls from the school in Benot were also being housed here.

"You mean held with the other hostages? I'd say that's affirmative, if you ask me," answered Sven.

Peterson agreed with him, as did several others.

"With the sun up, we don't have the luxury of the drones. But there was no major force headed this direction, so we're thinking we'd give you guys a few hours to rest up, get some grub, shower, and get your gear in order. We check out as soon as it becomes dark. Kelly, you and Gunnar and Sven need to have a conversation and get some of these men paid. Gunnar is expecting a very generous payday, and we'd like to keep them being so cooperative."

The team laughed.

"I know what he likes, and I brought lots of it," said Kelly.

Peterson turned to Sven, whispering, "I know you've been awake more than you've been asleep, Sven, but I do think we need to meet with Mr. Sabi to get a temperature read. Are you going to be able to go in with me and Kelly and maybe one of the drivers and pay him a visit?"

"Maybe we take Doctor Carr as well?"

"Sure, the more the merrier, I guess."

Andy was not delighted with this. He was hoping to have a date with his bed. He looked up at Peterson and held a pretend phone to his ear, raising his eyebrows. Peterson gave him a thumbs-up, which meant Andy was going to have the opportunity to call his wife when they got to town.

Andy took a quick shower and grabbed some food. He left his medic bag with T.J., and armed with his SIG Sauer and two knives as well as several chloroform packets, he was ready to go. All five of them piled into the truck, and Adaze headed toward town.

"So what's the deal with this guy? Who is he really, and who owns him?" Kelly asked.

Sven smiled back at her, gave her a wink, and said, "Oh, he's probably owned by some woman who leads him around by the nose. Isn't that the way all powerful men are handled?"

"You've got that right, Sven. I can see you've learned some things with your time in the bush." Kelly followed up that comment with a glare.

"Oh, but it would have been so much more fun if you'd been here."

She smiled in return. "I mean it. Who is he really, and who does he work for?"

Peterson filled her in on their conversation with Sabi before. "We're thinking that not much goes on in the way of security and operations that he doesn't know about. Maybe he works both ends, and he owes his loyalties to the highest bidder. So if there are church or missions that need help or assistance, they pay for guards that he hires out through the local police and fire department. But if somebody else comes along and pays more, then they get more guards or the guards for the other group are bought off and disappear."

"Kelly, we didn't get too far the last time we were here. I walked away with a sheaf of paperwork, which I've left back at the camp. He's a big one on paperwork," Andy added.

"Oh, they usually are."

Kelly was flirting with Sven very overtly. It made Andy feel a little uncomfortable.

"So we're going to ask him for permission to open up the clinic, right?" she asked.

"Yes," said Peterson. "And we're going to ask about location and see what he gives us. And then we're going to ask him some questions about the recent kidnappings and find out what his take is on them. What I'd like to see is if we can determine if he had anything to do with them, and I think we need to come to it from the point of being concerned about our safety. Like, is this a safe area?"

Kelly nodded her head in agreement.

They parked in the nearly vacant parking lot of the Ministry Building, leaving Adaze alone in the truck. The delightful lobby was air conditioned like a refrigerator. A guard directed them to the Commissioner of Health's office. This time, the door was closed. Walking inside, they asked for Sabi. The young receptionist placed her hand over the receiver and asked them what they wanted.

"We're here to see Mr. Sabi. We are the Americans who came by to see him last week," Peterson said.

"Just a moment. I will see if he's available." She hung up her call.

She slipped into Mr. Sabi's private office, closing the door behind her. After some discussion, she reappeared. "He will see you now."

Since Adaze was staying at the truck, the four of them again entered the office with only one chair. He offered it to them just like before. "Please, gentlemen, take a seat."

His eyes danced with delight, watching the men scramble make a decision who had the seniority to sit in the chair. That was Peterson. Mr. Sabi eyed Kelly suspiciously as she began to speak.

"Mr. Sabi, my name is Kelly Fielding, and I work for the State Department." She pulled out her badge, and the commissioner nodded with respect, sitting more upright. "So this is not private then. This is for my good friend, Uncle Sam?"

"It's a joint partnership. We are sponsoring several doctors here, who wish to set up a mission. They are concerned about their safety, and the State Department is equally concerned, so we are starting at the local level with you. We are willing to pay for security, which I understand you will provide, as well as a location for the clinic."

Mr. Sabi sat up even straighter, "You are well informed."

Kelly began the discussion about recent events. "One of the things State is the most concerned about are the recent tragedies that have occurred. We understand that, yesterday, a European businessman and his bodyguard were murdered on the road. We've been told, although we have no evidence, that it was a rogue militia group. It was our understanding that this gentleman frequented this area and had never had a problem before. So I ask you quite directly, is this area safe?"

Kelly had a way of staring right into a man's eyes until she got some kind of an answer, which usually revealed something more than what they were ready to reveal. Sven had told Andy that she was the best interrogator he had ever met.

Mr. Sabi thought carefully, examining his fingers on the blotter in front of him. He began, "It depends on what kind of security is involved. We like to give our local police and fire extra work. In case we don't need them, they can still earn a decent living on the side working for other interests of our town. But as far as safety, if you run across a very well-armed militia group—these people who owe no loyalty to any particular country—it's very difficult, in fact sometimes nearly impossible to ensure."

"So what you're saying is it's more expensive," answered Kelly bluntly without any emotion to her voice. "So how much would it cost to guarantee that a clinic would be able to operate without *any* kind of interference?"

"My dear, you do understand that not all of the security money will go to the men who are actually doing the guarding. Some of it will need to be paid to certain groups who promise not to attack the clinic. As long as the money is paid, the clinic is safe."

"And this is guaranteed?" she asked.

"Guaranteed."

"And what sum are we thinking?"

"I would have to check with my superiors, but I believe something in the neighborhood of ten thousand dollars a day might be able to be arranged? Do you suppose your 'uncle' would be willing to pay for this service?"

"Yes, I think we are in the right ballpark. But I need to know who was responsible for the two kidnappings first. I would like to know the location of the schoolgirls, the journalists, and the film crew who were taken seven days before. I need to know if they've been murdered, are being returned for ransom, or if they're still alive, and I need to know if they're in this country or not. Based on your answers, we will agree to do business or not."

"This will take some time to gather all the information."

"We do not have a lot of time. We're ready to make a deal now. If what you're saying is that someone else has to make the decision, please direct me to that person."

Sabi stiffened, unused to being talked to in this manner, especially by an American, but a woman as well.

"I am that person, and you will have your answer tomorrow." His eyes narrowed.

Kelly turned around and left the office without asking anyone else's permission. Peterson, Andy, and Sven followed her. Sven bowed to Mr. Sabi, "We'll be back tomorrow then?"

"I believe that will work. See you tomorrow, doctor." The commissioner was fuming.

"No, it's Sven Tolar."

CHAPTER 23

JUST BEFORE SUNRISE, Aimee got the call she'd been hoping to get for days.

"You sound naked," Andy whispered.

"Oh God! Andy! I feel like it's been a year since we've talked."

"Only five days, but I'm losing track of things. Look, sweetheart, this has to be another quick call, but I'm good. Nothing to report. Just wanted to hear your voice."

"I have the very best news."

"Really?"

"We're rich, Andy. Carmen left me a boatload of money. Honey, we can travel, fix up the house, and buy some investments. Andy, you can quit doing all that dangerous stuff. We can just be together, like we planned."

"But—"

"We'll never have to work again."

"Wait a minute. I didn't hear this right. You met with the attorney?"

"Yes, she passed day before yesterday. I visited with him yesterday morning and signed all the paperwork. I wasn't sure, at first, how I felt about it, but now that I've thought about what it could do for us, I see that it totally sets us free. You don't have to go on any of those dangerous missions anymore. I don't have to worry. I can get Logan into treatment again. It just opens up so many doors."

"But this is your money. She left it for you."

"That doesn't matter, Andy. It's our money."

"No, it's yours. It's not mine."

"I'm sharing it with you, so you don't have to do all that crazy stuff anymore."

"But I like what I do."

"Well, you could phase out. I mean, I wouldn't expect you to just quit. But you could."

Aimee heard nothing on the other end of the phone.

"Andy?"

"I don't want to quit."

"But you have to put your life on the line. It's dangerous, Andy. And you don't have to any longer."

"I don't do it to eat or for us to live. I do it because I want to. Don't you understand? Haven't you learned anything about us?"

"I don't like your tone, Andy. You're making me scared."

"Aimee. You have to get a dose of reality here. What else am I good at? I've trained to do this. I want to do this for the next, well, I'm not due to re-up for a couple of years, but I want to stay with it. I like this job. And I don't particularly like the idea of being a kept man."

"Don't be silly. That's nonsense."

"It's not. You're already telling me what you want me to do. Do I ever pressure you?"

"No, but—"

"I don't like the feel of this. I'm going to have to think about this whole thing."

"What about us?"

"You're part of it. You're who I come home to, Aimee. I'm doing it for you too."

"But wouldn't you rather be a man of leisure and spend all your time at the beach? Travel, see distant places, meet interesting people? Expand your knowledge of the world? Learn a bunch of languages, and invest in our future? Doesn't any of that sound like what we talked about?"

She was getting nervous about the conversation and knew she had gone about this all wrong. Now that it was fully out, there was no taking it back. And the answer she got back confirmed it.

"That's exactly what I do now, Aimee. You've got to be kidding me. I mean, it's great having all that money, but I've seen interesting people, traveled the world. I like being a force for good. If you ask me would I enjoy just spending my time at the beach all day or hanging out having cocktails and crab, I think I'd get bored."

"But we'd be together, Andy."

"But we're together now, sweetheart. I feel you here, right beside me. When I come home, it will be so great to be together again. We are a team now. And I want to be the support for the men I work with, men I care about. I don't think I could live with myself if I just sat around and did nothing just because I could. What kind of life is that?"

Her heart was racing and her blood pressure rising. She felt darkness in her chest, finding it hard to breathe. Black spots appeared in her eyes. She inhaled deeply and blew it out. Then did it again. That's when it hit her. Was he saying that his job was more important than their marriage?

"Unfortunately, I've got to go. And this sucks big time. I've probably said it all wrong, but I love you, Aimee. And if you love me, don't ask me to give up something I believe in doing. My work isn't done."

"I understand." She heard the whine in her voice and hated herself for it.

"We need to talk about this, and I can't do it now. I'm sorry if I rained on your parade, but I've got to go."

He hung up without saying good-bye. She felt like she'd been hit across the face. How could he be so cold? Was this the reason she was hesitant to accept the money? Did she know something like this would happen?

Andy had never spoken to her this way before. And, yes, he was right about a lot of things, but especially about her little special Happily Ever After bubble filled with unrealistic expectations. But she believed in things like magic, running in the direction of her dreams, making up stories and adventures, and being inspired. Was it a mistake, then, to be partnered with a man of action, as he called himself? Could they have made a mistake getting together?

All throughout her run with Sandy, it bothered her. The more steps she took, the more the hurt and anger festered. It wasn't fair, what he'd said. It was almost as if she'd done something bad. Why couldn't he celebrate what kind of freedom that money could bring to them? And did that mean—no—it couldn't be that! Did that mean that it would destroy them?

She hadn't considered the pride she heard in his voice. He didn't want to live off her money, that was clear as day.

Just as she entered the house, her phone rang.

"Aimee, I have some good news." Dr. Denby's voice should have given her relief, but she resented his happy demeanor.

"Oh, really? What?"

She cursed herself for being so lame. She was so knee deep in the conversation with Andy that she wasn't present to him. This had to do with Logan.

"We've found him. He was picked up late last night. The sheriff called me, and we were able to pick him up this morning. I've got him on a mandatory lockdown for seventy-two hours. I can hold him longer if you'll sign off on it."

"So he's at your center?"

"Yes. He's fighting a bit. I was thinking perhaps you should come over and see him. If you think it would do any good, I can try to find a permanent spot, get another scholarship for him, and see what we can do for thirty days. After that, he's going to have to put in more of an effort. But I just wanted to call you and let you know he's safe, and we have another crack at getting him on the right track."

"Thank you, doctor. Maybe I should do that. My plans for today just blew up on me, so I'll be over in an hour. Will that work?"

"Perfect."

"So how does this work? Will they allow you to keep him, or does he have to face charges?"

"I don't think they've filed anything. He's probably got one more chance. I'm not seeing his cooperation yet. Maybe you could convince him."

Well, she'd just perhaps blown up one relationship with the man she loved. She wasn't in the mood for this, but maybe it was exactly the right thing to do. She went to her bedroom and picked up the box of photographs her realtor had sent over. Maybe some of these would be useful, she thought.

All the way over, she thought about her conversation with Andy. The wakeup call was bitter. Buying the house and renovations to the house were done with her own money. It was her idea, and he went along with it. But it wasn't what he would have done, and maybe she should have paid more attention to it. The comment about not wanting to be a kept man left her hollow inside. She'd never thought that she was doing that. Never once did it occur to her that he might be sensitive to the money she inherited. And now, she'd just exacerbated it like one hundred percent.

She gripped the steering wheel and tightened her jaw. Hearing

Sandy move, she looked in the rearview mirror. That's when she got a good look at her face, streaked with lines and looking older, certainly not happy. It was the face like she'd seen on some of the wives—a face that scared her at first when she got introduced to the community. She'd been told it was hard, that loving a SEAL was not a casual thing. But for Aimee, it had never been like that.

But now she could see how complicated he was. And how completely caught unaware she was. What was she thinking?

The parking lot was full, so she had to drive around several times to find a spot. She grabbed Sandy's leash and prayed they'd let her take the dog into the hospital.

She'd been there the last time with Andy. She remembered that day. He'd been so caring, holding her hand, pressing her shoulders, and letting her know he shared her pain over her brother's problems. It had been such a difficult day, and Andy had been right there for her.

Like she was supposed to be for him.

A male attendant dressed in white greeted her.

"Ma'am, I'm afraid we don't allow dogs here. As much as we love them, not everyone does, and we have to think about the guests and patients who come."

"I don't have any place I can keep her. I'm here just for a quick meeting with one of your patients. Could you call Dr. Denby first, and can we ask him?"

"Well, it's policy—Yes, Dr. Denby? You have someone in the lobby to see you." He put his hand over the phone. "Who should I say is here?"

"Aimee Carr."

"Oh, okay. Well, she has a dog with her, and we can't—"

He focused on the ceiling as he was given instructions.

"Very well." He hung up the phone. "He's coming right up to talk to you now."

"Thank you."

Dr. Denby came with a young technician wearing a lab coat. "Hey there, Aimee. This is one of my students, and she's agreed to watch the dog for a few minutes while you visit with Logan. Meghan, this is Aimee. And who's this?" He bent down and petted Sandy, who tried to give him her paw.

"Sandy. She's very well behaved and would love it."

As the two walked out the front doors, Dr. Denby escorted Aimee back into the clinic. He held a chart under his arm.

"He's having a medical evaluation now. We're taking blood, getting some clean clothes for him, checking for head lice, all standard stuff, sorry."

"No, I completely understand."

"We get kind of detailed here. That way we know what we're dealing with. It appears he might have lost considerable weight since we saw him last. Did you notice the same?"

"Yes."

"So when you see him, don't react. We've also given him a haircut, and he hates it."

"He probably hates being detained."

"Definitely. Now, I'm going to give you two a chance, but if he gets violent, I'm going to stop it, okay?"

"Absolutely. Do you think he's healthy otherwise?"

"I'm not ready to say that. Something's going on, but we'll have to wait for the tests." He turned the corner and stopped in front of a door marked Examination Room 6. "Ready?"

"Just a second. I've just learned I've come into some money, and I'll have the ability to have him stay here, if you think it will work. I'm willing to invest in him, but only once. How do we do that?"

"We can put him on rotating lockdowns, voluntary. The ones I've seen work best stay about six months. If they do the program that way, it usually sticks. But it's a lot of money, Aimee. I won't lie."

"Let's do it, but only if you think he'll accept it and work on it. Otherwise, it's a waste. Again, I can only do this one time, doctor. Only once."

"I got you. That's a very generous offer. I'll do my very best. So are you ready?"

"As ready as I'll ever be." She was just about to put ten years searching for Logan behind her. She knew this was either an ending or a beginning. She vowed to be okay with it either way.

As soon as the door opened, Aimee saw the shriveled, scruffy figure of her brother. Like the way he'd looked at the doorway last night, his eyes were sunken in with dark grey circles beneath them. His cheeks sagged, and his eyes were partially glazed over. She thought the doctor might have given him something to calm him down but wasn't sure.

She sat across the table from him. "Logan? Do you remember me? I'm Aimee."

"I don't know you," he said.

"Yes, you do. You came by my house last night. And you made me this." She showed him the bracelet he'd left on her doorstep.

One hand came from under the table, his forefinger touching it, careful not to touch her skin.

"I wear it all the time, and I think of you."

He pulled his hand back under the table and angled away from her. "You shouldn't. You should forget about me."

"It's not that easy, Logan. None of us every forgot you for one day. Every single day, both mom and dad thought about you. They loved you so much. But you came back. You reached out, and now I'm here."

"Nobody can fix me."

"That's probably true, Logan. I know I can't. But I can love you. I know how to do that. I want to help you be able to feel it, too, if it's possible."

He turned in his seat, scowling up at Dr. Denby, who was standing next to Aimee. "This your idea?"

"Sort of." He shrugged. "Logan, you're being held on a seventy-two-hour order. But I'm going to recommend you try a thirty day stay and then decide if this is what you want or not. Because it has to be your decision. I'm not going to lie to you. I've been honest with Aimee when I told her that people who have done to themselves what you've done don't usually clean up on their own. Even our stats sort of suck."

"What's the point?"

"Well, to start with, there might be some underlying medical condition that's making your symptoms worse. I don't know. And we never got started because you walked away before the treatment was finished. I'm going to ask for more of a commitment from you this time."

"This must be your idea," he said to Aimee, sneering.

Aimee could feel her patience eluding her. It had been one ugly night, and this morning with the call with Andy making it worse, she didn't have the stomach for much more. She didn't hurt like she did before when she'd seen him. But she did care.

Maybe it was time to face reality.

"You know, Logan, you may not realize it, but you were loved. And Mom and Dad tried to get you help, but it was too much. It cost them almost everything they had at the time, not that money is everything. But you reached out to me, and I'd like to know why? What made you do this?" She held up the bracelet.

"I'm not sure. I like to walk the beach sometimes. I've seen you running there. I saw the wedding, that day. I stole some booze and grabbed a sandwich." He stopped then finished with, "I wanted to do something human. Most days, I feel like an animal."

The cold, icy crust covering her body melted. "Thank you, Logan. It is the most valuable piece of jewelry I own. I shall cherish it forever."

She let the tears run down her cheeks, let him see her and the hurt that was there. His eyes started to moisten, and then he looked away.

"If I never see you again, I just want to thank you for this gift. For showing up again. For giving me the chance to tell you that I love you. I've gotten to know some people who never got that chance, some of them waiting for twenty years or more. Now, some might find that cruel. But I find it inspiring. Because they have hope, Logan. That's something I want to help you find again, because you were the most positive person I knew growing up. My big brother."

Dr. Denby inserted himself. "You're being offered a miracle, Logan."

"Some say life is a gift. Some say it's a curse."

"What do you think?" Dr. Denby asked him.

"I've been on both sides of that argument." He looked down at Aimee's bracelet again. "I'd like to think of it as a gift, but I'm not sure I can handle it all the time. Sometimes people are just too damned happy. I hate that."

She saw the broken parts of his soul, the emptiness of his wandering.

"You're being given a chance. Do you want to take it?" the doctor asked.

"I don't like to make promises I can't keep."

"So how's that going for you, Logan?" he asked again.

Logan shrugged, briefly checking Aimee's expression. "Sure, I like gifts. Miracles. Why not?"

"But you have to want to get better," Aimee said. "And maybe you can't. But I'm going to help you this one time, and then I'm done. You stay here until you get better and stronger. Not perfect. But you don't run away this time. You stay as long as you like, and I'll pay for it, Logan. But if you leave, I won't be there a second time. Those are my rules. You have to agree to those rules."

At the end of their conversation, Logan consented to being voluntarily remanded to the clinic for four months, minimum, which Dr. Denby said could keep him out of jail unless he escaped. He'd be locked in his room at night but given relative freedom in a secured location during the day. He'd submit to blood and urine testing and attend classes. They'd do a full medical diagnosis and try to adjust what they could. He was told it might not work, but if he wanted it to, there was no limit to what he could achieve.

Just before Aimee left, he called out to her.

"Will you come visit me?"

"I will, if you ask me to. I won't come unless you ask, Logan. But I'll come as much as I can, if you ask."

Aimee left the clinic, collecting Sandy on the way, and felt settled for the first time in months. She'd been lucky enough to play by her heart and have the chance to do something good with her money. Now the next battle was going to be settling with Andy. Having some honest conversations.

She still had hope. Of all people, Logan gave her that hope.

CHAPTER 24

ANDY WAS SILENT on their way back to camp. Sven and Peterson were cracking off-color jokes, and Kelly was lowering the boom on them right and left. Sven seemed to enjoy getting her angry.

Andy wasn't in the mood.

"So what's going on with you, Dr. Carr?" Sven asked.

"Oh, you know. Got five minutes to talk to my new bride, and we sort of had a fight. I think that's what it was."

"She'll get over it," Peterson said, slapping Andy's knee.

"No, I think I'm the one who has to get over it. I reacted to something she said, and damned if I'm being stubborn, but I think I was right."

Kelly turned around in the front seat. "Really? A man who thinks he's right. I've never heard that before. Why, don't you know, all men are right?"

She turned her back on the second seat, with the three Amigos sitting side by side. They'd just gotten their fanny slapped, and nobody appreciated it.

"Maybe we better cool it for a bit. I think tensions are building, and we've got to have all our wits about us tonight," offered Peterson. "But I'll tell you, that's happened to me a time or two. It takes a little adjustment sometimes for the wives."

"We've lived together for a year. I've been on one deployment before."

"Oh well, then, my gosh, a whole year? Why you should have everything figured out by now." Kelly was downright nasty tonight.

Andy was starting to hate her. He'd never liked women who were sporting attitude with him because there was no real sport in it. He wasn't allowed to really fight back. It was an old wound.

For the rest of the five minutes it took to return to base, no one said a word. Andy wondered what Adaze was thinking. He was a man still feeling the pain of losing his wife. It was like all of them were on different pages in different books in different libraries.

Peterson retreated to make his phone call. Andy sullenly ambled over to his cot.

"How'd it go?"

"Drama wasn't one of my better subjects in high school. I don't get this guy, Sabi. I'm standing there, listening to him cajole and talk. I'm wondering to myself, what the hell are we doing here?"

"Whoa! Where'd that come from?"

"I'm a little short on patience today. I think I'm just probably tired. Mind if I catch some shuteye for a bit?"

"No, I'll leave you alone. You want some lunch?"

"Not really hungry. I'd rather sleep."

"Okay, I'll wake you if there's something else going on." Dallas left their room.

The other cot was for Sven, and Andy knew there was a fifty-percent chance he wouldn't be needing it tonight. It took mere seconds before he was in the pits of a deep, dark sleep.

WHEN ANDY AWOKE, Tucker was seated next to the cot with a plate of food.

"Come on, sport. You gotta eat something."

"I think I caught a bug."

"Yeah, that's what I heard. Well, this stuff is damned tasty. You should try some. One of the Africorps wives makes it. Pretty good for you too. Try it."

Andy knew he was sulking. He accepted the plate and realized Tucker was sent when he started eating and the old guy didn't leave.

"I got in a huge argument with Brandy before I left. I'm going to have to fix that first thing when I get back."

"Pretty remarkable you volunteered for this, with a new baby in the house. I can only imagine. You'll probably get *all* the midnight feedings and diaper changes for a year, and even then, it won't be enough."

"Some guys during my first ten all re-upped at the same time so they could get their bonus and buy a fishing boat together. Not only did it not go over with the wives they forgot to consult, two of them actually got divorced and wound up having to spend the boat money for attorney's fees and child support."

"That's a cluster fuck if I've heard one." Andy finished his meal. "You wouldn't be trying to make me feel better, now would you?"

"Oh, it kinda crossed my mind. You've done a great job with these new buds, and they like you, Andy. I think you've made a real contribution. I'm gonna have to get even for the suggestion I come over to do this little TDI. But besides that, we're friends, and it warms my heart to see you've found a place here. You know how Kyle likes to keep things tight. I can see Peterson has a ways to go, but he's alright. He's learning. He listens, and that's the most important part. Nothing worse than someone being stupid and putting everyone's lives at risk."

"He's pretty good, I agree with you there."

"So since Kyle's not your LPO anymore and I'm kind of senior here as far as years in, I thought, if you needed to, we could have a talk."

Andy didn't want to offend the big man, but he really didn't want to talk about the conversation he had with Aimee. But he decided to make a stab at it.

"Let me ask you this, Tucker. Did you ever find Brandy, when you guys were first getting together, like overly enthusiastic about really dumb shit?"

"You had an argument about *that?*"

Andy knew it was a feeble attempt. He shouldn't have tried, he knew better.

"Let me see, Brandy, yes, she can get worked up about stuff about the house, wanting to make it perfect. She went and had some plans drawn for a deck upstairs, the fencing for the rear yard, and heck, we didn't have more than two extra nickels at the end of the month. But damn it, somehow, she managed to get it done. Her dad was a big help. She found these three guys who love to build shit. They drew up the plans, got it through the city, and bingo, we had a beautiful deck, rear fencing, and a partial remodel. All I had to do was pay for materials. They do this pay-it-forward type of thing."

"So she solves problems."

"No, I'd say she always looks for the opportunities. She sees the good in everyone. I used to see her try to be nice to those bitches who were her best friend's girlfriends. She never fit in. She's a big girl, as you know. Those ladies would dis her in ways she never figured out, but it didn't matter. She was always cool about it. Didn't whine and complain." Tucker erupted in a belly laugh.

"What is it?"

"Well, she likes to get even. She has fun with that. People are always underestimating her, too, and it doesn't matter. She's naturally happy. I have to have someone like that by my side. I don't like having to eke out my itty-bitty emotions and proper thinking for approval. She loves me. She always will. And, man, the more we're together the more I love her right back."

Now Andy felt really bad. He'd been a total dick. It didn't matter if he was a poor SEAL or a rich SEAL. Being rich was going to be a whole lot better. Why the hell had he gotten so worked up?

"Thanks, man."

"For what? I didn't do anything."

Sven poked his head into the room. "We got a briefing starting now, Carr. We need all hands on."

THE INTEL RECEIVED during the last twenty-four hours confirmed that the film crew and the girls were being held at the abandoned school site. The whole team breathed a sigh of relief since the longer they were present in Benin, the more likely they'd run into someone who would want to pick a fight. But they had strength in numbers. Andy felt confident they had everything they needed.

Part of the team was to pack up and get ready to leave once they either did or did not recover the hostages. Gunnar was not happy he was going to lose three trucks, but Kelly made sure he was properly compensated. Adaze was happy to be one of the drivers delivering them across the border, since he'd get another bonus. He offered to bring back one of the trucks along with a couple of the Africacorps men.

Peterson let Tucker and Sven set up the mission and made some suggestions based on what he'd been told of the school. Diku had once had a child who attended the school, so he gave them good information on the most likely areas to search first. What was most concerning was that there were at least twenty armed guards, and Peterson had been told more were on the way. It was do it tonight or go away with nothing, possibly with injuries.

Tucker had Danny Begay and Armando positioned to pick off some of the guards with their long guns. Fredo was to blow up one of the guard huts where the drone had picked up the most bodies, but not in the other building with a heavy concentration of heat signatures, a former cafeteria, where they assumed the hostages were being held. It all had to be coordinated at the same split second. Then Tucker and his team would breach the building and start extracting hostages.

They were hoping everyone was healthy enough to walk. Diku, Adaze, and another brother were to bring the vehicles closer, all loaded up, so they could bypass the UNESCO camp and just make a line for the border. When they stopped at the Kandi camp to drop the girls, they could grab supplies or treat the injured.

Danny and Armando found rooftops with perfect line of sight to the yard outside the hut and the hostage area. They divided up the guards they could see, using their Invisios. Fredo and Dallas set charges all over the place. They wired an ammunition storage locker that had been left open, all around the old office building housing the guards, and a diesel storage tank used for fuel. Archie located the generator and, on the mark, would cut the power, leaving most of the camp in pure darkness. With their NV goggles, the SEALs would have a huge advantage.

Sven gave the signal. In rapid succession, six shots, sounding like three, took out six outside guards. Then they caught the two or three who ran outside afterwards. The charge was a little late and went off about a minute after the power was cut and the diesel tank exploded. But by that time, there was so much confusion that the element of surprise was no longer a factor.

Andy helped Tucker move out the girls, who were screaming and had to be calmed down. This was the part of the mission Andy wished they'd had the nurses. But as soon as the trucks arrived, they all climbed inside, helped by two of Diku's men. The six Dutch and American journalists were very weak and barely able to walk, but with help, they were loaded into the two remainder trucks, and when all three vehicles left the camp, less than five minutes had gone by.

Not one guard at the school was left alive.

Peterson got word that a force was coming up from the South. It was decided that they bypass the UNESCO site, where they'd planned on dropping off the girls, and to head to Kandi and return them to the two nurses, who could treat them.

The Africacorp drivers were phenomenal, and Andy wanted to make sure when he got stateside that the Navy knew how well they worked. They dodged obstacles, occasionally a cow or goat in the road, avoided potholes, and kept a speed of nearly fifty miles an hour all through the bush, cutting across two grassy savannahs without the benefit of a road beneath them.

Armando and Danny were riding in the rear of the last truck to watch for followers or choppers, but luck was on their side, and they made the rendezvous to the Kandi camp in record time.

All the guards had held, and several additional ones showed up. Kelly applied Uncle Sam's cash liberally, and when Sven hugged Flora and they all said good-bye to the schoolgirls, the whole place was erupting into a celebratory party. Diku said that word went out to several parents in Benot that their daughters were safe and were coming to pick them up.

Andy thanked the tall Africacorp leader, the one he wasn't sure he could trust.

"You come back, I be your driver again," he said in broken English.

"That's a promise, Diku. You did good. Uncle Sam thanks you. Stay out of trouble."

"Trouble? No, this is fun!" He laughed and ran to his crowd.

It took them another two hours to hit the Niger border. The border patrol was not out in full force, but there was a long line of lorries and commercial vehicles waiting to get through. The bottleneck was going to take an hour, which was way too long.

Kelly demanded they cut in line, and when deposited at the barricaded gate, several truckers behind them started honking.

Sven turned to Andy. "Amazing what that woman can do with a badge and some cash. Just watch her work," he whispered.

Seconds later, guards were removing the big barriers and the two trucks were allowed to pass. At the Niger border, the State Department had already given them clearance, and they were waved through without even stopping them.

Peterson turned to Adaze. "You make sure all these guys get back over the border together, or my ass will be on the line. We don't want any international incidents here."

Adaze grinned and gave Peterson the peace sign. "No problem. We were on a special mission saving baboons for UNESCO!"

For some reason, everyone thought that was hilarious, and nobody stopped laughing for nearly five minutes.

A cargo plane was waiting for them at the airstrip, the huge belly opening wide to accept the men, their equipment, and the hostages onto the plane. Andy watched through the tiny porthole as the big behemoth bellied up, took off, leaving the two white trucks and their African brothers-in-arms behind, waving.

It had been a week of very intense days with little sleep and nothing in the way of luxuries. But Sven passed out some Norwegian chocolates to every member of the team.

"Don't believe what they tell you. The best chocolates in the world come from Norway."

CHAPTER 25

AIMEE DIDN'T GET a call from Andy. Instead, she got a call from Peterson's wife.

"Hey, Aimee. You and I have got to get together and talk. My husband just loves Andy and what he's brought to this team."

"Thank you. I appreciate that."

"So I'm calling to let you know they'll be flying in tomorrow at three P.M. and to apologize that none of them had any time to call home. They've been in a big ol' bucket of bolts, and they'll probably arrive half deaf too. Andy is staying over in Norfolk and then driving home Saturday."

"Okay, thanks."

"I'm sure he'll call you when he lands."

"Yes, I suppose so." But Aimee suspected that the reason Andy didn't call was for something entirely different.

"We just wanted you to know how much we appreciate you and Andy. And I'm going to have to make sure you get invited to some of our wives' events. I've been remiss, and that's on me."

"Thank you. It's been pretty busy here with the wedding and everything. We live so far away."

"Well, maybe you two should consider buying a house here in Little Creek. It's a wonderful community. Very military friendly, of course. That way, you could get involved in more of the Team things."

It was the last thing Aimee wanted to do. With the additional funds, perhaps purchasing something for him to stay in when he had to go up to trainings or a place for her to go so she could be there when he returned made sense. But all those plans seemed so far away. She wasn't sure any of it would work out now. And she was exhausted. She just didn't want to make any more decisions until she had to.

She spent the rest of the day cleaning the house, changing the sheets on all three bedrooms upstairs, since Sandy usually liked to take her pick when Aimee was out shopping and had slept on all of them. She didn't mind the dog hair and smell everywhere, but it wasn't what Andy would like. It could also be one more thing for him to get angry about.

Shelley stopped by, bringing some flowers.

"Okay, what did I do wrong?" Aimee asked, slightly wary.

"Nonsense, silly. Why, are you in a streak of pissing people off? I hardly believe that about you."

If you only knew.

"I just brought them because. You've had a pretty big week. And now that Andy will be coming home—"

"How did you know?"

"One of my friends at school has a son on Team 4 with Andy." She walked up to Aimee and took her by the shoulders. "Are you okay?"

She hated that Shelley had that radar that could detect when she was on inner shaky ground. Despite her self-admonition, she began to cry.

"Oh, honey. I didn't mean to upset you, sweetheart."

Shelley was a good friend but a lousy hugger. Her skinny frame was just too bony and fragile. There was only one person in Aimee's world who could hug a woman like she should be hugged.

Shelley put the flowers down, took Aimee by the hand, and sat her down on the yellow couch so they could watch the bay together. "Tell me. I promise to only listen this time. I know I've been a pain and a half, and my advice has been shoved down your throat. You tell me. What's wrong?"

"I had a difficult call with Andy early this morning. And then I went down to Sarasota to visit Logan, and—"

"They found him?"

"Yes, he's in the treatment program there. He looks bad, Shelley. I just hope they can help him. But at least the money I get will be good for something."

"What did you say?"

"I meant, I can afford to help him out now. I couldn't have before."

Shelley stared out at the waves. "I shouldn't ask this, but is everything with you and Andy okay?"

"I think so. This was a hard trip. He was under lots of pressure."

"But certainly, you told him the good news?"

Aimee disentangled her fingers from Shelley's lap and smiled. "I did, and I was surprised with his reaction."

"I shouldn't pry."

"He doesn't want to be a 'kept man' as he put it. I thought he'd like to get off the Teams, retire. We could travel, do things around here, see the world a bit. Buy some property and fix it up."

"But? There's a but in there somewhere."

"There is. He likes his job."

"Nothing wrong with that."

"I think it's more important than me. I just realized that."

"No, I think you're wrong. I've seen the way he looks at you. He's completely nuts about you. You know, telephone calls can be strange, especially when they only have a couple of minutes to catch up. You probably just had a bad connection, that's all."

"Yes. It was a bad connection. I misunderstood him. So it won't be the happy homecoming like I expected. Instead, we have to talk some things out. I think we will."

"But you're worried about it."

"Think about it, Shelley. We live twelve hours away from his job. Who does that?"

"Airline pilots, senators, congressmen. Lots of people do. Professional athletes live clear across country sometimes."

"But it's a community. And it's important to him. For the first time, I feel like my pull here, to this house, might be coming between us. I don't think it means the same for him."

"It never does. A house is way more important to a woman than a man. A woman has to feel like she has a place of her own. I've read lots of books on that. Trust me, I know."

Aimee smiled at her friend. She would have said that they were identical personality types, but now she saw that Shelley was also just as upbeat and positive but far more realistic. It was hard to convey exactly what she was feeling. Maybe Shelley would never understand.

"It's more than the house. It's the disconnection to the community. That's the problem, and I didn't realize it until I spoke to him."

"Do you think you'd move up there?"

"No. I won't sell this house. This place is too special for me. He moved to Team 4 to be closer to here, but now I'm afraid it might still be too far. But we'll see. I just need to make sure it's what he wants to do, and I'd just been assuming before."

"And now with Logan in Sarasota, there's another reason you might want to stay here."

"And we both know how that could turn out too." Aimee leaned back on the couch, closing her eyes. "Argh. It's so complicated all of a sudden."

"Well, you have more choices now. Maybe one of them will work out. If not, I happen to know of a very deserving teacher who would love to inherit a small fortune." She followed it up with a smirk.

That did make Aimee laugh. "All right. Lecture's over. And I don't want to talk about anything sad. Bring me some good news."

"Oh, I forgot. I've got a new boyfriend. He's a single dad of one of my students. He's gorgeous, Aimee. You'd like him."

"We'll look forward to meeting him. You'll have to bring him by."

"I will once I feel I'm more secure. One look at you, and he might jump ship."

"Not a chance, Shelley. Come on, you were always the one they liked better."

"And you're a horrible liar."

SHE TOOK SANDY out for a run. On the way back, taking a new route, she passed a used bookstore she'd not noticed before. In the window was an old, blue IBM Selectric typewriter, surrounded by Hank Borges' books with a black and white picture of Hank sitting at the table, using that typewriter to write one of his novels. It was taken from his backside, so it showed the view from the living room of the house she owned. The beach in the background was identical to the beach she saw every day.

She left Sandy tied to a bike rack outside where she could see her from inside the store. A clerk came up to her.

"May I help you find something?"

"I was looking at that display in the window. The typewriter and Hank Borges' books."

"Yes. That's the very typewriter he wrote those books on. Right here in Sunset Beach."

"Did you know him?"

"No, he was way before my time. My mother met him a time or two. He was well liked."

"Did you ever see him with a woman?"

"No. I think he had a wife and children up north somewhere. I've never seen a picture of him with a woman before."

"How did you get the typewriter?"

"It belongs to the owner here. I think it was given to him when Hank died. It's for sale, if you're a fan."

"For sale?"

"Yes. Everything in this store is for sale. Even the store. The owner is moving back to be closer to family in New Jersey. He's ready to retire."

"How much for the typewriter?"

"He's asking forty bucks."

"Sold. Can I come by later and pick it up with the car?"

"Absolutely. Oh, Mr. Nichols will be delighted it went to a fan."

"Tell him I might be interested in the store too. But I have to talk to my husband first."

"That would be the best piece of news he's had all year. Can I take your number so he can call you?"

Aimee wrote her address and phone number down for the owner. "I promise to be back before dark."

THE NEXT MORNING, Aimee came downstairs with Sandy, ready for another run. She liked the look of the blue typewriter placed in the middle of her dining room table. Next to it, on the right, she had a stack of fresh white paper. To the left, she had a box ready to accept completed pages of a novel she had yet to write.

During her run, she passed by the bookstore, all of the surf shops not yet open, a diner serving breakfast, and several real estate offices in a row. Landscapers were leaf blowing sidewalks. The free bus from St. Pete to Clearwater passed by, nearly empty. The pulse of the beach community was beginning to increase with more and more snowbirds coming back to this special place every day. Signs began to pop up in the windows reading “Snowbirds Welcome” or “Snowbirds Specials” to attract the new inhabitants.

She was guarding herself, waiting to learn when Andy’d return. She asked herself whether she could give up all this, if he insisted she come live with him in Little Creek. She would want to say yes. But part of her knew that, if he made her give up something she loved so much, it wouldn’t last anyhow.

And then she understood how Andy felt about his Team of brothers.

CHAPTER 26

THE TWELVE-HOUR DRIVE from Norfolk to the Gulf Coast in Florida would give Andy lots of time to think, and he toyed with the idea of just coming home, unannounced. But that wouldn't be fair to her, to either of them.

He'd tried to sleep all the way home, but the hot and sticky ride in that transport wasn't ever comfortable, even with headphones, a dozen pillows, and blankets. At least the Navy equipped it with blankets.

He took a shower in the team building and headed out to the parking lot.

Aimee picked up on the first ring. "Hello?"

His heart melted the instant he heard her, just like the first time they'd met, when she belonged to someone else, when she wasn't his to take. Every fiber of his being screamed out that she was the one and how he thought that he would never be able to tell. But his body and soul knew. It had never wavered in that.

Just hearing her voice again seemed to bridge that gap, like the bridge that led to St. Pete and the Gulf communities beyond.

"I'm headed home. I'd offer to stop and pick up something from the store, but it would melt or go bad by the time I made it, but I'll ask again. Do you want anything on the way home?"

"Just you, Andy. You are the only thing I want in this whole wide world."

It was what he expected and didn't have any right to have. He never wanted to possess her, clip her wings, or make her do anything she didn't want to do. He liked that she was easily inspired. He wanted more than anything to be that inspiration.

But first, they had to have that talk.

"Can't wait, sweetheart. I'll be driving all night. See you in the morning. So sleep naked."

After they hung up, he smiled. She was easy to please, easier to love. His life would forever be a better one if she was by his side. And it would only work if she was happy too. So that's what they would talk about, explore together.

He listened to jazz all the way home. And before the sun was even warming a tiny part of the ocean at the horizon, he pulled onto Gulf Boulevard, which was completely devoid of traffic. He let the magic pull him back to the house on Sunset Beach.

He opened the living room door and was instantly greeted by a big yellow dog who barked at him.

"So much for a stealth entrance. Hello. What's your name?"

The big dog handed him her paw. Andy got on his knees and felt the fluffy fur around her ears and neck.

"That's Sandy," Aimee said from the top of the stairs.

He dropped his duty bag and ran up the stairs to greet her properly. Sandy followed right along, step by step. He took Aimee's face in his hands and pressed against her lips then luxuriated in the loving feel of her soft body. He'd forgotten how good she smelled, what her hair felt like when he laced his fingers through it.

She was crying.

"What's wrong?"

"I'm just so happy to see you. I thought—"

"Don't ever believe anything I tell you when I'm about to do battle," he whispered. "It's all bullshit."

"But—"

He cut her off with another kiss. "I'm sorry, Aimee. I was a complete asshole. This one was my fault."

"But—"

"It's all good. I need to sleep with the woman I love. You're my prize, my reason for coming home, sweetheart. Will you accept me, imperfect as I am?"

"Oh, Andy, always. I've never wavered. I'm sorry if I upset you."

"You know that saying on your wall? *The ocean heals everything.* That's the truth, Aimee. And you're right. This house is magic. You make it my magic."

She stripped off her nightie while he undressed. Then he slipped under the covers to lay on top of her, allowing her flesh and soft places to wear off all the rough parts of the past few days. He kissed her neck. He kissed that fragrant place between her breasts where she wore her perfume. She arched, bent her knees, and tilted her pelvis to accept him.

And Sandy hopped on the bed right next to them.

"So this is going to be a threesome from now on?"

Aimee was laughing so hard Andy thought perhaps he'd lost his opportunity to have a little romance.

"She sleeps on the bed too? Dog hair and everything?" he asked her.

"Yes. But we could convert the other bedroom into her room, if you like."

Andy got up, thought about it for a minute, and then answered, "Yes, I like." He called to the dog, walked her to the bedroom beside theirs, and closed the door.

While the dog whined and barked until sunrise, Andy and

Aimee rekindled the flame that had never really gone out. Wherever she wanted to live, he told her, is where they would live.

When they made love for the second time, she brought up the subject of buying him a little house in Virginia. "Some place for when you have to be there, some place where I can come visit and surprise you. As long as you come home to me."

"You'd do that for me?" he said as his rhythm increased.

"I'd do anything for you. I'd be your kept woman."

"Except you'd be paying for the house."

"I'd let you pay for the whipped cream and pancakes in the morning. That's only fair, Andy."

"Oh, pancakes and syrup all over your body. Hardly seems a fair trade."

"I negotiate well."

"I love the way you negotiate."

"So this will still be our home?"

"Of course. Always."

As long as she was okay with him staying on the teams, he'd drive that twelve-hour drive home after every mission if he had to, with or without a house in Virginia.

"Because, Aimee, I want to be part of your life when you're the happiest. And you're the happiest here, at Sunset Beach."

SECOND CHANCE REUNION

Sunset SEALs Book 6

SHARON HAMILTON

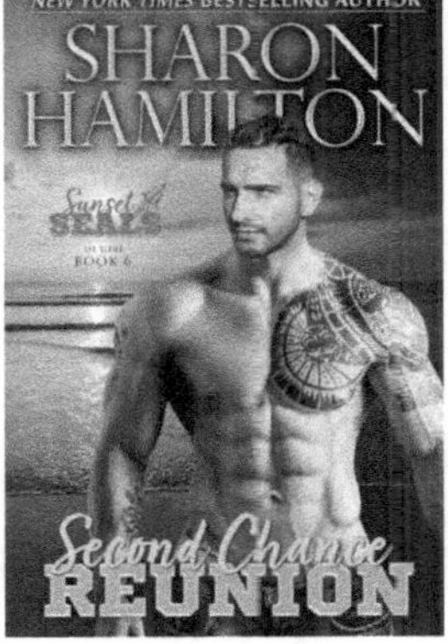

CHAPTER 1

Friday before Valentine's Weekend

DAMON HAMLIN STEWED over what to get Martel for Valentine's Day. They'd been apart for a month, and she'd be flying in to visit him for Valentine's Day, but she'd only be here that one day. Engaged, they planned on a June beach wedding, most of which she was handling. Not to mention, she needed to finish out the school year in Florida, saying good-bye to her parents and other teachers he knew she loved.

Because she was going to come live with him in San Diego, she was giving up her little house at Sunset Beach. And he worried it was perhaps asking too much.

What did she have to do to convince him she was actually joining him in San Diego? He wondered why he doubted things all of a sudden. Maybe it was because the next day after their night of romance, she intended to visit their daughter in Palo Alto—the baby she'd given up for adoption while he was off being a Boy Scout on his SEAL Team 3. Even though he didn't know about her until this year, he felt he should have known. He should have done a lot of things differently.

He'd made so many mistakes. *They'd* made a lot of mistakes together. But he still knew that Ainsley, their daughter, wasn't one of them. He would forever be grateful Martel decided to give her up for adoption rather than terminating the pregnancy—a decision she'd borne on her own. Strong, dedicated, and thinking straight, she could always be counted on to do the right thing. So he shouldn't worry or question her agreement to marry him, to give them a second chance to have that happily ever after, even though they'd blown the first one so badly.

Maybe it worried him that he wasn't worth what she trusted or saw in him. It was sort of imposter syndrome. Would she find out in time that he really wasn't the honorable man she thought him to be? He had been so weak and uncaring, so selfish, thinking the whole world revolved around him. He liked to tell himself it was because he had to focus on his demanding job—demanding emotionally as well as physically.

But that was a lie, because the job fit his limited capacity to think emotionally and deeply. It made him wonder if he ever would deserve her.

But she believed in him. That was for sure. He hoped to God he didn't disappoint her. He'd hurt her enough. She wasn't a fragile, breakable doll—she'd proven that overwhelmingly. She was strong. She loved strong. She never gave up, even when he did.

But she deserves more, doesn't she?

He couldn't tell her that he wished she'd spend all her time with him. He couldn't tell her he wished he could go with her to see their daughter. No, he had to earn that right. One thing at a time. What if the meeting caused her pain, so much pain that she didn't want to see his face again because it reminded her of the heavy decision she'd made twelve years ago? He knew it was going to be both good and hard for her at the same time.

And, God help him, he wouldn't be there to hold her hand. He'd be a phone call away while she boarded the plane and flew home to Florida to face the end of the school year all by herself. He should be there, but he couldn't be. He'd be on deployment.

Everything about his job had changed since he met her at that wedding in Florida. That second chance meeting where she just appeared, like magic—out of thin air, back into his life, and then soon back into his arms. He didn't even recognize her at first.

"What the fuck's the matter with you?" Calvin "Coop" Cooper asked him, slapping him on the back.

"I'm sorry?" He reared his head up to stare at the tall SEAL blocking the sun. The huge Adonis medic on their team had just taken one of his five-mile swims in the bay. He was just as ripped at thirty as he probably had been as a tadpole who nearly made the United States Olympic Swim Team.

"You look like you either ate too many of the Scupper pancakes or some bad seafood. Maybe something from the bottom of his chowder pot."

"That bad?" He sneered up at Coop.

The tall operator, almost the fastest swimmer on the entire platoon with hands that could palm a basketball no problem, hunkered down beside him and shook his head, as if to say, "clean up that brain of yours," and let him eat the consequences of being covered in droplets of salty bay water.

Well, he had it coming.

"I heard Martel was coming out tomorrow. You don't look like a man who's especially excited. I mean, if you were like Libby or one of the ladies, you'd be waxing yourself all over and getting a proper haircut and shave."

"Wouldn't do any good. It would grow back before tomorrow, Coop. You're the same way."

Coop rubbed the pelt on top of his head he called his hair, now beginning to thin. Soon, he'd have more hair on his chest and arms than on top. "That's probably true."

One of the things he loved the best about his SEAL buds was that they didn't have to talk much. There was this thing about syncing. Just sitting down next to a guy, and he could sort of tell what was going on. Lots of non-verbal communication.

Or maybe it was all horseshit. Damon chuckled.

"That's what I was looking for. You must be thinking about all the things you're going to do when she gets here. That's more like it."

"As a matter of fact, I was," he lied. But it was the game they played. It made no difference if it was bullshit or the truth. The rule was no lying to the women. The men, well, they could handle it, as long as it didn't put one of them in danger. Also, no lying about acting like a pussy or trying to get out of a deserved punishment. The only time SEALs lied to the women was if one of the wives asked if her husband was being unfaithful, and then no question, you had to lie. Every time. Not just sometimes, every time.

"As an older man married now nearly ten years, with three kids to chase around and a pretty wife who still looks hot in a bathing suit, I ask that you indulge me in your plans. Maybe I can learn something from your younger ones," Coop said with a big grin.

He asked not because he wanted to know, but because he wanted Damon to go there, hang around, remember who he was and what he had to do, and to stop moping and worrying about everything in the world he had no control over.

So he'd take a stab at it.

"I don't know what to get her for Valentine's Day."

"Roses are nice."

"Yeah. I thought about that."

"Hard to go wrong with those."

He wondered why the idea didn't make him feel better. Maybe

it was the romance he didn't feel he deserved. Or was he looking for something special? A band-aid on the chasm he'd created and now was repairing. The truth was, he felt like he wanted to apologize to her all the time. He couldn't help it.

"You know it's normal for engaged SEALs to go a little crazy from time to time. They start imagining things. It's one thing to earn your Trident and another altogether to step up to an altar and in front of everyone say, 'I do.'" Coop gave him a long look to make sure Damon got the message, like he'd stuck a pin with that note to his forehead.

"I'm not having cold feet." Fuck it. He was about to go deep, and he couldn't help it. "I don't think I deserve her. I've done so many shitty—"

"You shut the fuck up, Damon, or you'll be single for your natural life—or until some round gets you when you're thinking that. That doesn't do any good for anybody. Besides, it ain't up to you. It's the woman who chooses."

That was true enough.

"And Martel chose you, Damon. You're it. Now is not the time to consider some other story. You should have thought about that before you—"

"Don't bring it up." He really didn't want to hear that part.

"Oh, I didn't mean—" Coop shook his head. "Fuck, I must be losing it. I didn't mean the kid, Damon. I meant before you let her fall in love with you again. You had a choice in that. But once you opened that door and let her in, she tagged you. There's no getting around it. You're it. You got no more rights, man. It's chapel time, my friend. Has nothing to do with whether or not you deserve it. It's what she wants. And knowing Martel, she'll have it too."

"So now you see my problem."

"Ain't no problem, bro. You're screwed. Lovingly screwed. Grin and enjoy the ride."

"But there's a third person in our family I keep thinking about. I think about her all the time."

That shut Coop up. He cautiously continued. "Well, I haven't had that to deal with, that I know of, anyway. You made the mistake, the both of you made the mistake, but she wasn't one of them."

"That's what Martel says too."

"And that's the right way to look at it. You two should have been together, and you blew it. Now you do the rest of your life differently. You're playing a different game."

"So back to my original thoughts. What the fuck do I get her for Valentine's Day? Besides what I've already given her, I mean."

"You just give her everything you got. You let her know how special she is. Don't go wallowing around in that self-pity crap, Damon. She doesn't find that very sexy or attractive. I don't have to tell you that."

Damon agreed. But even if he plastered the road to his condo with rose petals a foot thick, it still wasn't enough.

"Do you write?" Coop asked.

"Not really."

"Draw?"

"Nope."

"Can you tell her a story?"

"I don't like to tell stories."

"So read her something. Ever heard of Rumi? He wrote some classic love poems. Libby has several books with them. Want me to ask her?"

"No, I can do the research. That's a nice thought, though. Do you think I should get a nice room at the Hotel Del?"

"Sure, if you can get one. Women like that. But it's going to cost you, if it's available. Valentine's is pretty big there."

"You're probably right."

"God, if I still had the Babemobile, I'd let you borrow that. Simple, just a big bed and a galley kitchen and a head."

"And more of your DNA in it than anything else in the world. No, thanks. That wouldn't work, Coop. What are you doing, trying to get me divorced before the wedding?" He was laughing now, at Coop's expense.

But the big-hearted man of steel was laughing too.

"Talk about pasts. See, I wasn't so bright, was I?"

"It worked out, though."

"As it will for you, son," he said as he put his arm around Damon's shoulders. "Can I buy you breakfast? I'm starved."

Well, he wasn't any closer to deciding what to get Martel for Valentine's Day, but the idea of a hearty breakfast with some decent coffee sounded perfect right now.

"Coop, you know just the right thing to say, don't you?" Damon said as they scrambled to their feet.

"I try. Goddammit, I try."

CHAPTER 2

MARTEL WAITED FOR the parents of one of her students. Her shared office seemed a little cramped and small today due to the clutter of papers and reference books she and her office mate and best friend, Kaitlyn, had collected over the school year. It was going to be a task to extricate herself from this little den where she had shared so much with Kate—the person she came to visit some six years ago and part of the reason she stayed in Florida, abandoning her California roots.

The space was filled with as many memories as papers and books.

This would be the last year she would be teaching here. It was the end of a long and enjoyable partnership with Kaitlyn. Combined, the two of them were the most popular teachers at the school. A part of her wanted to stay forever here, but her sensible, forward-thinking part knew she belonged in San Diego with Damon and the new life they would be restarting there.

At least, that's what she told herself. It was a day-by-day thing. Leaving the Gulf beach community sometimes felt like she was giving up something too precious to be able to recover from—but she'd done that already and survived. If she told herself this over and over again, eventually she'd not have those doubts. But sometimes it still felt like jumping from the skydiving plane into the blue unknown that beautiful day with Damon, flying through the sky in tandem with his careful guidance then coming to a safe landing. She hoped it would turn out that way. But often, hope needed help.

Tomorrow morning, she'd be off to San Diego to spend Valentine's Day with Damon, and then she'd fly to Palo Alto the day after to visit their daughter for the first time. She was excited, nervous, and now irritated as she tapped her fingers on the folder she'd prepared for the parent-teacher conference.

Often, she would meet with parents in the classroom, but in this instance, she needed the privacy of the office where she could close the door. The discussion she needed to have with the parents had to be in private due to the nature of the meeting. These talks weren't what she had expected when she got her teaching credential. She wasn't basking in the happy, fresh-faced adoring gazes from a room full of active young minds full of life and soaking up her every word. That was the part of teaching she loved.

This was the hard part. The part no teacher ever wanted to have.

A full twenty minutes late, the young couple appeared in her doorway. Mrs. Gibbs wore cut-off jeans a little too short for her hefty legs and a halter top because it was a warm day in February. Mr. Gibbs wore a dirty light green tee shirt with a construction logo on it and jeans equally as soiled. Even his hands were stained as he extended for the obligatory shake. The mother just sat down in the chair and asked Martel if she could smoke.

"I'm sorry, no. The whole campus is non-smoking, Mrs. Gibbs."

The young mother rolled her dirty blonde head back and forth, the French braid the only part of her appearance done with care. Martel immediately had a bad feeling about the outcome of the discussion she needed to have.

"So I have some concerning news, and I want to let you know that I have not spoken to the administrator about this yet, but I intend to. And based on our discussion here this afternoon, I may be speaking to other authorities as well."

"About what?" Mrs. Gibbs barked. Her frown was ugly. Her skin was over-baked from the sun and lined before her years. She was missing two teeth on her upper right side. She would have been pretty if she'd taken a little more care, Martel noted.

Mr. Gibbs sat stoically like he was about to get hit by a train.

"I think your daughter is exhibiting behavior I've seen before in young preteens who have experienced some kind of sexual abuse, and I—"

Mrs. Gibbs was on her feet. "No way, missy. You don't give me that crap. We may be poor, but we're good people. We don't abuse our children."

Martel knew they had five at home all under the age of ten. Her student, Cora, was their eldest.

"I didn't say you abuse your children, Mrs. Gibbs. Now, would you like to sit down, or should we move this discussion to the administrator's office?"

The young mother dutifully sat, her steely eyes struggling with thoughts Martel knew she didn't want to have. She and her husband avoided each other's attention.

"Let me explain. And then, maybe, the three of us can figure out what our next step is. First, I'm required by law to report anything I see that could be viewed as abuse to higher authorities. I'm sure you've noticed some of the bruises she has on her arms and legs. She came to school last week with a shiner and tried to cover it up with makeup. Several boys from the class teased her about it, and I sat her inside the classroom during recess and tried to have a discussion with her."

"You have no right to talk to our daughter without our permission," the mother started in again. "In fact, maybe we should pull her out and find another school."

"I'm not your enemy, Mrs. Gibbs. I'm trying to help Cora. I'm trying to help the two of you. I think we need to pay attention to several things I've observed."

"So, a kid can't be clumsy? She runs into things," said the woman who herself had a very large bruise at her wrist as if someone had yanked on it. Martel knew it was possible the mother didn't want to come to terms with just what was happening in their home for her own set of reasons.

"There's more than just the bruising." Martel tried to make eye contact with Cora's father but was unable to. His eyes were downcast. Martel's heart sank.

Mrs. Gibbs stood, nervously. "I gotta have a cigarette. Where can I go?"

"You can go sit in your car and have one, if you like."

"Gimme the keys," she said to her husband, again without looking him in the eyes. She held her hand out, and Martel saw the obvious signs of a knife cut nearly three inches long, extending from her wrist toward her elbow joint.

When Mrs. Gibbs left, the door remained open, which was a blessing, Martel thought. She heard sounds of birds who had built nests in the upper reaches of the hallway outside. There were sounds of a lawnmower and a leaf blower, children playing outside, and cars from a nearby expressway. She focused on the world going by outside, a world she wanted to run into and enjoy.

Mr. Gibbs was silent. He crossed his legs, balanced his chin on his fingers, and continued to stare at the ground.

"Are the two of you having troubles?" she asked him. She chastised herself for posing something perhaps too personal.

He gave her a half smile. "You could say that." He shifted his legs again. "My wife's a very disturbed woman. She tries. Good hearted. But she's damaged goods." For the first time, he peered back at her. "I didn't do any of that. I keep the kids away from her family as much as possible."

"Her wrist—"

"Yes, that happened about five years ago. She spent some time in the hospital after our third was born. She even tried to give the baby away."

Martel felt the hackles at the back of her neck rise. Perspiration dripped from her armpits and soaked her silk dress. A dull ache in her belly twisted her insides. She was flooded with visions of holding Ainsley, before she knew she was Ainsley, smelling her little pink face and fingers, heartbroken that she would probably never see her again. Her nineteen-year-old self had suffered, too, but in a much different way. It was still suffering. She'd cried herself to sleep the week before she delivered, wanting to meet her baby and not wanting to experience the separation she knew was coming, that had all been planned out. If she hadn't made those arrangements, she never would have been able to say good-bye and hand the baby over to the childless couple who took her.

The Newbergs.

She wanted to ask Mr. Gibbs the question she'd heard so often spoken when people talked about adoption. "How could you—" But she knew it was a different answer for every single person faced with the impossible choice. Polite conversations were had, even though people she talked to never knew she'd experienced it. She'd given her baby up, yet she'd found a way to live with that decision, telling herself it was for the best.

And it was. It really was.

But that was her story, just one of thousands every year.

So Martel didn't ask. Instead, she gave Mr. Gibbs the out he probably deserved. "Being a parent can be very difficult. And the two of you have so many. I know it must be a struggle, even on a good day."

"There aren't many good days anymore. Honestly, when I come home, I don't know if she'll be there. I think one day she'll just take off. No warning. Just disappear. She's not a very happy person."

"But your girls—all girls?"

"Yes, ma'am. We kept trying for a boy. I got the girls genes and no boys in me."

"Well, it takes two, you know."

"No, it's me. I can't have boys. I know I can't."

Martel was trying hard to stay positive, but her lower lip was quivering. She was about to burst into tears. She managed to get out, "Are you able to ask for help? There are agencies that do that, you know. Groups who help people who get overwhelmed with being parents. Classes you can take."

"Honey," he said, his angry grey eyes squinting at her, "I only got a fourth-grade education. My classroom days are over." He was sullen, leaning toward the doorway. "Where the hell has she gone?"

Martel could see Mrs. Gibbs talking to herself, walking across the lawn from the parking lot. "She's coming. I see her." Quickly, she drew out a pamphlet from her desk drawer and handed it to him. "This is a group from a Christian church who help with this sort of thing. No classes. Just help. And no money."

He assumed his half smile again. "I don't need anybody's goddamned money. I'm no charity case."

Martel nodded. "I can clearly see that." She let him meet her eyes. She wanted to smack him right across the mouth but worked very hard not to show it. But she did give him the stare just to make a point. "No shame in asking for help. Think of your girls."

Before he could tuck the pamphlet into his pocket, Mrs. Gibbs ripped it from his fingers. "What's this?"

"Just a suggestion for the both of you. I know raising children—"

"Do you have any kids?" Mrs. Gibbs interrupted.

That was a difficult question to answer.

"No."

"Then you can take your literature and shove it." Mrs. Gibbs threw it down on the desk. Martel quietly slipped it back into the drawer from where it came.

"Are you done?" Mr. Gibbs asked her.

"No, I was just beginning. Please sit," she directed the mother.

"This is a fucking waste of time," she said.

Martel took a drink of water, sat up straight, and continued. "I found Cora today with her pants down around her ankles, standing behind the field shed. She was letting two boys touch her down there. That's not the kind of behavior a fifth grader should be exhibiting. It means she's learned it from someone else, perhaps an older child or an adult. Probably a male. If I were her parents, I'd want to find out who that male is, and I'd want to get some help for Cora, or it may progress into something else much worse." She watched the shocked expression on both their faces. She was glad this was news and not something they expected. "Because this person might be preying on others, maybe one of your other girls too. This type of behavior is learned, and it has to stop."

Mrs. Gibbs burst into tears. Martel had struck a nerve, and the woman appeared to be reliving some pain from her past. She suspected it didn't have anything to do with Cora, either. And, for the first time, she saw Mr. Gibbs show some tenderness for his wife. He placed his arm around her shoulder and wouldn't let her shrug it off, even though she tried several times. Finally, she sunk into his shoulder and sobbed.

He whispered something to her. Mrs. Gibbs shook her head

violently in protest.

He caught Martel's eye as his wife calmed some. "So what's next? You call the cops? Because I have a past, when I was a dumb stupid kid," Mr. Gibbs said, settling back into his chair and crossing his arms.

"I honestly don't know how all that works, but yes, I have to inform my administrator. Then, yes, the police will be notified. And Child Protective Services will want to interview her. But I'll let them explain all that to you." She scanned between the two parents. Mrs. Gibbs was wiping her face, her eyes red and puffy. She was very fragile and barely able to breathe without strain. Martel reached across the desk, holding out her hand for the woman to take. "Can I get you something? Can I call someone? Do you want to talk to someone right now, Mrs. Gibbs?"

"No, I'm fine," she quipped. Her legs were crossed, and her foot was bouncing rapidly. "That sonofabitch." She turned to her husband. "Don't you lay a hand on him, Roger, or you'll have the lot of them after me and the girls. Don't you dare. We let the cops take care of him."

"So you know who might have done this?" Martel asked.

"I'm not admitting nothing," the mother said. "Not a word of this to the girls," she scolded her husband.

"Lorene, they probably already know. Where the fuck have you been?"

Martel realized she'd have to make a full report, and she wished she'd asked her administrator to sit in. This had been a huge mistake. But, if there was one thing she was thankful for, it was that she didn't think these two damaged parents were directly responsible for the abuse Cora suffered. But Martel guessed they were probably related to someone who was.

That was going to be very tough for all of them. But it was something that fit an ugly pattern she'd studied.

"Listen, I have no doubt someone will be in contact with you both very soon, maybe even tonight. Whatever help they offer, please take it. At least, that's my advice, for what it's worth."

"They're gonna take the kids away," Mrs. Gibbs whispered, covering her mouth with her fingers.

"They're going to want to protect them. Who is watching them now?"

"My mom."

"You need to go home and wait for the authorities."

"I'm supposed to get back to work, but I'll pack it in today."

"Does Cora come back to school on Monday?" Mrs. Gibbs asked.

"There's no reason she can't. She hasn't been a danger to anyone but herself. However, we do have to thoroughly investigate, so let's see what happens over the weekend. I think, for her own good, I'll keep her in with me during recess if she does. I don't want any bullying or teasing going on at her expense. And of course, I won't be saying anything to the other kids, just to my administrator. I do believe the school is a safe place for your daughter. And we'll keep a special eye on her. But I don't know what the administrator will want to do."

Mrs. Gibbs nodded.

"I have your phone number, and I'll call you this weekend, if you want. And here's my cell phone. Give me a call if you need anything."

Mr. Gibbs stood and shook Martel's hand again. "Can I have that brochure back?"

"You bet. Here you go."

After they left, she watched them hug in the parking lot, get into their car, and then drive away. Martel chose to believe the young couple were of the same mind with the same purpose. But that was just a guess on her part.

She called the administrator, and after they met, he agreed to call the Pinellas County sheriff's department, as well as Social Services. He told her to fill out her incident report at home over a glass of wine and email it to him when she finished. He admonished her to get it in this evening.

"Next time, don't tackle this by yourself. One of the counselors would have sat in with you."

"Yes, I couldn't find anyone, but you're right. I worried too many strangers in the room would cause a negative reaction. But I can see that was a mistake."

"Go home, Martel. But get me that report, agreed?"

"Absolutely."

HER HANDS SHOOK on the drive back to her bungalow. She clutched the steering wheel like it was a lifeline, digging her nails into the black leatherette covering.

She entered her living room, turned on some peaceful instrumental music, dumped her computer case and purse on the couch, kicked off her shoes, and poured herself a glass of white wine, taking one very long sip. She changed into a pair of sweats and treated her feet to her favorite pair of felt slippers.

The late afternoon sun melted low on the horizon, turning the sand and puffy clouds outside a deep rose-peach color. The bright glow reflected off her walls and warmed her face as she stood facing the sliding glass door overlooking the bay, sipping her wine. Her thoughts drifted back to the recollection she'd had of the baby in her arms all too briefly.

Now twelve years old, Ainsley was slightly older than Cora. The discovery of the abuse today had shaken her all the way to the bottoms of her feet. If she had a magic wand she could brush over the land, she'd make a perfect world for young girls like her daughter to live a normal life away from the fear of predators. She had to help nail this person or persons. It was a rescue she was embarking on, even though Cora belonged to another family. She cared enough to stay involved until the case was solved and then would need to care enough to walk away.

Like she'd done years ago.

She poured herself another glass of wine and sat at her computer, wrote her report, and emailed it to her administrator. Before she closed her laptop, she sent Damon an email.

'Can't wait to see you tomorrow and wish I could stay longer. Looking forward to a nice walk on your beach, discovering all the way its magic heals everything just like my beach does here in Florida. Packing now, drinking wine, and missing you terribly.'

While she was loading up her suitcase, she heard the ping of her cell phone with Damon's response.

'I can't wait. But I'm warning you, I might not ever let you go.'

'Music to my ears, my love.'

'Then let's do it. Let's run away.'

Damon's answer brought hot tears that spilled over her cheeks. Her delicious longing for him was causing her pain and, at the same time, filled her with joy.

'We will, Damon. First, we'll have the vows in June, the party with all your drunk SEAL friends, and you looking handsome in your dress whites. I want the spectacle of it all—at my beach at sunset.'

'Your wish is my command. Hurry.'

It was a glorious time to be alive, to be jumping out of that airplane and going for the freefall ride of her life. An adventure unlike any other she'd ever had.

After this weekend, she knew her life would never be the same.

CHAPTER 3

MARTEL'S FLIGHT WAS due in at noon, but this morning, Damon was commanded to the Team 3 building on base for an informational meeting on their next deployment, coming up sometime within the next month.

"Surprise, surprise. We got a sex trafficking ring still operating in Baja California, guys. I know that comes as a shock to you all, but that's what we've got. So dust off your tropical pink flamingo shirts and your rubber zoris, and start practicing being a tourist," Kyle Lansdowne said to the group.

Their State Department rep took over the floor next. He already wore a green and yellow pineapple shirt, sipping water from a glass with a purple paper umbrella sticking out of the top. He spoke to the group behind a pair of sunglasses.

"Carter Ridgeway here. I'm pleased to make your acquaintance. I don't want any of you to get the wrong idea. These rings that deal in drugs and girls—children, really—are all over the world. You throw a dart at the continent of Africa, South America, Mexico, even the United States, parts of Europe, Middle East, and beyond, and you'll probably hit the location of one of these rings. As soon as we get one put to bed, another takes its place."

It wasn't anything that surprised Damon.

"We have a different wrinkle in that we have issues at the border during the past three, four years, but now it's escalated to enormous proportions. We have a lack of manpower and changes in policy regarding undocumented workers. Add in the mix, we have drug dealers and coyotes who are making a fortune while we're all trying to sort out the most humanitarian way to deal with the problem. Which is what we stand for, gents. We want it to be safe and humane but effective. Meanwhile, the other side doesn't play by the same rules. So we're stuck."

Several comments were whispered around the room. Damon saw Kelly Fielding and Sven Tolar standing at the back of the building, sharing a coffee. They toasted him, and he nodded in return, which caused others to turn their heads and notice.

Ridgeway continued. "As a bit of background, I've been wearing my Special Agent badge now for ten years, and for the last five of those, I'm been taking stealth teams to various embassies all over the world, evacuating U.S. citizens undercover from hostile places where Americans shouldn't be, in my humble opinion. So it might surprise you to know that nearly ten thousand US citizens are still trapped in a few of these places. Some were NGOs, some were doing humanitarian missions, some sent by news agencies and churches. And some, believe it or not, are tourists."

The whole room erupted in whispers and light conversation.

"Now lately, we've seen an uptick in the desire for younger American girls and boys for the sex trafficking business. Those kids get sold all over the world, and once they are, they are really hard to find. We're talking less than thirty percent, maybe even lower, are recovered. In fact, we've been prioritizing groups to rescue based on the number of children these family units have traveling or living with them, because they've become very valuable targets for these cretins who deal in the flesh trade."

A number of their last SEAL Team 3 missions had involved the sex trafficking pirates in Africa and the Canary Islands. But the

Team had also been to Mexico on previous deployments before Damon joined up.

"You're gonna ask me how come all these people take their kids to these places and get caught. Some work in rural areas, villages where there isn't internet and barely cell phone service. Sometimes things can change so quickly that they actually travel by accident into the middle of a militia turf war. Or they think living with their friendlies will keep them safe, until someone's army comes through and decides to make an example of them. Two years ago, I rescued a whole family—they were ecotourists—who lived in the jungles in the Amazon for months before we could get them. These are good people, and they deserve to come home."

Kyle stepped forward and began adding to the presentation. "Special Agent Ridgeway uncovered a group in Honduras, an American soccer team down there for exhibition matches with local kids, kidnapped at gunpoint, a whole bus full of them, along with some local kids and international coaches, and successfully returned them home. At the end of that mission, he discovered parts of the ring escaped, infiltrating a huge migrant caravan, where there would be less scrutiny, and they were cherry-picking girls from that group, separating them from their parents and removing them quietly under everyone's noses.

"Ridgeway tracked them to Baja, where they've set up a complex of abandoned hotels and basic prisons to house their booty. He then requested help from our community. So our mission is to draw out as many of the leaders as possible and bring them to a black ops site State maintains near San Felipe at an abandoned Mexican air base perfect for extraction. From there, we'll be going down the finger toward Cabo to disrupt as much of their operation we can get our hands on. But it's only a matter of time before we'll run into Mexican Government resistance or from a faction in the government making money off the enterprise. We have some good partners we're working with in Mexico. It's much better in some ways and much worse because of the sheer numbers. But it only takes a few bad actors, and the missions get real complicated real quick."

Ridgeway continued. "You fellas have posed as fishing enthusiasts before, and that worked well. We asked for your Team because of your experience and familiarity with how these groups work. You successfully shut down the Cortez brothers' network. And this one and several others have replaced it, capitalizing from the vacuum created when you took the brothers out."

Damon saw lots of heads nodding. He could feel the Team getting pumped up with that old "force for good" pride he often felt himself.

"So here's one thing we have to be careful of. Their tactics have changed. If the cartel gets close to being captured, they murder all the victims and just disappear into the countryside, waiting to come back and strike once again with new prey later on, rather than stay and fight over the girls. The danger level has amped up significantly. We're losing a lot of Border Patrol agents, but now more than ever, children are being used and often discarded later, sort of like a disposable entry ticket into the US. Younger kids are used because they're easy to steal, easy to transport because they're small, generally more compliant than older children, and very easy to kill, unfortunately."

The room erupted in groans and curses.

Kyle completed the short meeting after some logistics were discussed. He introduced Sven Tolar and Kelly Fielding to the group of newbies. The legendary FSB warrior from Norway and the State Department liaison held hands and waved to the crowd.

"Damon, you be careful. I think these two want to come to your wedding, and they might piggyback on all Martel's hard planning. Watch 'em. If you're not careful, it will be a foursome."

The people in the room laughed.

It was going to be a warm day as he made it out to his Hummer. He'd worn a white long-sleeved shirt and his jeans. He took Coop's direction and had gotten a quick haircut last night, taking extra care to give himself a close shave this morning. He was headed to the airport.

He heard whistling behind him.

Fredo, T.J., and Tucker were clustered together, catcalling him.

"Lookin' very snappy there, son!" barked Tucker.

"Very tight and spiffy, tadpole," added T.J.

"Oh, you gonna get laid tonight for sure," Fredo finished.

This wasn't helping his case of nerves one bit. He turned without commenting, but they wouldn't stop. Finally, T.J. caught up to him.

"Bring her to the beach tonight. We've got a little pre-Valentine bonfire going on, in case you didn't hear."

"I'm sure I'll have other plans," Damon tossed back at the three. "You guys just want to look at her. I know you too well."

"We live for you single guys. Come on, give us a break," said Tucker.

"I'll ask her. You know she's only staying tonight. Tomorrow, she's leaving."

"Oh, I get it, she doesn't think you can last longer than one long night? Or is that all she can stand?" teased T.J.

The other two howled at the comment.

"You guys are assholes. She's gotta go up to the Bay Area to visit friends tomorrow. And she has to be at work on Monday. She'll be back." Damon hadn't told many about his past or about Ainsley. He definitely wasn't going to bring it up now.

"Or you might ditch the mission." Fredo winked, adding a nod for good measure.

“What did you get her? I wanna see,” T.J. whispered.

Damon stood tall, pressed his chest out, and grinned. “You’re lookin’ at it.”

“Oh, wow. Damon, my man, you gotta very long, painful evening coming up,” said Fredo. “That’s just not smart. You gotta work harder than that.”

“I can work very hard,” he smiled, raising his eyebrows.

“Not sure she’ll see it that way,” T.J. scowled.

He was now starting to get pissed off, so he stopped, put his hands on his hips, and lectured all three of them. He needed to put an end to their teasing.

“Look, it goes like this. Flowers? She’s traveling tomorrow, first to San Francisco and then back on the plane to Tampa on the red eye. I don’t think she wants to toss a sixty-dollar bouquet of roses in the trash, right?”

They nodded.

“Fancy lingerie? I don’t think we have time to properly enjoy that. I’ll wait until we have a whole week to ourselves to introduce some of that. Suggestions welcomed. And I’m taking up an offering, in case you are so inclined.”

All three of his buds had their arms crossed, now avidly listening… or pretending to.

“And what’s the point of getting a fancy hotel room? The Hotel Del is booked. So is the dining room, and I’m hoping we’ll be focusing on other things, not the quality of the drapes or the view. She wants to walk the beach and feel the sunset. I plan to give her both those things, and more.” He finished it off with a smile then added, “So fuck off!”

HE WAS MORE anxious than he wanted to be, sort of like the first time he deployed, which was silly because they’d spent lots of time together since they reconnected. He couldn’t shake loose the jitters, regardless. It was so important that everything be perfect. That's why he didn't want to plan anything. He was going to let her make all the decisions, since her big day was coming up tomorrow, when she got to meet Ainsley for the first time. God, how he wished he could be there with her.

So maybe Martel would be nervous, a little extra sensitive. That was to be expected, he thought. No biggie. Maybe she'd cry a little more when she talked about things or might take stuff in a strange way. Women were complicated, especially thoughtful women like Martel. Women who cared about people and weren't out there to just party. He didn't want to disappoint her. A nice, quiet evening with a good bottle of her favorite wine was all that was necessary. There would be time enough later on to get acquainted with the other guys, some of whom might come across rude or insensitive…

Oh fuck. I'm doomed!

No amount of self-talk was working today. He was going to sweat through this shirt, would be hugging her at the airport with huge basketball-sized sweat circles beneath his armpits. He could smell his aftershave burning off already, and the scent to follow wouldn't be nearly as pleasant. And he hadn't brought a fresh shirt. He should have thought about another tee shirt too. And now his pants felt a size too small. Had he gained weight? Would she think he looked flabby? He hadn't had time to get a proper tan, but the haircut she'd probably appreciate. Suddenly, he remembered she'd told him one time she liked his hair on the longer side.

Which way is it? he wondered as he entered the airport short term parking garage. He was a bit early, so perhaps he'd have a beer, and that might help—or a shot of Jack, maybe—but then he'd smell of alcohol, and she wouldn't like that either. Breathing into his palm, he wondered if his breath was bad but couldn't tell because his hand still smelled of aftershave.

He tweeted his Hummer locked and jogged across the concrete into the airport building itself. It was crowded and loud. He bumped into a young girl who dropped her teddy bear, which was quickly run over by a rolling suit carrier gripped in the hand of a man wearing a long green camo rain slicker. The man nearly tripped over his own feet as the suitcase stopped while his legs continued. He flipped his left arm out to the side to balance himself and slapped a paper coffee cup right out of a young woman's hand, which spilled down the front of her blouse and onto the gentleman in a suit walking beside her.

The woman, startled, dropped her cell phone on the travertine floor and watched it scoot nearly ten feet, hit the side of the lobby wall like a hockey puck, and took a ricochet shot right into the path of a ten-passenger electric transport vehicle barreling down the hallway to make a late gate assignment. The driver in a red vest tried to swerve to avoid running over the cell phone but clipped a handcart burdened with three precariously perched and overstuffed plastic garbage cans. One tipped off, spilling contents onto the pathway of a group of women Lacrosse players.

As papers and food wrappers spread out over the floor, someone's emotional support dog got loose and ran with its leash trailing to intercept a dirty diaper opened wide and fully exposed, resembling a melted chocolate croissant. The dog's owner pulled at the little mutt as he attempted to get away, dodging around and between oncoming pedestrian traffic. A toddler stepped right across the paper mess, including making a four-inch shoe-sized impression in the brown diaper detritus and then attempted to walk farther with it stuck to the bottom of his foot for several steps until he tripped and sat right in the smelly substance.

The toddler earned a nasty look from his mother, who

changed course with the little one in tow, the deflection causing her to bump into a luggage cart which toppled a dozen suitcases piled precariously high by an inexperienced young valet. One of the suitcases burst open, and several people nearly tripped over it, but one heavyset man carrying a guitar case stepped accidentally on a corner, which caused the case to flip into the air and then land a few feet away.

By this time, Damon had caught up to the case, having negotiated through the string of messes behind him that made the wide approach to the arrival lobby look more like there was some kind of protest going on. He didn't stop to right the case but quickly made his way up to the arrival lounge where there was a bar. He definitely was going to have that drink now, after he'd nearly talked himself out of it earlier.

Damon slipped in between two people with their backs turned to each other, one a woman and one a man, and ordered a neat shot. As he brought the glass to his lips, he heard a familiar, "Oh. My God. It's Damon!" from the woman on his right, which caused just enough of a jerk to his arm that he spilled some of the drink on the front of his white and very unforgiving shirt.

Dammit. Dammit. Dammit.

He slurped the rest of it quickly, smacked the glass back on the bar, and chanced a look.

It was as bad as he thought it was. Charlene, his ex, extended her rather large boobs in his direction, and he tried hard not to look, but it was no use. She was poured into her black very tight and very shiny skinny pants and wore ginormous four-inch heels and one of those fuzzy low-cut white sweaters that used to make him sneeze. He'd developed an allergy for sure to the Angora or arctic squirrel or whatever it was that those things were made out of.

Get. A. Grip.

"Well, if it isn't the old flame that still burns. And it's Valentine's Day. How perfect," she purred, batting her enhanced eyelashes with the red accents applied. "You know, I woke up this morning, and I was dreaming about you and that body of yours, Damon. We made a pretty good pair, don't you think?"

"Charlene. What a surprise." His stomach was flopping around like a near-dead fish.

"I'm off to Vegas. Wanna come?" she cooed. Her lips came dangerously close to his.

He backed up and stepped on the gentleman's shoe behind him. He had to get out of there.

"Those days are gone, I'm afraid. I'm here to pick up my—my *fiancée!*"

"Oh, how wonderful. I'd like to meet her."

"Not going to happen." He placed a five-dollar bill on the counter, checked the time, and noted it was still early, but he probably had enough time to wash the little light brown stain off the front of the shirt and, if he was lucky, dry it with the electric hand dryer. "I gotta run, but it was nice seeing you."

He heard the clickity clack of her heels behind him as she worked her little buns off to keep up with his long strides. This wasn't happening, he told himself. Now he was being chased by his ex, and he had alcohol on his breath and a stain on his once perfect shirt.

"Wait! Wait, Damon. I just wanted to tell you something."

He didn't pay attention. The loudspeaker was saying something about an arriving flight and the noise behind him blocked most of it out. He glanced at the monitor next to him until he found the flight information for Tampa.

Arrived early!

Due to the brief stop to check, Charlene had caught up to him. She placed her arms around his neck and pulled him into her chest and wouldn't let go.

"Charlene, please don't do that—" he'd started to say, but she interrupted him.

"Are you still a Navy SEAL, Damon? Because I have some great news. Jenna—"

He was searching the crowd. Several men were secretly smiling as he disentangled himself from her embrace, nearly peeling her arm from his neck as she tried one last time to grab his collar and practically ripped it.

"Stop—stop it, please, Charlene," he said, gripping her forearms and holding her firmly arm's length in front of him.

"Jenna is marrying a Navy SEAL, Damon. Isn't that great?"

He was having a hard time focusing. Did he see Martel's face in the crowd as he whirled around looking for the gate? He hoped not. Absentmindedly, he asked, "Jenna? Who—"

"My little sister. His name is Brian, and he's from Oregon. Big tall guy. A real stud, just like you," she giggled, trying to wrap her fingers around his forearms.

From behind him, he heard her voice.

"Damon?"

He quickly threw down Charlene's hands and did a one-eighty, coming face to face with Martel. Her forehead and brow wrinkled. Her mouth turned down into a frown as she leaned to the side to catch a glimpse of the blonde woman in the very tight black pants molesting him from behind.

Charlene didn't miss a beat. With one arm around his waist, the other shot out towards Martel, her red hearts charm bracelet shaking as she said, "I'm Charlene, Damon's ex. Nice to meet you, sweetie!" Charlene was hiding behind his torso, her chin resting on Damon's shoulder.

The look on Martel's face wasn't what he'd expected nor was it anything he wanted to see this Valentine's day. Her eyes focused on the stain on his shirt and followed down the length of his body and then back up again without lingering on anything in particular.

"You must be the welcoming committee. I'm Martel. I'm a *friend* of Damon's."

CHAPTER 4

MARTEL WAITED FOR Damon to clean up the mess he'd made of their meeting at the San Diego International Airport. She didn't return Charlene's happy banter and tried to ignore her altogether. She couldn't wait for the explanation he was going to stumble over, so she kept her emotions hidden and let her lack of reaction calm the waters. Charlene giggled, babbled along, and let her hands fly through the air like they were tambourines, the red hearts on her bracelet making little clicking noises.

She wondered what Damon ever saw in Charlene, which was a relief, because her former self might have gotten jealous. Today, she was just amused.

Oh, the choices we make!

She reminded herself not to be so hard on the early twenty-something Martel. She'd made some pretty poor choices too, after all. But the toughest choice of all was one of her best decisions.

Just from watching the three or four minutes between the two of them convinced her they were about as mismatched as two people could ever be. Damon was so nervous, or perhaps self-conscious, he didn't make eye contact. The two former partners would lightly toss word salads at each other until they'd just run out of things to say.

Martel was going to let them do just that.

Normally able to sleep on the plane, today's flight earlier was noisy, and her mind had been racing with the twenty or so to-do lists floating around inside her head. Some were about the wedding. Some were things she hoped she remembered to pack. Some had to do with Cora and her interchange the day before with Cora's parents. She wanted to be alone with Damon, not stuck in this airport with a thousand people crowding through it.

Charlene's nervous laughter wasn't all random. The woman snuck side glances at her to check her out.

As if she wouldn't notice.

Now Damon's ex was also talking about a mutual friend who was marrying a Navy SEAL. It was a warning beacon sent out to telegraph that Charlene was still loosely connected to the Brotherhood and probably wasn't going to leave Damon alone. This was one factor Martel hadn't counted on, but when she examined her insides, it was a minor annoyance and didn't really bother her.

Finally, Charlene's last good-bye and wink was laced with something a little dark. The woman's wounded pride was being a bully, trying to exaggerate that she was over Damon when clearly the opposite was true. Martel felt sorry for her but knew the gesture was really a veiled warning.

As Charlene's ass bounced down toward her gate, her destiny being Las Vegas, Damon put his arms around Martel's waist and turned her to face him. His sexy eyes were entirely hers to command.

"Now. Sweetheart. Love of my life. Martel." He turned her head with his thumb and forefinger at her chin. "Come here and let me show you how happy I am to have you here." His warm smile did start the process of making her panties wet. It didn't take much to just throw herself at him and plant a wet kiss on his soft lips.

"Thought you'd never ask."

"I need to get you home."

"Yes. You. Do." They walked arm in arm, heading to the luggage carousel. She let out a big sigh, glad to finally be in San Diego and clear of the talking parrot his ex reminded her of.

"Tough week?" he asked.

"Yes, you could say that." She stopped. "Damon, what was that all about?"

"What?"

"That woman. How did you—?"

"Don't ask. I'm still trying to figure out why. Sometimes you just do dumb stuff. You forgive me?"

"Nothing to forgive." She shook her head, began to laugh, and then rolled her shoulders. "You think you know someone, and they surprise you—"

"Come on, give me a break. I got those papers overseas, and you know what? I felt *liberated*. The guys were coming up and giving me the old heart-to-heart thing, and I was happy as sh—" He checked his feet. "I'm sorry about that."

"Unbelievable. Do you know how many hours I worried about your ex coming back into your life when we had to live separately for these months? I didn't expect this. I guess I feel liberated too." She gave him a quick smile and continued down the rampway.

"So you were saying there was a problem with your job at school?"

"Yes and no. I've got a problem with one of my students. I don't want to talk about it here, but we just had to refer one of my girls to Child Support Services and the police. It's just the beginning of what could be a very long and involved process."

"Oh wow. Sexual assault?" he whispered.

"Yup. Just a hunch, of course, and the first meeting I had with the parents revealed a lot. But I've just received minimal training. I'll leave it up to the experts. I sure hope we can resolve it quickly, but something tells me this is just the tip of the iceberg."

"That's too bad, especially for your last months of school there. Sounds like you don't suspect the father, or am I reading too much into this?"

"No, you're spot on, but again, it's just a hunch. They have all girls—six girls in the family. My guess is that it's someone, maybe more than one, from the wife's family." She looked up at him, his face in a deep, pensive frown. His concern made her love him even more. "But I'm not supposed to talk about it, so don't let me, okay?"

He adjusted his arm to grab her around the waist and squeezed her beside him as they continued walking toward the luggage area. "God, I missed you. It felt like half a year, and it was only, what, just shy of a month?"

"Twenty-five days. I crossed all of them off my calendar."

"How are the wedding plans coming? Or have you not had time?"

"I hired the caterer, but I'm getting the wedding cake from somewhere else. How many of your guy friends will be coming, do you know?"

"I haven't passed out any invites yet. A couple of the wives took pity on me when I talked about it. They made some 'save the date' post cards."

Martel giggled. "You're kidding, right?"

Damon shrugged. "Look, I don't do this DIY stuff. The married ladies love messing with us single guys, even the *engaged* single guys. I was going to do it today at the team meeting, but it ran over, and I had to get here."

"And you forgot to bring them. Fess up."

"Okay, yes, I forgot." His face had turned bright pink, having been caught in a white lie.

"So you know where your next mission is going to be?"

"Mexico. Baja, actually. We're looking for one particular bandido and his crew who have blended in and out of the migrant caravans, making tons of money along the way by convincing parents to give their daughters up for a better life in the U.S. Or telling them getting their daughters across the border will enhance their own chances for a successful crossing. It's so depressing to see this."

She stiffened.

Damon abruptly stopped, placed his palms under her jaw on each side. He kissed her tenderly, and whispered, "That didn't come out the way I wanted it to. We have some people actually *selling* their kids into sex rings too. Using them as an admission ticket. The coyotes work in packs, in tandem with other couples pretending to be parents who have let their daughters go with the handler, trying to convince the naïve parents they'll be safe. The whole thing is a very sorry situation. Breaks my heart, really."

She put the side of her face against his chest and listened to his beating heart, enjoying the warmth of his arms wrapped around her. Her familiar arousal was a welcome distraction to the harsh realities of the world in which they lived. "Thank you for doing what you can," she said into his chest.

He answered by kissing the top of her head.

DAMON ROLLED HER suitcase behind him as they strolled to the parking garage together.

"So did you know Charlene would be there? How did all that happen?"

"Just my unluck charm, I guess. She's between boyfriends again."

"Again? So you keep in touch?"

"Not really. I bump into her from time to time, that's all. She tries to hang around the Team 5 guys now."

"Oh yes, those rules again." Martel still didn't understand why an ex would be considered "off limits" but not a widow.

"It's a tight community. Even being careful, there's gossip, and there are some things a man and woman share when their marriage doesn't work out that has to stay private. Dirty laundry and all that. Those weren't my finest days. I don't need to be reminded of them."

She had nothing to add and didn't want to pry.

"I see on my phone the Gulf has been warm," he said as they entered the garage.

"I used to think San Diego was just as warm, but no way."

"We have a nice, clear weekend coming up. They're having another bonfire tonight, if you're interested. You can continue to get acquainted with some of the other wives."

"You steer me clear of anyone like Charlene, okay?"

"It's a deal." He unclipped the seatbelt from the side and placed it across her lap but lingered for a soft kiss. "Happy Valentine's Day, sweetheart. Just want you to know if you just want to stay in bed all afternoon and evening, I'm cool with that, too."

She watched him walk around the front of the Hummer and climb up into the driver's seat next to her. He was the sexiest man she'd ever met. Long after they'd lost touch after high school, she still dreamed about him. And just as those dreams started to fade away, they met at their mutual friends' wedding. What were the odds?

She felt silly spending so much time worrying about the chemistry between the two of them since they had to live apart. Their relationship was about as natural as it could be. This time it even felt more solid.

Damon was easy to love, and every minute she spent with him heightened her resolve to make things perfect. The problems always seemed to happen when she was all alone. The big man upstairs was telling her something alright.

She was *made* for Damon.

THE AFTERNOON SLEEPILY wound down. She had no appetite for strolling Coronado or spending hours at a seafood bar or restaurant with a view of the ocean. Her mind and desires were here and now, in his arms, in his bed, re-exploring all the reasons she was going to uproot herself and become a San Diego transplant.

Their prolonged lovemaking turned her bones to rubber. She could easily forget all her stress and worry, the apprehension of giving up a place she loved so strongly. It gave her focus. Each scorching hot kiss continued to obliterate her doubts. He was patient and relentless, taking her powerfully and not stopping until she'd reached the pinnacle of her passion first. She loved his control, the way his body and soul consumed hers. Left panting and without an ounce of resistance, the only thing she could do was surrender to him completely and try to match his ardor with the strength of her own.

It would be impossible to forget him again, and she hoped she would never have to try.

THEY ARRIVED AT the Team bonfire on the beach when the sky had turned deep navy blue and the stars were out. Jameson Daniels, one of Damon's brothers who used to be a fairly famous country star in Nashville, brought out his guitar, and his seven-year-old daughter, Charlotte, brought out hers, which was the size of a ukulele. The two of them sang for the group. Charlotte had a very strong and sweet voice.

After a handful of ballads, Charlotte was pulled away by some of the other SEAL children, so Jameson played a few songs he'd been working on.

"He's really good. I think I remember him," Martel said.

"You've met him before."

"Yes, but I mean, before—well, years ago. Something familiar about him."

Damon stared into her eyes with no expression.

"What?" she asked him.

"So maybe you were one of his groupies. He said he had a girl in every city. I'll bet you were Santa Rosa."

"I don't think so. Not sure we were big enough for the likes of him. You remember what it was like. Everyone was more into classic VWs and fast sports cars. Pickup trucks weren't considered cool. I don't ever remember listening to country growing up. You were into classic rock."

"Got that from my folks."

She watched Daniels tip his hat and quietly put away his guitar. His wife, Lizzy, now extremely big with another girl, they'd been told, gave him a big hug and kiss. Martel was touched nearly to the point of tears, watching their family unit. It was her vow that this time, the second time around, she would have what they had.

Damon introduced her again to several others on the team. She was disappointed Christy Lansdowne wasn't there. Kyle was trying to babysit his three and zoomed past them several times, frantically running back and forth in search of one or another of them.

Martel easily made the connection she'd hoped she would. This was now going to be her life. These were going to be the people she would depend on, learn about, and support.

She had expected to turn in early, but they took a moonlit stroll down the beach and then made love in the dunes.

"I hoped you wouldn't be disappointed I didn't buy you anything, Martel. I just wanted to be with you."

"It was the perfect Valentine's Day—one I'll remember forever. If this little trip was any longer, you probably wouldn't be able to get me to leave."

"And that," he said as he kissed her, "was exactly what I was going for."

On the way back to his rental, he added, "Make sure you tell Ainsley that I love her, okay? We created a little miracle, you and I."

"And we're just getting started," Martel whispered back. "I'll make sure she knows she's loved. That's the whole purpose of the meeting. We gave her the best start we could have. But I want her to know we did it out of love."

CHAPTER 5

IT WAS HARDER than Damon had thought saying good-bye the next day. Martel's plane ride was going to be a quick hour-long hop from San Diego to San Jose, where she would pick up a car and get checked into her hotel. And then she'd have that meeting with their daughter.

"You know I don't really want to go alone, Damon," Martel whispered as they drove to the airport.

"I do. But we're playing by the rules. Playing nice and careful. I get it. There's more to it than what either of us wants. We have her family to consider. I hope she lets me come next time."

"Same here. Maybe we rushed this too much. Seems like I'm making sausage here. Squeezing in a trip to see you, quick trip to see her, and then, wham, back at school with all the other stuff going on there. I should have taken a week off."

"But you got the invite, and they were specific on the date. So we had to do it this way. Besides, you won't be with your classroom next year, so you've got a lot of things to finish up. And you're planning a wedding. Just face it, sweetheart, you're going to be overmaxed for a few months. We'll relax on the honeymoon. I have one deployment coming up and maybe another one. These days, anything could happen. I could be back in Africa or South America next time. Who knows?"

"True. I just don't like to do anything this important so rushed," she gently suggested.

He felt her misgivings. He knew it was taxing her, having so many details hanging out in the breeze. She'd want to nail down every one.

"You could have just eliminated the trip to see me. But I'm glad you didn't." He watched her blush and shy smile, something he'd always love.

"I *had* to do that." And then, "But you're right, Damon. I've just got to embrace the rush. Keep my head on straight."

Damon knew she was nervous but would never admit it. That probably weighed on her as well. Ever the over-achiever, Martel had lists for everything and loved checking things off. She used big sticky notes on her wall for making project lists, like she was running a whole SEAL Team. It was kind of amusing to watch. But that's what made her such a good teacher, he noted.

As they pulled into the short-term parking area, he stopped the car and turned to her. People passed the car, traveling back and forth, bearing luggage and armfuls of carryon bags while the two of them sat in silence. "Martel, you're going to do just fine. Don't worry about anything. No way to know how it's going to turn out, so just be okay with however it does. Don't beat yourself up if it goes—differently."

He didn't want to put a negative connotation on it but needed to bring it up.

"But call me, okay? I don't want you stewing about something."

She gave him a timid smile. "Thanks. I do like planning everything out, don't I?"

He rolled his eyes and fanned his face with his fingers. "You think? Just know you can't control everything. On the teams, we plan for anything and everything and still it never goes the way we intend it. Never. There's nothing you can do but just enjoy meeting her and doing what you came to do: telling her that she is loved. *By both of us.* Hopefully making it so we can see her again, maybe together. That's all you can do."

"You're right. And we have a lot to be grateful for. The Newbergs have been wonderful. I want them to know that, too. It's such a gift they're even allowing me to see her."

"You did that. You chose nice people, Martel. Give yourself credit. Now they're treating you with the same respect you gave them."

"I want to do it right."

"You'll do it your way, Martel. I have no doubt it will be right. Come on, let's get you on the plane."

He wheeled her bag to the ticket counter, stood with her while she got her boarding pass, and checked her bag. Just outside the TSA checkpoint, they sat for a glass of wine and a beer, holding hands. He watched as several young men, looking like new Navy recruits, passed by wearing backpacks, acting like he did when he first reported to base after the training in Great Lakes. They behaved like kids on a football team. Excited, hiding their fears, trying to be a good friend to the guy on their right or left who was going through all the same jumble of emotions. Everyone wanted to be one of the ones who made it, not to have to report home and say they DORed—dropped on request. And yet, the odds were stacked against them. Always.

It would always be the same, class after class. Wave after wave of strong young men pushing their limits.

He knew what he was going to do later on this afternoon after her plane took off.

"I'll take pictures for you," she mumbled, ringing the top of her wine glass with her finger.

"Did you bring pictures of us?"

"I did. Got a nice one of us at Sunset Beach with the salmon-colored sky in the background, too." She smiled, removing her finger from the glass and folding her hands in her lap. "I brought pictures of my mom and dad, the house I grew up in. My dog. A picture of you from the yearbook I loved, the one in your basketball uniform. I'm standing next to you."

"I remember that picture. We'd just won the championship."

"You were the star. Always have been." Her eyes were warm and filled with tears.

He took her hand in both of his. "Hey, what's making you sad?"

"I'm worried about her questions."

"Well, just be honest with her. That's what we agreed, right?"

"What if I don't have an answer for a question she asks? You know, what if she asks me one of those tough ones?"

He put his arm around her shoulders and pulled her close. "They're all going to be tough questions. If they weren't, she wouldn't want to know anything about you. About us. And you'll have to make that okay, if that happens, Martel. Be prepared that she won't be that interested or scared to ask you anything. She's only twelve. Shoot, I was afraid of my own shadow at twelve."

Martel lay her head against him and thought about that for a bit. Then she slowly wound out of his arms and stood up, putting her computer bag strap over her shoulder. "I think it's time."

The long hug and even longer kiss didn't calm her nerves. He felt her heart beating like it was going to run down the hallway and out into oncoming traffic. Her hands were shaking and a little cold. Her smile was chaste and not full. He loved her so much and more every day. What could he do to help her?

Only one thing he could do.

"Martel, I just want to say how damn lucky I am that you came back into my life after those years when I was such an idiot. Just remember, you bring love to everything you do, honey. You make the world a better place just because you're in it. Go bring her some of that sunshine. She'll love meeting you. I hope she understands how lucky she is to have a person like you. Not everyone gets to have someone who loves them like you do. You can tell her from me, she and I, we are the lucky ones."

Her eyes were weeping, but she smiled through her tears.

"Thank you, Damon. It's all happening now. This is the big stuff, isn't it? I've thought about this day ever since her birth. I love you so much—" She grabbed him one last time then turn and walked into the TSA line without looking back.

He stood there, watching until she made her way to the rampway leading to the gates. At last, she turned and waved with a brave smile, holding her ticket over her head.

As she disappeared into the crowd, he felt like a piece of him had been torn out of his chest.

Damon drove to the Hotel Del Coronado and parked in an unmetered spot. He walked through the lush grounds, winding through an open-air restaurant and two-story bar area overlooking the ocean. He walked in front of it until he got onto the beach and then headed south.

When he was going through BUD/S, they had done their rubber boat exercises there on the beach, carrying them over their heads in crews of eight or ten or twelve. Sometimes the short ones, sometimes the tall ones, sometimes the mixed-up ones which were hardest on the tall guys like Damon.

He still had a patch at the back of his head where he could swear the hair had been rubbed off and would never really regrow. But maybe it was his imagination.

He remembered some of the faces of the guys who lay beside him, shivering in the cold early morning surf, the wet-n-sandys. It reminded him of the times when he'd look up at the stars and the moon and feel that cold pang of ocean creeping up onto his almost warmed but very wet uniform, boots and all, making him an icebox again, until the water would recede and his body's heater began to work overtime again to warm the water close to his skin. Then the surf claimed him again.

Over and over, it went. He never thought about how it stunk to be doing this. He just did it. In making it not significant, he could endure a lot more. It was always harder whenever he worried about surviving a phase.

He remembered how green his feet had been when he finally got to take his boots off after six days without showering, warmth, or sleep.

He remembered the line of blue, green, and red helmets, each with a name hand-painted by the recruit. These were the DOR guys, a reminder that some had chosen to go home or had decided the process wasn't worth the pain they were suffering. Sometimes, the guys just discovered their level of want or how far they had to test themselves. Some of these fellows he didn't know very well. Others, he did. Some were roommates or swim buddies. Then, one day, they were just gone. Nobody lingered around. They were either in or out. Some were made to chase the bell on the back of the pickup truck barreling down the beach, the instructors in their warm jackets yelling catcalls at them to ring the bell. He never got to the point where he'd suffer that humiliation.

Except it wasn't. To even try out for the teams was being a hero. So many hurdles had to be overcome just to get the chance. Part of it was luck, but most of it was not quitting. He wasn't very good at much, but he was good at not quitting, and so he became a recruit and eventually wore the Trident proudly.

He could still hear the shouts the instructors barked, the answering, shivering, miserable hoarse call-backs, and the grunts when someone fell or threw up or fell out of a boat and had to be hauled inside. He'd been on the last boat crew, relegated to an extra thirty-minute swim in the dirty inlet. Sometimes, he'd made the fastest boat crew. He'd been on the crew with foreign trainees who didn't try half as hard as the rest of them had to. He'd had to pick up some of the slack for some who were lazy, sick, or disheartened. It wasn't being soft. It was about being a team.

There was no other training in life like this training. And it didn't even begin to train him how to be a good person, husband, or father. While he was out there doing all that, he had been oblivious to what Martel was going through. Their baby was growing, and she was preparing to place her up for adoption. Martel was handling all the burdens, alone, no team to back her up. Just her mother, the nurses at the home she stayed at, and the grit that was Martel.

Because she wasn't a quitter either. And, like she said, she thought about meeting Ainsley every day since she gave birth to her. This was the day she'd finally do it. Cross that thing off her list. Stare into the eyes and face of the little girl she carried, they made together, the little girl who deserved to know she came from them, even though they were not her parents. Someone else stepped up to the plate and got to claim that one.

He and Martel just hadn't quit on her.

They didn't quit on the love that they'd once had and now had again. Even with the burden of the mistakes. It wasn't always going to be easy. They would never be perfect. But he knew, he was certain, they would never quit.

No matter what.

CHAPTER 6

THE TREE-LINED STREETS of old Palo Alto reminded Martel of the McDonald neighborhood in Santa Rosa where she'd lived during part of her childhood. Although the houses were much larger here on the peninsula, especially recently with the McMansions mushrooming from small bungalows in the trendy neighborhoods, the feel was the same. With the wider streets and old oaks, lush formal gardens lovingly tended, it was perhaps California's answer to Savannah, on a much smaller scale.

She'd ridden her bicycle to her music lessons and dance classes and been on teen boards at the Santa Rosa Youth Center, where the real action was. The dance parties and plays were her favorite, since she didn't do much with sports.

Later on, as her interest in boys developed, she watched basketball and football, even some soccer. The teen dances had become a problem with a downtown that was in search of itself and city leaders who didn't have the will to imprint a clear vision for the youth. She wondered if Palo Alto suffered the same fate.

The Newbergs lived in a brown shingled, mock Tudor style home on a quiet cul-de-sac street. At the end of the street, a quaint park/sitting area had been created, dotted with more than a dozen multicolored birdhouses mounted on poles. It appeared to be a neighborhood project, and the place was literally covered in little birds, mostly finches, landing and taking off, scaring off other birds and showing off their plumery. People had fashioned houses out of old boots, buckets and paint cans, galvanized watering cans, and old telephone boxes. One was even made out of a small pink Barbie house with glittering ribbons hanging down, blowing in the gentle late afternoon breeze.

She parked in a cut-out area of the lawn and walked toward the Newberg's simple but neatly manicured home. She heard a dog bark nearby when she rang the doorbell.

Ainsley answered the door, looking even more like Damon, her father, than the picture the Newbergs had given her a month ago. She was very tall for her age, her eyes a bright ocean blue, with a cute, upturned nose and a saddle of light brown freckles pouring all over her rosy cheeks. Her spun-gold blonde hair was tied in braids but mussed. Dressed in a basketball uniform, Martel guessed she'd either just come from practice or had been practicing in the front yard. She hadn't missed the basketball hoop attached to the double-car garage door frame.

She'd grown up fast, Martel guessed, because she wasn't entirely confident in her size, nearly Martel's height. Her feet were enormous. She sported athletic shoes with multicolored laces. Drawings of daisies and hearts adorned the sides in bright permanent markers.

"I don't wear them for games. For practice," she said, responding to the fact that Martel had been apparently gawking at them. Her voice was slightly raspy and uneven.

"Ainsley, they're beautiful. I was just admiring the patterns. You like to draw, I take it?"

"Not really," the teen shrugged. "I just didn't want them to look like basketball shoes."

A perfect explanation.

Not sure whether or not she should shake her hand, Martel

introduced herself. "I'm so happy you agreed to meet with me."

Ainsley shrugged again. "Sure. Why not? You gotta right."

And there it was, that little prick of a pin that burst her warm, friendly bubble. The air seeped out of the thought she could control this little drama play between them. It was Ainsley's show, and Martel was just here for the ride she'd allow her to take. Come what may. Damon had warned her about that.

Mark and Lori Newberg were standing behind Ainsley and invited her inside.

"Oh, sorry. Duh!" Ainsley said, standing aside to make room for her entry, making a face at her father, who mimicked her right back. Lori smiled and kept her eyes on Martel.

"Thank you, Lori and Mark. I really appreciate you setting this up."

"Of course," Lori said, with respect.

Martel felt a bond and trust between the two of them immediately. It didn't ease her nerves, however.

"Come on, Beans, let's get this group some refreshments," Mark said to Ainsley. "You want wine, beer, water, or soda?" He pointed in Martel's direction.

"I'll just have water."

"Fart or no-fart," asked Ainsley, her hands on her hips, one knee bent. She more resembled a young colt than a girl.

"I'm sorry?" Martel was confused.

"She means gas or no gas. Her spin on the little choice there," added Mark.

Martel laughed. "I see. Quite unusual. I can see she's her own person."

While everyone stared at Ainsley, the girl pulled her shirt from her chest, examined herself, and said, "Nope. No one else in there. I'm the only person in this body—today, anyway."

"I'll take the farted water, please, then." Martel answered.

"Make that two, Mark," yelled Lori.

"Coming right up!"

Lori motioned to a loveseat across from a leather-covered reading chair and matching leather couch at forty-five-degree angles. Martel sat in the loveseat and waited. Lori chose the large reading chair, crossed her legs, and leaned over her thigh.

"You can see we have our hands full. Ainsley is the center of our attention, the life of this family. It's never a dull moment." She tried to look overworked, but Martel knew otherwise.

"She's very bright. Quite a character."

"She and Mark play a lot of basketball together. He played in college some and helps out with the team. When she wanted to take ballet, he learned ballet himself so he could practice with her, help her with her lifts and stretches. That didn't last long, and I'm glad too. The sight of my husband in tights—well, he has skinny legs."

They both laughed.

"Sounds like they have a perfect relationship, Lori. I'm so pleased to see how happy she is."

"We're very proud of her. It's almost like she was meant for us. Having her in our lives is so perfect. I've thought about it many times, how similar she and Mark are in so many ways. People assume she's biological, not that it matters."

There was a little lump in Martel's throat forming. That pain in her gut that Damon had missed out on something wonderful. She drew in the thought she came up with many times like this when she was filled with regret: She'd done the right thing, and she hadn't been in any position to raise her daughter. These people were. And that was as it should be.

She inhaled and asked a question she'd always wanted to know. "What did she say when you told her about us?"

Just then, Ainsley and Mark returned to the room with coast-ers and tall glasses of mineral water, garnished with lime. Ainsley and Mark shared a flavored mineral water, still in the can. They sat side-by-side on the couch. Both crossed their legs in the same direction, same leg.

"You guys gossiping about me?" Ainsley asked.

"You tell them, sweetheart. She asked me what you said when we told you about the adoption."

"Oh, that." She scrunched up her lips, angled her head, and did a slow neck roll to the left. "The first thing I thought of was that Mom and Dad kidnapped me and that they told me so I could keep their secret in case the police came."

Martel nearly spit out her water. "You're kidding!"

"I thought someone would be very pissed, so I asked them about it. And they told me it was agreed to. I didn't understand it, but I didn't ask again, just in case they were lying to me."

Mark objected, pretending to be offended. "Hey, you really thought we were liars? Seriously, Ainsley?" The skin on his forehead lined as his eyebrows rose.

"I didn't understand how it worked. I didn't—" She stopped herself, creeping on territory that was becoming dangerous, but Martel caught the subtle flavor of her thoughts.

"Because you couldn't understand why anyone would want to give up their own child?" Martel finished for her.

No one spoke or moved.

Martel continued. "You know, Ainsley, I think about that every day. And meeting you here today is my reward. I think I did the right thing, don't you? Your life wouldn't be anything like this. You have the perfect parents, and I can see, they have the perfect daughter."

"Mom says you didn't even tell him. Why did you do that, Martel?"

The use of her name instantly turned something on inside her.

Her eyes watered, but she worked to keep them in check without spilling over. Her stomach began to flip-flop. Her parched mouth needed another drink, so she gulped down half the glass.

"Ainsley, I think it would be more appropriate to call her Miss Long. Although, you'll soon be Mrs. Hamlin, right?"

"Yes, in June." She looked at her daughter. "You can call me Martel, whatever you like to call me. I'm not offended by any of it."

The tiny white lie was eating a small hole in her gut, but she could handle it. Lori's tense expression softened. Mark's gaze was deflected, not engaging at all.

"Well, as long as I don't have to call you mom. She's my mom. He's my dad. That won't change, so I'll have to think about it. But you are a teacher, and your kids call you Miss Long, right?"

"To my face, yes. Some call me other names, I'm sure."

Ainsley grinned, showing off one tooth that had turned to the side and would require braces, and soon. Just like Martel had to do as a child.

"Your biological father is Damon Hamlin. I have a picture of the two of us here. Taken in Florida, where we met again and where we are going to get married." She handed the girl the photograph of the two of them at sunset.

Ainsley studied Damon's face. She turned to Mark. "He sorta looks like a blonder version of you, Dad. Should I be expecting another secret here?"

Mark took the photograph, his mouth showing the faint remnants of a curious smile. "I don't see it." Then he turned his head and looked at it from another angle. "Maybe, yeah, maybe a little bit."

He handed the photograph back to Martel.

"It's yours, if you want it, Ainsley. You don't have to accept it, but I planned on giving you a few pictures of our families, if you were curious."

She wrinkled her nose. "No thanks. No offense, but it's kind of creepy looking at people I'm related to and yet don't know. But I'll keep this one." She placed it on the coffee table in front of her, staring down at it.

"Completely understandable," Martel said as she put the other photographs back in her computer case and zipped it up. "My mother is passed, but my dad is still alive. We don't see each other much."

She was instantly annoyed at her comment, as if babbling along would take the gunpowder out of the room. This was starting to be hard. Ainsley's question still stuck in her heart like a fishhook. It was festering.

Ainsley reached for Mark's wrist to check the time. Lori gave her a scowl. Martel was disappointed their meeting might be cut short or Ainsley had lost interest, so she began words she'd rehearsed many times.

"Ainsley, I wanted to just tell you a couple of things, and then I guess you have to be off someplace else. I don't want to keep you or interfere with your life in any way."

"It's okay. We're good. I was just checking. Practice isn't for another hour."

"Okay, great." Martel placed her palms together, bringing her twin third fingers up to her lips and then began again. "When I found out I was pregnant, Damon had already gone off to the Navy, to his training to become a SEAL. You know what a SEAL is?"

"The bad-ass dudes with all the tats."

"Ainsley! That's not very nice!" Lori shouted, her back stiffening.

"Well, I see them on T.V. The movies always show them with full sleeves, muscles." She picked up their picture. "He's got some."

"They are elite military warriors, Ainsley," Mark inserted. "Very, very dangerous work, and only a few can qualify to be on these teams. They've done some incredible things, and we owe them a lot."

"I know that. I wasn't saying—"

"Don't forget to show your respect," Lori whispered.

"So why didn't this war hero come here and face me, huh?" Ainsley's eyes suddenly got angry and red.

"Well, I made the agreement with your parents. We decided I'd meet you first, and then we'd go from there. I—"

Ainsley was direct, interrupting. "So why didn't you ask to bring him? And where was he all these years?"

It was a question Martel hadn't been prepared for.

"I was young. My intention was never to interfere with your parents, Ainsley."

"But now that he knows, where is he?"

"Because I didn't give him a chance to. He's only learned about you since Christmas. I never told him."

"Why? Don't you think he would want to know?" she asked. Again, her eyes looked like they were about to burst. "You wouldn't like it if it was done to you, right?"

"No. You're right. I tried to find him, but I honestly didn't try very hard. My mind was made up. I was going to give you up for adoption. The most difficult decision I've ever made in my life, but it was the right one, Ainsley. He was off on his deployments and trainings, and when he didn't come look for me, well, I figured he'd moved on. I didn't want to interfere in his life either. But we met again at a wedding, and when we got close again, I told him."

"So was he pissed at you?"

"Ainsley watch your language, please," said Lori Newberg.

"No, the truth is, he was ashamed. He feels he abandoned us

both. It's been a difficult thing for him to bear, and I know he still struggles with it." Martel felt her voice quiver and her upper body shake. "I'll be the first to admit, we both know we made some mistakes. Lots of mistakes. But you were not one of them, sweetheart."

That seemed to leave Ainsley without a retort. Satisfied perhaps she'd lowered the pressure a bit, Martel gathered her thoughts carefully. "He asked me to tell you that he loves you, we both love you, and that he agrees I did the right thing by giving you to a loving family who could do all the things we couldn't do, so you could have a life you wouldn't have had with us. He wanted me to tell you we did it because we love you."

Ainsley sat back into the couch, crossing her arms over her chest. Her chin was low, edges of her mouth pointed down, and a worry line appeared at the bridge of her nose. She bit her lip in reflex and then said, "So, what do we do now?" She fussed with her clothes and averted her gaze. "Am I supposed to accept that I have four parents now instead of two?" Before Lori could run over to her, she continued, "What if that's not what *I* want?"

Lori was at her side, hugging her, holding her head against her chest. "Ainsley, sweetheart, I know it's confusing, but no, nothing's changed. Nobody is going to make you do anything. All of our lives stay the same. We'll always be your parents; we love you, and we're raising you. That's not going to change. I'm sorry. Maybe this wasn't a good idea—Mark?"

"It's up to you, kid. You don't ever have to see her again if you don't want to. That's the deal we made with her. You agreed on that basis. I believe her at her word. If that's what you want, that's exactly what you'll get. Miss Long is fine with that. The only one who has any decision to make is you, Ainsley. It's all up to you, and always has been."

"Well, I was curious," she began tentatively, "What kind of a person could have the heart to give their child away. I've thought about you a lot too, Miss Long. Except I didn't look at you in a good way at all. I thought you were some kind of monster. I still don't understand how you could do that. You're nicer than I imagined, but I don't want you to hurt my parents. I don't think I want to do anything to cause that to happen."

Martel was stunned with the truth, the anger in her young soul. It wasn't what she expected, but Damon had warned her. She was about to gather her things and suggest they terminate the meeting when Ainsley added, "I don't think I could ever be friends because I don't trust you." She reached across the table, picked up the picture of the two of them, and handed it back to Martel. "I don't want this. Maybe I will later, but not now."

Ainsley got up and ran upstairs. Martel heard a door slam shut.

And then familiar cold silence surrounded her, her broken heart in freefall.

CHAPTER 7

DAMON GRABBED A burger at the Scupper and joined several others from Team 3. They were inside the back room at the rear of the restaurant, where all the trophy pictures and flags were pinned, sort of the unofficial SEALs of Coronado clubhouse. Several of their members in past classes had spray-painted frog and tadpole pictures on the wall, along with some of the class logos, even class tee shirts were mounted and framed, as well as pictures of various campaigns in countries all over the world. Nothing was labeled or would mean anything to anyone else except those who knew these men by their faces.

He decided to slather his insides with the greasy but delicious fries and the double buffalo burger with extra cheese, along with a long neck, because he wasn't in Martel's company. She'd be horrified at his menu choice.

There was the usual smack talk, teasing someone who got engaged, someone who had a birthday, or someone who got their wife knocked up. It was low-level talk, mindless, irreverent, and didn't mean the disrespect it might sound to the untrained ear. They used it as a platform for basic communication when they really had nothing important to say. It was just touching and feels on the verbal side.

Several high school hotties swung back around after having

spotted them through the open doorway. Probably on a dare, these *too-young* ladies entered their den. One of them asked for their autograph. This kind of fraternization was discouraged, for obvious reasons, so one of the SEALs signed a small notebook as SEAL Team 3 and his name, which wasn't legible. In this way, the girls would leave quickly, without lingering any longer than necessary. It was handled in a way that wasn't rude but curtailed the meeting efficiently so that the appearance of something else was lessened.

But it was a problem. They were always a target. And to those who couldn't help themselves being in the limelight, couldn't help making names for themselves either by writing a tell-all book or going on a bunch of interviews, which also was discouraged, these encounters were mistakes. They were supposed to do the impossible—be invisible. But everyone had an opinion and a story about SEALs, so everyone clamored for their attention.

If he wanted to, Damon could go around posing or boasting about things he never did.

That disgusted him.

So it was back to the low-level smack talk.

"I understand Libby and the cheerleaders made you some Save The Date cards. How come you're not passing them around, you dork?" one of the newbies asked Damon.

"As a matter of fact,"—he pulled out one card and handed it to Cooper—"none of you assholes are invited."

That bought him some scorn. Coop examined the card, winked, and put it in his pocket. "We'll try," he mouthed across the table. "So Martel's back in Florida?" he then asked.

"Not sure, actually." Damon checked his phone. "I should hear any minute how the meeting went. You know, the meeting?"

Cooper nodded and sipped his ice water. He'd eaten all his lettuce and tomato and half his garden burger, served dry as toast, but none of the bread. He had a few sweet potato fries—toasted, not deep fried—left on his plate, and Damon grabbed one. It tasted like cardboard.

"Even when Libby's not around, you still eat like this?" he said to the team's lead medic.

"Hey, I'm the reason the family eats this way. It starts with me. Libby would have one of your buffalo burgers if it were left up to her, smeared an inch thick with mayonnaise." He tossed a fry in his mouth and wiggled his eyebrows. "But I got her trained." His eyes sparkled.

The rest of the younger SEALs, most of them single, added some very disrespectful comments to that. It had been a challenge all during dinner to see who could pose the best one-liner.

Fredo was sitting next to Coop. "No lie, Damon, Coop here knows about this shit. You want to have children? You start eating tofu and drinking gallons of water. I'm living proof of that."

Damon had heard the story of how Fredo had been despondent to learn he was sterile, and he had hidden it from his wife. Cooper had put him on a health regimen, and all of a sudden, Mia got pregnant with twins. It seemed to have reversed his sterility problem. The two SEALs were best friends but a very mismatched pair.

He didn't say it, but Damon knew he didn't have a sterility problem. Coop sent him a wink of understanding.

All of a sudden, all their phones vibrated or pinged, which meant something was up, and it was an emergency. Damon checked the message.

> *Emergency deployment in one hour. Team 3 building. Urgent DTI looking for volunteers. Please respond and then present if available.*

Damon pushed the confirmation letter "C" and saw Coop had

done the same. It was never optional for the medic or for Fredo, but some from their team might be with family for the Valentine holiday, and it sounded like they wanted a small group.

"Adios, Amigos," Coop said, standing, pulling up his khakis. "Duty calls."

Fredo, Damon, and several others stood as well and left the others to finish their beers.

"Hey, Coop, I got my girl coming in tomorrow from Connecticut," said one of the tadpoles. "Tell Kyle, okay?"

"Not a problem, but that's your story to tell. You go be with your girl. You need a full rotation to go on these, because they're not training missions, froglet," Coop said, patting the young SEAL's shoulder.

As they exited the Scupper and headed for their vehicles, Damon asked the two of them, "So it's Mexico, is it?"

"I'm guessing. Kelly Fielding and Ridgeway left yesterday. I'm thinking they got into some trouble. But it's just a guess," Coop whispered. "You didn't hear it from me."

"Got it. And holy shit. See you in a few," signed off Damon as he ran for Monica, his bright blue Hummer.

By the time he hit the Team 3 building with all his gear, he felt like he'd been running for the last hour straight. He'd already sweat through his fatigues. He liked to travel in those because they were indestructible, and sometimes they rode in transports that were drafty with uncomfortable seating arrangements. It was sometimes good to have an extra layer covering his lower limbs, and if he messed them up, they were easy to replace.

But he still hadn't heard from Martel. He decided he'd better give her a call.

Her voice was shaky when she answered.

"Hey there, so you're still standing. How was it?" He pushed his more optimistic side out first so his annoyance with her lack of contact didn't seep through. This was something he'd had to learn the hard way.

"It didn't go very well. I was trying to sort my thoughts before I called you. I've been crying for the past two hours."

Oh shit. Just what we need right now.

"Look, Martel, I'm really sorry to break this to you, but I'm off on an emergency run, so I'll be sort of MIA on you. Anything you need?"

"How long?"

"I have no idea. Hopefully not long. This isn't our regular workup. Something special."

She caught the implication. "I'm sorry I didn't—"

"Look, I got no time for this, honey. Sorry, but have to go. Just give me a brief rundown if you can. I've only got a minute or so before they call the meeting."

This was the bad thing about their quick deployments. They never came at opportune times, and they hadn't had much time to prepare, except they were training all the time between deployments.

"She got angry at me, Damon. She refused all the pictures. I guess I didn't handle it very well."

"Was there an argument?"

"No. She just had an attitude."

"Well, of course she would. Wouldn't you?"

"I was expecting—" Martel broke off in a sigh then a sniffle.

"Fantasyland. I told you about that. Hurts, doesn't it?"

"Yes, you did. I still walked right into it."

"She's got a right to feel how she feels. She'll either get over it or not. But you did what you wanted to do, right?"

"I guess."

"Come on, Martel, you didn't expect her to say, *'Oh, mama! So happy to see you at last!'* Right? I mean, come on. Give her some slack. But don't lie to yourself and don't lie to me, Martel. You did what you wanted. We don't have any right to anything else. You know that."

There was silence on the other end. This sucked all to hell and back a dozen times.

"Say something, please." He knew she'd beat herself up if she didn't and he got injured. Now her mood was infecting him, dammit.

"I don't like accepting that, but you are right. And I got to tell her we both loved her. She got to hear that. Maybe she didn't want to. Maybe that's what triggered it. Finally meeting me and hearing that we gave her up out of love. But I didn't lose it until I got back into my car and got down the end of the block so the Newbergs didn't see me. They apologized for her, but I told them I understood."

"I think you did perfect, sweetheart." He meant it. Martel was the bravest woman he'd met. "Just don't go telling yourself fairy tales, unless it's about my performance in bed, okay?"

Martel chuckled at that. "Right. I can do that all day and night long."

"You better. I'm sure going to be doing that."

"So I'm at the airport, heading back to Florida this afternoon. I changed my plans. I wanted to get out of here, so I'll be home late tonight Florida time, but way earlier than the red eye. I have some messages from my administrator I'm afraid to listen to, but I'll do it on the plane. Just wanted you to know."

"Awesome. I like you being back in Florida. Take a nice long walk on the beach for me. Go have banana pancakes and a good strong cappuccino. I'll call you when I can. We'll be in a different time zone but not sure which one. Love you, sweetheart."

"Love you back. Thanks for calling me. I needed to hear your voice. I didn't want to bring you down."

"No, that's what I'm here for. I'll tell you if it's a problem, trust me. You gotta lean on your team. That's the way we do it. No feeling lonely by yourself. You're part of the team, my team now, and we do this together. That's how it works. That's how we get through all this."

"I know. God, I miss you."

"Well, you could have stayed for Crissakes!"

"I know."

"You did your job. That part to be continued. Something tells me she'll reach out, if they let her. But it's out of our hands right now. You do see that, don't you?"

"I do."

The meeting was beginning.

"Have to go. Love you."

He was forced to hang up before he heard her response. He turned off one switch and turned on another. His attention was laser-focused on the mission in front of them and what part he would be playing.

Coop had been right. Kelly Fielding and Special Agent Ridgeway were missing, feared captured by the cartel they'd been sent to negotiate safe passage with so they could lead a team to apprehend a rival cartel leader later. She'd probably gone down there with tons of cash from Uncle Sam.

Damon guessed it wasn't enough. The cartels, all of them, were getting very rich already from Uncle Sam, the Mexican government, and the poor people being delivered inside the United States in the hundreds.

Things had changed, and the stakes had just gotten higher.

He settled down on the transport plane headed to Baja, adjusted his headset so he could listen to Margaritaville music, used his duty bag as a pillow, and tried to sleep.

They numbered ten, and a lot was expected of them. He'd been told it was probably one of the most dangerous missions he'd ever be on, a fact he neglected to tell Martel.

CHAPTER 8

AT THE AIRPORT, Martel listened to the first of three messages from her school administrator, Carlton Greene.

'Martel, we have a situation here, and I know you are in California for the Valentine's weekend, but I need you to call me back when you get a chance. I'm getting some pushback from a local attorney, and I need your input, if you don't mind.'

The second message was a bit stronger and came in about two hours later, which was late last night, very late for him in Florida.

'Martel, this is Administrator Greene again. I'd like to schedule a time before you return so I can speak to you. I have some questions, and as I said before, I know you are busy, but I'm running into something and need your urgent help. Please give me a call at your earliest convenience.'

And in the third one, which came in early this morning, Greene sounded near desperate. *'I'm going to simply insist I get a call back, Martel. We may be facing a full-scale lawsuit against the school, and you may also be, personally. So that things don't spin out of control, I have to have your cooperation or other steps will be taken.'*

That sounded like a threat.

She kicked herself for not checking her phone before the flight to San Jose today, but she'd been preoccupied, after all.

“Carlton Greene,” he said when she dialed his number, picking up before the second ring.

“I’m sorry I wasn’t able to return your call, Mr. Greene. I boarded a plane this morning, and then was in a meeting. How—”

He interrupted her. “The Gibbs family have retained a lawyer, and he’s making all sorts of threats against me, against the school, and against you. I want to avoid the publicity, but he’s demanding I set a meeting up with the both of us tomorrow first thing. I suspect he needs to serve papers, too, but he doesn’t need us to do that. He’s a bigshot, personal injury attorney from Tampa. I don’t like his tone nor his tactics. He *came over to my house last night!*”

“Oh, gee. I’m so sorry.”

“I told him you were out of town this weekend, but he insisted on coming over, even interrupting a nice Valentine’s dinner with my wife. The guy is a real jerk, a grandstander. Don’t quote me, but I want to get my ducks in a row before we make too many waves and before I have to call the District counsel’s office.”

“I don’t understand. What’s the complaint?”

“He claims their daughter has been bullied, harassed. It’s a sexual harassment issue now. That as a school district, and you in particular, didn’t protect their Cora, and so she’d been sexually assaulted on campus. I guess you got pretty graphic with them.”

“Well, I did tell them what I saw and why I was calling for the conference. As far as specifics, I don’t have any specifics except what I could see from a distance.”

“He wants assault charges brought against the boys. He wants names. Claims we’re trying to cover up the abuse by blaming the parents. He says that now they feel like victims too.”

“But that’s absurd.”

“You did call the sheriff’s office, right?”

“I did. I spoke to a young lady—I have the name back in my office. They were going to go out and interview the parents and the girl. Do you know, did that happen?" Martel asked.

"Apparently they refused to let the interview take place. They called their lawyer instead. Said you admitted she was assaulted on campus. I guess you did say that."

"Well, they challenged me in my opinion that she'd been exhibiting certain behaviors—"

"Yeah, I know. I know exactly what they're going to go after. Well, can you make a nine o'clock meeting if I can get our counsel there?"

"Sure. You'll have to call a sub for my class. I don't have the list here."

"That's no problem. We're already covering that. But you'll have to contact your union rep."

"My *union* rep? What for?"

"You're gonna need to get representation. Separate from the school district, your own attorney to represent you. Your union does that or will make recommendations."

"Nobody is going to be open today. It's Sunday. I think maybe you should hold the meeting after school. That would give us time to get our ducks in a row."

"Well, there's an issue with that. The other side probably doesn't want us prepared. But they're saying they don't want you teaching Cora's class tomorrow, endangering other students. I think he's going to be going after you personally, Martel."

She was going to be sick. Nothing like this had ever happened to her, nor to anyone she knew. "Endangering other students? Really? I was trying to let them know about that incident, not hiding it. I wanted them to seek counseling for her and gave them the courtesy of a heads-up before the sheriff or Child Protective Services showed up at their front door."

"I know. We discussed all this before you had your meeting. I didn't see this possibility. Wish I had."

That brought up another question. "So will I be placed on administrative leave then?"

"Possibly. I have to wait and see what counsel says."

Her spotless reputation was already trashed in her own mind. The upset over her meeting with Ainsley this morning was a distant second to this one. For the first time, she began to question whether or not she'd have a job after today. It might even become something of a criminal nature, although she doubted it.

"I'll be boarding in about an hour. I get in at ten, and by the time I get home, it will be close to midnight. You just call me with the where and when of the meeting, and I'll spend my minutes here right now and see if I can get in touch with the union. And, Mr. Greene, I'm so sorry for all this. I still think we made the right call. This wasn't the reaction I was anticipating when I spoke to them on Friday. When they left, they were totally focused on their daughter, or so it appeared. I was proud of how they were handling it as a couple. I even—"

Martel stopped mid-sentence.

"What?"

"I gave them my cell phone number and asked them to call anytime over the weekend if something came up. They planned on keeping Cora home on Monday. I wonder if the visit from the sheriff's department went badly."

"That's a question for counsel, if they can get that." Greene sighed. There was an extra weight to his concern. "If they go after you, they'll dig into everything. Everyone has something in their closet. Whatever it is, if this goes into a full trial situation, everything about your past will be on public view."

He was sounding like a man who had a past, Martel thought.

In any case, she certainly had one. And that would definitely alter the odds of any chance she'd have a relationship with Ainsley or her adoptive parents going forward, and even that was a stretch.

Her move to San Diego might be seen as her running away from some painful chapter for her in Florida, a gross mischaracterization.

But it could happen.

The timing was so wrong. Damon was gone. What a thing to drag him through when he returned. How would she be able to explain it to him?

She needed someone in her corner who could defang the aggressive Tampa attorney.

Her call to her union representative went to voice mail, of course. She tried to call Kaitlyn but didn't get an answer. She and her new husband, Greg, had gone to Disney World, and she wasn't going to be back in class until Wednesday.

So she called Aimee Carr, the wife of Andy, who had served with Damon on SEAL Team 3 and now lived in Sunset Beach.

Grateful she didn't ask too many questions, Aimee suggested she might have someone who could assist her in getting someone good. But she'd need until tomorrow.

There was no one else to call. With Damon and Kaitlyn gone, her mother passed, and her father more or less MIA, Martel was all alone.

Then she thought about Gran Karmody, the attorney who helped her set up the meeting with Ainsley. He was a grandfatherly type of old cuss and perhaps not as sleazy as it sounded like the Gibbs' attorney was, but he could be just the right kind of sly.

There was so much riding on this, she hesitated to call him, but did leave a message, finally. "I'm flying home tomorrow from my meeting with my daughter. She's beautiful, Mr. Karmody. But now it seems I have another unrelated problem. I need you to help me find someone who can represent me. Call me and we can talk."

That was all she could do, she thought as she boarded the plane for Tampa. She settled in her seat, looking out at the blue sky of San Jose, so close to where she'd been raised. Was she leaving California or going home? No answer came to mind as the plane took off, soaring into the air above San Francisco Bay, before taking a sharp turn inland, crossing over green valleys, orchards in the distance, the San Joaquin valley breadbasket, and beyond.

What if all the mistakes of her past became public gossip? She'd agreed to own up to all this, to move forward, learn from these mistakes, and create a compelling future with Damon.

But she never anticipated this. This had the potential to follow her all the way across country, affect her ability to work in California, do anything anywhere. It was like having to wear a scarlet letter. She'd be gobbled up in the social media explosion that was surely coming. She could even see the headline in the Tampa Bay Times,

Local Pinellas County teacher accused of abuse.

She was about to find out how strong she was and who her real friends and allies were.

CHAPTER 9

WHEN THE TRANSPORT landed at the former military base in Baja, it was still dark outside. These big behemoths were so loud that any planning or discussions were futile. The group who went consisted of Kyle, their LPO, Coop, Tucker, Trace, Jason, Fredo, Armando, Danny, T.J., and him. Jameson Daniels elected not to go because his wife was due to deliver any day. It was a good mix, with communications specialists, snipers, explosive experts, a drone specialist, two native Spanish speakers, and most of their most senior members.

They were transported to an abandoned housing project along the Sea of Cortez, a half hour bumpy ride from Cabo San Lucas, just outside of LaPaz. The project was part of a new resort that had bankrupted before the rest of the infrastructure and town itself were created. Grand vistas of the ocean and Mexican lands beyond were plentiful in the long view, but many of the thoroughfares that were to be four-laned expressways were reduced to two lanes and often only one. Night travel was extremely hazardous, and the vans carrying the team snaked around potholes and piles of abandoned construction equipment and materials at a very slow pace.

But what was problematic for their arrival was also a barrier for many of the locals, and it isolated the team from the curious.

While they were led to believe the road between the project and Cabo San Lucas, as well as Todos Santos, were not bad, many of them were dirt.

The completed building was three stories with a great hall/dining room on the main floor. The new condos, beautifully floored in glistening white marble, were above the ground floor. Between the ten of them, they were allowed use of the entire second and third floors, nearly fifteen suites.

Since the ownership of the land reverted back to the governor of the state of Baja California Sur, posing as potential buyers gave them a wide berth with little interference. Local staff were "borrowed" from the governor's resort on the mainland, oddly enough, so the prospective purchasers could have "the full ownership experience." If it was suspected these men were Navy SEALs, no one indicated such.

They traveled on their own with no escort, merely three rotating drivers who were undercover regular Navy Spanish speakers, running errands and transporting them by van. Their "fishing equipment" was stowed in surplus Coast Guard duty boxes from the seventies, long used by commercial fishermen in the San Diego area. They were a perfect disguise for some of their explosives and fire power, and the drivers, being military themselves, knew how to handle them.

A banker's box of real estate contracts and pro forma reports were provided, even including parcel maps and descriptions of the project itself. But most of the paperwork they brought were props to justify their cover, intended to calm the wagging tongues of the cook and maintenance staff. Kyle indicated they suspected a few of them would be plants, people who would report directly to the governor.

They were instructed to bunk in pairs. One large suite was designated as the equipment room. The lock on the door was quickly switched out to a keyless entry utilizing a combination code that noted date and time of access. Everyone's entrance and exit recorded with a camera Fredo installed inside the unit and one placed in the hallway outside the door.

He'd brought several other keyless pads and promised to get them working later that morning sometime.

There was only time for a quick team meeting over a buffet of fresh fruits, cold fish, lukewarm rice and beans and corn tortillas—a breakfast none of them had on a regular basis. One thing sorely missed was beer, so that was at the top of the sticky note hung in the kitchen. Cans of juice and bottled waters filled the one of the kitchen refrigerators.

When the prep staff left, Kyle spread out some maps and surveillance posters taken the day before when the mission had been approved.

"Carter Ridgeway and Kelly Fielding are being held at the Quantos Villa Ascension, home of the C.A.Sur or, as the DEA guys call them, California Surf Club, a relatively new cartel to form here in Baja. It's a large complex, heavily gated and armed twenty-four seven, with about five acres of lush landscaping and pools and cottages tucked away here and there. From the air, it masquerades as a tropical Mexican paradise with villas for wealthy tourists. Indeed, at one time, it was one of the most exclusive resorts on the west coast of Mexico. It's location to the mainland, as well as close proximity to the open sea of the Pacific Ocean, make it ideal for smuggling people and contraband in and out. They have a fleet of very fast pleasure boats. Some of them can outrun our Coasties."

The team studied the aerial photographs taken by drone.

"We spotted Kelly sitting outside a bungalow smoking a cigarette only once. Unbeknownst to their captors, both Kelly and Carter have embedded microchips which they can turn off and on with the touch of a finger to signal something. We get a weak signal from Ridgeway but clear on the other side of the complex, which makes sense. He may be being held in a metal shipping container, which could interfere with the transmission. We don't know if he's being tortured, but we do know they've both spotted groups of mostly male runners held in a secured lockdown location. They managed to get that information out before their capture."

"How do you know they're runners? You mean people being assisted to cross the border?" asked Jason.

"There are all kinds of human trafficking. Some pay a fee to be taken across the border, but others gain their freedom by carrying narcotics in their body cavities, their families back home being watched and held hostage until the mission is accomplished. Many of these will then release into the interior of the U.S. or come back down to help pay for another family member's passage, when they do it all over again, this time with their little sister or their mother or grandmother.

"They're like slaves, and the cartels pick them up in remote locations and drop them off similarly. Pickups are timed. If someone doesn't make their rendezvous, they're done. There's a high turnover, and nearly twenty percent of these don't survive the trip."

"So all this stems from this location?" asked Danny.

"This is one of hundreds all over Mexico. They own ranches and houses in California, Texas, Montana, and even Idaho where the drugs are stored and then distributed all over the U.S. There's so much demand that turf wars in the states are not heard of much. Turf wars in Mexico, now that's another thing."

"This location is where they pick up the drugs for land-based entries then. Is that right?" asked Damon.

"Yes. There are other warehouses near the marinas. It's such a lucrative venture that they can pose as wealthy Mexican and European tourists or landowners because they *are* wealthy landowners. They make billions. We have jokers coming all the way over here from the Middle East, direct from the poppy plantations and Kush regions to participate. It's a criminal conspiracy, partnership, and organization stronger than most governments. This cartel is only one of dozens. And Uncle Sam works with some of them. In fact, we've worked with this one before when they've helped us with some terrorist watch group individuals that slipped through our borders. They aren't exactly friendly with these groups, so they gladly take our money and help us catch them. Until yesterday. Yesterday, they moved from being an ally, admittedly a dangerous and not totally trustworthy ally, to being an enemy. Kelly and Carter walked right into it."

"What's the plan, Kyle?" asked Cooper. "How are you going to get around these armed guards?"

"That's a pretty big area for only ten of us," added T.J.

"We start a fire. Gentlemen, we're going to blow up one of their buildings, and it's going to be so big we're going to need a huge water tanker truck, rescue vehicles, and a boatload of crew to put it out." Kyle grinned.

"Do you happen to have one of those tankers?" asked Damon.

"We sure do. It's stored in that incomplete fire station right over there." Kyle pointed to the distinctive red brick building with large rollup bay doors. "And we think, given a large-enough emergency, they might run over here and commandeer this unit. Maybe ask for some manpower."

Damon was confused.

"I think we'll let them do it. And if not, well, we'll drive it over to them and offer our services."

They were released at dawn to get a couple of hours of sleep before they would go on their first rounds of exploratory. This would also give Kyle time to update his intel by calling the commander back in Coronado, just in case something had changed. Coop approached Kyle, with Damon right behind him, asking a question.

"You got tools here somewhere? I'm thinking I should maybe make sure that thing works out there or we'll be caught with our pants down around our ankles and no bride in sight."

"Whoa. That's an image I won't get out of my head anytime soon. But I get your point. Excellent idea. You feel like tickling her insides a bit?"

"Just wanna be sure. Depends on how long she's been standing. We're close to the ocean, salt water, you get the drill."

"Say no more. God, I'm glad I brought you!" Kyle shook his hand and sent him on his way.

Before Kyle could get distracted elsewhere, Damon asked him a burning question.

"You didn't say anything about our cells. Are we allowed?" he asked.

"You bet. This time, the gear isn't that sophisticated for that kind of stuff. Unless you have 'Badass Navy SEAL' all over your FB page or phone description, and you better not because that'll get you tossed, you're good."

"Thanks, Kyle." Damon headed for the stairs. "Oh, and Martel said she missed seeing Christy at the bonfire. She liked it."

"Oh, yeah? She fitting in already?"

"I think so, sir. But you know women. I mean, how do you ever know for sure?"

"Indeed, I do, Damon. Strangest, most beautiful creatures on this planet. Make you work so hard, hurt so hard, and want so hard. You're kicking and screaming and loving every minute of it. Guys who don't get that don't get loved."

No truer words were ever spoken. "Spoken by one who I'm

sure is."

"Thanks, Damon. Now you go get some rest, and we'll talk later. I understand she went to visit your little girl. I'd like to hear about it sometime. And tell the guys about the phones, 'cause I forgot to."

"Yessir." Damon was surprised Kyle knew about Martel's trip to Palo Alto but figured nothing much passed between the four amigos, as they were called: Kyle, Coop, Fredo, and Armando. All four pillars of the same fortress they called their platoon at SEAL Team 3.

Upstairs, he informed the other rooms about the cell phone use and entered his own. Jason had requested they room together since they were both about the same time on the teams, and they also had some adventures in Florida.

The suite was huge, each equipped with a king-sized bed. Jason sat with his cell phone in his lap.

"Pretty cool, isn't it?" the heavily inked Pacific Islander said, gesturing at the suite. "Heard you were talking about phones. Figured I'd get the scoop first before I go opening up a can of worms."

"Have at it. I'm going to."

He entered his room and partially closed the bedroom door, leaving a good foot-wide opening, then dialed Martel. He'd been concerned ever since her disturbing phone call. He willed himself to calm down as he waited for the rings.

But it went straight to voicemail.

"Hey, Babe. We're here, all safe and sound. I'm going to hit the sack for a couple of winks, and then we'll be on our way, exploring this *project*," he said with emphasis. "Nice weather so far. Not sure how available I'll be today, but keep trying and be sure to reach out to Christy or someone if you need help. I'm serious about that. Don't do stuff alone. You're pretty strong, but there comes a time when it all starts feeling like too much, and you just gotta step away and get some help."

Then he thought about something else. "You might give Lizzie Daniels a call, so you can let us know how if the baby's coming. Jameson stayed behind. I think you knew he'd do that."

He wrinkled his brow and finished up. "Love you, and wish you were here. The water is blue, and I've got this killer view and room. Jason is a poor substitute for the love of my life. Take care, be good, get some help if you're overwhelmed, and don't ever forget that I love you. More every day. You did good this morning, Martel. Everything will be okay. You'll see. Bye."

He hoped she'd find some comfort in his words, but he was always nervous about leaving long voicemails. It increased the chances that he would say something that would be taken the wrong way.

Kyle was right. Women were so complicated but incredible creatures. He wanted to feel that love from her forever.

CHAPTER 10

MARTEL PULLED UP to her rental and grabbed her suitcase. She noted people were putting their cans out for the early morning pickup, so she left her suitcase by her front door and struggled with the two plastic bins. One of them had a broken wheel, and it just wouldn't budge. She nearly toppled it.

"Hey, hey, let me get this, miss."

He was an older guy, maybe ten years older than her, with salt and pepper beard and hair, extremely handsome.

"Thank you," she said as he pulled the cans out of her grip. She waited for him to place them at the street.

"You just getting back?" he asked, noting her suitcase.

"Yes, a little Valentine's Day trip."

He nodded his head, hand over his mouth. "I'm your new neighbor, Carl Frame. I just bought the duplex next door. Going to be working on it."

She shook his hand. "I'm Martel," and left it at that. Placing her hand on the pull up grip, she thanked him again. "It's been a long day, so I'm going to crash."

He waved at her and began to walk away. "I'll take a rain-check."

It was an odd comment. She didn't owe him anything. But when she turned, he'd already gone.

She double checked all the doors and windows then checked her phone and saw she'd missed a call from Damon. She started listening to it when her phone rang.

"Hey there, little lady. Howz it going these days?" Martel was so happy to hear the lawyer's familiar southern accent, relieved he cared enough to call her at night.

"Mr. Karmody, thank you so much for calling. I didn't expect you until tomorrow."

"Well, I can't resist a pretty woman. You sounded a little stressed. Glad it wasn't too late. I considered that."

"No. This is better, much better."

"Normally, I like to have you come into my office, and we can have a proper chat, but I imagine you have school tomorrow, so try to be brief and how can I help you?"

"I'm not sure if you can. I mean, I don't know if you do that kind of law."

"What kind of law?"

"I might be sued for sexual abuse or just abuse or failure to watch out for one of my students."

"Holy cow. You don't mess around with little things, do you? How could something like that happen?"

"Well, I noticed something on campus a few days ago, and I wanted to report it to the sheriff. I'm *required* to report it, I should say. One of my students, a girl, was doing pre-sexual things, allowing things to be done to her."

"Missy, there's no such thing as pre-sexual in the eyes of the law. It's either sexual or not sexual. If it's even a little bit sexual, it's sexual. Get my drift?"

"I do, sir."

"And she was doing something with another girl or a boy?"

"Two boys."

"And what were they doing?"

"She was consensually, or it appeared to be consensual anyway, letting them touch her in her underwear, her panties."

"I see. And was there any penetration?"

"Oh god, I have no idea. I was clear across the yard. I don't think it could be. I don't think the boys knew what they were doing, but it looked like Cora—she's my student—did. And before I reported it to the authorities, and after checking with my administrator, I asked for a parent conference and met with them both on Friday after school."

"Okay. And what was the result?"

"Well, at first the mother had a complete defensive attitude. I told them that, to me, she exhibited adult behavior, and that, based on my training as a teacher and counselor, was a learned behavior, probably taught to her by an older person, man or woman. They didn't like hearing that or hearing what she was allowing the boys to do. I didn't get any indication it was against her will, but I just wanted someone to look into it, and I wanted them not to be blindsided by the sheriff coming to their front door."

"Okay. And this is normally the way it's handled?"

"We don't have a way it's handled. I relied on my administrator. He didn't ask to be part of the conversation. I told him what I thought was the right thing to do, and he agreed, so I set up the appointment."

"Well, now it's two against one as far as what you said and what they said or did. So now they're coming after you? Just why is that?"

"They've hired an attorney in Tampa and are treating it like she was raped on campus and neither me nor the school did anything to stop it and, in fact, encouraged it by not stopping it. I can see why they think that, but that wasn't the purpose of the meeting."

"Well, your administrator didn't do you any favors, but did the sheriff go to the house?"

"No one would let them in. And they're blaming me for that, too, like I damaged their reputation because the car came to the house, making all their neighbors think something wrong had happened."

"Fact of the matter is, something wrong probably did happen to her, from the sounds of it. But it's odd that they reacted that way. Who did they hire?"

"I'm sorry. I don't have all the information. My administrator said it was some personal injury attorney with a billboard on the freeway. He called me when I was up visiting with Damon and Ainsley, my daughter. Today, I got to meet her for the first time, Mr. Karmody."

"Oh, that's wonderful. How did that go? I'll bet she's so smart."

Martel hesitated, suddenly overcome with tears. With her lower lip quivering, she tried to get out, "Oh, not so well. She got angry with me. I jumped right from that into finding out about this attorney who's coming after me, so it's not been one of my better days."

She sniffled and found tissues to blow her nose.

"You poor dear. Are you still in California?"

"No, I'm back at my house. Just got in. Damon's on a deployment, an emergency."

"So you have that, too."

"I feel like a deer in the headlights. They don't want me in class. The attorney is demanding a morning meeting—"

"Wait a minute. Who doesn't want you in class?"

"The attorney said I shouldn't be around children because I don't do a good job of protecting them. My administrator agreed and has already gotten me a sub. I'm to meet with this attorney, and I don't know what to do."

"Your admin isn't doing you any favors. He's giving off the aura of guilt, like a no-confidence vote. Do you get along well with him?"

"Yes, we're fine. But he let something slip when he was talking to me, and I picked up on a weird vibe. He commented about them digging up dirt from our past and that social media could get heated and cruel. I just got the impression he had an issue he was wanting to hide. Not about Cora or anything at the school but from his past, perhaps a long time ago. Again, this is just a hunch."

"Kind of makes sense. Now, if you were to guess, who would you say has taught Cora these things? Do you think it's the father? They're usually the suspects. Is this his natural child?"

"I don't know, honestly, but I think she is. They look alike. He just doesn't seem like someone who would do that. But how would I know? They had a minor argument about her family. He was sort of pointing the finger at them, for some reason. The mother told him not to harm them, and I thought that was odd. The mom is kind of a mess, but the father seems hard working, a little depressed, but otherwise okay. She's on a downward spiral."

"If anyone asks you about her, keep your mouth shut, please."

"Sure. No problem. You mean I shouldn't have—"

"No, only thing you did wrong was not have your admin with you during the conference. But if he didn't insert himself or volunteer it, that can't be blamed on you. You were the one who called him first, I take it?"

"Yes. I told him, and then we agreed I'd talk to the parents and inform them. Together."

"You and the admin together?"

"No, I would talk to the parents together, not one at a time."

"Gotcha." He sighed and then posed another question. "Why are you worried about your past? You have nothing to hide."

"My daughter. Giving up my daughter for adoption. That wouldn't look very good if it came out in a lawsuit, would it?"

"There's no reason it would. Besides, the adoption was handled in Oregon. I don't think they'd know where to look. You haven't told anyone, have you?"

Martel's spirits collapsed again. It was getting so difficult to talk. "Only several of the wives on SEAL Team 3, my friend here who's also married to a SEAL. But not anyone else."

"These fellas are based in San Diego?"

"Yes."

"How big is SEAL Team 3?"

"Oh, I don't know the exact number, but I think about two hundred. Their platoon is much smaller, thirty-five or so. Maybe fifty. I don't know."

"I want you to stop talking about it, Martel. Especially with that administrator. I don't like what I'm hearing about him. Is it a him or her?"

"Him. He's very nice. I've never had any problems with him. Always very supportive of the teachers. I've done a good job of keeping that one to myself."

"Except for fifty or so men on SEAL Team 3 and their wives, maybe their children if they were listening. You see where I'm going?"

"Yes," she croaked, barely able to get it out. "I'm such an idiot."

"No, you're not an idiot, but there are a lot of things that could get sticky if not handled properly. We have to control the narrative. Usually, guilty people try to do that, like on TV. In your case, your past isn't indicative of who you are today. You didn't do anything wrong. You admittedly made a mistake, and I'll wager you've paid a high price for that."

"I have." She was tired, wanted to take a hot shower and just peel herself into bed. "Mr. Karmody, I'm exhausted. So, before I literally fall asleep on the phone, does this sound like something you'd be able to help me with? Or can you give me the name of someone else who could?"

"I think so. Your union should help, but you don't want them using their attorneys, even though they'll try to convince you of it. We can all work together. But I'm thinking about a lady I know who just salivates to go against attorneys like this gentleman you described, the ones who make a huge case out of a misunderstanding and cost everyone enormous sums of money, all for greed. But she's about as sharp as they come."

"So you'll call her then, or do I have to do it tomorrow?"

"You let me know what time your meeting is and where, and I'll make sure we both show up. If she can't, because I don't know anything about her schedule, I'll come. But I'm pretty sure she'll want to be there."

"You don't know how relieved that makes me feel."

"Well, we've got some homework to do. We need to find out who is doing the abuse, the source of it. If that comes out, I have a feeling this little ball of yarn will untangle itself."

"Wouldn't that be nice? Oh, thank you!"

"You go take your shower and turn in. I'll talk to you in the morning. Don't forget to let me know when the meeting is first thing."

"I promise. Thanks so much. I know this probably isn't something you do every day, but I just appreciate having someone on my side I can trust."

"Of course. And I don't take on any clients I don't believe in, either. If I'm not convinced they are innocent, I don't get involved. This shouldn't be happening to you. I want to help you fix it."

"How much will this cost?"

"If we have to hire a private detective, it could be sizeable.

We'll cross that bridge when we come to it. The bottom line is you're innocent, and we just have to do what we can to prove it."

After the call, she hesitated to listen to Damon's message but decided she needed that little bit of extra support. She took her shower, sat down on the couch overlooking the silver moonlight-created crystals of the calm bay this evening, and pressed play.

'Love you, and wish you were here. The water is blue, and I've got this killer view and room. Jason is a poor substitute for the love of my life. Take care, be good, get some help if you're overwhelmed, and don't ever forget that I love you. More every day. You did good this morning, Martel. Everything will be okay. You'll see. Bye.'

CHAPTER 11

THE TEAM WAS dropped off in two locations just outside Cabo San Lucas and were to rendezvous back in two hours. The location of the villa could be seen from downtown, nestled into foothills overlooking the lower part of the peninsula and Sea of Cortez. With specialized scopes, anyone up on the hillside would be able to see the faces of people below, so their vantage point to spot for operations against them was excellent.

But Coop had brought his drones, including one for use at night that could detect heat signatures. It wasn't as sophisticated as the ones the Feds were using, but they were smaller and could get in and out without detection since they were nearly silent. If they launched one, they were required to report it so there wasn't a mid-air accident, which had happened when there were too many operators with too many toys.

Damon was in Coop's group while the other four men went with Kyle into town from the other side.

"You make it look like you're just flying a little toy," Damon said as he watched the drone take off.

"Yeah, I don't think they use them much down here. That probably won't last, though. With the money they're making, they'll eventually set up a death drone system to keep out airspace intruders. But you never know. Sometimes, these guys fool you."

"That's the truth," agreed Damon.

"So you're gonna program it to just do circle reconnaissance?" asked Fredo.

"Yup."

Fredo explained earlier that they'd take the drone up to high altitude and then send it over the site before lowering it for a closer look. That way, the villa wouldn't know it was coming.

"I'll send the recording to the Feds so they can help with the analysis," said Coop.

"So when's the barbeque?" asked Jason.

Damon, Coop and Fredo chuckled.

"We'll see what she brings home. If it was me, I'd want it tonight. But we gotta know where we're going first."

"I don't like the idea of Kelly and Ridgeway being up there longer either," said Damon.

Fredo asked Coop another question. "Did Kyle say there had been any random demands for either of them?"

"Not sure. I haven't heard."

Coop's little plane had completely disappeared into the clouds overhead, but he still had a bird's eye view on his monitor. He scanned the horizon in front and then casually took a peek behind him.

"Jason and Damon, you guys act interested in rocks or something. Go look at that stone wall. Touch the soil. Let me know if anyone is watching me and this bird," asked Coop.

Both of them fanned out, scraping and tapping the ground like they were combing for shells at the beach. Damon did find several .38 casings and a red shotgun shell. They were about ten minutes outside of the beginnings of the outskirts of Cabo. "Probably a great place to do some target practice," he said.

"Kinda dumb, though. The whole place would hear it," said Fredo.

"Got anybody interested?" Coop asked over his shoulder. He tapped on his monitor a couple of times and shook his head.

"Not a soul," responded Jason.

"Nobody close by anyway," added Damon.

Coop tapped on the monitor again and then swore. Damon and Jason came running back to his side to ask what was wrong.

"So we're gonna act real disappointed here, because we just lost our little plane, okay?"

"Did you?" asked Jason.

"What does that look like?" Coop showed him the view of the complex, looking like a bunch of orange Monopoly houses clustered together with a large pool in the rear surrounded by a freeform lawn, smaller sand traps, and tiny lakes.

Damon knew Fredo relished a good acting job. He kicked the dirt and swore as well, placing his hands on his hips and shaking his head from side to side. "Son of a bitch, the guys have their own private golf course. That just sucks, man."

Damon couldn't think of anything so he just put his hand to his mouth, while Jason continued to search the horizon.

"You got it on autopilot then?" Damon asked.

"Yup. She'll do a cute little thirty-minute cycle. Then when she's done, she'll beep me, and I'll get her back up into the clouds and bring her back from the direction of town. Unless they've got something special, no one will ever know they've been mapped."

Fredo barked his command. "Everyone spread out and pretend we're looking for parts, okay? Like we think it exploded or something. Pieces. We're looking for pieces."

So while everyone searched, picking up interesting rocks and shell casings, the little bird was busily making them a map of the entire site. Damon was first to find a dead animal: a snake, and the head had been shot off. Coop had switched off the screen but was careful not to cut the power. He tucked the console in the back of his khakis and went on the search with the other three.

Damon heard the high-pitched beeping alarm of the monitor, which was Coop's cue to turn it back on, tap it again, even hold it up to his ear like he was listening for signs of life, then abruptly turn facing town, and shield his eyes as the drone made a perfect landing in front of him but coming from the opposite direction than the villa they were monitoring.

He unclipped the wing element, folded it in half on tiny hinges, and stored it, the body and other peripheral items in his backpack. Before zipping the bag up, Damon noticed he'd hit an arrow button on his monitor, the faint acknowledgement of something accepted, and then slid the monitor into a padded sleeve.

The four of them walked toward town. It was hard to tell where the road was at first, but slowly a worn section of red clay dirt appeared, along with a small curb. The newly formed road T-boned into a busier roadway that wove back and forth but generally headed toward town.

On the way, Fredo stuck his thumb out along the two-lane freeway, and a pickup truck bursting at the seams with family members in the four-door cab stopped and allowed them to ride in back with a goat that was tied to a hook mounted to the bed of the truck. It headed toward the Marina.

The ride was less than five minutes, but they exchanged waves and wished the family well. The men traveled the rest of the way on foot, toward the smell of sea water and a particular restaurant that specialized in crab tacos and boasted the largest margaritas in town.

It was their designated rendezvous point.

The restaurant didn't have any front doors, just a metal sliding grate that was pulled across the gaping entryway. Wicker tables and brightly colored chairs dotted throughout the inside of the place, closer to the fans and air conditioners. Outside under grass palapas, it was also very pleasant, and they could watch the population driving and walking past.

Kyle's group was slightly late but eventually arrived.

He sat close to Coop. "They're working on the upload you sent them. Said the pictures were excellent."

Coop patted his backpack. "She does real good work."

"Did you learn anything?" Damon asked his LPO.

"We have a minor wrinkle in that General Cortez is in residence at the present time. He didn't see us, but, well, I don't have Kelly yet to work something out with her people. If he cooperates, I think the price will go up from before."

Damon had been told that, on one mission, the general was awarded a bright cherry red Tesla at the border for his troubles in helping them with a mission. But the verbal promise Kyle made to him was also that one of his guys would marry the general's daughter. Luckily none of the bachelors from that trip were with them this time, but Kyle explained that they were to give him a wide berth.

"I'm not sure how he figures in here, but with the level of smuggling rising astronomically, it's no accident he's here, which means his prices are inflated should we need his protection."

"I've never met him," said Damon.

"He's hard to forget, even without his red Tesla," said T.J. "He likes his medals."

Kyle turned toward him. "He's got a house just over the border, and that's where the Tesla is stored. He also happens to have several beautiful daughters, and they would have to be to get any takers. I mean, who wants him for a father-in-law?"

"I feel sorry for the girls. They didn't ask to be born into that family," said Danny.

"You think he might know about Kelly and Ridgeway? Can

that be exploited any way?" asked Tucker.

"That's a good question, and I don't have an answer right now. Problem is, even though you two are native speakers, we don't know who the movers in town are. A lot could have happened since we were here last, so who knows what side Cortez is on." Kyle stood up to slip into the head.

Coop asked Trace and Tucker, "Was he alone or with his men?"

"He was with a handful of non-uniforms. Fairly clean-cut. Could be military or undercover, maybe cops, maybe government types. He's got an angle somewhere," answered Tucker. "He was definitely doing business."

"I think, if we run into him, we say it was intentional, flatter him a bit. Let him know there's something for him in it if he helps get her out alive. Them, I mean," barked Fredo. "You gotta figure people promise things all the time. We've never not paid him."

"Only when none of us came back to marry his daughter," said Armando coolly. He was wearing his shades, even though the palapas threw everything into near darkness. It was sort of his signature, part of his uniform.

Pitchers of beer and margaritas instantly appeared just as Kyle was returning from the rest room.

"Your little bird did good, Coop. The commander is pleased."

A group of very drunk American tourists, mostly college-aged men, passed by, attracting attention. "Dumb farts," he mumbled under his breath.

"Oh, come on, football jock like you—you never came down here for a good time, spring break and everything?" Fredo said.

"What you sayin', Fredo? They're probably not much older than I am. And as for college, well, take a gander. I don't think anyone here except Kyle ever went to college."

Danny Begay raised his hand. "Semester at the J.C. and I even managed to pull off a one-point-oh G.P.A. before I got expelled."

"See?" Damon said, defiantly.

"I got an AA degree in nutrition and weight training," said Tucker.

"Shrek, you're the highest educated one of us all then!" said Kyle, hand-slapping him a five.

"I took a cultural anthropology class at University of Hawaii just so my grandma would stop yelling at me. The teacher was right off a sailboat from Tahiti, and she wanted to surf, so I taught her how—for extra credit," Jason shrugged, pretending to be embarrassed.

"I rest my case, sir," Damon bowed onto the table toward Fredo.

The L.A. native wasn't pleased. His eyes were getting rheumy. Both he and Armando had consumed almost one entire pitcher of margaritas by themselves. Damon could see something was eating away at Fredo, and he thought perhaps he'd scratched something that was still bleeding, an old wound.

He was going to say something back, but Coop kicked him under the table. Then he asked Fredo if he'd been able to pick up any stray conversations, anything of interest. Kyle added his approval.

Fredo pressed his shoulders back, cracking his neck, then leaned forward, balancing his head on the tripod of his clasped hands over his elbows.

"There's a lot of stuff in the air. Lots of tourists, people who are not paying or tipping well, have little money, but sort of flaunt themselves at the local population, you know? They haggle and bargain, not because they need to, but just for the fun of depriving someone of money to feed their families."

Damon wondered if that was the source of the older SEAL's frustrations. He suspected it was more than that.

Armando added, "I've been hearing complaints too. Like people handing servers tips, peanut change, really, and smiling, expecting them to be so grateful. A lot of people here because it's a cheap place to go. There's a lack of respect. I've never seen it that way before."

"Yeah, and they're getting in the way. The locals are trying to make sure the tourists have a good time, and they're worried. We all know where the big money is. I think if the cartels had it their way, they'd send all the tourists away so they wouldn't have to worry about upsetting their uncle to the north," said Fredo. He gave a quick look at Damon but didn't hold eye contact. "Tension. I feel tension, Coop."

"Maybe that's why the massacres and holdups of the vacationers," added Kyle. "Maybe they're trying to discourage or depress tourism a little bit."

"But this is the bread and butter for the unconnected people," began Armando. "It's just that now, it's literally pennies compared to what they can make in the trafficking trade. I think some of them resent it."

"Well, it is their country," added Damon. "I can see how they'd feel disrespected because many tourists don't understand the culture or they have a fictional concept of it. Something they've seen on TV."

"It's more than that, Damon," Fredo said softly. His tone was lightening, indicating to Damon he'd been working on his attitude, keeping some of his emotions in check. "It's really more like they don't feel they need our dollars anymore. Or not these dollars. They're earning hundreds of times more than most the people coming to visit. I don't think they like hiding it."

"That's dangerous," whispered Kyle. "That's being drunk with power."

"Nobody treated them benevolently. Why should they return

the favor?" Armando said behind his shades. The comment made Damon shudder inside.

The balance of power was indeed changing. It was dangerous, unpredictable, and not likely to do anything but get worse over the coming months. Damon could see it wouldn't end well.

"All the more reason to get our people out now, because time is not on our side," he added.

"Most definitely," Fredo said, nodding his head solemnly. "Most definitely."

CHAPTER 12

CARLTON GREEN CALLED Martel before eight o'clock.

"The attorney for the Gibbs, a Mr. Manny Risso, wants a meeting in my office this morning at ten. Can you make it?"

"Sure," she said. There wasn't any choice in the matter. "This is just for the attorneys, right? The Gibbs won't be present?"

"Yes. He's going to be meeting with me afterward. He thought it would be best to informally meet with you before he files anything."

"Who is he considering suing, or do you know?" she asked him, beginning to have her first annoyance of the day. She knew it was going to be tough. Part of her resented it.

"Potentially against you and/or the school district."

Martel read between the lines that Green was jockeying for position to be excluded from the proceedings. Gran Karmody had been right about her administrator. She wanted to ask him why he wasn't named but decided to drop it for now. But she had to tell him about Karmody.

"Mr. Green, I'm going to be bringing in my attorney."

"Uh, well, this is informal, really. Nothing has been filed as of yet. He reassured me he was fact-finding."

"Then I definitely want my attorney there, since he'll be asking me questions, Mr. Green. You know that's the best way to do this.

The union would want it that way too."

"You have an attorney from the union already? That's kinda fast. They usually—"

"No, I haven't heard back from them. This gentleman will represent me and only me. I assume the school district will use their counsel."

"Well, if it comes to that. Don't you think that gives off a whiff of some wrongdoing here?" he asked. "If you just talked to him, maybe nothing further will happen. We certainly don't want to escalate things."

Martel wanted to give him a smart retort but knew it wasn't wise. "I don't think I did anything wrong. I was acting in the child's best interest, which indirectly was for the benefit of the parents as well. But I'll go over all that this morning. Let me get hold of my guy so he can be there on time."

"Suit yourself."

"Can I ask you why you won't be in the meeting?"

"We've managed to talk some, and he said he didn't think it was necessary."

"Okay. That's fine. I have no objection to that." She hesitated to bring up her concern about class this morning, even though she'd already decided to ready herself for it just in case.

"I can still go in. I mean, I'm prepared to teach this morning. I'll just need coverage for the meeting, if you can arrange that. But no need for a sub—"

"Already been arranged, Martel. Mr. Risso thought it would be a good defusing type of action, cooling down everyone's tempers."

So you're still setting me up.

Martel was feeling a little better about leaving in June.

Her next action was to call her attorney, who said he'd be there for sure, but wasn't sure about the woman he was referring to the case. "I want you waiting for me outside the school, so I don't have to hunt down the offices."

"No problem."

"I want you to dress up a bit, a little nicer than you normally go into school."

"Funny, I had thought to do the same."

"Olivia Noriega is a very bright shining star from Sarasota. I met her as a young law student when the class was working on a project pro bono."

"Okay. Has she worked on cases like mine?"

"I believe so."

"What was the project?" she asked.

"It concerned a woman who had been wrongly charged with child abuse and then convicted and had been separated from her family of five children while serving ten years. I helped them draw up and file petitions on the woman's behalf. They were successful because of how doggedly she took on this case. I'm going to see to it that she either gets appointed a judge or runs for public office. She's that good. I talked to her last night after you and I talked, and she's very interested. Now, don't get your hopes up about today, but she'll definitely help out."

"I look forward to meeting her."

"Who did you say the other attorney is?"

"Oh, let me think. Mr. Green told me it was Manny Risso. I don't know anything about him. Of course, I can count on one hand the number of attorneys I actually know."

"Manny Rizzo. That's good. That's really good. I'm sure Olivia will be pleased."

"Is he tough? My administrator says this is to be informal, that he'll have some questions for me, things that might affect whether or not he actually does file a lawsuit."

Gran Karmody laughed into the phone. "Sure. He wants to take the temperature of his case and get a hint of how he should write it up. As far as if he's good, I've never opposed him before, but I understand he can be quite charming. And he has a nice smile, according to that billboard in the Publix parking lot."

"Don't forget the bench."

"Yup, that too."

"So you aren't worried."

"Well, he just tried to pull off something very obvious, and we're going to stop that. He tried to get in there and interview you without representation, and he tried to get your administrator, who is scared to get involved, to grease the skids for him. It's a sleazy maneuver, and he'd never try it if he knew he was up against somebody good, so he's already made his first mistake—he's underestimated you, us, the situation. But don't worry, he'll quickly adjust."

"Okay, then. I'll see you at ten. Do I bring anything?"

"Just dress for success, like it was a big job interview. Look as perfect as you can be, which shouldn't be hard. And don't do a lot of talking. I'm going to step on your foot if you do too much of that. Save it for the judge, if it goes that far."

It was going to be a hot February day, not unusual for Florida, but she changed her mind on what she was going to wear. She took off the slate blue suit she had put on over her white long-sleeved blouse with the self-tie at her neck and put on a light blue seersucker suit over a short-sleeved silk blouse with a smooth neckline. She put on her mother's pearls, twisted her hair up to keep her neck cool, and felt much more comfortable.

Using the restroom before she left, she saw a light pinkish bleed on the toilet tissue and figured her period would be starting soon. She'd been slightly concerned that her period was late but chalked it up to the stress of her California visit. Now she could relax a bit with one less thing to worry about.

It never ceased to amuse her that, while she was readying herself for a big meeting, the rest of the people in the Sunset Beach area were on vacation. It was one of the things she loved about the Florida Gulf Coast, a much-needed reminder, especially this morning, about the fact that the whole rest of the world was operating at a different vibration. The pilgrimage to the white sand and surf had begun and would continue until the bright sunsets. She was going to have to find that same routine back in San Diego, because it was soothing, healing, and it kept her sane.

She saw parents with young children crossing Gulf Boulevard, wearing clothing they wouldn't be caught dead in elsewhere. Men normally dressed in business attire here could wear loud flamingo prints and straw hats, sunglasses, and flip flops, their arms laden with towels and coolers or pulling wagons with big wheels. The golf cart rental business was booming, since it was peak season. In this community, they were an adult form of four and six-seater bumper cars. People decorated them with lights, particularly when celebrating special events like Halloween, weddings, and bachelor parties. And unlike the Miami area, this part of the Florida Gulf Coast was a senior citizen paradise, a mini-Disneyland with endless warm days and shockingly beautiful sunsets.

It felt odd heading off to her school anticipating being served with a lawsuit.

She'd have to remember not to take things too seriously—at least not until she had to.

Gran Karmody was waiting for her in the parking lot, dressed in his signature white linen suit and string tie. Next to him stood a petite Latin woman with jet-black slightly wavy hair she wore back in a clip. She wore a stylish navy-blue suit and light-yellow shirt underneath with pumps that gave her a couple of inches extra height. Next to Mr. Karmody, she almost resembled some of the girls in her class. If Ainsley stood next to her, she'd tower over the woman.

Karmody was a little slow with the introductions, so she extended her hand, cutting him off.

"Olivia Noriega, nice to meet you." Her handshake was firm and all business. Her smile was genuine.

"Martel Long. Thank you for coming on such short notice." She asked, "Anything you need from me? We have about five minutes."

"Gran has filled me in. Only thing I want you to do is not to answer anything unless we say it's okay to do so. But don't make it obvious. Make it natural. And don't be nervous, no matter what you hear, okay?" the attractive attorney said.

"I always say walk in a couple of minutes early and catch him off guard a bit. Attorneys are always late."

"Good idea," said Olivia. "Do you have any questions, Miss Long?"

"Oh, please call me Martel."

"Fine. If you need to talk to us in private, you ask for that. Or ask to use the restroom, and I'll go with you, so don't be concerned if that happens."

"I pee a lot when I get nervous. It will probably happen."

"Perfectly natural," she said and gave Martel a wide, generous smile.

"Show the way, little lady," said Mr. Karmody.

Martel walked ahead of them, passing classrooms in session. She could hear the lessons being taught and the students answering, and she saw hands go up. She felt so much more comfortable in class. That was her environment, not the administrator's office.

They walked into the Attendance Office, and she greeted the school secretary seated behind the long counter. "Good morning, Shirley. We're here to meet in Mr. Green's office."

"Oh yes, dear. They're in there now." She leaned forward. "I think you can go in," she whispered, pushing her purple glasses back into her nose.

Martel turned left, crossing a series of teacher boxes, some worktables for students who had to spend study time in the administrator's office or who waited for parents to pick them up, the school nurse's office, on to the closed door of Mr. Green's office. She knocked.

Green was sweating already, reminding Martel that the office had always had trouble with the air conditioning system. His eyes darted behind her, studying the two attorney she'd brought, and then he focused back on Martel. "Manny's all ready for you." And then to the attorneys, he extended his hand, "I'm Carlton Green, the school administrator. Thanks for coming."

Gran Karmody was the first to speak. "Mr. Green, you have yourself a fine little school here. Nice and clean, I can see why my client loves teaching here."

Martel noted that Mr. Karmody was going to allow the misconception he was just a good old boy, a country lawyer in over his head. Green made a slight grunt, passing right by him and shaking Olivia Noriega's hand.

"Nice to meet you, Mr. Green. I'm Olivia Noriega."

"You're not from around here, are you?" Green asked.

"Not far. My office is in Sarasota."

Manny Risso, recognizable by his pencil-thin moustache from the famous billboard, was not much taller than Ms. Noriega, which surprised Martel. He appeared in the doorway and immediately lit up when he saw her.

"Olivia! Why, it's been too long."

Administrator Green appeared ill at ease and quickly retreated into one of the other little offices while the two attorneys briefly caught up.

"Manny and I were classmates in law school," she said to Martel, following it up with a pert smile.

"Well, this is most excellent. Most excellent. Great to be working with true professionals and old friends. Why that just makes it even better." He turned his back and entered Green's office. Martel and Olivia shared a look between them until Ms. Noriega rolled her eyes.

"After you, ladies," Mr. Karmody said.

Manny Risso sat in Carlton Green's chair, in front of the plaques he'd earned as Teacher of the Year and then Administrator of the Year. Other service club awards and pictures of him with students at science fairs and two Halloween carnivals, as well as a Rowdies game with several of the parents, served as a backdrop.

Except that Manny looked ridiculous sitting there. The chair was too low, and the desk came up mid chest such that he looked like a sixth grader sitting at his dad's desk. He had a yellow notepad already filled with a couple of pages of notes, folded back on itself. He spoke to Martel first.

"I think Carlton explained what we're doing here, Miss Long. This is just an informal meeting to go over some of the allegations—opinions, if you will—so we have a basis and context on which to start."

Before he could utter another word, Olivia inserted herself.

"Start what?"

Risso sat up straight, beginning to realize how undersized he was sitting at the large desk of a very large man. "Well, to check out the facts."

"Why don't you tell Gran and I what the facts are, as you see it, first. And then we'll respond."

"Well, obviously it's early, and we're still gathering the details. I thought Miss Long could fill—"

"We'd like to know what was communicated to you. You've had some discussions with Mr. Green, but you haven't communicated anything to our client. So why don't you fill us in?" she said, smiling.

Risso squirmed under the three sets of eyes on him, and Martel could see he hadn't quite prepared to do most of the talking but now was going to have to.

"Okay, we can start there. But I would like to get Miss Long's side of the story, if you don't mind."

Olivia Noriega re-crossed her legs and leaned forward, tapping a red polished forefinger on the edge of the dark oak desk. "Let me be blunt, if I may, Mr. Risso. We aren't here talking about suing your clients. Our only interest is two-fold. First, we'd like to see the young girl in question…" She turned to Martel.

"Cora Gibbs."

"We'd like to see Cora Gibbs and her home evaluated by the Pinellas County Sheriff. The reason is obvious. If there is some type of abuse going on, whether it's in the classroom or the home or elsewhere, we'd like to see her evaluated by a professional. We'd like the parents on the record in the evaluation. And second, after you give us your take on the whole situation from your client's standpoint, if our client wishes to and we advise it, she'll answer questions." She tapped the desk several more times. "But not until then."

She sat back in her chair, and, as an afterthought, plastered a smile on her face.

Risso's expression reflected the sudden realization he was headed straight toward a powerful locomotive, and he was driving a Volkswagen Beetle.

CHAPTER 13

KYLE HAD COORDINATED with the commander's team that they'd do a visual with their NVRs. They were also to take the other drone with the infrared camera and do a direct upload to Coronado so the Headshed could see in real time what they were up against. It wasn't to be a raid, per se. In fact, they were to get in and out without anyone being detected, unless conditions were stellar and they could remove both the hostages safely at the same time.

He told them State was negotiating with the Mexican government, but it was not being fruitful. Through diplomatic channels, they'd been told that the government officially had no ties to the group that took the two Americans and said they were trying to establish communication. But the days were ticking along. Two days were already too long.

Everyone agreed.

This was all standard, required channels since Ridgeway and Kelly were both federal employees, and Ridgeway's rank was nearly that of an ambassador. Only difference was that he couldn't order in troops or call an air strike independent of the dudes at Coronado.

They were sitting in their huge common area table back at the housing project, just after the domestics and cooks had left for the day. Damon thought the food was delicious, especially the artfully arranged fruit platters they munched on all day and well into the evening.

He was waiting for a chance to call Martel again. His first message went direct to voicemail.

"I don't get it, Kyle. How come there's no random demand, no contact with anyone in Baja," said T.J. "It's not like there will be some prisoner exchange."

"It's because they want something else," a heavily-accented voice boomed from the direction of the front door.

Damon turned around and saw Sven Tolar completely blocking the entrance. A former FSB, Norwegian Special Forces operator, Sven had stayed behind to meet with a small commando team Kelly's father-in-law had been organizing to work like a NGO, providing backup and intelligence for the Navy. He was to accompany Team 3 when they were tasked with a mission, but with Kelly's capture, he dropped everything and came as fast as he could on his own.

He was Kelly's fiancé.

"Was wondering if you'd show up," mumbled Tucker as he came over to give Tolar a brief hug and fist bump.

Tolar dropped his duty bag and joined them at the table, reviewing maps Kyle had spread out. "My theory is that they don't want to negotiate with the Americans. They can make more money negotiating with the other cartel who was here before. They follow a former Marine, Carlos Gutierrez, who comes from a wealthy family in Monterey and hung for a time with Delta Group as a special terrorist group search and destroy unit. Except he turned on Uncle Sam, started lining his pockets with gold and equipment, recruited half his team, and went AWOL."

"He's part of the California Surf Club, then," said Damon.

"That's them. I see you're focused on the villa," he said, pointing to it on the map. "Carlos knows the State Department isn't going to want to negotiate with him, because of the double cross he played on Uncle Sam. I think he's thinking he could get more by negotiations with the old Cortez brothers."

"The general?" said Kyle.

"Cousins. Same family. The general is a minor player, but he does have the ear of the President of Mexico, and he controls a sizeable militia, all state-owned but used to enhance the family's assets."

"And what value are they to Cortez?"

"Why, they save the U.S. Special Agents and curry favor with Washington D.C. That means more—like foreign aid, cooperation in Mexico's economic development plan, etc."

"And forfeit their holdings in Baja," said Trace.

"It's a small price to pay. They will get protection here. The turf war stops, and everyone goes back to their corners."

"It's kinda brilliant, if you think about it," said Kyle. "The Surf Club gets the girls and drugs between Baja and the US without having to watch their backs. They hand the Cortez group something they want, a direct line to elements in our government who might want peace and safety for its citizens on vacation. Not to mention lucrative contracts to partner and build more hotels all over the resort areas, not just Baja."

"Exactly," beamed Sven.

"Have you or anyone had any contact with either of them?" Kyle asked.

"Ridgeways has been disabled or temporarily removed," said Sven. "Not sure what that means."

Damon could see the burden of Kelly's kidnapping weighed heavy on him.

"Tonight, we're going for a look-see. I'm assuming you'll want to come." Kyle's tone was flat, his eyes downcast. There wasn't much anyone could say to make Sven feel better. Damon knew he just wanted to see with his own eyes she was okay.

"You sure we can't pull off an extraction?" Sven pleaded. "These things are fluid. They might make a deal, and then she'd be shipped out. I know the bosses will do everything they can to keep her alive, but the rank and file?" He shook his head. "They can be careless. And some of them don't have much of a moral code, if you know what I mean."

"We'll get her," said T.J., placing a hand on his shoulder. "She's one of us. She's kept a bunch of us alive more than once. Now, your sorry ass, I'm not so sure."

Everyone had a good laugh at that one.

"You go on up and take a shower, Sven. Take the room upstairs on the left, at the end next to mine. Everyone else's paired up, so you'll have the suite closest to the equipment room."

"What did I do? Is it my feet? My snoring?"

"It's your breath, Sven. You fish-eating Norwegians need to brush your teeth more often."

The men started to scatter. Kyle shouted instructions. "Get some rest. We head over there after nightfall, nineteen hundred. On foot."

The collective moan was laced with some heavy descriptions of sexual activity.

Damon approached Kyle. "I'm going to call Martel before it gets too late. She's gonna ask me how much longer we'll be here. I'm gonna tell her a month. Will that work?"

"Sounds about right."

Damon turned to go, but Kyle called out to him.

"Hey, anything going on between you and Fredo?"

"Not that I know of. I thought I was imagining things there for a bit this afternoon. I thought something might be going on at home."

"Okay, well, keep your distance."

"Why, what has he said?"

"I probably shouldn't have mentioned it. He's got a thing for kids. And, well—"

"I wasn't there, sir, because I didn't know about it." Damon had considered this briefly but didn't figure it was germane.

"Just leave him alone and don't engage. He'll toughen up."

"Toughen up? What does *he* have to toughen up about? He's got more kids than—"

"Watch it, Damon. Don't go comparing yourself to others, especially on this team. It's a dangerous occupation. If they feel you, as a newbie, need to be put down, they won't even think twice about it. He's senior around here, trying to make it to twenty like all the rest of the old guys here. You got four years on your first hitch. You're still in diapers, Damon, and don't forget it."

Damon realized he'd just been dressed down. It happened so fast it was over before he knew what was happening. He'd heard the stories about how there were highs and lows of any SEAL team. Some teams never gelled, like Team 4 in Virginia where Andy had gone. They'd lost guys they shouldn't have, including some on training exercises, which was a total waste. But they trained with everything live and real, so it happened.

Team 3 had been spared their share of problems, and that was mainly due to the solid core of the "old guys," as Kyle said it, who held everyone in check and who trained the tadpoles. They didn't have any superstars or whiners. They had lots of specialists in different fields, and there was a clear hierarchy of who was senior and who was learning. Kyle let them do that, as a good LPO should. Some were more heavy-handed, and if they lacked confidence, things could erupt and fracture or that glue would never form.

Damon hoped it was a temporary lull that just happened

sometimes. He'd heard his grandparents talk about being married for sixty years, and even they had good years and bad years, they said. The team was a family, after all. From year to year, not everyone loved everyone the same.

Fuck it.

Now he was starting to question himself. He'd ruled out Fredo's mocking and correction as just that time of the month, but maybe he hadn't been paying attention to things. Now it was going to dog him, too.

It was time to do something else. He ran up the stairs and heard Jason in the shower. He decided to call her first, so he'd have privacy, and then take his shower and hit the bed.

"Damon, oh, I can't believe it. I so needed to hear your voice tonight."

"Everything okay?"

"Well, I don't want to talk about it, actually. You shouldn't have to burden yourself with it. I'm getting some help. I'm not feeling all alone, so no need to worry."

He did hear the wiggle in her voice, that part that came from the back of her throat just before she started to cry.

"Better tell me now, Martel. Otherwise, I'm going to worry about it all night long."

"Don't be silly. It isn't anything I can't handle."

Damon felt the pressure of not having a lot of time to spend on the phone. Calls were supposed to be short. Otherwise, it set up a pattern in the cell towers and created curiosity, if anyone was listening. Long calls were always frowned upon anyway, because there was a lot of friction created between the older guys, who never had cell phones or facetime chats from home, and all the new "spoiled" SEALs who had all this fantastic equipment. They could talk to their naked wives and speak to their kids so that, when they got home, they'd recognize them. It had been that bad.

A lot of marriages were lost due to lack of communication. So it did make some angry, resentful.

"Tell me." He wanted to swear for emphasis.

"I think I told you I was having a parent-teacher conference because of some behavior I'd seen at school. I told you that, right?"

"Yeah, and you told me you weren't supposed to talk to me about it, so I quit asking. And you said it went well."

"It did. Until—"

"Until what?"

"Until they got a lawyer involved. A personal injury lawyer. And they're doing this dance about me not keeping her safe at school. *I'm* the one who demanded the conference. And I'm required to report things that I see, based on my admittedly limited experience, that don't look normal. It's not just what the school wants or I want. It's the law. I could have just let Child Services go over there unannounced or the sheriff, but I sat them down to explain what I'd seen and what was going to happen. I also asked them to take the advice of the professionals and get Cora some counseling, maybe the whole family."

"What did the sheriff say? Or am I not supposed to ask that question?"

"I can't get too much into the details, but this now is going to concern me, us, so I sort of feel obligated to tell you more than I could before."

"Okay. Look, maybe I should call you back tomorrow."

"You can do that."

Martel's voice faded, sounding like one of her students.

"Sweetheart, whatever it is, I can't imagine it can't be worked out. Besides, they love you there. That school is going to bend over backwards to protect you. There's no way they'd allow you to have to do battle with these parents and their asshole attorney all by yourself. Once they see that, they'll back off and go after someone else. An easier target. Someone who has something to hide. A secret past."

He heard silence on the other end of the phone.

CHAPTER 14

IT WAS LATE, but Martel didn't want to sit around the house tonight, especially alone. Her best friend, Kaitlyn, was nearing her seventh month and would be getting a sub for the remainder of the school year very soon. She had forgotten to tell her the reason for Martel's missing office hours and the sub.

But it was nearly nine o'clock, and Kaitlyn had told her that she often went to bed early these days because she was so big. She could call Aimee Carr, but that felt like she was going outside the school chain of command and might be a little sticky.

So it was Kaitlyn she called.

"Hey, kiddo. I was wondering if you'd gotten back. How was it? Did you get to meet her?"

"I did. She's beautiful, Kate. Big blue eyes just like Damon's. Has his build. She looks like a snickerdoodle with all the little brown freckles over the bridge of her nose and upper cheeks."

"Said by a true mother. Even ugly babies have fans."

They both laughed.

"So how was she to talk to?"

"Well, I think it's a lot to take in all at once. She was a little angry. There was some resentment there I didn't expect. Of course, that could be just my lack of experience. There are a couple of guys on Team 3 who were adopted, and Damon has told me some stories, but I think it's different for a girl and a guy. Or maybe I'm just making excuses."

"Sounds perfectly normal to me. I know I would be very sensitive to it. All these grownups making decisions that affected my life. Thank goodness the adoptive parents are nice."

"They're perfect. She's just like her adoptive dad, and most people they don't bother to tell because she looks and acts just like a clone of him. They're very close. So, yes, I made a lot of poor choices in getting pregnant in the first place but placing her with these people was a good choice. One of the best ones I've ever made."

"I'm glad to hear it."

Kaitlyn must have figured she had something on her mind because she let Martel speak next. That was one of the things Martel enjoyed so much about their friendship. They didn't push, pry, or judge.

"I was wondering if I could come over."

"Okay, this sounds serious. Things okay with Damon?"

"Yes," she lied. "He's on deployment right now, and I'm not supposed to say where, but you know what my favorite drink is, so…"

"Indeed. Strawberry margarita. I get it. I thought you said he was going later?"

"This is a temporary duty, an emergency."

"Okay, well, I hope it doesn't interfere with the timing of the wedding."

"It is what it is." Martel wasn't sure it was such a good idea to see her tonight. "You know, on second thought, maybe I should just take a bath, read a book, go to bed, and try to get some sleep. I really didn't sleep much Friday or Saturday nights, nor after I got home last night."

"And maybe that's why you think you need to have a talk. You could be just tired, Martel."

"You're probably right."

"They do know you're leaving at the end of the year."

"Yes. Mr. Green knows. I haven't said much to the other staff or teachers. Why?"

"Well, I wasn't sure. This morning, Green asked me if there had been anything bothering you, like, why did you fly to San Diego for just a couple of days and then fly all the way back. He wondered what the rush was and why you didn't take more time off."

"I don't think he's ever paid attention when I've asked for time off before. But did he ask you anything else or say anything?"

"Well, he said that he didn't think you'd been your easy-going self lately. He wondered if you were having some kind of personal problems."

"Oh dear. What did you say?"

"I knew you'd told him about the wedding, and I figured you'd told him about leaving at the end of the year. But I wasn't sure, so I just said you were anxious to see Damon and go over the wedding plans."

"And you didn't say anything about Ainsley?"

"Oh God, no. I would never do that."

"As far as you know, he doesn't know about her. Are you sure?"

"Oh, I'd remember if I'd told him that. Trust me, I would never talk about that. It's your story, not mine to tell. That would be unforgiveable."

"Okay. Thanks."

"So now you've got my brain going all haywire. How come you wanted to know about what he asked me? Is there some issue about you finishing out the school year?"

"Absolutely not."

"I saw your car today, but you weren't in class or in the office. Where were you?"

Martel had two choices. If she told Kaitlyn about today's meeting, their phone call would take an hour or more. She might as well go over to their house. If she didn't discuss it, she might not have an easy time falling asleep.

It wasn't hard to make her decision.

"I'll tell you what, let's go to dinner tomorrow night. Maybe catch an early one?"

"Greg's in bed, but I'll check with him and let you know tomorrow at class. Or are you going to class?"

"No, they've got a sub for me. I'm helping with some things for the district, a special project. I'll tell you more about it tomorrow. In the meantime, don't mention it to anybody. And please don't mention Ainsley to anybody, particularly anybody at school, okay?"

"You got it."

"Thanks."

"No problem. But, Martel, I'm genuinely worried about you. We've got the spare bedroom here, or you can stay up and watch TV all night. Don't be alone. Promise me you'll not stew about any of this?"

"I promise. I'll be fine. Thanks so much, Kate. I'll talk to you tomorrow."

It was nearly nine-thirty, and she was meeting Mr. Karmody tomorrow morning for breakfast. She threw one of her mother's quilts over her shoulders and, without changing her clothes, slipped off her pumps and walked barefoot out toward the surf. It was a full moon with a smudgy warm cream-colored glow commanding the whole sky. She could imagine it was a piece of vanilla cotton candy with a nightlight in the middle of it.

The water hadn't caught up to the temperatures of the warm

spring air, so it was jarring at first but didn't take long to get used to it. She could barely make out a couple sitting in the sand just far enough from the surf so that they wouldn't get wet. Someone else was walking their dog, which was illegal on this beach, but at this time of night, it wasn't patrolled. At her back, the glowing interiors of the beach houses began to make objects and the waves visible as her eyes adjusted.

She sat in the sand, watching the moon spread its magic over the whole scene.

Leaning forward against her legs, she rested the side of her face on her forearms piled onto her knees and kept that crouching position until she felt the warmth of her body filling up the space inside her quilt bubble. She inhaled the moist cool air and breathed in tandem with the waves.

She hoped she was making the right decision moving back to California. Aimee had convinced Andy to switch to an east coast team, but Martel knew Damon didn't want to do that. He liked Florida, but California was where he felt most comfortable. Andy had grown up on a farm in the central valley and didn't have the same allegiance.

But that wasn't it, she mused. She would be closer to Ainsley. Although at this point in time, she wasn't sure whether she'd be invited back to the Newberg home. Everything was so up in the air. Now her job was perhaps at stake. Certainly, her reputation was. There were so many things coming at her she felt like she was just in a reactive mode all the time. Not a well-planned out execution, like one of her lesson plans. She was the slowest person on the track team, and everyone needed her to hurry up so they wouldn't lose. And she didn't have the speed or the training the others had, so she was desperately trying to catch up.

She missed her mother, who was courage under fire. She'd know what to do and how to handle this overload. Her mother could have run a whole platoon all by herself.

She missed laughing with Phyllis, Kate's mother, who was probably up there dancing in Heaven with the jazz saxophonist—her fantasy love. The lady who told her to go find her daughter, to find that missing piece of her.

While confronting her past, dealing with a challenge in her present, and planning her flawless future, it was the women in her life that she missed. The ladies who bore their disappointments proudly, did the best they could do, and didn't worry about the rest. Martel wished her mother had met Ainsley, but she had a firm hand in Ainsley's life, even though her daughter might never know. It didn't make the gift of her love any less.

"Is this seat taken?" came a familiar male voice next to her. It was Carl Frame, her new neighbor.

"Oh, I was just going to go inside. So, yes, the beach is all yours."

His voice was pleasant. His face was handsome. He smelled good, especially for this hour of the night. Maybe that's what bothered her. He was trying too hard to be someone she really didn't need.

She began to scramble to her feet.

"Wait just a minute. Don't go."

If he came close to touching her, she'd scream. If he actually did touch her, she'd scream louder. "I'm not interested in striking up a conversation, Mr. Frame."

"Call me Carl."

She winced at that, closing one eye. "No, I'm afraid it has to be Mr. Frame. This place is very friendly, but not at nearly ten o'clock at night. It's not appropriate, so I'm leaving."

"You just looked so sad. I spotted you from my living room window, that's all. You looked like you could use some company. I was only trying to help."

"Well, I suppose anyone would look sad at this hour, shivering in the night air on an abandoned beach when they could go inside. But far from being sad, I was thinking. And I can't think when I'm talking, so I'm afraid I must insist that you leave me alone and let me get back to my place."

"Walk you safely there?"

The guy wouldn't quit. That set off the bells and alarms, made the hair at the back of her neck stiffen. The quilt draped around her shoulders would be no defense. She needed a weapon. She inhaled and, as loudly as she could, shouted, "Go away and leave me alone!"

A couple of dogs barked, and two porch lights came on. She was prepared to yell again if she even heard him following her. She ran all the way to her back door, which she'd left open, the last time she would do that, whirled around, and locked it. Then she ran to the front door and locked it as well. She turned off all the lights in the house and peered out her kitchen window to see if he was still out there.

She didn't see anyone on the beach, or her patio. But she did hear a sliding glass door shut and click locked.

She closed every blind and window covering she could find, shut her bedroom door and locked it from within, put the water on in the shower and then undressed, leaving her suit draped over her chair and her underwear where they lay on the bathroom floor. She found a long flannel nightgown that always managed to make her feel cozy, spreading it out on the bed.

The shower was heavenly. Even though she didn't have time to dry her hair, she still washed it and would deal with the tangles and odd cowlicks in the morning with some hairspray. She applied a facial scrub, then rewashed it with her scented gel face wash, used the lavender shower gel to make her skin squeaky clean, and shed all the negativity of the day. She was baptized in the heavenly lathers and scents, washing away all her sins and becoming fresh and new, just like the Easter Sunday when she'd gotten dunked and joined the church. This was the reset to her life she needed right now.

She loved the towel warmers the owner had installed, and tonight, as she wrapped and patted herself, they were nearly orgasmic. It felt good to stretch down and touch her toes, drying her lower legs, her thighs, and finally her upper thighs between her legs.

The towel came back light pink, one small stain that was unmistakable. Her belly didn't feel like it was going to erupt and release the monthly blood and fluid it automatically stored each month.

She checked her underwear on the floor, and it, too, had a thin band of pink, a small discharge of blood. Very watered-down blood. Spotting, really.

Just like she'd had with Ainsley when she first got pregnant.

CHAPTER 15

DAMON WASN'T THE only one who was annoyed at the five-mile run and the foothill hike. He just couldn't see expending that much energy when they could have had the vans drop them off much closer.

The explanation that Kyle didn't want the drivers to know what they were investigating just didn't sound reasonable enough for all the effort it was going to take. He thought, perhaps, they would have been better off conserving their strength. It wasn't that it was a five-mile run. It was a five-mile run near the hottest part of the afternoon, in more than eighty-degree weather. He saw huge clouds billowing up from the other side of the little mountain range to their East and prayed for rain, as a matter of fact.

Each of them brought a backpack, and instead of their regulation black duty bags, they'd been instructed to bring something a non-SEAL would use. Several guys used their daughters', covered with unicorns and pink rabbits. Kyle had borrowed Brandon's Captain America backpack, which was somehow fitting.

They ended their run toward the beach side then traveled through scrub brush, stunted desert trees, and cacti until they found a deep but narrow river that flowed out to sea. It came from up in the foothills and then meandered past the villa. If they followed along the banks, it would leave fewer footprints, even if their run had attracted attention. It wouldn't be of use now, but on the return trip, a little boat would do nicely, and they could just float back to the beach. He wondered if Kyle had considered using another method.

He stumbled several times, scraped his ankle on the sharp outcroppings, and kicked himself for not wearing socks he could pull up and protect his lower legs.

And there were bugs and poison cactus needles to avoid.

The base of the foothill the villa stood on was very gnarled and rocky, with cracks and cervices everywhere, as if it had been some ancient lava flow. Kyle pondered which way to approach the outcropping when Armando found a cave, which faced South, so the inside was well lit but cool. A smelly pool of green water had seeped in, no doubt remnants of a winter hurricane, as was prone in this region. During one such storm, one of these tributaries grew so fast that it overflowed and wiped out the first floors of several older hotels downtown as it traveled out to sea and disappeared. The town was still finding old mattresses, bedframes, and luggage the Sea of Cortez was trying to return. He'd seen a picture of an abandoned Coke machine and a half dozen refrigerators. It had also swept through a local truck dealership, and for weeks afterward, Ford pickups were finding themselves marooned on the beautiful beach, delighting all the tourist children.

Like everything else about Mexico, Damon always found something so totally unexpected and juxtaposed to something else that didn't belong there. He just prepared himself for the bizarre and macabre. There was a level of violence that he could almost smell, and it infected everything.

Maybe that's what I'm picking up. Fredo had been raised in East L.A. in a very tough, gang-infested neighborhood even back then. His father was murdered, and his mother sent him to join the Navy to get him out of L.A. He'd been running on the edges of beginning to get into trouble. The Navy completed the job his parents could no longer do. Damon knew Fredo was grateful for the chance to prove himself, finding a true family in the Brotherhood, and often spoke of it. Especially when someone's past came up. He was the conscience of the group, the one to remind everyone that their bond wasn't just lip service. It was everything.

But there was something dangerous going on with him this trip, perhaps harkening back to his Latino roots, and Damon was going to take Kyle's advice and steer clear of him.

In the cave, Kyle laid out a map he'd brought with him, a rough sketch of the surveillance footage sent back from Coronado on Coop's little bird.

"We're going to do some eyes-on surveillance of the villa since the likelihood is that we'll only have one shot at it. If it's too risky, we're to pull back. At the present time, there is no deal made on transferring the hostages out to someone else," Kyle began.

Damon and the others gathered around the sketches placed on a sticky page.

"She's here, we think, or at least that was the last sighting. Just like before, the last known signal from Ridgeway was from here. And it does look like a shipping container, which would explain the poor signal."

"You want us to scope out some good sniper locations if we need it later?" asked Armando.

"Exactly. You and Danny find four vantage points, two for each of you. Then you decide which ones will work, depending on what we find when we come back."

"Roger that," said Danny.

"Fredo, I want you and Damon to locate where and how you'll set up the charges."

Damon peered at Kyle, and then saw his smirk. He had decided to *force* them together, after giving him advice against it. He was about to object when he saw Kyle's slight shake of his head, so he shut up.

"You want massive or super massive?" Fredo asked.

"Whatever it is, I want you to blow a hole in the front gate big enough to get that water truck through and not get it stuck in the debris field."

Damon nodded. "What will they be protecting?" he asked.

Fredo pressed his stubby forefinger onto three other rectangular boxes near Ridgeway's location.

"What about the storeroom? Wouldn't they want to protect the guns and ammo?" he asked.

Cooper shook his head. "No, they'll do that underground, not on top where it's vulnerable to sunlight and surface explosions. They'd keep it cool, probably in a cave. I'm betting there is one here somewhere."

"I agree," said Kyle. "If we get them tasked with putting out the fire, and if they don't see or hear a big army or militia coming for them, they'll be focused on something else. The human cargo is where they make their money. Of course, they'd protect Kelly and Ridgeway too."

"Looks like she's over near the main part of the villa. You think they're actually putting her up in the house?" asked T.J.

Sven spoke up. "I imagine they need her in good shape, under house arrest, but they know she's State and a non-combatant. And if she's been beat up, the leverage they'll have to negotiate goes down."

"Precisely. Which means, Sven, I want you to smuggle in an Invisio to her, so we have ears."

Sven stood tall, putting his hands on his belt. "Well, I guess I could surrender to them, then, get it to her that way."

Several chuckled, but Kyle's expression was stern. "You are of no value to them, Sven. You wouldn't last an hour in there."

"I'll figure something."

"I want everyone looking at everything, anything we can use to our advantage. Tucker, Trace, and Jason, I want pictures if you can of what's in those squares. How many, ages, sex, how they're guarded. Coop, you be their cover, but you signal the shooters here if anybody gets into trouble. If you have to overtake anyone, make it quiet and very quick."

"What if we have to act, I mean, like tonight?" asked Sven. "We can't get back here in time if we have to jog again. We can't transport anyone if we don't have vehicles."

"We got vehicles, here and here. But, Coop, you see if they're operational."

"Hold on. I'm—"

"No, I'm not asking you to go around and try starting up the trucks, but just see if they're operational or look like they're being used. And then look to see if we can disable any of the ones we don't need, just in case."

"And I'm doing that while I'm watching these three?"

"I'm not gonna lay a hand on the kid," said Fredo. He winked at Damon. It sent a chill down his spine, but inside, he acknowledged the smack talk as a good sign.

"We might as well bury the charges while we're at it, Fredo," Damon thought.

"That's a good idea. Get it set up ahead of time. You're all right, kid."

Damon crossed himself and gave Fredo a bow. He got a finger for his troubles.

"So you want me to, what, clean my Sig?" T.J. asked.

"You're gonna be the runner in case someone needs help. You can back up any of the activities here, and if you have to, you can run radio to the base. Or call an SOS. I'm going to give you the sat phone, so you guard that thing with your life and stay hidden. You and I will be in good contact," answered Kyle.

"Got it. So where will you be?" T.J. asked.

"I'm gonna find that cave. And you older guys who've been down here before, you holler if you see anyone you recognize, hear?"

Everyone nodded. Kyle checked his watch.

"I have thirteen hundred oh five. Fredo, pass out the Invisios. Everyone, check your equipment. Anything you don't need from your packs, leave it here for now. I'm gonna make one call to make sure we're still a go and get a quick update. Oh, Fredo, you got plastic bags for burying those charges?"

"No, didn't bring any. What if I just use the backpack?"

"One of your boys is going to be mighty upset with you."

Damon examined the Hulk pack that obviously had belonged to one of Fredo's twins.

Fredo shrugged. "As long as I come home."

That put everyone into a quiet mood while they checked their specialized pockets, ammo, knives, and gear. Coop passed around a water bottle while Kyle headed to the mouth of the cave and made his call to the admiral.

Damon searched the faces of his team, saw the resolution written there, the focus, people tasked with doing what they were the best at but working together in a pinch. Trace and Tucker were still sweating from the run. Armando and Danny lovingly wiped down their long guns and carefully stored them on their backs. Cooper ate a granola bar. Jason held on to a carved piece of bone that always hung around his neck and whispered prayers to his ancestors. T.J. checked out a picture he kept of his wife and daughters and then stowed it in the zipper pocket over his heart.

Damon said a prayer, sending strength to Martel and whatever she was dealing with. In his mind, she was on the beach, walking, her long hair blowing in the breeze, holding her sandals casually in one hand while her skirts swished as she trekked through the surf. It wouldn't be long before she'd wear that white dress she'd picked out, and then maybe they could start their family, all over again.

And pick up the pieces of the last one.

"We're on. Nothing new, thank God," Kyle said. "Can everyone hear me?"

They nodded.

Kyle handed T.J. the phone. "Let's all be in position in fifteen minutes. We'll check in and then start our tasks."

CHAPTER 16

IT WOULD HAVE been a stretch to guess her mind would be off of the potential lawsuit, her visit with Ainsley, or her soon-to-be husband away doing dangerous things. Those three were pretty big in Martel's world.

But now there was a fourth.

And she wasn't stupid, either. If she was spotting, well, perhaps it would get stronger and then lead to heavy clotting, and so forth. She knew the stories. So, in addition to the possibility that she was pregnant, which she'd already thought about and dismissed previously, there was this strange déjà vu experience of this happening again. That she hadn't been paying attention. No, it wasn't a bit funny that the two of them were so fertile all it took was a few times together and, wham, she'd get pregnant. That conversation would have to be had much into the distance. Right now, it wasn't funny at all.

So how did she feel about this? Had she not learned her lesson? Her pregnancy had consumed the last remaining time she had with her mother before she passed. In fact, it was the reason she was not able to be at her bedside and say good-bye.

She'd altered forever the lives of three other people, not counting herself and Damon. Ainsley's life was arguably better for the adoption. So was the Newberg's life with the fulfillment of a dream of having a child. The full weight of her actions, or lack thereof, came falling down upon her. She was lucky the first time when she was able to find a loving home for her daughter, but Ainsley was right. It had been an afterthought. Did she look hard enough for Damon? Did he care enough about her? And wasn't it true, while she came to profess her love for her darling daughter that, in reality, Ainsley's feelings had been the least she'd cared about. It was all about raising a child by herself or not being sure what Damon would do or the horrible possibility she could have tried to trap Damon into marrying her. It was a choice she didn't want to make. She didn't want to be that kind of a woman.

Maybe I'm worse.

Her meeting exposed how blindsided she was because she hadn't thought about what Ainsley would think. Her goal had been to convince her that she did it out of love.

But wasn't that a lie?

The truth was, she had no right to have Ainsley in her life, and she was asking everyone to give her a pass—the Newbergs, Ainsley, even Damon.

She didn't deserve a pass. She didn't deserve everyone's understanding or their forgiveness, because she hadn't learned her lesson. She'd just perhaps done it again. How stupid and unthinking could she be?

So now what? She envisioned showing up for a trial, pregnant again, not married, and accused of not paying attention to the care of a child in her charge when she was at school. Wasn't this the same thing? Perhaps a light version of the same issue? Wouldn't she deserve any exploitation the opposing attorney might raise? Her last days as a teacher at the school she loved would be marred in shame and disrespect. It didn't matter that she loved Damon and they were engaged. That wasn't the point. It was that the rules, somehow, didn't apply to her. In her attempt to "fix" things, she was still asking for that passing grade when others had played the game in the right order. She was playing dangerous, loose with her morals, even looser with other people's feelings.

The thought that perhaps she was on the edge of a miscarriage didn't make it any better either. That was a convenient, albeit painful, copout.

How did she really feel about being pregnant again? And if it was so, how would she ever explain it to Damon or Ainsley?

It was hard getting showered, running her hands over her tender nipples, the smoothness of her soft belly, having that baptism of conscience as she anticipated having breakfast with Mr. Karmody. She'd have this little thought in the back of her head, the possibility, perhaps a hope, that new life was forming again, coming her way. And she'd think about this while chatting with Mr. Karmody about her future. The other part of her future.

On her way to the omelet house, she got a call from Kaitlyn.

"When I didn't hear from you, I worried. And when I decided to let you call me, I worried that was the best decision. So I'm calling you now because I'm worried, Martel. Tell me it's not justified."

She found herself laughing a couple notches below hysterically. She wanted to scream out the window, "Bring it all on!" But, of course, she wasn't going to do that. She was like an iceberg, one third above water, two-thirds below. The below was getting deeper and deeper.

"Martel?"

"I'm on my way to meet Gran Karmody over breakfast. If Greg is free, the offer of dinner is still on the table."

"He said he's got work. I think he just wants me to have a night off with my best friend."

"So let's meet early if you can. Five? Fergus Crab Shack?"

"Perfect. And did you sleep well last night?"

"I did. Took a nice, hot shower and fell into bed."

"He's the attorney who handled the meeting with Ainsley?"

"Yes."

"So does this have anything to do with her?"

"No. Nothing to do with Damon, either. It's a school thing. I'll brief you what I can tonight. In the meantime, not a word of this conversation or about Ainsley or what I did last weekend, okay? Please?"

"Of course. Well, until tonight."

"Thanks so much for calling, Kaitlyn."

Mr. Karmody was on the phone, pacing the parking lot when she arrived. He hung up and then greeted her. He still looked fresh in his white linen suit, but today, he had on a light blue shirt. His signature string tie still firmly balanced on his neck like a garotte.

"I've got a table inside," he motioned, directing her past the hostess to a corner by a window where the light was good.

"Olivia won't be joining us this morning. But I'm glad you could come. How are you holding up?"

She knew better than to tell the truth. "I'm fine. The worst part of these things is that they come out of nowhere, and they take time to work themselves out, don't they?" she said.

"You've got that right. Personalities, expectations, justice, respect. What is one thing to one person isn't to another. It's all a matter of interpretation."

"What did you two talk about after I left?" she asked.

"Olivia is quite confident they won't have much of a case or won't prevail. Unfortunately, that doesn't mean you'll be spared going through a few things, and I wanted to talk to you about this."

"Is this going to ruin my breakfast?"

"I don't think so. But in either case, I'm buying, so if you don't feel like finishing, don't worry."

"I was worried that the two of them had some history."

"I think it should be the Gibbs who should be worried. Olivia is a formidable attorney. He now knows it's not going to be a walk in the park. But before we get into all this, I want to make sure you understand how things are going to work."

"Sure."

He'd been playing with the plastic menu without looking at it, so when the waitress stopped by, he handed it back to her and asked Martel what she wanted. He ordered and then studied his hands folded on the table without making eye contact with Martel.

"You didn't give your permission to discuss your daughter, so I haven't talked about it with Olivia. But I'd like to."

"Sure. I'm fine with it"

"Okay, good. I'm going to run it by her how much we need to delve into it, but if they are looking for a fat settlement rather than a court hearing, her name might come up. I want you to be okay with that."

"No. I'm not okay with it. That's my personal business. It has nothing to do with them."

"I agree, but if they somehow get hold of that information, I want you to be prepared."

"It's not me that has to be prepared. It would be her parents. She's only twelve. I don't see where she would have any involvement at all."

"Newspaper reporters trying to find a juicy angle for their story. I'm sad to say teachers are getting a bum rap these days."

"I'm aware of that. But this is Florida. I doubt they'll hear about it in Palo Alto. Can't we keep them out of it completely?"

"As I think we should. So I'll talk to Olivia, now that I have your permission."

"What else?"

"She agrees with me. Somehow, we have to find out where the sexual abuse is coming from. She agrees with your assessment that her knowledge of sexual things is not natural and some adult is at fault. It's going to be important to help the sheriff find that person."

"Or persons."

"Yes, it could be."

"Will they share their findings? Or are they being kept from doing anything?"

"That's not up to the attorney or to the Gibbs. The law is very clear in the case of child sexual abuse. The child comes first. There are limits to what the law can do, though. But the child is supposed to be protected first and foremost. So they can't stop an investigation forever. They can delay it, and if they get too much in the way, they can be arrested. Not that we want that."

"So, Mr. Karmody, what's your point? I don't understand."

He looked down at his big hands again, chewing on his lower lip and frowning. "We might have to hire a private investigator. We need someone who knows how to dig into court and other records, see if there is anything in the family history that will give some indication of who's at fault."

"Okay."

"It can be expensive."

Martel knew it was coming down to that.

"How much?"

"Five, ten thousand dollars easily. Goes up from there. The bottom line is that we have to walk the very narrow path of showing Cora has been damaged by some association and, because of that, unwittingly invited the attention at school. That you had no idea to be careful with her or to watch her more closely. You could not be held to a higher standard than a normal other teacher would. In fact, you went out of your way to be transparent, which

I think is obvious."

"And if it's not done right, it will backfire. Make enemies out of the parents."

"Or Cora herself. We don't want her embellishing her story, making you more the target. You can see our problem. Unfortunately, resources aren't what they should be, so the sheriff's department isn't known for their skill in this arena."

"Great."

"They have more work than they have people to do the job. Have you ever seen a wrestling match? One of those big events on TV?"

"In passing. It's not my thing."

"Nor mine. But have you ever watched the referee? Now, do you think they ever are in control? I mean, they don't really stop the fight, do they? Most those guys are half the size of the wrestlers, anyway. And some of it is just show. I'm not saying the sheriff's department is like that, but they are more like referees. They gather up all the information for charges to be filed. Someone has to become the target of the investigation. That shouldn't be Cora. It needs to fall on the shoulders of the sicko who can't stop. And it shouldn't be you, either."

Martel nodded her agreement. "So the detective will do some of the legwork for the sheriff and help them build a case, if there is one."

"That's right. And if you think about it, getting some help for that little girl is paramount. We need to get her the support system that will help her heal. We aren't looking to tear the family apart. But it depends on who did what to whom. Get my drift?"

"I do. And I don't think the father is involved."

"Olivia agrees with me on that too. She thinks your hunch about the wife's family would be a good place to start. That is, if you're willing."

"Do I have a choice?"

"Oh, you do. You most definitely do. You could wait until the school gets served with a complaint, naming you as well. By the time things get filed, they become concrete. Sides start forming. It's why Manny wanted to meet with you 'informally,'" he said, using his fingers in the quote marks, "to get enough facts he could use to make a compelling case. It was sleazy, but it was also smart."

"Well, I've been saving for the wedding. I could invest about five thousand dollars in this, if you think it's money well spent. How much more for your fees, for Olivia's fees?"

"I'm not going to charge you. I think you're looking at another five thousand dollars for her, minimum. That's what I'd propose to do, give her a retainer, and let her work with the private detective to see if they can dig up something on that family."

Martel looked at her breakfast and wasn't going to be able to eat a bite. She wasn't sure what had made her sick, but she knew one thing. The catered dinner in a gazebo out at the beach and the rows of rented white chairs became a distant memory. Since it didn't matter much to Damon anyhow, a potluck dinner at Aimee and Andy's house, cases of wine from the Liquor Warehouse, no bridesmaids or groomsmen, and a cake she could probably bake herself was looking pretty good.

Those beautiful, perfect weddings at exotic destinations were for other people who made different choices with their lives. Maybe she'd get to go to Ainsley's wedding someday where she'd have all that.

She could wait that long.

CHAPTER 17

FREDO AND DAMON waited under the shade of a large outcropping of sandstone, populated with desert plants. They were roughly twenty feet from the left side of the enormous solid metal gate that swung open, so they had adjusted their spot to make sure they weren't caught in it. They could hear guards walking the interior perimeter of the plaster walls lined with broken bottles and barbed wire.

Fredo indicated they were in place a whole two minutes early. Danny and others started whispering their checks as well.

Damon nodded toward the wall. "What are they saying?"

"I think they're talking about where they're going to take their group. I guess these must be part of the Coyote brigade."

"Probably do it all. Cross train. They guard, watch over the hostages, and lead the group over the border, you think?"

"Makes sense. They must have hundreds of these guys. You know they busted a team from Romania with affiliation to the Cortez cartel?"

"The ones they're trying to move out?"

Fredo nodded.

"What would they be doing there?"

"Same as here. Picking up people who want to get out, enslaving them to be mules for them and owing them money if they can't pay up front."

"That's sick, man."

Just then, Fredo put a hand to Damon's chest to make him be still. He listened to the conversation.

"Shit, tonight's a big meeting. Someone from Casa Cortez is in town to negotiate."

Damon was completely still, not even moving a muscle so that Fredo could hear everything. Then they heard Kyle's voice.

"I was going to tell you to cut the chatter, but what the hell did you say, Fredo?"

"Someone's coming tonight. Someone big from Cortez."

"Unfortunate," came the whisper back. "Moves up our timeline. This is no longer a fire. This has just turned into a rescue mission. Bone Frogs, you get those containers scoped out. If no one's there, you let me know pronto. I want pictures, body count."

"Roger that," said Tucker.

"Sven?"

"Working on it. Not there yet."

Damon knew Jason was going to give Kyle a piece of his mind when this was all over. He was barely thirty, not a Bone Frog at all.

Fredo unpacked his equipment, laying the blocks of explosive clay a foot apart, like he was organizing a large solitaire game, in two neat rows. He left the plastic covering on the soft bricks but peeled the top layer off, prying it loose with a plastic knife. He asked Damon to cut ten cords about a foot long and fray the ends slightly. With a small plastic-looking drill bit, he made two holes in the top of every block.

"You using it all up?"

"Might as well. I sure as heck don't want to be running across the desert again with this shit."

He got a reprimand again. "Cut the goddamn chatter."

Fredo motioned with fingers to his eyes and pointed to the piano hinges on the outside of the metal gate. He then indicated Damon should do just as he was doing, digging a pit big enough for a backpack to fit and be covered on the other side. He handed him another folding shovel and indicated there was a straight line extending from the hinge to the pit he was digging, showing that it centered on the weakest part of the gate.

Damon carefully waited in the foliage at the side until he was certain no one was coming along the approach and quietly ran across, positioning himself at the other side, then began digging. He was careful not to let the red clay soil, which was extremely dry, form a cloud of dirt that could be seen by anyone with scopes.

They heard Tucker and Trace confirm there were mostly boys housed in very close proximity, wall to wall mattresses. They appeared to be about thirteen to fifteen years of age. Just kids, really. But they were big enough to carry a fairly heavy load.

"They've been issued brand new backpacks with water, food. They've got a shithole around the corner, and one of the kids brought his backpack," said Tucker.

"Girls and boys, younger kids, in the other house. I'm going to check on Ridgeway," Coop whispered."

"Sure would be nice if I could get a tracking device on that backpack," said Fredo.

"Well, why don't you hop the fence and bring it over to me, then," said Tucker.

"Fuck, that's me. Headed your way now, Fredo." T.J. was coming over to pick up and deliver the little needle with the chip inside.

"Too late for this one, but there will be others," said Tucker.

"How did they get inside?" Damon asked Fredo.

"The gate kind of gaps open when you remove the latch. We walked in."

"Too social," whispered Kyle.

Fredo rolled his eyes. Just then, T.J. appeared from the shadows. Fredo stopped connecting the blocks with the cord and removed the pin from his breast pocket. He showed T.J. how to weave it into an inseam so no one would see it. He gave him two more just for good measure.

"Put this on Ridgeway."

T.J. nodded and disappeared as fast as he appeared.

Fredo laid five of the bricks side by side in the unzipped backpack with a piece of Styrofoam as a spacer, the cords in place, then held them all together with a bungee cord with plastic hook ends. With the last brick, he attached the timer, which he could auto turn on. It was set to go off in ten minutes once activated. He motioned with his fingers splayed. Damon had seen him do this several times before during their workups.

Gingerly, Fredo removed a nylon bag from an outer pocket of the pack, unfolded it, and placed the other bricks and spacers in it. He pointed to the other hole and Damon carried the explosives like a tray of tea and cookies to the second hinge. He laid the packs side by side, like he'd seen Fredo do, then strapped them together with the bungee, and made sure all the tops were indeed connected. If one was disconnected, it could throw the timing off or knock the other cords loose, and they could have a one-block dud.

Fredo attached his timer and then placed the bag against a large rock slightly larger than his hand, angling the bag until it was partway leaning against the piano hinge. Damon knew this was to make sure the angle of the blast kicked the hinge loose from the bottom. Due to the weight of the gate, that would be all it took for it to become completely disabled.

He gave Damon a thumbs-up, zipped up the bag, and motioned for him to cover it with soil.

Coop indicated Ridgeway was in poor shape, lying bloody and unconscious. Checking his signs, he reported that, if he didn't make it to a hospital soon, he wasn't going to make it at all.

"Faint pulse. Dehydrated. Two bad wounds on his right thigh. He's not walking. Possibly a fractured foot and ankle. I got the tracer on him. Administering antibiotics, and I hope he doesn't wake up screaming."

"Got you covered, Coop," whispered Danny.

"Charges in place. Set for ten once activated," added Fredo.

"You guys get out of there," Kyle barked. "Get around to the back so the walls will protect you."

"I got to be twenty feet away, Kyle," said Fredo.

"I got him." Damon grabbed the remote. "Kids need a dad."

Fredo was visibly touched but didn't interfere with the transfer.

"Damon, you get the hell out once it blows."

Sven's voice came over the com. "Kelly's been drugged but in good shape. Are we doing this tonight?"

"We are. T.J., that was the last piece of the puzzle. Danny and Armando, on your marks?"

Both indicated they were ready.

"So you want me to make the call?" T.J. asked.

"Let's do it and get a SITREP."

They all heard T.J. tell the commander someone from the Cortez cartel was headed over to negotiate.

A few seconds later, they heard all clear. "We are to wait for the new visitor and nightfall. And then it's up to you. They've already got eyes on us. I'll signal them."

"So now we wait," said Kyle. "Anyone want to tell me their plans for Mother's Day?"

Several laughed. Damon stared at the roadway, listening for a vibration. Fredo stuck by his side for now. He removed his Invisio and indicated Damon should do the same.

"You're all right, kid."

"Tell me that when I don't screw up."

"All you gotta do is push the button. How hard can that be?"

"Then you do it."

"I was going to."

They heard the sounds of trucks. They both replaced their earpieces, and Fredo whispered, "We got trucks coming. Danny? Armando?"

"We got one nice, shiny black SUV, heavily armored, followed by another," reported Armando.

Two? He motioned to Fredo.

"Then we got some covered troop carriers. Yo, the gate fellas," Armando warned. "We got four oncoming."

Damon pushed Fredo to the back while he hid in the bushes under the overhang. The sun was beginning to set, but it was still too light out. He was concerned that too much could be seen without the cover of darkness. But, if the former marines were equipped in any way, they'd have IRVs, just like the SEALs did, so it wasn't to their advantage. Main thing was to get the hostages out before they could be taken away.

He thought about what Martel was doing right now. He had intended to recommend they go to Mexico for their honeymoon, but he was nixing that the longer he was here. He would sure look forward to Florida, the sunsets, and the beach. All he had to do was push the button when the signal was given.

The first SUV stopped at the gate. Two drivers in black sunglasses and suits got out, followed by a couple of Dobermans, big black Dobermans. On a whistle command, the Dobermans started sniffing the gate and around the plaster walls. One was on the right, and one was headed straight for him.

"We got a dog tracking Damon," he heard over the Invisio, followed by some pretty hefty swearing.

Damon didn't want to tell them he'd been bitten by a Dobie

when he was young and never trusted them. In fact, he didn't like dogs at all, which most of the SEALs thought was odd. This guy meant business as he tracked his scent from the outside of the hinge on the gate to just outside the thicket where he was holed up in.

"Get up on the rock, Damon," whispered Armando.

Damon tried to get his footing but slipped and fell on his belly. The dog abruptly stopped and started barking.

"They're not inside yet. Gates are still closed," Armando updated everyone.

"If you have to, just blow it," said Kyle.

One of the troop carriers unloaded six or seven armed men, who followed behind the dog. The beast was well trained and wasn't going to attack until commanded to do so. His bark was piercing. Damon could hear shouting from inside the gated perimeter as more men came running.

He knew better than to hide the trigger device in his pants, so he pressed the button and tossed it into the brush.

"We got ten. Nice knowing ya," Damon said. He considered what his future looked like. He was either going to be shot, mauled by a dog, or blown into a thousand pieces by his own hand. The choice wasn't a difficult one. He'd take death by his own hand any day. But those dogs could do a lot of damage to him in ten minutes.

He tossed the Invisio into the brush so he could at least look like he was not part of a team. He'd forgotten to tell them this, but they'd figure it out. They didn't have to hear him screaming his lungs out anyway as the dogs ripped the legs from his torso.

He slowly removed his KA-BAR and knew he could take care of the first dog but not both of them. A lot of men were running toward him now, and it was close, but he was still in the kill zone. In slow motion, the SUV doors opened. Damon said a prayer for that piece of luck. General Cortez was standing right next to the gate, speaking with someone else, and he guessed it was part of the Surf Club, maybe Carlos Guitteriez himself.

He hoped the team didn't come run to his aid, but instead get Kelly and Ridgeway out, hop in a truck, and get the hell out of Dodge.

In slow motion, like it was a rolling thunder, he saw the larger of the two dogs leap in his direction, the Doberman's body completely covering his, as the snout went for his jugular. Behind him, Damon could barely see the two hinges of the gate explode, sending one side up into the air about twenty feet, and the other slicing across the horizon, taking the top off the first Suburban.

The blast ruined his hearing, leaving him with an electronic buzz that nearly split his head. It must have been disorienting to the dog, too, because he lay very still. Damon sat up and discovered a metal tie bar from the gate's outer surface had given the dog a lethal blow, severing his spinal cord.

Incredibly, that dog had saved his life.

The wholesale bursting body parts spurting blood and guts all over the ground and chaos that erupted in complete radio silence was surreal. And where the general had been, all that was left were his two well-polished boots, still standing as if he was in a salute, fragments of the general's lower legs protruding out the top in ragged peaks, oozing red blood. The other individual was nowhere to be found.

He heard a motor running and wanted to stand up, but he'd been injured. Trying to put his weight on his leg, the pain was excruciating, and he passed out like a pussy.

CHAPTER 18

GREG DROPPED KAITLYN off at the crab shack. "Do you mind bringing her home?" he asked. "I don't want her driving now."

"Don't you know? When you get pregnant, you forget how to do everything!" Kaitlyn said, trying to get her big ass up on one of the stools.

"Please, Martel. It would mean a lot to me," he begged, even putting his hands together.

"No problem. We'll not be long. I'm tired." Greg gave her a peck on the cheek, then kissed his wife, and left.

"I'm sorry, sweetie, I know you were looking forward to that margarita, and now I've just spoiled it."

She couldn't tell her best friend that, as of today, she wouldn't be doing any more drinking until she knew the results of a blood test she'd had on the way home from breakfast with Mr. Karmody.

"No worries, Kate. I'm not really in the mood anyway." She sighed and gulped down half of the oversized glass of ice water. One thing she hadn't gotten used to was the slight sulfur taste of the Florida water. It almost made her gag.

Kaitlyn watched her, the curious grin crossing her pink cheeks. Her eyes sparkled as if she was going to hear some really good gossip. Martel didn't know where to start.

"You can't tell anyone, not even Greg."

At first, Kaitlyn angled her head, frowning. "Oh dear. That bad?"

"It could be." She felt the hot tears collecting in her lower lids. She tried to will them to stop, but it was no use, and she gasped into an ugly, snorting cry that turned heads.

If she noticed, Kaitlyn paid no attention to the reaction of the crowd. She reached across the table and seized Martel's hand. "Your fingers are ice cold. What is going on with you?"

She halfway decided to break her own rules and have a margarita anyway, but she held firm.

Just where do I begin?

As usual, Kate wasn't going to pry. She was going to wait until Martel was collected and wanted to share. She massaged her knuckles and gave her an adoring look, like some of her students did.

"I have a girl in my glass who appears to have been involved in some sexual activity. And it's spilled over onto the class. She's using her new-found experience, kind of flaunting it in front of a couple of the boys in my class. And, well, I caught her and two boys out behind the field house being inappropriate."

Kate's eyes narrowed as she bored into Martel's stare. "How inappropriate?"

"She let them put their hands down her pants, you know, touch her there. I guess she wanted to impress them or something. She was acting out something she'd been taught and not by another child. Probably an adult. That's the way it works."

"Yes, I know. So you reported it?"

"I reported it to Carlton Green, and we discussed having a parent-teacher conference with the girl's parents before I called the authorities. That way they'd have some kind of idea what they could expect. I didn't want them blindsided by all of it, and, well, frankly, I was also checking out their reaction in case I would have to also report that I thought they were involved."

"Oh. My. God," she said, putting her hand over her mouth. "And are they?"

"I don't know, Kate. My gut tells me no."

"So this is what Green was doing on Monday, meeting with you and the representatives of the child?"

"They obtained a lawyer. They're saying that I didn't keep their daughter safe. That somehow, I'm to blame, that I allowed the boys to abuse her and didn't stop it."

"That's nuts. Someone got to them. So what does Green say?"

"He's kinda wishy-washy. It's like he doesn't want the controversy to come up in the first place. I get the impression that if someone's going to fall over this, it won't be him."

"Have you called your union rep?"

"Three times. No answer."

"You poor thing. So you're in this alone? Well, with Damon being gone, I guess you are. What can I do to help?"

"Nothing. I've hired my own attorney. He thinks it would help if we could identify who the real perpetrator is. So we're maybe hiring a private detective."

"Ouch. That's going to be expensive, isn't it?"

"Lucky thing I was saving up for the wedding."

"No, you can't do that. You can't sacrifice your wedding, Martel. That's just wrong."

"But with this hanging over my head, without it being resolved, how will I ever get a good job in a decent school, either here or in California? And there's the cost. I don't even want to know what Damon will say about all this."

"Oh, he loves you. Don't worry about that."

"He's away on deployment. I told you where."

Kate nodded.

"It's supposed to be very stressful. Oddly enough, they are investigating some sex trafficking cartels there. Very lucrative business helping people cross the border, charging an arm and a leg, and the cartels make them work it off in various terrible ways. Even children."

"I've heard. It's terrible. So rampant now."

"I've told you more than I'm supposed to, about both Damon's work and my situation. If I get sued, I could lose my job and my ability to get another job. The financial setback would be horrible, but worst of all, what kind of an introduction would that have to Ainsley? How would she ever believe in me?"

"Love finds a way, Martel. You know this."

"I've lost those rose-colored glasses, Kate. I really have. I used to be such a Pollyanna about things, always believing the best in people, always believing the best things happen to good people. Here, I thought I was helping them, I wanted them to know about their daughter so she can get some counseling. But it's blown up into a legal affair where it has to be someone else's fault. And it is, truth be told, just that I'm not that someone."

The waitress had come by several times, and neither of them had even looked at the menu.

"I don't think we're very hungry," Kaitlyn said to the woman.

"Suit yourself, but it's going to get crowded tonight. If I need the table, I'm going to have to ask you to leave."

"How about two bowls of soup? You have some chowder and French bread?" asked Martel.

"Cup or bowl?"

"Bowls." Kate nodded her agreement.

"Coming right up." She took the menus and hustled away to wait on someone else.

"Have you told Damon yet?"

"He knows something's up. But it wasn't until this morning

that I found out how much it was going to cost me. He won't be pleased, but I do think we'll have to put the wedding on hold or just do a barn dance or something very easy and inexpensive."

"That actually sounds more like his style, anyway."

"He was letting me do the beach wedding, but no, it wasn't his idea. I just wanted a perfect wedding, like yours."

"It was perfect, wasn't it? But that's because you were there, Martel. You and the kids from the school. That was so cute. Now they're getting into the baby and everything. It's really sweet how all of this is unfolding."

Martel was happy for her, but their two lives didn't have any resemblance of each other. Kaitlyn did everything perfectly. She had the fairy tale wedding with the handsome prince. She had the love and support of the whole school. All the other teachers loved her. The children adored her, and parents tried to get their kids in her class.

Martel was loved and considered a good teacher, but she didn't have that level of respect. Her life was lived under a little rain cloud. She'd given up Ainsley and missed out on ten good years with Damon because she hadn't fought hard enough for them. It was a mistake to take such a passive role in all that. Now there was so much to regret.

All based on the decisions she'd made when she was young. It had changed the whole trajectory of her life.

They hardly spoke all the way to Kate's house. Greg came out and helped her get out of the car, her belly becoming a real obstacle now. Martel remembered those days, when she'd take long walks in the woods and talk to her baby. She told her all about their family, even though she'd never get to meet them. She taught her to listen to the birds and to smell the leaves after it rained, as it always did in Oregon. She'd sit in her car with the windows open looking at the rough surf. An angry surf. Not like Sunset Beach. It was dangerous and relentless, powerful and strong. It made her feel strong as she carried the child she knew was not going to be part of her life. She willed that her daughter would be just as strong but make better choices.

Yes, Ainsley might be one of those, like Kaitlyn, who would have everything, the fairy tale all the way through. She hoped she would learn to appreciate all her gifts and celebrate her life like Martel had.

And someday, maybe she'd forgive her.

She didn't have any reason to expect it but all the reasons in the world to hope it would happen.

CHAPTER 19

DAMON WOKE UP in a hospital bed. He was confused at first, but then the last painful memories of the Mexico trip came flashing by—the explosion, the carnage, even the bizarre celebration of the Day of the Dead when everyone dressed up in skulls, sugar skulls. They worshiped ten-foot-high ghosts and horned creatures who cavorted with the living and coaxed them into their deaths. He'd had all those vivid dreams, but now he was back, amongst the living.

Someone had brought some flowers by, which was nice. Several of the SEAL kids drew pictures. He examined them carefully, pulling himself up on the bar strung across the bed. What caught his eye first was that someone had drawn him on crutches.

He flipped the sheets over and felt the warm bandage covering his upper thigh. He'd either broken his upper femur or his hip. Either one was bad. He guessed it was his hip.

Next to the flowers, one of his brothers brought him some Jack Daniels. He wouldn't mind a drink right now, but he was still on an I.V., and he hadn't been shown how to walk. He didn't want to risk crashing to the floor and maybe breaking his other one.

He lay back, realizing it was exhausting just sitting up. How long had he been there? He must have been unconscious all the way home, because he didn't remember any of it. He did remember the general's boots with parts of his legs sticking out the top, greenstick fractures that would never heal, even if they could find the rest of his body.

Then he remembered the dog. How warm and almost protective that animal was, as he was lunging for his neck. He touched his neck and felt a bruise there. But nothing like what would have occurred if that dog had survived. He hadn't even gotten far enough to break the skin.

"Well, look at what we have here. Mr. Hamlin is up and awake. Is he hungry this morning?"

For some reason, he didn't understand why she was talking that way. Was there someone else in here too? He turned around and, no, just saw the wall with all the monitors on it. He was alone with the nurse. He didn't find her attractive or cute at all. He wanted to throw something at her because she was too pert, too happy, happy, happy. Didn't she know he'd almost died?

His ears still rang too. He tried to talk, and his tongue curled over on itself until he relaxed and tried again, with the same result. It was the strangest thing.

"You're having a reaction to the anesthetic from the surgery to give you a new hip."

"New hip?"

"You've got a brand-new beautiful hip with a titanium ball and new ball socket. And the doctor says you were lucky. It could have been both hips or the injury could have been higher and then you might not have survived."

"Higher?" He couldn't remember any of it.

"Your memory will come back in no time. Some people sleep for days after a trauma like this. Do you remember what hit you?"

"A fuckin' door. A huge solid metal door about as long as this room and five times thicker."

"A flying door. I'll bet that will be an interesting story over beers at the Scupper. You'll have some tall tales like all the other guys there."

"I blew up a general, a Mexican general, too."

"Well, I'm sure you didn't mean it. You should say a prayer for his soul, may he rest in peace."

"No way. I want him to rot in Hell. He was a bad dude." Damon was feeling punchy and then realized she'd put something into the plastic tube that went right into the back of his hand. "Hey, that's not very—he wanted me to marry his daughter so I blew him up. But I already got a girl—I got two girls, as a matter of fact—"

And then the darkness consumed him.

THE NEXT TIME he woke up he had a splitting headache, more like a migraine. He didn't dare move a muscle, even opening his eyes would risk a blinding flash of yellow light and a pain so great he'd nearly poked his eyes out once to be rid of it.

A rough hand peeled up his eyelid and peered down at him. "Hello, Damon," said Coop.

"Don't touch me. I have a headache."

"Not to worry. Sex is the furthest thing from my mind. Besides your hairy ass is just too, well, it's just too hairy. It doesn't turn me on at all."

Through the foggy dreams with all the bouncing sugar skulls, pictures of little children with their teeth filed to points and blood dripping down their chests haunted him. Just who was he messing around with his eyes, his chart, even making notes in it.

"Hey, that's *my* chart. It's for my doctor, and besides, you're no doctor."

"Why yes, it is. And no, I'm not a doctor. I'm the one who stopped the bleeding so you had a chance to live and hassle all the staff here and be an asshole to me. Your guardian angel. I'm the one who saved your life."

"And I'm the one who blew up a general, and don't you forget it."

"No, I'll never forget that as long as I live. Did you see his boots? They were still shiny."

"I know!" Damon was beginning to warm back up to Coop. Maybe it was the drugs making him think the medic was being a dickhead.

"How did my hip get broken?"

"You mean, how did you manage to blow yourself up and at the last-minute grab a dog to save your sorry life?"

"What was it that happened?"

"The rod that went through the dog went right into your hip and sheared off the top of it. If it had been a few inches up and over toward the middle, and if you hadn't been so freakin scared and shriveled, you might not be able to father any children. But you can breathe a sigh of relief. You can breed to your heart's content. You're checked out. You're fine."

"You handled my junk?"

Coop stood next to the bed with his arms folded. "Nah. I didn't. But I think they would have said something if you were missing anything else."

"Did everyone make it out alive?"

That made Coop sit on the bed and give him a serious look. "We lost Special Agent Ridgeway. But he was half-dead when we found him anyhow. Kelly made it, though. Everyone else made it out in good shape, without a scratch.

"And I bagged a general."

"You bagged a general and a capo. An up-and-coming capo. The head of the Guittierez family in Baja. You rid the planet of a couple of real bad dudes."

"Hey, thanks, man. I'm sorry if I said some scary stuff a few minutes ago. I've had some very weird dreams."

"Damon, you earned your spot on this one. Kyle, everyone is pleased. He's going to come talk to you. But my man, that's one helluva wound and repair. Your days jumping out of airplanes might be over."

"That's bullshit and you know it."

"Ain't up to me. Up to the Navy doctors."

"I want to stay a SEAL. I'm not ready to get out. Don't you let them talk about it like that. You tell them—all of them—I'm staying. I will haunt all you guys down at the SEAL Team 3 building every day and make your lives so miserable you'll wish I died in the explosion."

"Even SEALs have paperwork to do. You can still do that. You could go be an instructor and laugh at froglets and tadpoles and try to get them all to quit. Somebody actually did that once. You could be that guy. I could see it."

"The whole class quit?"

"Yessir. He got relegated to making welcome packets for SEAL graduations, you know, the little programs for the families?"

"And that's where they want to put me. A war hero. A man who sacrificed his hip for the cause, for his brothers."

"Yes, and for blowing up a dog and a general and others. They first give you the medals, and then they give you the desk and the paperwork. You'll see, it isn't that bad."

"Hell no!" Damon shouted.

Coop just laughed at him. "Yeah, that's what I told Kyle. There was no way that was going to happen."

And then he left.

He heard his phone ring and nearly fell out of bed looking for it. When the orderly brought him his tray of food, he asked them to find his phone. He had been sitting on it, but because of the painkillers in his system, his butt didn't feel the vibration.

It had been Martel!

The food smelled divine, but Martel came first.

"Oh God, Damon, they said you broke your hip. I wish I could just fly out there and be with you, sweetheart. Are you in any pain? How did you break your hip? Did anyone else get hurt? Was it an accident?"

"Wait a minute, Martel. I can't think that fast right now. They've got me so high I'm having nightmares, seeing skeletons and little children with filed teeth. But the long and the short of it is I blew myself up."

He sensed she was confused as to what to say. But then she slowly let out the question, "How did you manage to do that?"

"Well, Fredo showed me what to do. Our timing was off. I was in the process of being eaten by a dog or something. But I was pinned under this monster, and that's what saved my life. Seriously."

"Oh wow. You're really out of it, Damon. So you're not in any pain, then?"

"Not much. I'm about to have my first meal, though." He lifted the white plastic lid. "And it's *mystery meat!* Mashed potatoes and some peas and carrots. I have chocolate pudding for dessert."

She giggled. How he loved to hear her giggle.

"Well, *bon appetite*! Maybe I should call back later?"

"Can you come out? That would be great if you could. I haven't seen you in so long."

"Damon, I was just out there not more than a week ago."

"Yeah, but that's too long. You should just move out here, forget the school. None of this transition bullshit. I want to live with you, Martel. I don't want you clear across the country. What made us think that was a good idea?"

"But I always had this fantasy of getting married at the beach at sunset. Everyone being there. But I'm afraid we'll have to scale back our plans a little."

"Oh? Something else happen?"

"I'll tell you later. Right now, why don't you enjoy your mystery meat, and let's figure it out. Maybe you could come out and stay with me a few months so I can say good-bye."

"Good-bye to whom?"

"Kaitlyn, the beach, the ocean, the vibe of it all."

"Martel, that's nuts. You don't say good-bye to oceans or beaches. Those are inanimate objects. And as for Kaitlyn, she can get on a plane and come visit, or you can go out there and visit. You're not saying good-bye. You're saying hello to San Diego, to me, to the Brotherhood here, to the new school and job I'm sure you'll get. You have a lot to look forward to, but your life is here with me. I don't want to do this any other way."

He must have touched the hang-up button, because when he waited for her answer, there wasn't anyone there.

CHAPTER 20

MARTEL TOOK THE luxury of sleeping in late. At nearly ten o'clock, she finally peeled herself out of bed and made it to the shower. The nausea in the mornings was getting worse and worse, and she knew it would continue until the third month when, miraculously, she'd start to feel full of energy. Or at least that's what had happened the first time.

The pregnancy test came back positive. She didn't want to tell Damon until they could meet in person, and right now, that was looking not for a week or more. He had to learn how to walk up stairs, get in and out of a car by himself, and how to maneuver with a cane as his protection.

And he was in physical therapy three days a week. The progress he was making was very good, he'd told her. She knew how critical to his healing it was to continue that.

He pressed her several times about the wedding plans, and she withheld that from him as well, figuring it would make more sense after she told him they were going to have another child. She didn't like keeping secrets, but without their face-to-face meetings, it was better this way. And, if he couldn't visit within the next two weeks, well then, she'd tell him. That was the agreement she'd made with herself.

Her administrator let her know that the Gibbs had withdrawn

Cora from the school. He quizzed her on what their thoughts might be in regard to them filing a lawsuit, and she told him the absolute truth. She knew nothing. They'd discussed her leaving early, and she offered, if that was what he wanted. But he didn't seem to be pushing her in that direction, so she planned on going back to class on Monday. Her sub had been a student teacher under her two years ago, so she was able to keep up with the class progress.

Once dressed, she made some non-caffeinated tea and was going to go sit out at the beach when she heard the mailman open the creaky box and deposit something. So she picked up the envelopes, sat on the couch overlooking the wide swath of beach, and opened them one by one.

There were a couple of bills, a bank statement, and a letter written by perhaps one of her students. Upon close examination, she discovered it had been postmarked from Palo Alto. All of a sudden, Martel's hands began to shake, and her breathing became shallow.

Ainsley had put a daisy sticker on the back flap of the brown envelope. Martel had not heard anything since that day when they'd met, but the more days that went by left her hopeful. She knew if the decision had been made that Ainsley wanted nothing to do with her or Damon, Mrs. Bergman would have called and stated it so.

The flap gave way, and Martel pulled out a letter on brown matching paper, along with a picture of Ainsley accepting an award for Most Valuable Player for her junior high school basketball team.

She knew Damon would be delighted.

Dear Ms. Long,

I wanted to apologize for my behavior when we met last

month. I've talked a lot about it with my parents, and we agreed that I should perhaps make another effort to talk to you again. I really didn't want to, at first, but Mom suggested it when I kept bringing up our meeting. Something had bothered me about that meeting. I still don't know why, but I found myself getting angrier and angrier with you. I'm not angry that you placed me with my parents. It was something else. I'm writing this letter because I didn't want you to think you did something wrong.

I have spring break coming up in two weeks, and our school will be closed for a week. I was wondering if I might come out to Florida with my mom and visit you. I've seen all these pictures about the beach, and it looks pretty. I've never been to Florida.

Don't feel like you have to say yes to this. I won't be mad. I know you'll be busy teaching, but it would be nice to see where you're going to marry Damon, and maybe I could help with addressing the envelopes or something. If he came out to visit, maybe I could meet him too.

I'm making a wedding present for you guys. It isn't much, but I hope you'll like it.

My mom wanted to know if there were any good motels nearby, not anything fancy, but maybe something within walking distance.

And she says you can call her if you want to meet again. I understand you are probably busy, so I won't expect you'll say yes, but just know that I enjoyed meeting you and would like to get to know you better.

Your friend,
Ainsley.

By the time she got to the end, Martel had lost it. She was having a good, warm but very ugly cry again. Ainsley'd signed the letter "your friend" which touched her greatly. She imagined that Ainsley had struggled with how to close the letter, and that had come to mind after agonizing over it for some time. When she signed her name, she used daisies for the dotted "I" letter, and the "y" was followed by switchbacks with curlicues everywhere, even adding hearts and flowers.

She checked her clock and discovered it was a little before eight in California. Ainsley would be on her way to school or at school soon. Maybe this would be a good time to talk to Lori Newberg.

She dialed her number and got her voicemail.

"Hey, Lori, I just got Ainsley's lovely letter, and I was delighted to hear she was interested in coming out to Florida for a visit. I would be most honored and delighted to put you up in my house. It's very small and not very fancy, but it's right on the beach, and the price is right. I don't have a second bedroom, but I have a very comfortable leather couch in the living room that makes into a sleeper. And you two are welcome to use my bedroom if you want privacy.

"Hope you are doing well, and thanks so much for the letter. You can tell her it meant a lot to me. Hope you guys can come but let me know either way. Take care, Martel."

She'd agreed to meet with Aimee today, so she locked up the house and walked down the beach until she came to their backyard with the gazebo and hot tub facing the gulf. Knocking on the kitchen door, she heard pleasant music from the inside.

"Hey, Martel!" Aimee was dressed in an old shirt of Andy's, which was smudged with paint. She slipped it off and threw it over a chair, inviting her inside. Their large and friendly Golden Retriever tried to pry her way between the two of them. She sat on

Martel's feet, begging for pets.

"This is Sandy. She has to be involved in everything now. Notice she helps me paint," Aimee pointed out several places where the dog had gotten too close to a freshly painted off-white surface.

"So what are you painting now? Which room?"

"One of the bedrooms upstairs. We're trying to finish it as a guest room but to double as an office. I've decided to start trying my hand at writing."

"Really?"

"Come see."

She held Sandy's collar while she closed the door behind them. Martel followed her upstairs. The room had access to the balcony overlooking the gulf. On two sides of the room were built in bookshelves, which Aimee had just finished painting. There was an old oak desk facing out, taking up space on the stationary side of the sliding glass door. In the middle of the desk was a blue IBM Selectric typewriter.

"This belonged to Hank Borges, the science fiction writer who wrote many books right here in this very house, except he used the dining room as his office. This is where he and Carmen fell in love. And guess what, she wrote books after his death."

"Carmen is the lady who left the house to you?"

"Not exactly. I bought it, but yes, she left her estate to me. So, in a way, I got the house money back. It feels like a never-ending circle, doesn't it?"

"Something. Definitely something. Is it in the air, or is it the house? Or maybe a ghost!"

"I know. I felt it the first time I came in here. I don't think it's a ghost. It's just a very creative vortex or something. I don't want to study it too much for fear of scaring it away."

"It is a spirit then. That's how you see it?" Martel asked.

"No, I don't see it. I *feel* it. I sit down at the typewriter, feel the keys underneath my fingers, and something just connects. It's almost like I can't stop."

"What are you writing?"

"Novels about falling in love at the beach. You know, the fairy tale everyone wants but no one really gets?"

"Some people do, I think." Martel was recalling the conversation she'd had with herself about Kaitlyn.

"Anyway, it's very healing here. Something about these four walls is healing to me. I feel like creating. I've heard about houses like this. There are several in England, famous writers and poets lived in them, passed them down from one to another, a solid chain of creativity through hundreds of years. I think I've found one here. It was dormant, and then one day, Carmen stepped inside, and it transformed Hank's life."

Martel watched Aimee, grinning.

"You don't believe me, do you?"

"No, I do. I've just never experienced it before. I'm happy for you."

"Oh, all right. I'm boring you, aren't I?"

"Not at all."

Sandy sat next to where Martel was standing, leaning into her. She brushed the top of the golden dog's head. The room was lit from the large window but seemed to have another glow all its own, too.

"You like this room, Sandy?" she said to the dog, who looked back adoringly at her.

"She likes to sit by the window and watch people walk on the beach. When she's left alone, she always comes here."

They went downstairs, where Aimee had prepared a green salad for both of them. "You want some coffee or wine?" she asked.

"No, thanks. Water would be great."

"So how are the wedding plans coming. You reserved the gazebo at Sunset Beach?"

"I did. But something's come up, and I think I'm going to let it go."

"Oh dear. What happened?"

"I'm not at liberty to talk about it, but I've run into some extra expenses, and me without a job for next year, I just thought it would be good to cut back. Besides, Damon hasn't really been sending out the invitations, so it's kind of stupid to spend a lot of money on a party where not many people will come."

"You could use it to help purchase something back in Coronado when you move there."

"Exactly. I just re-thought the expense of it." She didn't want to lie to her friend, but there was no safe way of letting her know.

"I offered to let you use this house for your reception. I don't see why you couldn't get married out here at the beach and have the reception here. We did it. It was perfect. The offer still stands."

"Are you sure?"

"Of course. I'll even have it catered. Let me do that for the two of you."

"I couldn't ask you to do that. That's way over the top."

"Nonsense. If you have it catered, it won't drive you crazy with all the work. They come in, prepare, then clean up, and you're left with a beautiful house with wonderful memories. You don't have to spend a week to clean up after, either. Seriously, it's the only way to go."

"Well then, I accept. On one condition."

"Sure, what?"

"I want Damon's approval first."

"He's coming out here?"

"He is. In about two weeks." She didn't want to discuss Ainsley's possible visit yet so left it at that.

"I'm so excited. I hope he likes it."

MARTEL LEFT AIMEE'S house feeling very light and hopeful. On the way back to her place, she got a call from her attorney.

"Our private investigator has come up with some past arrest records for Mrs. Gibbs' father and two uncles. They all center around child sexual abuse. Unfortunately, it goes back generations. It's heartbreaking. She probably grew up in it and was a victim herself."

"It fits the pattern, doesn't it?" Martel said. "I feel so sorry for those kids in that family."

"We have some choices, so I need to know. You could report your suspicions. Child Protective Services will have to investigate, but it could hit the paper and get lots of publicity."

"Is that what you'd do?"

"I would."

"I think I want that too. Main thing is to get Cora some help. The whole family is going to need help."

"Always a possibility when it hits the paper, they'll mention how the investigation started. I just want you to be okay with the extra scrutiny."

"I want what's good for Cora. This isn't for me. It's for Cora."

"Brave little lady, if you ask me. I'll email you some of the investigator's findings, the arrest records, which are public record, but you have to know the dates and things to put them on the trail. There are several unsolved cases, too. We'd be helping the sheriff's department."

"Let's do it. I'm driving home right now. So does that solve the potential lawsuit with their attorney?"

"Only a matter of days now. I think you're almost in the clear."

"That's the best news I've had in a long time. Thank you so much."

"Not quite out of the woods yet but nearing the clearing, as we say. Don't forget to make that call."

"Nothing could tear me away from that mission. Thanks once again."

Her phone pinged, and she read the text message from Damon.

'Got approval for early release and leave. When should I come?'

She didn't have to think more than five seconds. She texted him back, *'How about tomorrow?'*

CHAPTER 21

Two Weeks Later

DAMON CHANGED HIS clothes three times before they left for the Tampa Airport, each time fussing with his balance, using the cane he'd been told to use to help support his new hip.

"You're fine. Don't keep doing that, Damon. She's not going to notice any of this," Martel insisted. "I don't want you to hurt yourself."

He'd started with khakis then some long Chinos, the relaxed fit jeans. His canvas slip-ons would go with either of these. He opted for a clean white button-down long-sleeved shirt. While Martel put away the two pairs of pants he didn't wear, he sorted through the three jackets he had, deciding on the dark grey one.

"Come on. Honestly, Damon, you're worse than any of my girlfriends ever were. As long as you smell good and don't look all wild and scary, she's going to like you just fine."

"Do I smell good? Tell me honestly."

She approached, delicately pulling his shirt toward her. Her forefinger ran across his lower lip as she leaned into him and kissed him. It was natural to wrap his arms around her, pull her into his chest, and feel all the wonderful ways she filled all the vacant and painful parts of him. How could he have ever let her go? he wondered. What a complete idiot to have missed all those years. But she was here now, and he was going to make sure she never got away again.

His body responded with the delicious slow arousal that always had been there, from the first time he'd ever kissed her. With how she showed she needed him like tugging on the top button of his shirt or the way her fingers traced the arch of his ear or the satisfied look on her sweet face when she shattered beneath him, Martel always brought her A game. The more he spent time with her the more he couldn't live without her.

"I asked you if I smelled okay," he said between kisses.

"I'm thinking about it," her soft pink lips purred. She inhaled and her eyelids fluttered just a bit. "Oh my. I'm wet, Damon."

"That happens when you're pregnant too?"

"Why wouldn't it? I feel it. Why wouldn't I get ready for you? All those pheromones, all those ancient mating rituals through time that we're part of."

"So is it worth it to be late?"

"Maybe just a quickie, if you can."

"I can do it anyway you like it, sweetheart."

She had her clothes off within seconds. He removed his for the fourth time, knelt, and kissed her belly button.

"Now I get to have all this, to watch you grow, Martel. This time I get to have everythin."

He kissed her again there. "Thank you. Thank you bringing me this gift."

She lazily sorted through the top of his head as he stroked her wetness.

"I wish we had more time," she sighed.

"Honey, we got all the time in the world."

She turned to present her rear to him, and he slipped inside smoothly, feeling the early fullness in her breasts, one hand gently placed on her abdomen as he stroked her carefully, kissed her neck, and felt the ripple of her spine triggering his own arousal.

"I can never get enough, Martel. I never could. I still can't."

Her muscles contracted and fluttered. She reached behind, pulled her butt cheeks apart, and gave him deeper access, and he took every bit she would give him. "I can't wait to fuck you when you're huge."

"I get horny when I'm pregnant. I want it all the time, Damon," she whispered.

"Music to my ears, sweetheart. I'm going to make sure I'm here for you every time you want it."

Their quick interlude was over too soon but lingered still as he helped her get dressed and they drove to the airport, holding hands and kissing as he helped her out of the car and placed his palm on her ass and rubbed. It was divine being in love with her, made even more special by the fact that she was carrying his child. Again.

Not everything was settled with Martel's school situation, but with the potential lawsuit dropped, and the arrest of the mother's relatives, charged also with Cora's abuse, he could see some of her excitement for teaching and for the remainder of her school year coming back. Her teaching was as important to her as his being on the SEAL team. And, as long as he healed properly, and didn't get given a medical, they'd both be able to do what they loved to do, and do it in San Diego.

He'd stopped to buy some flowers this morning. As they stood in the lobby area waiting for the passengers to arrive on their way to baggage claim, he held those flowers, a spring bouquet with apricot daffodils.

As Martel greeted Mrs. Newberg, Damon saw Ainsley—her face almost like looking into a mirror and seeing his own face there. She was embarrassed, too, looked down at the flowers and then back at him, smiling, happy, tall, and strong. She was a beautiful young woman who was only going to be more beautiful as the years descended upon her. He extended his hand, and she took the flowers he offered. His heart beat so loud surely they all could hear it.

"And here you are. I get to meet you at last. I'm so proud, Ainsley. Thank you for agreeing to meet me."

"Of course," she said with a shrug, except she didn't convince him that she was casual about it. He felt it was as heartfelt for her as it was for him. She would always be a miracle to him, and he'd remember this day for the rest of his life.

Martel and Lori Newberg smugly smiled between themselves, having shared something he wasn't privy to.

How could he be so lucky that he could get to know this beautiful young lady with poise and grace, her long blonde hair like spun gold, with the clearest blue eyes he'd ever seen. He was completely enamored by her.

"Damon, this is Lori Newberg, Ainsley's mom."

Yes, she is her mother. "Thank you and so lovely to meet you."

"You're not at all like what I thought you'd be," she said.

"I know, you thought I'd be a big wild guy with tats all over his body and scars on his face or something?"

She giggled. "Something like that." She looked at Ainsley. "Right?"

"He does sort of look like Dad. Wait until you meet him. You'll get along with him, I know," she said.

Damon still couldn't take his eyes off her. "I'm speechless. I really am," he said.

"We'd better get downstairs and get their luggage before they put it in the lost and found, Damon. Can I peel you away for just a few more minutes until we gather everything up?"

"Of course. Here, let me take those," he said as he reached for her backpack and Lori's carryon bag.

"We're good. Help us with the heavy stuff," Lori Newberg said.

Downstairs at the claim, their bags were making their way around the carousel. Ainsley pointed out their luggage, and Damon retrieved them both, grabbed his cane and they headed for the short-term garage.

He listened to the ladies' happy banter, enjoying being in their presence. In just under an hour, they were turning off the freeway toward the beaches.

"Look at all that blue water, Mom. And all the boats!" Ainsley said.

"Really gorgeous. I can understand why you like it so much."

"I fell in love with this place the instant I took my first look at the Gulf and the white sand beach. I'm going to miss it, but I have so many happy memories here," Martel said.

He looked at her animated face. "And now you're about to make more memories, sweetheart." She smiled back at him.

At the house, all four of them stared through the sliding glass door onto the beach and glittering bay beyond.

"Come on, Ainsley, take a walk with me," he said to her.

"Okay. Mom, you want to come?"

"No, you go ahead. Take a walk with Damon. I'll stay here and get our things settled."

Damon observed her long gait as they headed down the beach toward the hard sand and the surf beyond. "We often do this at sunset. Wait until you see that. Really magical."

"There's no one here. I expected it to be crowded from all the news reports I've seen."

"A well-kept secret, my dear. Not everywhere looks like Miami. We like this sleepy little coastal community. The pace isn't too fast. It's quaint, in a way. All the normal people are here. That's what I keep telling Martel all the time."

"I always wanted to know what you thought when you first found out about me."

"I saw these pictures of Martel, month by month, and I couldn't believe it. I thought she'd had a baby with someone else, to be honest. She sat down and she told me, and then she showed me your picture in your school basketball uniform." Damon stopped. "It was a miracle, Ainsley. I couldn't believe it."

She liked that, Damon noted.

"What did you think when your parents told you about the adoption?"

"I didn't believe it at first. But then they explained that they chose me, that I was special. I always felt special."

"You are special."

"But they made sure every day was special for me."

"You're one lucky little girl. You have lots of people who love you, Ainsley."

"It's nice to finally get to meet you. And Mom says you're going to have another child?"

"We are. You'll be a big sister."

"Are you totally okay with all this? I mean, I'm going to still call them my parents, because they are. Does that make you feel bad?"

Damon smiled back. "Do I wish I'd done things differently? Yes. I think everyone always knows when they could have done things better. But the main thing is that we're all together now. And I get such enjoyment just being able to share a little piece of you. Thank you, Ainsley. I'll always be here for you. I'm never going away again."

LOVE'S TREASURE

Sunset SEALs Book 7

SHARON HAMILTON

CHAPTER 1

Ned Silver and the rest of his SEAL Team 3 buddies were unceremoniously dumped at the Coronado airport by a military-contracted flight. A group of women, parents, and children welcomed them just outside the chain-link fence near the visitors' reception area. The team had just returned from a short trip to Baja California. Hugs, giggles, and some tears were shed by the audience present to welcome their homecoming heroes. The team had only been gone three months, but that didn't interfere with the ardor or exuberance of their greetings.

None of them were there for Ned.

He slapped backs of some of his teammates, slung his duty bag over his right shoulder, waved at several faces in the greeting party he knew, passed by the rest of the family grouping, and gave a salute to two Lieutenant Commanders and their team handler. Then it was off to the parking lot to climb into his Hummer and crash at his condo with the tiny slice of ocean view so small he could measure it in inches.

He planned to call Madison, who was probably waiting tables and tending bar at the Salty Dog, but he wanted to organize his thoughts first.

His emotional state was flat. Not that he didn't *feel* things, but he just didn't have the energy to react to them. He didn't talk. He didn't smile. He didn't stare, and he'd tried to sleep during the bumpy flight from Cabo to Coronado but gave up unsuccessfully, turning it into a jostling, noisy meditation even his ear buds and Two Steps From Hell cranked up to nearly max volume couldn't drown out. Only good thing about it was that the noise made conversation impossible, while his closed eyes signaled he didn't want anyone to try.

As Ned approached the Hummer and climbed inside, he carefully pulled out his cell phone. Staring down at the dial face, he wondered if Madison would be able to hear his ring over the din of the usual noise on a Friday night at the Salty Dog. He imagined there would be live music, and the place would be packed, most customers looking for the snow crab special and happy hour pricing.

She picked up on the first ring.

"I got a little vibration on my fanny and could just tell it was you. So when the heck are you getting out here to Florida? I need you. How about driving for four days straight?" she asked in her fresh voice.

It was such a relief to hear her while he was standing on US soil.

"You can tell it's my call just by the way it tickles your fanny? Is that what you're saying?"

"Something like that. There's more to that story of course. But you'll have to stand in front of me naked before you're gonna hear it. I'm just wondering when that's going to happen."

"If you close your eyes, we could do it now. But if you want the real thing, I was planning on flying out tomorrow morning. I kind of need to sleep off some crummy shit, Madison. These deployments to Mexico never get any better. I wonder what the heck we're doing there. But I'm home, and that's all that matters."

She went cold stone quiet. He heard clanging in the background—dishes and their Cajun cook dressing down some poor kitchen help.

"Did I scare you off, Maddie?" he asked, thinking he might have offended her in some way.

"Not possible. Just thinking about you being here tomorrow has my panties soaking wet."

"I love the sound of that, sweetheart."

She paused, gave him an enormous sigh, and added, "Gotta distract myself with customers. Love hearing your voice, Ned. Can't wait until tomorrow. We've got a lot to talk about. And, of course, I'm requesting the use of your naked body, as much as you are up to, that is."

He chuckled. He liked that. "You know, I was kind of tired, but if you'd promise to talk to me the whole way, I might be able to drive straight through. What would it be? Forty-eight hours?"

He knew it didn't make sense but was all he could muster.

"I like the idea of you snuggling in your own bed tonight, getting all of those restorative juices back up and running and anticipating being here tomorrow. Oh, I almost forgot—bring some extra gear, Ned, if you have anything fancy to play with. Noonan's got a big new dive coming up, and we have to go deeper to get it." She ended her sentence with a sultry whisper.

"I like deeper."

"Yes. You. Do. And so do I. But any little extra gadgets or dive prototypes your bosses are testing might be helpful in this circumstance. And that's all I'm going to say. Night, sailor boy."

She signed off with a kiss, and now Ned was going to have to battle his hard-on all the way to his condo.

Madison had been the only woman he'd fallen head-over-heels for at first glance. Ned had never believed in such a phenomenon before he met her. She was all the right kind of long and lean in all the perfect places, muscular and strong where she needed to be.

He lay awake at night thinking about what she looked like swimming above him, with her darned pink flippers and the skin-tight wetsuit that accentuated her curves. Her blonde hair was usually tied in a long braid during dives, but he'd seen it floating all around her head like a golden cloud. She was the perfect vision of the perfect woman who Ned didn't have any right to claim for his own. But he was so glad that he did.

But the best part was she made him feel like Triton or Poseidon himself on his golden throne when she was beside him. She brought out all the best parts of him, and she kissed away and bandaged up his many flaws. He felt braver, more relaxed, and happier than he'd ever been before. He prayed they'd have time to explore and make this relationship into something lasting. That was his goal this visit—to build on what they'd started and make it permanent.

But just as fast as her vision appeared, it disappeared, and his chest filled with some dark foreboding left over from a difficult mission in Mexico. And they were all getting hard—each one worse than the next. Something had been eating away at the Team. Everything seemed to be off-kilter, out of sync. There were fights amongst the men—small disagreements at work irritating him. He found he didn't have the patience to deal with the group dynamics. He began to wonder if he still fit in.

Has it come to that?

One of the things he had learned from the older team guys, including Kyle, was that the time to get out was when it wasn't fun anymore. Was it now a challenge because he wanted to do different things with his life since meeting Madison? He'd put in a good ten years. He had an exemplary record and was told he'd be up for promotion soon, if he wanted it. Kyle had encouraged him to go to OCS. But Ned wasn't sure the Navy was his real future any longer. He'd enjoyed it, but less now. Perhaps the end of the road had come.

Ned worried what Madison would think or whether he should even tell her until he was sure. They'd made plans to be together after this last deployment, and that spark was still there he'd missed these past two months. But there hadn't been a formal commitment made. It was loosely assumed. That's the way most of Ned's life had been run.

He was conflicted. With this new relationship, his life was more complicated.

Am I really ready for this? Is this what I really want? Am I making the right decision in waiting, or should I just say "fuck it" and do it?

He felt like he was in two places at the same time. He let his mind wander all the way home.

Would Madison be in favor of him leaving the teams? Or would she distrust a decision abandoning a good paying job, leadership potential, and a real chance in a permanent career for the life of a beach bum, perhaps helping her tend the Salty Dog? Yes, they might run into some serious cash with his treasure dive. But that wasn't a sure thing. And he wanted a sure thing before he made that life commitment to Madison.

The story of the old barge that sank off the Florida coast, along with hundreds of other ships that had also perished there over time, piqued his thirst for adventure and love of history. They'd been contracted by a family to find a missing artifact, a dog collar, which had sentimental value to the family and belonged to the cook's dog, Otis. In that story was an old romance, a story of love lost. Of course, with the backdrop of the Civil War brewing and the age of piracy having just passed its heyday, it was already full of intrigue and danger. But adding the fact that they found a Spanish Galleon during their search made it an even greater story.

He'd been called up on deployment without having his rightfully earned time to do the exploration and had missed out on some of the adventure.

If Madison was correct, maybe old Noonan had discovered something else. It was always possible. But his visit back to Florida didn't have anything to do with buried treasure. It was really all about Madison. She was the real treasure in his life.

He laid everything out on his bed, packed and unpacked several shirts, shorts, and all his flip-flops. He really didn't have much left, except for the bolted armory box in his closet. It would not be possible to bring all his weapons since he was going to fly. Perhaps he could talk one of the other SEALs he met in Florida to drive them out for him. But that was a small problem. A minuscule problem at that.

You shouldn't be concerned about little things, Ned. Only the big stuff counts.

He walked through his apartment one more time after he showered, put on his pajama bottoms, stared at the bare walls—still empty since he never had time to decorate and never entertained. There was a definite look of a bachelor pad here; no trace of a woman existed. Even a used nighty or some underwear would make him feel better, but it just wasn't there. This was not where his love was, where he wanted to be, where he needed to be to survive. This was the place he crashed, restored himself in between deployments, and hoped the rest of his life showed up.

He placed his final choices inside his duffel bag, including a few pieces of gear he picked up at one of the scuba dive shows he'd attended in San Diego, the book of poetry his mother had given him, a few pictures of her and his dad, and a handful of things from his childhood in a small box, and zipped the whole package up.

It felt like he was never coming back, or perhaps the man who would walk in the door the next time would be different than the man standing here now. Whichever way it flowed, he was just going to go with it, see where his heart took him, and let fate and the mermaid take hold of his hand and lead him down that blue watery path.

BEFORE TURNING IN, he called his mother.

"Oh, Ned, I'm so happy you're safe and going back out there again. I had such a lovely time. I just keep seeing those beautiful sunsets, that white beach, Madison's mother's colorful paintings in the house, her caftan, and all her eclectic friends. I felt like I was twenty years old."

"I noticed. And I'm glad. I think you should fly out there again."

"Well, your aunt is adjusting quite well, and with each passing week, she seems to recognize me less and less, so there is that possibility now, but I'll visit more often. Amberley has invited me to stay with her if I want it. It would just be temporary."

Ned was glad to hear the happiness in her voice. She was beginning to explore outside her small world in San Diego after Ned's father's death. It was a healthy sign.

"I think that's a fine idea."

"Really? You really do?"

"I know I was quite harsh with you the first time I saw you there. It was a shock. No one told me you were coming. But after I saw how everyone fit in, I realized I was just the last one to accept what everyone else already knew."

"I was not happy with how that happened. But I'm glad you found your peace with it. I don't think there was any other way that it would've worked for me, except to just jump in. You know, dive in headfirst like you do."

"No, we don't dive in headfirst, Mom. We jump in with our flippers first. We sort of slip into the water seat. That's the way we do it. You dive in headfirst and, all of a sudden, you've lost all your gear."

His mother laughed. It was great to hear the mirth in her voice.

"Oh, Ned, I think the way you describe things is marvelous. Of course, it would be me who would think about jumping in head first. I've always been risk averse."

"Not so, Mom. Remember, you married old Jake, the pirate. That was a leap of faith if ever I heard one."

She chuckled. "Now you've made me spit out my tea!"

They ended their call with a promise to meet up in Florida again in a few weeks' time. Ned let his mother know that he was considering leaving the Navy. She was cautious in her response but said she trusted him.

Ned wasn't sure he could trust himself.

Before retiring, he checked his voicemail and chose to listen to Noonan's message, since Madison had already spilled the beans.

"I'll be picking you up in Tampa. But I just couldn't wait. Ned, this is the call I always wanted to make to your dad. But now I have the honor to give it to you instead. We're going to be fucking rich, my boy! And Otis's collar led me right to it!"

CHAPTER 2

THE AIRPORT WAS as busy as it always was. San Diego, a huge military hub, was dotted with uniforms of all branches. Wives, husbands, and loved ones greeted soldiers coming home, including an occasional honor guard standing to attention to receive coffins sadly returning. Young men and women said their goodbyes to young brides, husbands, and children. Pregnant wives and children waited impatiently for the sight of that one special person to come bounding down the corridors of the airport and into their arms. Young women, also in fatigues, said goodbye to their children and families, arms wrapped around each other in groups of two or three, heading off to an occupation somewhere. Ned saw these service men and women as members of his tribe, and he was honored to be counted among them.

He was offered a first-class upgrade because of his military ID and sat next to an attractive young woman heading back to Dallas and her home nearby. He always loved listening to Texas accents, especially on women. She was about ten years his senior, very well educated, and delightful to sit next to. She was well-versed in many subjects—especially travel and world affairs—and had a nice manner without being overly opinionated. He liked that. There were a lot of things ruminating inside him he wasn't sure he was ready to open a discussion about.

"What do you do in Dallas, if I may ask?" He wasn't sure it was the right thing to do, but she'd been very pleasant and didn't ask him a single question. She'd made comments about his tats and suggested she knew he had a dangerous job. He liked that too. It made him trust her, even if just a little bit. She wasn't pushy.

The question elicited a measured smile, more like a smirk, followed by a sigh as she rolled her eyes. He knew he wasn't going to like what she had to say next.

"Actually, I'm a psychologist. I pegged you for a military man, because I work with a lot of vets. Sadly, I work in suicide prevention."

Her sparkly green eyes studied him carefully as he decided what face to show her. This was uncharted waters.

"Wow. I tip my cap to you, ma'am. I'm not sure I could do that. I mean, I'm there for my buddies, people I know, but I'm not sure I could ever do that for strangers. But you're right. It is a problem. And I'm glad you're addressing it."

"You know, I find that most of the really tragic suicides are not people that run around all crazy and freaked out all the time. That's not a psych or medical term, by the way. It's a favorite term of my mothers, from her hippy days." She smiled, which disarmed him. Finding words all of a sudden became awkward.

"I use freaked out a lot. On the Teams." Ned immediately wished he could take those words back and realized he had breached the wall he meant to avoid. He hadn't wanted to tell her he was a SEAL. But he continued anyway.

"Oops, my loose tongue gave myself away, I guess. I'm with a Team at Coronado."

"I was just there, working with a group of Navy recruits, giving a couple of lectures. I also was contracted to do some assessments of a unit that suffered heavy casualties in a rescue operation. I believe some of your SEAL brothers were in that operation, if I could be so bold as to say that."

He knew about the tragic rescue operation where half of SEAL Team 5 Charlie platoon was gunned down in an ambush in West Africa. It was not part of the globe he looked forward to going back to anytime soon. Mexico was almost as bad to him.

"You're talking about the guys on SEAL Team 5?"

She nodded, a tiny frown line exposed between her eyebrows. "As I said, most of the damage happens internally. You guys are trained to hide it. And you must, in combat situations. I know platoon leaders who suffer nightmares for twenty years or more afterwards, when they lose guys or even have guys that are injured or permanently disabled. Choosing who to send and who to keep back has to be done in a non-emotional way. However, the results can wind up causing an extreme emotional reaction."

Ned looked straight ahead, not willing to reveal anything of that emotional side. He'd seen one man fall in his ten years as a SEAL and heard about others, people he knew, guys he really liked. Even a couple of assholes got wounded, and he still felt sorry for them.

But he wasn't going to be confide any of this. It just wasn't right, wasn't something he felt he could reveal to someone, no matter how professional they appeared, how reasonable they were, even if it might benefit him or bring some comfort. He'd remain tough, even though he knew that was bullshit.

She must have sensed she'd hit a nerve. She quietly removed herself from the conversation and returned to her magazine. Ned was relieved.

When they landed in Dallas, she slipped him her card and promised that she would return the phone call if ever he wanted to chat or ask questions about her work. She always considered her work with individual vets, especially the elite core, to be just service done *gratis*.

"It was very nice to talk to you. I enjoyed it," he lied. "And now I realize I don't even know your name." Ned scanned her business card and tried, "Sherine?"

"That's the name my mother gave me. I don't necessarily like it, but I'm sticking with it." She extended her hand. "You have yourself a nice weekend, Sailor. I hope you don't miss your next flight. Dallas/Fort Worth is known for plucking people from their dreamy vacations and making them spend it in an uncomfortable chair for hours, sometimes all night. If that starts to happen,"—she leaned over and whispered softly—"let them get you a room. That's the least they could do." After they shook hands, she added, "Thank you for your service, and I know that's trite, but I mean it. You're one of the good guys."

Before he could answer, she was halfway down the hallway. The view of her graceful frame moving down the corridor towards baggage claim and the tram was not unpleasant.

Ned checked the gate for his connecting flight to Tampa and headed the opposite direction. He tucked her business card into his wallet and began to anticipate seeing Madison.

Hours later, his connecting plane took a hard landing, like one of those monster transports he was used to. It caused some of the overheads to spill their contents on the vulnerable passengers below. Ned assisted getting the bags safely stowed away, lending a hand to the attendants, even though the plane was still making its way down the runway to the gate.

The instant Ned walked from the downstairs baggage claim to the outside pickup area, the warm Florida evening caressing him all over, he was suddenly filled with joy. This was the place he belonged now. He chuckled that he'd been so nervous. But now he knew, this was it. It almost didn't matter what Madison said. He wanted to spend the rest of his life here.

The pirate was there to pick him up as had been previously

arranged. The old man ran with a limp and nearly body slammed Ned, which was borderline humiliating. The crusty friend of his recently passed father was difficult to shake.

As Ned tried to extricate himself, the pirate kept his right arm around his neck and whispered in his ear, "Ned, my boy. Hope you got my message. We're going to be so stinkin' rich you'll get tired of spending all the money. I wish your father were alive to experience it all. But we've hit the mother lode!"

CHAPTER 3

MADISON KEPT CHECKING her cell phone, waiting for the call from Ned informing her that he had arrived. The Salty Dog was chock-full of snowbirds this evening, people who were fleeing the bad weather of the Northeast, Midwest, and even wildfires in California and Oregon.

She was training another new girl but kept an eye on a second bartender the owner had added. She suspected him of stealing from the till. She knew it was a common occurrence for bartenders, but that didn't make it right. It cheated everyone, and she had no patience for it.

Her mother was dressed in what she called her "highbrow hippie attire", the look she probably wore in her twenties. Now in her mid-fifties, Amberley's long, gray flowing curls and all the bright colors she could muster made her just as disarming as a twenty-something walking through the Salty Dog in a bikini.

She probably did that too.

But that was her mother—always looking to cause a stir, a lasting impression, impossible not to forgive when she erred, and double impossible not to laugh with. In fact, Madison hadn't met a single person who could be considered her enemy. Amberley got along with everyone.

The entertainment this evening was a pair of young songwriters, each wearing guitars that looked too big for their small frames. But their voices were very melodic, and although it was nothing you could dance to, the music was all original and very good. The crowd wasn't going to allow it to dampen their mood. The duo might as well have been screeching out soul music, the crowd was so enthusiastic.

She felt her phone flutter it in her back pocket.

"So you're here!" she squealed.

"In the flesh, Madison. Surviving another raucous ride with the pirate, who doesn't drive as good as he pilots a boat. But I don't think he's drunk."

In the background, Madison you could hear old Noonan La Fontaine's voice barking, "Not yet at least!"

"Well, just tell him to slow down, because I have plans for you, and it will be greatly interfered with if you're all bruised and bloodied. Tell him to get you here in one piece."

"Yes, ma'am."

Madison signed off quickly after noticing a fight developing at the end of the bar between two seventy-year-old men fighting over the same white-haired woman.

A couple of the owners' security guards were able to lend a hand, but the two men were quite difficult to separate. It was enhancing the entertainment value of the whole place. The police were called, and the two were removed from the premises, leaving the woman to fend for herself.

Madison approached her, considering offering assistance. "I guess nobody asked you if you have a way home?" she asked the frightened woman.

"I've got Carl's set of keys, luckily. But I don't have his house key. I guess I'll be spending the night in a motel."

"I certainly hope this sort of thing doesn't happen all the time. Are these guys friends?"

"Funny you should say that," the woman answered. "They're actually brothers. My mistake for dating both of them and marrying one of them very briefly. None of us expected to meet up again in Florida, but as they say, things happen in the Gulf. I was not prepared for this."

The woman straightened her dress, took down her hair and re-clipped it up at the top of her head again. Madison had an idea.

"Do you see that attractive woman over there sitting with several people at that table?"

The woman nodded quickly.

"Her name is Amberley, and she's my mother. She's usually a great shoulder to cry on, knows all the eligible locals, and is a great friend. She collects people like stray cats and turns them into prized possessions."

"She's your mother, you say?"

"Unbelievable, right?"

"Now that you tell me, the two of you actually look quite a lot alike. I'm sorry I didn't see the resemblance. You are sure she'd be okay with a stranger crashing her little foursome?"

"The more the merrier. She'll tell you the same thing if you ask her."

Madison followed the woman as she introduced herself to her mother and three others seated at the table, all men. One guy stood, bowed slightly, and brought a chair for her. That made the odds shift a bit, two women for three men. Madison figured that was about right.

Ned's rock-solid frame sauntered in through the double doors open to the night air. The sight of him always gave her butterflies and sucked the wind right out of her. His lithe body, with muscles that could fill out a pair of jeans very well, made a beeline for her with a gait and swagger that only a tall man could afford. He stared right at her, and her heart skipped a couple of beats as he crossed the hushed room.

"Well, look what old Noonan dragged in this evening."

He stepped up on the bar rail, leaned over, grabbed her face in his huge hands, and planted a deep, wet kiss on her lips. "Miss me?"

Madison loved the way he made her swoon. "Of course. More than breathing. More than life itself. So how was it?"

This tour in Mexico had been unlike several others the Team had taken, and Madison wasn't quite sure what they'd run into, but Ned had never been on a deployment, short or long, where he didn't call home every day. Yet for this one, she had to do most of the calling or she suspected she wouldn't have spoken to him at all.

Ned's expression went dark. He was good at drawing out the face armor, that part of him that was so difficult to read, especially when his mouth smiled but his eyes looked dead. He was trying very hard to look cheerful, but she knew something was wrong.

"It went okay. I'm glad it's over. And that's all I wanna say tonight, if you don't mind." Ned was very clear in dishing out ground rules. Madison didn't want to risk crossing any of those lines. He'd talk about it when he was good and ready, and not before then.

"Hey, Ned, this is me. This is paradise, your home," she reminded him.

That did the trick. He rewarded her with a broad smile.

"Any chance you could get off early?" he asked.

"Not much. But if you want, you can take my car. I'll catch a ride home with one of the other girls. You can shower, unpack—maybe walk the beach a bit until I'm done here. We are a bit short-staffed tonight, as always. We've already put down one fight, and I'm hoping the crowd will settle down a bit. I'm cutting off a few people, requesting a couple get a taxi and go home, and pretty soon will stop taking orders for dinner."

"Nope." Now he was dancing with that playfulness she loved. "I'm going to sit right over there near your mother, eavesdrop, and watch you scrub down those counters, bend over to pick up beer bottles, and lean over the counter with that very awesome but way too small T-shirt you've got on there."

"So I'll consider myself monitored then, is that right?"

"Abso-fuckin-lutely."

It had been over two months since Ned's arms had encircled her waist, since she'd experienced how artfully, delicately he undressed her, playing her body like a finely-tuned violin. Whatever darkness or questions she had about his demeanor were completely obliterated as they took their time, got reacquainted, and connected both spiritually and physically. He lovingly shattered all her fears except one.

She'd be desperate without him.

She told herself over again that these weeks of separation were things she had to get used to, that it wouldn't interfere with her happiness, her daily life. Now, in Ned's arms, she felt like he had brought her back to life—resuscitated after a long sleep under water. The magic of their love overcame the impossible odds. She'd been so wrong about this. And just like all the other times he'd been deployed, the leaving was getting more and more difficult. She suspected that this one would hurt more than the rest but tried to convince herself otherwise. Now she understood.

She'd been wrong.

They didn't make it home for hours. After they made love, he lay back against the pillow, watching the moon darting behind large white clouds on the horizon. Madison placed her cheek over his left upper rib cage, rubbing her hand up and down the ripples of his abs. She felt safe, secure, and never wanted to leave his side.

Seconds later, Otis jumped up on the bed and attempted to

bury himself in the soft covers between them, making little squeaky moans that had them both giggling.

"Why, you little rascal. Look at you!" Ned laughed.

As if embarrassed by his own boldness, Otis ducked his head beneath a flap of sheet beneath Madison's upper chest.

"He's my constant companion. After you left, he made the adjustment easily coming over to my place. I don't think he'd hurt anyone, but he's a heck of a watch dog," she added. In babytalk, she whispered, "We were good for each other, weren't we, Otis?"

The dog lifted his head, stared back and forth between the two of them, and then attempted to bury himself again in the covers.

"I'm surprised he didn't bark at me. I've been gone so long in this dog's life."

"I think he's a keeper, Ned. I leave him inside now most the time, only let him out for brief potty breaks or when he sees something he wants to chase. Have to be careful though, or I'll be running down the beach while Otis is in search of a pelican or egret."

"We'll take him to the dog park later, after I figure out what's going on here. Glad you're taking care of my girl, Otis." he said as he scratched the top of the dog's head around his ears.

The dog accepted the praise and, as if working on a checklist in his head, jumped off the bed to pursue something else in the house.

"Independent, too," Ned commented.

"Very. Still a little unpredictable but loyal. I think he's grateful after being a street dog for who knows how long. I'm glad you befriended him."

She adjusted herself against Ned's hard body, which was sweating like a turbine, blood infusing into his muscles and regulating his heartbeat, which had gone from racing to nearly normal, just like hers. She knew he had questions for her.

So did she.

"Tell me about this new dive of Noonan's. He was all excited about striking it rich, and I practically had to put duct tape over him in the airport for fear of him telling everybody at the baggage claim about it," Ned chuckled.

"That's Noonan. Except this time, I think he really has found something. He wanted to wait until you came before he explained it to both of us. He just couldn't hold it any longer. But yes, he thinks we're all going to be buying houses on the beach. Can you believe it?"

"I guess if he hadn't been such a good friend of my father's, I might believe him more. I don't think he's conning us, Madison. I just wish he'd be a little more discreet about it. And he normally is. I hope he's got it all locked up this time." Ned's eyes stared from under worried brow lines.

"After the first dive, when we had to fend off those jerks who tried to take it all away, I would've thought the old captain would be a little more careful. So I think you're right, Ned. We better talk to him right away and make sure he doesn't blow it for all of us. And I think it would be best coming from you."

"I suppose, after all these years of looking and then finally getting something, it's a temptation that's hard to resist. But I thought he catalogued all those things the last time. I know he got paid something by the big boys he brought in. Not that I was expecting much, but I haven't seen a dime. Have you?" he asked.

"He got enough to pay off the boat. But, no. Nothing so far. He said there were expenses and he'd explain. Mother says he's a man of his word." Madison wanted to trust him, and it didn't take much convincing to ease off her questions of the old crusty friend of her mother's.

"This appears to be a new find, and I don't think he's obligated to share it with anyone except you and me."

Madison nodded agreement and then laid her head back on the pillow next to Ned's. She thought about what it would feel like to be rich. She wondered, would it change them? Would he become a different person? Would she? Would it bring more danger than it was worth in the long run?

She decided now was a good time to begin some of her questions. Lacing her fingers through his hair, she asked, "How much time do you have here, Ned? How long do I have you for?"

He hesitated before answering then cleared his throat and began. "I've been giving it a lot of thought. And I want to talk to you about that too. But if Noonan's right, then maybe living here would be my destiny. I've asked for two months' leave. That should give us enough time to sort all this out. After that, I'll have to make a decision about going back to Coronado."

Her heart was dancing in a cascade of rose petals.

His warm eyes saw all the way to her soul. "I felt when I arrived tonight that I had come home."

"You have."

"What if I don't have to leave?"

"What about the Team, Ned?"

"The Team—all the Teams—will still be there. But maybe I won't."

Madison's breath hitched as if she'd been punched in the stomach. "Don't say that!"

"Look at the chances for happiness we all don't take? None of us knows how long we're going to live, Maddie. I'm not afraid of that. But I do have some control over where I spend my days—however many I have left. And who I get to spend it with."

Her eyes filled with tears, and she let them fall back into her hairline and into the pillow below. He said a lot in those few words, but he had not asked her to marry him. She was hopeful that would be part of the picture, but she didn't want to ask. She wanted to hear it without having to request he say so.

She preferred to dream about what it would be like to wake up every single morning with him at her side. Not just for a few stolen evenings or days or weeks at a time, but *forever.*

She was going to keep her hopes up but still protect her heart. Her mother had always been the one to believe in fairytales, but Madison grounded herself in reality. Now all of a sudden, their roles were reversing.

"Talk to me, Madison. Tell me how that makes you feel." He kissed the side of her face and then pulled back after noticing her tears. "Have I hurt you somehow?"

"Not in the least, my love. It's just all so overwhelming. But I do like having you here, and I wish you never had to leave. So if you're looking for some kind of encouragement about perhaps leaving the Teams, I'll happily be your cheerleader."

"I'd love that, Maddie. Let's see what Noonan has to present to us. I want this to be a decision we make together. I want to make a life with you, Madison. I can't be a Boy Scout forever."

It wasn't the whole enchilada, but it was pretty darned close. She wasn't sure about the new dive being a dominant factor in his decision, because it really was his decision to make whether or not he remained a SEAL. What she wanted to hear was that his love for her was all he needed, and it wasn't there.

Yet.

But yes, it was close. She allowed herself to feel giddy. She knew pressuring him or asking for an outright commitment might not get the result she was hoping for. So she turned and said, "You'll always be a Boy Scout, Ned. You can't help but save the world. It's just that people in Florida need some saving to. And I love the idea of never watching you run off to some dangerous place to save others when there's so much you could do here."

"Sweetheart, something tells me we're in for a big adventure.

We better buckle up and get ready for the ride of our lives."

His passionate kiss transported her to a cloud floating in the sunset overlooking the Gulf of Mexico. Maybe her mother was right.

Maybe miracles really do happen.

CHAPTER 4

SLEEP DEPRIVED, NED brought Madison to the restaurant they arranged to meet Noonan at. This was the morning of his big reveal, and Ned hoped pulling himself out of a bed he could lazily spend the next twenty-four hours in was worth it.

Normally, he'd be irritated with his two or three hours of sleep, but last night had been the best kind of tug-of-war. It took a couple hours before he could finally relax and really enjoy the bedtime play. That was always one of the highlights of being with her. Her energy drove him forward, bringing out more passion than he'd experienced before. He would've loved her anyway, of course, but this was just icing on the cake.

He wished he didn't have to wait to explore what moving here to Florida would mean for them both. This new dive had altered his plans somewhat. But he'd give Noonan time, especially if it involved some adventure and the possibility of finding a fortune to stake their new life on.

Madison snuggled closer to him, reached over, and grabbed his orange juice, having finished her own first. He pretended to be territorial of the sweet liquid but followed it up with a smile. She could strip him of everything he owned, and he'd still die a happy man.

"Do you know, Ned, I could get used to this? I kind of like that discussion we had last night."

Her big blue eyes looked up at him, and he was hooked all over again, wishing they'd spent an extra hour or two at home in bed before showering and getting down here.

"I'll have to adjust to sharing my O.J."

"Small price to pay, right?" she said, brightly.

"I don't ever want to get *used* to this. I want it to be fresh and exciting and something different every single day."

She gave him back a puzzled expression.

"Oh, excuse me," he quickly added. "I didn't mean a different position every day. That's not what I meant. What I mean is…"

She placed her palm over his lips. "I know what you mean. I feel the same way too."

How did he get so lucky?

She was so easy to love, firm and stubborn in all the right ways, funny as heck when the mood struck her. So damn sexy and logical at the same time. He was reminded of that math teacher in high school who wore big black horn-rimmed glasses but had a knockout figure, cute little upturned nose, and pert lips. She used to drive him crazy, and at those very moments, when he was at his peak of intoxication and fantasy, she would call on him to answer a question he never heard.

Just then, Noonan La Fontaine darkened the restaurant entrance, searched from side to side, and spotted them in the corner. He was carrying a briefcase, but all the rest of him was pure pirate captain. He didn't dress up. In fact, as he sat down, Ned realized he probably was wearing the same clothes he wore picking him up at the airport the day before.

"So how are you two love birds?" Noonan sat the briefcase on his left in the booth, leaning across the table. The waitress filled his coffee cup without him asking.

When neither of them jumped to give Noonan an answer, he waived his fingers in front of their eyes and remarked, "Oh! I get it now. This won't take too long, so you'll have plenty of time for a nap this afternoon. But first, we eat, and then we talk about some business."

"Is this the same site we were at before? Or have you located something else?" Ned asked, ignoring Noonan's instructions.

"We've harvested almost everything from that site, and of course, we're not allowed to disturb too much of the seafloor for environmental reasons. Now it's up to the archaeologists to do their research. There turned out not to be very much silver after all. Most everything will be placed in the University's Museum collection for future study. Lots of interesting tools, utensils, and such, but not much as far as silver or gold bullion. The Galleon and what was left of the barge are not ours any longer."

Ned was surprised at this, and it must have shown on his face.

"What happened?" Madison asked.

"Lawyers! How I hate them. Contract fine print. The University has a ton of them. And tree-huggers, environmentalists combing over every splinter down there."

"There are no forests down there," said Madison.

"You'd be correct. But there are kelp forests, no trees. Doesn't mean they don't look for them, though. Some group claimed the site was home to an endangered starfish colony, if you can believe such foolishness. How can you endanger a starfish? They grow back arms and legs, and you can grow new starfish from amputated legs just like cactus! These scientists are nuts. Fuck science!"

"Sorry to hear that," Ned whispered. He glanced around the room to see if he'd stirred up any interest amongst the other patrons and found none. "Keep it down, okay?"

Noonan interrupted him. "You remember Travis and Gary, don't you?"

"Just get to the stuff we can understand, will you?" Ned insisted, lowering his voice and requesting Noonan do the same.

"I had to give up before I used all my proceeds fighting them off. So it's done. I gave them the site. Washed my hands of it."

"Done? As in all done, Noonan?" Ned asked.

"I know you are telling yourself how could I turn over the site? Well, I'm not, really. The part that landed at the bottom with the figurehead? It's not the most important part. It probably was a huge weather event, likely a hurricane that occurred soon after the ship went down, separating the two halves."

Noonan leaned forward and whispered, "I've located the stern. It lies nearly twelve miles from the original crash site, and I think it was towed there originally, perhaps as part of a salvage operation to be re-explored later. Something happened, either natural or man-made. It looks like someone tried to cover parts of the wreck up with rocks and boulders, or somehow an event occurred that rained down these rocks, but over time, the entire hull has been filled with sand."

He gulped his coffee and tapped his fingers on the table, surveying the restaurant one more time before he dug into his briefcase and pulled out a leather pouch. Inside was a cleaned and partially eaten-away mesh of fine chain, with clusters of large stones the size of his fingernails.

The dog collar.

"How the hell…?" Ned started.

"Someone found it maybe more than a hundred years ago. It had been cleaned and dried, partially repaired. See?" He showed where portions of the links were replaced with new material.

"But how did it get preserved so well?" Ned asked, fingering the collar.

"It was buried in a jaw that remained relatively air-tight, in a crypt, probably interred with the guy who found it. He didn't fare as well as the collar did, I'm afraid to report."

"How did it get back in the ocean? That's where you found it, right, Noonan?"

"Yes. Old sly Davey Jones went and took it back. This nameless soul's remains were reclaimed to the Bay in the crypt he was buried in, during the great hurricane of 1863."

Noonan pulled out some large photographs, which were grainy at best, and handed them over.

"I had these taken last week before I called you, Ned."

Ned looked over the poor-quality, colorless image.

"This looks deep, at least deeper than the other one," he mumbled.

"And that's exactly why no one has found it. In fact, I even suspect there's been a minor earthquake below, because only portions of this vessel can even be seen. Take a look at this, though." He pointed to a dark pile of rocks, not like piles of cannonballs but angled pieces of rock, almost as if the ocean had found concrete from an abandoned roadway.

Ned pointed to one enormous dark grey structure, the crypt. "I don't see a single thing in this picture that makes me think of anything about a shipwreck. Why do you think this is the hull of a buried ship?"

"Oh! Very astute!" He demonstrated a number of dark gray striations in the bed floor. "These are not only draglines, but I believe they will show evidence of the ship's mast. See how long and perfectly straight they are? If she was bottom or stern-heavy, the mast might have been placed toward the rear, not in the center or towards the bow. I think this ship was made for hauling heavy cargo." Noonan's eyes were wild with excitement. He searched between both Ned's and Madison's faces.

Ned was still confused. "But how is the ship's mast, made of wood, lasting three hundred years?"

"Because this particular vessel I traced back to the lady. Remember the figurehead that we found, a unique identifier and unlike anything else we'd seen? Remember?"

"How can we forget?" Madison answered.

Noonan continued. "I checked with the University of Florida maritime archives, because I felt like perhaps some academic had done some kind of vessel research and didn't realize that we had one of these here in Florida."

"One of what?" asked Ned.

"This ship did not come from Spain or Portugal or England. This ship was a privateer, a pirate ship. I think it was originally built or remodeled not in one of the great shipyards in England or Spain, but it was a homegrown variety, perhaps built in the Bahamas, Antigua, or the Caribbean. It puzzled me when I saw the lady with..." Noonan demonstrated with his hands how the statue had extremely large breasts.

"I'll admit, that was a bit strange. They were oversized to put it mildly," said Ned.

Madison frowned at him.

"We're talking about an artifact. Who knows why it was made that way, Maddie?" Ned returned.

"And you would be correct!" Noonan barked, clapping his hands in front of him. "There's a whole story about that. In the late 1700s, Captain Falkland, who was the youngest son of a British admiral, left the family suddenly to seek his fame and fortune by asking for a charter from the Spanish crown. He wanted to be a privateer but was turned down by the Spanish court. In doing so, he also became an enemy of his own family and the English."

"Why would he give up a naval career since he was already a successful captain and a nobleman?" asked Ned.

"Yes, I thought the same thing. Then I read historical records at the museum and discovered, during this period, Spain was not willing to risk a row with the English. There had been a very fragile truce negotiated, codified by a public, high society wedding between an extremely rich merchant in Barcelona and the daughter of an English nobleman at court. And something went very wrong."

Ned sat back, watching Noonan's presentation growing to the boiling point. He knew Noonan's style of giving directions was always laced with a story, a really good sea story. He didn't disbelieve his friend. He only wished the old pirate would get to the point quicker.

Ned decided to demonstrate that by checking his watch, which immediately brought the desired reaction from his father's best friend.

"Hear me out, son," Noonan whispered. "I'm about to make you a very rich man. For that, I beg you to give me a little more indulgence."

"Go on."

"You see, as it turns out, this nobleman's daughter was endowed with a very large upper torso, similar to our lady. For all I know, it could be a portrait of her. The privateer was in love with her." Noonan shook his head from side to side. "I'm sure his affection was returned, but it was a double rejection for the young captain, since his love had been tragically betrothed over his objections, setting off a whole chain reaction of other consequences I'll get to later. Both countries were at the brink of war, and merchants on both sides were desperate to keep the peace, which was good for business. That was the reason he would not be granted his charter to go after the plunder he felt was due him in the Bahamas. But that was *not* the reason Captain Falkland wanted the ship."

"The Bahamas? And what was his reason?" Ned asked.

"Because it was his ship. He designed and retrofitted it for his life of piracy. And he was the captain when it was wrecked."

"His love married the merchant's son, and—"

"No, no, that's not what happened. Captain Falkland was going to target ships docking in the Bahamas, the British Virgin Islands, Antigua, and other places. It turned out that he also had several close friends who'd been conscripted in the most brutal manner to serve on British ships guarding important ports for the English in the Caribbean. He planned to return the favor by stealing them back into a life of piracy, since after their abduction, they were dead to the world anyway. He went there looking for manpower."

Madison leaned into Ned, resting her cheek on his shoulder. He drew his arm up and around her and kissed the top of her head.

"When can we get to the love story?" she sighed.

"I'm almost there, Dear," Noonan said, patting her hands on the table. "Although, it's a sad one, sorry to say."

"So tell me how this ship wound up in the bottom of the Gulf of Mexico, off of the Florida coast then, if all his operations took place in the Caribbean."

"Because, my friends, he was running away. Her father was looking for him, after his daughter was found to be with child, and this child is suspected of being the offspring of the young captain-turned-rogue. The rest of the story is that she stowed away to join Captain Falkland, in the Caribbean, and was never heard from again. The legend goes that she died in childbirth, and to erect a monument to her passing, he had the figurehead created and lashed it to the front of his pirate ship."

"Noonan, maybe it's because I just came over after more than two months of difficult action plans, and my brain is probably not working up to speed. But I'm confused. All these threads are making my head hurt," murmured Ned.

Noonan struggled to draw out the drama further, but even the pirate was getting tired.

Their waitress brought them the omelets they had earlier ordered, refills on coffee, and a whole pitcher of fresh squeezed orange juice. Everyone remained quiet.

"I want to hear about the metal mast," said Ned. "To my knowledge, during those days—unless we're talking about something much, much more recent—metal wasn't used. It was considered dangerous. It attracted lightning, and it was too heavy."

"That's where you're wrong, son. Yes, it was not used commonly, but metal masts were used in places that had access to a particular kind of metal."

"What do you mean, Noonan?" Ned asked.

"In the middle 1700s, gold was discovered in Mexico but also in Columbia as well. Other minerals were also found such as copper, tin, and huge deposits of silver. Since gold and silver were so heavy, anyone who might use them to embellish a ship would be adding extra tonnage to the draw. However, just like how we soup up cars today, some privateers created very intricate and complex designs using plating—converting regular cargo ships into first-class works of art. It was thought some privateers earned so much money in the trades all through the 1700s and 1800s, they would occasionally pour themselves sheets of gold or silver and hammer them into place over their masts. When these caught the light of the sun, they almost appeared like a ship approaching that was on fire. It scared everyone in their wake."

"I've never heard that before, but I can just imagine. So you think this hulk was one of those custom hot rod ships?" asked Madison.

"I do, and I have the proof." He tapped on the long striations in the black-and-white photograph. "It took something rather heavy, if it was dragged, to make lines like this. It could even be these are the actual pieces of the ship's mast, creating a sort of small ridge and valley, the characteristics of the gold or silver metal affecting what kind of plant and animal life attached to it."

"Fascinating. And these pictures, these are your proof?" ask Ned.

"They are, and I also have this."

Noonan punched his hand into his briefcase and pulled out a man's sock containing some kind of artifact. He looked behind him and then scanned the room before he laid the object on the table. It sounded like it was dense, probably metal.

He slipped the sock off and revealed a shiny, six-inch-long half-tube of silver.

Ned was shocked.

"It didn't look like this when I picked it up. I got lucky with a basket and dredged the bottom, and this came up with several other pieces of crude red clay pottery, containing iron remnants that, of course, created lots of associated layers of sea etching. I soaked it for two days in a special cocktail, peeled off some of the sea crust and debris, and eventually got down to the silver itself. Once I removed all the detritus, I was able to polish what was left. And you will see the filigree etched inside silver, the shape of the tube, and the fact that the edges are smooth, and contain holes for fixing this piece to another rounded object like a mast pole. I believe this is one of perhaps hundreds of pieces that adorned the ship."

"So what's the catch?" Madison asked.

"The catch?" Noonan barked, irritated. He slipped the object back into his navy-blue sock and tucked it away safely in his briefcase.

"Yes, the catch. You've already found this, and surely, you've laid claim to it. You have lined out people with specialized equipment ready to assist with the dive," she explained. "And just who were your divers and photographers for this?"

"Students. They have no idea we found anything except more artifacts for the University. No idea at all. I had to tow the crypt behind my boat and open it later without prying eyes."

"Oh, boy. We have a couple more Travis characters out there, then," remarked Ned.

"Nope, they've gone. Back home. It was just a Spring Break project, a scuba training project, that's all."

"So you can claim this?" Madison asked.

"It's a technical problem for me, because I was given permission to dive for architectural reasons and happened to find what we thought was a galleon. However, the gold and silver that normally would be carried by a galleon, we could never find. We found some gold and silver and jewelry remnants, but it wasn't really the mother lode we thought we had."

Ned waited for further explanation.

Noonan nodded. "You are due a few thousand dollars, but not the millions I hoped. My partners had to be paid back first, since there wasn't much to salvage. And that was always something that puzzled me and a mistake I didn't want to repeat. The portion of the ship we found didn't have any of this rigging on it, which I thought was logical at first. After all, it's quite common for these wooden timbers to be destroyed, like you pointed out, Ned, damaged by all the storms and currents until they disappear. But when I researched the statue and read the stories about the privateer's silver ship with the mast plated in silver, I knew I had to find the other half of the hull."

"So how did you find it?" asked Madison.

"I calculated the currents and also the records of weather conditions during those years, and I found one hurricane record that we might consider a Category 5 if it were to occur today. It came right across the islands here, long before there were many European inhabitants. There were Native Americans who traveled to the beaches for fishing parties, but I could not find any notation of the storm other than checking old records from the geological survey office. Since they weren't looking for shipwrecks or buried treasure, the record of the Category 5 hurricane hitting an uninhabited island was barely a footnote in history."

"Voila. The hurricane of 1863," Ned whispered.

"Exactly."

"But the damage to the sea bed could be extensive in that size storm," Ned added.

"Of course. And I calculated that the force of the storm would be enough to carry tonnage certain distances, plotting the minimum and the maximum amount they would travel. I also was under the assumption that these heavy pieces of metal would remain together or were somehow connected or lashed and, in this case, obviously screwed to timbers or railings or other parts of the ship instead of being thrown all over the seafloor, and I was right. It remained relatively intact."

"You haven't dived this site?" Ned asked.

"That's correct. And I haven't filed a claim, either. Since this is a deeper dive, I wanted people I could trust to go down and take a look first. Then I'll wade through the legal technicalities of whether or not this find needs to be shared with the family who originally hired me to find the dog collar, which is only a coincidence, or if I could claim the treasure for our own. I'm going to have my maritime attorney look into it. And I want to be fair with them. I'm not looking to cut them out, just want to maintain something for us."

"So this debris field is much deeper than the other site?" asked Madison.

"I believe it's between two hundred and two hundred fifty feet deep. We are going to need special equipment. Ned, I was hoping you could help us out with that."

"I've told you before I can't bring anything the Navy gave me. That's strictly forbidden, but I know some guys who freelance, and I think we can get ourselves hooked up with some prototypes the Navy doesn't have yet. Maybe they'll take their payment in terms of percentage of the find. But that requires us explaining to them what we think we found, which is dangerous."

"And, Ned, I'm going to rely on you and your best judgment to find me characters or partners we can trust. We had trouble with criminal elements the first time, but now this site is way more significant. It might attract a whole new class of criminal element. We're going to have to keep this very quiet."

"Then take my recommendation and stop shooting your mouth off excitedly, Noonan. I've been telling you this since I arrived," Ned reminded him.

He could feel Madison shaking next to him, and he knew she was having some fear issues. He was also concerned about their lack of numbers as far as protection. He didn't like the idea of having to hire too many people onto the dive, since it increased the chances of leaks occurring, which could jeopardize the whole project. But without the additional help, it would be impossible to control the security of this type of operation.

At the same time, Ned was excited about the possibility of finding the rest of the plates of silver covering the mast of the ship. He knew in his bones that it was going to add up to be a substantial fortune—once they located and brought them up.

"What do you say?" Noonan chuckled, scooping up a forkful of omelet he'd allowed to get nearly cold with all his storytelling.

"Well, Noonan, I think you've got yourself one Navy SEAL and a mermaid, if Madison's agreeable."

Madison nodded, her eyebrows raised and her shoulders rounded. She didn't quite exude the confidence that Ned had, but he could tell she was in.

"And I think I can find you maybe ten guys who might be perfect for this type of caper—men of action, who aren't afraid to protect what's theirs, guys who would be loyal. But the first thing I've got to tell you, Noonan, is this must be a legal dive. We can't get involved in something that is claimed by somebody else or by some foreign entity. You know that happens with shipwrecks."

Noonan sat back in the booth and crossed his arms in front of him. "I swear to you that I will make sure we don't get you guys stuck in something it would cost them their billet. It will be legal, and I'm going to be transparent with you all every step of the way."

Ned wasn't sure if Noonan was telling the truth or just making a hopeful exaggeration, but he still thought it would be safe enough to trust him. For the rest, they'd be looking for good luck. He'd built a career on the Teams based on that one factor alone, since most operations were shitstorms anyway, no matter how much advanced planning was done.

He felt Madison's blood pressure spike up again so asked about it. "Are you sure you're in, Maddie?"

"I can't help myself, Ned. If I don't try, I know I'll regret it the rest of my life."

CHAPTER 5

"WELL, WHAT YOU'RE telling me, Madison, is very exciting. But are you guys sure you're not getting involved in some kind of mess that will get you into trouble?" her mother asked.

"I've known Noonan longer than Ned has, not that I trust him completely. I think you'd say the same, Mother. He certainly has had a lot more experience than all of us combined. He's researched it. He's been doing treasure dives for—what?—thirty or forty years?"

"I think Noonan teased me one time that he could see little baby Noonan's on the beach, digging for shells or using a metal detector to find coins. I thought it was funny at the time, but shortly after that, we had a big falling out. That image still sticks with me to this day." Both women laughed. "He's an odd duck, definitely an acquired taste, but harmless for all the right reasons and trustworthy as far as he knows. His research is good, Maddie, but he sometimes cuts corners."

"But he's honest."

"Yes. He's honest. He tries to be with the facts he has to work with." She frowned and stared out at the ocean. "Just make sure you guys cover all your bases and are extremely careful. Let Ned handle the security. Noonan's just the pilot."

Madison knew that was sage advice.

"Now what did you really come over for, sweetie?" her mother asked, her eyes flashing with mystery and intrigue. Her depth of perception astounded Madison. She could never get away with any secrets, especially involving affairs of the heart. Her mother could pry her deepest thoughts from her just by that look in her eye. And she was a flawless guesser.

"During the dive, we'll be staying on one of the ships for three or four days. We're assembling the team now. Ned is drawing from his ranks in San Diego, from the Teams. I'm reaching out to some of my performance friends who are very experienced at working on dive charters. I hope to God they can cook too!"

Her mother had a belly laugh at that one, clasping her hands together. "You're a good cook, Maddie."

"Mom." She was stern with her answer and wanted to make sure it was clear. "I'm on the dive team period. I don't stay in the kitchen on this one. There's too much to see, and we're going deeper this time." She remembered Ned's admonition. "Remember, this is all confidential."

Amberley stood up, tossing her hair over her shoulder. "Then don't tell me anything more."

Madison rose to take her in her arms. "Mother, you're being ridiculous. You know how careful we must be. I promise to watch my tongue. But nothing. You can't say anything to anyone, understood?"

"I'll manage to keep myself on my best behavior. I promise." Her lower lip mimicked a pout Madison knew she must have given her mother when she was a toddler. "Sounds like you've got your hands full. I can only imagine the entertainment on board. Navy SEALs, your show buddies. That could be a very interesting combination."

"Ned is going to try to pick married guys."

"Oh, sure. That ought to work." Amberley winked at her

daughter.

"We need people we can trust. What they do in their off time is their business. As long as we have their loyalty, that's what we're looking for."

"So you need help with Otis, then."

"Well, yes. Would it be possible for me to bring him over here, so he's not left alone in the bungalow all day long, since I don't want you to have to be running back-and-forth between our two houses? I'd just like him to have a safe place to be and be given food and water regularly."

"The street urchin who found a home in your hearts. I think that's very sweet, and of course, I'd be happy to watch him over here. Does he still sleep with you on the bed?"

"Absolutely. And he'll keep you up all night if you don't let him."

Amberley stretched her arms to the ceiling and then bent over to touch the floor with her palms touching her toes. Madison was impressed that her mother was still so limber without doing any formal exercise, except walking. Lately, she hadn't either, and if it wasn't for the heavy lifting she was doing at the Salty Dog, she would be in worse shape than her mother. It kind of tickled her.

"So the man of the hour dropped you off, and when is he coming back?"

Madison looked at her watch. "Soon. Unfortunately, and the timing of this is horrible, my car is making all kinds of noises, so he's taking it over to the mechanic to take a look at it. I'm hoping for the best, but fearing the worst."

"I hate cars. That's why I stick to shopping within golf cart distance. If I need to go somewhere else, I'm going to be either hitchhiking or getting a ride with a friend."

"Tell me you've stopped hitchhiking, Mother."

"All in good time, dear. Soon. How about that?"

"It's dangerous! You read the stories, I'm sure. That's just not smart, Mom."

"Don't lecture me, Maddie. Life is dangerous. Every part of it."

"But—"

"Oh, come on. I much prefer driving my cart. No need to worry." She held her hands at her hips, staring right back. "Really."

"Well, I imagine it saves you a ton of money. No fill-ups."

"Exactly." She added, "Besides, the darn thing is so much fun to drive. Nobody expects this gray-haired woman to be driving a golf cart, often with people falling or hanging over all over it. It gives the young kids, you know, the teenagers, a double take."

Madison resigned herself to failure when it came to arguing further with her mother. She accepted the fact that Amberley refused to be run by fear, and it had always been this way.

There was a long silence between them, as Amberley sat back down on the couch, put her feet up on the cloth ottoman, and leaned back to face the ceiling. "I think there's something you're not telling me, sweetheart." She sat up again, stared into Madison's face, and demanded, "Spill it."

Madison was mortified that her secret had been discovered. She thought she'd been so good at covering things up, at least lately, but ever since Ned came back, her skills and techniques were rusty. Everything in her life had been thrown off-kilter, not that she was complaining, but just everything was off.

Her mother's intuition was always spot on, and she would feel like an undersized fish that had to be thrown back into the water if she didn't just come out with it. So she took a deep breath, blew it out, and repeated it one more time. Then she began.

"You probably think I'm pretty naïve, but I have a couple of things that are bothering me about Ned and me."

"Only a couple?" Amberly's eyes were wide and questioning.

"He's come out here and asked for time off. The Team isn't

deployed right now, of course, but he's asked for two months, and he expressed the opinion that perhaps he won't go back."

"Oh my God!" Her mother's expression was hard to read. "Isn't that good news, Maddie?"

"I-I just can't tell you right now. I can't determine how I feel about it. And I just don't know why."

Amberley took her hand and gently caressed it. "Even a good change can be hard. Adjustments. Maybe you just have to get used to him being around all the time. Or"—she paused—"is that the problem?" Her mom angled her head and studied her face. "So has there been talk about him staying here with you permanently, as in getting married, settling down, raising a family?"

Madison wished she could give her a different answer, but the truth was going to have to work. "It's what I've been telling myself I've wanted ever since he walked into my life. I just don't know, Mom."

Her mother's touch was gentle. "Sweetheart, I can't help you there. It's your life. Your choices. Answer me this. Did he actually say something specifically about marriage or not?"

"Not specifically, and maybe that's what bothers me the most. He knows I love him, and I know he loves me, and he talks about us being together forever, but I keep waiting for, you know, the formal proposal. Am I wrong to not get my heart set on something until I hear that?"

"You would have to ask me that question, wouldn't you? I'm afraid I'm no help to you here. I wish it weren't so."

"I don't understand what you mean, Mother."

"Well, when I was your age, that was the last thing I ever wanted—to be married, tied down, raising a family. But then when you came along, I guess that shifted many things, but it didn't mean that I wanted to get married, settle down, and be a wife. Not with your father. I was certain I wanted to raise you on my own. There was never any question about that."

Madison knew exactly what her mother meant. The only person in the world that her mother would have stayed with her entire life was Ned's father, Jake Silver. However, Madison wasn't going to make her admit it tonight. But she still had a question.

"Mom, is it wrong to want at all? I worry that I'll pressure him too much, that'll make him feel cornered, or we'll stop being fun, and would you just listen to what I said!"

She was even frustrated with herself, pulling at her hair, then scrambling to her feet, and pacing back and forth. "I've told myself hundreds and hundreds of times that I wasn't at all interested in being someone's sometimes wife nor was I interested in being someone's wife at all. I rather thought I'd follow in your footsteps, but I was open to whatever the sea dragged in. I certainly wasn't going to go searching for it."

"You're talking about the ring and the ceremony. Not the falling in love part, right?" her mother drilled her for an answer.

"Exactly. Maybe you did your job too well. You did it. So could I. I'm convinced of it. But I still want the whole Happily Ever After when it is all said and done. Is that wrong?"

"Of course not. You have a right to want anything at all. But a woman should never chase. She might like to *be* chased, but she should never chase. However, I'm not sure that answers your question. And maybe I don't have a good answer for you, but I wish I did."

"Do you think I should ask him? Should I just hint that I'd like to know if, in his mind, this was going to be the relationship of his life like it is for me?"

Amberley carefully answered her with a whisper. "Only if you can handle the answer. Go ahead. Ask him. But be ready for the truth when he answers you. If you're sure, and I mean one hundred percent sure, you can live with the answer, then satisfy that curiosity, ask him, and see what he says."

"What if he feels pressured, then?"

She shrugged. "That depends how you ask him, my dear. There is a nice way to do this, you know. You show respect for yourself by asking him. Come from that place. Not the needy place, which isn't real, anyway. But only when you're good and ready. Not until then, Maddie."

Her mother released her hand. Madison stared at her lap. Her head was nodding, yes, but she still wasn't sure. "I wish I knew what to do, Mom. I really want this to work."

"Of course you do, sweetheart. It will all work out one way or the other. It is an important direction and decision in your life. Probably the most important one. Unfortunately, these decisions have to be made without the benefit of years of experience. If I told you what I thought the right answer would be, that's based on years of knowledge. I've fought a lot of wars over this—relationships being lonely or being happy. You will have all this experience one day but don't have now. That's what makes it so unfair."

"Yes. I can see the logic in that."

"But I give you this, and perhaps this non-answer will help. He's a man of action, just like his father was, and he doesn't want to be told what and how to do things. But he does want to be sold on something that he doesn't think he can create all by himself. Men are afraid of things like that when it comes to relationships. That's why so many of them are afraid of women. On top of all that, you have to make him think that it's all his idea."

Her mother's advice hit her chest like a ton of bricks. She was no more sure of what she should do next than she was when she sat down the first time. All she knew was that she loved Ned and wanted to bring joy and laughter into his somber life. She was certain she could do that. But she wasn't going to beg. She wanted to be his choice, someone he couldn't live without, because that's how she felt about him.

"Thanks for giving me something to think about, Mom. I do know a couple of things about myself that just popped into my head. I won't beg, and neither will I wait in line."

Amberley beamed with fresh light from within her soul. "That's my girl!"

The two women hugged.

"Here's one last piece of unsolicited advice. Don't do what I did. Don't let him get away."

Just then, Ned burst through Amberly's front door. "Well, it's official. Your car is dying, and it's about time we bought you a new one. Since we're waiting on Noonan anyhow, I think that's what we should do tomorrow. What do you think?"

"Why, Ned Silver, are you buying Madison a car?" Amberley asked.

"I guess I did say that, didn't I? Well, how about I take it out of my share of the proceeds? A gift in exchange for putting up with me here these next few weeks. What do you think, Madison?"

"We could always borrow Mom's golf cart."

CHAPTER 6

NOONAN CHARTERED ANOTHER dive boat, the Lucky Strike. It was also approximately seventy feet long but had accommodations for four. Between the two vessels, they could sleep up to twenty people, including the old captain himself.

"I only want people you can vouch for. We have a lot of work to do bringing up, charting, and cleaning the artifacts, but we also must be mindful of our security concerns. I want us kept discreet and safe. Your SEAL brothers seem like they'd be the perfect fit."

"I'm gonna have to check with my LPO on whether or not they can spare the number of men you're asking for. If Kyle says I've got to go outside the teams for our crew, then my task is going to be a little more difficult. But I promise you, Noonan, we'll use only good people that I personally vouch for."

Noonan also informed him he asked Madison to find a few divers that she'd worked with before at SeaWorld. "Two to four would be the perfect number. Not only would we eat better, sometimes women notice things underwater than a man doesn't. Madison knows several ladies who have hired on to help as boat crew on some of these treasure dives in the past."

"She told me, and I completely agree. You won't find a protest here, and neither will some of my guys."

He and Madison were going to spend a few hours in the morning searching for a car, a small SUV of some sort. They were both hoping the dealerships would be interested in taking her old car in trade, fully disclosing its mechanical defects.

But first, he had to make that call to Kyle.

"Geez, Ned. I think I've said it dozens of times, there must be something in the water there on the Gulf coast. You guys get into some crazy schemes, not to mention everybody falling in love all the time. I'm not sure I should ever go there, happily married man that I am."

Ned was pleased he'd found Kyle in a good mood. Their last short deployment had seen lots of upset and friction amongst the members of the team, and Kyle had used every bit of patience he possessed to keep war from breaking out.

Ned had never experienced these issues to such a degree before. He chalked it up to new rules of engagement being imposed upon them by the Navy, their State Department overseers, and upper management—officers who no longer worked the active ops and perhaps had lost their taste for blood, along with some of their courage.

It was a common complaint amongst Team guys these days. Kyle had confidentially revealed to him that, if Ned wanted a leadership role, it would probably be one of the biggest issues he'd face. He'd have to keep the head shed upstairs satisfied while not allowing them to infect his guys in the unit.

Perhaps Kyle had reached his limit. Maybe his time with the Teams was waning. If so, he'd be sorely missed. The whole platoon looked up to Kyle Lansdowne. It had taken a dozen or more years for him to earn that.

Ned decided to get right to the point, sticking to the script he'd written in his mind. "So how many can I recruit?"

"And you're talking something one hundred percent legal? I mean, no clandestine operations, no unusual fire power, no specialized naval equipment taken in secret?"

"No. That's not it. What we're looking for is boat crew. Smart good guys who can help us with security, experienced divers extremely comfortable researching the shipwreck we're going after. I'm not allowed to say much, but I hear your concern. I can guarantee that everything we're doing will be abiding by the law."

"Ned, I don't know exactly when our next little vacay is, but I think a little Florida R&R probably wouldn't hurt any of the guys. Are you going outside Team 3?"

"I may have to. I was thinking Andy and maybe boatman Wilson Nez, Danny's cousin. And I was going to ask Danny as well. You know I hang with Damon quite a bit, Tucker, TJ, and others. I was even thinking of Zak, if he wanted a little adventure, though he might be too busy with the winery."

"You're going to need certified divers, Ned, so some of the retired guys might not work. Depends."

"Okay. Then I'll give you a list before I make the final selection, and if you got anybody on that list who isn't solid or for some reason you don't want to be invited, I will honor that."

"I appreciate that, son. But it is your gig."

"Out of respect to you, Kyle. That's important."

With that bit of encouragement under his belt, Ned began the long process of creating his roster. Kyle approved it within minutes after the email was sent to him. He began making his phone calls, needing to be cryptic while explaining that it was necessary.

It took him less time than he thought to round up a crew of twelve solid guys, including one of the best dive instructors, Crater Meade, who had his own long list of successful treasure hunts. Pieces of eight and other artifacts littered his office at the dive shop.

Although Meade was technically a civilian instructor, sometimes the BUD/s instructors would add him to the training faculty, especially if a newly reorganized Team was needing extra skills with an eye to training for a mission that was going to be almost entirely water bound.

Madison made her calls as well and was waiting answers. She readied herself for their car shopping adventure.

Ned needed to impart some car shopping advice. "If you see something you really like, Maddie, I want you to look like you don't. The worst thing you can do is to let the salesman know that you're absolutely in love with a particular car."

"I know how it works," she said. He could tell she was slightly annoyed with the process. Ned knew it would be more of a challenge than she thought. In the end, his instruction was useless.

Even with the early warning, they bought the first white VW compact SUV she drove. She even told the salesman, "I think I'm done here. Let's get this one. Okay, Ned?"

And that was that. He was unable to negotiate more than a few hundred dollars for her trade-in, which was a crying shame. He made her promise she wouldn't let any of the other Team Guys she was going to meet know about what they'd bought or how they negotiated.

Maddie also threw in another little surprise. "My mother advanced me some money, so we can pay her back from our plunder. Is that how you say it?"

Ned laughed. "Close enough, sweetheart. As long as you're happy, I'm happy too."

By early afternoon the next day, Ned's whole team had been selected, with only one change. Kyle agreed on all of Ned's choices. Andy Carr from Seal Team 4 would join along with Jason Kealoha, Damon Hamblin, TJ Talbot, and Tucker Hudson, who were all enthusiastic about the possibility of making some extra money. He wasn't sure Jake, Lucas, or Zak would be interested, but in the end, all three agreed. Zak reminded him that it had been a while since he'd done any kind of operation but he had kept his dive certification active and was looking forward to the challenge.

Crater Meade was a little more difficult to convince. He was making big bucks already with civilian dive trainings and recruiting new instructors for his school. He had also planned a surfing trip to Australia and Fiji, which would now have to be postponed.

But in spite of it all, he said yes.

Danny Begay was thrilled with the opportunity to work with his cousin Wilson Nez.

Everyone was scheduled to arrive over the next twenty-four hours. Ned told them their expenses and airfare would be reimbursed at the end of the trip. He also asked them to bring equipment suitable for a two hundred fifty-foot dive, as well as any other specialty equipment, cameras, or electronics that might be useful. Crater was helpful in obtaining some specialized equipment they would need. Those outside Kyle's command were asked to get permission from their respective teams.

Madison found a large Airbnb House close to the beach for the guys. She then rented a house several doors down from her own bungalow for the girls. It would be tight quarters on the Gulf, but there was no reason why they couldn't spread out a little bit and enjoy the beach before the adventure.

All the next day, Ned delivered back and forth several of the members as they arrived. All the girls arrived in one car driving from Orlando, about two hours away.

That evening, the group circled for a bonfire, barbecuing steaks and veggie burgers, and getting acquainted. Ned could already see several illicit hookups in the making, things he was going to have to watch closely.

They got to bed way too late but stayed to do clean up then took a long moonlit walk down the beach. He could tell Madison was nervous. Hell, he was too. But tonight, it was all about enjoying the cool breeze coming off the Gulf, holding hands, and letting the sounds of the ocean rock them both to sleep.

CHAPTER 7

MADISON ESCORTED HER team picks to their new quarters a few houses from her bungalow. Each of the three ladies had their own tiny bedroom, since the house was converted from a modest two-bedroom home to a short-term vacation rental. The market for beach property had soared through the roof, and she felt herself lucky to even find a place so close. She explained this to them when she demonstrated that, unfortunately, they'd all be sharing the same bath.

Georgia Allen was Madison's oldest friend, a Southern girl raised in Florida and South Carolina, with bright red hair and penetrating green eyes. She'd been the performance team's leader when they did five shows a day together at SeaWorld before Madison moved over to the Gulf and gave up her "water dancing" routines for the Salty Dog and the company of her eccentric mother and her quirky friends.

"We'll be in the water so much and then on the dive. I could care less about pampering in a bathroom. And no makeup! What a blessing," she said in her soft Southern accent.

Serena Brooks had been raised in Southern California, where she attended college in the greater L.A. region on a volleyball scholarship. She stood six foot three and had nearly made the U.S. Olympic Volleyball Team a decade ago, before she fell in love with synchronized performance swimming and moved to Florida to work at SeaWorld. An injury took her off the schedule for several weeks, but she continued to train and supplemented her income during her performance seasons by doing charter crewing for dive captains, similar to Madison's experience. Maddie was delighted she was able to join them because she was an excellent cook and was expected to take charge of the galley.

"I'll be all right as long as you don't use up all the hot water. That I gotta have every morning, no matter what."

"We'll make sure, right, ladies?" Madison asked the group.

Liz Fong, from Hawaii, spoke up, "You just heard Georgia doesn't even shower, so we're cool."

"I didn't say that," protested Georgia.

"Well, it sounded like it," Liz insisted. "But just to show I'm still a nice girl, I'll let you go first."

Liz liked to call herself the human cannonball since she was the shortest of the former group and usually would be tossed in the air while doing tumbling routines. She had only been in Orlando for about four years but was already looking for a change of scenery and more than a little adventure to her life. The idea of crewing with a dozen or so SEALs and former SEALs, plus the prospect of earning a small fortune, was exactly what she'd been looking for.

Even Ned's insistence that all the divers were either married or had someone didn't faze her in the slightest. Liz was also an excellent oriental cook, having grown up working in her parent's family restaurant on Kauai as soon as she could hold a rag. But she let it be known she didn't expect to be stuck solely in the kitchen.

"The house comes with a golf cart, but we can ride together if you meet me at my place," Madison began. "I'm at 701 Gulf. Now, I'll give you a chance to get settled. Noonan wants to have a preliminary meeting in two hours down at the Blue Water Sports

Club, about two miles south of here. So come on down to my place no later than an hour from now, okay?"

"What about a car?" asked Georgia. "You got one of those we can borrow? I understand rental rates are outrageous here."

"They are. And often there isn't anything available. Let me work on that, but as of right now, no, no car. Most of what we'll be doing we'll be doing together, anyhow, so I wouldn't worry. Serena, you and I can do the food shopping this afternoon, unless Noonan wants to get involved. Usually, the men handle the alcohol. Since you're the designated cook, we'll have to come up with some menu plans this afternoon."

Serena nodded. "I already worked on a few anticipating that. Also, I have to check out the equipment before we take off too. Just in case I need something. Usually, these boats are pretty bare."

"You'll have that chance today after the meeting. Both the Bones and the Lucky Strike will be there. My guess is we'll be on the Strike, since the galley is twice as large," Madison answered her.

"Works for me," Serena responded. "I brought a few tools of my own."

"Okay, meet me down at my place in about an hour, then. I have to run a short errand but will be back shortly. You all have my number. If you have questions, just text me. There should be an extra set of sheets and towels in each of your closets. Speak up now if you need additional blankets as it can get a little chilly on the shore if we get some wind. Depending on how things go, we might be coming back here two or three times during the contract, but I'm not positive. We've leased the place for three months, which Noonan thinks is more than enough time to get the job done. But I don't know exactly how long you'll actually be living here. I'd take everything with you when we take off tomorrow morning."

Satisfied everyone was set and unloaded, Madison drove back to her place to finish packing. Ned would be meeting her at the Sports Club dock site later with everyone else.

She picked up Otis, placing him and his dry as well as wet food in her new little SUV and headed to her mother's house. Otis was nervous at first, peering out the window with a forlorn look, pacing back and forth on the second seat bench. But just as they turned into her mother's driveway, he began to calm down and slouched over onto his legs folded in front of him. Madison connected his leash, tucked the bowls under her arm while holding the bags of food, and directed Otis to follow her to her mother's front step.

He sat, waiting for her mom to answer the door. Without being asked, he stepped through the doorway.

"Would you look at that? Already feeling at home, I guess," said her mother. She pulled the bags of food from her daughter's arms as Madison disconnected the leash.

Bending over, Madison spoke directly to Otis. "We're going to be gone for a few days, Otis. I want you to be good. This nice lady took very good care of me, and she'll do the same for you too. I have it on good authority she likes to spoil her pets, so you'll have an easy time of it."

The mutt looked up at her adoringly, seated, as if to attention.

Madison padded his head, scratching the hair between his ears. "That's a good boy."

"When do I—?"

"You feed him about the same time you have breakfast and dinner. And then take him outside at least twice before bedtime. I told you he'll sleep on the bed with you, I think."

"I've not had a dog in so long. Hope I don't kick him off the bed," her mother added.

"Happens in our house all the time, especially now that Ned is back. Don't worry about it."

She said goodbye to her mother with a hug and gave Otis another pat, turned, and drove back to her little house to meet up with the ladies. As she got out of the car, she could already hear their music blaring over the narrow alleyway on the beachside of the island.

She thought it was a little early for a dance party.

She might have been in a more festive mood, but she knew a lot more about the risks than they did. There may come a time when she'd have to explain to them that two people had lost their lives on the previous dive. Since they were experienced crew, she didn't think she needed to mention unsavory characters who liked to hang around watering holes looking for information they could sell or use. Or that just the preliminary research Ned and Noonan had done might have put them all at risk, inadvertently.

The three newcomers knocked on her door just as she was zipping up her pack. She greeted them and motioned for them to sit in the living room. "Just gathering some maps and a couple of sketch tablets. I'm almost done. Help yourself to the refrigerator."

She had her back turned as Georgia made her way to the kitchen.

Georgia sighed. "It's water or beer. I'm guessing water?"

"Bingo," whispered Serena.

"I've brought my own water," added Liz.

Georgia handed a bottle of water to Serena. "What about you, Madison?" she asked.

"I'm good. Have a bottle already," she said, holding up her light pink glass water container on a strap.

"They have a desalinated supply on board, or do you know?" asked Serena.

"I know the Bones doesn't have one. Not sure about the Strike, but I'd guess it does. Will you find out and let us know?" Madison answered.

The ladies pulled up to the club, following Madison to the rear by the pier. Several tables had been placed together. Noonan was talking to Ned and several of the men while others sat and awaited the start of the meeting. They stood when the ladies entered the area.

Liz Fong took a seat next to Crater Meade, whom she'd gotten acquainted with the night before at the get-together. Serena and Georgia sat together, close to where Madison was standing. Ned joined her, giving her a kiss on the cheek.

Noonan barked out the meeting orders and then lowered his voice as he read off his notes.

"Most of you don't know all the details of this dive, so I'm going to spell it out and then give you a chance to bail now. Otherwise, I'm handing out consent forms, a notice of non-responsibility, and insurance options. It's important you read over this document carefully so you know your rights and the risks involved.

No one spoke, so Noonan continued.

"I've consulted my maritime attorney, and we are a go on making application for a claim. However, I want to be sure the full coordinates of the project—I don't want to encroach on anyone else's claim, and I want to give us as much room to explore as we can legally get. We're looking for silver. In this case, we are hoping to find a supply of tubes of silver. And we're looking for plates of silver. Not plates you eat from, but plates that would be attached to a mast, to a special railing, something to enhance the beauty of a corsair, a rogue ship sometime before the Civil War, perhaps closer to the Revolutionary War."

He showed the silver tube without letting anyone touch it. He held out several pieces of plate, roughly molded and hammered. Some were decorated in etched filigrees. Others bore rough pour markings or unfinished adornments.

"I want you to explore in teams of three or four. We're going to determine the size of the field and then work off a grid. Everything we find gets catalogued and marked down. I know I don't have to tell you this, since you're all experienced, but no one takes home a trophy. Not until the claim is filed."

T.J. Talbot raised his hand.

"Yessir?"

"You don't have a claim to dive for this? What guarantees do we have we won't get into trouble trespassing on someone else's land or claim?"

"That's a fair question, son," Noonan answered. "I've catalogued a few items, like these here I've shown you today. But the instant I file a claim to bring up silver, the State of Florida will have their hands in everything we do. We need to make sure what we're diving around has not already been claimed, either as a historical treasure or a claim filed but now abandoned for salvage. We'll want to identify the vessel or vessels to determine their origin and their payload. But, if I'm right, these are individual wrecks of vessels avoiding the long arm of the law. Ownership may be hard to verify."

"That would be you have no permission, then," T.J. stated.

"Technically, yes."

"What's our protection, because I was told that would be in place," T.J. insisted. "I made a promise to my LPO and my wife that I wasn't going to do anything illegal, and I'm sticking to that plan."

"I'll see to it that you do. But right now, from my research, I find no claim of this wreck I'm wanting to investigate. In this case, we know the ship was lost at sea somewhere around 1862 or 1863 because it never reached its destination. But no one knows where it went down. The only thing I've determined is that it is at least ten miles, probably more like fifteen, off the Gulf Coast of Florida. Beyond that, we have to establish that we have the rights to keep what we find or at least a significant portion of it. That's the chance I'm offering you. The moment we discover something is illegal about removing anything from the site is the moment we stop. Is that understood, son?"

"Yes, that covers it. So what do you think we have here?"

"I think we have a clever and rogue pirate, once a decorated naval officer, who possibly was a wanted man for crimes he probably didn't commit. He operated under the noses of the French, the British, the Portuguese, and Spanish. His home base might have been somewhere near the islands of Antigua, Barbados, or Bahamas. In fact, I think this ship was made on one of those islands."

Judging from how quiet the patio went, everyone sat to rapt attention. Madison knew more than many of the other crew members chosen, but even to her, the story Noonan was painting was exciting.

"I think I even know the name of the gentleman, the captain of this ship that went down. You're going to have to make a decision, because after that, there's no turning back. Ask yourself if you want to be part of this or not. Either way, we won't discuss anything about the project until you've read over and signed this document."

Many of the people on the patio had heard tall tales of getting rich from the treasures lying at the bottom of the ocean. They'd just never placed themselves in the center of those stories.

Until today.

CHAPTER 8

NED WAS PREPARING to head home for an early turn-in after preparing maps, coordinates of where they were estimating the site was located, and reading over the rules for recovery of artifacts and treasure. The good news was that it was nearly fifteen miles off the coast, which made permissions more likely if they had a connection to a research institution or school. Noonan had worked with the University of Florida, so they would have to be brought in carefully. Everything had to be by the book legal since the SEALs would be risking their careers if it weren't so. And even though portions of the find would have to be shared with the institution and the State of Florida, there would still be enough to make a small fortune for all of them.

But there was bad news, and Ned knew he was going to have to tell Madison and the others about it soon. He also wanted to hear from the maritime attorney himself before he could proceed, since it was a new wrinkle.

Ned felt like a dumbass for not questioning the towing ashore and opening of the crypt Noonan admitted to doing. He should have known right away that there were Federal laws against tampering with gravesites, human remains, and desecration of historical relics. Noonan should have known about those laws, yet he ignored them. Was Noonan being deceitful or just trying to cut corners in his fever to obtain treasure?

The bottom line for Ned was that it didn't matter whether it was done on purpose or not, Ned couldn't be a party to grave-robbing, and he couldn't get the others involved, either.

Going out to the Gulf of Mexico—regardless of other claims, distance from shore, registration of wrecked vessels—without knowing the consequences of the discovery and opening of a crypt would be aiding and abetting a third-degree felony. Noonan had said not to worry about it, that it was being taken care of. However, Ned was hired to worry about all those things, and he didn't trust an attorney he'd never met before, nor did he completely trust his father's old pal. But his fondness for Noonan had perhaps colored his feelings, and now Ned himself had fallen victim to the treasure-fever Noonan had.

The pirate captain was due to return to their little rented office across the street from the fishing club and the pier any minute now. All this was weighed on him the more he thought about it. He had kicked himself across Gulf Boulevard and back again, slammed against all four walls of the little office in his mind when the old man opened the door, giving him a huge grin.

"There he is. You wrap it up?" Noonan asked him.

"Just about. But I got one huge problem to go over with you, and I discovered lots of things I wasn't aware of as I read over all these salvage laws. My ass, as well as my reputation with my colleagues, is on the line here. I'm a man of my word, and I still intend to keep it."

"What's got you all riled up? Show me."

"There's no 'show me.' It's something you know about full well. You opened someone's grave, Noonan. You desecrated a body. That's against the law."

"Oh, that. My attorney is handling that."

Noonan didn't seem to be phased one bit.

"That's just not good enough, Noonan. I'm going to call a halt to this whole thing if I don't get some answers I can verify."

"Go ahead. You can call him."

"I will. But first, I want you to tell me how you plan on 'taking care' of the issue, because I don't see any solution in front of me."

"Sit down, Ned."

They both took a seat.

"You're right. I shouldn't have opened it. At the time, I didn't know what it was. But I knew it was hollow from the sounds it made when the kids tapped on it. Our detector couldn't pick up anything inside. It was encased in lead, I discovered after I opened it. But it was much too light for a solid piece of concrete or for a safe. And there was lots of debris all around. You saw the pictures, Ned."

"I remember. I agree, nothing could have told you what it was. But you pulled it out of the water without permission, nonetheless. Like you did the masthead, the lady."

"Yes, I did. And the lady is now sitting in the University's Museum for all to see. Quite an attractive and well-received display, I'm told."

The old man's eyes twinkled, and Ned knew exactly what Noonan was implying.

"Give me some answers, man. I gotta have them now, or I'm pulling the plug on this whole thing. I'm going to have to eat crow to men of honor who will never trust me again. They all got leave and traveled here on their own dime. And now I must tell them you violated the law. Worse, I knew it and didn't let them know about this."

"No, that's on me. And for your information, I was going to tell them."

"Goddammit, Noonan. *Telling* them isn't the issue. The issue is we can't be a party to your committing a felony. If we're involved in the coverup, we're just as at fault. We could lose our Tridents over it. That's on *me!* How could you do this to me, to Madison, to all of us, Noonan?"

"Listen. Things wash up on the beach all the time. Hurricanes have wiped out whole cemeteries in the past all over the East Coast, in this state, as well as others. They find shit all the time, floating in the water, washed up on land. Sometimes ships run right through them when things float out to sea and find their way to shipping lanes. Japanese glass fishing globes have washed up in San Francisco Bay after having traveled clear across the Pacific."

"Where is the crypt? Where is Falkland?"

"Martin already took care of it. He reported it, said it had been found by someone who didn't want to come forward, which is certainly true, and he was doing the right thing by allowing the authorities to examine it. You're gonna hear a news report about it sometime soon, coming straight from the Coroner's Office. It's been disposed of and is now safely out of my hands."

"And what if Martin decides to turn you in, Noonan?"

"He can't. He's my attorney."

"He can't help you break the law, Noonan."

"I didn't knowingly break the law, Ned. Only you and Madison know about the collar. I intend to give it to the family in North Carolina after all this is over with. It has nothing to do with the site, except that the man's grave landed right on top, perhaps protecting that site for over a hundred years as a pure unrelated coincidence."

"I have to hear it from Martin himself."

"Suit yourself. I'll get him on the phone if I can."

"Better tonight than tomorrow. Because tomorrow, we must tell the guys and gals or end this whole caper."

"Don't be so hasty. Talk to Martin first. I'll arrange a meeting with him tomorrow morning in person, as well. He drew up all the disclosures, the releases here. He wouldn't have done that if he knew he was violating the law or helping me to do so. You ask him about that."

"I will."

Ned wasn't feeling any better about this whole situation. In fact, he was feeling much worse. Again, he blamed himself, but now anger toward Noonan was boiling in his stomach. Some of his experiences with his father came flooding back to his memory, compounding the situation. It was like he was being taken advantage of by that dick of a father all over again, just as he was starting to put some of those feelings to bed.

"Martin. I'm sorry to call you so late, but..."

Noonan listened to the attorney. Ned could hear a long-winded interrupt, which sounded suspicious.

"Oh, I completely understand. Can you call me after his game is over? It's very important. I need to talk to you tonight."

Noonan signed off and ended the call. "He's at his son's soccer game, but it's at the end of the second half, and he says he'll call me when he can get some privacy. He's in the bleachers."

"Fair enough," Ned answered. "So we wait."

"Show me what you've done while we're waiting."

Ned brought out the maps. He'd marked the tide timetables and weather conditions for the next week. He'd compiled a folder with all the expenses of the rental diving equipment, the cost of leasing the Lucky Strike, supplies for operating both vessels, additional safety equipment, communication devices and readers, extra lines, tanks, scuba gear, and emergency supplies in case of an injury, the marine biologist report on expected plants and wildlife, including a certification there were no endangered reefs or international sites or toxic cleanup projects in nearly the whole eastern half of the Gulf of Mexico, where oil rigs had caused problems in the past. Much of this was paid for by Ned's own money, and the amount was adding up quickly.

"We're at over twenty thousand dollars, not including the Strike," Noonan mumbled under his breath. "I can give you some money for Madison's shopping adventure with Serena today. I'm assuming…"

"I gave her my card, but I don't have the receipt yet," Ned interrupted.

"Thanks. You're doing a great job of keeping the costs down for me. I've got savings to cover all this, so you won't have to wait."

"I appreciate that, Noonan. This isn't like me. I can't believe I went full speed without questioning all this stuff. Man, I'm losing it," Ned added, shaking his head. "Your attorney better be honest."

"He is. Maritime law is all he does. Went to law school in Norway, also interned with several large European shipping firms. He knows his stuff and has Merchant Marine companies as some of his clients."

Just then, Noonan's cell phone rang. Before he picked up, he pointed to Ned. "Do not talk about the collar. Anything else you want to ask, go ahead. No mention of the collar."

"Damnit."

"Ned, I gotta have your word."

"Okay. But I better get a straight answer."

Noonan answered the call, thanking Martin for returning it. "My partner here is worried about the crypt and how that was handled. Can you explain it to him, like you did to me? He wants to be reassured nothing about that will come back to bite any of us, even slightly."

Noonan listened and then passed the phone to Ned.

"Martin? This is Ned Silver…"

"You old Jake's son?"

"I am."

"Your dad was right proud of you, son. Said you got all the good parts from your mama, and he was damned grateful for that."

"Thank you, sir." Ned felt far from thankful but was going to give the man a chance.

"I was best man at the coroner's wedding to his third wife about ten years ago, but we go way back to high school. I told him I had an anonymous call from someone who had uncovered a body encased in a box. Not a murder, mind you, but in a burial box. We wanted to turn it in, but the caller didn't want to get involved. I asked if they could do that. He wanted to examine the remains, see if there was some sort of foul play first, but he called me yesterday and told me they had closed the investigation and the man, at least they are assuming it was a man from the bone structure, would be re-buried since they didn't have the resources to find his family that far back. He said DNA samples could not be obtained, so that was that."

"I want to make sure none of that taint comes back on me or on the guys and gals we've hired to help Noonan with his exploration."

"No, you're good. I got a coroner's report emailed to me this morning, and I guess I could let you see it. I can't give you a copy. Son, this sort of thing happens all the time. At least it wasn't a murder, because that would have been another story completely."

"I'd like to see that report, if you don't mind. This whole thing has got me spooked. Sort of a bad luck omen, if you know what I mean?"

"Noonan did the right thing by telling me about it. The coroner said the box was consistent with the way burials were done above ground over a hundred fifty years ago in this county. It probably was lost years ago and just took a while to resurface. We've got records of cemeteries pulled to the sea all over Florida.

Not a damned thing we can do."

"Should I come to your office in the morning then? About what time?"

"I'm coming in at eight. Meet me after my secretary arrives at eight-thirty, if you can. I'll put the coffee on."

CHAPTER 9

MADISON MISSED OTIS already, so called her mother to make sure the mutt wasn't misbehaving.

"Are you kidding? He's wonderful, Maddie. I gave him some instructions on how to paint a floral landscape, not that it will do him much good, but he did manage to get some acrylic in his whiskers. He didn't like the taste much."

That cheered Madison up. "I expect great things from Otis," she said. "Can't wait to see what he paints in the sand next time we take him for a walk."

"You might not get him back. I'm growing rather fond of him already. He might just decide to stay here. But you could always visit. I promise you that."

She heard Ned's truck pull into the driveway and signed off. "I know I don't have to say it, but take lots of pictures. I'll be missing him something terrible when we're out on the Gulf."

"Will do. You're leaving in the morning?"

"We are. Supposed to, anyway. There are so many last-minute details, and we're on a race against time due to some weather concerns. Also, we've got this big crew here who are anxious to get started."

"Well, be safe. Best of luck. If you can, send pictures yourself."

"And I probably won't do that," Madison said as she watched

Ned come through the door. "Now I really need to go. Ned's home."

She could see right away something wasn't right with Ned.

"Uh-oh. I know that look. You're scaring me," she sighed.

Ned gave her a quick hug and then stood facing the ocean, which was smooth as glass in the early evening moonlight.

"Do we need to take a walk on the beach?" she tried.

"No," he said to the glass door. Then he abruptly turned. "But I'm worried about a couple of things." He stared into her eyes. "The biggest problem I have is that I have to keep something from the team guys. I don't like having to do that."

"Keep what? We have no secrets."

"The collar. We can't mention the collar or where it came from. I'm trying to figure out a way that I can let them know about what Noonan found, as in the box, but not tell them about the collar. They should know, Maddie."

"I trust your gut instincts, Ned. Do whatever you think is right," she answered. With her hands around his waist, she rocked with him in tandem, trying to release the tension he was rigidly holding all over his body. "It can't be that bad to let them know, unless..."

"Noonan doesn't want me to. He thinks it complicates things, and it will. We might lose the entire crew."

"Why?"

"Because it's a felony to disturb a grave or human remains. I discovered that when I was going over some of the protocol for the survey and exploration. We could go to prison for disturbing that man's grave."

"The grave that the hurricane unearthed, you mean?" Madison stood with her hands on her hips. "It's not like he went to a cemetery and started digging someone up. That didn't happen. It was Mother Nature."

Ned angled his chin, shaking his head. "I didn't see a footnote stating that if a diver didn't know it was a grave and disturbed it, then it was okay. No such rule about that, Maddie. I don't want any of my guys to get in trouble for my fuck up."

"But you didn't know that—and Noonan had no clue what was in that box—unless he really did. In that case, he's been lying to us." Madison frowned and released her arms from his hips. "Are you saying you don't trust Noonan now? He's hiding something? Where is the coffin, anyhow?"

"It's a crypt, or was. It's been turned over to the coroner's office. The remains are going to be buried in an unmarked grave. After over a century, with the water seepage, DNA testing wasn't possible."

"Did you help Noonan actually do that? Did you see the remains?" she asked.

"Hell no, Maddie. I wouldn't touch that for anything. But I'm kicking myself all over the place that I didn't think to ask more questions before we had the guys come out here. That's my fault. And I feel I should own up to it."

"Then you should. Better that they decide they don't want to get involved than to risk them finding out afterwards that you knew something and didn't reveal it to them in time to make a different decision. You would expect the same from them, right?"

"I would. And I promised Kyle and all the guys that everything was above board. I just didn't think about the issue of the dead body. I feel stupid about that. I let them down."

"No, Ned. That's your good and honest nature kicking you in the gut. You've got to act on that. I don't think you have a choice." This was one of the reasons she loved him so.

He nodded. "You're right, of course. But I'm checking with the attorney in the morning first, and then I'll talk to everyone and make sure there are no second thoughts. But the hardest thing is going to be not having the story spread to too many other places or the news could get hold of it, and then our dive would no longer be a secret."

"Maybe it was folly to think we could keep it under wraps, Ned," Madison whispered. She was hoping he took it as a suggestion, a comment, and not a criticism. She felt how on edge he was.

"I must make this right, honey. I just won't be able to live with myself otherwise. It will be my job to convince both the attorney and Noonan that this information has to be revealed. If not, then it falls to me to curtail the whole mission. I'm just going to have to admit that I made a mistake and now I'm trying to fix it."

She didn't envy his task, but she was certain it was the right thing to do.

THE GROUP GATHERED at the SEAL house, or so it had been nicknamed, sharing takeout from one of the great pizza kitchens on the island. Ned and Madison were the first to leave, and they told everyone to plan to have their gear ready by noon. Ned apologized at the late start but indicated there were some additional details he had to take care of first.

As they drove back to Madison's, she knew that the group would take advantage of the fact that they didn't have to get up at dawn, which is what they had planned, so some partying was in order. Ned told her that not everyone would be in favor of that and would elect to call home instead, but he wanted them well rested when he had the little talk.

She agreed with his approach and told him so.

"I have no doubts you'll do the right thing. You'll figure it out, now that we know," she said.

She requested to accompany Ned and Noonan's meeting at Mr. Zinski's office, and he agreed. She called the ladies, letting them know she'd be available by phone in case they needed her.

And she offered to lend her keys to Serena in case she needed anything they'd neglected to pick up earlier. The gesture was greatly appreciated, and they agreed on a spot she could leave behind her keys.

They showered and turned in early, but the sleep was fitful, both of them tossing and waking each other up several times.

Madison knew part of her feeling uncomfortable was the fact that Otis wasn't there with them on the bed. She'd forgotten what a comfort he'd been when Ned was away. Now she missed him even more.

Just before they fell asleep, Ned got a text from Noonan stating he was not going to be able to attend the meeting but would catch up with him afterwards.

"Figures," Ned whispered. "Just my fucking luck." Madison pretended to be already asleep.

IT WAS A gorgeous Friday morning in Clearwater, where Martin Zinski's office was located. The lobby had a sweeping view of the Gulf, the huge beach and community below, and the little boats out on the water streaking across the blue expanse like tiny comets in an early evening sky.

Ned could see immediately that Zinski was indeed a heavyweight in maritime law and commented so. His business was booming, and they both were impressed by the organization. The office bustled with several junior associates and clerks brightly doing worthwhile work they obviously loved.

They were shown to the conference room around the corner, which had a two-sided version of the large window from the lobby.

"Geez. I can't even remember my name; this is so impressive. All my meeting notes just flew out of my head," Ned muttered.

"I agree. It's stunning," she answered.

Martin Zinski's handshake was tight, and Madison noticed Ned wince slightly, trying to mask his surprise. She could see this also caught him off guard. On top of that, the attorney was probably no more than about five foot five inches. He was fit and trim, graying at his temples. He didn't resemble anyone old Jake, Ned's dad, would have ever known or Noonan either for that matter. This realization was almost as distracting as the setting.

"Thank you for coming in. I'm really slammed. Where's Noonan?" Zinski barked.

Ned rubbed his palm with his other hand. "He texted me and said he couldn't make it. I'm guessing he wants to let you do all the talking."

"That's just like the man. But never mind. I'm hoping I can assuage your fears without him."

Ned was waiting to be convinced. As Zinski opened up a thick file, Ned added, "I'm a man of my word. I should have asked about the legal issues of Noonan hauling this crypt back to the pier. Should have been the first thing that came to my mind, but it wasn't. Now I've got twelve men and three women ready to help us with the project, and I'm inclined to pull the plug on the whole operation. I can't ruin my career in the Navy—I'm a fuckin' SEAL—sorry…"

"No, no. I understand," Zinski blurted. "Let me…"

"These Team guys would never let me step into something without assurances I gave them first. Turns out, I didn't know everything I should have. I even gave my own LPO a guarantee of sorts that everything was going to be done by the book—proper and legal. He released these guys, or acted to help get them released, so it's on him too. I can't have everyone going off without some 'out-of-this-world-type' exceptional piece of information changing my mind about this mission being scrapped, Mr. Zinski."

"I get it." He turned to Madison, nodding. "Sorry I didn't introduce myself to you. That was rude. Pleasure to meet you. You are Amberley's daughter, right?"

This also surprised her. "Yes. Boy, you're well informed," Maddie said with a smile.

Zinski shook his head. "Not really. Small town. That helps a lot."

He directed his attention back to his file folder and produced a piece of paper with the letterhead of the Pinellas County office of the coroner.

"This," he said, tapping the document, "should be all you need to see. He says right in there that an unknown, unrelated person accidentally found this grave and wanted to do the right thing by turning it over to the authorities and enlisted my help. They examined the contents, which were nearly destroyed except for several of the long bones, which had partially turned to stone and were crusted with what we call sea concrete—deposits of organisms we find everywhere here. Cause of death was indeterminate, no apparent evidence of foul play, and it was consistent with other types of crypts that have washed up on our lovely shores for decades. The remains were logged, catalogued without any active DNA, photographed, and will be buried again within the next few days. That, my friend, is the end of this long story."

"But what if the facts turn out to be otherwise?" Ned asked.

"Is this a crypt? Do you believe this is a crypt?" He showed the pictures of the broken concrete and lead liner from the burial vault.

"Appears to be."

"Are there remains there?"

Ned examined closer, and there did appear to be one long thigh bone with some smaller ones, all laying parallel to each other, none of them with marks or striations on them, and not broken, altered, or sawed. "I think so."

"We have no I.D. We have no DNA. What we really have is a biohazard that has to be disposed of. We have no cause to believe the man was carrying something contagious, do we?"

Ned shook his head. "No."

"So we dispose of the biohazard quickly after cataloguing it and keep the public safe. It was the responsible thing to do since there doesn't appear to have been any kind of crime or foul play."

"But it's against the law to tamper with dead bodies."

"Are you saying Noonan chose to tamper with it?" Zinski looked hard into Ned's eyes. "It's an important question, Ned."

"I don't know how he could. There's barely anything there."

"Right again. Now we could make up all kinds of theories, but on the basis of what? We have no other evidence pointing us to the direction other than an accidental find. Noonan did the right thing by reporting it. In this case, he doesn't have to reveal his name, and I'll make sure that never happens, as well. He doesn't want or need the notoriety. As his attorney, since it isn't required, I'm going to honor that."

Zinski blinked several times but didn't take his eyes off Ned.

"I want to tell the others about the body." It was out of his mouth so fast she was sure he hadn't thought to choose his words carefully.

Zinski shrugged. "Fine by me. I'm not asking you or any of them to lie about it. It's just that there's no need to reveal it until after you've done your dive, because it has nothing to do with it. But if you go around talking about it, well, all bets are off. You might as well all go home. So no, I don't mind that you tell the team. Make sure they understand they undermine the whole operation in the way that story gets told. It's not illegal to stumble upon a dead body. It's illegal to try to cover it up without alerting authorities. There's a huge difference between the two."

CHAPTER 10

NED WAS NERVOUS, and he knew he wasn't exuding confidence like he should have been. He noted Madison was discreetly watching him, as if noticing a crack in his armor and waiting for something to fall apart. That irritated him no end. It was why he had always preferred the lonely, uncomplicated life of a single SEAL, since he didn't have to explain his actions to anyone else—anyone else who would care about him, that is. His mother had been like a shadow those past few years as his father wasted away and prepared to leave this world.

He'd seen the upsets and marriages crumble while men in his platoon were deployed in godless countries, witnessing unspeakable horrors. Or when they were trying to overcome ridiculous odds: their small Team against bands of roving hired mercenaries, cutthroats, and villains who would even make Stalin look like a cat sitter instead of the butcher he was. In the middle of all that shit, they'd have an argument with their wife about the kids or the car payment or how they didn't feel loved and why couldn't they call more often. There were good Team wives, and there were those who never should have signed up for this duty. Guys who should have known the pressures would be too much for certain women. He'd seen guys shot trying to cool down an argument in the middle of a firefight.

They'd laugh about it afterwards, but it left scars, all of it. Ned considered himself lucky never to have gotten snagged. He'd always figured he would be a good husband and father when he had time to garden, work on his truck, or put new sod in the backyard—the easy stuff of life. Not this stuff.

But all that was before Madison, and now she was a factor, someone he opened up to. By doing so, he brought her along too. So whatever happened on this dive, it was not only going to affect the men he felt he could die for and his leaders—the good, the bad and the ugly—but it would affect Madison.

He told himself he'd had years of practice controlling his nerves, thinking clearly, and strategizing to accomplish missions. Kyle had noticed it and recommended him for OCS. So he must have been doing something right.

Most days, he just did the best he could.

With the stakes so high, he felt the pressure. *"Pressure makes the weak shatter and the strong become stronger. No other way it works,"* his LPO had said more than once to the Team before an op. Kyle was a good example for him. He went out every time. He chose the guys who would do certain dangerous jobs, knowing there'd be a good chance they'd get injured or worse, and he had to do it anyway. Or when something went wrong and he had to order someone to put their life on the line, do something he shouldn't have to ever be tasked to do, and lead him to that opportunity to prove they all were heroes. He had to get everyone home, safe, as intact as they could be.

The dangerous injuries were the scars no one could see, just like that pretty lady on the plane described. The good doctors understood the fighting man and his unique needs. They were constantly testing themselves, looking for that weak link. Close to breaking, they had to pull it off like a hero. If it came to that, Ned had always hoped that he would die with dignity, a hero, show some of the younger guys how to do that just like he trained them to dress a near-mortal wound before evacuation or how to carry their equipment so they didn't stumble over something and kill themselves by accident. They all taught each other everything.

These men and women he was going to speak with in a few minutes were looking for him to do the same today. It didn't matter that the air was warm, the water was crystalline and bright blue, or that billions in gold and silver still slept in the grip of the beautiful Gulf of Mexico just waiting for the right person to come along and claim it all. The dangers were all around, whether it be the sea life, pirates, or just plain criminal elements. Florida didn't look like some inner city with graffiti tatted and tagged everywhere.

It looked like paradise, but it was still dangerous as hell.

Wilson and Danny, the two Navajo boys from Arizona, came up to him for a private conversation. The group was assembling at the office, which had been a last-minute change Noonan made in case things got hot and they needed secrecy.

Ned had never noticed that, although the two were first cousins, they looked like twins.

Wilson spoke first.

"Hey, man, I really appreciate you including me in this op. It's one hell of an adventure. Danny will tell you I've worked really hard on my diving and took any class I could to stay up on my certification, even though, if I did my job well, I'd be the one in the boat picking up all the rest of you frogs. You never know, so I kept it going so I could compete if I had to rescue someone."

"I've heard about you. You're our motor man too. I kinda like having someone to second Noonan's opinions on the equipment on these boats. You see something that is about to fail or doesn't look right, you let me know, understood?" Ned answered.

"Oh, roger that. And if you want me to tweak anything, well, I won't tweak anything I'm afraid of breaking. I'm not that kind of mechanic."

"Nah, that wouldn't do. Fifteen miles is too far, especially with our equipment, to have to swim back to shore. And we may have to anchor the dive boats and take the dinghies. I understand you can soup them up something special, Wilson."

"Yes, I can. I sure can." Wilson, who was nearly a foot shorter than Ned, stood like he was two feet taller instead. He held out his hand for a shake, and Ned pushed it aside.

"Thank me when we get back to land safely and the mission is accomplished. Otherwise, I might be the one you blame for getting you into a clusterfuck."

Danny had a belly laugh over that one. With his arm around his cousin, he said, "He can get us out of Dodge so fast they won't even know we were there."

Ned loved having them on the Team because of their grateful attitude. They never took their opportunities for granted and worked everything the hard way.

He surveyed the group, and as Madison and her girls entered the cramped office, greeting Noonan with hugs that made him cringe, everyone was accounted for.

"Okay, listen up, everyone."

Noonan hung back in the corner, his arms across his chest, a grey shadow crossing his forehead down across his nose and chin.

"First, I'm going to need to collect your consent and bio forms, and we'll get to your questions in a minute. Mother Nature gave us a little time, and now there isn't any rain in the forecast for the next seven days. That's a good omen as they say."

The group mumbled a general agreement.

"But I got something serious I have to discuss with you, and I'm not going to lie. Some of you are going to be pissed."

The grumbling immediately stopped. The only sounds in the room were traffic noises from outside.

Half the room was still waking up. Several men had deep creases in their forehead at the prospect of having to listen to something they'd wished they didn't have to. Most everyone else had clenched their jaw, bracing for the final instructions, the last-minute changes. The SEALs were used to this. The ladies, Ned surmised, not so much.

"It's come up that we had a little issue a few days ago. I'm going to apologize to all of you. I was not made aware of it until yesterday, or I would have mentioned it sooner. But I need to tell you about it, and I need to make sure you are still in on this operation. Everyone has to be solid, understood?"

Most everyone nodded silently.

Tucker Hudson, the biggest man there, affectionately nicknamed "Shrek" by most of the wives and girlfriends of Team Guys, as well as his own wife, had to take issue with it right off the bat.

"Goddammit, Ned. Just fuckin' get to the point. I could care less how you feel about it. Give me the crap and let me make the decision. Stop treating us like we're teenagers afraid of cutting ourselves shaving."

T.J. and Jake Green laughed. T.J. punched him in the arm.

The women bore shocked expressions, and not from the foul language, either. Even Maddie looked scared.

"Okay, here it is," Ned began. He gave a wink to Madison before he continued. "Noonan here discovered a crypt that had been washed out to sea sometime in the last hundred plus years—probably remaining there since about 1863 or so. We have record of a hurricane that came through these parts before there were many European settlers. The Native American population inhabited these parts for centuries before. I discovered that this crypt did contain remains of someone we can't identify. Noonan hauled it out of the Gulf before he knew what it was, and that's what created the problem."

"That's it?" T.J. barked. "That's the shit?"

"Hear me out, T.J. It's a federal crime to tamper with human remains. Noonan did the right thing, the responsible thing. Through his attorney, he reported the find, and the attorney arranged for the crypt to be turned into the coroner's office here. After careful review, they've cleared any issue they might have had about the body, foul play, as this sort of thing has happened over the years—actually, over decades."

"What do you mean 'cleared'?" Liz asked, using her fingers as quote signs.

"The body was anonymously surrendered to the coroner. Under the circumstances, Noonan didn't have to give his name, and we want it to remain that way. Our concern is that it might interfere with the dive, not that the two are related. Do some of you understand now?"

"So what's there to decide?" Jason asked. "They're not looking for Noonan, right? He's not a fugitive, isn't that correct?"

"That's right. It's case closed. But you might hear of it on the news. We want all of you to make sure and not contribute to the conversation or the accuracy of any reporting that might come up. But the most important thing is, I wanted to tell you because if any of you are uncomfortable now and want to back off, I will understand. You can leave."

"But what does this have to do with the dive in the first place?" asked Andy Carr.

"It was on the sea floor, right on top of what we believe to be the remnants of the wreck. We don't think it had anything to do with the wreck. It just happened to land there, but we really don't know."

"So Noonan's cleared of any wrongdoing, right?" Damon

asked.

"Yes, that's right."

Ned looked at the two Navajo boys, who were extremely closed mouthed and showed no emotion. He knew a little about their culture, because he'd read about the invasions in the South Pacific and how it affected the Navajo Code Talkers who had to navigate through floating bodies during that bloody campaign. Many of the men had to go through purging ceremonies or were sent special herbs by their families at home to ward off the evil spirits they believed came from the dead. He didn't want to call them out to embarrass them, but he knew it was something they would be thinking about.

"If any of you would prefer not to dive the site because of this, no problem." Ned didn't make eye contact with Danny or Wilson.

"Are we sure there aren't any more graves, Ned?" asked Georgia.

Ned shrugged. He hadn't thought about that. "To be honest, I can't say. But we don't see anything from the pictures we've reviewed that looks like what's already been removed. We wouldn't be asking you to go down there otherwise."

There was a pause while everyone worked on their private thoughts. Ned added, "Of course, if we find anything that appears to be human remains, we have to stop, catalog it, and report it. We are not allowed to remove anything without that protocol. But first, we comb the site grid by grid, make a final determination how much area we're talking about, and search the perimeters to make sure we've looked at everything. We document everything because artifacts and historical objects have to be recorded, so that when they are turned over—in this case, to the University of Florida—they have a reference point to the conditions of where they were found. A map, if you will, of how they lived on the ocean floor."

Tucker uncrossed his arms and swore. "Fuck it. I've seen dead bodies before. I've even caused some of them myself. As long as I'm not going to be hauled away for touching this stuff, makes no difference to me whether it's a crypt or an oil drum. But I sure as hell am going to look ten times closer. That's a fact."

Several others stated their agreement. T.J. said he just wanted to get out there in the water and stop wasting time. He palmed his disclosure sheet into Ned's chest. "Here, this is my answer," T.J. said, turned, and walked to a far wall.

One by one, everyone, even Danny and Wilson turned in their slips, without a single defection.

CHAPTER 11

MADISON RODE ALONG with the other ladies and several of the Team Guys on the Lucky Strike, piloted by Wilson Nez. The ship was much faster than the Bones, and at regular intervals, Wilson led them on a circular tour of some of the tiny islands that dotted the Gulf, being careful to avoid the shallow parts. The entire west coast of Florida was bordered by a shelf, containing some very shallow areas. The average depth was some six hundred plus feet, but the site they were working on was a mere two hundred fifty or so.

The beauty of the water mating with the horizon was highlighted by the gentle sun and a touch of clouds, which tended to keep everything on the cooler side. It was ideal diving conditions. And if the weather held, it would also make for some ideal starry nights and calm waters—always a welcome occurrence since they would need their sleep.

Danny, Wilson's cousin, was fascinated with the variety of sea life, including dolphins, who liked to run alongside and race with the ship, and sea turtles, looking like dark green ink spots on the otherwise clear turquoise water.

Sport fishing was allowed in these waters for selected species, but no one but Noonan had an active permit. Jason Kealoha had indicated they could be catching their own food and having fish fry every night, but everyone knew it was important not to get caught doing anything without proper permission. It would be explored the next time they came back to port. If the weather held, they'd be done with the mapping and preliminary photography work in three days' time. That was the goal. Then they could seek out their permissions and return to do the actual recovers and exploration.

Everyone had their attention focused on two things: the appearance of other boats in their vicinity and what particular areas they wanted to come back to that drew more interest than others.

Ned was co-piloting with Noonan in the Barry Bones. Madison noticed that one of the motors was smoking slightly and made a mental note to let Noonan know about it.

Noonan slowed down, searching his sonar for the coordinates he'd logged. The Lucky Strike followed behind at a good distance, giving the Bones room to slow down quickly if they needed to or double back and re-approach a particular area.

The ocean floor showed up littered with debris from oil drums to solid evidence of other small craft or sport fishing vessels ruined by some of the strong hurricanes frequenting this area. But there were dozens of dark areas that were quite large, which indicated a literal vessel graveyard. She was surprised they didn't see any other vessels with the naked eye. Damon and Jason took turns scanning the horizon with their small binoculars, very new tech and highly specialized with add-ons, and which could also go IR at night, all courtesy of Uncle Sam. It was just some of the equipment most of the SEALs had as standard issue. Four of the men brought their re-breathing units as well, just in case.

Danny and Wilson also brought along Wilson's drone, a piece he was working on and hoping to one day sell to the military. It had a twenty-mile range and could send a signal to their computer on board, which could print out color copies with a tiny printer no bigger than an iPad.

Madison was fascinated with the device when Wilson showed it at the get-together two days ago.

He also told her that the tiny device on the drone would even calculate the wind speed and the temperature. It had a memory so that, as it traveled, it began to make an all-weather map, even locating some possible underwater elevations, although that was still being perfected.

She was amazed how inventive he was.

Both teams were issued coms they used on missions, their Invisios, so they could talk back and forth without tagging a cell site. There had been a lot of major smack talk going on all during the trip, although she couldn't hear a word of it. Based on the looks she got, the laughing and basic chatter she knew that she was being targeted in some of their comments. But she also knew none of the ladies would escape the fun play and mock ridicule that was just part of their community and came out at every bonfire or family party. Her friends had thick enough skin to handle it.

Serena was whipping up something in the galley for dinner that smelled like a seafood stew and cornbread. She and Georgia were having a catch up on their love lives while Liz had her nose in a romance book. Zak was trying to help but got delegated to cutting up onions, tomatoes, and celery. She could hear him describe their winery and all the catering they'd done for weddings and special events over the ten years they'd been in business.

"How'd you lose your eye, Zak?" Georgia asked.

"On a mission. Cape Verde, off the coast of Africa. We were protecting the U.S. Ambassador. I got shot. A fragment lodged in there and took my eye. But I still got one left. I requalified expert on everything I used to shoot before, but they still rolled me out on a medical. We got a little settlement, so heck, we bought a piece of land, an old winery site."

"I might be looking for a job," Serena said, "After all this is over. Or maybe I'll have enough money to buy a little place—where did you say that was?"

"Healdsburg, California. Dry Creek," said Zak.

"I could run a little Airbnb and cook for those nice folks coming to visit from my old stomping grounds."

"Very popular, if you can find a place reasonable enough. Amy and I work our buns off. But now the kids are older and able to carry some of the load. They don't get their allowance unless they finish their chores."

"See, that's a good thing right there. You're doing right by those kids by making them work. Can't give them everything they want. That's not healthy. I mean, I grew up in the gym. My older brother had basketball dreams. Everything was basketball. My dad had been a good college player at a small school, but my brother, he had the real talent. They left me alone. I learned to walk on a shiny basketball court. The first time I ran across a game, I not only got trampled but came home with a black eye too. Boy, the kids on the street really gave me a hard time about that."

"Did your brother play later on?"

"No, sir, Mr. Zak. A stray bullet stopped his basketball dreams. Stopped everything for him and for the whole family. That's when I threw myself into volleyball, and I never looked back or thought about anything else until I was out of college."

"Sorry to hear that, Serena. That must have been tough."

"It was. But you know what they say. It makes you tough. All of us kids got a big dose of reality from that. No more sugar plum fairies and princesses. We had to work our way out of the neighborhood by playing ball. And since I could jump but couldn't shoot worth a darn, I spiked and blocked the hell out of that ball and broke a few noses along the way."

Georgia giggled as she scooped Zak's chopped mixture into a

bowl. "I'll bet you liked to pancake those pretty blonde girls, didn't you, Serena?"

"Oh, you're bad, my red-haired sista. But it has a ring of truth to it, come to think of it."

Everyone laughed. Madison was glad they didn't know she had overheard them. She had a case of terminal blondeness.

Suddenly, Damon and Jason pointed toward the stern of the ship, where Madison could only see a flat line horizon. But the two men had spotted something. Damon used his earpiece to notify the crew on the Bones. Madison waited with bated breath.

"What is it?" she asked Jason.

"We got someone following us, I think. They were popping up and down from the horizon, trying to escape detection, but when Noonan slowed down, they didn't react in time and blew it. I saw it briefly before I lost the line of sight."

Wilson appeared next to them. "Can I see?" he asked, holding out his hand for the scope. He yelled at Danny, who had temporarily taken the helm. "Slow down, Danny. Let me see if I can see this thing."

"There it is," pointed Damon. "It's a big one. About this size, maybe bigger. And fast too. Look at the wake."

Madison knew Ned and Noonan wouldn't be happy. "What did they say?"

Wilson was running down the half flight of stairs to the bunk rooms, past the galley, returning with the black case he carried the drone in. Over his shoulder, he whispered, "Ned said to get the bird up there, but don't make it obvious."

Madison watched as Wilson adjusted the wing into the slots in the body of the drone, heard the familiar click and the flipped the locator switch. He got out a small laptop, which he'd told Madison was dedicated to the drone so they had enough battery and storage for good pictures. The green screen went from static to focusing on the floor and his running shoes. Then he excused himself past Madison and asked Danny to slow so he could launch. He sent it due north so it would travel perpendicular to the suspicious vessel. He quickly adjusted his screen until he got a clear picture and then increased the climb to an elevation the ship wouldn't be able to see with their bare eyes.

Placing it on magnification, he got a shot of the ship, which had also slowed down. On deck were four men, and luckily, no one had power scopes, so there was a chance they didn't see the drone launch. He shot several pictures, getting a photo of the vessel I.D. and the name and registry.

"Fuckin Bahamian," muttered Jason. "She's powerful, all right, but I think we could outrun her."

"We could. The Bones would never make it. Go let them know. I'm sending Ned the link to the shots right now."

Danny was twisting around to try to see what had shown up on the screen. "You really think he's tailing us? He looks like he's veering off east of us now."

"Son of a gun," said Damon while using his binoculars. "I think he knows we saw him. He's doing a decoy run."

"Uh-oh," yelled Wilson. "I see three more vessels. We got a fucking flotilla out there, about a mile behind, east of them."

All of a sudden, the warm sunny day became dark and dangerous. Madison knew this wasn't good news at all. Their secret search wasn't secret any longer.

CHAPTER 12

THIS WASN'T SUPPOSED to happen, Ned thought. They were nearly ten miles off shore, and thank goodness they hadn't yet reached the site. They had been zigzagging, not traveling in a straight line, to disguise their final destination in case someone flew overhead or, as in this case, a faster ship overtook them.

Noonan was sweating profusely, both because of the sun and the danger that had suddenly popped up.

"I'm heading north, Ned. You tell me if they stay semi-engaged."

"Jason said they were rolling the horizon, trying to stay out of sight. Noonan, I think we got ourselves some trouble."

"Shit. Yes, I agree. But no uniforms, right? It's not a fuckin' gunboat, right?"

Ned chuckled in spite of his own concern. "No, Noonan. Just calm down and take it casual. Breathe. Heading north is a good thing. We'll slowly maintain toward land in case we have to go for it."

"The Bones isn't made for this," mumbled Noonan.

"She'll be fine."

When word came that there were three other boats behind the one that had been shadowing them, Noonan barked for a beer.

Ned gave him an ice water instead and earned a nasty look. He shouted down to the galley where Jake and Lucas were making sandwiches for everyone. "Jake, I need a cold wet towel."

Noonan was sitting now, wiping his forehead as the sweat poured down him profusely. He wasn't in the sun, as the Bones had a fairly generous upper deck canopy, and with the breeze, it wasn't unpleasant, but it was obvious to everyone he was struggling a bit. Ned hoped it wasn't anything medical, but just like his dad, Noonan wasn't known for taking very good care of himself.

Jake brought the towel up from below. "What's cooking? We got a tail, I hear?"

"I'm afraid so," said Ned as he wrapped the towel across Noonan's shoulders, stuffing it around his neck and into the collar of his flamingo shirt. Noonan leapt to his feet and, with a jerking motion, ripped the towel off him with his right arm while his left hand gripped the wheel. He tossed the cotton towel into the spray alongside the boat.

"Dammit. I don't need to turn into an ice cube. Get me a fuckin' beer."

Ned couldn't recall Noonan ever being so angry, but he was sorry to see this change in demeanor, which was suddenly now a medical symptom, not a feature of his personality. Unfortunately, it reminded him of his dad, because Noonan wouldn't take any advice, wouldn't allow anyone to help him, and screamed at anyone who didn't do what he requested.

Now Ned could see there was indeed a medical component. The vein in Noonan's neck on the left side was stressing, protruding as if it was going to burst open and spray all of them. Ned grabbed his right hand and took his pulse.

"T.J.! Get your ass up here!" he shouted to the other Team 3 medic.

Breathless, T.J. arrived shirtless, still holding a fan of playing cards to his chest so Tucker wouldn't see his hand. Ned grabbed the cards, beginning to ignite T.J.'s anger, until he took a good look at Noonan.

"Noonan, I'm taking you below decks. We can do it hard or easy. Or I could toss you overboard and let the guys behind us pick you up. Your choice."

The big medic didn't give their captain any time at all to think. He hoisted him up, held him backward in a body slam position, and dragged him, kicking and trying to get purchase with his hands at anything he could grab onto.

"Get your fuckin' hands off me!"

"Not having that. You want me to make you pass out? I can do it very easily." As the old captain's legs and arms continued to fight against T.J., Jake grabbed his ankles, holding them so tight that Noonan began to howl. They dragged him down the stairs and into his stateroom, the largest compartment on the boat. Jake sat on the old man's chest to keep him flat on his back. Ned could barely see Noonan's face, but it was obvious his lips were turning blue.

T.J. opened his medic kit, bypassed the blood pressure cuff and went straight for the adrenaline, administered it quickly and then applied the cuff. The results were staggeringly quick. His face lost the ashen, gray look, and his lips began to turn deep red. Tucker brought another cool towel, this time not dripping wet, and dabbed Noonan's forehead, face, and neck.

Noonan's eyes began to water as they darted from side to side. What Ned saw in those eyes wasn't pain or suffering from the effects of a heart attack he'd just had or they'd just avoided. It was shame. He was afraid to show his fear of dying, being taken out by his own lifestyle. Ned was sure of that.

He'd seen that on his dad's face too.

Ned turned his back on Noonan and the men taking care of him, confident that the worst had passed. He buzzed Danny Begay on his com.

"Where the hell you guys headed, Ned? I'm having a hard time keeping up with your pattern. And you've got something going on with one of your engines. Smoking like my Grandma Emma Two Toes."

Ned appreciated the comedy. He loved that about the Teams. When things were the most desperate, they'd see something and burst out laughing so hard they forgot they were too close to death to not laugh in Dr. Death's face.

"Noonan's had a heart attack, I think. He's down in his cabin. T.J. and Jake are working on him. Tucker too."

"Oh, shit. Let me get Wilson to take over then. Is he going to be okay?"

"For now. I'm going to recommend we get him to the hospital, so that means we're taking the quickest way back. You guys stay here, and I'll catch up with you tomorrow, if I can."

"Nope. Not doing that, Ned. We're following you just in case you have an engine failure and need a ride. You probably haven't seen the footage yet. Should have come through on your phone."

"Been kinda busy."

"I get it. Wilson's drone did everything but look up their social security records and blood type," answered Danny.

"I'm going to call D.C. and make a report, see if we can identify that craft and the owners. Tell me what you saw. Are they military? Any uniforms? Noonan was most afraid of that bunch."

"I'm guessing no. If they'd wanted to highjack the boat, they'd have done it before we got so far out to sea. And besides, who would want that bucket of bolts? How's he feeling?"

"Sheepish. Angry at the world. Embarrassed too. We definitely need to find out whose crosshairs we got in front of. It was not a coincidence, Danny."

Ned made a sweeping arch, having made some good ground in

the few minutes they'd been turning back. He swung behind a small cluster of islands, or perhaps one large island with just the peaks sticking out of the water. The water was dangerously shallow there. The larger boat the bad guys had would need to be careful not to get snagged on something as it had a bigger draw. The Lucky Strike was like a fast-moving tank and would plow through anything and had even less displacement than the Bones. It was newer and made of more lightweight material. And that added to her speed.

Danny buzzed again in Ned's ear. "I got an idea. Mind if I place a call to the tribal council? We got some guys with better-than-top-level access to some criminal databases, on a much smaller scale than your FBI contacts. I may not be the best swimmer, since most of us were never taught as kids on the res, but my contacts might be able to help find these idiots faster than your team in D.C."

"Sure, go ahead." Ned didn't want to be disrespectful, but he just couldn't help himself. "So, Danny, I got a question for you. How the hell did you get your Trident? And how did you manage to get invited on my dive team?"

"Oh, my bad."

Ned began to laugh. "No, seriously. How'd you do it?"

"One of my BUD/S instructors was Dine. He took me to the complex one night during pool comp and wouldn't let me leave until I passed. Trust me, I wanted to kill him with my bare hands when it was all over. I don't know by how much, but I passed. I was near drowned, but I passed."

Then out of the corner of Ned's eye he saw the big dangerous-looking behemoth swerve away in the opposite direction, speed up, and then disappear over the horizon in mere seconds.

Danny squawked in Ned's ear again. "See? There's another reason I'm on this team," Danny persisted.

"I'm going to regret this. I just know it."

"That was no boat. That goddamned thing was a spaceship. We got those on the res too. You know that, right?"

"Good one. Okay, we're gonna head back slower, so I don't blow up Noonan's rig. I'll call ahead for medical to be waiting for us at the pier."

"Roger that. Wilson's put the drone back to bed so I can help the ladies down in the galley. We'll have dinner ready by the time we hit Treasure Island."

T.J. climbed up from quarters and reported to Ned that Noonan was sleeping and his blood pressure was approaching normal range.

"Can you call Bay Care and have someone meet us at the Sports Club?"

"Will do. Bay Care?"

"They have a hospital just over the causeway with a first-class emergency and cardiac unit. That's where I want him to go. We'll settle up who stays behind and watches the gear later. First, I have to make sure Noonan gets treatment."

"Roger that."

T.J. scanned the horizon for the other vessels and shook his head. "All clear for now."

"Thanks, T.J. You getting hungry?"

"I'm always hungry. I understand Serena and Georgia have cooked us a nice meal."

"I've been told the same." After a short pause, Ned shook his head again, laughing.

"I fail to see the humor, Ned. Wanna let me in?"

"I think we'll call this Operation Dinner Cruise."

"Now that's funny."

But T.J. didn't laugh.

When they arrived, Noonan was met by the Bay Care Paramedics team and whisked off to emergency. T.J. offered to go with him so Ned could stay behind with Madison.

She fell into his arms, still shaking, but Ned made no mistake. He needed her now more than the other way around. And that was funny how that worked, he thought.

"Is Noonan going to be okay?" she asked.

"I think so. He needs to take better care of himself, but I think, like any good alley cat, he still has a few more lives left."

"I'll get my mother to go visit him after the dust settles. Will he be long in the hospital?"

"Depends on what they find. I'm guessing they'll keep him a day or two at the most, unless something else is going on or he needs surgery. But that might be what has to happen, Maddie. Your mom could be a big help with that, if it should come to it."

"You know she'll do anything to boost his spirits."

Several minutes later, the crew gathered on the Lucky Strike, trying to relax, but also trying not to attract more attention than was necessary. They'd already drawn a crowd with Noonan being transported to the hospital.

Zak brought some of his wine from California, which paired nicely with the Cajun fish dish Serena had made. Ned knew Noonan wouldn't have tolerated the heat levels, but the Team loved it. Ginger brought out a whole pound of Amish butter to slather over their steaming hot cornbread that melted in their mouths.

Then they had strawberry shortcake with huge fresh Plant strawberries, only in season for a few weeks out of the year.

The whole meal was simple but certainly hit the spot. As night fell and the stars came out, Wilson brought out his guitar and sang some cowboy songs he'd learned at the mission school, taught to him by a Jesuit priest.

Ned noted how well their team had bonded already, made up from a diverse collection of members from different cultures, living and working in various parts of the country. It was voluntary, but everyone agreed to stay on board until the next morning when new plans would be discussed.

Jason Kealoha expressed his desire to perform his Haka traditional Maori dance ritual. Before he could begin, just the act of stomping his legs, readying his huge frame for the movements caused the Strike to wobble from side to side. It took several men to stop the dance from ever starting.

It was just not the way anyone wanted to end the evening.

Ned and Madison planned to turn in early as several of their group talked into the night. Guards were posted on regular shifts. T.J. returned with news Noonan would be prepped for surgery tomorrow to correct a heart blockage.

"I'm glad we were there. If he'd have been way out there by himself, I don't think he'd have made it back," T.J. said.

"Is he still talking about the dive?" asked Tucker.

Ned already knew the answer. He was leading Madison down the stairs to their tiny cabin.

"Non-stop," said T.J.

Madison paused. "He's in his element, surrounded by people who have to attend to him. They're a captive audience, and he has lots and lots of stories!" she added.

Ned didn't want to spend any time thinking about what their plan B was. All that could wait until tomorrow. It was an exciting day. One could even say a perfect day. He knew just the way to bookend it.

And yes, the two of them would rock the boat big time.

CHAPTER 13

NED WAS AWAKENED for his shift, which began at 0600. They had spent the night in Ned's cabin on the Barry Bones.

Madison got up with him, bringing her lightweight blanket and pillow. Together, they sat on the bridge, watching the sunrise.

"As many times as I've watched the sun come up on the Gulf, I never tire of it. The sunsets either," she said. It seemed like such a natural and beautiful way to begin a day. She never wanted to be without it. They got to witness miracles every day.

"We're in the tropics. Very unpredictable," Ned answered, agreeing with her. "I totally get why people come for a vacation and stay their whole lives. Like there's some kind of magic here, just as Kyle said."

"Everything is so unpredictable, but it's beautiful in that it's always fresh and surprising here. The warm air, like this morning, just swirls around me and makes me feel safe and whole."

"Or the illusion of," reminded Ned.

"But I feel like I can still relax. And I know there's always danger lurking. But the land, the water, and the clouds—it's like they conspire to take my mind places it's never been before. That's what I mean by different and surprising. You certainly don't want me to worry more, do you, Ned?"

"Nope. That's my job."

That brought silence between them as the full force of the sun hit their faces and then the gentle ocean breeze cooled them off.

In the next berth over, Danny and Wilson were drinking coffee and whispering from the bridge of the Lucky Strike. Wilson waved, and she returned his greeting.

Several club workers arrived early and didn't take much interest. There was very little traffic on Gulf Boulevard, and the water was calm. It was as if all the excitement of the day before, with Noonan's heart attack and the chase involving the unknown parties, was washed away since no evidence of them lingered in the early morning light fog.

Ned's cell rang. He adjusted his arms around Madison's waist, readjusted the blanket, and put it to his ear. It was a call from 202 area code. D.C.

"Ned Silver speaking."

Madison could hear the caller's voice.

"You asked for support in identifying ownership of a certain Martin Starliner, and we've located the records," the young woman on the other end of the line said.

"That's great. Let me—"

"First, this vessel was reported stolen four months ago in the Bahamas. It's owned by a British couple who still maintain the open claim. There is a reward for the successful return of the craft."

"So the people who came after us are not the owners?"

"Came after you? Are you sure?"

"Looked like it to me, ma'am."

"For the moment, let's assume not. Our records show that it remains missing. Your pictures are the first concrete evidence the vessel hasn't been destroyed or parted off and sold to pirates for use in their drug trade in Africa and the Mediterranean. You say you saw this boat last night in Florida? A place called Treasure

Island? That's kind of a strange coincidence."

"We get that a lot here. Big vacation resort area. People from all over the world. On the Gulf."

"How did you come across it? You saw it with your own eyes?"

"We did. We were about ten plus miles out, and we noticed them pop up on the horizon behind us. It was part of a flotilla of three other boats that were too far away to get any identifiers. I think they were chasing us. This triggered a medical emergency with one of our older passengers, our captain, and we had to head back to shore. Right now, we're tethered privately at the Blue Water Sports Club, while we await the treatment of our dive captain. Next door and only a short walk away is the Treasure Island Marina."

"And where did the craft, the *Jilly Jean* go?"

"They kept going deeper into the Gulf."

"Could it be that's where they were headed, not following you?"

"Could be."

Madison could tell Ned didn't want to give her more detail.

"Okay, I'll initiate the report. I can reach you on this number if I need further information on something, then? You would be the contact person?"

"Yes, ma'am."

"How many in your party, and what was the purpose of your outing?"

Ned was quick on the reflex answer. "We're a group of old friends just messing around, reliving our college days. Boats, blue water, fishing, and swimming—things we all like to do and never get enough time to satisfy."

He was very clever, and Madison smiled at him, giving him encouragement for his performance.

It seemed to work.

"I'm going to relay this to the insurance representative and the Coast Guard. We'll reach out to the consulate in the Bahamas to locate the owners. You make sure to contact us again if you see this craft a second time. I'll text you the owners' contact information, as there is a reward posted."

"That's interesting. How much?"

"It depends on the condition of the vessel, but this is a two-million-dollar speed-yacht, a custom special hybrid craft. We'll leave all that up to the adjuster. The information will be in a text message directly to your device."

"Is that it? Aren't you going to send someone to interview us?" Ned asked.

"We have your contact file, Mr. Silver. We'll be in touch. Thank you for the information."

"Let me ask this question, then. Am I to assume that the people who have possession of this vessel are involved in some sort of illegal trade or activity, like drugs or high seas piracy?"

"Most definitely, yes."

"Can you give us any information on suspects or at least what kind of illegal activity they have engaged in, other than stealing the boat?"

"Perhaps the adjustor will have that information. Often these fast boats are used as transport for human smuggling and drug running, since they can outrun anything with the exception of the Coast Guard cutters. We find them abandoned all over the world now."

"I feel they were directly trying to target me and my crew, personally. Are we in any danger?"

"You maintain contact with us. Please let us know if you see the vessel again, but I'd stay away from them. Do not approach. I'd consider them dangerous, so I'd do everything you can to avoid them. Especially if they're running a group of them together.

We understand that, in your line of work, your naval history, this might seem like something difficult to do. But, for your own good and for the health and safety of your friends, I'd refrain from trying to engage them. I don't want to offend you, but we don't need any acts of heroism with this bunch. We need you to stay as far away as possible, and let us investigate and do our jobs here."

"Once again, ma'am, we have no intention of trying to contact them, but can we have some indication of who these people are? Some names? Nationalities? Surely you have something on them, with this kind of theft."

"We're working on it. We'll be in touch, Mr. Silver. Try to enjoy the rest of your vacation."

Madison heard the phone disconnect before Ned could sign off.

"Don't you find that strange?" he asked her.

"You sure you called the right department?"

"It was our liaison number, the number we're supposed to call when we've witnessed a domestic crime. Shit. Maybe that call was a mistake. I better get hold of Zinski."

In the middle of their breakfast, the Team got word that Noonan had survived the surgery, which had taken less than the five hours originally set aside. He would be staying in the hospital an additional two to three days, and he wasn't allowed visitors until the attending physician was sure the risk of infection was significantly lessened and his heart was beating normally.

One by one, members of the team asked Madison in private what Ned had revealed was the future of the mission, now that Noonan was temporarily out of the picture. They all knew that perhaps he'd never be able to re-join the party.

Madison told the truth. She wished she knew, as well. She knew it was weighing on Ned tremendously and that any efforts she might make to talk things over would only add to the pressure he was feeling. She knew he was working on it. He'd made two calls to the attorney's office before they ate and hadn't been able to reach him.

Meanwhile, costs were adding up. This was not Ned's op. He wanted to be able to release everyone quickly if they had no path forward, at least for now, and he'd told her so. But he was still playing a wait and see game, and he didn't want to disrupt a mission that might still have a prayer of going forward. It just wasn't his call.

T.J. and Tucker had gone to the hospital on Ned's direction, to make sure Noonan had some protection while he lay immobilized, in and out of consciousness.

The crew began cleanup of the galley, routine maintenance of the vessel, and checking the dive equipment, which was a constant job on any of these chartered adventures. Every day started out at ground zero so that nothing got missed or taken for granted.

Wilson found a local diesel mechanic to take a look over the dual motors, trying to assess if it was reliable to take out or not. The SWCC guy hovered over the mechanic so close, asking questions, that the two almost got into a fight.

Just after noon, Ned finally got the call he was expecting. He took it in private, pacing up and down the pier out of anyone's earshot.

Madison double and triple crossed her fingers.

CHAPTER 14

ZINSKI WAS ALREADY aware of Noonan's condition.

"This leaves you in a pickle, Ned."

"You think? I get the strange feeling—call it my sixth sense—that something is about to go down. Something big. I'm just not sure where we stand. Should I send everyone home, wait until Noonan is fully recovered, or go ahead in his absence?"

"If he were conscious, would he give you the power to go forward?"

"I think so. Problem is, I've not done this as often as he has. He had a buddy last year who was murdered. But Gary knew all the ins and outs and had been on hundreds of dives."

"Related to this?"

"No. Those were low life, petty criminals one of our crew met through a drug buy. This time, Noonan didn't vet anyone but me and Madison. And he trusted me to get the right crew. But do I have the authority?"

"Off the top of my head, I'd say yes. If you reasonably think he'd want the project to go on, people on the outside would deem that a smart and rational decision for the betterment of all. There's a university that's going to benefit as well, you know. So that's part of the picture—your philanthropic hero button, as it were."

"I'd rather have a little dose of certainty, please. I've got patches and pins galore, thank you very much."

Zinski chuckled. "I'll bet you do." He sighed while Ned waited for his recommendation. Ned wanted to get the green light. They could figure out how to do the dive, and Madison would be a great help, but he really wanted Zinski's blessing first. Without it, Ned was going to send everyone home and risk the ire of Noonan when he recovered and found out what he'd done.

"Your call, sir. But I really need your advice." Ned purposely laid it on thick.

"I'd say go for it. But I also wouldn't string it out more than a handful of days, maybe three or four max. Keep a captain's log of every detail, every event just in case something goes sideways, and you'll have a record to fall back on. Wouldn't hurt to stress in your notes that you're trying to carry on what Noonan had asked you to do before his heart attack."

"We don't have our University of Florida liaison set up yet, and I don't know who he used there. Do you?"

"I can't assume it's the same person or department. They switch out all the time. Just intending to include them when—and specifically say you expect this to happen—Noonan recovers, you'll turn over what you must and catalog the rest. Noonan had a family in North Carolina who originally tasked him with his first dive. He seemed to be very loyal to them, so you could mention that. Let's play it that you are just going to do the best you can and Noonan will fix everything later on. Does that make sense?"

"Sure it does. But what happens if he doesn't recover?"

"At best we have a problem. At worst, we have a huge problem, maybe even a lawsuit."

"And what about those guys sniffing around?"

"You definitely follow the orders the lady at the FBI gave you, Ned. You stay out of their way and report the sighting of the vehicle. Let the feds pick them up. That's a huge crime they committed. Kinda dumb, if you ask me."

"Sounds like we should get going right away. Get in and out before anyone knows we've been there."

"I think that's best. And don't let anyone keep anything. You've got to control that. You are tight with everyone, right?"

"Madison is friends with the ladies. I've spilled blood with all the other guys or had friends who did. All except one guy, Crater Meade, who owns a local dive shop. He's a certified instructor and even trains SEALs for the Navy. I don't know him, but Noonan chose him, and he's giving us a big discount on some of the equipment. I think he's okay."

"I don't know why that name is familiar to me, but it doesn't send up any red flags. I may have met him a time or two. So, Ned, are you ready and are you sure about what you're going to do?"

Ned didn't want to lie to the man, but in this case, it was necessary.

"Martin, I think Noonan would be delighted to know we're moving forward. One thing you can do for us is get someone posted outside Noonan's room as a precaution. I have two former teammates there now standing guard. But I need them on the boat with their equipment, not standing in some hallway eating hospital food."

"I have a husband-and-wife team who are excellent. Which hospital?"

Ned gave him the room number and all the other details. They promised to stay in touch, each of them promising to let the other know if there was a new development.

Ned thanked him and signed off. He took several minutes, tactical breathing, working to lower his pulse rate, as he watched the calm waters of the bay and the puffy salmon-colored clouds growing like mushrooms from the horizon.

Noonan, you get better. Not time to show up at old Jake's door-

step. You're needed down here. You'll have time for all your hellos and partying later. This is not that time. Give me a hand. Help me decide how to do this. I need you. I really do.

Just saying those words in his mind gave him more courage. He placed the phone in his pocket, turned, and approached the Bones with an extra spring in his step.

Madison was the first worried face he encountered. "Pack up and get ready. We're off as soon as we can. Now go tell everyone. Help me out, okay?"

She beamed. "Absolutely! You got everything straightened out?"

"Nearly. To acceptable risk levels anyway. Did you work Noonan's grid pattern for your past dives?"

"Only about two dozen times. I even know where he stores his paperwork and maps from past dives. He's got logs and a map closet in his cabin. I can show you."

He grabbed her and placed a big kiss on her cheek. "That's all I wanted to hear, sweetheart. I'm going to need you to take the lead on much of that. I'm calling for T.J. and Tucker to return to the boat ASAP. I'd like to get out of here within the hour. Can we do that?"

"We most definitely can. Both boats are clean, the equipment checked. Wilson even got Noonan's engines serviced, so we're good to go."

"Excellent. You spread the word while I call in the boys."

THEIR FUEL WAS topped off and fresh water onboarded. Serena purchased some items from the head chef at the Sports Club to replace what they'd used. In one hour and thirty, they were heading out to the belly of the Gulf of Mexico, looking to lift up her skirts and recover her secrets. As the barrier islands disappeared from view, Ned was suddenly hopeful. The dread he was carrying had lifted. He wished his father's old friend well.

He knew he was going to make both men proud. One was clear across the country in California, sleeping off a hard and probably disappointing life. The other one was in the shop being repaired. With any luck, Ned felt he had a shot at redemption for both of them.

CHAPTER 15

MADISON SPREAD OUT Noonan's logs and maps over his old lumpy bed, showing Ned how they had organized the grid pattern from start to finish. He had marked with a pencil sketch where he thought the wreck and debris field was located. Long lines extended south from the bulk of the site. The location of the crypt was noted with the explanation "Concrete Box of unknown origin." Ned had suggested they continue to use that term so no one slipped up later.

"See, these lines are where he said the drag occurred," Madison explained. "Some event moved the hull, we hope loaded down with precious cargo, until it buried itself again in the sea bed. I think he would make sure a double team would follow those lines to where they entered the floor, perhaps excavate down to see if we could find any of those encrusted timbers or the mast. We'd also be looking for semi-circular casings, but the shape isn't as important as how it tests on the metal detector. If it tests for a precious metal, then we work that site in more detail."

"You want me to make the assignments? Do we start with pairs at the corners?" he asked.

"No, we start here, at the end of the drag marks, and go outward, north, south, east and west, until we've made a square, further delineating a grid pattern until there is no evidence of the debris field left and it just reverts to virgin sea bed."

Ned nodded.

"You can make the assignments, though. Pick this center section for the most experienced divers. I think Crater and I could partner that. You could take the upper quadrants with your swim buddy, and so forth. Pair people together who would work in tandem. One takes notes and pictures. The other one excavates and explores, and they trade off in twenty-minute shifts so no one gets bored and misses anything."

"Fantastic. I think I'm beginning to see how it's done. When everyone brings back their drawings and photos, we get a look at the whole field, right?"

"Yes, that's where the pattern is discovered. And hence the theory of what caused the wreck or identifying the ship itself. And it could be more than one. We saw that before on the barge dive, remember?"

On a separate map, Madison drew the proposed grid, starting with deep "skid" marks. Ned labeled the teams for each area, leaving Madison and Crater for the middle section. They presented it to the others after they'd found Noonan's coordinates, dropped anchors, and gathered everyone in the spacious Lucky Strike main deck lounge.

The coms and other equipment were tested and re-tested by each buddy in the teams. Wilson would stay on the bridge of the Strike, while Danny would man the Bones. Liz partnered with Jake Green, but the other two ladies remained in the galley to prepare lunch and to prep for dinner to follow several hours later.

The dive lines and monitoring equipment were only connected to the Strike. The Bones had taken on more as a supply vehicle, except for the storage of maps and items Noonan had in his cabin. But all the more sophisticated equipment and sensors were housed on the Strike.

Madison and Crater descended down into the deep first, followed by the other pairs. Lucas was to remain up top on the Strike to help keep a lookout for approaching vessels and to help Wilson and Danny monitor traffic. If anything was needed, he would be the errand boy for now.

Crater and Madison roved side by side with Crater holding the metal detector until they found the deep grooves Noonan had photographed. In one of them was a piece of silver plate, distinguishable by the screaming of the detector. Madison tried to pry it from the sea bed, with no luck. Crater handed her the machine and used a specialized part hatchet, part crowbar custom tool to get leverage on the object and broke a piece of it off. The shiny edge of the fragment was revealed, and there was no doubt that it was silver.

Madison dropped it into the basket attached with a belt to her hip. She then motioned for the others to pace off four big steps and work in all four directions. Soon, the chatter from the coms was lighting up the enthusiasm as more and more items were called out and identified. They found coils of metal, glass jars, tools, hardware, and some broken earthenware pottery. Ned reminded them they were under strict orders to leave everything on the floor except for the remnants of silver plate they might need to plead their case for further exploration. It was going to be hard to sell Noonan's theory of golden or silver-plated masts, so a photograph was deemed not adequate.

T.J. and Ned found the remnants of a rounded door handle, covered in a thick white crust. They also photographed and studied what appeared to be a pile of lumber that had at one time been lashed together with rope, now reduced to several long strings. As Ned tried to place one in his basket, it turned to putty and eventually disappeared completely.

The twenty minutes went by fast. Teams switched roles and

worked until the edges of the site could be determined. Each group photographed the four corners of their grid using plastic L-shaped markers Madison had given them.

After nearly an hour, they heard Wilson's voice over the com.

"And I have a sighting of a dark blue or black yacht—looks to be a hundred foot or more. It's crossing our path. He doesn't appear to want to come over. And now, he's waving."

"Make sure you get pictures, Wilson," demanded Ned. "See if you can get their call letters on the side."

"I can't read them. I'd get the drone, but he's too close."

"What's he doing?" asked Tucker.

"Stopping, dammit."

"Keep your distance," Ned barked.

"We're sitting ducks," Danny added.

Lucas broke into the conversation. "Hey, guys. I think they mean to board us. He's talking to someone on a radio or sat phone."

"Wilson?" Ned called out. "Get that fucking drone out now. I want a recording of this from overhead. Send a copy to your own devices just in case."

"Roger that, Ned."

"Lucas, give our friends at the Coast Guard a call, let the ladies know what's going on, and then help Wilson out at the bridge. Danny, you okay? If you have to run a decoy, you do it. There's a Luger and some extra rounds in the captain's locker under the wheel, but you'll have to break the lock to get at it. You do that if you feel you need to."

"I'm on it, Ned. If I have to ditch, do I have permission?"

Madison's heart sank with that last comment from Ned. Was he actually asking him to make a run for it armed with only a handgun? His boat could easily be overcome, putting Danny in grave danger.

"Use your best judgment. But you'll have to explain it to Noonan."

"Ned, we're not staying down here, are we?" asked Crater. "If we got potential bad guys up top, we shouldn't be left so vulnerable. We gotta get back on board."

"I'm one step ahead of you, Crater. I prefer they not know we're down here until we've made the calls."

Madison opened her basket and placed the silver piece in her dive pack. She let the basket float to the floor, since it was obvious their collection time was over.

"Don't lose your notes, but make sure you tuck them inside your wetsuits, out of sight. Store your cameras securely and try to hide them, if you can."

Ned and T.J. began the ascent. On their way, they heard Wilson confirm he'd launched the bird, sending photographs downloading to his laptop. At the same time, he'd rigged it to send off a distress signal, which would be picked up by any civil defense, law enforcement, or coast guard receiver within a ten-mile radius.

"Good thinking, Wilson. Glad you're with us. T.J. and I are on our way. If you don't mind, Madison, you and Liz come up last."

"Got it," Liz acknowledged.

Ned climbed onto the deck at the stern, making as little splash as he could manage, and then helped T.J. with his equipment. He stored the detector in one of the compartments under the rear seating.

As others followed suit behind him, Ned watched their audience, who had not approached, regardless of what Lucas had claimed. The sleek yacht the group was using wasn't the same vessel they'd seen yesterday, but this one was even nicer, slightly larger and more modern. It looked brand new.

Wilson approached with his controller and asked for Ned's

email to send images to. Ned also gave him the FBI contact information he'd been given over the phone. There wasn't any way they could send an explanation, but he hoped the pictures themselves would flag someone.

As Liz and Madison surfaced and stowed their equipment, three additional yachts appeared from the north, including the large black one reported stolen from the Bahamas.

He leaned over and whispered to Wilson, "Get that one, quick."

He watched as the screen showed the drone's call signs and even got a closeup of the occupants standing on the bridge. One was a woman.

"My com still working? Just nod your head if you can still hear me?" Ned watched as everyone acknowledged. "We're gonna get out of Dodge, just turn around and leave quietly without a confrontation. If they come after us, we'll keep moving east toward the shore. Danny, if it becomes a chase, you split off if you feel comfortable.

"Roger that."

"Gentlemen. Start your engines."

Wilson said something over the com to his cousin as a farewell in Navajo, Ned guessed.

It hit him right in the pit of his stomach. He was responsible for these good men. He prayed they could get back without incident.

As the four crafts began to follow, Wilson sped up. The Bones couldn't keep up their pace and began to drift back. As the cousins turned and waved to each other, Danny swerved off to the side and headed for a small sandbar off in the distance. He wouldn't be able to outrun them to shore, but he could make it to the sandbar before they were forced to slow down to keep from running aground.

Madison pressed her palm against Ned's back as they all watched one vehicle follow Danny, but the other three were closing in on the Lucky Strike.

"Ned, you take the wheel. I must bring in my drone."

"Can it follow?" Ned asked.

"It has time, but I'm getting ahead of its range. She'll drop from the sky if that happens.

Tucker barked an answer. "Send her over to Danny. You can crash her there on that island."

"Now that's a clever thought," Wilson said, adjusting the controls and then pushing the little craft in Danny's direction. Seconds after the bird disappeared from view, there was a large explosion and fireball from the direction of the sandbar as Ned and the rest of the team watched the Bones shatter into a million shards of light.

CHAPTER 16

"DANNY!" WILSON YELLED.

Without asking, he circled back to head toward the island. The boat careened, nearly ending on its side, but successfully made the turn. Madison and everyone up top hung on to anything they could to avoid being tossed overboard. Liz fell on top of Andy and Jason. They all heard the sounds of pans and dishes and even humans being tossed about the small galley space below. Serena let out a scream and then cursed at the top of her lungs.

Ned was down the stairway, followed by Jake and Andy, helping Zak and the ladies recover from the disaster.

Wilson had clenched his jaw, bent over, and punched the power, determined to get to Danny.

Crater jumped to the bridge and tried to grab the wheel from Wilson's hands. As the two struggled, Crater yelled, "You turn around. You can't do anything for him. We *have* to get to shore. You don't want to mess with these people!"

Tucker Hudson, in one long leap, reached the bridge and picked Crater up. He was going to toss him overboard when Jason and T.J. stopped him.

"You fuckin' traitor!" Tucker said as he extricated himself from his buddies. The dive shop owner had been dumped on his ass, sprawling down the steps and onto the upper deck. Tucker was preparing to back it up with some serious physical pain for the man everyone now suspected of sabotaging their mission.

Ned's shirt was bloody when he popped up from the galley, but he otherwise seemed unhurt. "Tucker! Knock it off. He'll get his due."

"You want me to cuff him?" asked Damon. "I got zip ties."

"Get them," Ned shouted over the noise of the motor and the boat slicing through the waters of the Gulf.

Ned stared down at Crater, in total shock. "You knew about all this? How could you do this, Crater?"

The man's bloody lip upturned as he hung his head. He accepted the ties, placing his wrists together and allowing Damon to lash him to one of the chairs bolted to the decking. "No one was supposed to get hurt, okay? They were just supposed to scare you off."

"And then take our finds. That's fuckin' stealing," said Ned.

"Stupid Noonan. He was warned. You can't stand up to these guys."

"So now it's Noonan's fault?" Liz's voice was shrill. She held a pan, her elbow bloodied, looking like she was going to smash Crater's head in. "What a coward. You're a despicable human being."

Wilson kept hard charging until, all of a sudden, they ran right over their own debris field. Bits of fiberglass were flying through the late morning air. But there was no sign of Danny.

Madison looked behind them. One boat remained headed in their direction, but the other three were turning away. Ned focused on the beach, looking for Danny, when she grabbed his hand. "They're turning back. Ned, they're not coming after us. Just one boat—"

Wilson took a hard right turn to avoid hitting Danny, who was floating in the water face down. Madison lost her footing and fell overboard.

The water was warm, and for a split second, she forgot that she was in the middle of a chase, that Danny was perhaps badly injured or worse, and they were being pursued by a boatload of drug smugglers or pirates. Sounds of a motor became louder, and it was then she noticed the sleek black boat headed straight for her.

She paddled, trying desperately to get out of the way, but she knew she wasn't going to be fast enough. There was no possibility she could do anything to stop the yacht from running her over, and the captain didn't have nearly enough time to stop. In a slow-motion dream-like trance, she braced herself for the pain of metal blades slicing through her flesh and did the only thing she could think of.

She dove down deep into the water. Hoping to God she was fast enough, she kept pushing with downward strokes, anticipating losing one or both legs, or perhaps just a foot at the ankle. Her imagination ran wild as any minute now her body was going to be in excruciating, horrible pain. She hoped it was followed by a quick death, not torn apart and still alive to feel every bite as sharks devoured her body.

And there it was, that pressure on her ankle, just one ankle. Her right ankle. But it wasn't a shark bite. It was someone's hand, grabbing hold of her leg and pulling her up. Did this mean her head was now in the path of the engine? So maybe this was better. Get it over with. No lingering agonizing death. She screamed until she realized she was completely out of breath.

Up out of the water, she was dragged. She kicked, trying to dive back in, but even though she thrashed, gulped in air and screamed, scratched and pushed, rolled over and over like a fish, she was restrained. Someone pulled her thigh, hand over hand.

Then the top of her wet suit, pulling her, sliding her across the deck of the boat.

"No!" she continued to scream and felt her heel land in the soft flesh of someone's face. She kicked again, and this time felt warm liquid, blood, coming from the face of her attacker.

Another set of hands was on her body now, and she couldn't kick. A large body, a man's body had covered hers, immobilizing her, making it impossible for her to fight. They restrained her hands next.

Then someone said, "Madison, Goddammit. Stop fighting me. You're hurting me!"

Ned?

His face was bloody. His left eye was swelling, reaching the size of a hardboiled egg. His lip was split and draining red phlegm. His blue shirt was stained red and pink. He was trying to say something, but he was breathing so hard, he couldn't get a word out.

"Oh, Ned. Did they hurt you too?" she screamed.

Someone laughed in the distance. Ned gasped and started to choke, laughing. He spit out blood and gave her a smile through the wounds in his face.

"No, honey. But you did, Madison. You hurt me. You have a wicked, wicked kick. Beautiful legs, lovely to look at, but bad all the way to the bone. I just never knew how much I loved you until just now."

He fell back, laughing. Several other people stood over her, also smiling or chuckling. Someone gave her a cool towel. She righted herself, looking at all the blood spread over the deck, making it slippery. But she persisted, sitting up and placing the cool towel against his eye.

"I'm so sorry, Ned. I thought—"

"It doesn't matter Madison. We're okay. The cavalry has arrived, and we're safe."

"Danny?"

"Knocked out of breath, maybe a broken rib. Just guessing. But he'll be fine."

"How did you stop the boat?"

He laughed again, his elbow slipping on his own blood until he fell back against the deck again and let himself laugh more.

"It doesn't matter. It would take too long, and I don't have the energy."

"But—"

"Madison, just stop. Stop asking questions. Everyone's safe, and we got some of the bad guys anyway."

"Who's we?"

"Oh God, Madison. The Coasties. The ones you think look so sexy in their uniforms?"

"I did not say that."

"Oh, yes, you did. In your sleep, you've said it many times. I remember, because I don't wear a uniform, unless it's something official. But you like uniforms, don't you?" He gave her a smirk.

When she couldn't think of anything to say, she asked another question. "But how did you—?"

"If you don't stop with the questions, I'm not going to ask you to marry me."

Behind her, she heard clapping and a couple cheers. But his words got her attention. She wasn't going to say another word.

CHAPTER 17

THEIR DREAMS OF ending up rich and famous went up in smoke, just like the Barry Bones. Ned did feel badly about that but convinced himself it was Danny's fault, not his. That didn't make a bit of difference to Noonan, who could barely speak to him. His favorite words were, "What in the world were you thinking, going after all that shit without me?"

And even if he'd been tired of saying, "You were hooked up in the hospital after having your chest cracked," it would continue to do no good. Noonan was grieving, not about the treasure that wasn't there, but about the old Bones. He walked around the Salty Dog, down the street, over at the office they were shutting down across the street from the club. His maps and logs were gone. Noonan said he felt like he'd died that day in the water, so much of his past was lost.

The Salty Dog was the only place to meet him. It was where the conversations were too loud, the music even louder, and as the evening wore on, no one was making any sense talking to anyone. You could be with a person all night long and not remember a thing either of you said.

Noonan had been so convinced of the existence of this ship with the golden or silver mast he was willing to risk it all to see if it was there. And he very nearly did risk it all. He'd kept the threats on his life, on their lives, away from them so he didn't have to feel the rejection when they told him no.

But that would have been the right answer, he told Ned. If someone had said "No" sooner, Noonan would still have that ship. He could still pretend he was a pirate, full of adventure. He could still pretend that, if he could just lay his hands on the wheel of the Bones one more time, he'd find it. Find enough to put him in the lap of luxury, not smelling of fish and beer, sitting with his buddies, all jockeying for position to avoid picking up the tab.

"Well, we did get something out of it, Noonan."

"Not much. That wasn't my fault, either."

"No, it's never your fault, Noonan. But we did get the insurance finder's fee."

"You watch. They'll find a way to wiggle out of that too. You want to bet how much it will be?" he asked Ned.

"Sure. What are you willing to lose?"

He pulled out the dog collar that Otis had worn at one time—the first one, not the imitation, he was fond of saying. "I'll bet the whole farm there won't be more than twenty bucks."

"That's not fair, Noonan. Now you're just being a sour puss. Besides, I don't want that old thing."

Noonan put the collar back in his pocket. "It's hard when you're so old no one wants anything of yours. I remember when the ladies wanted all of me. Couldn't get enough of me, in fact. Beautiful ladies, like Amberley. Your father loved her too. You know that."

"Of course, I know that. You only tell me just about every day. So what are we going to bet, then? Let's make it realistic. A proper wager."

"Didn't you hear me? No one wants anything I've got, Ned. That's a problem."

"I know something you've got that I'd like to have."

"You don't say?" Noonan took another drag on his beer. He watched Madison wipe down the bar with a dishrag. "You promised you'd marry her, Ned. You remember that?"

"Yes, I did. And I will."

"When? When your ship sails in? When you get that treasure I've been looking for my whole life?"

"I want to be worthy of who she is. I want to be the man she thinks I am. This mission we went on, I fell for it. You conned me, didn't you?"

"No. I believed in it all along. I honestly thought there was a wreck with a silver masthead, embellished door handles, silver-plated dishes, grates on the storage areas. Maybe the anchor! But it's there, somewhere."

"Ah, so then you're going to look for another crypt, right?"

Noonan nearly spit out his beer. "After the next hurricane. But anyway, we were going to make a wager. I couldn't take anything from you, but what is it that you want of mine?"

"Memories."

"Excuse me?"

"Memories. Of Jake, my dad. I want to know what he was like. What he was like when he was happy, because he was never happy around me. I was the reason he couldn't have the life he wanted to have, was supposed to have."

"Don't say that. He had your mother. And what a prize she is, too. You're lucky to have such a mother."

Ned fingered the droplets of condensation on his beer. He was apprehensive to ask the question he'd always wanted to ask Noonan. Now was the time to be the kind of man Madison wanted and thought him to be.

"Why, Noonan, didn't he show me his happy side? Why did I bring him so much pain? What did I do to deserve that?"

In spite of himself, he did feel that deep, deep pain in his heart for the father he never got to know.

"I don't know, Ned. He always told me such wonderful things about you. He loved you very much. He loved your mother too. What he was unhappy about was that he wasn't good enough for Amberley. He knew he didn't deserve her. And he knew he could make your mother happy by giving her you. It was just the best he could do."

"Let's have that bet, then. If we get less than $1000 on the finder fee, you win. If we get more, I win."

"And what do you want of mine?"

"I don't want that dog collar. I want you to tell me stories about my dad. I want you to tell me the stories he should have told me. You can do it for him, or do it for me, makes no difference. But I'd like the gift of those memories, something I can think about instead of that grey, stiff old buzzard I saw that last day before we put him in the ground."

Noonan flicked a tear from his right eye and cleared his throat. "Okay, fair is fair. And if I'm the winner, I get to be your best man, stand by you at your wedding day. I get to be old Jake for a day. How about that?"

NED WAS PREPARING to leave for San Diego. He'd told Madison just one more deployment and then he'd make a decision. She was okay with it being his choice. She understood that about him. But she told him she didn't want to move to California, because everything magical was in Florida. She never wanted to live far from the beach, the warm beach, and she never wanted to have to work so damned hard she'd not be able to enjoy it.

He was fine with that.

"When I get back, the first thing we'll do is plan the wedding. I want you to pick out all kinds of pictures of how you want it to look like. I want as big or as little a wedding as you want. I want you to think about where you want to go on our first night married. Because when I'm gone, I can't think about things like that, so you'll have to think about them for me, okay?"

"It's a deal."

The postman rang their doorbell and had a certified letter addressed to him. There was another one addressed to Madison. It was from the insurance adjuster.

He was going to receive one hundred thousand dollars. They were also giving fifty thousand dollars to everyone on that dive trip—all seventeen of them, including Madison and Noonan.

"Amazing. Looks like we got the treasure after all," he said to her, swinging her around as if they were on a dance floor. "But you know what's even better?"

She smiled. "Tell me. I'm dying to know!"

"I won the bet."

"Who did you bet?"

"Noonan."

"What did you win?"

Ned smoothed his thumbs over her lower lip, slipped his fingers behind her ears, and pulled her to him. "It means I get to hear all the stories about my dad."

"That's what you asked for?"

"Indeed, I did."

"Ned Silver, I think you're the most amazing man I've ever met."

FINDING HOME

Sunset SEALs Book 8

SHARON HAMILTON

CHAPTER 1

NAVY SEAL JASON Kealoha walked in the orange glow on the white sugar sand beach aptly named Sunset Beach, Florida. It wasn't anything like Hawaii, where he was raised, but there was a vibe and a peacefulness here in Florida that he remembered from his childhood in Kauai.

One of the sad memories, however, was the skirmishes that existed sometimes between the races: the Samoans, the Native Hawaiians, the Haole, the Chinese, the Indo-Chinese Polynesians, and mixtures in between. He had friends in school who had Chinese fathers and Japanese mothers whose relations wouldn't speak to each other at family gatherings.

Old ways die slow.

He had girls in his high school classes who outweighed him by a hundred pounds and friends he played rugby with who were both men and women, and they played fierce, were highly competitive, and reflected their ancestral warrior backgrounds.

His blended culture accepted all sizes, and yet frequently fights erupted over those very same differences. In the end, they were all one family. Just like their hatreds of certain things, they practiced fierce love.

In Florida, it was similar. So many people from different countries spoke a patchwork of Pidgin languages almost like it was in the islands. Cultural roots went back thousands of years. Refugees and vagabond travelers descended upon the state from both exotic as well as ordinary places in the world, mostly for the weather, but also because it was much more affordable than other parts of the US. It was a melting pot of ideas, cultures, religions, and everything in between.

But one thing he found in Florida he had not found other places was that everybody liked to laugh. That was something the two communities had in common. His Hawaiian heritage had taught him the value of laughter, especially as a healing or mask of pain.

It was nearly 90 degrees, and the bright orange and yellow, purple-streaked sky looked ominous with huge clouds that were going to turn dark. He didn't see any lightning, but at the first crack of thunder, he would quickly move indoors, not wanting to become a statistic he'd been warned about. After all, this was the lightning capital of the whole world—as if God's finger touched the ground here so often that it showed.

His and Kiley's quick wedding on Kauai was beautiful, a mixture of the Hawaiian ceremonies, festivals and songs of his childhood and the western influence on his father's side, what Jason called his watered-down or "Hawaii Lite" type of ceremony. His uncle Keoki, his father's older brother, who lived with them, even sharing a bed with his mother, insisted on using a Methodist minister in deference to Jason's deceased father, since all the children on that side had been raised in a small Methodist school, now gone. The unfortunate new shepherd of their tiny lava-stone church in Hanalei, bursting to the seams with family partially seated in the graveyard next door to the church, had to share the stage with his mother's favorite three-hundred-pound female caller, who had sung to her all night long as she was giving birth to Jason.

Kiley had thought the music idea beautiful, so he let his mother have her way.

Jason hadn't saved enough to buy her a proper ring, so he bought her one perfect pearl and promised she could select a setting or have it made into a necklace. All that was going to change today.

When his treasure dive insurance payoff happened in Florida, he finally had enough to buy her that diamond ring he figured he owed her. He'd been practicing a song he was going to sing with his ukulele, and he wanted to do this right. Because, although he was an enormous, tatted rugby-playing fierce Māori warrior, he was raised as a gentleman. A Hawaiian gentleman with manners, someone who cared about other people's feelings, especially the precious women in his life.

It was the one thing unfinished about their relationship. Afterall, she was already with child.

Kiley had adjusted to Florida living and didn't want to move to Coronado, which was the only problem remaining with their marriage. The flying back and forth cost them dearly, and he tried to catch a military transport plane any chance he could get.

She'd decided, after he insisted, not to return to Portland and her job at the newspaper there. Although her series of stories in the paper brought down a very dangerous human trafficking ring run by local politicians connected to organized crime, several had slipped through the cracks and disappeared. It was general opinion that she would be safer in Florida from now on, especially if she was no longer writing articles for the paper and stirring things up in Oregon.

Florida was, after all, about as far away from Portland as one could get. And yet, Jason knew that didn't guarantee much of anything. The long arm of evildoers in places where they had served as SEALs occasionally extended to the United States from even farther distances.

No place was really safe.

Kiley had said she would meet him out by the beach after she finished cleaning the kitchen. And she insisted that he go out by himself. He had barbecued pig in Andy and Aimee's pit barbecue, all four families dividing up the succulent animal. He prepared a fruit salad with fresh pineapple, papaya, and mangoes he'd found at the local farmers market. The rule in their household was that if he cooked, Kiley would clean up. And he usually made a big mess. So she was going to be awhile.

He heard the chanting, the singing in the back of his head. He reached back, closed his eyes, inhaled the warm breeze, and pretended to smell the flowers of Kauai. The more he focused on it, the more he smelled them. Plumerias and orchids, the very soil, the volcanic soil of Hawaii, even smelled like flowers to him.

When he opened his eyes, Kiley was standing in front of him.

She handed him a glass of champagne. Tapping her glass to his with a ring, she said, "Here's to us, Jason. And all the sunsets and warm evenings and balmy strolls down the beach we can jam into our perfect lives here. This is the place you will come after your deployments, the refuge I found here, the place where you buried Thomas, the place you were told stories about. Now we are going to make stories here. This is where we belong."

He watched, distracted by her big eyes as they both sipped from their glasses, tasting the sweet elixir. He nodded, and then he remembered the pregnancy.

"Kiley! The baby!"

"Relax, Jason. Just one. Can't I have just one special glass tonight? I feel hopelessly romantic and so blessed. I want to celebrate without anything, except this," she said as she twirled around, her hands reaching out to the orange sky. "This perfect life of ours."

"Are you sure?" he insisted.

"I asked the doctor today when I called to inquire. He said just one and only one."

Jason sighed, knowing she wouldn't lie to him but still not liking the idea. Then he studied her glowing face. His heart jumped several beats, running away with the rest of him.

"Kiley, I would live anywhere with you. And based on your past history, I think it's necessary that I follow you no matter where you go. But please, please let's stay in one place. Let's stay here. Otherwise, when I'm done with the teams, I want to go back to the islands."

"I need you, Jason. And, as much as I love Hawaii, this place *calls* to me, I'm *connected* here. I never felt connected any other place I've lived."

"Then the God of the green and the God of the blue sky and the God of the sunsets has grabbed your soul, protecting it, and all three of them forbid you to leave."

She raised her eyebrows. "Indeed? You know this for sure?"

Was she mocking him? He played along with her. "I would never lie to you, sweetheart."

She chuckled as she placed her arm around his waist. They faced the gentle surf rolling in. The foamy edges mimicked petticoats on a woman's skirt, dancing and hissing all around their feet. As the sky darkened and the stars began to come out, they finished their glasses and just remained there standing, looking to the horizon, as if searching for a ship or some new adventure coming their way.

Jason knew she felt it too. It was more than just their new baby.

"Is this as pretty as Hawaii?" she asked him, looking up to his face.

He instantly knew the answer to that. He didn't want to say, but he decided it was best to be honest.

"It's different. Florida is beautiful in a different way. Hawaii is just—lush. That's all I can say. It smells like flowers. It has the songs of the ancients in the breeze. Old sailors tell stories about singing they would hear as they entered her ports. Back in those days, ships only traveled by sail, without benefit of a motor. So they would glide into the white sand beaches. The wind would send them the scent of flowers and the songs as people waited to welcome them with torches, drums, and chanting. I think there was so much chanting over the centuries that it would be impossible to stamp out that sound—an echo that will remain for eons. And when you live there long enough, you begin to hear it as if the hills and the surf and the horizon are singing to you too."

"You did promise that you'd take me there again before the baby comes."

"Yes, Kiley, and I think we should do it soon. I want to give the baby the blessings of the old ones."

"That sounds lovely, but what are you talking about? And when?"

"I'm going to get an ETA on our next mission, but I'm hoping, even if we have to leave sooner, maybe I can sit out the next rotation. I've also been thinking, Kiley, if this is where you want to stay and you're absolutely sure, perhaps I should consider joining Team 4. That way, I'd be with Andy and some of my other friends and not be quite so far away."

"But wouldn't you miss Kyle and all the guys on Team 3?

"Well, I'm not married to them, am I?"

"No. You belong to me," she whispered, the edges of her lips arching up into a coy smile.

Jason could hardly contain himself. It was time. He dropped to his knees, held both of her hands in his, and scanned her beautiful face contoured in the orange glow of the sunset.

"Kiley Worthington Kealoha, I am yours completely, and you are my island girl forever. I didn't have this before, but now I do, so I want to make this right in all the possible ways it's right for me. This is a symbol of my love for you."

He removed the ring from his pocket and held it up to her.

Her face erupted in shock. "Oh. My. Gosh! This is so beautiful, Jason, but so unnecessary. This must have cost you all your bonus money."

"No, not all. But that's irrelevant. Will you promise to love this poor traveler, this flawed military man, who desperately wants to make a huge family with you, who will love and protect you and all our keiki forever and ever?"

"But can we afford this, Jason?"

He was beginning to feel annoyed. "I didn't steal it, Kiley. I paid for it with the money from the boat recovery, remember?"

"But we were saving that for a house."

He looked down at the ring she still hadn't taken. He hadn't expected this reaction. "You want me to take it back? I didn't get the biggest diamond like I wanted to get. I bought you something I thought you'd love, and we still have money left over. You tell me what to do, honey, because I'm all confused here."

His mouth was parched, his heart thumped furiously, and his stomach was filled with butterflies. All the singing had stopped. He didn't even hear the ocean any longer.

Her eyes began to tear up. Her shoulders dropped. She leaned over, placed both palms at the sides of his face, and bent down. Just before their lips touched, she whispered to him, "It would be my pleasure to wear your beautiful ring, Jason. And I promise to bring you as many keikis as you desire."

After the first kiss, she pulled back slightly and whispered, "But, just tell me, sweetheart, how many are we talking about?"

"As many as you want. As many as your belly can hold."

"That's a lot of diaper changing, getting pregnant, nursing, and learning..."

He interrupted her, whispering to her lips again, "And a lot of steamy nights and beautiful bright mornings making love, making those keiki with you, and watching them grow inside you, making you glow."

Even at sunset, he could tell she was blushing.

"Oh my, Jason," she began as he slipped the ring on her left finger. She dropped to her knees. With one hand on her tummy and placing one of his there as well, she cupped the back of his neck, drew his face into hers, and said, "If she's a girl, I'm so thankful she will feel the love coursing through us as we taste and explore. If he's a boy, you're going to teach him how to thoroughly pleasure a woman to distraction."

The kiss went on for several minutes. He inhaled and hurriedly picked her up and ran to their bungalow.

He heard the cackles of the ancients floating over the waves, some of the sea birds imitating their chants. The closer he got to their house the stronger the scent of flowers filled his head. His heart was full to bursting.

Along with another huge body part.

He intended to go slow so he didn't hurt the baby growing inside her. He was going to make sure it lasted all night long.

And then he'd watch her sleeping, nude body rest in the morning light until she wanted him all over again.

Until she heard the music too.

CHAPTER 2

KILEY WOKE UP on the airplane. To her right was the hulking form of her husband. In repose—at least when he didn't snore or have some sort of a bad dream—he slept like a baby, his full lips creased into a line, his tanned and smooth skin relaxed on his forehead and on the bridge of his nose. His daily stubble was constant, and he had taken to shaving about every three or four days now, so it didn't chafe his skin. She liked the rugged look of her man. Just watching him got her excited.

Even the sound of his breathing turned her on.

She felt the nose of the plane dip gently into the white fluffy clouds several seconds before the announcement came over the loudspeaker, indicating they were preparing to land. Green verdant islands appeared out of nowhere, surrounded by turquoise and light turquoise rings surrounding the white shoreline.

Kauai was the rainiest of all islands, she'd been told, but its lush green mountains weren't the tallest in the chain. It just happened to be the one that got all the storms coming from the north. It rained on Kauai double what it did on some of the others.

Like a butterfly, the plane circled two times and then began to land.

As soon as the announcement had been made, Jason stirred, righted himself, uncrossed his ankles, and blinked. She held up her water glass, and he hungrily drank from it, finishing it off.

The cabin attendant came by with one last chance to discard rubbish and check for fastened seat belts. Jason had to be reminded to put his seat in the upright position. Less than five minutes later, they were on the ground, with a smooth landing she was grateful for.

Kiley knew there was going to be a big to-do made of their arrival, and she liked his family, all the while missing the life she never had with her own. But of the few memories she did have, she was grateful for the fact that her parents had spent some happy years at Sunset Beach, Florida, which had given her the perfect hideout from the mob in Portland. It became the place where she could breathe and relax, the place where her life began.

And it was where she met Jason on the beach one moonlit night.

There was still a bit of unease in her belly, now that she was carrying a child, even though she knew Jason's relatives would be very welcoming. Her biggest fear was that she didn't want to break some protocol, offend them in some way, or do something that was inappropriate in their culture. She wanted to show them the respect she had for them and the way they raised their Hawaiian boy.

She dismissed these thoughts as silly, reasoning that they'd be the most forgiving of any, certainly not like her own family of origin, cold and at times cruel.

Jason insisted on carrying her computer laptop case and the bag of t-shirts from the Tampa Airport she'd picked up before the flight. He had warned her that if she was buying t-shirts for the men in his family, she'd have to purchase large ones. If it was for the women in his family, she needed to buy a 4 to 5X. And that included all his aunties and the marriage singer who had been the first one to greet Jason into the world while his mother was in labor. Jason's mother was not one of the huge women, although she was much larger than Kiley.

A sea of tanned, round faces greeted them with smiles as soon as they walked down the hallway exiting the terminal enroute to baggage claim. Little kids were jumping up and down dressed in bright Hawaiian print dresses and shirts. There were several younger twenty-something women dressed in traditional Hawaiian garb with layers upon layers of wonderful smelling Hawaiian leis. The beautiful Polynesian girls wore their hair long, reaching their waist. They held armfuls of sweet-smelling leis and presented Kiley with nearly a dozen of them.

She looked up at Jason, who gave her a wink.

"I can hardly see you through the flowers. But you know what? It looks good on you," he said.

The audience laughed and clapped as he kissed her on the cheek.

Jason's younger nieces and nephews monopolized him, dancing around him and making him get down on his knees to hug them or shake hands. He extended his arms, trying to smack several of the little boys who were poking and teasing him. He was like the pied piper with half a dozen little kids surrounding him. Then he passed out silver dollars and packets of chocolate made by one of the chocolate companies in Belleair Beach. He stood, carefully bringing out several boxes of multicolored chocolates for his mother and the aunties.

The shopping tab at the chocolate factory had cost them nearly three hundred dollars.

But it was worth it, Kiley knew.

Jason's family had a line of cars ringing the pickup area, and after everyone was loaded and their bags were stowed, Kiley and Jason discovered they almost were shoved into different cars. Jason pulled her out and directed she ride with him in his mother's truck.

"You are going to have to get used to saying no," he said to her quietly as he closed the door.

From the front seat, his mother barked, "No? What is that word?"

She sped up, and the caravan of cars kept tight formation behind her.

Jason turned to her. "Kiley, I mean it. They're going to want you to go everywhere with them, and they'll compete for your time—take all of it if you let them. Even the children. The aunties will sing, and everyone will fuss over you—it might take some getting used to, but it is our way of welcoming you to the clan. And the dancing. You'll have hula instructions. You saw some of it at the wedding, remember?"

"Not easy to forget that part, Jason."

"But this time is different. Now you are family. Then you were *becoming* family, and they were on their best behavior," he said as he made eye contact with his mother in the rearview mirror.

"Jason, how dare you!" His mother launched into something in a tongue that Kiley could not understand. Jason shot her back a retort, and then they both threw their heads back and laughed, perfectly timed.

"You must remind me, dear Kiley," Mrs. Kealoha started, "that if I start to speak in our tongue you cannot understand me. It's natural for me to speak in three or four different languages during supper or an outing of some kind, depending on who shows up, so I forget. Remind me to speak Haole English, okay?"

"It's a deal, ma'am."

"Ma'am? Jason, who in the heck is she talking about?" his mother growled, feigning anger.

"That's a term of respect, Mama. You are a very important person in our lives and you know it."

Kiley watched him survey the land as they traveled out of the airport and headed up the highway to the north shore. "My goodness, in just these few months, I see many, many new buildings. I think life is good here. You are becoming more prosperous in Kauai."

"I think so. We have many investors from overseas coming in. Unfortunately, their arrival makes it difficult for people without a lot of money to purchase a home because they've driven the prices up so high. To be honest with you, most of the family wishes for a recession. Otherwise, they'll never be able to afford a house. But that's okay."

Jason turned to Kiley. "We live semi-communally—twelve, thirteen, or fourteen people in a two-or three-bedroom home. Most of us rent. It is no shame in not owning property, but we do have to sleep in shifts."

Jason's mother cackled. "Now who's telling stories? Don't lie to her, Jason. It's not that bad. We are together. We have enough, and we live in the most beautiful land in the whole world. It's been said more than once that this is paradise."

Kiley felt the same way about Indian Rocks Beach and Sunset Beach in Florida. But she kept her mouth shut. Every man's paradise was his own. And as long as Jason was with her, she could live in New York City itself and be happy.

"So where is Papa?" asked Jason, referring to his uncle, showing respect for his mother.

"Oh, the hotel. You know the hotel. Those Haole bastards. They don't know what a good man your uncle is. They work him to death. That's why he's so skinny."

Kiley could see that Jason was concerned about it, his face turning into one big frown.

"Is he going to take some time off while we're here, at least?"

"Yes, I think so, for sure on your naming day. But as far as other times, I think he will probably have an attack of sickness of some kind. That's usually how he gets around asking for days off. He never uses his sick time. So occasionally if he does this, they look the other way."

"Why do they insist on treating him so poorly?" he asked.

"Jason, you know the answer to this. You learned it years ago when you were in high school, remember? They treat him this way because *he lets them*. He doesn't like confrontation."

They drove up north on the two-lane highway, past tourist shopping centers and strip malls, nothing too tall except an occasional high-rise condo.

"I had always expected Kauai to look like Honolulu with large hotel complexes," Kiley mentioned to Jason.

"Most of the hotels were built as per royal decree long ago: *no taller than the height of a palm tree*. That had been one of the last acts of our Queen Lili'uokalani before she abdicated her kingdom. Our people, no longer subjects to a queen now dead many years, still abide by that rule. It is very difficult to get a variance for a developer of hotel property, unless it includes low-income housing for the local population," he answered.

Everywhere Kiley looked the hillsides were bright green. She saw large white birds circling the cliffs with waterfalls almost appearing to descend from the clouds. Kiley counted eight before they made it to their destination up in the Hanalei Valley.

She remembered the subdivision just before the turn off to his parents' home, and it looked the same, dotted with golf carts and tourists, an occasional tourist bus or two, with letters written all over it in Japanese or Korean characters. During the ride, she had never seen so many ice cream and shaved ice vendors.

Time seemed to stand still. There was no rushing around, and the traffic was horribly tangled and slow. The island traveled on one speed and one speed only, no matter the urgency.

Once they drove up the red volcanic dirt road to their little home, Jason opened the sliding door to the van and helped Kiley out. She felt soreness in her back from sitting so long and not being able to walk.

"Is there a place where we can go take a walk later on? I feel like I need to move. I just—I've been cooped up in a little metal capsule all day, and I need to stretch and move my legs," she asked him.

"Absolutely. I'm going to put everything else on hold until I take you down to the beach in my father's old pickup truck. Just like how it was when I was in high school. Even the same pickup truck."

"Really?"

"I'm actually surprised, too, it hasn't become one with the soil," he laughed. "I'll take you down to the beach. We'll walk and take a little swim. It's not a very wide area, and its steep with some serious undertow, but you're going to love the way it looks. Palm trees lean over the edge of the bay almost touching the water. I'll bring a couple snorkel masks too. Do you know where your bathing suit is?"

Kiley scanned the four suitcases they had brought, realizing that two of them were filled with gifts. But she couldn't remember which ones contained her clothes and which one contained his.

"I'm not sure. But let's pull them inside, and then I'll go through them and find it. If I remember correctly, it's somewhere at the bottom of one of the big cases."

He shrugged. "Of course. It always is."

The children were scolded as they ran in and out of their bedroom, not leaving them alone. Someone handed Kiley a skewer of barbecue chicken, which was rather spicy. Someone else handed her a skewer full of barbecued pineapple. Someone else handed her a huge tropical drink with an umbrella garnish, and she declined. After pointing to her belly, the young woman returned with a non-alcoholic drink.

"This is for you and the baby. No alcohol." Her beautiful smile lit up the room, and Jason thanked her.

"Thank you, Lana. My goodness, how you've grown in a year. Are you still in high school or have you graduated this year?" he added.

"Uncle Jason, I am in ninth grade. You shouldn't tell my mother that I look old enough to drive. She'd be furious. But when I wear lipstick and eye make-up, I do look twenty-five, I think. Don't you agree?"

Before Jason could answer her, Kiley rescued him, "Yes, Lana, you do. You look beautiful, and no one would ever guess you're in ninth grade."

The young girl beamed, turned around, and left the room. They changed into their suits. Jason picked up a couple of snorkels he found in his mother's garage along with two towels with Hawaiian fish designs on them. He opened the door to his dad's very rusty pickup truck, came around the front, then jumped inside the cab, and turned the keys to start the engine.

"He leaves the keys inside the truck all the time?" she asked, swiping away the smoke cloud they were engulfed in.

"My uncle forgets where he puts them. So we all agreed that Papa's truck has keys left in it at all times. Then he doesn't have to go spend time to find them."

"I understand now."

The sun was still bright, and with the time change, Kiley was feeling like it had already turned evening. Her energy level was sapped. But it felt good to get in the water, to sit and put on her flippers, and place the snorkel gear around her neck. Jason took her hand and carefully walked with her backwards into the surf up to their waists, and then they sat down butt first. The warm water felt heavenly and gently soothed her muscles and salved her aches and pains as they swam south along the shoreline.

Turning onto his back, Jason treaded water, still holding her hand. "You want to be careful of this undertow. It gets stronger as the day goes on. We've had some very sad rescues here. So I'm going to keep hanging on if you don't mind. We'll head a little bit south and out of the bay to where the undertow is less dramatic."

She nodded, spit into her glass and washed it with water, and then placed it over her eyes and nose, putting the mouthpiece between her teeth. Together, holding hands, they leisurely drifted several feet until she began to see a large gray school of fish coming toward them. They stopped their forward movement, floating on the water's surface. Within several seconds, the fish surrounded them, begging for handouts and brushing their bright yellow fins against their bodies, their big blue eyes and flat noses expressionless but somehow looking curious. She had seen fish like this on a plate at a dinner once, so it was a rather different experience for Kiley to see them in the wild.

The two of them drifted farther south until they ran across a huge school of bright turquoise fish with odd-shaped, protruding bellies, their scales laced with iridescent colors of hot pink, raspberry, and burgundy, almost making a plaid pattern on their sides. The fish were about three times larger than the yellow angel fish, all appearing curious and extremely tame, and hovered around her free hand as if knowing that hands gave food as she sculled her way and continued floating.

As they made their way back, she turned and floated on her back, looking up at the sky. In the beautiful late afternoon air, she smelled flowers and enjoyed the gentle sounds of the ocean, a few birds off in the distance, the pounding of the water on the sand, and the happy voices of little children laughing somewhere echoing in a canyon.

She understood how people would call it paradise.

On the way back to the truck, she asked him a couple of questions.

"How old were you when you learned to swim?" she asked.

"I can't remember *not* swimming, to be honest. I think my mother probably brought me into the water as a baby. I floated. When I saw my first fish, my dad says I was hooked on snorkeling. I went to bed with my snorkel on for days after he bought one for me."

"You know what, that's what Ned told me about when he grew up in San Diego. He said his father bought him a mask, and he wore it to bed for about a week."

"It's hard to imagine as a child when you don't see the fish from the top. But once you put your face in the water, the whole world opens up, doesn't it?"

"It does. I can just imagine what it would be like as a child to experience that."

"Our child will."

His comment warmed her all over.

"Tell me about this gathering this evening. Is there any chance we could go to bed early? I mean I'm tired, but I don't want to be ungrateful or seem unfriendly to your family. It's the pregnancy and the long travel. I feel I need to rest."

"Of course. I'm sure everyone understands, and I'm good with that. I will make sure you are given that space. We usually stay up a bit and sing, so if you feel like coming out, we'll probably have a bonfire. But you don't have to. You just rest. You listen to the songs and pretend that you understand the words. You dream about your future, Kiley, the future of us two becoming three."

"I can't think of any better way to fall asleep, my love."

CHAPTER 3

"I LIKE THE name Leilani. It just sounds Hawaiian," Kiley said.

Jason wrinkled his nose and cocked his head to the left, squeezing his eyes shut. "But it's so common. It's like Tom or Harry. It's what everybody thinks of as being a Hawaiian girl's name. Don't you want something unusual, something exotic?"

"I think Leilani is exotic and unusual. At least it's unusual compared to other names that I've seen kids I grew up with in Portland or Florida."

"Okay, then if we're settled on Leilani for a girl's name, I'd like to use Luki for the boy's name. I heard it in one of my dreams."

"Well, that reminds me of Loki, the Viking god of the underworld—isn't that it?"

"Beats me." Jason shrugged his shoulders. He was sure he'd heard the name before, but he liked Luki. "My father whispered the name Makoa to me in a dream as well. Which one do you like better, or should we let the elders decide?"

"We can't?"

"We can, but many in our culture bring the names either from ancestors or from dreams or from the clouds. Makoa means fearless, courageous."

"I like that much better than Luki, which sounds to me like the name of a cat or rabbit, not the son of a warrior," she sighed.

"Would you have me make him a used car salesman?"

She showed him a nasty face. "Wait. They have Hawaiian names for used car salesmen?"

He could hardly contain himself; he was laughing so hard inside. She was looking up at him seriously. She'd fallen for it. "Yes, in Hawaiian, it's called," and he waited, drawing it out further, "used car salesman."

She hit him in the chest with her towel. "You're impossible."

"I'm rather proud of that. So it's settled then? Unless the family insists on something else."

"Well, what if we change our mind after the ceremony this evening? Or they try to force a name on us that means banana slug or something."

"Now look who's being ridiculous. Besides, once the ceremony is over, we can't. If she's a girl, she will be named Leilani, at least for her middle name. She can have her American name, her *Portland* name," he said using his fingers as quote marks. "We can choose that together, but she will have this Hawaiian name with her as her middle name forever."

"And if he's a boy, then he will be Makoa."

"Like Thomas Makoa Kealoha. I think that sounds pretty Hawaiian, strong. I don't want to saddle our son with a name that has twenty-six letters in it. One of my friends in grammar school had one of those, and he was the last person in the class to learn how to spell his name properly. That's what some of our ancestors used to do."

"Okay then, it's settled." She finished dressing, and the two of them came into his mother's kitchen where she had laid out a huge spread. She'd made her famous oversized cinnamon rolls, an egg frittata mixture, a huge fruit salad, and fresh Hawaiian coffee. His uncle had already set himself a place and had started eating before they arrived. Jason was able to have a long talk with him last night and cherished the moments they spent together.

"Hi, Dad," Kiley said to his uncle. It made his mother smile.

The older man's eyes grew huge, and he stopped his fork in midair, as if at a loss for words. Holding the fork just in front of his mouth, he said, "Jason, you chose wisely. This girl is going to do you proud. I hope you can come by the hotel today. I'll buy you lunch."

"We'll see, Uncle Keoki. I want to make sure Mom has everything for the ceremony."

"Oh, for heaven's sake, Jason." Uncle pointed his fork at Jason's mother in the kitchen. "She's not going to let you do anything. And, Kiley, don't even ask her. Don't ask the aunties either. They fuss and gossip and tell stories and distort everything in the family way out of proportion. You'd think they were talking about someone else's family, not ours. Give yourself a few years before you have to become immersed in that, okay?"

Kiley smiled and took a seat at the table where Jason's mother had directed her to. Jason sat next to her.

"Don't listen to him. If Jason had listened to him or his dad growing up, he wouldn't know anything about his culture or background. He wouldn't know the dances or the songs."

"I'm not against all that," said his uncle. "I just don't go all crazy about it. I mean, we are part of the United States now. We're not an independent country and haven't been for over a hundred years, Emma. I think you guys are doing a good thing by keeping our culture alive, but I'm not going to pounce around, paint my face up, and pretend that I'm some kind of an ancient warrior. That would look funny."

He scraped the plate, stood, and brought it over to the sink, handing it to his wife. He placed a peck on her cheek and began to leave.

"I admit, Uncle Keoki, it would look funny on you. But what I wouldn't give to see it," Jason said with a smirk.

"Well, you have the muscles and the tats, and you embrace it. I applaud you for that. I, on the other hand, have to keep my job. And if I go running around looking like someone from an insane asylum, I will be fired. The guests will think me a little too exotic, a little too unusual for their tastes. They don't need to dream about getting murdered in their beds with a machete. We want Hawaiian culture, especially this part." He used his two forefingers to forcibly make his lips upturn in a huge clown grin, like that on the character The Joker.

Kiley nearly spit out her coffee. All Jason could do was shake his head.

JASON DROVE THEM south past the airport and then farther around to the backside of the island, still populated with occasional pineapple and papaya plantations. Although developments were encroaching on the beach side, most of the locals lived up in the mountains, where the air was cooler and less humid. It also was a lot less busy. And unlike many of the "lowlanders," everyone on the hill had an unobstructed ocean view. He drove Kiley up a winding road to the very top of the ridge line, an ancient Hawaiian burial grounds built atop an extinct volcano overlooking the resorts down below. He could see the island of Oahu and just the tip of Maui, and he pointed them out to Kiley.

"This is just beautiful. Look at the colors. The blue is so blue. I thought only the Caribbean was this blue," Kiley said.

"Oh, there are turquoise, yellow, black, and peach-colored beaches all over Southeast Asia and Indochina. I've been to some beaches in Cambodia that were just mind-blowing. You have no idea, Kiley, what a beautiful world this is. Dangerous sometimes, as often those places are, but beautiful. We're so lucky."

"I like your family, Jason. I like how they make fun of each other, I like how they laugh, and I like how they celebrate. I think maybe that's what was wrong with my family. They kept focusing on what wasn't working instead of what was there to be enjoyed. It was depressing growing up."

"I'm sorry for that. Children shouldn't be raised that way. In our culture, being serious is a crime," he said and then smiled. "Well, it should be," he added.

He was happy Kiley had taken to the beautiful scenery around her and the way they all lived in the middle of it. She didn't care for the tourists or the busy bumper-to-bumper highway, but like everyone who lived there, if she didn't like what was going on at one portion of the island, all she had to do was drive to the other side and have an entirely different climate and view. The one thing that always happened to Jason whenever he had done that, though, was he would run into the same people he was running away from on the other side of the island.

But that was how it was, and he accepted it. He was glad Kiley did too.

EMMA KEALOHA BROUGHT in a white moon dress she had worn for Jason's naming ceremony nearly thirty years ago.

"I want you to wear this tonight, Kiley, if you don't mind."

Kiley was touched and delighted as she held the cotton fabric delicately in her fingers. "Thank you. This means so much to me."

Jason watched his mother smile, step forward, and give her a hug. The two women were getting along extremely well, and it was all happening exactly the way he hoped it would.

"Thanks, Mom," he said as he put his arm around her and kissed the top of her head.

Kiley held the dress up to her shoulders and noticed the hemline dragged on the floor about two inches. "Oh dear, what do we do? I don't want to trip over it or ruin it by tearing it."

"Not a problem," his mother said as she took the dress from Kiley's arms and raced through the door, calling out the names of several aunties who were in the kitchen putting together food.

Jason took her in his arms. "You see, in this household, you're a guest. And you don't do anything. They will whip up a new dress in no time at all if we had to, but I'm sure she's going to eyeball that hemline so you won't be stepping all over it."

Kiley stood in front of him shaking her head. "This family is just amazing."

The ceremony was going to be at sunset, which gave them just enough time to run over to visit the large chain hotel where Jason's uncle worked. And, of course, there was the promise of a nice seafood buffet lunch. That was a huge call for Jason. They only did the seafood buffet on Fridays, so he always found some excuse growing up to drop in and say hello to his father or his uncle, since they both worked for the corporation, around lunchtime on Fridays.

The lobby had been redecorated with a colorful print that mimicked an old green and cream-colored Hawaiian quilt. The walls were decorated in attractive chalk drawings of Polynesian women, landscapes, little huts surrounded by palm trees or flowers, and quilts in bright geometric patterns. The most famous, a pineapple quilt, was hand stitched and hung, all twenty square feet of it, from the ceiling on the wall behind the registration desk. Jason realized a lot of money had been spent on the hotel by the chain. He hoped this signaled an investment in his uncle's future as well.

His uncle walked out from one of the side doors behind the registration desk, wearing khaki pants and a matching pattern Hawaiian open-collared short-sleeve shirt, as did all the men. He also wore flip-flops, as did many of the other men. As a young boy growing up, he used to love to look over the counter at banks and see how many of the tellers, either men or women, were barefoot and wearing swimming trunks.

"Ah, so he has brought the lovely Kiley to visit me. Welcome to my palace," he said as he stepped aside and swept his left arm in front of him to show off the beautiful lobby.

"It's gorgeous. It's—it is a palace," Kiley remarked, searching the walls, the floor, and the people coming in and out. She closed her eyes and smelled the scent of flowers.

"I'm sorry we don't have enough real flowers to make that scent you're smelling. We have it infused into the air system. I happen to think it's even nicer than the real thing. Just wanted to disclose."

Kiley opened her eyes and smiled. "I love it. I love everything about it. So far, everything I've seen here is just unbelievably beautiful and perfect. No wonder you like working in such a beautiful place. This rivals any of the hotels near me."

"I thank you for that. I think so too. It does help with the long hours and the getting home late after everyone's in bed. And sometimes on the weekends. But as general manager, there's a lot of responsibility. I won't do this forever, but right now, it's a good job for me."

Jason could see in his uncle's eyes, as well as the way he held his body erect, that he was proud of what he did and that such a large organization found their trust in him. It was something new he hadn't seen before. Jason liked it.

"You know, Uncle Keoki, I have to say you're looking younger, and yet there's something about you that's grown up."

Uncle looked nonplussed, frowned, and shook his head. "I have no idea what you're talking about, but I'll take it."

And then they all laughed.

He led them into the dining room, which was also a showplace for older Hawaiian tapestries. Some of them looked to be extremely old and in disrepair, probably of significant historical value. Large display cases on the side housed an old Hawaiian patterned china with the name of a hotel that used to sit on the site where this big chain was now.

"A hurricane took this old place and leveled it to the ground. There wasn't a single piece of lumber or stone that remained. It was wiped off the face of the earth. That's what happens here sometimes. We didn't have storm standards in those days. It was such a delicate and beautiful hotel, decorated like a giant wedding cake," his uncle said, tears forming in his eyes.

"We all grieved for it," added Jason.

"But the new owners who rebuilt did a wonderful job trying to replicate some of the original plantation features of the old one. And of course, they added hurricane-rated windows and roofs to make sure it would last at least a couple of hundred years, like the other one did," said his uncle.

Jason added, "These dishes were saved because the housekeeping staff came in the middle of the storm and rescued all that they could grab."

"Yes, or they all would have perished, washed out to sea. We'd be diving and finding them at the bottom of the ocean or halfway to Japan by now. The staff even managed to save a lot of the silver. So this is our wall of miracles," Jason's uncle said.

They were seated next to a large picture window overlooking the pool area with a distant view of Hanalei Bay. The squared pattern of various shades of green looked like a patchwork quilt itself, a splendid display of ancient farming techniques done in the old days by hand.

"So today we have the seafood buffet, which I recommend," his uncle said. "Make sure you have the Hawaiian lobster, it's smaller than your Eastern lobsters, but we think even more tasty.

We have any kind of shellfish you want," he leaned forward and whispered, "even some fish that aren't from Hawaii. But don't tell anybody."

It was difficult for Kiley to recognize some of the dishes, so Jason and his father took to explaining the names in Hawaiian, which only confused her further. She didn't seem to mind that her husband and his uncle were having a good time messing with her.

"Just take a little bit of everything, Kiley. You really can't go wrong. And you can go back as many times as you like if you find something you want more of. We have a dessert tray they'll bring out later, so be sure you leave room for that. We have a world-class pastry chef here all the way from Paris," he said.

Jason noted how Kiley enjoyed the opulence of the room, the whole atmosphere of being there, just as much as she enjoyed the food. She seemed to be in a perpetual state of awe.

In an adjacent room, a meeting was going on. Several men in suits sat around a large table, being served by two young Hawaiian waitresses in muumuus with flowers in their hair. As they walked past the room, several of the gentlemen looked up, nodded toward Jason's uncle, and then refocused on their meeting.

"We have a lot of nonprofit groups that meet here—Rotary and whatnot. I am very proud to say that I think this is the finest place on the North Shore, at least to have a business lunch. That room is filled all the time. Most of the other hotels can't say the same."

"Are these business leaders then, Mr. Kealoha?" Kiley asked.

"You must call me Keoki. It's Emma and Keoki. No Mr. and Mrs. Kealoha. No more," he said as he shook his forefinger back and forth from side to side.

She glanced at Jason's expression to see how he reacted to the Mr. and Mrs. reference. Jason kept it tight and didn't flinch a muscle.

"Okay, Keoki. So these are men from a service club then?"

"Not exactly, more like a union. They are mostly attorneys, some from the other islands and a few from the mainland."

They said goodbye, and Jason told his uncle he looked forward to the naming ceremony later on in the evening. "You're not going to miss it, are you?" he asked him. "If you're not there, I'm going to drive up here and grab you and bring you home. Is that understood?"

"I get your meaning, and unfortunately, I was not supposed to have the day off. However, I think I will have an attack of ulcerative colitis in about," he checked his watch, "two hours?"

"Very well, Uncle Keoki. We need you there. We need the whole family there."

"Yes, we do," his uncle said, putting his arm on both of their shoulders.

CHAPTER 4

KILEY AND JASON stood in the center of a wide circle of friends and family, in the backyard of his mother's house. The crowd was mostly dressed in white, linen short-sleeved shirts for the men and boys, long white dresses or gathered skirts for the ladies and girls. The circle of family had clasped hands and grew quiet as dusk fell upon them.

Kiley knew the ceremony was about to begin.

Jason had explained to her that the naming ritual was very important in his immediate family, since—like everything else they did—they had created their own brand of celebration and the reasons for it.

"It will help the child come forward at the time of their birth," he'd told her. "They will follow the sound of your voice, especially, Kiley. They'll know they come from proud ancestry and their Hawaiian name will be familiar to them as a greeting to complete the transformation of being born. They will know that they are expected and welcomed."

She was struck with the beauty and the symbolism of this ritual, which didn't wait for the birth but started long before, during their baby's journey into the waking world. The newborn would not come as a stranger but like a celebrated already-existing member of the entire family.

There was so much still she needed to learn about Jason's culture, and she never tired of the stories he told her.

He also relayed that there were lots of ways to choose a name and that every family member adopted their own form of selection, so Kiley and Jason did the same.

The singer who had been present at Jason's birth wandered around the inside of the circle, encircling the two of them as she told stories through her song. Her lilting voice, still full and melodic even with her advanced age, blended with the strumming of the ukulele's own unique voice. At various times during her song, the audience was encouraged to chant or add something, often harmonizing to insert another rich layer to her melodies.

Tucking her ukulele under her right arm, she picked up two small bouquets of white flowers set in a crystal vase of water next to them. The smaller bouquet she reserved in her left hand while she handed the larger one, made up of daylilies, white lilacs, gardenias, blooming ginger, and plumeria blossoms, to Kiley.

Her light brown face bore all the laugh lines of the living, the experiences of being a trusted elder and spiritual guide for the family. She eyed the transfer of the flowers to Kiley's hands, bowed her head, and said, "Now we shall give your child, if she is female, a name we can call to her on her birthing day."

Kiley felt her hand shake as she held the bouquet, waiting for further instructions. She glanced up to Jason's strong face looking down on her. While she stared into his eyes, feeling all the love and emotions pouring down upon her, she heard the singer ask her question.

"Have you selected a name that came to you through ancestry, recommended by an elder, or heard in a dream?" she asked Kiley.

"Yes, I heard the name in my dreams."

It was a true statement. Kiley had been thinking nonstop about what name she'd like to call her daughter, ever since Jason told her they would be making this trip to Hawaii.

"You will now place your hands upon the child, both of you," the singer instructed.

Jason's enormous palms settled evenly at each side of Kiley's navel. She placed her hands on top of his and immediately felt connected, as if the young child growing inside her was listening carefully. She was not far enough along to begin feeling the baby's movement, but it definitely was some sort of connection between them.

"Will you call your child's chosen name now, please?" the singer asked.

Kiley took a deep breath, watching Jason's lips, and together, they said, "Leilani."

A hush came over the crowd as she stood, witnessing the love and acceptance of her husband, his willingness to be this child's father and protector. It was the beginning of their family, with their child born under the ancient customs that meant so much to them all.

And, as their hands continued to warm her belly, she was given the vision that, indeed, she was carrying a girl, almost as if the baby herself spoke to her. She wondered if Jason felt it too.

The singer began a soft lullaby, a gentle song for the baby's health and peaceful sleep. As she had done earlier, she swayed back and forth, moving around them both while she sang. Their hands remained in place, Kiley's fingers locked in Jason's, also gripping the delicate white flowers.

The singer then gave the small bouquet to Jason and, placing her instrument under her arm again, asked the same words. "Have you selected a name through ancestry, recommendation from an elder, or something you heard spoken in a dream?"

Jason nodded and then whispered, "Yes. I heard the name spoken to me in a dream."

Anticipating what was to come next, Jason repositioned his hands on Kiley's belly, this time holding the small bouquet. Kiley drew strength from his eyes, from his honest lips, and the way his enormous chest rose and fell. The singer once again asked Jason to repeat the name he had heard in his dream.

"Makoa. I will name him Thomas Makoa Kealoha."

The crowd buzzed with excitement and approval. Again, while their hands warmed Kiley's belly, the singer played to the perimeter of the group, walking in circles, nodding, addressing, and smiling at people she knew, people she had seen born, and people she had watched grow. Some of her songs and stanzas were repeated by several of the audience, mostly women, as she passed them by.

When the music stopped, the singer repeated words in Hawaiian Kiley took as a benediction. She declared the ceremony complete, resulting in shouts from the audience she could not understand, as well as clapping and even some whistling. People ran from the circle to the two of them, embraced them, gave them both flower leis, and welcomed them and their soon-to-be-born child to the family.

Kiley then realized this seemed to be an even more important custom than their marriage vows taken nearly a year ago.

The feast afterwards was not like anything Kiley had been to before. It resembled a Renaissance Faire, with people meandering around platters of food, even a pit-roasted pig, covering several tables at the edges, accompanied by the sounds of music and more chanting. The large lawn area was kept free from chairs so that those who wished to dance or sing in pairs or small groups could do so.

A line of women performed the beautiful hula, and then they were joined by a string of young girls doing the same motions in tandem in front of them. Men performed the Haka, this time without Jason's animated movements. They had songs they sang to each other, their parents, or loved ones, and different songs they sang to their children as well. It worried Kiley a little bit that every single person in the family sang or danced or both.

Kiley couldn't do either.

But in her beautiful hand-me-down white dress lent to her by Jason's mother, covered in heavily scented plumeria leis, she felt like a bride all over again.

As the orange and purple sunset turned dark gray, a scattering of stars skidded across the sky, sometimes obscured by tissue paper clouds that temporarily blocked and then enhanced their shine. It was as if God had thrown fairy dust over the whole world in celebration. The night's sky became so dark the stars seemed to be ten times brighter than she'd ever seen before.

Jason's mother and uncle lit torches and presented one to each of the partygoers for safe journeys home as they bid farewell. Again, Kiley was hugged and kissed and whispered to, while Jason continued to grip her hand. She was grateful for that moral support.

After several minutes, the crowd had seeped back into the gardens and walkways of the Hanalei valley. Emma and her consort, Keoki, returned to their house, leaving Jason and Kiley alone. He directed her toward a wooden bench large enough for both of them and sat, placing her on his lap, balancing her on his thigh. Kiley held both bouquets of flowers, inhaling them again.

"I feel like tomorrow morning, even if I take a shower, I will still be covered in this beautiful scent."

"You're probably right."

"That was so—what is the word I'm looking for, Jason?"

"Magical. It felt like ancient magic to me. Did you hear the chanting coming from the ocean?"

She hung her head. "Sorry, no. But how in the world would I

be able to tell? Everyone was singing."

"You'll hear it, in time. No reason to rush things, sweetheart."

She leaned into his chest, seeking warmth as the air began to turn chilly. "I don't know what I expected, but it was magnificent."

"I'm going to Roger that."

She gave him a mock glare, lifting her head from his chest. Then she softened. "I know our little one paid attention. I could feel it."

"So did he or she tell you whether we're having a boy or a girl?"

"You mean like maybe I was told a secret? Do you think it would be wise for me to reveal it?"

"I did have something to do with it. It's safe to tell me, if you know. But we'll know soon enough."

Kiley ruminated over that for a few seconds, not sure if she should reveal what she felt inside.

"But seriously, you think he or she was listening? I just was wondering if—"

She interrupted him. "I think, Jason," she said as she placed his hands on her belly one more time, "we're going to have a little girl. That's honestly what I think she told me."

Jason's arms surrounded her, those strong arms that she fell into that first night they spent the evening together at the beach in her bungalow. It had been a long, fearful few months, and for the first time in a long time, that night she had felt protected and safe. She felt that way again this evening.

"I guess I need to have you help me with her first name, since we have Leilani as her middle name, her Hawaiian name."

"Something will come. I think you'll dream it. Or she'll tell you. Trust me on that. I've heard all my aunties say so."

CHAPTER 5

Jason and Kiley's Hawaiian trip had to be cut short due to SEAL Team 3 conducting another rescue in Baja California, Mexico. Kyle called Jason in the middle of the night, and it took them two hours to get their plane reservations changed so they could return to San Diego immediately. Kiley would have to go on to Florida without him.

Their flight didn't leave until late in the day, catching the red-eye back to San Diego. That left just enough time to say goodbye to Jason's Uncle Keoki. They agreed to meet at the hotel for breakfast on the way to the airport.

"You didn't tell me that your uncle was staying with your mom, Jason. What's up with that?" Kiley asked.

"Well, what do you think it looks like? I don't ask questions. I'd have to approve for the sake of my mom, even if I didn't. He's been like a father to me, not that he had any choice in the matter." He chuckled as Kiley got the inference.

"Oh, I can imagine what your mom has put him through. It's just the romantic in me that wants to know. Do you think they had a close relationship before your father died? And how long have they lived together?"

"I think he moved in about five years after Dad passed. He is the older brother, but I think he's in better shape than my dad was.

Side by side, most people thought they were twins. Since Keoki never married, there might have been some kind of infatuation with my mom, but I doubt it ever went outside the marriage. We just don't do that."

"Good to hear. I'll file that one away," Kiley said, not looking him in the eyes.

"He knew my mom needed help raising us. I think he felt it was his responsibility to pick up where my father left off. And my father would have done the same if it were reversed. But Keoki didn't have any baggage, no girlfriends or children, so he got to have all of that, being part of our nuclear family. My mom adores him. I honestly think she gets along with him better than she did my dad."

"Really?" Kiley's expression was one of shock.

"You be careful not to tell anybody I said that. But my sisters and I have discussed it very, very quietly. And so now you know. But we will never speak about this again, understood?"

"I got it. You can count on me. And if somebody brings it up?"

"Well, it's like what Kyle tells us when we're on a mission and we're not supposed to be soldiers. His command is 'don't engage.' So I'm giving you the same command. Don't engage, Kiley, sweetheart."

He gave her a sparky grin, trying to make light of a situation that could get sticky if someone wanted to make it that way, sending the whole conversation in the file drawer in Kiley's basement, hopefully never to return or see the light of day.

"Well, I like your Uncle Keoki. And I notice sometimes you slip up and call him Dad. She calls him her husband. I guess he is, isn't he?"

"As far as I'm concerned, yes, he is. I have no idea if they've done the ceremony or not. It doesn't matter really. I'm glad she has someone, and I'm glad they are happy together." He was not happy the subject hadn't been properly buried. Kiley was so stubborn. She just wouldn't put it to bed.

"Do you think they—"

"Kiley, I said quit it! I don't want to know, and I don't care. You shouldn't care either. Don't go asking those kinds of questions." He was frosty, and since his efforts at being lighthearted and friendly with her didn't work, he decided to try the direct approach. It really was for all their benefits that she forgot they'd ever had this conversation. Time would tell if that would actually occur.

"Do you suppose your uncle got in trouble for being sick yesterday?"

"I think the staff there is extremely loyal to him. They must be seeing they're working him into the grave. He covers for everybody, so why not? Why not take a day off? He's just one of those guys who's always there. So responsible. I think perhaps putting in all the extra hours makes him feel better, because he makes a whopping good salary for a job on the island, since it's expensive to vacation here, but getting a job? They don't pay worth crap."

"You think he feels guilty taking a big paycheck when so many other people make so little?"

"Exactly."

"I think that's why I like him. I love your family. I love their values, the way they live their life, how they help each other. They're just good people. We would say 'salt of the earth' in California, or something like that."

"He's a sardine, and he puts on his shark tank suit and swims with the sharks. He's a chameleon. He fits in wherever. You saw him waving to those businessmen. He's very well-respected. Not for being a heavyweight, but just for being a guy you could count on."

"Well, I'm happy for him. And I'm happy for your mom too. I

imagine she struggled a lot less once he came to the household."

"Kiley, when are you going to give this up? I don't want to talk about their relationship. I don't want to talk about whether they're married or what the arrangement is. I certainly don't want you to turn the music down to see if you can hear anything coming out of their bedroom. You did that last night, didn't you?"

Kiley squinted and put her hand up to her eyes. "Was it that obvious?"

"Yes, it was. And I thought you'd just forget about it if I didn't say anything. You have to forget about it. Please, Kiley."

"Roger that, S.O. Jason Kealoha. I got you loud and clear."

A large group of Japanese tourists were boarding their bus, probably headed straight to Lihue Airport. Jason parked in his uncle's employee parking spot, took Kiley's hand, and ran around the back side of the bus into the lobby. He crossed the huge room in several long strides, Kiley bouncing and taking little short bird steps to keep up with him but falling slightly behind with each one. He grabbed her arm and gave her a boost, supporting her body so she could move faster.

Echoing across the lobby, he heard his uncle's voice.

"Ah, there he is. And there she is," Uncle Keoki said as they entered the dining room. "Are you in a hurry? If you are, the buffet is the best thing to do."

"I don't want to eat that much food," Kiley said.

"You know, Uncle Keoki, if I never eat another bite of food all day—maybe even all day tomorrow, as well—I'm still not going to get rid of this paunch I've got. I came here for three days, and I've gained eight pounds. How does that happen?"

"Emma's a great cook. You know this. Out of those two-dozen cinnamon rolls she made, how many of them did you eat yourself, Jason?" His uncle grinned from ear to ear, probably already knowing the answer before he asked the question.

"I lost count."

"You never could lie to me, Jason Kealoha. I have it on good authority, plus I watched you devour more than half of these, that you ate at least ten. That makes me sick just thinking about it. Of course, you don't have any room for anything else. You have to work off all those carbs and all that sugar."

"You're right. I think just some scrambled eggs and some coffee with cream." He turned to Kiley. "Does that sound about good for you, or do you want something more?"

"Oh please. No more. Every time I burp, I taste that pig. It was delicious, but it's going to be with me for days."

"Very well, let's sit, and I'll have them bring our coffee." His uncle pointed to another table in front of a smaller window this time, with a golf course view instead of the ocean view they had before. To the left of the golf course was the clubhouse pavilion and a packed parking lot. It wasn't lost on Jason that there were no less than five black stretch Suburbans parked there.

"I think they must be having a big-time golf championship or something. I've never seen so many cars so early in the morning," he whispered to Kiley.

She crooked her neck and peered out of the window over his shoulder. "You're right. Almost looks like a political convention, doesn't it?"

That's when Jason noticed several mic'd up armed security guards keeping watch over the vehicles while the occupants were otherwise engaged.

Private security detail. They weren't Secret Service.

His uncle returned, and not more than two minutes later, they were served scrambled eggs and bacon, a side of fruit, and thick slices of hot buttered Hawaiian toast. All he could do was look at all the food in front of him and shake his head.

"Just eat what you want," his uncle said. "Don't worry about it.

They don't do anything small here. I think that's why everybody loves coming."

"We noticed all the limos over there at the clubhouse," Kiley said. "You got somebody running for election having a day of golf?"

"Oh, those people… not exactly. You know how it is with the rich and powerful. They don't like to be disturbed, and they like complete anonymity, which is impossible on an island since everybody gossips about everybody. But they don't know that. It's another meeting like the one you saw yesterday. I think they're probably getting ready to make some kind of a land purchase, probably not here. But if they did it over on Oahu, everybody over there would know about it. So over here, they're kind of incognito. I don't even know who half the people are. Some of them are new. I noticed a couple of fellas from overseas as well. But they're just having a meeting, and then they're going to play some golf. They usually screw around for a few hours, and then they'll head out tonight."

"Are they staying at the hotel?"

"No, they never do, not this crowd. Maybe some of their staff will. One of the fellas has a huge plantation up in the hills. He has a house that's probably bigger than most of the little hotels around here. They usually stay there. It's got a whole bunch of private security and little cabins dotting the property. It's more like a private resort. I guess the guy was a hedge fund trader or something at one time, and he's a multi-billionaire. He keeps things around that property very tight. I don't know anybody who's spent any time there. And that's the God's truth."

They finished their eggs, and Kiley once again expressed her appreciation for the celebration, and the fact that she got to meet so many of the relatives she hadn't met last year for their wedding. "I was just saying to Jason that I think this celebration was even more important than our wedding. I had no idea that that's the way your culture is."

"I think we tend to celebrate what's the most important. A man and woman can decide to be together, but when they make a child, that's when everything changes, doesn't it?" His uncle said to Jason.

"That's true. Very true."

"Well, I've got to be handling some things at the front desk, and we have two on the cleaning staff who didn't show up today, so I've got to see if I can get someone from one of the other shifts to show up. Our systems in our hotel completely break down if we have problems with the cleaning staff. I'm the general manager, but don't get me wrong, it's the hotel cleaning crew who really runs this place. Trust me on that."

Jason chuckled and then pushed his dish aside, took another sip of coffee, and shook his uncle's hand. He helped Kiley stand, and together, they raced out to the lobby. As Uncle Keoki headed behind the desk, Jason called out to him. "Is it okay if I leave the truck here? We'll just take a cab to the airport?"

"Of course. Leave the keys in it. I'll drive it home tonight."

Jason gave him the peace sign, and after stopping to grab their luggage from the truck, they headed to Lihue Airport.

"Nobody will steal his truck?" Kiley asked.

"Have you taken a closer look at it? It's got rust all around the headlights. We affectionately say that it's got breast cancer. It's got rust eating away along the wheel wells where mud and water from the roadway splashes up. I think that truck has nearly 400,000 miles on it. I doubt that it's worth anything at all. He'll drive that thing until something breaks, and then he'll just leave it. We find vehicles all over the island that people just drive, park, and abandon. Sometimes tourists come for the summer, and they buy a cheap car because it's way cheaper than renting, and then they just leave it behind. It's ridiculous but that's what happens. We have a regular tow crew that goes around and inspects cars for rust damage. It's a big problem here. And even garaging your vehicles doesn't take care of all the salt water and the rust."

Kiley smiled and shook her head. "Jason, this feels like another world completely. I never expected to feel this way about Hawaii. But I'll grant you, it's very attractive."

"Well, things can be arranged, if you change your mind about Florida."

She hesitated then answered him carefully. "Why don't we talk about it when you get back from wherever you're going?"

"Suits me just fine."

"And I wouldn't put in for the transfer just yet. Let's talk and make some strategy, okay?"

"Fair enough. But, Kiley, I think it would be best if the baby were born in San Diego rather than here on the island. The medical facility there might be superior, not that I'm expecting complications."

She agreed.

As their cab arrived, Kiley slipped in the back seat, and Jason landed next to her, closing the door behind him. He gave instructions to the cab driver, and they were off in a cloud of smoke.

She had been looking out the window at the green, little peekaboo bits of the blue Pacific Ocean as the highway traffic was light this morning. Jason knew she was thinking about something. He liked that she was considering what it might feel like to live here. He already knew she would love it. It would take some getting used to, of course, but he knew she would. And it had to be her choice completely.

Kiley turned to face him. "I'm going to think about it, Jason. The only thing that's a problem is that it's too far away. Not exactly what anyone would call a decent commute. There's no way

I'd want you doing that every month. Or, even worse, we wouldn't see each other as often."

"Well, there's two things wrong with that assumption. First, SEAL Team 1 is based in Hawaii. The sub-crew. I could transfer, if they'd have me. They work with those little single-man subs. Not sure I'm the right size for them, though."

"And the second reason?"

"It's about the same distance as it is to Florida—just slightly more."

"No way."

"I'm giving it to you straight, Sweetheart. You go look it up."

"Hmm," she mused.

"It just seemed longer because we came from Florida, not San Diego, that's why," he added.

"You'd be willing to make all those changes?"

"Can't do it for a while. The team here in Hawaii is a different gig. Spots are limited. They probably don't need the same number of medics, either, than on the other teams. But it's not impossible. It would be far easier to transfer to Little Creek and hook up with Team 4."

She was listening to him, mulling it over, processing the possibility.

"Kiley, write down all your questions, and then we'll have a long talk when I get back. I'm hoping this will be short. Otherwise, I was going to ask to bow out of this next one, right? But Kyle says it will be short. A quick extraction."

"I've heard that before, Jason. There's no such thing."

He shrugged, agreeing with her. "Anything can happen, and usually does. But if it all goes as planned, it will be short."

"It'll give me time while you're away. I need to ask our landlady about extending again. Maybe she'll let us buy it? Do you suppose?"

"Buy the house at Sunset Beach and have us live in Hawaii? You mean like for a rental?"

He noticed how confused she was getting.

"It's a lot to consider, but if you want something bad enough, we'll make it happen. Besides, what exactly did you have in mind doing during this next rotation?"

"I'd planned to arrange the house to get ready for the baby. I like making decisions when I'm alone. I'm going to focus on staying healthy, getting lots of rest, working a little bit on some fix-up projects. Maybe I'll help Aimee a bit just to stay moving, and I promise you I'm going to walk the beach every single day."

"Excellent. And as soon as I get to someplace where I can, I promise to call you as much as I'm allowed."

"I thought I'd tour a couple of maternity wards, maybe start pregnancy classes. It will take my mind off what you're doing."

"That all sounds good, sweetheart. I'm really looking forward to helping with whatever decisions you make."

A picture flashed in Jason's head. He saw their daughter laughing, throwing sand, and jumping into the waves at the beach.

"Do you suppose our little *wahine* will like living on Kauai?"

CHAPTER 6

KILEY TOOK AN Uber from the Tampa Airport back to Indian Rocks Beach and the shelter of her rented bungalow. She hauled her two big suitcases, the other two going back to San Diego with Jason, over the threshold and into the living room. She was going to catch up on some TV, unpack, and do laundry.

Her phone rang, and she didn't recognize the number.

"Well, as I live and breathe. She actually answered her phone!" Corbin Newman's voice had the same syrupy texture, but this time when Kiley talked to him, her stomach began to heave. It wasn't all due to her pregnancy either.

"No. The answer's no. And the more you talk the more *no* it will be," she shouted.

"Holy cow, Kiley. How do you know what I'm calling for? I heard—well, Carmen spilled the beans—that you're pregnant. Congratulations."

"Since when do you care?"

Corbin had been her editor at the Columbia Passage newspaper, where Kiley had worked as an investigative reporter prior to moving to the Gulf Coast of Florida. Her stories on human trafficking, encouraged by Corbin, were what landed her in hot water and placed a target the size of the Empire State Building on her back.

"Oh, so you're apologizing then?"

"Sure, Kiley. I'll apologize for anything. I just wanted to hear your voice, just to see how you're doing. Do you have any free time to look over a couple of articles I've got going? We're following up, you know, on some of this trafficking business. I thought you'd be interested."

"Absolutely not. I'm done with all that."

She felt her blood pressure rise and ran to the kitchen to pour a glass of cold water. She also sprinkled tap water on her face. Corbin Newman II was the absolute last person in the world she wanted to talk to. And it would be a shame if she missed Jason's call because Corbin had tied up her line.

"Look, I'm expecting an important call, so I'm afraid I'm going to have to cut this short. I really have nothing to say to you. And I'm not interested in any more work."

"Even if I get Natalia and Carmen to help you out?"

"What do you mean 'help me out?'" she asked.

"Natalia, the Ukrainian girl that rescued Carmen, has agreed to help us delve further into the smuggling ring. The mayor is awaiting trial, as well as several in his police detail. The big guys, I mean the *really* big guys with money, they're gone. Took off in their jets or yachts or whatever, and they're gone. The Portland Police, the FBI, nobody has time to find them. Where in the world would they start looking?"

"I'm just glad, Corbin, that I got out of there with my life."

She let her words slice through the air with crisp, exacting, unmistakable detail. She hoped he felt threatened.

"Kiley, now, there's no cause for that—"

"Are you really that stupid to think I would actually want to go back into that snake pit you call the Columbia Passage and risk my life? For what? I don't need a do-over, thank you very much. I got my life back. Now I'd like to live it."

"We can hire protection for you, if you should need it."

"'*If I should need it.*' Honestly, Corbin, Carmen needs her head examined. She'll get them both killed as one of the loose ends the mob must take care of to give themselves some wiggle room. I, on the other hand, want a safe place to live. For me. For Jason. And for our child who is coming in approximately five months if everything goes well. I don't need the protection because I don't plan on being anywhere near those cretins who steal the souls of the young and sell them to devils who are addicted to creating evil and love paying for the privilege of indulging in that lifestyle. It's all sick, and I want nothing to do with it."

"When you say *goes well*, are you having issues?"

"Corbin, I am none of your business. Please stop even slightly entertaining the idea that I would be interested in working with anybody from your newspaper. I don't care what the reason."

"You know we've got Colin Riley helping us as well. He's found a home for Natalia, and Carmen thinks we should involve him. He has quite an impressive organization and nearly unlimited funds. We've already hired their security people to watch over the office and several of our key players. He may have limited time left, since his health is not good. Carmen is worried that if we don't act, we'll lose the opportunity—an opportunity to do some good for some people who are powerless against these crime families."

"I'm powerless to change it. That's why I'm out. I don't have to get involved anymore, so I don't want to. I value my life and my baby's life. I want you to leave me alone. As a matter of fact, if you don't stop calling me, I'm going to call the police. You know, here in Florida, they take these sorts of things much more seriously than they do in Portland. In case you haven't heard."

"Well, I'm going to send over an email anyway—"

"Don't. I'm asking you to leave me alone."

She heard his exasperation in the long sigh he uttered. "You know, it's my civic responsibility to cover news, to tell people the things they need to know that makes a difference. We don't make things up or write 'stories' of how we wish things were. We just report what's going on. Unfiltered. Just the facts."

"I think you're lying to me, Corbin."

"People hear what they want to hear. We can't report what we want to report. We have to expose the truth, and you were doing that. Saving lives, Kiley."

"You're right. And now I'm getting ready to be a mother. I want to be a wife and a mother. I don't want to save the world. Give it to some other Girl Scout. That's not me any longer."

"But you must admit, most people have no clue, and they don't understand how deeply ingrained in our fabric of society human trafficking is. They think it's something that happens in a third-world country somewhere far, far away. But you and I know that the well-connected get to do whatever the hell they want to do. Look at all the recent arrests of several prominent socialite men and women. I rest my case."

Corbin Newman III was good at wearing people down. But in Kiley's case, he was infuriating her further.

"You've got thirty seconds to finish up, and then I'm calling the police if you're not off the line. Do not send me anything. I don't want to hear from you again. Have a nice life, Corbin. Get that scoop without getting half your staff or yourself killed in the process. But leave me out of it."

Kiley didn't really have to, but she watched her wristwatch count down to the thirty seconds, and without hearing a further sound on the other end of the line, she hung up.

She whirled around the kitchen, picked up the glass of water, gripping it tightly, and raised it above her head, about ready to throw it at the sliding glass door leading to the ocean. It took every ounce of strength in her to not toss that glass.

Corbin was going to be a thorn in her side, skilled at needling her exactly where he could find purchase. He treated people like commodities, not like humans with real feelings. He hid behind his executive position, his Ivy League upbringing, and the family he married into and then divorced out of, receiving a big settlement which set him up for life. He was a man who was used to massaging the system, getting his way, and looking more successful than he really was. The bottom line was that all the people who worked for him worked their buns off.

Corbin took all the credit.

She wasn't going to calm down, couldn't calm down. Watching some idiotic show on the television while she did laundry and folded her clothes just wasn't going to cut it. She thought about calling Aimee Carr and dumping on her, but that would be just as manipulative as Corbin was trying to be. She knew better than to try to call Jason. She was going to have to wait for that. She thought about calling her former roommate, Megan, who still lived in Portland at their beautiful flat overlooking the Columbia River.

But nobody and no one was going to be able to take away the boiling oily black pit in her stomach that oozed venom and hatred all the way down to her ankles.

She ran to the bedroom, ripping off her clothes and planning to jump in the shower, when she looked at the sign over their bed. *The beach heals everything.* That sign she'd carried with her all throughout her semester abroad in Paris and various other cities she explored during that time at Lewis & Clark. She had it in their flat in Portland while she wrote her newspaper articles. It had been a relic, a remnant of happier days when her parents were still alive. The family had a brief few years down at St. Pete Beach, and it almost looked to Kiley during that time that maybe things would work out. Happiness almost showered them in the bright light Jason's family possessed.

But in the end, it was all an illusion.

With her blouse open and her pants slid halfway over one hip, she looked up at the sign again. And then she completed disrobing, this time with intention.

Naked, she rummaged through her dresser to find her one-piece bathing suit, not wanting to draw too much attention to the small belly that was growing. She grabbed a beach towel, flip-flops, sunglasses, and her Ward's Seafood baseball cap. Locking the front door, she exited through the slider and latched it with her key. She stowed the key underneath the frog pot to the left of the door handle.

Nearly stumbling, she crossed the patio, making sure that she hadn't drawn anyone's attention, and then headed straight to the water. About ten feet before the surf, she threw everything on the ground, disgusted. She'd left her cell phone back inside the house, which annoyed her, but she decided she just needed to get in the water, perhaps float for a little bit, listen to nothing else but the sounds of water in her ears, and try to chill for thirty seconds.

And if that worked, maybe she could do it for a minute, she thought as she approached the surf. Maybe she could do five minutes, longer even. Her heart pounded in her chest. She hadn't noticed that her right hand had balled into a fist, her red nails digging into her palm.

The wide sugar-sand beach was very sparsely populated today, the afternoon sun a little too warm at this late part of the day before it would cool. The snowbirds hadn't yet returned from their summers up north. It was a transition time at the Gulf, in between the crazy tourists who would brave the heat of Florida in the summer and the long-timers who owned investment property and knew better than arrive before fall.

Kiley agreed. The fall was the very best time to be there.

She continued walking out to face the rest of her life, as if the ocean held everything that was important to her. She kept her gait slow and balanced until she was waist-high in the foamy surf. An airplane sputtered overhead, pulling behind it a red banner advertising a local taco bar that had recently opened up on the island. Nobody was floating in the water. Nobody was surfing, since the waves were way too calm.

She had stopped time itself as she stood there. The undulation of the huge body of water in front of her pushed and pulled her back and forth as if she was a baby in a swing, lulling her to sleep. The ocean was taking over everything, telling her stories of all the people it had touched.

She remembered the snorkeling they did the day before yesterday, the parties, the naming ceremony that nearly brought her to tears as she thought about it now, still smelling the barbeque and the smoke from their bonfires. She remembered how she felt when she heard about Emma and Keoki. She saw the children in her mind, the singer with her ukulele tucked under one arm.

Part of her wished she could go back there and stand in the middle of Jason's family, where they'd smother her in flowers, shower her with kisses, and sing so loud she couldn't think of anything else. All her worry and her cares disappeared, just like magic.

It was magic.

She heard splashing to her right, and several yards away, three teenage boys were pushing each other down in the water, scooping saltwater into each other's faces, laughing, and all falling down. They swam out to catch a small wave before it broke on them. She completed her turn and scanned the beach. There was no jogging group this afternoon and no fishermen, which was odd. She did see one older gentleman in a fat tire bicycle riding on the hardpan of the beach, his white hair tied in a ponytail.

What was he thinking, she wondered. Did he worry about things, did he sometimes run scared from issues that were way over his head like Kiley had done? Was he inquisitive? Stubborn? Did somebody at home love him like Jason loved her? She wondered if he had children or if he'd ever married. She wondered if he had a dog, or maybe he was a cat lover.

"What am I doing?"

Then, just like Jason said would happen, she heard chanting. The singer's voice was the most prominent, but there was a group behind her. They were chanting in perfect rhythm to the movement of the ocean pushing and pulling her at will. After several minutes went by, her feet had sunk into the soft sand all the way above her ankles. Carefully, she removed one foot and then the other, not wanting to have a sudden fall.

Here, she was free. Here, it was safe—or safe for now. This was refuge. This was where they could raise their child and have many others. But one thing would always remain, and that was if Jason remained a SEAL, there were going to be stretches of time when she was going to be all alone. Of course she had her friends Andy and Aimee Carr, Ned and Madison, Martel and Damon. They were good friends, and they would do just about anything to help her. Aimee was buying a bookstore, and Kiley had thought about helping her catalog, purchase used books, display them, and run the shop.

In her mind, she saw their children learning to read, surrounded by thousands of books—books that had been loved and cherished by people long gone, downsizing, or who had changed their minds and now read something else. All that had been her plan, something she was looking forward to. But now she had another choice. Was this original plan going to be enough for her?

If they were on the rainy island, there would always be Jason's family surrounding her. They would never let her go. They would never let her be alone, especially during his deployments. That way, he could stay with SEAL Team 3 and wouldn't have to move commands. Or she could stay in San Diego, although she felt no connection there. Even though it was a busy area and there'd be lots of brothers from the SEAL teams and their wives, the huge support system that they had made up, it still wouldn't be the same thing as Jason's family protecting her.

She didn't want to make a decision, so she did what she'd intended to do when she put her suit on. She walked farther into the ocean, leaned forward, did a gliding breaststroke and kick, picked up some speed, then rolled over on her back. With her arms and legs dangling out to the sides just like she used to do when she was a child, she floated.

The sounds of the water in her ears drowned out everything else, even the beating of her own heart.

"This is what we do to relax, little one," she said to the baby. "This place will protect you. It's going to be the first lesson I teach you. The beach does heal everything."

CHAPTER 7

THE TEAM 3 briefing was held, as was custom, in their building in Coronado. Kyle took the center stage, pacing back and forth after posting several large maps of Baja California, Mexico behind him on the bulletin board. He also had a projector and several slides prepared for the meeting.

Jason sat next to his other Team 3 medics, Tucker Hudson and Calvin Cooper. He turned to Coop, asking, “Is it true this is going to be a short stint?”

“That’s what I’m told,” Coop said. “But you know how that goes.”

All three of them nodded agreement.

Kyle flipped on the projector, and a handsome businessman in a suit with a handlebar mustache flashed onto the white screen behind Kyle.

“We have a new player this time around, gents. His name is Carlos Gutiérrez. We believe he was sent by the Sinaloa Cartel to set up shop in wake of several takedowns and murders that have taken place in this area. As you know, there is a war going on south of us, a very dangerous and fluid situation. Just so happens we’re going to drive right through the middle of it but *not get involved.*”

Several groans peppered the air.

"Let me repeat that one more time so there is no confusion about this. We are *not* going to get involved. In fact, if there's a way we can off-road around it through several of the small villages south of Mexicali, we will do so. But Mother Nature might have other plans, and if we have to stick to the highway, we'll do it."

Their LPO surveyed the group of some twenty-five team members. It was larger than Jason had expected.

"We're headed down here to San Felípe." He pointed to the dot at the northern end of the Sea of Cortés where the peninsula attached to the mainland. "This is probably going to be the largest town you'll see this time. Used to be a sleepy little fishing village frequented by sports fishermen and tourists on a budget. Now, it's a small mecca of cartel and human smuggling activity due to its proximity to the sea. Profits from their successful enterprises have built this place, its schools and government buildings."

Kyle paced again, stopping to add another note.

"We're going to take off here as soon as we can load up. It will take us about four and a half hours to get there, barring any unforeseen issues. But San Felípe is our destination."

The metal chairs squeaked. There weren't many comments this early in the morning. Jason wished he'd stopped to pick up a coffee on the way, because nobody made it this morning in the building.

"We're going to take four vehicles, and I will send a handful of you in by private plane. We have assets on loan from the State Department, and that would be a more convenient way of getting fire power over the border, rather than risk running into bad guys in between here and San Felípe. It is a major drug smuggling route that we'll be traveling, so keep your eyes and ears open. Large trucks travel back and forth commercially between the two countries, but that doesn't mean a truck loaded with produce can't also bring in young girls. The cartel in this area was always involved in the drug trade. But they discovered very quickly that human trafficking was more profitable."

As Jason listened, he wondered if and when this would ever change. It was the same story over and over again with different characters leaving their mark for a brief moment in time and then disappearing. But the illegal trade remained constant and, even with temporary setbacks, was almost bulletproof.

Almost as if it were designed that way.

"We are informed that, by mutual agreement, this particular group has allowed others to control the border mess. They want to stick to large hauls, semis filled with people and drugs, rather than small shipments. They're making their money on the big runs. I'm sure you've heard about some of the drug busts in the paper and on TV. We've been told that amounts to barely one percent of the actual trade getting through. Trying to stamp it out is now a matter of national security."

Jason could feel the anger of the group rising. They all had the same calling, to protect the innocent as best they could. There was so much left to be done.

"I figure I'm going to need a couple dozen of you, and we'll set out your travel assignments a little bit later. We're staying in a condo complex that was taken over by the feds and kind of roughed up in a drug bust. Uncle Sam has completed some of the units and done some construction and repair of damage caused by the numerous ops and raids done by others in closing down that facility. So now it's ours to use. But, for all intents and purposes, it doesn't look like a government-owned property. It looks like a group of private investors bought it and are fixing it up to sell. At least that's what we want everyone to think."

Coop raised his hand. Kyle nodded in his direction.

"We're not going to be moving around the peninsula at all? We'll just be staying right there in San Felípe?" he asked.

"No, I didn't say that. We'll probably bring some inflatables. We have to remain mobile in case we run into hostages we have to extract."

Coop nodded acknowledgement.

"A few miles south of the city, in the Sea of Cortés, is a place they call Guardian Angel Island. It has a long history of being a very sleepy and poor fishing village. Accommodations are scarce, which is why we're not staying there because we'd stick out like a sore thumb. Sadly, the waters in the surrounding area are not as lush with fish as they used to be. So the village is basically dying. However, we do believe there have been some stash houses where contraband has been stored, possibly even where boats carrying human slaves are temporarily hidden.

"We're going to check out the island by boat. It's extremely primitive. Power is, at best, iffy. But it has the advantage for the cartels of affording an escape either to the Baja side or the mainland. Of course, they could head south through the Sea of Cortés and the Pacific beyond. In other words, we'll probably have to do a night survey. And we don't have any intel on trade routes or who we can trust in the village. We go in blind there, so be careful. We don't have anyone on the inside. But it's been a confirmed staging area, run by the parties in San Felípe."

Kyle walked over to the picture of the businessman he'd shown earlier. "This man has a beautiful house in San Felípe—a fortress. It has a gorgeous view of the Sea of Cortés, sleeps nearly twenty, and can house a small militia. He's just finished remodeling it. We believe he lives there full time and that the house was awarded to him when he was made boss.

"One more thing needs repeating, and you've heard it many times before. Our government does not want us to engage in killing or hurting innocent Mexican nationals. Government officials, even if they're dirty, are completely hands-off as well. But we have permission with the head shed to get this guy and bring him to the border, so the FBI can question him. We're not to hurt him or kill him. We're here to have him answer questions since he won't come voluntarily."

The crowd chuckled.

"So you're going to want to make sure you have a duffel bag with your side arms and your long guns, your medic kits, and any other specialized devices including drones—those of you who are going to carry them. I want it all stored in stackable units one man can carry by himself, and I want them brought to the airstrip in exactly one hour thirty minutes. I have a list of those men I want to see get on the plane, courtesy of Uncle Sam, and you fellas will check in for us and prepare for our arrival a few hours from now. This is a State Department official flight, with special diplomatic immunity, so the cargo holds on this plane will not be checked nor do you have to go through customs."

Several in the crowd were mumbling, and Kyle stopped them.

"We're going to have to do this quick. I want you guys to be on the road before 0700 if we can. The plane will take off, and the four trucks will head south. We travel to Tijuana first, then cross over to Mexicali, and follow the highway if we can to San Felípe. Our plane will be landing in a private airstrip, and we'll all meet up at the rendezvous."

Kyle dismissed the group, and Jason began separating and sorting the bags he brought, as well as retrieving items he was going to need from the team lockers. He consulted with Coop and T.J. and Tucker. They always duplicated several essential items in their medic kits but spread out additional equipment between the four of them, sharing the load.

"I understand congratulations are in order, you old fart," said Coop. "Libby was delighted."

"Hey, thanks. Kiley's working on that little bump, about four months along, feeling a little tired, but I think she's going to get her energy back here pretty soon."

"Yep, that's usually when it starts to kick in," said Tucker.

"So she's at your old place here in Coronado?" asked Coop.

"Nope. We're working all that out. Right now, she's back in Florida. We're kind of looking at all our options. Haven't made any permanent decisions. We're going to *reconvene the committee*," he said and grinned to the other medics, "once we get back from this mission."

"So how does that work then, if I may ask," whispered T.J. "You're going to fly back and forth and share diaper duties with her from Florida?"

His face was scrunched up like a prune.

Jason tried to be patient. "No, we're going to have to decide what to do. I'm staying put right now, but there's a possibility I'll request a transfer."

All three of them reacted. T.J. swore.

"Shit, Jason. We're not losing another one, are we?" said Coop.

"I don't know. We just got back from the naming ceremony on Kauai. She kind of likes it there."

"And how would you manage that? Shannon likes lots of places, but I can't have her living on the other side of the country or across the ocean," T.J. added.

Jason found him to be the most direct and insistent inquisitor of the whole group. He wanted to put the subject to bed so tried again to reason with his Team buddy. "Well, there's the little subgroup. Not sure I'm up for that."

"Well hell, Jason. You got about as much chance fitting into one of those things as I do," Tucker barked, his tatted arms crossing his enormous chest. "If you ask me, she needs to move *here*. Don't go do something stupid."

The other two medics objected to Tucker's language.

"He didn't ask you," interrupted T.J.

"Hold it, sport. Just watch that tongue of yours, please," said Coop. "Remember what Kyle said, we stay away from all the drama, right?"

"I'm just trying to lobby so that we get to keep this guy," Tucker objected. "I mean, these guys go out to Florida and fall in love. Then, you know, we lose Andy. I think we're losing Damon too eventually, so I guess maybe you'll be next. But Florida's still a hell of ways away from Little Creek. What's the matter with finding a nice house here in San Diego? It's near the ocean and got the same beaches and sun."

Kyle's angry shout for them to shut up and get ready had the four medics separate immediately and quietly focus on getting their gear properly stored, like they'd been told.

Jason was grateful for the save. He was going to have to do a better job of explaining their situation—once he figured it out, that was.

JASON SAT BETWEEN Tucker and Coop in the first van. Travel across the border to Tijuana was uneventful, as was the long and dry highway to Mexicali. But the closer they got to Mexicali, the more traffic they saw coming west, toward the United States' border.

They stopped to pick up some local grub for lunch. Cooper and T.J. decided to brave the sidewalk vendors and ate tamales with tomatillo sauce, along with several other fried fish delicacies. Jason wasn't going to touch anything off a food vendor, since on one prior trip, he got horribly ill, which nearly sent him home.

Nothing was remarkable of the city except that it was busy with commerce. The cars were newer than those they'd seen on the road. They saw groups of school children dressed in uniforms being accompanied by nuns or playing in the schoolyard as they drove by. Jason knew that it only looked like a normal, family town complete with four or five church spires and bells that were constantly ringing. The underlying community was far from normal and extremely dangerous for an American.

They pretended not to be interested in some of the things they observed, including drug dealing being done right in front of them on a street corner. Since the drivers were being switched out, those who had driven the last two-plus hours got to order a beer. Tucker was propositioned by three prostitutes who admired his girth. The team had fun with that, at Tucker's expense.

The "old guy" as they all affectionally called him sauntered up to Jason.

"God, I'm getting too old for this. I used to kind of like it, you know?" he said.

"I get it. You grew up, Tucker. You fell in love, and you grew up. That's what happens, right?"

"Damn straight. I'm looking at this group of guys—Kyle didn't send anybody single, did he?"

Cooper leaned in front of them. "Excuse me there, team historian Hudson, there aren't many single SEALs. You know that. When was the last time we actually got a newbie who wasn't at least engaged?"

"We all were single when we upped," T.J. said.

"Yeah, but it didn't take us long, did it, T.J.?" said Kyle as he approached the group.

Everyone got quiet, remembering their fallen team member, Frankie, leaving behind a pregnant wife. And T.J. married her.

"God, I'm sorry, man," Kyle said, slapping T.J.'s shoulder.

T.J. nodded his head and shrugged him off. "And life goes on."

It was the understatement of the day.

Kyle gave the order to load back up, and soon, they were headed out of town to the south toward San Felípe. They kept to the highway because black storm clouds were rapidly developing on the horizon.

About twenty miles north of the city, they encountered a long line of backed up traffic. It appeared a semi had blown a tire, crossed the center divider, and slammed into a passenger vehicle. The three medics grabbed their kits and ran for the passenger van with Arizona plates. Jason identified the family as possibly Amish, since the woman was wearing a hair cap and the girls were clothed in dresses instead of pants, their hair tightly woven into one long braid going down the center of their back.

It appeared one of the girls had suffered a broken arm, which T.J. was immobilizing. The youngest boy had hit his head pretty severely, blood running down his face and dripping on his white shirt. Coop attended to him, using some super glue to close the wound temporarily, and recommended they stop in Mexicali to be checked by a physician. It would be an easy drive for them, and they could also have the other two children seen by medical personnel.

The mother objected. "But how are we going to get there? Our car is destroyed. I'm going to have to file this with the insurance, and they're going to ask me to notify the police."

"I don't really want to get the police involved," said the father of the two injured children.

The man was right. He'd done a good job of swerving to avoid a direct head-on hit by the semi, but the last panel on their van was completely smashed in, the tire blown, the metal frame so twisted the door was inoperable, and all the back windows had blown out. Jason knew it wasn't an option to drive the family to Mexicali themselves, so he looked to the crowd on the opposite side of the road to see if he could locate someone who might be able to escort them. Kyle had already identified a cargo carrier, who was towing an empty climate-controlled horse trailer from Texas. It wouldn't be as comfortable as the van they'd been driving in, but it would certainly be much better than sitting in the back of a pickup truck or in a cattle car.

The children were treated as best they could, and Jason gave the mother instructions on not allowing her son to fall asleep until they got to Mexicali, because he suspected he'd had a pretty bad concussion.

"Thank you all so much," the mother said in return.

She tried to give Kyle a little wad of dollars, and he turned it down.

"No, ma'am, we don't accept money. I'm sorry. And don't go flashing that around. You don't live around here, do you?"

Her husband spoke up. "We came for a visit. Our church sponsored a small mission in San Felípe, and we were delivering some things from the ward that they couldn't buy here. Plus," he looked at his wife and then frowned as he examined his children again, "we were considering volunteering with the mission. But that's going to have to be on hold for now. So thank you."

Kyle addressed him again, "Well, the reason I asked is, you don't want to show money here. And as soon as they get your van moved and the truck gets on its way, you're going to see some Federales show up, and you definitely don't want to show your money to them. There are many honest law enforcement agents here, but any show of wealth and you'd just be increasing your risk of having problems. So we'll help you transfer your things to the trailer, and this gentleman over here will take you across the border. He says he will take you in to town to the hospital. How does that sound?"

They both nodded agreement.

Jason didn't understand how people were so naïve as to drive long stretches of roadway in a foreign country without proper tools for protection, bringing children and exposing them to the danger as well. He thought to himself, maybe he'd seen too much.

And yes, he definitely had seen too much. But that was what he was here for, to make sure that other people didn't have to.

CHAPTER 8

KILEY WRAPPED THE towel around her. Picking up her things, she scampered to her bungalow, unlocked the sliding glass door and keeping the key inside for the night. She made sure the slider was locked. She double checked the front door and made sure it was also locked. These had all been things she had promised Jason she would do.

Tomorrow morning, she'd get up early and take her walk on the beach, also a promise she'd made to him.

Her conversation with her former editor had annoyed her so much that it obliterated her appetite. But she knew she still had to eat, so she heated up some cream of mushroom soup, changed out of her swimsuit into some fuzzy loungewear, put on her massaging socks with the aloe vera cream infused in them, and sat back on the leather couch to watch the sunset and have her soup.

She wasn't interested in the news. Any news.

A light on her phone caught her attention, and she saw it was Jason. Then she noted the two messages he'd left before.

"I'm so sorry, sweetheart. I went for a swim. And of course, I didn't take my phone, so I didn't realize you'd called until just now."

"I got to get you one of those fancy new sat phones they're handing out to some of the military higher ups. The darn things are so indestructible you could practically drive a semi over them and they'd still be working. Supposed to be completely waterproof, too."

"Yeah, but then I'd look like some important person myself, and that's just too high profile for me, Jason. Besides, something like that is probably bigger than my forearm."

He chuckled, and just the sound of that spun the world in the right direction for her.

"God, it feels so good to hear your voice," she said.

"Ditto that, sweetheart. Obviously, you got home safe if you're swimming in the ocean. House is okay? Everybody else is okay? You're feeling good?"

"You mean, how's the baby?" she teased. "The baby's fine. I'm a little tired still, but the swim in the water was good for me. I haven't had a chance to talk to anybody else except Corbin. That son of a bitch is still trying to get me to go back to the paper."

She heard him take a huge inhale and hold his breath.

"Not to worry, Jason," she quickly inserted. "I am so over doing that. I am never going back in his offices again. I mean they'd have to give me a gold or platinum award for being the reporter of the century before I'd ever walk into their place again. It's just wrong him chasing after me."

"Is he chasing after you? Or is he asking you to do a story?"

"With Corbin, it's one and the same. And honestly, Jason, I don't think he cares about either really. He just wants headlines. He wants to shake things up. He sees himself as a Bob Woodward, but he doesn't have the balls to go out and do the stuff they did to uncover Deep Throat. I just have no respect for the man. And he's even using Carmen and Natalia to try to get to me, although I haven't heard from either one, and the answer will still be no, Jason. You don't have to worry about that."

"Good. Look, I don't want to waste our time with you telling me about your former boss. I only have a few minutes, and then I've got to get some shut eye so we can be ready early in the morning. We're here at our location in that country we talked about—"

"I got it," she said.

"And I verified that the timing is going to be what it is, you remember? We talked about it."

"Yup, all clear here."

"I mainly just wanted to confirm those things, make sure you got home safely, and see how you were feeling."

"You're three for three, Jason."

"I encourage you to stay connected with the ladies there while I'm away. I think you, Aimee, Martel, and Madison should do what we do when we get together, just stay connected, make sure they know where you are. Okay?"

"Yes. You've given me the lecture before. What else?"

"I can't help but fantasize, in fact maybe I'm having visions of living here, and I know it's not all settled… I just want to say the more I think about it, the more I like that option, Kiley. And I want you to use the time to do your research. So when I get home we can look at all the pros and cons, okay?"

"Yes, I agree. I promise I'll do that. As far as getting together with Aimee and Martel and Madison, they're all so darn busy. I thought maybe Martel was out there in San Diego. I haven't seen anybody at their house."

"Nope. Damon's here with us. As far as I know, Martel is still in Florida. He's having kittens over here hoping he gets home in time for the baby. Kyle told me he talked Damon out of going over to 5, but he probably won't re-up. He's got three years left. I guess they've had a change of heart on all that too."

"Can't say as I blame them. Makes it easier."

"I know. Please make the effort, Kiley, to stay in contact with them, more than you usually do. I'm sure Aimee will know where they are."

"Will do. So do you think it'll be okay for me to take those early morning walks by myself?"

"Well, I'd rather see you do it with somebody else, but I think it's okay. I mean, the crowds aren't there, right?"

"Oh, the beach is deserted. And it's so nice out. It's just between seasons, you know?"

"Yeah. But it doesn't smell like flowers, does it?" he whispered.

She paused and wondered if she should tell him her vision. She decided to go for it.

"Don't be angry with me, but I think, when I was swimming, I think I heard some chanting."

"Then it's happening. It's starting to become part of your life now, and that's going to come straight to the baby too. We believe in that."

"I was a little surprised at first, thought I was hearing birds, but it was very clear. I heard something that sounded like your mom's singer and a whole chorus behind her. It was beautiful."

"Honey, I think that's the best thing you could have said to me tonight. You make sure you get to bed early and take it easy for a few days. Get some rest and then connect with your friends. You could also give Christy and a couple of the ladies back in San Diego a call too if you wanted to."

"I will."

"Just don't be a ghost. Make sure you let people know where you are. That's the best safety advice I can give you. And I don't expect you'll need it, but it's always good to plan for it. That's what we do. It takes the odds a little bit away from the bad guys."

"Jason, listen. I. Got. The. Message!"

KILEY TOOK A long shower after she put her dishes in the dishwasher. She changed into one of her favorite flannel nighties and put her moisturizing socks back on. She bent over closer to the mirror in the bathroom, examining her face for fine lines and wrinkles, some kind of indication that her face was changing because she was pregnant. But she couldn't see anything. Jason had told her she looked glowing and healthy. She just didn't see it.

Pulling back the covers, she had considered picking up one of her romance novels and falling asleep with it, but even that felt too tiring. She knew she'd only get through the first two pages before it would be a struggle, and she'd be fighting to stay awake for another half an hour later, so what was the point? She turned off the bedside light. She scrunched herself down in the sheets, pulled Jason's pillow from his side of the bed, and propped it underneath her head and neck so she could be completely infused with his scent.

Bushes outside on their patio beat against the glass window of the bedroom, indicating perhaps a storm coming or the weather falling back into its normal hurricane pattern. This year, the storms had been infrequent and very light. They were due for a whopper.

She closed her eyes and remembered the ceremony, the walks on the beach, the view from the top of the old extinct volcano, the smell of the flowers, and the singing. She remembered the feel of the water as she floated in it. Florida was not all that different from Hawaii, except for the population count. Florida was pretty packed, at least along the coast. With no mountains like Kauai had, the similarities between the two completely ended. She'd read somewhere that the highest elevation in any part of Florida was still less than about 450 feet. No wonder people thought someday it would sink into the ocean.

But just as Hawaii was Jason's refuge, the source of a happy childhood for him, the place of his birth, the home of his ancestors, and the land where his family resided, Florida was important to Kiley for similar reasons. Although she'd been a vagabond uprooted by her family as they moved and despite her love of travel, their short stint at Sunset Beach had been the highlight of her life. And like Jason, even though Kiley's roots were very shallow, this was the place where she felt connected to her own family.

She told herself not to rush. She had a lot of things to do in the next few days to keep her busy, and Jason was right about connecting with Aimee, trying to find Martel, and going to visit with Madison over at the Salty Dog. She could use a few laughs and the camaraderie of Friday and Saturday night crowds that jammed that bar. Although she wouldn't drink alcohol with her pregnancy, she'd done it many times before, and she could pretend. Heck, if she could visualize chanting in the background, she certainly could remember how good it tasted to have a huge strawberry margarita, sitting on a stool, talking to a stranger at Madison's bar.

And then she remembered the baby and her instructions to her. More and more, Kiley became certain that she was having a girl. It was secretly turning out the way she'd always wanted it to be. Still, if she was having a boy, she knew she'd be delighted with that as well. She felt the connection between the two of them forming a very strong bond, and maybe it was the fact that she never had a sister or she never got to be close to her mother, but she vowed to end that lonely cycle and make sure her daughter never experienced the pain Kiley did growing up.

It was all good.

"Leilani, you're going to love the beach. I've got a sign that I'm going to put in your nursery. It doesn't matter whether it's in Hawaii, San Diego, or Florida. The beach heals everything. That's the first lesson I'm going to teach you."

CHAPTER 9

THE TEAM DIDN'T even get the opportunity to watch the sunrise on their first morning in San Felípe, since they got up before the dawn and loaded two inflatables. While several stayed back at the condo complex to monitor radio traffic and be their backup, should they need it, fourteen went with Kyle and Jason. They were headed out to explore the island in the middle of the Sea of Cortés, called Guardian Angel.

There was no jungle in this arid part of Mexico. Although technically still the tropics, the terrain was craggy and resembled high desert. Rocky outcroppings showed layers of ancient volcanic activity, which dislodged the old seabed into stiff peaks of light brown without a stick of greenery on it. It was in stark contrast to what Jason had been experiencing the last few days in Hawaii.

They'd loaded everything they could into two of the vans, strapped the inflatables to the roof, and off-roaded it down through a winding canyon that eventually led to a small tributary. Depending on the rainfall, which was rare, that tributary could bring them to the sea itself.

As they neared the bottom, they had to watch their noise level. The canyon walls echoed and distorted their voices, sometimes magnifying it and thus revealing their presence. It was unlike anything Jason had ever seen before.

Walking past the dry remnants of the tributary, they arrived at the sea, being fairly sure no one had seen them enter the water.

Each boat carried eight men, who sat on the edges, their equipment placed in the center at their feet for quick and easy access. A tiny outboard motor got them to Guardian Angel Island just as the horizon was starting to turn a pinkish orange. Both inflatables made a silent landing on the smooth-pebbled beach without a grain of sand anywhere.

Jason and T.J. hauled their boat up out of the water and stowed it under an outcropping in the shade. The other boat was positioned right next to it. They left very little except extra food and water under a tarp large enough to camouflage both the boats.

Kyle pulled out a plastic map showing full topographical detail and locations of points of interest. He motioned to a trail they could see between another outcropping nearby. There were no footprints or signs of man on the trail, indicating no one had been there recently. There were, however, swirling tracks indicating snakes or lizards had. It was about the most desolate place Jason had ever seen.

They hiked the path until it began to rise up over the outcroppings and then followed switchbacks going back and forth as they descended to the small desert floor. Looking down and south, into the valley below, the land appeared to be shaped by an old volcanic crater. The only forms of plant life were tall cactus rising as much as twenty feet into the air. Jason noted those as being a good source for water should they need it in an emergency. Smaller creeping sagebrush appeared in sparse patches between the rocks. Several tall palm trees also dotted the canyon floor.

There were no structures, corrals, houses, or places where livestock would be living. Nothing lived there except for birds, some of whom nested in the cactus and no doubt drew their water source from the spindly towers. They loudly proclaimed their outrage at these humans who dared to invade their habitat. Some birds watched down from washed-out alcoves or small caves and would swoop down and fly just a foot above the heads of the team.

But suddenly, as they traversed to the bottom of the crater's canyon, they heard the unmistakable sounds of sea lions.

Jason knew that meant they were close to the water's edge again, and as soon as they finished the climb on the other side of the crater, sure enough, bathing in the grayish pebbles was a colony of sea lions, at least four-hundred strong. At any time, two-thirds of the sea lions were resting on the shore, while the rest of them frolicked in the water. Careful not to alert them, the team bypassed in a wide arc to connect with another set of trails that led toward the tiny fishing village they were looking for to the south.

Jason, T.J., and Cooper all brought their small medic packs. Others brought food and water. Fredo and Armando carried other specialized gadgets and equipment, including a couple small drones. Armando and two others brought their long guns, broken down and stowed in specialized packs never out of their sight. All of them brought grappling gear, supplies for their own personal use, and sufficient gear to set up a small campsite should that be needed. Normally delegated to Fredo, Kyle carried the coms.

At the next ridge, they stopped for a water break and passed around some energy bars. Several pulled out a canteen flask and drank coffee. Jason loved the smell of it but knew his stomach wouldn't be able to handle it this morning.

"What a difference between this place and down at Cabo. It's like two different countries," said Danny Begay. "This looks more like Afghanistan than Mexico."

"That's because we landed on the hot, north side of the island. The population, what little there is, is on the south side where there is more rainfall," said Kyle.

"But unlike some of the waters farther down toward Cabo, this place looks like the Dead Sea. I didn't see a single fish, did anyone?" Damon asked.

"I'll bet the whales come in here in the spring. It looks like good whale country. Nothing to bother them. I'm guessing you'd see a lot of them then. But that's probably it," said Fredo.

"And then you'd get some dolphins," said Armando.

"I think the more south you go, you'll find all the wildlife. These sea lions, they love the sun, and they don't want to be anywhere close to people, so this place is perfect for them," added Jason. "You don't want to get anywhere close to them, though. Those bulls can be deadly, and they can get to nearly two thousand pounds. I've heard some are the size and weight of compact cars."

"Roger that," said T.J.

Kyle gave the order to gear back up and head south, following him. Again, they walked nearly single file through the narrow canyons of long-extinct and dried rivulets. Still there was no evidence of wildlife other than a bird carcass occasionally or a snake or lizard skin. Once in a while, they spotted evidence of an old campfire, littered with beer cans and trash. Coop quickly dug a hole and buried the trash in the sand while the team stopped to watch him.

Straightening up his lanky frame, he shrugged. "I can't help it. The Boy Scout in me is not going to let me leave that garbage there. I mean who comes all the way out here and then leaves their fucking beer cans?"

His attitude drew chuckles from the rest of the crowd. Jason had never pegged Coop for an environmentalist, but he agreed with the repair and knew Coop had a great love of the outdoors and worked to take care of it.

"We'll see if we can pick that stuff up on the way back if that'll make you feel better," said Kyle.

"You going to get the birds too?" Fredo questioned him, his forehead and nose bunching in disgust. "I mean, beer cans, they could be houses for little creatures, insects. There's got to be insects here, right?" he asked.

"I'm not going to leave beer bottles here. No way. And the carcasses, well, they'll break down," Coop pushed right back at him.

"I just think you should be consistent. I mean, if you're going to pick up the garbage, then pick up the bird carcasses too. You know, make the place a better place for you and me, all that stuff?" Fredo said with attitude.

"Don't start on me, Frodo," Cooper shot back.

Jason thought they might even get into a wrestling match. The two were the best of friends, but they argued constantly. Jason remembered during their single days that it was much worse than he was hearing today.

Kyle stepped in, as he always did in this situation, because someone had to. "Come on, ladies. Put your lipstick on, adjust your knickers, and let's get over to the other side."

Another forty-five minutes later, they bellied up to a ridgeline overlooking another barren expanse. But two or three miles inland from the beautiful turquoise and white beach shoreline, there were little shacks, a marina with several fishing boats, and a dozen more abandoned boats anchored and listing in the bay. Several scrawny palm trees dotted the streets and occasionally were tended to by a green lawn. They also heard a donkey braying and the sound of chickens.

"I guess that's what you call a sleepy little Mexican fishing village, right, Fredo?" Coop asked.

Jason knew their chiding was beginning to wear on the group. It certainly didn't do anything to calm his nerves. He didn't like the conflict.

"I've seen things that look like that in Nebraska too. You've got some towns out there population six and a half. I think these people here have you beat," Fredo responded.

"Yeah, but they grow their own food in Nebraska. Everything grows there, not like here. You'd see corn fields. Those people could grow corn anywhere. I'll bet if they sent a family of Nebraskan farmers to the moon, they'd grow corn there too! Even here. I know they could," he said.

"What's the plan, Kyle?" Armando asked, slicing right across the conversation and skillfully stopping the bleeding.

"I just want to get eyes on the village and look for evidence of police, some official representation. One thing State wasn't sure about is if there was a garrison nearby. In this part of the country, troops are often transported from town to town without any permanent station or location. I just need to know if they're here or if anybody has advance knowledge of them coming."

"How do we approach getting down there? Obviously, we aren't going to walk in there single file like we have been, right?" asked Jason.

Kyle gave directions for the men to break up into groups, approach the shore, and then walk into several palapas that were food stands, pop-up restaurants manned by family vendors. He asked Jason and T.J. to talk to some of the fishermen about what they were catching and if there was a boat they could rent.

"If we can get ourselves a fishing boat here, we'll have a good reason to come back and not blow our cover. It doesn't look like they're very busy, and I don't see any tourists. Do you?" asked Kyle.

Jason shook his head.

The group split up as directed. T.J. mumbled his disgust at the bare scenery. "I need to get my butt in the water. Damn, Fredo was right. This is like Afghanistan, isn't it?"

"Yeah, we'll get some time in, T.J. Don't worry about it. Myself, I like that quiet water where we left the dinghies. That's my kind of quiet place. Here, it's not really set up for swimming."

Unlike most fishing villages Jason had been in, the first thing that always hit you was the smell of fish. While there was the distinct smell of rotting something, it definitely wasn't fish, which told him there wasn't much of the sport. As they approached the edge of the bay, there was a small trench that had been hand dug. Bleeding guts and waste animal parts were flowing into the water, leaving a reddish-purple stain in the otherwise bright turquoise water. He followed the ditch until it was buried, ending in a line of corrugated shacks.

T.J. pointed to the buildings.

"I think they've got themselves a little slaughterhouse there. Maybe they're cleaning fish, I don't know. You want to go check it out or should we inquire about a boat first?" he asked Jason.

"Let's check and see if we can find a boat first," he answered.

Several small children ran up to them, one little boy pointing to Jason's heavily tatted torso, the Polynesian designs and patterns almost appearing to dance as he moved his muscled body. He looked at T.J. for a translation, who shrugged his shoulders.

"Beats me. I don't speak Spanish. I don't know what the hell they're saying, except I think I heard the word lizard in there somewhere." He laughed.

Jason drilled him with a stare followed by a growl. Standing firm in front of the boys, he flexed his pecs, rolled his eyes back, crouched, and started doing one of his Māori dances. The boys instantly disappeared, running in all directions.

"Hey, way to not draw attention to yourself, big guy. Or did you forget we're supposed to be stealth, on a secret mission?" T.J. said with his hands on his hips.

"Fuck you. You think I should have worn a long-sleeved shirt and covered up all my artwork? If so, Kyle would have mentioned it."

"Okay, I concede. Your point is taken."

"I'm thinking he chose me precisely for that."

"I already said you're right. Now shut the fuck up. Let's go talk to these guys over here."

Three older men sat on a metal bench rusting in the shallow water, their feet dangling in the surf, mending a fishing net. One of them smoked a pipe. Jason greeted them all and immediately noticed that between all three they probably owned a combined total of ten teeth. Their skin was leathery and brown from being out in the sun all day. Although skinny for their age, they were not weak.

"Buenos días," Jason tried to say in as close to a Spanish accent as he could muster.

All three of the men nodded and issued a greeting in return that neither T.J. nor Jason could understand.

Then he tried to indicate the shape of a boat and pointed to several out in the marina and then pointed to himself and to T.J. and several of the other men they could still see wandering through the village. He waited for the three older men to confer between themselves, and then they spoke back to him in Spanish. So Jason repeated the gesture again—pointing to himself and T.J. and the other men, then the boats, then to himself again, pressing a palm to his chest.

This time, the older gentlemen seemed to understand. One ran up to the metal shed, asking to wait with gestures while he retrieved someone who might be able to help them. Or, at least, that's what Jason thought.

The fellow he brought was obviously former military. In impeccable shape, his hair was clipped tight and high on his misshapen skull. He had tats on his chest that had faded, indicating he'd probably received them while incarcerated. His eyes drilled into Jason as if the mere fact that he was six inches shorter than the Polynesian giant and was way outmatched in tats offended him.

"You want a boat?" he said in decent English with a sneer.

"Yes, if there's one to hire. We would like to do some fishing," Jason said.

The man searched the ground around where T.J. and Jason stood, looked at their backpacks while shaking his head, and squinted as he said, "Where's your fishing gear? Or do you need to rent that too, soldier boy?"

Jason was alarmed the newcomer had pegged him so quickly. He could feel T.J. straining, holding in laughter.

"I always rent the equipment with the boat. You have such a boat? Yes or no? And if not, where can we get one?" he said to the man.

"*Señor*, I will make the arrangements. But not today. You come back next week sometime? And I feel I must warn you, we have no fish. Nothing you can eat. The fish are all gone now. Pollution from your country, no?"

Jason knew he wanted to pick some kind of a fight, but he didn't take the bait. He was about to suggest they go back to their group and reconsider their strategy, when T.J. interrupted his thoughts.

"Not tomorrow? Maybe the next day?" T.J. asked him. "Next week won't work. Too late."

The man looked between both of the SEALs, probably weighing something about odds and trying to answer his internal questions, and then took a step back.

"I will see what I can do. You can stay in my village if you like. We have a cantina. We make our own beer here. I will know later tonight if you stay and have something to eat. You come back and see me up there." He pointed to the shed. "Or tonight at the cantina. And I will let you know."

Jason grabbed T.J.'s arm. "Come on, sport. Let's go check out what the rest of the guys are doing."

T.J. nodded in the direction of the gentleman from the shed and said, "We thank you for your kindness. We brought our own food. But we may see you tomorrow."

With that, they walked up the small swale through pebbles that turned into larger rocks and then sandy soil dotted with failing foliage. It was probably not the welcome they expected, and they had possibly not been as successful as Kyle would like, but it did look like one way or the other, they'd get their boat.

Jason hoped the other teams had had more luck.

CHAPTER 10

KILEY CONNECTED WITH Aimee and Madison. Madison had learned of an art exhibit she wanted to go see in downtown Tampa. The three of them met at the Salty Dog, and they all piled into Aimee's car and headed over the causeway to the city.

"I haven't done something like this in ages, it seems," said Aimee.

"In college, we used to go to galleries all the time. This whole area has beautiful exhibits, and I've always wanted to see the Highwaymen paintings," said Madison.

"Why do they call them the Highwaymen?" Kiley asked.

"Because they were Black men who couldn't find work in the fifties and sixties or couldn't find anything but menial labor jobs that didn't pay well, so they learned to paint," said Madison. "They used to stand by the sides of the highway and sell their paintings for like twenty-five or thirty-five dollars. People would stop and buy them. They painted them on a special kind of wood, not canvas, so it was inexpensive for them to do it. Back then, it was called 'fast painting,' because they often would do several in one day. They even sold them with the paint still wet!"

"I never knew that the Highwaymen were in Florida," said Aimee. "I've heard about them, and I saw some of the pictures in a documentary, but I didn't realize it was Florida they were painting."

"Yeah, and people who are lucky enough to have an original Highwaymen painting, well, they're worth thousands of dollars now. Real collector's items," added Madison. "They're very sought after, because most of the original painters are gone."

"Has your mom seen their exhibit over at Fort Pierce?" Aimee asked.

"Oh, she not only has visited, but she knew some of the guys."

Aimee rolled her eyes.

Madison shrugged and then added, "Yes, I run across that a lot. I never ask my mom about her past anymore. But I think she probably knew some *quite* well."

Kiley knew that Madison's mother had been the love of Jake Silver's life. In a strange twist of fate, Jake's son, Ned, had married Madison, falling in love with her before he even knew the story. Amberly was a painter herself and loved entertaining artists, writers, poets, and musicians at her house on the beach frequently.

"I'll bet you've met some of them, Maddie. It would be just like your mother to invite them to her legendary parties. She'd help them get discovered too. I can see that in her," Kiley confessed.

"Could be."

They parked in the city parking lot right across from the gallery. The tickets had been given to Madison complimentary by one of the tourists who frequented the Salty Dog and wasn't able to use them. But all three of the ladies placed money in the donation box which was set up to benefit the families of some of the Highwaymen who had passed on.

Walking through the exhibit, Kiley loved the vibrant colors, the deep sunset vistas, the different blues of the sky and the water, the foliage. The painters were known for doing mostly landscapes, but occasionally, they'd come across a painting done by a relative of one of the original Highwaymen as some of their children started to paint portraits. But most of the paintings were holding true to the style that had been developed seventy years ago, born from the love of art and turned into a way of life for these men and their families for generations to come.

She noticed one beautiful blue ocean painting, and upon checking the picture of the artist below, noticed it was a woman.

"So there's a woman who's a Highwayman? Is that right?" Kiley asked.

"Yes, Mary Ann Carroll, First Lady of the Highwaymen," said a young gallery guide behind them. She wore a black pleated skirt and a white short-sleeve blouse with the logo of the gallery on the front. She also wore white gloves for handling the paintings.

"She was married to one of the original Highwaymen, and he taught her. So she joined the group. She's actually quite good, don't you think?"

Kiley loved the painting.

"Are they all gone now?" she asked.

"All but one. But most of their children paint, and some grandchildren too. The Highwaymen taught their families, and so this is a regular industry for their progeny. No painter paints the same picture, and you'll see the same scene painted differently over and over again even by the same painter. They're all unique, something slightly different about each one."

The three wives meandered through the gallery, and Kiley purchased a paperback book showing pictures of some of the artists and their families and some of the paintings. It chronicled the history of how the group got started and where some of their paintings lived today.

Reading the back of the book, she showed Madison and Aimee. "Look, there's one hanging in the White House. And they have three or four in the Smithsonian. Isn't that cool?"

Afterward, the three had lunch together at a local burger place.

Aimee asked Kiley about her trip to Hawaii.

"It was beautiful. It's the only place other than here where I could see myself living. I mean, it's got palm trees everywhere, it's green, and it rains every day. It's just a gorgeous place. I don't know what I expected, but I think I was in such a daze for the wedding last year that I wasn't paying attention. The Hanalei Valley was spectacular. Jason's family is very traditional Hawaiian, and the naming ceremony was just awesome. Magical."

Madison was curious. "When you say naming ceremony, you mean they pick the name for your child?"

"No, it's a process. It's different for every couple. Some people dream it, some people have it recommended to them by an elder, but it's a very sacred thing, naming the baby before the baby's born. And the theory is that when they're born and before, they're welcomed to this world, I mean, *formally* welcomed."

Aimee's reaction was immediate. "What a concept. That sounds very spiritual, beautiful. What a wonderful thing to experience."

Kiley agreed. "I'm a lucky woman."

"So Jason's going to be in Mexico for very long?" Madison asked.

"No, otherwise he would have asked to sit this one out, with the baby coming and all. I'm hoping he'll be back in less than a month. We'll see. They've arrived, I know that. And I don't know too much about the operation, of course."

"Of course," Aimee said.

"How are Ned and Andy doing with Team 4? Are they happy there?"

"Aimee and I were just talking about how we need to do a girl's weekend up there at Little Creek. You know the two of them got an apartment together?"

"That's right. How's that going?"

Both the girls laughed. Madison could hardly speak she was laughing so hard. "I don't think they've had anybody in there to clean up after them for, what would you say?" She looked at Aimee and squinted.

"My bet?" answered Aimee, "Not more than once in the six months since they've been there."

Kiley put her hand over her mouth to stifle her laugh. "Oh my God, you guys better take a week off to go do that then."

"See that's the thing, we've asked them to pick a date, and we said we'd come up and help them straighten the place, maybe decorate, clean, and get themselves situated. The bottom line is, I don't think they want us to come." Madison pouted, and then everyone laughed again.

Aimee had to explain. "They don't say it that way exactly, Kiley, but they just can never find a date because they're so busy. Or they're coming down here to visit us. It's kind of like they get to be in boy's school again. They go out and do things together, the two of them, and I think they're a good influence on each other. Andy seems to really like his LPO, and they have some good rotations coming up. But to be honest, I can't wait till they detach," said Aimee.

"I think Jason's going to want to stay in for a while. We're checking out our options. It's a long way between here and San Diego. Even Hawaii would be nice, but we really don't know. We're going to talk when he gets back."

"You can't be serious, commuting between Hawaii and California?" asked Madison.

"Funny thing is, same distance from Florida."

"You're kidding. I didn't know that," said Aimee.

"Why doesn't he transfer to Team 4 in Little Creek?" asked Madison.

"It's part of what we're thinking about. Yeah. It's a possibility."

"How are you feeling?" asked Aimee.

"I'm tired a lot. So I'm going to use the next few weeks to get caught up on my sleep, and hopefully, by the time he gets home, I'll be back to my old self, except I'll be a little bigger."

"Well, you look beautiful." Aimee squeezed her hand. "I'm sure Jason has told you that. You look very happy, Kiley. I'm so glad things have worked out for you guys."

CHAPTER 11

KYLE HAD BEEN given information by Kelly Fielding of an American man who ran a veterinary stand in the village. He'd been a trained veterinarian in San Diego prior but had gotten caught up in a sting operation when some of his employees were selling tranquilizers for pets to some of the homeless population down there. He was able to stay out of a long-term jail sentence, but he lost his practice and his certifications.

He'd always wanted to just retire in a little Mexican fishing village, so he took what equipment he was allowed to bring, picked up his Mexican girlfriend and their child, left the United States, and was never going to return. But Kelly knew a good asset properly buried, and that's when she gave Kyle the information.

"I know it's tough down there. Small community, especially on the island. And you're up against some huge players. Those guys never show their faces. But the fear factor is strong, and to be honest with you, most people would probably prefer to just be left alone, but you and I both know there's no place on this planet where that can happen anymore, Kyle. Every place is overrun with people trying to take advantage of others."

"Well, Kelly, that's the first I've heard of you speak this way, almost sounding like you're going political." Kyle looked up at Jason and T.J., who had been sitting in his bedroom, listening on the speaker.

"It just is something that I am feeling overwhelmed with at this point. I've had some close calls. They seem to happen more frequently, and I'm getting tired. I haven't really had a family life, and Sven is trying to encourage me to retire, live simply somewhere, and just give up everything. I can't do that yet. I still have people like you and others who I try to protect, to get information for, but man. It's getting tough."

Jason felt for the talented State Department asset, even though nobody was really sure who was paying her salary. But if it hadn't been for Kelly, they would be minus several men on their team, including Kyle. While she sometimes had to bend the rules, the nice thing was that everybody else bent to Kelly's wishes when she said something needed to be done. It was a good but rare thing to have a honest, street-smart asset who was creative in her thinking and just trying to do good without drawing attention to herself. Damn lucky to have such a liaison.

"I'll look up this fellow. Should I just show up at the guy's place of business, his little clinic here in San Felípe, now that you've given me all that?" asked Kyle.

"For his own safety and yours, it would be better if you picked a way to meet him socially, I think I'm going to notify him that you're going to try to reach him and to be looking for some kind of strange American contact, seemingly coming out of the blue. That way, he'll trust you. And, in case his home or business is being watched or you're being watched, we won't expose the both of you at the same time."

Kyle looked up at Jason. "I've got a better idea, Kelly. How about you tell him to look for a huge Pacific Islander guy with tattoos all over him, who looks like he should be wrestling in the WWE? I'm whispering because he's sitting right here, and I don't want to give him any ideas. He'd probably make a lot more money."

"You've got that right, Kyle. I know exactly who you're talking about. Hello there, Jason."

"Hello, ma'am, and it's good to have your help."

"Kyle tells me you struck out on Guardian Angel. Give me your impression of the place."

"Honest to God, there was just nothing for T.J. and I to work with. I mean just nothing. Normally there's so much business going on in a fishing village down by the water, that's where all the deals are done, but this place is deserted."

"I'm not sure that's a normal thing for this island, but San Felípe would be busy like that. Guardian Angel Island is really a dropping off place, but if it's quiet, then they're preparing for something, you can count on it. When the locals avoid coming out, it means it's bad."

"Kinda felt depressing, if you ask me," answered Jason.

"You probably didn't have time to look at it very carefully, but there's talk about tunnels and caves and things there, and next time you go, I suggest you start at midnight and work until dawn and not meet any people. But you'll get your boat, and if you don't, I'll make sure somehow you get one. I got to figure out how I'm going to do that. You're way out there in the middle of nowhere. Which was the plan."

Kyle leaned into the phone, removing it from Jason's fingers. "Well, Kelly, we're going to walk through the town. We're going to go tourist shopping, let off a little bit of steam, and let the guys do some swimming. We're putting the island on hold for right now until I hear back from you. But I think we need to brighten our spirits a little bit. It's a little dismal down here. Hot as hell. Feels like nothing should even be alive here."

"Well, don't be deceived by the people, the traffic, or the apparent lack of commerce going on in San Felípe. It's a very dangerous place, and it's not getting any better."

JASON PICKED OUT a couple of bright flowered hand-stitched tops to take home to Kiley, buying them in extra-large sizes so she could wear them during her pregnancy. He liked her in pink and red, but he also found a beautiful turquoise blue one that he thought maybe she'd like. Each of the smocks were crafted as dresses but cut short and hemmed. The colorful stitching was done in exquisite detail, depicting bright flowers and vines. Kiley loved wearing Hawaiian and Floridian prints, so Jason felt she'd enjoy wearing something from Mexico. It too had wonderful beaches and great weather near the resort areas. He was going to have to leave out the part about what he saw and how dangerous it was, just like he always did when he came back from an op. This was his way of telling her, "Hey, I did it. I'm back. No big deal. Our life goes on."

Just like all the other SEALs did when they came back home.

Damon peered over Jason's shoulder. "Those are nice. Now if I get those for Martel, she'd punch my lights out. Kiley's going to be appreciative of you getting her a huge smock like that?"

"Yeah, I'm hoping so. Why wouldn't she like it?"

"Haven't you had that little discussion yet about 'do I look fat?'"

Jason didn't figure Kiley had any issues about her weight, had never mentioned it.

"Well, it is her first pregnancy, and everything's all new and exciting. I don't think she has thought about that part yet. But I get you. I've got sisters, and they want to get back into their skinny clothes just as soon as they can. So yeah, you probably would deserve getting your lights punched out. I think I get a free pass for a while, maybe just this once."

"Jason, you're a smart man."

"So how is Martel doing? Kiley was hoping to hook up with her, but she said the house has been dark, nobody there."

"She's gone up to Palo Alto to visit Ainsley. The Newbergs agreed she could stay for a few days at a local motel and visit with her, and she's very excited about the new baby. We aren't going to have her come out to Florida right away. I'm still trying to convince Martel to have the baby in San Diego. But we're running out of time."

"So how long do you have left?"

"About a month. Pretty soon she's not going to be able to fly. So I just hope I get back in time. And I've talked to her on the phone. She really wants to stay in Palo Alto as long as I'm okay with it. It's a little expensive, all the hotels there are expensive, but you know she's missed out on so much of that bonding with our daughter. I think she's trying to include her in the whole pregnancy. In a way, it heals some of her own wounds about giving Ainsley up for adoption."

"Those adoptive parents are just amazing. Did you ever think you'd have a relationship with the daughter you gave up?"

"Well, of course, I had the easy part, or the bad part, depending on your perspective. I'm the one who left and didn't contact Martel back. She's the one who had to make the decision. I wasn't anywhere around."

Damon continued to explore some of the trinkets, the fabric, and painted gourds this particular vendor was selling.

"But yeah, we are pretty lucky, and I think Ainsley's lucky as well. In a way, she has four parents. And we all get along. As long as that continues, we're going to be good with it. And it's only right that she get to know something about her new little brother or sister."

Jason looked over all the things that the vendor was selling. "Other than smocks, I have no clue what I should be buying for people."

"Jason, just don't. Just don't even go there. Stick with what you got. I think it's perfect. But I'll tell you one thing you might want to do. There's this little shop down the street I could show you if you want. They sell blown glass made out of recycled bottles. You might want to pick up something pretty for Kiley. It's not something we will be able to travel with very easily, but we can make accommodations."

"Are they fragile? And how big are they?" Jason asked.

"Oh, you can get them big, I mean, you know, like really big." He showed with his two hands that the size could be two or three feet. "But they're made from bottles. Bottles are thick, not like crystal. I'd suggest getting something, you know, about the size of the palm of your hand? That way you can put it on a string and hang it in the window or put it on your Christmas tree. You'll see. You'll like them."

The two SEALs picked up two others and headed down the dusty cobblestoned street toward the little shop Damon was looking for. Jason and the others entered the metal shack just as it began to rain. He hadn't noticed the clouds in the sky, and the rain was quite timid, so he knew it wasn't going to last. But the sound on the corrugated stall was almost musical, he thought, like the sound of a piano playing with tacks on the keys, out of tune.

The shopkeeper had created wind chimes out of cut rings of glass from bottles of all colors and shapes, and the melodies were beautiful. He was fascinated with their vibrancy and the way the light from outside shone through the window and splashed color all over the walls. In one corner, the shopkeeper had a cabinet filled with hearts of different sizes, starting from small marble-sized hearts all the way up to enormous hearts that were made into flower vases.

Jason picked a red heart that was about five inches across with a glass loop on it, admiring the mottled surface, the bubbles, and the swirling red and white colors in it. He asked the price and got an answer in Spanish he couldn't understand. The shopkeeper wrote it down on a piece of paper for him.

"U.S.?"

She shook her head and wrote down another figure, which he gladly paid in one-dollar bills. He thought, as he held his prize up to the light, that ten dollars was way underpriced, so instead of haggling, he gave her a tip of two dollars and felt good about it. She wrapped the heart in a newspaper, placed it in a brown paper bag, and handed it to him.

He thought about what that heart was going to look like dangling from a fishing line, sending warm red images all throughout the room.

That's when he knew the heart wasn't for Kiley. It was for his daughter.

CHAPTER 12

KILEY'S PEACEFUL AND beautiful morning ritual of walking on the beach was rudely interrupted by a phone call. She cursed to herself, remembering that, almost without thinking, she'd slipped the phone into her pocket before she left the house. Realizing it was her own fault, she looked at the number and knew right away who it was.

"Carmen? Is that you?"

"Yes, Kiley, it's me. I am calling to ask a favor."

Here it comes, she thought. Here comes the pitch, the opportunity, the something she would never in a million years want to miss. That was what they were going to tell her right now. Carmen was Corbin's secret weapon. He knew it was far easier for Kiley to turn him down than to turn one of her best friends at the paper down. Carmen's call was not unexpected.

"I told Corbin I wasn't interested in anything at all there. I'm going to distance myself and completely separate myself from that life. I wish you guys all the luck, but I'm not available."

"Yeah but you need to know a couple of things."

"It's always just a couple of things, and then it's a couple things more, and then you're asking for my help, and then I get embroiled, and then I can't get out again. I told you, and I told Corbin, I am not jumping back in. I've made a promise to Jason.

I'm pregnant. I don't want to spend any of my time thinking about all those things I used to write about. And don't get me wrong, I still care; it's just that I don't have the capacity to do anything."

Carmen was obviously flustered. But there was something else, a wavering in her voice, and yes, Kiley had to admit, she sounded scared. Kiley took several deep breaths and then told Carmen to do her ask. She knew it was a mistake before the words came out of her mouth.

"Well, it looks like the group is revving back up. I mean revving back up big time. It's almost like they got an infusion of some protection deal. Natalia has gotten death threats, and they've had to locate some of her relatives in Ukraine. You remember, she was able to track a few of them down after she got her freedom?"

"I remember." It had been one of the happier moments of the whole saga.

"Unfortunately, not all her relatives are safe. She's lost touch with one of her cousins who was working on getting us some information for the ongoing story. We fear she's been locked up some place, or worse."

"I'm sorry for all this, Carmen, but I don't see where I fit in. There's nothing I can do from here, and I'm not going to go to Portland. I'm done with that life. I told you when I left you guys, go at it and risk your own necks, but I'm done. I did what I could, I helped bring the mayor and all those other cronies of his down—"

"Well, they released the mayor today. They've made a statement saying they're not going to prosecute. They are getting all the low-level players, but the investors, the foreign agents, and mob guys are all gone. Completely disappeared. And as a matter of fact, the mayor's going to launch an investigation into the district attorney's office here, who's not very popular anyway, threatening to fire the lot of them. He's using the unhappy public with a DA that doesn't often view things the same way they do, and he's going to champion getting rid of this guy so he can somehow work his way back into everyone's good graces."

"But I thought he lost his law license. I thought he was no longer able to hold public office."

"He can't be elected to public office. But he can be appointed. Oh, Kiley, it would take me hours to tell you what's happened since you were on this beat."

"But he was arrested!"

"That's true, but he's still being the champion of the people. And from what I can see, he's really ramping up. He's not apologetic at all. He's going to blame everyone else he can, claim he was made a victim. He says he wants to clean house and is running an anti-corruption campaign. Can you believe that?"

"That takes some balls."

"Probably more like money. There's still big money in trafficking. Did you really think they'd just walk away with their tails between their legs?"

"No, but—"

"And he's even told Corbin this morning that, by the time he's done, he'll own the paper."

Kiley knew the millionaire heiress widow who really owned the paper would not be happy if she had to do a proxy fight with the former mayor and his representatives. It would be near impossible for the paper to survive if it was accused of dirty dealing. The public wouldn't support it. That's why most newspapers now print what the public pays to see, not what is the news.

"I'll bet it's doom and gloom over there these days."

"Got that right."

While it would certainly mean Corbin's firing, the owner was smart, and Kiley didn't think it would affect Carmen or Natalia, especially if they jumped to another paper before the shit hit the fan.

"Carmen, this is a large tangled web. I have no clue what to do with these people. I'm not even connected to anybody who can."

"But the people read your stories, Kiley. And when I write them or we have a couple of newbies on staff take a stab at it, the online paper does terrible. Like nobody reads it. Nobody comments. With you not here, it's all dead."

"Well, for me, it is. It's just not something that I can do and stay healthy, not to mention I've promised Jason. I've said this to you now three times during this conversation. I've told Corbin. I've promised him that I won't go back. And I'm going to keep that promise. He's on deployment right now, and I'm not going to do anything to upset him while he's on a mission. So you need to get it straight that I'm not your person. You need somebody much more powerful. Have you tried talking to Colin Riley and his group? They can do an awful lot of good, and with his money, he could have a greater influence than I ever could."

"He's in the hospital, Kiley. I thought they'd told you. Nobody's quite sure if he's going to ever be the same again, but it appears he's had a stroke."

Kiley wondered why she'd not heard this. But then again, she had left strict instructions that she was off of everybody's phone list. She didn't listen to the news, and they'd been in Hawaii where the news was different. Nobody cared what was happening in Portland any more than they cared what was happening in San Diego.

"I'm so sorry. That's too bad. So how is Jenna and everybody else there?"

"It's like a ghost town here. Everybody's just kind of biding their time. People are spinning off, taking other jobs. Most of my research team is working at Starbucks now where they get medical insurance and their hourly wage at minimum is higher than what we pay. That and they get to go home sometimes. I could really use some help."

Kiley was touched by Carmen's honesty and her beg, but she still held firm.

"You're going to have to figure out another way, Carmen. You could do one thing for me, though. Why don't you go see Colin Riley and give him a message for me. Tell him I'm pregnant, and ask if I can see him perhaps. Ask him if he even wants visitors."

"I will. Natalia and I were going to try to go see him soon, maybe this afternoon. But I don't think they're allowing anybody but family members in. Are you serious about coming to visit him?"

"To say goodbye? I probably would feel pretty lousy if I didn't. But there's no way in hell I'm going to get involved in any of those stories, Carmen. If they found another way to start business again, then they must have somebody pretty powerful backing them up."

"They do. They've got a plan, Kiley. I don't even know if I should say this over the phone. But Natalia uncovered a source that told her their plan is very shocking."

Kiley knew she was going to regret asking. She just knew because every bone in her body started tweaking, her ears rang, her stomach did flip flops. Whatever it was Carmen was going to tell her, she imagined that big steel wall coming down. She had no protection against the news that was coming. She took a deep breath and then violated every rule she'd set for herself and promised to Jason.

"Okay, tell me then."

"I can't tell you. I'm going to have to email it to you."

Dammit! Dammit! Dammit! Kiley said to herself. She should not have asked. She'd gotten hooked—just like she used to do anything for chocolate as a child. She knew better. She had her baby to think about.

"I'll send it tonight. You look it over, and you just tell me what you think I should do. I'm trying to be respectful of Colin Riley and his health situation, so it would be irresponsible for me to talk to any of his team without getting his approval first. And this news could kill him. I know that Sven, Kelly, and Jenna are all off doing their things, but they're supposed to return tomorrow, and they're going to have a family powwow concerning Riley and his health. So we have a short window, very short, but it's there."

Kiley was done asking any more questions. She tried and failed to not be curious. It was like not trying to breathe.

"Natalia uncovered this yesterday. Corbin doesn't even know about it yet, except for the fact that Mayor Whitman is working to get his job back—a job he can't have. But he's gunning for something else, and I want you to read about some of the things we discovered."

"Carmen, you just ruined my fucking morning."

CHAPTER 13

KYLE, JASON, AND a team of eight used the off-road location to launch their inflatable. It was a perfect night for an operation that needed to stay completely secret. They painted their faces for the moonless night, and they'd been instructed to bring dive gear to be able to explore some underground pools showing up on satellite footage Kyle was sent.

Due to the location of the island in the Sea of Cortés, it was the perfect spot to use for smuggling. With a relatively small island population, lack of interference from the U.S. Navy or the Coast Guard, and the proximity to the border states of California and Oregon, risks of being discovered or caught were minimized. All the cartels needed to do was deal with Mexican officials.

Kyle had briefed them the night before.

"Border patrol has intercepted caravans and interviewed migrants who talk about the island, so we've been sent to check out possible underground caves where contraband and smuggling activity could be conducted. The island is the site of a volcanic crater, possibly hollow on the inside. That's what we're going to check out, especially now that we have the satellite imagery to back it up."

They went light on the firepower but were not totally unprotected since every man had a side arm of their choice. Jason had his SIG SAUER, which was always his go to weapon.

Armed with night vision scopes, they launched from the completely dark lagoon feeding into the larger body of water and slowly rowed several hundred yards until they were out in the middle of the Sea of Cortés itself. Their outboard motor would most certainly wake people up on shore, but without lights and out in the middle of the open sea, there would be no way anyone would be able to pinpoint their location. At least that's what they were counting on.

It took them over an hour to reach Guardian Angel Island at their slow speed. Even in the pitch dark of night, Jason could still see the huge white rock standing tall and menacing, the barren surface reflecting off some light source behind them. Were it a full moon, the crater would glow like an iceberg.

Upon landing, they pulled the boats underneath the ledge overhang as they had done before, covering them again with sandy brown colored tarps so they'd be invisible even from the air.

Instead of going through the canyons to the right as they had done the day before, they took a path which led them wading through surf up to their knees. As they rounded the rocky shore, they discovered a small sliver of beach.

From the outside, it looked like the beach was only large enough for the length of one or two men, but as they walked up onto the sand, they saw it had fanned out a lot in the back and was surrounded by rocky walls, creating a cove or inlet effect. The rocks in front protected what was behind them.

Jason also noted the area was like a wind tunnel, with tropical breezes being captured, whipping around, causing small sandstorms from the shedding rocks around them, and then blowing away. At several times during one particularly heavy gust of wind, they heard what sounded like whistles.

Kyle led them toward the sounds, where a small cave appeared. Kyle peered inside and then waved behind him for the rest of the team to follow. As they explored farther, the white sand sloped and revealed with their NV goggles a turquoise pool of water, with fingers extending under the rocks in multiple directions.

Part of the area was covered with a rock layer with large holes punched in it. Jason knew right away what they were.

"See those holes that look drilled into the ceiling?" he whispered. "Those are from lava tubes being flushed out by sea water, sending rocks and debris out like mini bombs. I've seen these in Hawaii. This would all be in sunlight in the middle of the day."

"Good to know. Adds credibility to the theory people could be housed here temporarily and no one would be able to see them from the outside. Perfectly camouflaged," said Kyle in addition.

Jason was thinking that someone could easily, if they had the right provisions, live here for several days.

"Partially protected from wind too," Coop whispered.

Kyle put his fingers to his lips as several of the SEALs started making other comments. At Kyle's direction, Fredo began searching the perimeter, looking for anything that might indicate some kind of an electronic component, a trip, an alarm, or camera. A couple of the other men actually scaled up the cave walls carefully, avoiding making a slide or showering the team below with pebbles and dust.

Fredo turned to Kyle as the two climbers repelled back down. "There's nothing here. I don't see a darn thing. I don't see how they could, but I don't see any kind of listening device, unless it's very small and I missed it. But I doubt it would transmit through that rock. I think we're good."

"Okay then," Kyle said. "So I'm splitting you up into twos and threes. Jason, you and Cooper dive down some of these holes I'm seeing in the pool, and see if there's another compartment or pool on the other side. I just kind of want an idea of what's there, okay?"

"Roger that, Kyle," Jason responded and began to remove his dive gear. Coop sat beside him and started to do the same.

"If you find anything, take pictures and let me know over your coms. We certainly don't want to walk into some kind of a drug stash, which will be heavily guarded. I want you to report back if you see any footprints whatsoever. And please, let's try walking in each other's footprints if we can."

"I'm going to photograph the floor first before anyone jumps in," said Fredo.

"Good idea. Mind your things. We don't want to leave anything that indicates we were ever here."

Several of the team acknowledged.

"Coop, you and Jason, start with that one over there. It looks like it has a huge bridge just underneath the water. My bet would be on that area having the best chance for having a large hidden compartment."

"Roger that." The two SEALs parked their packs on the dry sand, stripped off their khakis and shoes, left their t-shirts on, grabbed their flippers and scuba gear, and began to descend under the water's edge. Jason pointed forward, and Cooper allowed him to go first. He knew Cooper was a world-class swimmer, almost making it to the Olympics, but Jason had years of experience cave diving in Hawaii and French Polynesia growing up.

Taking air, they continued through the passage that narrowed and then flared out again, just like the area they had come from. It was all underwater, with sometimes large air bubbles skidding along the ceiling of the cave, until they came to a hole in the cave wall, blasting out bubbles like a small furnace. Jason put his hand up to them and found the bubbles were warm.

They continued on until they found a drop off where the water suddenly grew cold and they could not see the bottom. The water's color had changed to a deep navy blue. Along the sides of the pool, there was a sandy shore, and there was evidence of backpacks, bed rolls, provisions, and even an old fire scattered in one corner. Cooper snapped photos of the provisions before they started to open the bags and peer inside.

Jason lifted out American MRE rations and several magazines for a 9mm gun, as well as a small medical kit. The bullets were hollow pointed. That indicated to Jason that this wasn't just a recreational or fishing expedition with a couple of friends. These people had firepower intended to stop a man.

But even as they further searched the belongings, they could not find a weapon. They also did not find a radio, any instructions, or maps. Several feet away, they smelled a shallow latrine that had been dug. And it had been used recently from the strength of it.

Jason sat on one of the large boulders overlooking the pool. He flipped off his mask and breathed the stale air inside the cave. It was steamy but not too warm. It definitely was something a human could survive in for a few days anyway, barring any great drop in temperature at night, which he doubted.

"U.S. military MREs?" Cooper said. "I don't recognize the backpack, and I don't recognize the bedroll. I think those came from Mexico. Or Central America. You suppose they're just lookouts, and this is like their little stash for when they're on an assignment?" Cooper asked.

"I don't know. I'm kind of spooked by the fact that I don't see any footprints," said Jason.

He stood and examined the sand leading to the pool. That's when he saw ridges on the smooth surface, as if a sheet of water had completely flooded the area. He heard water dripping and walked across the bar toward the sound. And there was a trickle of a waterfall, seeping from the top. The stones and part of the crumbling walls to the right and left of the small seepage were smooth and completely dry. Even cracks between rocks were smooth and carved out. That led Jason to the only conclusion he could come to, and he voiced it.

"This area floods. This whole wall has been washed with water. Depending on the rain or high tide or something, this washes down over this wall and completely obliterates any footprints or elements in the sand. There are different kind of rocks on the other side of the pool, so I'm thinking this is just in the middle. Part of this island is hollow inside."

They did a perimeter check, taking pictures of everything they noted. They considered whether to bring the backpack and some of the items with them and decided to just photograph it and leave them in place so that perhaps no one would guess they'd been there.

The beach surrounding the pool was high ground and looked like normal sand. No one had traveled on it for years.

"That it on chronicling all this?" Coop asked.

"I got dozens of pictures. Why don't you go explore that pool and see if there's anything of interest in the bottom—if you can find it."

Again, Coop dove into the water, turned on his underwater video and light, and scanned the walls below sea level. Jason stayed on top to monitor just in case someone arrived.

Cooper's fins were the last part Jason could see as he dove deep to locate the bottom of the hole. Then he burst up out of the water, thrashing about in the water, holding a human femur bone.

Jason examined the bone and then looked at Cooper. "What have you found?"

Cooper slipped off his mask, trying to catch his breath. "They're all at the bottom, Jason. There's a whole pile of them. All sizes."

Jason knew that at one time, women and children had perished here. The thought churned his stomach, but still, he was glad he was chosen for this mission. Whoever had caused their demise would pay for this.

CHAPTER 14

KILEY ANXIOUSLY AWAITED the arrival of the documents Carmen had sent. She had been checking her phone when she got a ping on her computer. Opening her laptop, she noticed the screen was frozen from an update that had occurred early in the morning. She quickly jumped into restoring some of the apps, and one disabled app caught her attention. It was her newsfeed link, NewsNow!.

She had purposely disabled it when she left Portland, so she could control the volume of project-interrupting alerts she expected to come her way. But now, she considered perhaps she should reopen it.

The one thing she didn't feel good about was that it was not what she'd promised Jason. She'd given her word to stay out, completely out. Checking her gut, this was not keeping her promise. But on another level, she had left a job—and she'd done a good job too—but she'd left her job incomplete. She left feeling there was sufficient momentum for others to complete the rest of the details left unfinished. That's what she told herself to justify her leaving.

It was true. They'd taken down one huge wing of the human trafficking and drug trade in the Portland area, and she'd believed that those still on the ground battling this war had the confidence and resources to finish it, shut it down forever.

She'd been wrong. It was a costly mistake for several of the players standing. She'd perhaps made her decision prematurely.

With the knowledge that Colin Riley was now in the hospital, the prospects for anybody being able to continue the work had greatly diminished. It wasn't impossible, but without Riley's contacts, coordination, and money, the pressure to close everything down would be diminished. Their grip slipped away by the day.

And there was the problem. Because she had been a reporter, an investigative reporter. Not supposed to be *making* news but *reporting* news. It had morphed into reporting about things that needed to change in society. And the public was hungry for it. They wanted stories of recovery; they wanted stories of people who were doing something to take care of the issues plaguing most American large cities like Portland. Portland was filled with families, wonderful people who did many philanthropic things for the community. It was very proud of its heritage and background and the role that it played in the development and history of the West Coast, even the international stage as many leaders went on to assist forming organizations like the U.N. and its precursor, the League of Nations.

But it also had become, over time, a place where other opposing forces-forces who wanted to dismantle the very fabric of their community could safely hide. Now those forces had come out in the open. And one or two or ten or twenty police or FBI raids in an effort to control and combat some of the evils seeping in were becoming more and more difficult. Nothing was working.

Many of Jason's friends had told her they didn't see how even a paramilitary operation run by the government, which was certainly illegal under current laws, could do the job. And government programs were, at best, very costly with little results except at a campaign stump. What Kiley knew worked was a combination of having the public support, understanding the situation, using force where it was needed, and having the resources to be able to take care of those damaged, extracting the bad players, and having the guts to see the operation through. The problem with most inner-city operations was that administrations would change, somebody would make a mistake or take their foot off the gas pedal, and then all of a sudden, the task force was either corrupted or shut down.

There was no history in general, and there were places that were well run and shining examples of what could be done with the city and population partnership, but most cities didn't have a long-term solution to these huge problems invading their town. Everything was an experiment. The population were guinea pigs. And for the political leaders, they were votes.

It wasn't a justification, she thought to herself, to say perhaps she needed to investigate what she could do. That didn't mean she'd be on the streets or involved in any direct way like she had been before. It just meant that, if she saw the web that had been created and understood the blockages to getting things done, perhaps she could make some suggestions.

Would that make her a target? If she wasn't writing articles, if her byline wasn't splashed all over everywhere and picked up by other national news media, maybe she could just stay under the radar, have her baby, and remain in Florida safely.

But the other issue was with Jason in Mexico and an indeterminate date he was to return, she was all alone, about to embark on probably the most important project of her life, the birth of their child. And she wouldn't do anything to jeopardize that.

Kiley knew she was stubborn. She tended to root for the underdog. She knew she would continue to do that, even though sometimes she'd lose. It was a question of what the stakes were. She wouldn't do anything to lose Jason or the baby. She would defend her friends. She would defend her right to say and do and think and publish what she wanted. She hadn't stopped being an investigative reporter because she was afraid. It was because she had made that promise. It was because she acknowledged that doing that would put herself, her baby, and perhaps Jason's career at risk.

And that she wouldn't do.

She checked her phone again and noticed the several Messenger notes coming across. When she first turned on her computer, there had been four messages. Now there were thirty-five. Something big was about to happen.

Checking on the newsfeed app on her cell, it also had been disabled with the last update. She turned it back on, and immediately, her phone blew up with emails from other sources and news flashes. She knew that would dissipate in time, but she had a lot of reading to do. And she wanted to be informed before she made her next decision. She also needed to frame her concerns and needs to Jason when he called, and she needed to do it in a way that didn't upset him.

She scanned several of the text messages Carmen had sent her, trying to look at Carmen's comments first before she clicked on the links to take her to the stories. There were several from her old paper, but other papers from Seattle to San Francisco to San Diego were also picking up news feeds about political activities going on in Portland. The bottom line was the former mayor, Whitman, had been released from prison, but this had been in the works for several weeks. His attorney had claimed the police and the FBI had conspired to close his operations in the city because of politics. And since politics seemingly entered into everything these days, the public was buying it. He claimed he was a victim. He'd been conned into participating because he was a force for good, not bad. He claimed he was falsely accused and tried.

Kiley knew the mayor was dirty. She had seen his name on the deeds and documents for some of the buildings where the young women were brought in and groomed and then sold to the highest bidder. These were innocents, many times, picked up in villages or sold to traffickers by their parents with the promise of a better life in the United States. And the truth was sad. Most of these women either didn't make it to the United States or were shipped elsewhere, never to be heard from again. Only a select few came to Portland and were tended to by Natalia, the Ukrainian woman trafficked and sold to the cartel by her grandmother, who had a change of heart and helped Carmen and Kiley take down the organization that she worked for.

Kiley was shocked the public would buy such a lie, but former Mayor Whitman was good with his pressers, had a team of fantastic attorneys specializing in criminal defense, and claimed victory after he'd only spent a few months in prison. The strategy had been set in place before he even served time and planned during his trial. While the public was championing the fact that he was going to be convicted, his legal team was strategizing the way they were going to get him out.

In the middle of her reading, she received a call from Carmen.

"Okay, Kiley, I've made contact with Colin's family. As you know, Jenna and Kelly are on their way. The hospital has given us permission for you to see him, so I'm just calling to let you know that time is of the essence. I'd recommend you come out to say goodbye tonight if you can, or you will miss your chance."

This put her in the difficult spot she'd been worried about.

"But you haven't told me the important thing. I asked you and I asked you this specifically, Carmen, does he want to see me?"

"He does, and you can," Carmen said, without an ounce of

hesitation. "That's all I can say at this point. He is gravely ill, in and out of consciousness, and he could recover, but it's not likely at this point. I'm sticking my neck out here, Kiley, just by telling you. That's personal information I got from the staff, and they could be fired over this. I have not told Jenna or Kelly, and I'm not going to tell them. I'm going to let the medical staff do their job."

"But if they come and they see me there, am I going to look like an intruder trying to get a story? The optics of that are just horrible, indefensible."

"No, Kiley. You're going there to say goodbye. That's what you said. You're not working on the story. Right?"

Kiley was furious at the way Carmen phrased everything. She suspected that not everything was as true as she had said, but they were friends. Carmen had stepped into the arena, given her all, and was risking her own neck, whereas Kiley was going to try to stay out of it. That pushed her in the direction of trusting her friend. She hoped she didn't regret that decision.

"Against my best judgment and contrary to the promises I made to my husband, I'll book a flight tonight, if I can. I'll text you the details. Can you be there to pick me up? No limos or sending anyone else. I want you there, Carmen. Only you."

"Absolutely. I think you're doing the right thing. Colin will be happy to see you. And don't forget, there are women and children out there who need our help. That's our purpose here."

Of all the things Carmen could say to completely stick the fork in her all the way, that was it. No denying women and children were being abused. And Kiley just couldn't let herself be okay with letting that happen.

"Oh God, forgive me, Jason," she whispered just after she hung up the phone.

CHAPTER 15

When Coop and Jason made their way back to the rest of the team, Coop threw the femur at Kyle's feet.

"And there's a whole lot more where that one came from," he spat.

Different team members had their own way of expressing disgust, but the most common was a string of expletives they would never say in front of their wives or their mothers.

"Holy shit, Coop," Kyle said, picking up the dripping long bone. "Where was this thing? I know you traveled under water for part of this, but was this in water or on the sand or somewhere else?"

Jason spoke up next. "There are several small caves back there. The place is like Swiss Cheese, with all these lava tubes and such. One large cave had a pool where the water looked extremely deep." Jason backed up and motioned for Coop to continue.

"It was about forty feet down. I saw this huge pile of what I thought were white rocks. When I got closer, and it was kind of hard to see because I had my night vision goggles on, they were not rocks, but a huge pile of bones. We didn't measure. But among these bones are all different sizes. Like smaller, very small. We all know what that means."

Jason pulled two other femurs from his dive pack, obviously

one belonging to a child.

T.J. uttered, "Fuck me!"

After that, a hush descended over the crowd.

Kyle was speechless.

Jason knew every single man in that room felt their heart had just sunk to their feet. The second emotion was going to be anger, just like his was. He was noting the fact that if there had been any guards or lookouts anywhere near where that pit was, they would've been very unlucky.

Kyle took the smaller bones, examining them. "We got marks here and here." He demonstrated, and Jason and Coop nodded.

"We saw the same."

"Well, this deserves a call back to Norfolk. I'm going to have to proceed with caution here. There are certain protocols we have to follow involving the retrieval of body parts, human remains. Since we don't know whether these are American human remains or Mexican nationals or belonging to someone else, we should proceed with caution. You've got pictures?" he asked.

"Already uploaded them to the Team site," said Coop.

"So I'm going to get some advice. I certainly don't want to get my tit in a wringer over a pile of bones at the bottom of an island lagoon in the middle of the Sea of Cortés at the edges of a turf war between two drug cartels. That doesn't sound like the kind of vacation I signed up for, you get my drift, gents?" Kyle finished.

There wasn't a man in the room who disagreed.

THE WAY BACK to San Felípe was deadly quiet, each man absorbed in his thoughts. After the report that Cooper and Jason made, Kyle and two other witnesses followed them back over. Upon further exploration, they confirmed that indeed the pile of bones in the bottom of the pit was at least ten feet deep. It could have been even deeper. However, most of them bore varying degrees of injuries, anything from machete marks to fractures. The one thing that was missing in this pile of bones were skulls. And that was the freakiest thing of all. What the hell were they doing with all the skulls?

Several of the smaller bones were brought out and laid on the sand so that they could document them. Cooper was instructed to take one sample from each age group, perhaps take a piece of a pelvic bone if he could find something small enough to carry, indicating men or women. The head shed was going to want to know for sure that it was men and women or possibly women and children. Not that it made a difference. It still was a genocide site, according to Jason's own personal view. And nobody else in the group would disagree.

Earlier plans they'd made about going out at a local restaurant, having a nice meal, blowing off steam, and turning in early had been rerouted. Most of the men on the team, except Coop and a couple of others who didn't drink, wanted to skip the meal and just take the alcohol. It was one of those nights that always made the service they provided their country difficult. It would have lasting effects on them, and they would dream about it probably forever.

Jason decided the best thing for him to do was to take a swim in the Sea of Cortés. Cooper agreed to come with him, as well as Armando and Danny Begay. He ripped off his clothes, putting on his swim trunks and flip flops, and didn't bother to bring anything else but a towel.

He went downstairs to the common area, waiting just outside the patio door for the other men to arrive. Kyle was on the telephone calling his superiors, perhaps calling Christy. He heard T.J. talking to Shannon in hushed tones, and several others, quietly wiping tears from their eyes, made the connections they needed to feel human. Jason wondered what used to happen in the days when men couldn't call home or call someone else for moral support or help. He was grateful he was serving in these days and not the days of his father's life.

Today could've been one of those he could recall years later as being one of the worst days of his SEAL life. But the day when he held Thomas in his arms as he was dying, his best friend, that was worse. It wasn't good to stack his bad news neatly in a pile to help keep track, but it also wasn't healthy to deny that it existed. He chose to view them with stoic, completely unemotional reverence, thereby honoring those who were lost too soon. That way the past didn't ruin the future for him.

He wouldn't let it.

He recalled the sign over their bed Kiley had dragged with her all over Europe, from Portland to Florida—*The Beach Heals Everything*. That was going to be his go-to place today, his refuge. He hoped to God this part of the sea was clean, not filled with oil and diesel like the waters of Coronado. He just wanted to float until the memories faded away.

The men joined him at the picnic table he was sitting on, and all four of them headed down the sand to the blue water in front of them. Young boys were renting beach chairs for tourists, kayaks and double-hulled kayaks the hucksters tried to offer them, but they waved them all away and headed straight for the water after dropping their towels in a pile.

It became kind of a race between he and Armando, who was a very good swimmer, but then Cooper, damn his ass, beat them all. The guy was a fish. Even though he grew up in Nebraska.

Instead of doing what he really wanted to do, which was to float, he allowed Cooper to run the swim. All three tried to keep up with him, and for the most part, everybody did. They swam for about twenty minutes in one direction. On the return, Coop really stepped it up a couple notches, and Danny dropped back. He and Armando held tight to Cooper's backside until finally Jason could not take it any longer. He stopped, and then he realized Armando had stopped some five hundred feet back. Jason waited for him to catch up.

"Damn, I think he must be exorcising some mighty big demons today, don't you think?" asked Armando.

"I think you're right, Armando. I know working it out of me is a good thing. I hope to never live any place that isn't close to the ocean. You grew up in Puerto Rico?"

"That's right. The beach was my time. It was my backyard, my front yard, it was the place I went when nobody was home, because my mom worked and my dad did too. And then after my dad—"

Jason knew Armando's father had been a policeman and was gunned down on the job. After all these years, it was still hard for him to talk about it. Jason felt guilty, his visions of his father was that of a monkey man dancing around, laughing making fun of him. It was a completely different culture and type of relationship between the two of them than Armando had.

"Hey, sorry, man. I didn't mean to bring us there."

"It is what it is. Some of us get to carry a little extra burden. My mother always says God never gives you more than you can handle. I'd like to think I'm stronger, especially after Gina. It's just been a rough year, man, and Sambra and I are just getting situated, so I am careful what I share."

Jason had thought the same. "I completely understand. Same for me."

"So I go back to the ocean, because that's where I begin to feel alive and happy again."

"Damn, Armani, we are way more alike than I knew. You're strong, one of the strongest men I've met here."

"I think we get stronger because of the shit we see and do. I'm learning to cope with all kinds of things I had no idea I could."

"You know, Armando," Jason said as he paddled around his buddy splashing water, "If I could be half the father you are to Artemis when my baby comes, I'll be doing good. I think you're a damn fine person. I think every man on this team is worth giving my life for. Not that I'm seeking it. But that's the way it is, isn't it?"

"Yep. We try to be there for our families, and then we have this job, doing things no one else will do, seeing stuff a person shouldn't have to see. Isn't fair, is it, Jason?"

Jason shook his head. "Nope, nothing fair about it."

Their fourth, Danny, zipped past the two SEALs in a competition to make it to where Cooper was hollering, yelling at them for being pussies. Jason kicked his legs into gear and swam as fast as he could, arriving at the shore completely exhausted. He lay on the wet sand and then slowly rose and walked to the complex.

When they returned to the condo, someone had ordered trays of Mexican foods and a ton of alcohol. In one corner stood a case of mineral waters and a plastic bag filled with limes for Cooper and the non-drinkers in the group. Jason got the message right away that this meant there was no going out on the town, but they were going to stay here together, probably get some rest, maybe play some games, and turn in early. Kyle had told them that they would be taking their off day tomorrow.

While they were munching on the food, Fredo mixed margaritas in the blender in the kitchen. Several men found puzzles they began to put together—one of them a picture of kittens.

In the game closet was also a game called Butt Darts. And that became an instant hit. Each man wore a belt with a little target on the back made of Velcro, and the point of the game was to have someone pitch a whiffle ball in the air and then they all had to try to get the ball stuck to their butts. It caused a lot of take downs and very aggressive wrestling. A lamp was broken, a table overturned, and two or three drinks spilled. But it was good, clean fun, great competition, and it was the mind shift everyone needed.

"Luci gave me some news from home," Danny said. "She told me that Griffin learned how to use a slingshot and got Ali in his left eye. It's swollen up so big he's having to miss school. Can you believe it?"

Several of the men clapped and then drank to Griffin's ingenuity. Ali was the little Iraqi boy that Danny and Luci adopted, and Danny had taught how to use a slingshot, which wound up being one of the ways he escaped from Ali's father's captors. But the problem was that he had deadly aim at it, and Griffin usually was peppered with bruises because he was Ali's favorite target. Griffin was approximately three years younger.

Jason studied the faces of the other men on his team. They had hearts that were so big and so inclusive that they would do anything for their kids and their wives and their families, without thinking of themselves. That quality was far more important than how they were trained to efficiently take down bad guys. They were lethal weapons, but they were a force for good.

Just as the sun was setting, Kyle called for one more swim in the ocean.

Jason listened for the voices of his ancestors. He listened for the sounds of the singing, and he couldn't find them. He knew they were there. He just couldn't hear them. He tried to think about the flowers, the green hills, the way his mother laughed, and the way his uncle liked to walk around with his skinny legs and bare feet in his shorts. He thought about his little nieces and nephews, and he thought about Kiley, waiting for him, waiting to become a mother.

He thought if he paddled on his back with his eyes facing the heavens, closing them, and just floating, he might be able to transport himself to Hawaii. Or maybe Florida.

Something caught his attention as he heard the call of a seabird. It did sound like a child crying or someone yelling at first. He looked up toward the horizon and saw a beautiful thunder cloud rising from the center, obscuring the setting sun.

That's when he started to hear the singing. But it was faint, very faint.

He decided he would have to try harder. And he needed to talk to Kiley. He needed to feel that connection to the woman waiting to love him when he came home.

CHAPTER 16

CARMEN MET KILEY at the Portland Airport, just as agreed.

"I'm going to head us straight to the hospital, Kiley," Carmen said. "I want you to get there so you can have your little greet with Colin Riley. The news is not good on his condition, and I think it's better if you see him even before Kelly and Sven and Jenna arrive. I wish they hadn't taken off like they did."

"Well, this was totally unexpected, right?"

"It was. But he's never been very well. And usually not all three are gone at once. But yes, this happened quite suddenly."

A dark thought crossed Kiley's mind. "You don't think he was somehow poisoned or given something that would cause a stroke?"

"God, I don't know. I got my hands full just trying to track all the other stuff going on. You won't believe what's happening here, Kiley. You wouldn't recognize this place now."

"So what is Corbin letting you do, or not do?"

"Oh, he's given me carte blanche to do things, although I do believe he's getting some pushback from our owner. She's recently run into a bit of a financial bind. Our business news section chief heard that through the grapevine. But nothing in print."

She maneuvered around cars and took the onramp to the freeway toward downtown Portland.

"That probably wouldn't sit well with your boss, Carmen. Or does he know?"

"Of course he knows. Our newspaper is like a sieve. There really are no secrets. It's not a leak; it's common knowledge. We have to confirm it before we can print it."

"Wish everyone did that. One thing I loved about the paper."

Carmen glared at her. "Having a change of heart? Gee, that was easy."

"I didn't say that. Don't put words in my mouth." Kiley made a note to be more careful and to keep her opinions to herself.

"I don't know. Maybe she's considering selling the paper. But that's not anything I have any time to explore. It's just another one of the destabilizing factors that's going on. It's like everything's blowing up, Kiley."

"I really didn't want to jump into all this, Carmen. I'm only here to see Mr. Riley. I'm really not interested in getting involved in the day-to-day war, but if there's something I can do or see that can help you guys out, I'll try. But I'm already way out on a skinny branch here, because I promised Jason I wouldn't do this. And here I am."

"Well, you need to talk to Natalia. Maybe after you have a sit down with her, you'll feel different. But I understand. And I'm just helping you out in the off chance that you'll change your mind. That's my job. Corbin wants me to convince you to stay. Just being upfront about this, full disclosure and all that. But I know you probably won't."

Carmen continued to wind their way through the downtown traffic until they came to the five-story parking garage adjacent to the Mercy General Hospital complex and parked.

"You can leave all your things here. It's pretty safe."

"Just my suitcase, but I want to leave it in the trunk if you don't mind. I'm taking my laptop. I'm never separated from my laptop," Kiley insisted.

They ran to the garage elevators and then across the walkway, which traversed a four-lane freeway, into the hospital complex itself. Just the smell of the hospital put Kiley's nerves on edge. Every time she had come, it was for something bad, someone like her parents passing away, friends, Jason with a couple of his injuries. It was never good to be in a hospital. And she knew about saying goodbye. She'd been there too.

This was different, she thought as she tried to calm her nerves. This man was special, and she would not be able to live with herself if she couldn't at least tell her husband and some of the SEALs who worked with him that she had said goodbye. She tried to leave messages for Brandy and several of the other wives, including Christy, but had to resort to voicemail. She'd taken off so fast she wasn't able to reach anybody in person live.

Carmen knew how to get up to the ICU floor through the back way, a service elevator. That route took them past fewer nurses' stations, and when they got to the sixth floor, she pulled Kiley's arm, and they ran down the hallway, stopping before turning a corner. Carmen peered around to check on the station and then motioned for Kiley to quickly follow behind her. As they ran past, the station was temporarily unmanned.

They slipped into Colin Riley's private room, which was completely dark, except for a glow coming through the large picture window, displaying a beautiful pink and orange sunset.

She timidly followed behind Carmen, who approached Mr. Riley's bed. He was asleep, an IV and other tubes crisscrossing around the backside of his bed, his face slightly pinkish and swollen. He also had one leg uncovered by the blankets, very swollen and slightly purple.

Kiley looked at Carmen and frowned. "What's with the leg?" she whispered.

Carmen shook her head and shrugged. "Must have something to do with it, but it wasn't like this yesterday. I don't know."

Mr. Riley opened his eyes, and his right hand came up in front of his body as he splayed his fingers and said something to the two women, something Kiley couldn't understand.

Then he pulled three of his fingers toward him, curling as if motioning Kiley to move forward. "Thank you for coming. You must be careful," said Mr. Riley in a barely audible voice.

Kiley sat next to him and gripped his hand with both of hers. "I'm so sorry it took so long to get here. I understand Sven and Kelly and Jenna are on their way, Mr. Riley. I just wanted to express my gratitude and to lend my support."

"You need to be careful. I think they're trying to eliminate me."

"Mr. Riley, somebody did this to you?" Kiley asked him, turning and glaring at Carmen.

"It's a poison. I had one of the nurses research. I was hit on the foot with something sharp. It's a poison, a toxin, and it causes strokes. My body is weak. I don't know if I can survive. But you must tell the girls. You must tell Sven. You must help them."

"Who did this then?" Kiley asked again.

"I think the Russians. Ukrainians perhaps? There are all kinds of mercenaries out there, making lots of money. You exposed them, Kiley. You made them run and hide. You must be careful not to become a target again."

Kiley thought about the words that Colin Riley said to her. She wondered why Carmen had never mentioned it. She wondered if anybody else knew this information. That was going to be the first thing she was going to check out when she left this room.

"What is it you want me to do?" she asked.

"I have a will that is stored in my safe at the house, the safe that's in my office. I believe that Jenna has the combination, but my attorney in Portland also has it. I just drafted it two weeks ago. My attorney needs to make sure that it is completely followed. I bequeath everything to my girls."

Jenna was Colin Riley's natural daughter and Kelly Fielding was his daughter-in-law, married to his deceased son. But he considered her just as much part of his family as Jenna.

"They are coming I think tonight or tomorrow. You should tell them. It should come from you."

"I have it on good authority this toxin takes thirty-six hours to shut down everything inside me. I will not be alive in the morning. Everything you need is in that safe, Kiley. You are the only person I trust to get this to my daughters, to Sven. And then I want you to go home."

"You heard about my news then?" Kiley asked, smiling, hoping it would cheer him up.

For the first time since their meeting, Colin Riley returned her smile, the blue around his lips becoming more and more prominent, almost a death smile. "Yes, sweetheart. You and Jason will make wonderful parents. I wish that Jason could work with my team. There are several of his teammates who would really enhance our operation. I'd love to get Tucker, and I think he's ready. I can't convince them. Maybe you could help?"

Kiley knew that was way outside of her wheelhouse, and she didn't want to promise so she deflected.

"When it comes to talking to the team guys, I let my husband do that. But I will make sure and let him know what your wishes are."

"Now go. Before they find you. I don't want you to be harmed in any way. You have much to live for, Kiley. There is much that you have done, and yet there's still so much more to do. Go, escape from this place, be safe, and if I'm lucky enough to see my children before I pass, so be it. But I want to die knowing that you are safe."

CHAPTER 17

THE CALL CAME in very early. There would be no day off today. Kyle informed them a team was to immediately go to Carlos Gutiérrez' home in San Felípe.

"We have authorization to do some eyes-on surveillance. We've got drones we're sending, but we need to get you guys inside his complex somehow. If possible, we'd like to get him offloaded and onto a naval ship or plane to bring him back to San Diego so he can be questioned. With the findings that you've located, it backs up some of the information we've been given prior, and we're to insert ourselves, but be very careful not to harm anyone unnecessarily."

The team, eating breakfast, groaned. Jason knew this was extremely unpopular, whenever the boundaries were fuzzy. Fuzzy boundaries got team guys killed. Fuzzy boundaries got team guys booted off the teams. Fuzzy boundaries could also cause international incidents. And of all those three items, the one that was the most important to the government, to the Navy, was the last one.

"So here's my take on what we're supposed to do. We're going to try to get this guy, maybe lure him out somehow without bloodshed if we can. But really what we're there to find is evidence that he could be implicated in the smuggling operation. His fortress is well guarded. It's at the top of a hill, and they can see toward the sea and all the surrounding areas, for miles. It's going to be hard for somebody to sneak in there without being noticed. We're not going to parachute at night, because there's too much going on in San Felípe, and we don't want you shot down like some kind of an enemy drone or something. They have that capability. We're going to be careful, but how we're going to do it? I'm working out as we speak. But if we can't get him outside, we need to get inside his fortress."

More brief questions were answered. No matter what happened next, breakfast was clearly over. It was time to get ready for action.

"I'm taking a couple of you to meet with the veterinarian, Kelly's friend, and we're going to see if there's some kind of logical way we can get inside, and even he may not know how."

Several more questions were raised, but at the end of the discussion, Kyle told them to be ready by noon. And to expect to go well until dark before they would be returning back.

"I want you armed, but I want it stowed, out of sight. I don't want anybody to show a weapon unless they have to kill somebody. You got it?"

It was clear. Jason knew everybody had done this before. And the plan hadn't been formally hatched, it was being created while they were getting ready for it. This was not one of those ops where they could train over and over and over again. It was all going to be new territory. They were going to be up against many other men. Kyle had said Gutiérrez had at least thirty security personnel at the complex. But there probably would be more.

Kyle tasked Cooper and Jason to go with him to meet the veterinarian, so they took one of the vans and headed downtown, and although Kelly had told them not to reach him at his place of work, Kyle was going to use Jason to create the excuse.

"I would feel better doing this if we could find a cat or a dog or something to walk into the clinic with," Kyle said. "But I don't want to go through all that. We don't have a lot of time."

"I thought Kelly said we should try to find him socially?" Jason interrupted.

"She did. Won't be able to reach her today. They're all headed toward Portland. Coming from Europe. Riley's not expected to live very much longer. So she's out of the picture for a couple of days. We'll know further tonight."

"Colin Riley is not going to make it then?" Cooper asked.

"No. At least that's what Kelly's been told."

"That's a damn shame. Wonder what will happen with his group?" Jason asked.

"Well, they'll be up and running. You aren't going to stop those guys, Bryce and all those. Shoot, I'm going to be talking like crazy to try to keep some of you guys from joining up with them. But it is what it is, and he was not a healthy man, so things happen. Life goes on. They've got Sven, and they've got the two girls. I think they can put their heads together and create a force for good. They've got his money. It's just going to take a while. So there's a gap. We used them a lot, but now, they're not going to be there for us. Anyway we've got bigger fish to fry. And we've got to get hold of this Gutiérrez guy and see if we can find some evidence linking him to what's been happening on the island."

The clinic was in a strip mall off in a back-alley street, behind a popular restaurant but situated in-between a discount hardware store catering to locals and a uniform shop of some kind. While the street in front of it that the restaurant was on was a main thoroughfare, this alleyway was very seedy looking, and Jason knew that, at night, it would be extremely dangerous.

The door to the front was locked. They buzzed a doorbell, and electronically the door opened. Kyle pushed Jason in front, so he was the person approaching the reception desk. An attractive younger woman with a flowered headband greeted him behind the glass window. Jason noted that it was very thick, obviously bullet-proof.

"You speak English?" he asked.

"Sí, sí, señor."

"I'm here to visit Dr. Pennington. He asked me to stop by for a consult. He has seen my horse, and I have some questions. I was just in the area and thought I'd talk to him."

Inside, Jason's stomach was rumbling. He felt so stupid coming up with that kind of an excuse. He hadn't seen a single horse since they had arrived in San Felipe. He could feel Cooper and Kyle chuckling under their breath even though he didn't want to look at them.

The woman raised her eyebrows. "Your name please, señor?"

"Jason Fielding. I'm a friend of Kelly's."

"Let me see if he can see you. I'm not sure he's here at the moment. I'll be right back," she said and left the office.

Jason discovered he'd been stooping way over because the countertop was so low. He slowly turned around, straightening his frame in the process, and sure enough, Kyle and Cooper were smiling, showing him huge cheesy grins, their arms crossed their chest.

"I didn't take you for a cowboy, Jason," said Kyle, laughing.

"Just shut up. I'm doing the best I can. I didn't know what to say."

"Nah, it's all good. You're doing fine." Kyle added.

The receptionist returned to her cubicle. "Dr. Pennington will be right out. He said he wished to speak to the fellow who has the tats?" She frowned as she glanced over all three of the men standing in her waiting room.

"Fine by me," said Kyle.

"Wait here, and he'll come out."

Dr. Pennington was a silver-haired, good-looking man, about sixty years old. His face was well-tanned, and he had bright blue eyes. He was fit, very slim, and looked out of place operating out of a clinic in a back street like this. But all of them knew his background and understood.

The doctor shook hands with Jason first, and then Jason introduced him to Kyle.

"I'm going to bring you to the back, just in case someone else comes in." He waved to his receptionist, who buzzed the door open.

Barking dogs greeted them as they wandered down a hallway toward the back behind Dr. Pennington. They passed two treatment rooms and then a full surgery operating room at the very back. He opened the door to the room with a key, let all three in, and then locked the door behind them. Over the window of the operating room, he slid a covering down to make their meeting private.

"So Kelly says you're going to be investigating Mr. Gutiérrez? You know what the hell you're doing?" the doctor asked.

"I wouldn't say we know everything we're doing, but we're fairly trained," answered Kyle. "I guess what I need from you is how I can get my men inside his complex. You know anything about what he has delivered, who works there or any excuse we can use to get in?"

"He has lots of allies in the city here, and because he's the source of a lot of revenue for people, they're going to protect him, so be careful who you trust—especially against any suspected U.S. or drug enforcement official. But I do know he comes down to San Felípe on a regular basis to attend meetings and have dinner with friends. Of course, he brings his security detail. He doesn't try to hide it, and it's really impossible to miss. Everybody knows who he is. Everybody stays away, unless they have business with him. And those who have business with him don't talk. I'm not sure how much help I can be except to tell you if you happen to catch him downtown, that might be your best bet. But unless he invites you in, you aren't going to get inside. I mean there's just no way."

Pennington was extremely matter-of-fact, spoke his truth without any show of emotion, and laid it out for them very clearly.

"So does he have a favorite as far as restaurants?" Kyle asked.

"He likes the dance clubs. He likes the girls there. We've got the Pink Flamingo and the Potted Orange. Kitten Cabin is an especially favorite one of his."

"Kitten Cabin?"

"It's a live burlesque and strip show, male and female, so it's like probably the least likely place I'd ever go, but he seems to like that. I've seen his entourage in front of it several times as I've made it home."

"Sounds lovely."

Pennington shrugged. "Better than cockfighting or bull fighting, I suppose."

"No movie theater?" Kyle joked.

"Nope. Things are pretty basic here. They cater to a lot of tourists as well. I think he likes to have meetings in places like that because your average Joe isn't going to be there. You know what I mean."

"Thanks." Kyle stared at his feet and then asked another question. "Kelly said he had recently remodeled his place. Do you know the contractor who did the work? Is there any work still to be done?"

"The only thing I think they're still doing is some outside work. I heard people talking about needing a gardening crew or someone installing lawns or sprinklers. But I think most of that is all complete. He used the contracting firm of Construction General, and he's a pretty good guy. Also an American, but he married the daughter of the owner of the company. You might be able to talk to him. I don't think he's involved in Gutiérrez' business, but you never know."

Kyle was considering what Pennington had said.

"So you do know you're taking your life in your hands if you ask the wrong person, right? That's all I can do to help you. If I think of anything else, how do I reach you?"

Kyle wrote his cell down on a piece of paper for him, and Pennington slipped it in his shirt pocket.

"Any idea where the construction office is?" Jason asked.

"He doesn't have a building downtown. It's about half a mile outside of San Felípe. He has a large ranch there, and the office is in the front. You can't miss it. It's got pink walls, and I take care of three of his horses there. He's quite a horseman."

Jason added "He sounds like the best chance of getting in through the front. What do you think, Kyle?"

"I thank you, Dr. Pennington. And good luck to you. I'm sure going to tell Kelly how helpful you were. You stay safe."

"While I may be a convicted felon, I'm still a patriot. And I hate drugs, so anything I can do to help these kids out there and whatever else is going on, I'm in it, as long as I can protect my family. Mexico has been good to me. I don't mind it one bit."

CHAPTER 18

"OUT WITH IT, Carmen. This is not what I expected. What aren't you telling me?" Kiley was furious that she'd been brought to Portland without all the information she had very clearly asked Carmen upfront.

"I just wanted to get you here. I needed to get you here. We have to have your support."

"Am I going to have to start looking around behind me, watching my back? I thought we were friends, Carmen. I agreed to come see Colin, I agreed to help you with what I could, perhaps information or contacts, but I never agreed to become part of this war that's going on. You have to understand that."

"I do. And if I had anywhere else to turn, I would, Kiley."

"Goddamn it, Carmen. I knew I shouldn't have trusted you. So what is the story? I'm here. I might as well hear the whole thing. Just give me the dirt on it."

"Let's get over to my place where we can be alone. I've got food and stuff over there. I'll make you a nice dinner, and we'll talk."

"I'm going home tomorrow. You know, my ticket says I'm leaving tomorrow morning."

"I understand. And I've told Natalia that too."

"Natalia? Why is it that she has to know when I'm going to be here and when I'm going home? This doesn't have anything to do with Natalia. It's between me and Colin Riley. Me and you."

"You're right of course, but all the same, she's going to come over this evening, and I think you need to hear what she has to say."

"You didn't promise her that I was going to help you, did you?"

"No. I didn't. I just thought that if you heard—"

Kiley put her hands up to her ears. "I don't want to listen to any more of this until we get to your place. This is not something I'm going to do. And if you don't abide by my wishes, I'm going to leave tonight."

"But Sven and the girls, they're all arriving. Don't you want to talk to them too?"

"If I have a chance in the morning to do so, I will. But it's not dependent on them, Carmen."

"But you heard what Mr. Riley asked. How can you abandon his request? I mean, he's on his deathbed, and he asked you to do something? Are you telling me you're not going to do it?"

"I can give them instructions over the phone, Carmen. But my place is in Florida. And you heard what he said. I'm in danger here. What about that don't you understand? It's one thing for you to be going out after the story, but it's another thing to pull me back in. I don't want to do this."

"Very well, I get it. I didn't think you'd do it."

For the remainder of the short trip to Carmen's house, they didn't speak a word.

Once inside, the two girls ran up two flights of steps to the landing where Carmen's apartment door was. She used her key to open it, and Kiley lugged her suitcase and laptop inside, leaving it over by the living room couch.

Carmen's apartment had a beautiful view of the city below and the waterways and shipping lanes in the distance.

"Wow, I guess the days of slumming in an efficiency studio are over. You've done well for yourself," Kiley said.

"Not really. You know I had a boyfriend there for a while, but things didn't quite work out. This is just on a lease, but the strength of his financial statement is what got us the lease. When it comes up, I'm going to have to find something else. But it's nice while it lasts."

Kiley sat down as Carmen began pulling things out of the refrigerator and her cabinets to prepare a dinner for them.

"Okay, I have some hamburger here. I've got a couple of frozen lasagnas, some mac and cheese, or I have soup—I have lots of good, organic soup. You want a sandwich or something?" Carmen asked.

"Whatever's easiest. I'm really not very hungry," said Kiley. "Listen, I'm going to give Jason a call and just let him know where I am. Okay?"

"Sure, it'll only take me about fifteen minutes to get this all done for us. So you kick your feet up and just relax."

Kiley started to dial Jason's number when they heard a knock on the door. Carmen came running from the kitchen, checking her watch. "She's early."

"Who?" Kiley asked.

"Natalia. I told you she's coming over." Carmen opened the door wide and stepped back. Natalia came rushing inside. Behind her stood two men.

Kiley's shock must have been visible to all in the room. She put her cell phone away, but didn't clear Jason's number in case she needed to call him.

Natalia was the first to speak. She first addressed Carmen and then turned to Kiley.

"I am so sorry, Carmen, Kiley. I have brought some friends,

who think they can help me locate my family. My two cousins have been kidnapped, and my mother's brother is missing. Other members of my family are missing as well. These two men were referred to me by someone I trust. They are from my country."

Kiley didn't like the looks of either of them.

Both men were well-built, looking more like thugs or security detail, than anything else. They were in their thirties, had short-crop hairstyles, no facial hair, and wore identical dark gray suit coats and black pants, like it was a uniform. Kiley also noticed that both men wore shoes that appeared to be steel-toed. That completed her assessment. They were not helpful citizens. They were security.

Slowly, Kiley stood. "What is this, Natalia? Carmen?"

"I have no idea," whispered Carmen, who came over next to Kiley, shaking like a leaf.

Natalia approached them, and Kiley stopped her. "You stay right there. I want to know what's going on, and I'd like these two gentlemen to leave the room please."

She reached into her purse and pushed send on the call to Jason, but she left the phone in her purse.

"I'm afraid that will not be possible," one of the two men said in an accent. "We have orders to bring you downtown, to meet with someone who has a favor to ask of you. Natalia is correct about one thing. If we do not have your cooperation, members of her family will be harmed. There is no choice. And, Ms. Carmen, you must come with us as well."

"This is a free country. I'm not going to go with you," Carmen barked. "Natalia? What have you gotten me into?"

"As I said, I am sorry. I thought I was doing something good, and these gentlemen agreed to help me to free my family. They just want to ask questions. I'm sure they do not wish you any harm."

Carmen became even more frosty. "Were you born, like, yesterday? These are the same people you dealt with before, you know this. You know what these people do."

"Yes, but that was before they had members of my family. I have talked to them. I know they are being held. This is not a game, Carmen. If you can cooperate just a little bit, I think all will be well."

"And how the hell is that supposed to happen?" asked Kiley. "I'm not even involved in any of this anymore. I have nothing to do with your family. Why have you brought me here?"

One of the gentlemen smiled and held out his hand. "You will please accompany me to downtown. I mean you no harm, but you are the person we must deal with. As a courtesy, we will include your friend here, Carmen. She has been most valuable to us."

Carmen burst into a tirade. "You motherfuckers, you used Natalia to get to me? And you used me to get to Kiley? What in the fuck are you guys doing? I want to know—no, I demand to know where we are going and who we are meeting with. I am not going to leave this place until I know that."

Carmen, every 5' 4" bit of her, was furious, shaking. Her hands were on her hips. The two men looked at each other. One stepped forward, and although Carmen tried to back up, he grabbed her by the collarbone, pressed, and she fainted into his arms. He picked her up and began to leave the apartment. The other gentleman turned to Kiley. "I can do the same for you if you refuse. But it will be better for you if you don't."

Kiley glared at Natalia. "You're as bad as they are. Aiding and abetting after you've lived through it, after you spent a lifetime—"

The gentleman who asked Kiley to accompany him swung his arm in front and slapped Kiley across the face. The last thing she noticed before the room got black was that he hadn't let her hit the ground. He caught her just before.

She was worried, not for herself but for the baby she carried. She hoped Jason had heard it all.

CHAPTER 19

ON THE WAY back to the condo, Jason turned his phone back on. He was shocked to see a message from Kiley.

He started to listen to it and then, after several seconds, turned the speakerphone on so Coop and Kyle could listen at the same time. What they heard was so disturbing that all three men were left in shock.

The message ran out, until either the battery on the phone stopped or somebody manually turned it off. The last three and a half minutes were muffled sounds of people talking, moving something around, Russian conversation, and Ukrainian dialogue in the background. Even the traffic sounds were muffled. Finally, just before the phone turned off, there was a very clear message. Someone had discovered that the phone had been running and flipped it.

"Where is she?" asked Kyle.

"How should I know? But she's talking about Carmen and Natalia. And you heard the accent of those guys. The only thing I can think of is she went back to Portland. She defied me, Kyle. I told her not to do this." Jason was beside himself. "I have to go. I can't stay here any longer. She's in danger."

Kyle sounded more levelheaded than he was. "The best I can do, Sport, is try to get some local liaisons. I wish I could get a…

Let me try to get hold of Sven or Kelly—see if they're close. But honest, Jason, I can't release you yet."

"Fuck!"

"You know I can't, Jason. But I fuckin' promise we'll get somebody to look in on her. Do you have any idea where in Portland she would be?"

Jason didn't have a clue. "I'm not from there, I know she had a flat down by the river, but she gave that to her roommate. Sounds like they were at Carmen's place, and I don't know where she lives."

Kyle had an idea. "What about their editor? Would he know?"

"That's a possibility."

Coop nudged him. "You better call him right now. You have his number?"

"Yes, I do." From the second seat of the van, Jason was able to dial the number for the paper, and he asked for Corbin Newman. He turned on his speaker phone.

"Hello, Editor's Desk. Can I help you?"

Jason wasn't going to run through any niceties with the man. "Hey, asshole, they've got Kiley. If anything happens to her, I'm going to come and personally skin you alive and hang you outside your fucking office building."

"Whoa, whoa, whoa, wait a minute. Who is this?" asked Newman.

"It's Jason Kealoha. Kiley's in Portland. I just got a message from her, and somebody's kidnapped her. I need to know where the fuck Carmen lives so I can send people over to get her if they can. I'm going to need your hundred percent cooperation, Mr. Newman, or I will personally make sure that you pay, along with everybody else in that filthy city responsible for this."

"Wait a minute, Jason. I understand you're upset. But—"

"Upset doesn't even begin to describe how I feel. If anything should happen to Kiley, like I said, I will sue your ass, the paper, I will make sure you never get to print another word anywhere. I'll make sure you can't even sign Christmas cards, and I will land you in jail or end you, do you understand me?"

"Jason, I'm clueless about any of this. I know Carmen was working on something, and yes, we were trying to get Kiley to come back and help us out with some more articles. We put a lot of bad guys away. But you know they've substituted other people in their place, and they're back at it again. We just wanted some background, and we thought Kiley could help us."

"Yeah, but she promised me she wouldn't get involved. She promised me she was done with all of that. What did you tell her to make her change her mind? Did you threaten her?"

"Absolutely not. She came to say goodbye to Colin Riley. That's why she came to Portland. I don't think she intended to get involved in anything else."

"So you know where Carmen lives then?"

"Yes, I can look it up. Of course. I'd be happy to help that way."

"Okay then. I'm going to get the cops, and perhaps one other person is going to give you a call, and get that information. I want you to be as cooperative as if you were going to earn a million dollars off of this deal. I want you to not hold back a single bit. You tell them everything when they show up. You make sure everybody knows what the score is. I don't want them walking into anything that's going to be a surprise, okay?"

"You got it, Jason, I'm on your side. I have absolutely no hidden agenda. I just want to do the same thing you do. I want the truth, and I want people to know."

"Fuck you and your truth. I want to find Kiley."

"Okay, I get it. Look, honest, I'm a hundred percent on your side." There was a pause and then Corbin added, "Hey, congratulations on the baby."

"You fucking son of a bitch. You are an insect, and I am going to smash you. You don't have a right to any of the knowledge of my family or anything we're doing. You have no right. You're not part of our lives, our future. After this is all over, you're going to stay away, and I'm never going to hear from you again. Neither is Kiley. You get it?"

"Okay, so that was perhaps unfortunate—" Newman began but was interrupted.

"Yeah. You're an asshole alright."

They had arrived at the condo. Jason was still steaming, beside himself, twisted and broken inside, feeling helpless to do anything. As soon as Kyle walked through the door, his phone rang.

After a few seconds, Kyle once again put his phone on speaker, "It's Sven," he whispered to the group.

"So what the hell is going on, Kyle? I mean, I get this frantic call from Brandy Hudson, something about Kiley. What is she doing in Portland?"

Jason stepped forward and spoke into Kyle's phone. "Kiley came to say goodbye to Riley. Did you guys get there? Have you talked to him?"

"I'm sorry, man. We got here just after he'd passed. The girls are still in the room with him. But I was told by the staff here that two women had come by and had a chance to see him, and they knew who Carmen was, and from the description, and after that call from Brandy, it sounded like Kiley was the other one. How the hell did she get here and do you know anything about why? What's going on?"

"I just found out about it. We're still in Mexico. But there's something more, Sven, and I have no right to ask you to do this, now with Colin and everything. But they've kidnapped Kiley, and I think they have Carmen as well. I don't know where they are, but

I can get you an address where Carmen was living. I just—I don't know where to start, but I was wondering if you and the guys could maybe get a triangulation on her cell phone, something like that or track where it was, where the signal was coming from?"

"Sure, but slow down, Jason."

Jason rambled, not stopping to listen to anyone. He knew Kyle was about to snatch the phone from his hands. "Somebody who turned it off would probably be smart enough to take the chip out, but perhaps it would reveal their last location? I don't know what else to do. I'm here in Mexico. We're supposed to go on an op here tonight, and I can't even think straight. If something happens to her—"

Kyle was standing to Jason's back and patted his shoulders, asking with his outstretched hand for the phone. "Come on, man. Give it to me. You're scaring everyone, Jason."

Cooper directed Jason to sit down, and someone handed him a beer. Kyle continued discussing the situation, what they knew of it, to Sven.

"So that's what we got, Sven. I think if I can get Jason sent home, I'll try that. I just don't know how many days that's going to take me. I can't just release him and have him go AWOL. You know what that would mean."

"I do. Okay, let me see what I can do. Who do I call?"

Kyle gave him the phone number for Corbin Newman at the paper. He told him what Kiley's cell phone number was so that they could try tracing it.

"I do have somebody I can call. Take me about thirty minutes, but he should be able to give me a location. I'll call Bryce and several of the other guys and see if we can go launch a team. No promises, but God, I'll do the best I can."

"I know the whole team is grateful to you, Sven, and I wish the timing weren't so bad—"

"You don't have to even say that. Colin's gone. There's nothing I can do for him here. I think Kelly and Jenna will understand when I tell them. So let me go do what I can, and I'll call you back when I've got some news."

"Thanks, man."

Kyle exhaled, blowing out all his breath, then calmly walked over to Jason, his face long, his hand still gripping the cell phone. "I wish like hell I could send you home, kid. I just can't. And I think you better stay here. I don't want you launching any kind of an op right now. But I got to have your complete promise that you won't leave on me. I know you could. I know you could probably overpower anybody here that tried to stop you, but I'm telling you right now, Jason, you can't do that. You have to stay here with the team. And we're going to do everything we can to put in motion every asset we have to find her. You're just going to have to put all the negative stuff out of your mind. And that sucks. And in your position, I may not be able to do it, but I need you to do it, Jason."

Jason knew he deserved the dressing down, the public reminder of how precarious his position was. Normally, he had a very calm box he could put himself in, where he could remain with ice water in his veins, no emotion, stoic, a rock. Today, that box was failing him. Everything inside him was failing. He didn't want to think about fucking songs or chanting or stupid celebrations. His whole world was blowing up.

What was the purpose of running around acting like a monkey, trying to pluck magic from the clouds, listening to the old ones? They were useless to him now. The most important person in his life was in trouble, and he was way past being able to help her. If he couldn't keep his woman safe, what good was he?

The waiting was hard. Kyle sent teams to scour some of the hangouts where they knew Gutiérrez liked to party. They checked in on a regular basis, including one group who was monitoring the gates at the villa he owned. Nobody had seen him. It was as if the guy knew there were all kinds of eyes looking for him, and he was going to stay put behind the safety of his own fortress.

But all of a sudden, Kyle got calls from several of the team who informed them that there was a caravan of black Suburbans streaking down from the house, headed toward San Felípe proper.

Everybody was on the lookout for him, and when he showed up at the Pink Flamingo, that told Kyle they had a chance. The reports came back that he traveled with eight bodyguards. Kyle consulted with the head shed, requesting orders for what was coming down. He was trying to clarify whether this was a snatch-and-grab, removing Gutiérrez to San Diego, or an interrogation of some kind done locally.

Then they received satellite images sent from Norfolk. A drone had picked up some of the activity in the courtyard of Gutiérrez' compound. As the camera swung around, giving full detail in anticipation of a future raid, off to the side, in front of a long storage building that was suspected of holding ammunition and equipment, was what looked like a tall picket fence with oddly shaped figurines of some kind mounted on top.

As the drone honed in on the fence, what came to light shocked them all. Someone had taken two dozen skulls at least, mounted them on poles, and left them in Gutiérrez' yard just outside the barracks. Perhaps this was a reminder to all those who worked for him of what was to befall them if they betrayed him.

Based on this information, it was determined that he was directly related to the atrocities the team had found in the pools on the island. There were still a lot of blanks to fill in, but that meant they could go get this guy.

Jason sat while the rest of the team began to cheer, anxious to go rid the world of one more motherfucker.

But of course, there was only one person in the world who mattered to Jason. And she wasn't here to celebrate.

"Not yet," he mumbled to himself.

CHAPTER 20

KILEY AWOKE TO the sounds of an angry woman cursing and kicking and objecting to being handled.

"Goddammit, I said don't touch me, you cretin! You lay a hand on me and I'll come back and scalp you alive!"

Before she opened her eyes, Kiley smiled, with a certain understanding that she was flanked on her left by her best friend.

Carmen.

And thank God she was salty. Thank God she wasn't a wallflower that Kiley had to prop up. Because she didn't have the energy. Her lip hurt. Her eye hurt. The whole side of her face hurt. In fact, she thought maybe he broke her cheekbone. The force of that man's arm literally felt like he'd taken her head off.

Very slowly, because she knew the pain would be agonizing, and she was right, she opened her eyes. Or at least, she opened her left eye, because her right eye was swollen shut. It even hurt to turn to her left and look at Carmen.

"Just like the old days at the paper, right, Carmen?" she said in a grumble. "Those assholes in the newsroom, the way they used to treat the female interns? You remember all that when we were first starting out?"

"Yeah. And we outlasted them all, didn't we, Kiley?"

"But look at us now. I mean, you're covered in blood." She

scanned Carmen from head to toe, and her white blouse was covered in ribbons of dark red blood. Her nose had been running and was caked with dark purple and crimson phlegm from a direct hit. Her eyebrow was cut and still oozing slightly. She was a mess.

"You should talk. God, you look like you've been in a wrestling match. And you lost. I don't even think I'd recognize you if you were walking down the street."

"Yeah, well, go look at yourself in the mirror, and you tell me if you're any different." Kiley inhaled, looked straight ahead at the desk they were parked in front of, and then she started to laugh. She couldn't help it, and her ribs hurt too. It hurt so bad, but it felt so good to laugh. Then she heard Carmen start to laugh, and the two of them giggled like they'd put dog poop on the teacher's chair and he just sat in it.

"Do you suppose it's all worth it, Kiley, in the end? Do you think they have any fucking clue how bad it is out there? Is it worth us risking our necks to do this?"

"You know the answer to that, Carmen. You're like I am. You can't wait and see innocent people get taken advantage of. It's no different for the team guys. They do the same thing."

"You've got to get me one of those guys. I need a man like that real bad. I'm sorry. I'm done with these assholes who only want one thing, and now, when you get successful and have some creds, it's like the reverse of what it used to be. They sleep with you so they can get the opportunities. It sucks. It totally sucks."

Kiley figured they would get it all straight eventually. But today was perhaps not the day. Today was the day they had to think about how they were going to get out of this situation.

"So, Carmen, where's all my stuff, my laptop, my purse?"

"I think it's back at my apartment. Sorry. I wasn't exactly conscious at the time."

"Well, I saw the way he carried you in like a sack of potatoes. I got hit too you know."

Carmen looked at her like she had green ears. "You think? How could I not notice?"

"Well, if they ever can catch these guys, they'll go to jail for sure. You can't beat a woman up like this and get away with it."

They both thought about that for a few minutes and began a discussion. Men were getting away with it every single day. Traffickers, husbands sometimes, boyfriends, anybody who could abuse someone who's not quite as strong as they were did it. It had become so common that there were some people that even thought you shouldn't report it anymore. And that was wrong.

"I was wrong about you, Carmen. It was still a stupid decision for me to come, but we've got to figure this out. I'm done being angry. We've got to put our heads together and figure out how we're going to get out of here."

They were each lashed to heavy, wooden straight back chairs, impossible to roll over on their side. They weren't even able to tip those chairs, unless they wanted to hurt themselves. Both had moving straps cinched around their laps, and Kiley was a little concerned about the strap on her lap, being pregnant. But she was able to scooch back farther so that the bulk of the strap landed across her upper thigh. Their hands were lashed behind them, and from the feel of her own wrists as well as looking at Carmen's, Kiley knew she was secured with zip ties.

Her feet were strapped to the legs of the chair, and her shirt had been ripped partially open. She didn't want to think about it, but probably somebody had decided to take a little advantage of her when she was passed out. Or perhaps they were checking for a wire. She studied the rest of her body as best she could and didn't feel like she got raped, and she didn't feel like she was recovering from a drug of some kind, which boded well for the baby.

She wondered if Jason got her message and what he would

think.

"So you think all my stuff's over at the apartment?" Kiley asked her again.

Carmen nodded. "I think my stuff is too."

"Where's Natalia then? Is she in this, or do you think she was being forced like she said."

"No, I don't think she's involved in it, I think they gave her no choice. Who knows, in the same situation, you and I might have done the same. I can't hold that against her. But she helped us out before. Maybe she'll do it again. We'll see."

Just then someone walked in through the door and slammed it behind. A young American looking man in a business suit sat behind the desk. Kiley recognized him immediately as one of the former mayor's members of his housing task force. No doubt, he was feeling emboldened by the former mayor's triumphant attempt to return. Kiley knew that evil never did win in the end, but she let him feel all full of himself for a few minutes. Eventually, he'd rot in a cell just like everybody else of his ilk.

"So, ladies, we have a situation here. This was not our choice, and I apologize for the heavy-handed way in which you have been treated."

Carmen started off right off the bat. "You son of a bitch, then get us untied right now and give us some clean rags so we can wash up. And you know what? Kiley's pregnant, so if she miscarries or has a problem with this pregnancy, you're going to have a murder charge on your hands. Don't hide behind that little voice of yours that says 'oh, it was somebody else's fault.' You guys are responsible. Do the manly thing and release her or at least let her clean herself up. This isn't healthy for her or the baby."

The young man raised his eyebrows. Kiley was hoping that he might not recognize her. But she knew that was too good to be true.

"So, Kiley, you've gotten married, and now you're having a baby? How nice. Now you have one more thing to live for, right?"

She decided not to answer him or give him the satisfaction of answering him.

"I really would like to let you take a shower and change, and I think we can get you some clean clothes here, but what I need first is, I need you to write a story. And since both of you are such excellent writers and have such a following, especially you, Kiley, I'm going to suggest that you write a fairy tale. Something that you know isn't true, but you're willing to do it to save your lives and the life of your baby," he said as he nodded to Kiley's tummy.

"Perhaps the lives of Natalia's family in Ukraine? Other women who could be under our control and who might also be in danger. You've really stirred up a hornet's nest here, and all we want, it's very simple, is that you make it right. You fix it. The public will welcome your opinions, and we'd like you to write the biggest *mea culpa* of your life. Like your life depends on it, because it does."

Kiley's stomach groaned. She felt like she was going to be sick.

"I want you to say that you made the whole damn thing up, that you and a bunch of women friends staged it because you hate men, I want you to make it really juicy. But you're the creatives here, not me. You write it however you want. But it has to say that you made it up and that the organization you tried to take down was fictional. You were writing a story, not news facts."

"It would never work," said Kiley. "Nobody would buy that. You're asking for a creative retraction. You'll never convince the public it was sincere."

The young man leaned forward, his elbows and forearms flat against the desk. He peered across the wooden top at Kiley. "I said, make a compelling story. *Make* them believe you."

Carmen shook her head. "I don't think I could write such a story. I'm not that good anyway. If I wrote fiction, I'd sure as hell do that. Who wants to do this anymore? All this is crap."

Kiley was surprised to hear this, but continued to listen.

"If I wrote romance or something like that, I wouldn't get tied up and put in some guy's trunk for heaven's sakes. This is bullshit. You're looking at the wrong people here, sport."

"That would be very unfortunate. Very unlucky for you. I suggest you start strategizing."

"How about you let her take a shower? You can keep me tied up if you like. How about you let her get herself cleaned up? How about you untie her so you don't kill her baby before you even get started?"

Carmen was like a junk yard dog with a bone, and she was not going to give up. Kiley was proud of her.

"We'll see, I'm going to check with my superiors about a couple of things that are needing attention, but you guys talk about it for a few minutes. Mull it over, see if there isn't some kind of a way you can bring yourself to save yourself and your baby, to save Natalia and her relatives."

At the doorway, he turned to address them. Kiley couldn't see him because she was lashed too tightly to the chair.

"You think about it real hard, and when I come back, I'd like to know what you're going to do."

With that, he closed the door.

"Shit. Damn me for ever dreaming I could write fiction. Now I get my big opportunity and I have to write the kind of fiction that I hate. I have to write something like it's the truth and make it all up. That's crap," said Carmen.

Kiley laughed. "That's all fiction is. I think they make it all up, don't they? Someday, you and I could sit down by the beach and we could spin some stories about our time on the paper—all the assholes we had to deal with, the stories we thought were not stories that turned out to be huge stories, the jerks we interviewed who turned out later to be dirty. Or the people who we came across whose stories we really wanted to tell and we weren't allowed to?"

"That would be pleasant, Carmen. I'd like that, I think."

"We could write whatever we want someday. But first, we have to get over this hurdle here."

Kiley thought of something. "I suppose we could come up with a series? We could say it's going to take four or five series to really land it home and make it seem real? What do you think about that? Do you think he'd buy it?"

Carmen was still shaking her head, looking out the window at the town below. "I couldn't pull it off. That's all I know. I couldn't do it. But you probably could."

"I think what we need to do is to stall them. I think we need to try to string it out, because I think eventually somebody's going to come find us."

"Who? Nobody knows where we are. How are they going to find us?"

"Well, think about it, Carmen. They knew I was coming here to see you, Corbin knew that maybe I'd be staying with you, right? And wouldn't they just figure it out from there? There're cameras all over, aren't there?"

"I don't know. But you're right, it is a good idea to string it out a little bit. You don't have your laptop, though, do you?"

"Well, that could delay us a bit. I could demand that I have my past articles, which is all on my laptop. I could say that I need to reference it in order to do a good job. What about that?"

"Okay, so they get your laptop, then what?"

"It would take them a few minutes to get over there and then back here? So maybe by that time the police or somebody—I mean

Corbin has to have some inkling what's going on by now. Surely someone has contacted him. I did get a message to Jason, too."

"You sent a message to Jason?"

"Yes, I did."

"In Mexico?"

"Yes, I think he's still in Mexico."

"How's he going to get here if he's in Mexico?"

"Well, I don't know. But he could tell somebody. He could call the police. I don't know. But if Jason knows, that's good, isn't it?"

"I didn't realize that, Kiley. Boy, I guess I've partnered with the right person after all, didn't I? You're always thinking, aren't you?"

Kiley thought about that. Her year with Jason had been full of all kinds of events, part of it had been his training her to be conscious of things around her. Of course she violated that hugely by coming to Portland, but he had taught her to think of her resources and to always look for something she could use so she could leave a trace behind so people could find her. She didn't want to get into all the gory details, but even if she was physically attacked, she knew there were certain things she could do to make sure that person's DNA was found and they were caught. It made her feel less afraid to know how to take care of herself, to fight back.

Yet, in this instance, it wasn't enough. And she vowed, if she survived this, that she would take much better care of herself. She knew she was going to have to do that not only for herself but for their daughter.

They waited in silence for a few minutes, both of them lost in thought. Then Kiley spoke up next.

"Did I tell you what our daughter's name is going to be?"

"No."

"Leilani. Her name's going to be Leilani."

CHAPTER 21

KYLE LEFT ARMANDO and Cooper to stay behind while the rest of the team went to retrieve Gutiérrez without a firefight. If the extraction was successful, he would be transported to the private airstrip for a quick flight, courtesy of the Navy, to Coronado, for interrogation.

Jason got a call from Sven that they had located Carmen's apartment, neutralized two men guarding Natalia, and held her in custody for her own safety. He reported he had been given the office location where Carmen and Kiley were being held.

"She's helped us with information on her relatives in Ukraine. We're going to mobilize a small unit to go in and make sure the hostages are released. I've already been in touch with Kelly's sources on the ground."

"Thank you, Sven. Please let us know when you find Kiley. Let me know she's okay, unharmed."

Jason continued to pace back and forth. He agreed with Kyle. It was right to leave him behind. What he didn't like was that two others had to stay back to babysit him. But they also had equipment and coms to monitor, and that had to be done at the complex, not in the field.

Roughly an hour later, Kyle called. The three heard on speaker phone that they had captured Gutiérrez, who had been partying in a private room upstairs at the club and was, therefore, not heavily guarded. Danny and Damon transported the cartel boss to a waiting plane in the private landing strip for a short flight to Coronado before his men even knew he was missing.

They would regroup and return to the complex shortly.

"Any news from Sven?" Kyle asked.

"They have the location where they believe Kiley is being held. Natalia helped them with that, and her guards have been captured and will be turned over to Mexican authorities. We're just waiting to hear they've found the two girls, Kyle."

"How are you doing, Jason?"

"I'm good. Glad we got the guy, Kyle. Just one more hurdle to go."

"We're hoping to get some decent intelligence out of him, enough to do another sweep. That's another team's job. So far, we're at one hundred percent. You hang in there. See you in a few."

Jason's phone rang again.

"It's Sven," he told Coop and Armando as he placed it up to his ear.

"Jason, Oh, it's so good to hear your voice, sweetheart!" Kiley's soft purr sent a bolt of electricity throughout his body.

"Kiley! Is everything okay? Did they hurt you? And how is—"

"I'm fine. Everything is good, Jason. I look a little beat up, Carmen too."

"What happened?" Jason's heart was pounding. He wanted to be home so bad it hurt.

"I guess we got in trouble with our smart mouths, Carmen more than I."

They heard Carmen in the background, objecting to the description. "You should have seen her, Jason. Unstoppable!" they heard her shout from a distance.

"When are you coming home?"

"I have a ticket for tomorrow morning, if I can get them to allow me to fly. We're here with the Portland Police and FBI. We got records, Jason. There's enough here for charges to indict the whole group all over again, and enough for at least a dozen serial stories—"

"Which Carmen is going to write. Or you can write, but it's her byline, not yours, sweetheart. You promised."

"I did, and I'm so sorry I didn't keep my promise, but no worries on the serials. I think I'll shift to fiction, maybe romance."

"I like the sound of that. I'm in need of a little romance at the present time."

"Are you guys coming home soon?"

"I think so. I'll let you know when it's a sure thing. Wish you were coming to San Diego, sweetheart."

"My ticket says Tampa. You get your LPO to release you and Damon so you can both do daddy duty."

"As soon as I can, I'm there. You make sure Aimee and Madison take good care of you."

ALTHOUGH THEY TALKED daily, it was more than a week before Jason could be released to Florida. Aimee insisted on a small party at their house, just a few friends, including Madison's mother and Noonan LaFontaine. They spent time out by the firepit after stuffing themselves on another roast pig.

Andy, Jason, and Ned took a quick dip in the ocean, which had become customary to end the evening.

Then Jason and Kiley took a slow walk back to the bungalow.

"I really do owe you an apology," she said as he took her in his arms.

"It all worked out, but God you had me scared. Tell me, please, you've learned your lesson, Kiley."

"I think so. I learned something else, though."

"What's that?"

"I've learned where I belong."

"And where is that?"

"First, I belong with you. I could live with you anywhere. But—"

"Uh-oh. Have you made a decision without asking me? And please don't tell me you love Portland now."

She smiled, placing her arms up over his shoulders, the length of her body deliciously pressing against his. He could feel her bump!

"Hawaii was your home, your family home and where you come from. I've lived in Northern California, Portland, traveled in Europe—I've thought about living anywhere, but it's here, Jason, where I belong. In Florida. This is where we met, at Sunset Beach. This is where our paths crossed, right here. This is where our daughter was conceived. This is the place I belong. We belong. Now, it's your decision what you do with your Team. They'd love to have you on Team 4, but even for Ned and Andy, that won't be forever. This is where they'll return when they're done. And that's what I want to do too. So where you work, that's going to be up to you."

Jason was touched she'd left that decision for him.

"What if I went to work for Riley's company? They'll be starting that up."

"I'll support anything you decide to do, Jason. And we'll visit Hawaii as much as we can. We'll visit Sven and Jenna and Kelly too, wherever they take the company."

"Then it's agreed. Florida, it is. It was supposed to be Florida all along. We just had to go through all this to discover it. If I re-up for another four years, we can do that early, we'll use the bonus and the rest of the treasure money for a house. Probably not on the beach, but somewhere close."

"I like that idea, if you're game for another four years with Kyle and the boys. But don't do it for the money. I could rent a house forever and never own if I could just live here."

He was grateful for everything his ancestors had given him. He was grateful Thomas had brought him to this place to help him travel on to his next life. He knew there would be adjustments to be made, problems to solve. But they were the perfect pair.

And soon to be a family, another great adventure!

ABOUT THE AUTHOR

NYT and USA/Today Bestselling Author Sharon Hamilton's SEAL Brotherhood series have earned her author rankings of #1 in Romantic Suspense, Military Romance and Contemporary Romance. Her other *Brotherhood* stand-alone series are: Bad Boys of SEAL Team 3, Band of Bachelors, True Blue SEALs, Nashville SEALs, Bone Frog Brotherhood, Sunset SEALs, Bone Frog Bachelor Series and SEAL Brotherhood Legacy Series. She is a contributing author to the very popular Shadow SEALs multi-author series.

Her SEALs and former SEALs have invested in two wineries, a lavender farm and a brewery in Sonoma County, which have become part of the new stories. They also have expanded to include Veteran-benefit projects on the Florida Gulf Coast, as well as projects in Africa and the Maldives. One of the SEAL wives has even launched her own women's fiction series. But old characters, as well as children of these SEAL heroes keep returning to all the newer books.

Sharon also writes sexy paranormals in two series: Golden Vampires of Tuscany and The Guardians.

A lifelong organic vegetable and flower gardener, Sharon and her husband lived for fifty years in the Wine Country of Northern California, where many of her stories take place. Recently, they have moved to the beautiful Gulf Coast of Florida, with stories of shipwrecks, the white sugar-sand beaches of Sunset, Treasure Island and Indian Rocks Beaches.

She loves hearing from fans through her website:
authorsharonhamilton.com

Find out more about Sharon, her upcoming releases, appearances and news when you sign up for Sharon's newsletter.

Facebook:
facebook.com/SharonHamiltonAuthor

Twitter:
twitter.com/sharonlhamilton

Pinterest:
pinterest.com/AuthorSharonH

Amazon:
amazon.com/Sharon-Hamilton/e/B004FQQMAC

BookBub:
bookbub.com/authors/sharon-hamilton

Youtube:
youtube.com/channel/UCDInkxXFpXp_4Vnq08ZxMBQ

Soundcloud:
soundcloud.com/sharon-hamilton-1

Sharon Hamilton's Rockin' Romance Readers:
facebook.com/groups/sealteamromance

Sharon Hamilton's Goodreads Group:
goodreads.com/group/show/199125-sharon-hamilton-readers-group

Visit Sharon's Online Store:
sharon-hamilton-author.myshopify.com

Join Sharon's Review Teams:

eBook Reviews:
sharonhamiltonassistant@gmail.com

Audio Reviews:
sharonhamiltonassistant@gmail.com

***Life** is one fool thing after another.*

***Love** is two fool things after each other.*

REVIEWS

PRAISE FOR THE GOLDEN VAMPIRES OF TUSCANY SERIES

"Well to say the least I was thoroughly surprise. I have read many Vampire books, from Ann Rice to Kym Grosso and few other Authors, so yes I do like Vampires, not the super scary ones from the old days, but the new ones are far more interesting far more human than one can remember. I found Honeymoon Bite a totally engrossing book, I was not able to put it down, page after page I found delight, love, understanding, well that is until the bad bad Vamp started being really bad. But seeing someone love another person so much that they would do anything to protect them, well that had me going, then well there was more and for a while I thought it was the end of a beautiful love story that spanned not only time but, spanned Italy and California. Won't divulge how it ended, but I did shed a few tears after screaming but Sharon Hamilton did not let me down, she took me on amazing trip that I loved, look forward to reading another Vampire book of hers."

"An excellent paranormal romance that was exciting, romantic, entertaining and very satisfying to read. It had me anticipating what would happen next many times over, so much so I could not put it down and even finished it up in a day. The vampires in this book were different from your average vampire, but I enjoy different variations and changes to the same old stuff. It made for a more unpredictable read and more adventurous to explore! Vampire lovers, any paranormal readers and even those who love the romance genre will enjoy Honeymoon Bite."

"This is the first non-Seal book of this author's I have read and I loved it. There is a cast-like hierarchy in this vampire community with humans at the very bottom and Golden vampires at the top. Lionel is a dark vampire who are servants of the Goldens. Phoebe is a Golden who has not decided if she will remain human or accept the turning to become a vampire. Either way she and Lionel can never be together since it is forbidden.

I enjoyed this story and I am looking forward to the next installment."

"A hauntingly romantic read. Old love lost and new love found. Family, heart, intrigue and vampires. Grabbed my attention and couldn't put down. Would definitely recommend."

PRAISE FOR THE SEAL BROTHERHOOD SERIES

"Fans of Navy SEAL romance, I found a new author to feed your addiction. Finely written and loaded delicious with moments, Sharon Hamilton's storytelling satisfies like a thick bar of chocolate." —Marliss Melton, bestselling author of the *Team Twelve* Navy SEALs series

"Sharon Hamilton does an EXCELLENT job of fitting all the characters into a brotherhood of SEALS that may not be real but sure makes you feel that you have entered the circle and security of their world. The stories intertwine with each book before…and each book after and THAT is what makes Sharon Hamilton's SEAL Brotherhood Series so very interesting. You won't want to put down ANY of her books and they will keep you reading into the night when you should be sleeping. Start with this book…and you will not want to stop until you've read the whole series and then…you will be waiting for Sharon to write the next one." (5 Star Review)

"Kyle and Christy explode all over the pages in this first book, *[Accidental SEAL]*, in a whole new series of SEALs. If the twist and turns don't get your heart jumping, then maybe the suspense will. This is a must read for those that are looking for love and adventure with a little sloppy love thrown in for good measure." (5 Star Review)

PRAISE FOR THE BAD BOYS OF SEAL TEAM 3 SERIES

"I love reading this series! Once you start these books, you can hardly put them down. The mix of romance and suspense keeps you turning the pages one right after another! Can't wait until the next book!" (5 Star Review)

"I love all of Sharon's Seal books, but *[SEAL's Code]* may just be her best to date. Danny and Luci's journey is filled with a wonderful insight into the Native American life. It is a love story that will fill you with warmth and contentment. You will enjoy Danny's journey to become a SEAL and his reasons for it. Good job Sharon!" (5 Star Review)

PRAISE FOR THE BAND OF BACHELORS SERIES

"[Lucas] was the first book in the Band of Bachelors series and it was a phenomenal start. I loved how we got to see the other SEALs we all love and we got a look at Lucas and Marcy. They had an instant attraction, and their love was very intense. This book had it all, suspense, steamy romance, humor, everything you want in a riveting, outstanding read. I can't wait to read the next book in this series." (5 Star Review)

PRAISE FOR THE TRUE BLUE SEALS SERIES

"Keep the tissues box nearby as you read *True Blue SEALs: Zak* by Sharon Hamilton. I imagine more than I wish to that the circumstances surrounding Zak and Amy are all too real for returning military personnel and their families. Ms. Hamilton has put us right in the middle of struggles and successes that these two high school sweethearts endure. I have read several of Sharon Hamilton's military romances but will say this is the most emotionally intense of the ones that I have read. This is a well-written, realistic story with authentic characters that will have you rooting for them and proud of those who serve to keep us safe. This is an author who writes amazing stories that you love and cry with the characters. Fans of Jessica Scott and Marliss Melton will want to add Sharon Hamilton to their list of realistic military romance writers." (5 Star Review)

"Dear FATHER IN HEAVEN,

If I may respectfully say so sometimes you are a strange God. Though you love all mankind,

It seems you have special predilections too.

You seem to love those men who can stand up alone who face impossible odds, Who challenge every bully and every tyrant ~

Those men who know the heat and loneliness of Calvary. Possibly you cherish men of this stamp because you recognize the mark of your only son in them.

Since this unique group of men known as the SEALs know Calvary and suffering, teach them now the mystery of the resurrection ~ that they are indestructible, that they will live forever because of their deep faith in you.

And when they do come to heaven, may I respectfully warn you, Dear Father, they also know how to celebrate. So please be ready for them when they insert under your pearly gates.

Bless them, their devoted Families and their Country on this glorious occasion.

We ask this through the merits of your Son, Christ Jesus the Lord, Amen."

By Reverend E.J. McMalhon S.J. LCDR, CHC, USN
Awards Ceremony SEAL Team One
1975 At NAB, Coronado

www.ingramcontent.com/pod-product-compliance
Lightning Source LLC
Chambersburg PA
CBHW050118030726
47505CB00007B/1918